THE SCOTTISH ENLIGHTENMENT
AN ANTHOLOGY

The
Scottish Enlightenment

AN ANTHOLOGY
edited and introduced by
Alexander Broadie

CANONGATE
CLASSICS
80

First published as a Canongate Classic in 1997 by
Canongate Books Ltd, 14 High Street, Edinburgh
EH1 1TE. Editorial arrangement and Introduction
copyright © Alexander Broadie 1997.

The publishers gratefully acknowledge general
subsidy from the Scottish Arts Council towards
the Canongate Classics series and a specific grant
towards the publication of this volume.

Typeset in 9.5pt Plantin by Hewer Text Composition Services, Edinburgh. Printed and bound
in Great Britain by Caledonian International,
Bishopbriggs.

10 9 8 7 6 5 4 3 2

British Library Cataloguing-in-Publication
A catalogue record is available on request
from the British Library

ISBN 0 86241 738 4

Contents

Preface

To select material for a Scottish Enlightenment Anthology requires hard choices regarding not only authors but also fields. Some major fields within the Scottish Enlightenment are not represented in this Anthology. Seminal writings on engineering and chemistry, by James Watt and Joseph Black, have been omitted because the relevant writings are technically difficult and would require considerable commentary to make them generally accessible. Neither have I included anything of the fictional or poetical writings of the day, though fiction and poetry are certainly media for the exploration of human nature, a field of central concern to the enlightened thinkers of Scotland. Such media are not however in general the best way to participate in debates, to develop lines of argument for or against given theses, and it is to writings of such a nature, which are found in academic fields such as philosophy and science, that I have turned for excerpts. Nevertheless I have presented, within the constraints of space, excerpts illustrative of a wide range of fields, since the sheer breadth of achievement of the Scottish Enlightenment is itself one of its glories. At the same time the selected authors have been given ample room to develop their arguments – this is not an anthology of sound bites.

In line with the rather common Enlightenment view that philosophy is a central discipline and particularly the part of philosophy that focuses upon human nature, the Anthology starts with that topic, drawing its material from Hume, greatest of Scotland's Enlightenment philosophers, and from the school of common sense. Thereafter Parts III, IV and V, covering ethics, aesthetics and religion, can be seen as providing in a variety of ways further content to the concept of human nature, by probing our moral and aesthetic judgments to determine the nature of their relation to feelings, and to determine the extent to which it makes sense to speak of moral and aesthetic qualities as existing independently of our feelings and judgments. The excerpts in these Parts include a number of seminal passages by

Hutcheson, Hume, Smith and Reid. As regards the philosophy of the Scottish Enlightenment these four are self-selecting. In Part V on religion Hume again has a voice. Miracles were commonly cited as evidence for the existence of God, and in a famous article, Hume sought to argue against the value of the evidence provided by reports of miracles. This article is given in full in Part V, along with an excerpt from a counterblast by George Campbell. Hugh Blair's sermon 'On our imperfect knowledge of a future state', delivered at the High Kirk of St Giles in Edinburgh, is also given in full, as an example of Scottish Enlightenment pulpit oratory at its best. In Parts VI–XI many of the authors excerpted were self-selecting, such as Smith and Steuart on economics, Millar and Ferguson on social theory, Erskine and Kames on law, William Robertson on history, Hutton on geology and Maclaurin on Newtonianism. Though many others could have been selected, a line has to be drawn somewhere.

Some of the excerpts are taken from works that are readily accessible, and some might think this a sufficient reason to exclude them, but I preferred not to exclude them from an Anthology intended to represent the best of the work done in the Scottish Enlightenment, especially when those excerpts provide an important part of the context within which other valuable works are to be understood and assessed. Nevertheless I am conscious of the fact that it is possible to compile an admirable Scottish Enlightenment Anthology containing only excerpts that are of the highest quality and that are also not readily accessible. Indeed an indefinitely large number of admirable Scottish Enlightenment Anthologies, all of them constructed on perfectly reasonable principles and yet differing totally from each other in their content, could easily be constructed. It was also necessary to decide whether to modernise the spelling and punctuation of these eighteenth-century texts. I have not modernised, though I recognise that there are arguments on both sides.

Any selection is bound to reflect the interests and even the ideological stance of the compiler. An evangelical theologian and a historian of technology would not compile the same Anthology. My own interests and ideological stance are simply stated – I am a philosopher with a particular sympathy for the Scottish school of common sense – and these personal facts are plainly reflected in the choice of excerpts. Some perspectives are of course better than others at yielding insights into the true nature of the Scottish Enlightenment and, for reasons I indicate in Part I, I believe philosophers to be particularly well placed to discern what really happened. But as my friends out there are sure to reply: 'He would believe that, wouldn't he.'

As compiler of a wide-ranging Anthology I have sought wide-ranging help, and am deeply indebted to'the wise counsel given me by Professors Christopher Berry, William Gordon, Andrew Skinner, David Walker and Paul Wood regarding suitable texts and to Dr Donald Withrington who provided invaluable material on Sir John Sinclair's *Statistical Account of Scotland*. Miss P. S. Martin proffered advice, much of it promptly accepted, on stylistic matters. For all this help so generously given I am truly grateful.

Alexander Broadie
Glasgow 1997

PART I
INTRODUCTION
WHAT WAS
THE SCOTTISH ENLIGHTENMENT?

I

To understand the Scottish Enlightenment it is necessary both to grasp the concept of Enlightenment, and also to appreciate the fittingness of the application of the concept to eighteenth-century Scotland. I shall begin by discussing the concept and shall then turn to its specifically Scottish dimension.

Much the most influential account of the nature of Enlightenment that has come down to us from the Age of Enlightenment was written not by a Scot but by a German, Immanuel Kant (1724–1804). Since I shall be stressing the fact that the Scottish Enlightenment was the Scottish contribution to a more than Europe-wide movement, it is appropriate to consider the concept of Enlightenment as expounded by perhaps the greatest philosopher of the European movement, particularly in view of the fact that Kant's account accords closely with events in Scotland and in view also of the extent to which Scottish philosophers influenced him.[1] In 1785 he wrote a short essay in response to a request from the Berlinische Monatsschrift for an answer to the question 'What is Enlightenment?'[2] He defined Enlightenment as 'man's release from his self-incurred tutelage', tutelage being the inability to make use of one's understanding without direction from another. It is self-incurred if failure to use one's own understanding is due to laziness and cowardice. Kant therefore suggests as a motto for the Enlightenment: 'Sapere aude – Dare to know' or, as he paraphrases the Latin injunction: 'Have courage to use your own reason.'

In Enlightenment, therefore, the autonomy of reason is centre-stage. We think in an enlightened way when it is we who are generating the ideas. Instead of doing no more than

[1] Manfred Kuehn, *Scottish Common Sense in Germany,*
1768–1800
[2] Isaac Kramnick (ed.), *The Portable Enlightenment
Reader*, pp.1–7

following intellectual pathways cut by others, giving our assent to their ideas without any contribution of our own, we are engaged in thinking creatively. This suggests that enlightened thinking is not to be identified by its content so much as by its form. It is not *what* we think that makes our thinking enlightened but the *way* we think. In particular the enlightened thinker accepts things not merely on the authority of another but on his own authority and in the light of his own thinking on the matter.

For Kant there is a social dimension to Enlightenment, for Enlightenment requires freedom, not only freedom of will but also freedom to operate in a certain way in society, and indeed he believes that once such freedom is granted Enlightenment should come easily. The freedom Kant has in mind is the freedom that a man of letters has to publish his thoughts, to lay them open to public criticism by others and to respond publicly to their criticism. This is not at all like the freedom that a soldier might take to himself to disobey orders, or like the freedom that a pastor might take to himself to preach what he believes even if it is contrary to the teachings of the Church, or like the freedom that a citizen might take to himself to refuse to pay taxes when payment is rightfully demanded. Such freedoms work against the discipline that has to be maintained in practical matters if there is to be social stability, and since there can be no Enlightenment in time of social chaos they also work against the possibility of Enlightenment.

The freedom that Kant has in mind is, then, simply the freedom of a man of letters to put his ideas into the public domain for public discussion. In an enlightened age a soldier would be free to dispute in public the tactics or the strategy developed by his superiors even though he would not be free to disobey orders, the citizen would be free to dispute in public the wisdom of some given form of tax even though he would not be free to break the law regarding payment of that tax, and so on. In each case therefore the citizen who is free to dispute in public is also bound to obey those in authority. This is not to imply that Enlightenment has no practical results. It is bound to have, but the results flow from this essential feature of the situation, that there has been free, public debate on the practical issues, regarding say government policy, or professional ethics. Ideas have been tested in the intellectual market place and have passed that test. That they have passed is a powerful inducement to those in authority to implement them. In an enlightened state they would be implemented.

The two central elements of Kant's analysis, those concerning free discussion in the public domain and reliance upon one's own reason, are at the heart of most accounts of the nature of the Enlightenment, and certainly accord well with the experience of the Enlightenment in Scotland. To get a sense of the significance of these ideas it is important to see what it is with which Enlightenment is being contrasted. As against the employment of one's own reason there is the lazy and cowardly acceptance of ideas and beliefs on the authority of another. The unenlightened person says 'yes' to an idea, not because he has thought it through and sees that it is true, but because someone whom he accepts as an authority has told him it is true. But to accept something merely on the word of another is an exercise of faith. One form of such an exercise is religious faith; it is, in most of its forms, based on reports, now unverifiable, of miracles, and on reports, now unverifiable, that God spoke to human beings. On the other hand science is based not on faith but on reason. Scientists think things through for themselves. It is true that they accept many things on trust, for in general they trust the word of other scientists, and if they did not do so then science would make hardly any progress. But the propositions they accept on trust are not accepted only and always on trust, for if a scientist is at all sceptical about another scientist's report he can confirm or disconfirm the report by testing it. In this respect the scientist sceptical about another scientist's report is unlike the religious person who has become sceptical about a proposition he had previously accepted on the authority of the Bible, that God had spoken to Abraham or that Lazarus had risen from the dead, for it is now too late to test reports such as these.

There is no doubt that, during the Enlightenment, religion in general, and Christianity in particular, were subjected to rational scrutiny as never before. And while the enlightened were not predominantly anti-religious, some were, and many held religious views which were anaemic compared with the common stance of previous ages, for they held that only doctrines sanctioned by reason were to be believed, and that the *magnum mysterium* of religion, in so far as this was taken to be beyond the bounds of reason, was to be rejected. There was, therefore, in keeping with the idea that reality was fundamentally rational, a tendency towards the demystification of religion, and the affirmation of a rational religion or natural religion, a natural religion being one congenial to our rational nature. It was this need for such sanction as reason could provide that prompted a substantial literature on the reasonableness of Christianity (this last phrase being the title of an influential work by the English philosopher John Locke (1632–1704)).

Not only Christianity was at issue in these Enlightenment discussions. Judaism and Islam were also, as well as religions of India and the Far East, knowledge of which was feeding into the anthropological literature of the eighteenth century, along with accounts of the languages and customs of these distant peoples. Nevertheless it was for obvious reasons primarily Christianity that was at issue when the enlightened thinkers of Western Europe discussed religion, and the predominant position was that true religion, and therefore Christianity so far as it embodied religious truth, could be worked out by reason. There are many possible views concerning how much of Christianity can be worked out by reason. Some held that little if anything could be, while others thought that reason could go a considerable distance in the direction of the reconstruction of Christianity.

We find the full range of positions among the leaders of the Scottish Enlightenment. David Hume was probably an atheist, and if not an atheist then at least highly sceptical about the claims of religion; Hugh Blair and Thomas Reid on the other hand were deeply committed Christians and, as ministers of the Kirk, accustomed to preach their Christianity from the pulpit. Intermediate between these positions were deists, who maintained at least that a creator God existed, but who expressed also scepticism of one degree or another concerning those truths of revealed religion that can be accepted only on faith and cannot be demonstrated by reason. There is room for discussion about where James Hutton, the greatest geologist of the Age of Enlightenment, should be placed on the theist/atheist spectrum. His teaching on geological time gave rise to a strongly hostile response from a significant group within the Kirk who saw him as contradicting fundamental Christian teaching, though Hutton tells us that through proper consideration of the Earth we shall be led 'to acknowledge an order, not unworthy of Divine wisdom'. And though there were serious attempts to arraign Henry Home, Lord Kames, before the Kirk in view of his beliefs, no one doubted that he was deeply committed to Christian truth; the doubts all concerned his loyalty to the Kirk's vision of that truth.

The contrast between science and religion is at the heart of the rhetorical significance of the term 'Enlightenment' itself (*Aufklärung* in Germany, *Lumières* in France, *Ilustración* in Spain and *Illuminismo* in Italy). The term was used self-consciously by those who saw themselves as enlightened, as living in the light, in contrast with those who lived in darkness, the benighted ones. 'Enlightenment' was therefore a term of self-congratulation, and when those who were enlightened congratulated themselves on living in the light the denizens of darkness whom they most saw themselves as unlike were the 'schoolmen', the theologians of the Middle Ages, who relied on faith rather than reason, and whose favourite argument was the argument from authority. A given proposition is true. What is the evidence? It is that Aristotle assented to it, or St Augustine did, or John of Damascus, and so on. This view of the medieval theologians is demonstrably false, and it is worth while spelling out what makes it so, for by that means we shall be able to focus on the distinctive feature of the Age of Enlightenment that made that Age enlightened and the Middle Ages not.

Medieval theologians recognised the authority of certain texts, above all the Bible, but also the writings of Aristotle, and there were other authoritative texts also. The theologians were accustomed to use the fact that an authoritative text affirmed a given proposition as a reason for saying that the proposition was true. But they also used other sorts of arguments, arguments that do not rely upon the authority of others, but instead rely upon sheer rational insight and upon the authority of one's senses. And even when quoting an authority there was still a question as to how the authority was to be interpreted, and there was often deep disagreement on such matters. So the schoolmen argued with each other in the public domain, as men of letters do. It is true that they were told what they had to believe as members of their faith community, but they sought a rational basis for these beliefs wherever possible, though arguing among themselves over what religious propositions could be supported by reason (and arguing about how strong the support was when it was available); and they did not regard themselves as trumped if they were contradicted by an authoritative text, for they could then argue about whether that text meant what it was thought to mean.

These debates were often conducted in public. That is to say, the theologians wrote their arguments down and passed them round for others to judge them. Furthermore they had, in Kant's phrase, 'the courage to use their own reason'; they did not simply reheat and retail the same old arguments. Those debates therefore have characteristics not unlike the debates of the enlightened thinkers of the eighteenth century.

But there is a crucial difference. It concerns freedom. As we saw, Kant regards as a characteristic feature of Enlightenment the unlimited freedom of the man of letters to say his say in public. The only tribunal that matters is the tribunal of human reason, in particular the reason of other men of letters. In an enlightened society the fact that a person in authority does not like the conclusions drawn by the men of letters, has no bearing on whether they have the right to pronounce their views in public. The Age of Enlightenment is therefore an age of toleration; above all, those in authority tolerate the men of letters. For the authorities not to tolerate them is for there to be external constraints placed upon the voice of reason, whereas in the Age of Enlightenment the only constraint on that voice is internal, a judgment by the tribunal of human reason itself.

In the Middle Ages there was no such toleration by those in authority. Far from the medieval theologians having unlimited freedom to dispute in public, a false theological move would have been a dangerous, even a deadly, act for them. They were free to an extent; but there were many propositions they could not safely defend, and here we have the whole range of medieval heresies to turn to for propositions that marked the limit of the toleration of the free expression of reason in the Middle Ages. Since toleration is a necessary part of Enlightenment the medieval period was not an Age of Enlightenment. It is not a coincidence that John Locke's *Letters Concerning Toleration* (1689, 1690, 1692), which demanded religious toleration for all theists who had not declared loyalty to another country, ushered in a period of intense interest in the idea of toleration. In a sense toleration was the moral space within which the Enlightenment developed. David Hume observes: 'So true it is, that however other nations may rival us in poetry, and excel us in some other agreeable arts, the improvements in reason and philosophy can only be owing to a land of toleration and of liberty.'[1]

In respect of the freedom of the man of letters to follow his reason whithersoever it takes him, and to do so in public, Scotland of the eighteenth century was immeasurably more tolerant than was society in the Middle Ages. There were of course many intolerant people who would gladly have prevented certain men of letters publishing their views. But to speak of the Enlightenment is to speak not of a society in which all citizens

[1] David Hume, *A Treatise of Human Nature*, Introduction, p. xvii

are tolerant, but of a society whose citizens are tolerated when they exercise their reason in public discussion, and are tolerated even by those in authority who do not like what they hear. Of course no society is, or perhaps can be, perfectly tolerant or perfectly enlightened. This is a matter of relativities. Scotland in the eighteenth century was enlightened compared with the countries of Western Europe during the Middle Ages.

Edinburgh's treatment of David Hume, a noted sceptic on matters of religion, and accused even of a lack of warmth in the cause of virtue, bears testimony to the comparatively high level of toleration. His attempt to gain the moral philosophy chair in Edinburgh in 1745 came to grief partly because twelve of the fifteen ministers called upon to vote on Hume's candidacy voted against him, and the evidence suggests that they did so because, in light of what they believed to be his doctrines on morality and religion, they thought that Hume was simply unfit to hold the chair.[1] However neither they nor the country's political leaders attempted to prevent him publishing his thoughts, as contrasted with the obstacles which would certainly have been raised in the Middle Ages in many cities. Furthermore Hume had formidable allies, such as Lord Elibank and Lord Tinwall within the ranks of the 'literati' (as active participants in the Scottish Enlightenment described themselves) who put up a strong fight on Hume's behalf. The fact that he lost, therefore, has to be kept in perspective, since he had his supporters as well as his opponents and he continued to expound his views.

The case of Hume is particularly important in this context since his position was extreme in the area of religion in that he was, at least by repute, an atheist. That reputation is possibly unfair, for it could be argued that he maintained not that belief in a personal God is false, but that such a belief is not supported by sound argument. It is true that he argues against arguments for theism, but it has been claimed that Hume's sceptical philosophy points, more widely, to the conclusion that statements about the existence and attributes of a personal God are simply not within the competence of human reason to settle. This position leaves the field open to faith, and accords well with some versions of

1 See Roger L. Emerson, 'The "affair" at Edinburgh
  and the "project" at Glasgow: the politics of Hume's
  attempt to become a professor', in *Hume and Hume's
  Connexions*, eds M. A. Stewart and John P. Wright; also
  M. A. Stewart, *The Kirk and the Infidel*

Calvinism. In so far as his position is that reason cannot decide the religious questions at issue, then Hume's is not an atheistic position. Nevertheless he did have a reputation, widespread within the Kirk but also beyond, for atheism. Despite this he continued to write and to publish, and his views were common knowledge, even if there was disagreement as to their precise import. In addition he was an enthusiastic member of all the best clubs of Edinburgh, and his wide circle of friends included almost all the prominent literati. He was, in short, more than just tolerated; for many people Hume's presence in Edinburgh was a matter for rejoicing.

II

I have now discussed the most influential account of the nature of Enlightenment that has come down to us from the Age of Enlightenment, and I should like next to focus more precisely upon the Enlightenment in Scotland. As a first step let us note that Scotland's situation at the start of the eighteenth century has prompted many to ask how this of all countries could, just then, have moved towards the accomplishment of so much. Historians point especially to three aspects of the country's life which collectively ought to have been more than sufficient to prevent Scotland making any significant cultural advance. They point to the country's loss of its court when the crowns of Scotland and England were united in 1603 and the one centre of royal patronage for the two countries was thereafter in London. They point also to the country's loss of its parliament when the parliaments of Scotland and England were united in 1707 under the Acts of Union, and the one centre of parliamentary patronage for the two countries was thereafter in London. And thirdly they point to the Darien Scheme at the very end of the seventeenth century, which aimed to establish a colony in central America, and which instead caused a nationwide economic disaster at home. How was it possible early in the eighteenth century for this small impoverished country, far from the great centres of European culture and lacking the great centres of patronage of a nation state, to begin to mount so stunning a cultural performance?

However, these features of the Scottish scene represent a very small part of the whole scene, and against them it is necessary to set a number of facts. Of these the most important is that the country had universities in St Andrews (founded 1411/12), Glasgow (1451), Aberdeen (1495) and Edinburgh (1583), universities that, even during the second half of the seventeenth century and the early part of the eighteenth, the pre-Enlightenment period, provided their students with an education, including a scientific education, at a standard equal to that found at the great universities on the continent. One aspect of the quality of the universities during that period, as at previous times, was their enthusiastic receptivity to new ideas in philosophy, theology, law, medicine, mathematics and science. I am speaking of pre-eminent contributions to pre-Enlightenment culture such as the philosophy and mathematics of René Descartes (1596–1650), the mathematics and physics of Isaac Newton (1642–1727), and the juridical ideas of men such as the great German jurist Samuel Pufendorf (1632–94) whose work was the subject of a commentary by Gershom Carmichael (1672–1729), first professor of moral philosophy at Glasgow University and the teacher of Francis Hutcheson (1694–1746), who would in due course succeed him in the moral philosophy chair.

Chairs of law were not founded in the Scottish universities until the eighteenth century. For example, at Edinburgh University the regius chair of public law and the law of nature and nations was founded in 1707, the chair of civil law followed in 1710 and of Scots law in 1722, while at Glasgow University the chair of civil law was founded in 1713 and filled one year later.[1] Nevertheless, even before the foundation of the chairs, law was taught in the universities, and indeed during the pre-Enlightenment period Scotland boasted an intellectually lively legal community led by men such as Sir James Dalrymple (later Viscount Stair) (1616–95) and Sir George Mackenzie of Rosehaugh (1636–91), the latter a philosopher by training and, for some years while regent master in philosophy at Glasgow University, also by profession. Both men were highly innovative, Stair in civil, and Mackenzie in criminal, law. Stair's *The Institutions of the Laws of Scotland* (1681) was a major landmark in Scottish legal thinking. It is a creative work in which the law of Scotland is presented, as never previously, in a clear, systematic, and philosophically sound and rigorous fashion; more than any other text it formed the basis for Scottish discussions on law during the century of the Enlightenment. Sir George Mackenzie was a Lord Advocate with a reputation as a tough enforcer of the criminal law, as is evidenced by his nickname 'Bluidy Mackenzie' which was bestowed in light of the manner of

1 John Cairns, 'Rhetoric, language, and Roman law: Legal education and improvement in eighteenth-century Scotland'

his prosecution of covenanters. His *Laws and Customs of Scotland in Matters Criminal* was the first ever textbook of the criminal law of Scotland. He also published an *Institutions of the Law of Scotland* which became a standard textbook in the eighteenth century.

By the end of the seventeenth century, students in the Scottish universities were reading Stair and Mackenzie, and were learning from them that, while the tables of the law brought down from Mount Sinai taught us moral principles, those same principles could be learned from an appropriately slanted investigation of nature. Such rational exercises resulted in the body of natural law theory, and that theory, which has great intellectual and moral strength, would in due course play a major role in Scottish Enlightenment legal writings. It should be added that the intellectual and moral strength of Scottish law, as represented especially by the works of Stair and Mackenzie, was no doubt one explanation of the provision for the continued separate identity of Scots law that was written into the 1707 Acts of Union.

As well as the lawyers there were also the Scottish scientists of the pre-Enlightenment period. They included the physician and scientific experimenter David Gregory (1627–1720) from Drumoak near Aberdeen, famous as the inventor of a powerful artillery piece (though not one ever built and fired in battle), and his brother James Gregory (1638–75), likewise from Drumoak, the first professor of mathematics at Edinburgh University, who made original contributions to the theory of trigonometric functions and who worked out the theory of the reflecting telescope. Also prominent in the scientific community was Sir Robert Sibbald (1641–1723), co-founder, with the distinguished physician Andrew Balfour (1630–94), of Edinburgh's Physic Garden, founded near Holyrood in 1670. The Physic Garden formed the basis of the Royal Botanic Gardens of Edinburgh and contributed to Edinburgh's reputation as a centre for medical studies since the main purpose of the Garden was to ensure a regular supply of medicinal plants. Sibbald was also a founder member of the Royal College of Physicians of Edinburgh, and one of the earliest presidents of the College. Archibald Pitcairne (1652–1713), professor of medicine at Edinburgh after holding a similar post at Leiden, was another founder member of the College. They and many others (including other members of the extraordinary Gregory dynasty) worked in Scotland at the cutting edge of European science in the fields of medicine, botany, mathematics and physics, and of course did a great deal to enhance the international reputation of the Scottish universities. The world-beating qualities of the Scottish scientific community in the eighteenth century were not at all matched by its predecessor in the seventeenth, but all the same the achievements of that earlier generation of scientists were not negligible.

During this same period there were also distinguished religious thinkers. Among them were Robert Leighton (1611–84), principal of Edinburgh University (1653–61) and episcopalian archbishop of Glasgow (1669-74); and Gilbert Burnet (1643-1715), episcopalian minister, professor of divinity at Glasgow and author of *Vindication of the Authority, Constitution, and Laws of the Church and State in Scotland*, and a *History of the Reformation*. After a year spent in the Netherlands as adviser to Prince William of Orange, he returned to England in 1688 with William and was appointed bishop of Salisbury. His theology had led him previously, in days of bitter controversy in Scotland, to adopt the role of peacemaker between the Scottish episcopal church and the presbyterians. Henry Scougall (1650–78), another significant religious thinker of the eighteenth century, was professor at King's College, Aberdeen, and author of the influential work of mystical piety *The Life of the Soul of God in Man* (first published 1677). These were humane and reasonable men who, in a century of strong theological debate and of murderous religious repression, kept alive the Scottish tradition of thoughtful enquiry into the religious dimension of the human spirit.

These points, relating to the intellectual liveliness of the nation during the pre-Enlightenment period and centring on the nation's respect for educational values, are a counterweight to the fact that in the early eighteenth century Scotland was without two traditional centres of large-scale patronage and was in a poor economic condition. In short, there were also ways in which the country was not at all in a poor condition, and these other ways, all of which concern a vigorous search for the best expression of civilised, humane values, can be seen in retrospect as creating a space within which just such a phenomenon as the Scottish Enlightenment could come to fruition. This is not to suggest that there is nothing more that need be said by way of explanation; even less is it to suggest that the Enlightenment in Scotland was not a historic moment of brilliant originality. But at least these facts make the occurrence of the Scottish Enlightenment less astonishing than it would have been if it had taken place immediately following a period of cultural aridity.

There may also have been features of the earlier culture against which the enlightened thinkers, the literati, were reacting; and those earlier features may have continued into the period of the Enlightenment and helped to sustain it by continually presenting it with something against which to react. Indeed it is easy to demonstrate that there were cultural features in Scotland, particularly relating to elements or segments in the national Church, which continually stimulated the Enlightenment by opposing it. This consideration has to be handled with care. It is true that some of the literati were committed to a religion within or mainly within the bounds of reason and therefore were drawn to deism rather than theism, that is, they held to the existence of a God that is the cause of the world even if not to the existence of the loving, just, and merciful God of the Bible. Some others from among the literati were in modern terms agnostic or even atheistic. But as against this, and aside from the fact that some of the literati were deeply committed believers with a traditional outlook, there is also the fact, recently investigated, that a number of essentially Calvinist moral and social positions are to be found in a duly modulated form in the writings of Enlightenment authors, particularly David Hume, who are not commonly thought of as sympathetic to Calvinist theology.[1]

I have been commenting on the relations between the Enlightenment in Scotland and the country's cultural achievements during the preceding half century or so. There are also questions to be answered regarding the relations, during the century of Enlightenment, between Scottish culture and cultural events occurring elsewhere: for example, investigations into fields such as philosophy, law, economics and medicine, in France and the Netherlands especially. These questions remind us that the Scottish Enlightenment was the Scottish part of a much wider Enlightenment movement that included figures of the stature of Charles-Louis Montesquieu (1689–1755), François-Marie Voltaire (1694–1778), Jean-Jacques Rousseau (1712–78), Immanuel Kant and Benjamin Franklin (1706–90). Scotland in the Age of Enlightenment was no more separated from contemporary cultural events elsewhere in Europe, America and beyond than the Scotland of the pre-Enlightenment period had been from the wider cultural scene. It can readily be shown that contemporary cultural events elsewhere, in conjunction with Scotland's own political, religious and educational traditions, the cultural context within which the Scottish Enlightenment

1 Roger L. Emerson, 'Calvinism and the Scottish Enlightenment', pp. 19–28

occurred, by which it was nourished and to which it made a distinctive contribution.

III

The majority of those who formed the Scottish Enlightenment were university professors, ministers of the kirk, and lawyers, in short the teachers, preachers and pleaders who dominated the Scottish cultural scene during the eighteenth century. These three roles are not mutually exclusive in theory, nor were they in practice.

Among the literati were the philosophers Francis Hutcheson, David Hume, Thomas Reid and Dugald Stewart, the latter two being leading figures in the Scottish school of common sense philosophy. The leading economists were Adam Smith and Sir James Steuart, though David Hume, who was on friendly terms with both Smith and Steuart, also made major contributions to economics. The social theorists included John Millar and Adam Ferguson, with Adam Smith's masterpiece on economics, *An Inquiry into the Nature and Causes of the Wealth of Nations*, also containing valuable insights in the field of social theory. The lawyers of the period, including Lord Kames, Lord Monboddo and John Erskine, built significantly upon the work of Stair and Mackenzie; and the historian William Robertson made full use of the large amount of data concerning distant peoples that was beginning to arrive from the Americas and the Far East – this was a time when the ship's logs of Captain James Cook concerning his travels to the islands of the South Pacific were beginning to circulate. Another crucial feature of the Enlightenment in Scotland was the work of the rhetoricians, such as George Turnbull of Aberdeen whose studies of discourse probably went deeper than those of any of his contemporaries, and Hugh Blair, famous preacher at the High Kirk of St Giles in Edinburgh, and first professor of rhetoric and belles lettres at Edinburgh University.

The scientists include William Cullen from Hamilton, who in 1747 became the first professor of chemistry in Britain when he was appointed to the chair in Glasgow; Alexander Monro primus and Alexander Monro secundus, a father-and-son team, medical professors at Edinburgh, who helped to make Edinburgh a medical centre of Europe-wide significance; and Colin Maclaurin, one of the great Newtonians of the age. Joseph Black, who held chairs successively at Glasgow and Edinburgh, developed the theories of specific heat and of latent heat, and worked closely with James

Watt whose invention of an improved version of the Newcomen steam engine had a major impact on the industrial revolution. In 1769 John Robison, a student of Joseph Black's at Glasgow, discovered the inverse square law of electric force. And James Hutton was the greatest geologist of the age.

Scores more literati could be named, as also could other cultural fields. Where the line should be drawn between the enlightened and the non-enlightened is not at all clear, nor could it be, in the absence of a clear definition. But among other major contributors to the spirit of the Age of Enlightenment in Scotland are Robert Burns (1759–96); and James Macpherson (1736–96) whose *Poems of Ossian* divided critical opinion regarding their authenticity. We should also include biographer and diarist James Boswell (1740–95), and novelist Henry Mackenzie (1745–1832) who was also a founder member of the Royal Society of Edinburgh. The portraitists Allan Ramsay junior (1713–84) and Henry Raeburn (1756–1823), were leading figures of the Enlightenment in Edinburgh, as were members of the Adam family of architects, the greatest of whom, Robert Adam (1728–92), was responsible for Register House and much of Charlotte Square in Edinburgh, and Culzean Castle in Ayrshire.

The Scottish Enlightenment would not have existed without the great figures such as those just mentioned, but the Enlightenment was a good deal more than those great figures. The literati operated in a social context of a kind that enabled them to develop their talents, to gain an audience, to climb to the top, and in many cases to produce changes in the society that provided the ladders.

In some ways they constituted a society of their own, a liberal minded, tolerant 'republic of letters', a phrase characteristic of the Enlightenment. But, though citizens of that republic, they were also integrated into the wider society. They were, in short, highly sociable; they sought out and enjoyed society, and one aspect of their sociability was their clubability. They founded many clubs, for example, the Literary Society in Glasgow whose membership included Joseph Black, William Cullen, Adam Smith, Thomas Reid, and James Watt; and the Rankenian Club in Edinburgh, which included William Wishart (Principal of Edinburgh University), John Stevenson (professor of logic at Edinburgh), George Turnbull and Colin Maclaurin. Also in Edinburgh was the Select Society founded by the painter Allan Ramsay junior whose membership included David Hume, Adam Smith, Hugh Blair, Robert Dundas (President of the Court of Session), William Cullen, Adam Ferguson and Lord Kames. Equally distinguished was Edinburgh's Philosophical Society, this last becoming the Royal Society of Edinburgh in 1783. And in Aberdeen we find, among others, the Philosophical Society, which included in its membership Thomas Reid, George Campbell, Alexander Gerard (first professor of moral philosophy at Marischal College) and James Beattie (professor of moral philosophy and logic at Marischal College).

These clubs were a central feature of the Scottish Enlightenment, providing a context for discussions and debates between philosophers, theologians, lawyers and scientists – thinkers representing the whole gamut of Enlightenment interests. At meetings of such societies Thomas Reid could try out his philosophy of common sense, which would in due course have a major impact on philosophers in France, Spain and North America, and Adam Smith could receive from prosperous merchants of Glasgow a well-informed response to his ideas on free trade, a response which would in due course see light of day both in his *Wealth of Nations* and also in government policy. Certain papers presented at these clubs, for example James Hutton's presentation of his theory of the Earth to the Royal Society of Edinburgh in 1785, are now recognised as among the crowning achievements of the Enlightenment in Europe.

A consequence of the mixture of interests in the societies was that the individuals exposed to so wide a range of subjects were by modern standards very broadly educated. The generalist education made available in this way is well symbolised by the fact that the *Encyclopaedia Britannica*, whose first edition was printed and published in Edinburgh in instalments between 1768 and 1771, was a product of the Scottish Enlightenment, and by the fact that a substantial part of it was the work of one man, the polymath William Smellie, friend of Robert Burns and a member of the Society of Antiquaries.

IV

I have spoken about the concept of Enlightenment as a process in which reason is exercised in free public debate, and if reason leads then one might expect real progress. There would surely be progress in the field of the natural sciences once reason were given its head, and ancient authorities did not act as a deadweight round the necks of scientists. There would surely be progress in other areas also, for example, in matters of religion, with the establishment of a rational religion which might gain universal acceptance, for we can respond affirmatively to sound arguments when they are presented to us in a clear style. Likewise in political matters; if political debates are carried on, in an environment of toleration, before the tribunal of human reason, and are therefore not slanging matches between opponents armed first with slogans and then with steel weapons, there might be progress towards the resolution of political disputes. Progress will surely come in other areas also, in response to the Enlightenment exercise of free civilised public debate before the tribunal of reason. That is, the Enlightenment will produce improvement.

But most of the leading literati, perhaps reflecting in this matter their Calvinist background and therefore the Calvinist belief in our fallen state, recognised that improvement or progress, if it comes, will be slow, and they recognised that any position gained has to be defended if it is to be retained. Society cannot risk ever sitting back on its laurels after congratulating itself on having made progress. Hume, Smith, Millar, Ferguson and others who wrote on this matter did not see us as on the way to a worldly perfection; they held out no hope of a terrestrial utopia but instead attended to features of human psychology and of society that tend to produce instability.

One example will suffice here. That Adam Smith's *Wealth of Nations* is concerned with improvement is signalled by him in the opening sentence where he makes reference to an improvement in the productive power of labour. He sees such improvement, and therefore sees economic growth, as coming with increased application of the principle of the division of labour. Of course, economic growth is a good thing but the very principle (that of division of labour) that produces economic growth can also undermine it if precautions are not taken. The endless repetition by very many workers of very simple tasks is the inevitable consequence of the systematic application of the principle, and sheer mind-numbness results from performance of those repetitions. Yet society is harmed economically if it has a workforce many of whose members are stunted in mind. Smith therefore proposed that there be educational provision to correct the damage done by the systematic application of an economic principle. Educational provision, which is crucial if scientists and engineers are to be trained to an appropriate standard for work in a progressive commercial society, is therefore also crucial if an underclass of depressed and disgruntled workers is not to emerge as a product of that same society. Smith foresaw the problem and he worked out the solution.

Smith was also fully alive to the fact that stunting the minds of workers, indeed of any human beings, is simply morally unacceptable whether or not also economically undesirable. It was in fact his view that, generally, morality and economics go hand in hand, at least to the extent that maltreatment of the workforce is not only bad morality but also bad economics. A further aspect of the historic situation, to which Smith's essentially humane outlook is immediately relevant, concerns the industrial revolution. That revolution was made possible not only by the systematic application of the principle of division of labour but also by technological and engineering developments pioneered in Scotland by, among others, Smith's friend James Watt, who was helped by the close professional contact he maintained with Joseph Black while Black was carrying out research into chemical problems relating to heat. For Adam Smith the hideous deterioration in working conditions and living conditions that were introduced into the commercial society as a byproduct of the industrial revolution is just the kind of morally unacceptable outcome that should be foreseen by economists, and having foreseen it they should work out how to avert it, providing therefore an economic response to a moral problem.

Implicit in these comments is a concept of an interrelation between the three disciplines of ethics, economics and engineering. Solutions to engineering problems have immediate economic consequences, which themselves have to be judged in terms of ethical criteria. The three form a system of thought, a unity of disciplines. There was in fact a rather common view during the Enlightenment that the sciences as a whole form a unity, and the classic statement of this view was provided within the Scottish Enlightenment by Hume.

Hume held that by one route or another all the sciences lead back to what he terms 'the science of man'; put otherwise, human nature is a principle of unity for the sciences taken as a whole. The rational structure supporting this insight is the following: each of the sciences attempts a systematic representation of part of nature. The nature to be represented is of course nature from a human perspective, nature as seen by us. For Hume, nature is not simply something out there to which nothing is added by our inspection of it; on the contrary, nature is in large measure a product of our own imaginative activity. We make the world we live in. That the natural order is not something absolute that can continue without us human beings who perceive it and interact with it implies that all the natural sciences are inextricably linked to human nature. It is only because human nature functions as it does that the natural order is as it seems to us. Human nature is therefore a principle of unity for all the sciences.

One aspect of this unity, which lies at the heart of Hume's philosophy, is the fact that we cannot help seeing the natural order in terms of causal connections. We see events as having causes and as having effects, even if we cannot always say what the causes are, or the effects. A flame is placed close to a piece of wood; the wood becomes hot and bursts into flames, not by chance but of necessity. We kick a stone and the stone immediately moves, not by chance but of necessity. This necessity, which is always present when one event causes another, seems to be an element or a feature of the world, something independent of ourselves the spectators. But on Hume's analysis the necessity is to be accounted for entirely in terms of features of the spectator. We observe regularities: a pebble is struck and it moves, it is struck a second time and moves again, struck a third time and moves again. In due course the mind becomes accustomed to expect the pebble to move when struck; on seeing the strike, the mind, by custom, forms a belief that the pebble will then move. On Hume's analysis the necessity we say exists in nature is no more than the feeling of expectation we form, by a custom of the mind, as a result of repeatedly observing a given sequence of events. But if an essential component of causality is the necessary connection between a cause and its effect, and if this necessary connection is a product of the human mind and, finally, if natural science is concerned with the investigation of causal relations in nature, Hume is surely right to conclude that all the natural sciences have a relation, greater or less, to human nature. And as regards the so-called moral sciences, such as the disciplines of ethics, aesthetics and politics, it is plain that the principles of these disciplines are, in the deepest way possible, dependent upon features of human nature, particularly our sense of beauty and of the sublime.

It was considerations such as these that led Hume to conclude: 'There is no question of importance, whose decision is not compriz'd in the science of man; and there is none, which can be decided with any certainty, before we become acquainted with that science.'[1] Philosophers of the Scottish Enlightenment disagreed about many things, but in general they agreed with Hume's contention concerning the special relation in which the

1 Hume, *A Treatise of Human Nature*, Introduction, p. xvi

science of man stands to all the other sciences. Thomas Reid, the first great figure of the Scottish school of common sense philosophy, disagreed with Hume about most things, but fully concurred on this one, and was followed on this matter by other members of the school, such as Dugald Stewart and William Hamilton. The philosophical focus of the Scottish Enlightenment was therefore beyond doubt the human mind. Thus Reid's three great works, all of them written at least in part in opposition to Hume, who therefore can be seen as setting Reid's agenda, were *An Inquiry into the Human Mind on the Principles of Common Sense*, *Essays on the Intellectual Powers of Man* and *Essays on the Active Powers of the Human Mind*.

Thomas Reid emphasised the limits of scientific enquiry into the human mind, but he said a great deal up to those limits. We think, we remember, we reason, we will, and so on, and all such acts are acts of mind. This is not a definition of mind, for a definition would tell us what mind is in essence, and not merely what sorts of acts it can perform. Body, on the other hand, is what is extended, solid, moveable and divisible. For Reid, the first and crucial step towards an understanding of mind is to see both that the various acts of mind, such as remembering and reasoning, cannot truly be ascribed to body, and also that the various attributes of body cannot truly be ascribed to mind.

Yet, as Reid points out, we speak about some things as being in the mind and about other things as being external to the mind, and this suggests that mind is spatial, for how can something be in the mind unless the mind is conceived of as a space in which things can be? And how can something be external to mind unless mind is a bit of space that excludes those things said to be external to it? And if mind is spatial it is surely extended, though Reid has said that mind, unlike body, is not extended.

But words can be a trap. There are ways of being in something without being spatially in it. For example, I have an idea in my mind just now. It is not spatially in it, but in it in the sense that I am thinking about something. To have an idea about something, or for something to be in one's mind, is to be thinking about that thing, or imagining it, or conceiving it, and so on. Hence to talk about ideas being in the mind is to speak about the relation between an agent (the mind) and its various operations.

The human mind can hardly make a move without bringing common sense principles to bear, and nothing in Reid's philosophy was more influential than his account of such principles. As Reid puts the point: 'There are, therefore, common principles, which are the foundation of all reasoning and of all science. Such common principles seldom admit of direct proof, nor do they need it. Men need not to be taught them; for they are such as all men of common understanding know; or such, at least, as they give a ready assent to, as soon as they are proposed and understood.'[1] These principles are part of the original constitution of our nature. A human being who lacked them would not have a recognisably human belief system. Nowhere does Reid produce a definitive list of such principles; they are to be found not by generating them systematically from some single principle, but in an ad hoc fashion, on the basis of attention to people's behaviour (as opposed to their affirmations), and on the basis of scrutiny of language, for nothing more clearly displays our belief system than the structure of our language. Attention to language is a most important part of Reid's methodology.

A further way to learn about the mind is by what we should now call introspection. As regards this means of investigating our mental operations Reid draws attention to two obstacles. The first is that there is a natural human tendency always to focus outwards, via the senses, rather than inwards to the mind itself, and this tendency has to be overcome if it is the mind's own operations that are under investigation. Secondly, mental operations are, in most cases, operations upon objects, for we never just see, think, imagine or wonder; we see something, think about something, imagine something, wonder about something – in every case there is an object, a something, which the mind is operating on. Upon the removal of the object the mental operation ceases. But if we try to attend to the operation and therefore direct our attention away from the object of the operation, then of course the object that sustains the operation ceases to be an object for us, and as a consequence the operation itself ceases and is not there to be attended to.

Investigation of the mind leads to the discovery of many powers, and these have traditionally been listed under two heads, understanding and will. Reid, however, is concerned to stress that though it is possible to make distinctions between the powers which are exercised when we perceive, remember, judge and reason, and the powers which are exercised when we will, desire, love or are angry, these powers are in practice inextricably

1 Thomas Reid, *Essays on the Intellectual Powers*, Essay 1,
   ch. 2, in *The Works of Thomas Reid*, vol. 1, p. 230

linked, so that there is no exercise of will without exercise of the understanding, nor vice versa.

Reid has a strong sense of the unity of the human mind. It is true that he attends in detail to a great many mental powers, and in different ways stresses the immense complexity of the mind and the multiplicity of the parts of it. But this does not in any way speak against the unity of mind; on the contrary it speaks for the richness of the unity.

Human nature was explored not only from a philosophical perspective but also from a linguistic, for explorations of grammar, rhetoric and literary style were seen as contributing to the understanding of human nature. The underlying insight was that our nature is expressed in detail and with clarity in our language. The larger grammatical features of our language were held to be indicative of our fundamental beliefs about the world. The tenses of verbs reflect our beliefs about the temporality of the world; the distinction between nouns and adjectives reflects our beliefs about the distinction between things and their qualities; the fact that active verbs have subjects, of the first, second or third person, reflects our belief that actions are performed by agents, and so on. From reflection upon the structure of language we can learn a great deal about the fundamental belief system of the language user. Furthermore it is through language that we learn of the deeper subtleties of a person's emotions, and can study those subtleties in poetry and fiction. The Scottish literati wrote extensively on language: James Burnett, Lord Monboddo, produced a multi-volume study *Of the Origin and Progress of Language*; Adam Smith wrote on the origins of language and on varieties of literary style; Hugh Blair gave a brilliant series of lectures on literary style; and George Campbell wrote a magisterial philosophical study of rhetoric.

For example, Campbell raises a question concerning the relation between rhetoric, grammar and logic, the three arts known collectively in the Middle Ages as the trivium, or the 'trivial' arts. Campbell distinguishes between the body and the soul of a piece of discourse, respectively the words of the discourse and its sense. Grammar is related to the words of the discourse as logic is related to its sense, for grammar states the rules for constructing well-formed sentences, and logic, which is the science that pre-eminently aims at truth, attends to sense since a sentence is true in virtue of its sense. Rhetoric is, however, as Campbell emphasises, not simply a combination of grammar and logic; rather it presupposes them. The orator must use well-formed sentences and should speak truly, but that is not enough, for questions of style have to be addressed. There are different ways of presenting the truth and the expert in rhetoric knows which way will be most effective at persuading the audience; he has an eye to style, to the bewitching phrase, to the cumulative effect of phrases, and so on. While therefore grammar aims at correctness of speech, and logic at truth, rhetoric aims at eloquence. There is an ordering relation here; rhetoric depends on logic, which depends upon grammar. One consequence of this position is that Campbell does not take sides in the long running dispute between logic and rhetoric. Traditionally, philosophers have seen rhetoric as an enemy of logic, as more interested in persuasion than in truth. Campbell on the other hand thinks that the best way to persuade people, and the way that is at the heart of rhetoric, is to tell the truth and to present well-expressed, sound arguments in support of the truth.

Human nature was also studied from a historical perspective. Any attempt to discover universal principles of human behaviour must respect the historical data, for principles which are truly universal will be found to operate at other times as well as in other places, and in that case it is necessary to test the hypothesis that certain features of, say, human motivation are indeed not peculiar to the present age but are to be found in all other ages for which there are data. In this way historians make a contribution to the study of human nature. In his own lifetime Hume's six-volume *History of England* achieved greater popularity than his other writings, including his overtly philosophical works. Nevertheless his interest in history was philosophical not antiquarian, as is made plain by his statement concerning the utility of history:

> Mankind are so much the same, in all times and places, that history informs us of nothing new or strange in this particular. Its chief use is only to discover the constant and universal principles of human nature, by showing men in all varieties of circumstances and situations, and furnishing us with materials from which we may form our observations and become acquainted with the regular springs of human action and endeavour. These records of wars, intrigues, factions, and revolutions, are so many collections of experiments, by which the politician or moral philosopher fixes the principles of his science.[1]

1 David Hume, *An Enquiry concerning Human Understanding*, section 8, part 1, pp. 83-4

The reference in the last sentence to the moral philosopher's use of experiments is particularly interesting in the light of the subtitle of Hume's philosophical magnum opus, *A Treatise of Human Nature: being an attempt to introduce the experimental method reasoning into moral subjects.* The experimental method involves placing substances in particular circumstances and observing what happens to them. Historians are peculiarly well placed to carry out such observations where the substances in question are human beings. They can observe people in a thousand past circumstances, observe their behaviour, and by such means gain new insights into human nature or at least confirm, or otherwise, new hypotheses.

Adam Smith also was a historian of the first rank. Apart from his *History of Astronomy* (see excerpt 44) and his history of historians in his *Lectures on Rhetoric and Belles Lettres* (see excerpt 38), the *Wealth of Nations* is written, in part, from a historical perspective. This fact is signalled by its account of the four-stage history of society, which conjectures that human beings passed from a hunter-gatherer stage, through a pastoral stage and then an agricultural stage, to the commercial stage at which we are now. But aside from the four-stage theory, which is an example of what Dugald Stewart was later to call 'conjectural history', many of the arguments Smith deploys in support of his claims concerning the dynamic of the commercial society are of a non-conjectural historical nature. For example he presents an account of the historical development of cities in order, in part, to demonstrate the principles of change that have operated in them, and to argue for the form that economic behaviour will take in cities, given that they have reached their present state by taking the particular route they have taken. For Smith a society's history is part of its environment, and we cannot understand either its behaviour or the behaviour of its citizens if we do not know their history.

Dugald Stewart's concept of conjectural history has wide application within the Scottish Enlightenment, as witness the range of topics on which the literati produced conjectural histories, topics including the earliest forms of society and of government, the religious beliefs of ancient peoples, early interpretations of the motions of heavenly bodies, and the origin of languages. Granted that these topics concern matters beyond the experience of the literati, how did they know so much about them? As regards human culture of the prehistoric past, we do the best we can by asking ourselves how beings such as ourselves would have behaved given certain circumstances. We thus argue from what we know about at first hand, namely human nature as manifested in ourselves and in those we know at first hand, to what we do not know about at first hand or by testimony. As Dugald Stewart was aware, this procedure makes a large assumption which has to be brought into the open, and which he formulates as follows: it has 'long been received as an incontrovertible logical maxim that the capacities of the human mind have been in all ages the same, and that the diversity of phenomena exhibited by our species is the result merely of the different circumstances in which men are placed'.[1]

The significance of this maxim for conjectural history is obvious. If we do not suppose the capacities of the human mind to be invariant through time and space we cannot calculate the behaviour of people in other times and places. Without the support of Stewart's 'incontrovertible logical maxim', conjectural history would be pure guesswork. But how is the support itself to be supported? On what interpretation, if any, is the maxim true? One problem concerns the danger of assuming the maxim in the course of trying to prove it. The question whether human nature is invariant appears to be amenable to experiential confirmation. We look to see how people behave in a wide variety of circumstances, and note the regularities of behaviour. The problem is however that, in relation to the space and time in which the human race has lived, any individual person has a very narrow experience of people, and accordingly is tempted to supplement this meagre experience with facts which are significantly speculative or conjectural. But conjecture which has any sort of scientifically respectable basis can be made only on the assumption that human nature is invariant – and we have come full circle.

In light of this problem it is not surprising that our conjectural historians delved into reports of primitive peoples in the Americas, Polynesia and Asia. The American tribes were treated as a sort of window onto the distant, the prehistoric, past. But this employment of the data about native American tribes involves conjecture. What is the evidence that modern primitive people are like ancient primitive people? Perhaps, after all, the primitives of fifty thousand years ago were as unlike the native Americans

---

1 Dugald Stewart, *Dissertation: Exhibiting the Progress of Metaphysical, Ethical and Political Philosophy, since the Revival of Letters in Europe*, in Dugald Stewart, *The Collected Works*, ed. W. Hamilton, vol. 1, p. 69

as the native Americans were unlike the Scottish literati. Let us say therefore that the maxim on which conjectural history is based is less an 'incontrovertible logical maxim' than a scientific hypothesis or theory. On an obvious interpretation it is itself a piece of conjecture. Whether, and how far, we should trust it depends in part on the level of generality or abstraction of 'the capacities of the human mind' that is at issue when Stewart says of them that they are always the same. The more content is poured into the concept of human nature or of 'capacities of the human mind' the less plausible the hypothesis becomes.

Regarding Hume's famous remark: 'Mankind are so much the same, in all times and places, that history informs us of nothing new or strange in this particular',[1] if the sameness to which this dictum refers concerns the fact that we usually deliberate before acting, that we aim to do what, in our judgment, is good, and so on for other equally high-level generalisations, then the claim is no doubt plausible. But those generalisations are of little use in enabling us to determine how people in the distant past, in societies that were no doubt radically different from ours, would have responded to given circumstances. Knowing that they would have deliberated and would then have acted for what they conceived to be the best, tells us nothing if we do not know what in particular they conceived to be good. And in the absence of historical records how are we to gain knowledge of these things? We can only conjecture, but conjecture yields only opinion, not historical knowledge.

It might however be wondered to what extent Dugald Stewart, one of the great biographers of the Scottish Enlightenment, is interested in historical knowledge. He set a hare running with his notorious remark: 'In most cases, it is of more importance to ascertain the progress that is most simple, than the progress that is most agreeable to fact; for paradoxical as the proposition may appear, it is certainly true, that the real progress is not always the most natural' (excerpt 39). That Stewart is apparently dismissive of what is 'most agreeable to fact' surely indicates an unhistorical approach to history. But Stewart is concerned as much with *why* things happened as with what happened. It is not that he despises the facts, but rather that individual facts are not interesting; what are interesting are facts as perceived within a context that explains them. Once we have the explanation we can give an infinitely

---

1 Hume, *An Enquiry concerning Human Understanding*, section 8, part 1, p. 83

richer description of the facts. A description of what happened can make clear that the event in question is an effect of something, and the description of the event can therefore make reference to causal factors. The more detailed the description of the cause the richer the account thereby given of the effect itself.

Explanations of human acts depend crucially upon the perspicuous deployment of a theory of human nature, including an account of the way human passions, prompted by particular circumstances, lead to particular sorts of act rather than others. When we know universal truths on these matters we can start explaining past events, and thus see the universal truth embodied in the singular events. Historical knowledge worthy of the name is not knowledge of 'one damn fact after another'; it is knowledge of the explanation of those facts and therefore of the universal in the singular. When Stewart affirms that it is more important to ascertain the progress that is most simple rather than the progress that is most agreeable to fact, he is saying not that the truth does not interest him, but that the important thing for the historian is to bring the facts under general principles. Piling on the details, giving a more and more complicated description of something, is pointless unless we bring to bear the principles that enable us to understand the event. Once we understand it, we can say what is important in the event and what is not. In that sense, we are in a position to simplify the picture by omitting the elements or features that do not contribute to historical understanding. This is a thoroughly philosophical approach to history, and is an illustration of the fact that, in the Scottish Enlightenment, philosophy was in the driving seat.

It is also plainly in the driving seat in Adam Smith's discussion, in his *Lectures on Rhetoric and Belles Lettres*, of the relation between historical writing and the investigation of human nature (see excerpt 38). There are, according to Smith, distinctive features of the style of historical writing that distinguish it from other styles, particularly from the rhetorical and the didactic. The contrast is important, but equally it has to be borne in mind that for Smith 'narration makes a considerable part of every oration', and that by 'narration' he means the recounting of historical events. The orator puts his rhetoric to work in the light of his account of past events, and here Smith has in mind particularly the rhetoric of the politician speaking before a political assembly and of the barrister or advocate addressing a jury. Both types of person are concerned with what has happened and what should be done about it, what political action should now be taken and what verdict the jury should reach. In short, the political decision and the verdict both have to be determined in the light of history. It is not surprising therefore that Smith judges it necessary to explain the historical style before expounding in detail the rhetorical.

The difference between the two styles lies in the role of persuasion. Persuasion can make its mark on a literary composition in at least two ways. Smith contrasts the speaker's intention to give every argument its due weight with his intention to persuade, by stating as strongly as he can the arguments that support the position he espouses, while at the same time making light of those arguments which support the opposite position. In the former case we have an example of didactic composition, and in the latter we have an example of rhetoric. In the case of didactic composition the proof 'is a strict one applied to our reason and sound judgment'. In the case of rhetoric the proof is 'adapted to affect our passion'. The two styles have this in common, that they are each in two parts, one part being a proposition which is laid down and the other being the proof offered in order to persuade us of the proposition, whether by appeal to reason alone or to our passions. A composition in the historical style does not answer to either description, since it has one part only; it is a narration of facts, and does not include proofs brought to bear in support of the claim that the facts are indeed facts and not fictions. Of course historical writings often contain evidence to support the given account of events, but the proofs are not part of the narration.

Historians will no doubt baulk at the distinction being made here, and say that, on the contrary, proof is an essential part of their stock in trade, and that they are not in the business of stating dogmatically: 'This is what happened', for historians are as committed to saying what the evidence is for the claim that this *is* what happened as they are to saying what happened. But the dispute here is terminological only. Smith makes a distinction between saying what happened and saying what the evidence is, and states that a composition that performs both tasks is a didactic or rhetorical composition, and one that performs the first task only is historical.

Of course the fact that historical narration does not include evidence does not imply that truth is not important to it. It aims at the truth, not merely at entertainment. As Smith bluntly puts it: 'The facts must be real.' But it is not enough that they be real. They must be facts about human beings, human beings being special in view of the fullness with which we can enter sympathetically into their positions. Relying on psychological insights that he develops in detail in *The Theory of Moral Sentiments* (see excerpt 7), Smith remarks: 'We enter into their misfortunes, grieve when they grieve, rejoice when they rejoice, and in a word feel for them in some respect as if we ourselves were in the same condition.' The historical style is not well served if no explanation is given for these human facts, explanations in terms of causes. Smith hints at a practical agenda in saying that the causes point out to us by what manner and method we may produce similar good effects or avoid similar bad ones.

That practical consideration regarding causes is matched by another, equally practical, though satisfying a different agenda. In his *History of Astronomy* (see excerpt 44) Smith discusses the motivation for thinking scientifically about the world, and his discussion centres on the three states of surprise, wonder and admiration. We are full of expectations as we look out upon the world. We see what we see and, in the light of past experience, that is, from custom or habit formed by experience, we have expectations about what will happen next. The mind moves smoothly from the present event to an idea of its natural successor. Occasionally our expectation is proved false, and we feel a gap between the first event and the surprising second event. What fits into the gap is something we need to know in order to understand why our expectation was not satisfied. The good scientist is good at plugging that gap, by discovering the missing part of the causal story. In this sense Smith sees the historian as a scientist, delivering up insights into human nature, and Smith's 'history of historians' (see the third of the three lectures in excerpt 38) is best read in that light.

Human nature was the subject not only of the philosophers and historians of the Scottish Enlightenment, but also of its portrait painters. The greatest of the period, Allan Ramsay (1713–84) and Henry Raeburn (1756–1823), have not been matched by any other Scottish portraitists, though David Martin (1737–97) who was Raeburn's teacher, Archibald Skirving (1749–1819), and George Watson (1767–1837) at the end of the period, produced very fine portraits; as also did James Tassie (1735–99) working in the medium of glass-paste and producing on his medallions some of the most enduring images of the age. Unlike the philosophers, who spoke of human nature in respect of its universal qualities, the painters were intent upon representing human nature as individuated in the characters of their sitters in all their immediacy. Hume's sociability and the richness of his inner life are conveyed in the finest image we have of him, a portrait by Allan Ramsay of 1766. Raeburn likewise produced strongly evocative portraits of major figures of the Enlightenment, such as Robertson, Reid, Ferguson, Hutton and Dugald Stewart. He not only painted the philosophers; he knew them personally and was familiar with their writings, including their writings on perception. There is evidence that his art was influenced by those writings, particularly Reid's (see excerpt 13) concerning the painter's need to paint not what is signified by the various patterns of light and shade, but instead the light and shade themselves and to leave it to the spectator to interpret the patterns that the painter has put on canvas.[1]

It is demonstrable therefore that human nature was investigated from philosophical, linguistic, historical and aesthetic perspectives. It can also be shown that there was a determined effort to carry out the investigation in what may be called a scientific spirit, and as far as possible to employ the methods of the natural sciences in the course of the investigations of human nature. When Hume spoke of a science of man, he was thinking of human beings as part of nature, and therefore most appropriately to be investigated by the means proper to the study of nature; hence his description of the *Treatise of Human Nature* as 'an attempt to introduce the experimental method of reasoning into moral subjects'. In a broad sense of the term 'scientific' Hume's approach was therefore scientific. In this respect he was followed by Smith, Reid, Millar, Ferguson, and many others, who were of course familiar with scientific methods of enquiry and scientific perspectives, through their close and active association with scientists such as Cullen, Black, Watt and Hutton. The Scottish Enlightenment was a wondrous performance, a moment when universal features of the human spirit, finding their voice as rarely before, burst forth upon Western culture with an awesome intensity. Hume's judgment was impeccable: 'I believe this is the historical Age and this [Scotland] the historical Nation.'[2]

1 Duncan Macmillan, *Scottish Art 1460–1990*, pp. 157–8
2 Letter to William Strahan, August 1770, printed in
  David Hume, *The Letters of David Hume*, ed. J. Y. T.
  Greig, vol.2, p. 230

PART II
HUMAN NATURE

ONE

DAVID HUME
The Science of Man

. . . even the rabble without doors may judge from the noise and clamour, which they hear, that all goes not well within.

The noise and clamour to which Hume refers is that of philosophers in dispute. His rejection of the systems under dispute is based on a close investigation of the premises and inferences of those systems. His aim is to build a philosophy upon an entirely new foundation, whose starting point is human nature and whose method is scientific. Since he proposes to employ a scientific method, and since it will be used in the investigation of human nature, it is not surprising that Hume describes his goal as a 'science of man'.

It is plain that, for Hume, the science of man that he proposes to construct requires a methodology which is equally applicable to other sciences, for example, physics. If we are to study the human mind we require 'careful and exact experiments, and the observation of those particular effects, which result from its different circumstances and situations'. Hume, impressed with a scientific methodology which, in the hands of Sir Isaac Newton and Robert Boyle, had produced spectacular successes in other fields, proposed to apply the same methodology to the study of man.

There are, as Hume acknowledges, limits to the scientific enquiry into the human mind, for we can never discover the 'ultimate original qualities' of human nature. But this does not mark off the science of man from the scientific study of the rest of nature, for we can never discover the ultimate original qualities of anything whatever in the order of nature. To discover these qualities it is necessary to go beyond experience, but, as Hume puts the point in an affirmation of one of his basic principles, no one 'can go beyond experience, or establish any principles which are not founded on that authority'.

Hume emphasises the unitariness of the sciences. His words: 'we in effect propose a compleat system of the sciences' have to be taken seriously. And the unifying principle for the sciences is human nature itself, the subject of the *Treatise*.

A.B.

A Treatise of Human Nature

Introduction

Nothing is more usual and more natural for those, who pretend to discover any thing new to the world in philosophy and the sciences, than to insinuate the praises of their own systems, by decrying all those, which have been advanced before them. And indeed were they content with lamenting that ignorance, which we still lie under in the most important questions, that can come before the tribunal of human reason, there are few, who have an acquaintance with the sciences, that would not readily agree with them. 'Tis easy for one of judgment and learning, to perceive the weak foundation even of those systems, which have obtained the greatest credit, and have carried their pretensions highest to accurate and profound reasoning. Principles taken upon trust, consequences lamely deduced from them, want of coherence in the parts, and of evidence in the whole, these are every where to be met with in the systems of the most eminent philosophers, and seem to have drawn disgrace upon philosophy itself.

Nor is there requir'd such profound knowledge to discover the present imperfect condition of the sciences, but even the rabble without doors may judge from the noise and clamour, which they hear, that all goes not well within. There is nothing which is not the subject of debate, and in which men of learning are not of contrary opinions. The most trivial question escapes not our controversy, and in the most momentous we are not able to give any certain decision. Disputes are multiplied, as if every thing was uncertain; and these disputes are managed with the greatest warmth, as if every thing was certain. Amidst all this bustle 'tis not reason, which carries the prize, but eloquence; and no man needs ever despair of gaining proselytes to the most extravagant hypothesis, who has art enough to represent it in any favourable colours. The victory is not gained by the men at arms, who manage the pike and the sword; but by the trumpeters, drummers, and musicians of the army.

From hence in my opinion arises that common prejudice against metaphysical reasonings of all kinds, even amongst those, who profess themselves scholars, and have a just value for every other part of literature. By metaphysical reasonings, they do not understand those on any particular branch of science, but every kind of argument, which is any way abstruse, and requires some attention to be comprehended. We have so often lost our labour in such researches, that we commonly reject them without hesitation, and resolve, if we must for ever be a prey to errors and delusions, that they shall at least be natural and entertaining. And indeed nothing but the most determined scepticism, along with a great degree of indolence, can justify this aversion to metaphysics. For if truth be at all within the reach of human capacity, 'tis certain it must lie very deep and abstruse; and to hope we shall arrive at it without pains, while the greatest geniuses have failed with the utmost pains, must certainly be esteemed sufficiently vain and presumptuous. I pretend to no such advantage in the philosophy I am going to unfold, and would esteem it a strong presumption against it, were it so very easy and obvious.

'Tis evident, that all the sciences have a relation, greater or less, to human nature; and that however wide any of them may seem to run from it, they still return back by one passage or another. Even *Mathematics, Natural Philosophy, and Natural Religion*, are in some measure dependent on the science of Man; since they lie under the cognizance of men, and are judged of by their powers and faculties. 'Tis impossible to tell what changes and improvements we might make in these sciences were we thoroughly acquainted with the extent and force of human understanding, and cou'd explain the nature of the ideas we employ, and of the operations we perform in our reasonings. And these improvements are the more to be hoped for in natural religion, as it is not content with instructing us in the nature of superior powers, but carries its views farther, to their disposition towards us, and our duties towards them; and consequently we ourselves are not only the beings, that reason, but also one of the objects, concerning which we reason.

If therefore the sciences of Mathematics, Natural Philosophy, and Natural Religion, have such a dependence on the knowledge of man, what may be expected in the other sciences, whose connexion with human nature is more close and intimate? The sole end of logic is to explain the principles and operations of our reasoning faculty, and the nature of our ideas: morals and criticism regard our tastes and sentiments: and politics consider men as united in society, and dependent on each other. In these four sciences of *Logic, Morals, Criticism, and Politics*, is comprehended almost every thing, which it can any way import us to be acquainted with, or which can tend either to the improvement or ornament of the human mind.

Here then is the only expedient, from which we can hope for success in our philosophical researches, to leave the tedious lingring method, which we have hitherto followed, and instead of taking now and then a castle or village on the frontier, to march up directly to the capital or center of these sciences, to human nature itself; which being once masters of, we may every where else hope for an easy victory. From this station we may extend our conquests over all those sciences, which more intimately concern human life, and may afterwards proceed at leisure to discover more fully those, which are the objects of pure curiosity. There is no question of importance, whose decision is not compriz'd in the science of man; and there is none, which can be decided with any certainty, before we become acquainted with that science. In pretending therefore to explain the principles of human nature, we in effect propose a compleat system of the sciences, built on a foundation almost entirely new, and the only one upon which they can stand with any security.

And as the science of man is the only solid foundation for the other sciences, so the only solid foundation we can give to this science itself must be laid on experience and observation. 'Tis no astonishing reflection to consider, that the application of experimental philosophy to moral subjects should come after that to natural at the distance of above a whole century; since we find in fact, that there was about the same interval betwixt the origins of these sciences; and that reckoning from Thales to Socrates, the space of time is nearly equal to that betwixt my Lord Bacon[1] and some late philosophers in *England*, who have begun to put the science of man on a new footing, and have engaged the attention, and excited the curiosity of the public. So true it is, that however other nations may rival us in poetry, and excel us in some other agreeable arts, the improvements in reason and philosophy can only be owing to a land of toleration and of liberty.

Nor ought we to think, that this latter improvement in the science of man will do less honour to our native country than the former in natural philosophy, but ought rather to esteem it a greater glory, upon account of the greater importance of that science, as well as the necessity it lay under of such a reformation. For to me it seems evident, that the essence of the mind being equally unknown to us with that of external bodies,

1 Mr. *Locke*, my Lord *Shaftsbury*, Dr. *Mandeville*, Mr. *Hutchinson*, Dr. *Butler*, &c.

it must be equally impossible to form any notion of its powers and qualities otherwise than from careful and exact experiments, and the observation of those particular effects, which result from its different circumstances and situations. And tho' we must endeavour to render all our principles as universal as possible, by tracing up our experiments to the utmost, and explaining all effects from the simplest and fewest causes, 'tis still certain we cannot go beyond experience; and any hypothesis, that pretends to discover the ultimate original qualities of human nature, ought at first to be rejected as presumptuous and chimerical.

I do not think a philosopher, who would apply himself so earnestly to the explaining the ultimate principles of the soul, would show himself a great master in that very science of human nature, which he pretends to explain, or very knowing in what is naturally satisfactory to the mind of man. For nothing is more certain, than that despair has almost the same effect upon us with enjoyment, and that we are no sooner acquainted with the impossibility of satisfying any desire, than the desire itself vanishes. When we see, that we have arrived at the utmost extent of human reason, we sit down contented; tho' we be perfectly satisfied in the main of our ignorance, and perceive that we can give no reason for our most general and most refined principles, beside our experience of their reality; which is the reason of the mere vulgar, and what it required no study at first to have discovered for the most particular and most extraordinary phænomenon. And as this impossibility of making any farther progress is enough to satisfy the reader, so the writer may derive a more delicate satisfaction from the free confession of his ignorance, and from his prudence in avoiding that error, into which so many have fallen, of imposing their conjectures and hypotheses on the world for the most certain principles. When this mutual contentment and satisfaction can be obtained betwixt the master and scholar, I know not what more we can require of our philosophy.

But if this impossibility of explaining ultimate principles should be esteemed a defect in the science of man, I will venture to affirm, that 'tis a defect common to it with all the sciences, and all the arts, in which we can employ ourselves, whether they be such as are cultivated in the schools of the philosophers, or practised in the shops of the meanest artizans. None of them can go beyond experience, or establish any principles which are not founded on that authority. Moral philosophy has, indeed, this peculiar disadvantage, which is not found in natural, that in collecting its experiments, it cannot make them purposely, with premeditation, and after such a manner as to satisfy itself concerning every particular difficulty which may arise. When I am at a loss to know the effects of one body upon another in any situation, I need only put them in that situation, and observe what results from it. But should I endeavour to clear up after the same manner any doubt in moral philosophy, by placing myself in the same case with that which I consider, 'tis evident this reflection and premeditation would so disturb the operation of my natural principles, as must render it impossible to form any just conclusion from the phænomenon. We must therefore glean up our experiments in this science from a cautious observation of human life, and take them as they appear in the common course of the world, by men's behaviour in company, in affairs, and in their pleasures. Where experiments of this kind are judiciously collected and compared, we may hope to establish on them a science, which will not be inferior in certainty, and will be much superior in utility to any other of human comprehension.

Source: David Hume, *A Treatise of Human Nature*, ed. L. A. Selby-Bigge, 2nd edn by P. H. Nidditch, Oxford 1975, pp. xiii–xix

TWO

DUGALD STEWART
The Unity of the Sciences

Dugald Stewart takes up the theme, stressed in excerpt I, of the unity of the sciences and the centrality of the science of man. But he develops the theme in a way not found in Hume's *Treatise*, though Hume would probably have approved of the way Stewart handles it.

The starting point is the fact that all human pursuits, whether speculative or active, are connected with the science of the human mind, for our power of understanding is at work in all our thinking and acting, and the power of understanding is a proper object of investigation in the science of the human mind. We relate to the world as scientists trying to understand it and as agents trying to change it, and in an obvious sense understanding must precede acts of agency. For in order to act on the world a person must have a concept of how the world is and of how it ought to be and of what has to be done to transform what ought to be into what is, and he cannot have that (or any other) concept without having a power of understanding. It is plain to Stewart that, in our search for an understanding of our world, an insight into the power of understanding itself can only be of help to us, never a hindrance.

Stewart gives this point a distinctive twist. He notices that scientists are not content with knowing only one corner of science, but on the contrary are curious about other parts also. And their curiosity is fed by the recognition that there is indeed a unity of science of such a kind that knowledge of one part can make a helpful difference to one's thinking in other areas. This point has immediate implications for education; in particular it indicates the need for a general as opposed to a specialist education. A century and a half before George Davie's *Democratic Intellect* was stressing the merits of the generalist approach in Scottish education as against the specialist approach in English education, Dugald

Stewart had already placed generalism in education on a firm philosophical basis.

In all this, Stewart has a large agenda. Writing of 'the great aim of an enlightened and benevolent philosophy', he tells us that it is 'to diffuse, as widely as possible, that degree of cultivation which may enable the bulk of a people to possess all the intellectual and moral improvement of which their nature is susceptible'. There is, of course, a view which has persisted through Western philosophy that what we should aim at is happiness, and a question naturally arises as to whether a generalist or specialist education best serves this aim. Stewart, alive to the dangers of a 'partial and injudicious education', argues that a specialist education can actually diminish an individual's happiness, by failing to respect the holistic nature of the mind. It produces a lop-sided individual who is further removed from intellectual perfection than is a person who has not progressed so far but has progressed on a wider front.

A further advantage of the philosophical study of the powers of the mind is, on Stewart's view, that such a study could constitute a bulwark against scepticism. The more liberal spirit of enquiry of enlightened times led to an attack on prejudice and superstition, but the enlightened movement went too far by attacking truths as well as falsehoods. Most especially it noted the power of education to mould minds and concluded that through and through we are the product of the education system. Yet, as Stewart argues, we cannot possibly be nothing more than products of our education, for if we did not have certain mental powers as original features of our constitution, we would simply not be educable. Stewart was as much interested in what the pupil contributes to his own education as in what the teacher contributes.

A.B.

Of the Utility of
the Philosophy of the Human Mind

I It has been often remarked, that there is a *mutual connexion between the different arts and sciences:* and that the improvements which are made in one branch of human knowledge, frequently throw light on others, to which it has apparently a very remote relation. The modern discoveries in astronomy and in pure mathematics, have contributed to bring the art of navigation to a degree of perfection formerly unknown. The rapid progress which has been lately made in astronomy, anatomy, and botany, has been chiefly owing to the aid which these sciences have received from the art of the optician.

Although, however, the different departments of science and of art mutually reflect light on each other, it is not always necessary either for the philosopher or the artist to aim at the acquisition of general knowledge. Both of them may safely take many principles for granted, without being able to demonstrate their truth. A seaman, though ignorant of mathematics, may apply, with correctness and dexterity, the rules for finding the longitude. An astronomer or a botanist, though ignorant of optics, may avail himself of the use of the telescope or the microscope.

These observations are daily exemplified in the case of the artist; who has seldom either inclination or leisure to speculate concerning the principles of his art. It is rarely, however, we meet with a man of science who has confined his studies wholly to one branch of knowledge. That curiosity, which he has been accustomed to indulge in the course of his favourite pursuit, will naturally extend itself to every remarkable object which falls under his observation, and can scarcely fail to be a source of perpetual dissatisfaction to his mind, till it has been so far gratified as to enable him to explain all the various phenomena which his professional habits are every day presenting to his view.

II *All the pursuits of life are connected with the study of the Intellectual Powers.* – As every particular science is in this manner connected with others, to which it naturally directs the attention, so *all the pursuits of life*, whether they terminate in speculation or action, *are connected with* that general science which has *the human mind* for its object. The powers of the understanding are instruments which all men employ; and his curiosity must be small indeed, who passes through life in a total ignorance of faculties which his wants and necessities force him habitually to exercise, and which so remarkably distinguish man from the lower animals. The active principles of our nature, which, by their various modifications and combinations, give rise to all the moral differences among men, are fitted, in a still higher degree, if possible, to interest those who are either disposed to reflect on their own characters, or to observe, with attention, the characters of others. The phenomena resulting from these faculties and principles of the mind, are every moment soliciting our notice, and open to our examination a field of discovery as inexhaustible as the phenomena of the material world, and exhibiting not less striking marks of divine wisdom.

III *Advantages of a successful analysis of them.* – While all the sciences and all the pursuits of life have this common tendency to lead our inquiries to the philosophy of human nature, *this* last *branch of knowledge borrows its principles from no other science whatever*. Hence there is (1) something in the study of it which is peculiarly *gratifying* to a reflecting and inquisitive mind, and (2) something in the conclusions to which it leads on which the mind rests with peculiar *satisfaction*. (3) Till once our opinions are in some degree fixed with respect to it, we abandon ourselves, with reluctance, to particular scientific investigations; and (4) on the other hand, a general knowledge of such of its principles as are most fitted to excite the curiosity not only *prepares us for engaging in other pursuits* with more liberal and comprehensive views, but *leaves us at liberty to prosecute* them with a more undivided and concentrated attention.

It is not, however, merely as a subject of speculative curiosity that the principles of the human mind deserve a careful examination. The advantages to be expected from a successful analysis of it are various; and some of them of such importance, as to render it astonishing, that, amidst all the success with which the subordinate sciences have been cultivated, this, which comprehends the principles of all of them, should be still suffered to remain in its infancy.

I shall endeavour to illustrate a few of these advantages, beginning with what appears to me to be the most important of any; (5) the light which a philosophical analysis of the principles of the mind would necessarily throw on the subjects of intellectual and moral education.

IV *The most essential objects of education* are the two following: *First*, to cultivate all the various principles of our nature, both speculative and active, in such a manner as to bring them to the greatest perfection of which they are susceptible; and, *secondly*, by watching over the impressions and associations which the mind receives in early life, to secure it against the influence of prevailing errors; and, as far as possible, to engage its prepossessions on the side of truth. It is only upon a philosophical analysis of the mind, that a systematical plan can be founded for the accomplishment of either of these purposes.

There are few individuals whose education has been conducted in every respect with attention and judgment. Almost every man of reflection is conscious, when he arrives at maturity, of many defects in his mental powers, and of many inconvenient habits, which might have been prevented or remedied in his infancy or youth. Such a *consciousness* is the first step towards improvement; and the person who feels it, if he is possessed of resolution and steadiness, will not scruple to begin, even in advanced years, a new course of education for himself. The degree of reflection and observation, indeed, which is necessary for this purpose, cannot be expected from any one at a very early period of life, as *these are the last powers of the mind which unfold themselves;* but it is never too late to think of the improvement of our faculties; and much progress may be made in the art of applying them successfully to their proper objects, or in obviating the inconveniences resulting from their imperfection, not only in manhood, but in old age.

It is not, however, to the mistakes of our early instructors, that all our intellectual defects are to be ascribed. There is no profession or pursuit which has not habits peculiar to itself, and which does not leave some powers of the mind dormant, while it exercises and improves the rest. If we wish, therefore, to cultivate the mind to the extent of its capacity, we must not rest satisfied with that employment which its faculties receive from our particular situation in life. It is not in the awkward and professional form of *a mechanic*, who has strengthened particular muscles of his body by the habits of his trade, that we are to look for the perfection of our animal nature; neither is it among men of confined pursuits, whether speculative or active, that we are to expect to find the human mind in its highest state of cultivation. A variety of exercises is necessary to preserve the animal frame in vigour and beauty; and a variety of those occupations which literature and science afford, added to a promiscuous intercourse with the world, in the habits of conversation and business, is no less necessary for the improvement of the understanding. I acknowledge, that there are some professions in which a man of very confined acquisitions may arrive at the first eminence, and in which *he will* perhaps *be* the *more likely to excel, the more he has concentrated the whole force of his mind to one particular object.* But such a person, however distinguished in his own sphere, is educated merely to be a literary artisan, and neither attains the perfection nor the happiness of his nature. 'That education only can be considered as complete and generous, which' (in the language of Milton) 'fits a man to perform justly, skilfully, and magnanimously, all the offices, both private and public, of peace and of war.' – *Tractate of Education.*

I hope it will not be supposed, from the foregoing observations, that they are meant to recommend an indiscriminate attention to all the objects of speculation and of action. Nothing can be more evident, than the necessity of limiting the field of our exertion, if we wish to benefit society by our labours. But it is perfectly consistent with the most intense application to our favourite pursuit, to cultivate that general acquaintance with letters and with the world which may be sufficient to enlarge the mind, and to preserve it from any danger of contracting the pedantry of a particular profession. In many cases, (as was already remarked) the sciences reflect light on each other; and the general acquisitions which we have made in other pursuits, may furnish us with useful helps for the farther prosecution of our own. But even in those instances in which the case is otherwise, and in which these liberal accomplishments must be purchased by the sacrifice of a part of our professional eminence, the acquisition of them will amply repay any loss we may sustain. It ought not to be the leading object of any one, to become an eminent metaphysician, mathematician, or poet, but to render himself happy as an individual, and an agreeable, a respectable, and a useful member of society. A man who loses his sight, improves the sensibility of his touch; but who would consent, for such a recompense, to part with the pleasures which he receives from the eye?

V *Farther advantages resulting from a knowledge of our capacities.* – It is almost unnecessary for me to remark, how much individuals would be assisted in the proper and liberal culture of the mind, if they were previously led to take a comprehensive survey of human nature in all its parts; of its various faculties, and powers, and sources of enjoyment, and of the effects which are produced on these principles by particular situations. It is such a knowledge alone of the capacities of the mind, that (1) can enable a person to judge of his own acquisitions, and (2) to employ the most effectual means for supplying his defects and removing his inconvenient habits. (3) Without some degree of it, every man is in danger of contracting bad habits before he is aware, and (4) of suffering some of his powers to go to decay, for want of proper exercise.

VI *True principles on which Education should be conducted considered*. – If the business of early education were more thoroughly and more generally understood, it would be less necessary for individuals, when they arrive at maturity, to form plans of improvement for themselves. But education never can be systematically directed to its proper objects, till we have obtained, not only an accurate analysis of the general principles of our nature, and an account of the most important laws which regulate their operation; but an explanation of the various modifications and combinations of these principles, which produce that diversity of talents, genius, and character, we observe among men. To instruct youth in the languages and in the sciences is comparatively of little importance, if we are inattentive to the habits they acquire, and are not careful in giving to all their different faculties, and all their different principles of action, a proper degree of employment. Abstracting entirely from the culture of their moral powers, how extensive and difficult is the business of conducting their intellectual improvement! To watch over the associations which they form in their tender years; to give them early habits of mental activity; to rouse their curiosity, and to direct it to proper objects; to exercise their ingenuity and invention: to cultivate in their minds a turn for speculation, and at the same time preserve their attention alive to the objects around them; to awaken their sensibilities to the beauties of nature, and to inspire them with a relish for intellectual enjoyment; – these form but a part of the business of education, and yet the execution even of this part requires an acquaintance with the general principles of our nature, which seldom falls to the share of those to whom the instruction of youth is commonly entrusted. Nor will such a theoretical knowledge of the human mind as I have now described, be always sufficient in practice. An uncommon degree of sagacity is frequently requisite in order to accommodate general rules to particular tempers and characters. In whatever way we choose to account for it, whether by original organization or by the operation of moral causes in very early infancy, no fact can be more undeniable, than that there are important differences discernible in the minds of children, previous to that period at which, in general, their intellectual education commences. There is, too, a certain hereditary character (whether resulting from physical constitution, or caught from imitation and the influence of situation) which appears remarkably in particular families. One race, for a succession of generations, is distinguished by a genius for the abstract sciences, while it is deficient in vivacity, in imagination, and in taste: another is no less distinguished for wit, and gaiety, and fancy; while it appears incapable of patient attention or of profound research. The system of education which is proper to be adopted in particular cases, *ought* undoubtedly *to have* some *reference to these circumstances*, and to be calculated, as much as possible, to develope and to cherish those intellectual and active principles in which a natural deficiency is most to be apprehended. Montesquieu, and other speculative politicians, have insisted much on the reference which education and laws should have to climate. I shall not take upon me to say how far their conclusions on this subject are just; but I am fully persuaded, that there is a foundation in philosophy and good sense for accommodating, at a very early period of life, the education of individuals to those particular turns of mind to which, from hereditary propensities, or from moral situation, they may be presumed to have a natural tendency.

VII *Why such different opinions upon this subject.* – There are few subjects more hackneyed than that of education; and yet there is *none, upon which the opinions of the world are still more divided*. Nor is this surprising; for most of those who have speculated concerning it, have confined their attention chiefly to incidental questions about the comparative advantages of public or private instruction, or the utility of particular languages or sciences; without attempting a previous examination of those faculties and principles of the mind, which it is the great object of education to improve. Many excellent detached observations, indeed, both on the intellectual and moral powers, are to be collected from the writings of ancient and modern authors; but I do not know, that in any language an attempt has been made to analyse and illustrate the principles of human nature, in order to lay a philosophical foundation for their proper culture.

I have even heard some very ingenious and intelligent men dispute the propriety of so systematical a plan of instruction. The most successful and splendid exertions, both in the sciences and arts, (it has been frequently remarked,) have been made by individuals, in whose minds the seeds of genius were allowed to shoot up, wild and free; while, from the most careful and skilful tuition, seldom anything results above mediocrity. I shall not, at present enter into any discussions with respect to the certainty of the fact on which this opinion is founded. Supposing the fact to be completely established, it must still be remembered, that *originality of genius* does not always imply vigour and comprehensiveness, and liberality of mind; and that it is desirable only, in so far as it is compatible with these more valuable qualities. I have already hinted, that there are some pursuits, in which, as they require the exertions only of a small number of our faculties, an individual, who has a natural turn for them, will be more likely to distinguish himself, by being suffered to follow his original bias, than if his attention were distracted by a more liberal course of study. But wherever such men are to be found, they must be considered, on the most favourable supposition, as having sacrificed, to a certain degree, the perfection and the happiness of their nature, to the amusement or instruction of others. It is, too, in times of general darkness and barbarism, that what is commonly called originality of genius most frequently appears; and surely the great aim of an enlightened and benevolent philosophy, is not to rear a small number of individuals, who may be regarded as prodigies in an ignorant and admiring age, but to diffuse, as widely as possible, that degree of cultivation which may enable the bulk of a people to possess all the intellectual and moral improvement of which their nature is susceptible. 'Original genius' (says Voltaire) 'occurs but seldom in a nation where the literary taste is formed. The number of cultivated minds which there abound, like the trees in a thick and flourishing forest, prevent any single individual from rearing his head far above the rest. Where trade is in few hands, we meet with a small number of overgrown fortunes in the midst of a general poverty: in proportion as it extends, opulence becomes general, and great fortunes rare. It is, precisely, because there is at present much light, and much cultivation, in France, that we are led to complain of the want of superior genius.'

VIII *Objection to the advantages of Education answered.* – To what purpose, indeed, it may be said all this labour? Is not the importance of every thing to man, to be ultimately estimated by its tendency to promote his *happiness?* And is not our daily experience sufficient to convince us, that this is, in general, *by no means proportioned to the culture which his nature has received?* – Nay, is there not some ground for suspecting, that the lower orders of men enjoy, on the whole, a more enviable condition, than their more enlightened and refined superiors?

The truth, I apprehend, is, that happiness, in so far as it arises from the mind itself, will be always proportioned to the degree of perfection which its powers have attained; but that in cultivating these powers, with a view to this most important of all objects, it is essentially necessary that such a degree of attention be bestowed on all of them, as may preserve them in that state of relative strength, which appears to be agreeable to the intentions of nature. In consequence of an *exclusive* attention to the culture of the imagination, the taste, the reasoning faculty, or any of the active principles, it is possible that the pleasure of human life may be diminished, or its pains increased; but the inconveniences which are experienced in such cases, are not to be ascribed to education, but to a *partial* and *injudicious education*. In such cases, it is possible, that the poet, the metaphysician, or the man of taste and refinement, may appear to disadvantage, when compared with the vulgar; for such is the benevolent appointment of Providence with respect to the lower orders, that, although not one principle of their nature be completely unfolded, the whole of these principles preserve among themselves that balance which is favourable to the tranquillity of their minds, and to a prudent and steady conduct in the limited sphere which is assigned to them, far more completely, than in those of their superiors, whose education has been conducted on an erroneous or imperfect system: but all this, far from weakening the force of the foregoing observations, only serves to demonstrate how impossible it always will be, to form a rational plan for the improvement of the mind, without an accurate and comprehensive knowledge of the principles of the human constitution.

The remarks which have been already made, are sufficient to illustrate the *dangerous consequences* which are likely to result from *a partial and injudicious cultivation of the mind;* and, at the same time, to point out the *utility of the intellectual philosophy,* in enabling us to preserve a proper balance among all its various faculties, principles of action, and capacities of enjoyment. Many additional observations might be offered, on the tendency which an accurate analysis of its powers might, probably, have to suggest rules for their further improvement, and for a more successful application of them to their proper purposes: but this subject I shall not prosecute at present, as the illustration of it is one of the leading objects of the following work. – That the memory, the imagination, or the reasoning faculty, are to be instantly strengthened in consequence of our speculations concerning their nature, it would be absurd to suppose; but it is surely far from being unreasonable to think, that *an acquaintance with the laws* which regulate these powers, *may suggest some useful rules* for their gradual cultivation: for remedying their defects, in the case of individuals, and even for extending those limits, which nature seems, at first view, to have assigned them.

To how great a degree of perfection the intellectual and moral nature of man is capable of being raised by cultivation, it is difficult to conceive. The effects of early, continued, and systematical education in the case of those children who are trained, for the sake of gain, to feats of strength and agility, justify, perhaps, the most sanguine views which it is possible for a philosopher to form, with respect to the improvement of the species.

IX *The necessity, force and natural effects of authority*. – I now proceed to consider, how far the philosophy of mind may be useful in accomplishing *the second object of education* [see p. 46]; by assisting us in the management of early impressions and associations.

By far the greater part of the opinions on which we act in life, are not the result of our own investigations; but are adopted implicitly, in infancy and youth, upon the *authority* of others. Even the great principles of morality, although implanted in every heart, are commonly aided and cherished, at least to a certain degree, by the care of our instructors. – All this is undoubtedly agreeable to the intentions of nature; and, indeed, were the case otherwise, society could not subsist; for nothing can be more evident, than that the bulk of mankind, condemned as they are to laborious occupations, which are incompatible with intellectual improvement, are perfectly incapable of forming their own opinions on some of the most important subjects that can employ the human mind. It is evident, at the same time, that as no system of education is perfect, a variety of *prejudices must*, in this way, *take an early hold of our belief;* so as to acquire over it an influence not inferior to that of the most incontrovertible truths. When a child hears, either a speculative absurdity, or an erroneous principle of action, recommended and enforced daily, by the same voice which first conveyed to it those simple and sublime lessons of morality and religion which are congenial to its nature, is it to be wondered at, that, in future life, it should find it so difficult to eradicate prejudices which have twined their roots with all the essential principles of the human frame? – If such, however, be the obvious intentions of nature, with respect to those orders of men who are employed in bodily labour, it is equally clear, that she meant to impose it as a double obligation on those who receive the advantages of a liberal education, to examine, with the most scrupulous care, the foundation of all those received opinions, which have any connexion with morality, or with human happiness. If the multitude must be led, it is of consequence, surely, that it should be led by enlightened conductors; by men who are able to distinguish truth from error; and to draw the line between those prejudices which are innocent or salutary, (if indeed there are any prejudices which are really salutary,) and those which are hostile to the interests of virtue and of mankind.

X *Preliminary step in entering upon the study of metaphysical science.* – In such a state of society as that in which we live, the *prejudices* of a moral, a political, and a religious nature, which we *imbibe in early life*, are so various, and at the same time so intimately blended with the belief we entertain of the most sacred and important truths, that the great part of the life of a philosopher must necessarily be devoted, not so much to the acquisition of new knowledge, as *to unlearn the errors to which he had been taught to give an implicit assent, before the dawn of reason and reflection.* And unless he submit in this manner to bring all his opinions to the test of a severe examination, his ingenuity, and his learning, instead of enlightening the world, will only enable him to give an additional currency, and an additional authority, to establish errors. To attempt such a struggle against early prejudices, is, indeed, the professed aim of all philosophers; but how few are to be found who have force of mind sufficient for accomplishing their object; and who, in freeing themselves from one set of errors, do not allow themselves to be carried away with another! To succeed in it completely, Lord Bacon seems to have thought, (in one of the most remarkable passages of his writings), to be more than can well be expected from human frailty. 'Nemo adhuc tanta mentis constantia inventus est, ut decreverit, et sibi imposuerit, theorias et notiones communes penitus abolere, et intellectum abrasum et æquum ad particularia, de integro, applicare. Itaque illa ratio humana, quam habemus, ex multa fide, et multo etiam casu, necnon ex puerilibus, quas primo hausimus, notionibus, farrago quædam est, et congeries. Quod siquis, ætata matura, et sensibus integris, et mente repurgata, se ad experientiam, et ad particularia de integro applicet, de eo melias sperandum est.'[1]

XI Nor is it merely in order to free the mind from the influence

---

[1] 'No one has yet appeared of such strength of mind
as to resolve and lay it down for a law to himself
utterly to reject theories and popular opinions, and
unprejudiced to apply his mind clear and impartial

of error, that it is useful to examine the foundation of established opinions. It is *such an examination alone*, that, in an inquisitive age like the present, *can secure a philosopher from the danger of unlimited scepticism*. To this extreme, indeed, the complexion of the times is more likely to give him a tendency, than to implicit credulity. In the former ages of ignorance and superstition, the intimate association which had been formed, in the prevailing systems of education, between truth and error, had given to the latter an ascendant over the minds of men, which it could never have acquired, if divested of such an alliance. The case has, of late years, been most remarkably reversed; the common sense of mankind, in consequence of the growth of a more liberal spirit of inquiry, has revolted against many of those absurdities, which had so long held human reason in captivity; and it was, perhaps, more than could reasonably have been expected, that, in the first moments of their emancipation, philosophers should have stopped short, at the precise boundary, which cooler reflection, and more moderate views, would have prescribed. The fact is, that they have passed far beyond it; and that, in their zeal to destroy prejudices, they have attempted to tear up by the roots, many of the best and happiest and most essential principles of our nature. Having remarked the powerful influence of education over the mind, they have concluded, that man is wholly a factitious being; not recollecting, that this very susceptibility of education presupposes certain original principles, which are common to the whole species; and that, as error can only take a permanent hold of a candid mind by being grafted on truths, which it is unwilling or unable to eradicate; even the influence, which false and absurd opinions occasionally acquire over the belief, instead of being an argument for universal scepticism, is the most decisive argument against it; inasmuch as it shows, that there are some truths so incorporated and identified with our nature, that they can reconcile us even to the absurdities and contradictions with which we suppose them to be inseparably connected. The sceptical philosophers, for example, of the present age, have frequently attempted to hold up to ridicule, those contemptible and puerile

to facts. For human reason, such as we have it, is a
mixture and accumulation of credulity, of casualties,
and of the childish notions which we first received.
But if any one of unimpaired faculties and of purified
mind, would, commencing a new course, apply himself
to experience and to facts, good hopes might be
entertained of him.'

superstitions, which have disgraced the creeds of some of the most enlightened nations; and which have not only commanded the assent, but the reverence, of men of the most accomplished understandings. But these histories of human imbecility are, in truth, the strongest testimonies which can be produced, to prove, how wonderful is the influence of the fundamental principles of morality over the belief; when they are able to sanctify, in the apprehensions of mankind, every extravagant opinion, and every unmeaning ceremony, which early education has taught us to associate with them.

XII *How far implicit credulity and unlimited scepticism related.* – That *implicit credulity* is a mark of a feeble mind, will not be disputed; but it may not perhaps be as generally acknowledged, that the case is the same with *unlimited scepticism:* on the contrary, we are sometimes apt to ascribe this disposition to a more than ordinary vigour of intellect. Such a prejudice was by no means unnatural at that period in the history of modern Europe, when reason first began to throw off the yoke of authority; and when it unquestionably required a superiority of understanding, as well as of intrepidity, for an individual to resist the contagion of prevailing superstition. But in the present age, in which the tendency of fashionable opinions is directly opposite to those of the vulgar; the philosophical creed, or the philosophical scepticism of by far the greater number of those who value themselves on an emancipation from popular errors, arises from the very same weakness with the credulity of the multitude: nor is it going too far to say, with Rousseau, that 'He who, in the end of the eighteenth century, has brought himself to abandon all his early principles without discrimination, would probably have been a bigot in the days of the League.' In the midst of these contrary impulses of fashionable and of vulgar prejudices, he alone evinces the superiority and the strength of his mind, who is able to disentangle truth from error; and to oppose the clear conclusions of his own unbiassed faculties, to the united clamours of superstition, and of false philosophy. – Such are the men, whom nature marks out to be the lights of the world; to fix the wavering opinions of the multitude, and to impress their own characters on that of their age.

For securing the mind completely from the weaknesses I have now been describing, and enabling it to maintain a steady course of inquiry, between implicit credulity and unlimited scepticism, the most important of all qualities is a sincere and devoted attachment to truth; which seldom fails to be accompanied with a manly confidence in the clear conclusions of human reason. It is such a confidence, united (as it generally is) with personal intrepidity, which forms what the French writers call force of character; one of the rarest endowments, it must be confessed, of our species: but which, of all endowments, is the most essential for rendering a philosopher happy in himself, and a blessing to mankind.

There is, I think, good reason for hoping, that the sceptical tendency of the present age, will be only a temporary evil. While it continues, however, it is an evil of the most alarming nature; and, as it extends, in general, not only to religion and morality, but, in some measure, also to politics, and the conduct of life, it is equally fatal to the comfort of the individual, and to the improvement of society. Even in its most inoffensive form, when it happens to be united with a peaceable disposition and a benevolent heart, it cannot fail to have the effect of damping every active and patriotic exertion. Convinced that truth is placed beyond the reach of the human faculties; and doubtful how far the prejudices we despise may not be essential to the well being of society, we resolve to abandon completely all speculative inquiries; and suffering ourselves to be carried quietly along with the stream of popular opinions, and of fashionable manners, determine to amuse ourselves, the best way we can, with business or pleasure, during our short passage through this scene of illusions. But he who thinks more favourably of the human powers, and who believes that reason was given to man to direct him to his duty and his happiness, will despise the suggestion of this timid philosophy; and while he is conscious that he is guided in his inquiries only by the love of truth, will rest assured that their result will be equally favourable to his own comfort, and to the best interests of mankind. What, indeed, will be the particular effects in the first instance, of that general diffusion of knowledge, which the art of printing must sooner or later produce, and of that spirit of reformation with which it cannot fail to be accompanied, it is beyond the reach of human sagacity to conjecture; but unless we choose to abandon ourselves entirely to a desponding scepticism, we must hope and believe, that the progress of human reason can never be a source of permanent disorder to the world; and that they alone have cause to apprehend the consequences, who are led, by the imperfection of our present institutions, to feel themselves interested in perpetuating the prejudices, and follies, of their species.

XIII *Value of correct early impressions.* – From the observations

which have been made, it sufficiently appears, that, in order
to secure the mind, on the one hand, from the influence of
prejudice, and, on the other, from a tendency to unlimited
scepticism, it is necessary that it should be able to distinguish
the original and universal principles and laws of human nature
from the adventitious effect of local situation. But if in the case
of an individual who has received an imperfect or erroneous
education, such a knowledge puts it in his power to correct,
to a certain degree, his own bad habits, and to surmount his
own speculative errors; it enables him to be useful, in a much
higher degree, to those whose education he has an opportunity
of superintending from early infancy. Such, and so permanent,
is the *effect of first impressions on the character*, that, although a
philosopher may succeed, by perseverance, in freeing his reason
from the prejudices with which it was entangled, they will still
retain some hold of his imagination and his affections; and,
therefore, however enlightened his understanding may be in his
hours of speculation, his philosophical opinions will frequently
lose their influence over his mind, in those very situations in
which their practical assistance is most required; when his temper
is soured by misfortune, or when he engages in the pursuits of
life, and exposes himself to the contagion of popular errors. His
opinions are supported merely by speculative arguments; and,
instead of being connected with any of the active principles
of his nature, are counteracted and thwarted by some of the
most powerful of them. How different would the case be if
education were conducted from the beginning with attention
and judgment! Were the same pains taken to impress truth on
the mind in early infancy that is often taken to inculcate error,
the great principles of our conduct would not only be juster
than they are, but, in consequence of the aid which they would
receive from the imagination and the heart, trained to conspire
with them in the same direction, they would render us happier
in ourselves, and would influence our practice more powerfully
and more habitually. There is surely nothing in error which is
more congenial to the mind than truth. On the contrary, when
exhibited separately and alone to the understanding, it shocks
our reason and provokes our ridicule; and it is only (as I had
occasion already to remark) by an alliance with truths, which
we find it difficult to renounce, that it can obtain our assent or
command our reverence. What advantages then might be derived
from a proper attention to early impressions and associations,
in giving support to those principles which are connected with

human happiness! The long reign of error in the world, and the influence it maintains, even in an age of liberal inquiry, far from being favourable to the supposition, that human reason is destined to be for ever the sport of prejudice and absurdity, demonstrates the tendency which there is to permanence in established opinions and in established institutions, and promises an eternal stability to true philosophy, when it shall once have acquired the ascendant, and when proper means shall be employed to support it by a more perfect system of education.

Let us suppose, for a moment, that this happy era were arrived, and that all the prepossessions of childhood and youth were directed to support the pure and sublime truths of an enlightened morality. With what ardour and with what transport would the understanding, when arrived at maturity, proceed in the search of truth; when, instead of being obliged to struggle, at every step, with early prejudices, its office was merely to add the force of philosophical conviction to impressions which are equally delightful to the imagination and dear to the heart! The prepossessions of childhood would, through the whole of life, be gradually acquiring strength from the enlargement of our knowledge, and, in their turn, would fortify the conclusions of our reason against the sceptical suggestions of disappointment or melancholy.

Our daily experience may convince us how susceptible the tender mind is of deep impressions, and what important and *permanent effects* are produced on the characters and the happiness *of* individuals, by the casual *associations formed in childhood* among the various ideas, feelings, and affections with which they were habitually occupied. It is the business of education, not to counteract this constitution of nature, but to give it a proper direction; and the miserable consequences to which it leads, when under an improper regulation, only show what an important instrument of human improvement it might be rendered in more skilful hands. If it be possible to interest the imagination and the heart in favour of error, it is, at least, no less possible to interest them in favour of truth. If it be possible to extinguish all the most generous and heroic feelings of our nature, by teaching us to connect the idea of them with those of guilt and impiety, it is surely equally possible to cherish and strengthen them, by establishing the natural alliance between our duty and our happiness. If it be possible for the influence of fashion to veil the native deformity of vice, and to give to low and criminal indulgences the appearance of spirit, of elegance, and of gaiety, can we doubt of the possibility of connecting, in the tender mind, these pleasing associations with pursuits that are truly worthy and honourable? There are few men to be found among those who have received the advantages of a liberal education, who do not retain, through life, that admiration of the heroic ages of Greece and Rome with which the classical authors once inspired them. It is, in truth, a fortunate prepossession on the whole, and one of which I should be sorry to counteract the influence. But are there not others of equal importance to morality and to happiness, with which the mind might, at the same period of life, be inspired? If the first conceptions, for example, which an infant formed of the Deity, and its first moral perceptions, were associated with the early impressions produced on the heart by the beauties of nature, or the charms of poetical description, those serious thoughts which are resorted to by most men, merely as a source of consolation in adversity, and which, on that very account, are frequently tinctured with some degree of gloom, would recur spontaneously to the mind in its best and happiest hours, and would insensibly blend themselves with all its purest and most refined enjoyments.

In those parts of Europe where the prevailing opinions involve the greatest variety of errors and corruptions, it is, I believe, a common idea with many respectable and enlightened men, that in every country it is most prudent to conduct the religious instruction of youth upon the plan which is prescribed by the national establishment, in order that the pupil, according to the vigour or feebleness of his mind, may either shake off, in future life, the prejudices of the nursery, or die in the popular persuasion. This idea, I own, appears to me to be equally ill-founded and dangerous. If religious opinions have, as will not be disputed, a powerful influence on the happiness and on the conduct of mankind, does not humanity require of us to rescue as many victims as possible from the hands of bigotry, and to save them from the cruel alternative of remaining under the gloom of a depressing superstition, or of being distracted by a perpetual conflict between the heart and the understanding? It is *an enlightened education alone*, that, in most countries of Europe, *can save the young philosopher* (1) from that anxiety and despondence which every man of sensibility, who, in his childhood, has imbibed the popular opinions, must necessarily experience when he first begins to examine their foundation; and, what is of still greater importance, which can save him, during life, (2) from that occasional scepticism to which all men are liable, whose systems fluctuate with the inequalities of their spirits and the variations of the atmosphere.

XIV I shall conclude this subject with remarking, that, although in all moral and religious systems there is a great mixture of important truth, and although it is in consequence of this alliance that errors and absurdities are enabled to preserve their hold of the belief, yet it is commonly found, that, *in proportion as* an established *creed is complicated in its dogmas* and in its ceremonies, and in proportion to the number of accessory ideas which it has grafted upon the truth, *the more difficult is it* for those who have adopted it in childhood *to emancipate* themselves completely *from its influence;* and in those cases in which they at last succeed, the greater is their danger of abandoning, along with their errors, all the truths which they had been taught to connect with them. The Roman Catholic system is shaken off with much greater difficulty than those which are taught in the Reformed churches; but when it loses its hold of the mind, it much more frequently prepares the way for unlimited scepticism. The causes of this I may, perhaps, have an opportunity of pointing out, in treating of the *association of ideas.*

I have now finished all that I think necessary to offer at present on the *application of the philosophy of mind to the subject of education.* To some readers, I am afraid, that what I have advanced on the subject will appear to border upon enthusiasm; and I will not attempt to justify myself against the charge. I am well aware of the tendency which speculative men sometimes have to magnify the effects of education, as well as to entertain too sanguine views of the improvement of the world; and I am ready to acknowledge, that there are instances of individuals whose vigour of mind is sufficient to overcome everything that is pernicious in their early habits: but I am fully persuaded that these instances are rare, and that by far the greater part of mankind continue, through life, to pursue the same track into which they have been thrown by the accidental circumstances of situation, instruction, and example.

Source: Dugald Stewart, *Elements of the Philosophy of the Human Mind*, London 1867, Introduction, ch. 2, pp. 9–24

THREE

DAVID HUME
The Theory of Ideas

Hume's science of human nature is based upon a distinction between two sorts of 'perception'. I see an object, and later I recall what I have seen. I hear a sound and later think about the sound. I am sad and later think about my sadness. In these three pairs of perception something is first really present to me and is then re-presented, that is, is presented again, but this time only in my mind. The first perception is termed an 'impression' and the second an 'idea'. Hume attends to two differences between them. One difference is that the first perception has greater 'liveliness' or 'vivacity' than the second, so that for example the auditory experience of actually listening to a piece of music is livelier than is the performance I later hear in my 'mind's ear'.

But this difference is not secure for, as Hume acknowledges, when a person is dreaming or feverish his thought of a previous perception can come close to attaining the degree of liveliness of the original perception. Another way of distinguishing impressions from ideas must therefore be found. And Hume finds it in the very fact that there is a temporal ordering between impressions and ideas. The impression, the livelier perception, must come first. Thus I cannot form an idea of a given musical note unless I have first heard that note, nor of the taste of pineapple unless first I have actually had such a taste-experience. In each case the description given by another person will not produce in me the correct idea; my own experience is essential. I can of course form a complex idea of something that I have not previously experienced. But the complex idea is composed of simple ideas, and each of them must be of something simple that I have previously experienced. I imagine a chair – it really is a product of my imagination in the sense that I have never before seen a chair that resembled my idea – but the parts of the idea, the colours and so on, must have been previously seen by me.

The doctrine that a simple idea is preceded by a simple impression which resembles the idea is the basis of Hume's entire system: 'This then is the first principle I establish in the science of human nature.' It provides him with a procedure for dealing with a wide range of questions. In each case Hume proceeds from the fact that we have an idea, for example, an idea of causality, or of the external world, of the self, or of morality, and he asks: 'What is the impression from which this idea is derived?' And in each case he finds that the origin of the idea is not at all what previous philosophers had taken it to be.

In section IV Hume discusses the principle of association of ideas. He believes our ideas to be attracted to each other in a systematic way rather than coming together to form complex ideas randomly, and in this there is a hint of Hume's Newtonianism. As with many other of the literati, Hume studied Newton's system, the central principle of which is the law of gravity, that every particle of matter in the universe attracts every other particle with a force that varies directly as the product of their mass and inversely as the square of the distance between them. For Hume, simple ideas are mental analogues of Newtonian particles of matter, and as the latter attract each other according to a certain ratio, so also do Humean simple ideas. Hume believed therefore in a kind of mental gravity, though he did not of course offer a mathematical formula corresponding to Newton's law of gravity.

A.B.

Of the Understanding

PART I *Of Ideas, their Origin, Composition, Connexion, Abstraction, etc*

SECTION I *Of the origin of our ideas*

All the perceptions of the human mind resolve themselves into two distinct kinds, which I shall call Impressions and Ideas. The difference betwixt these consists in the degrees of force and liveliness, with which they strike upon the mind, and make their way into our thought or consciousness. Those perceptions, which enter with most force and violence, we may name *impressions*; and under this name I comprehend all our sensations, passions and emotions, as they make their first appearance in the soul. By *ideas* I mean the faint images of these in thinking and reasoning; such as, for instance, are all the perceptions excited by the present discourse, excepting only, those which arise from the sight and touch, and excepting the immediate pleasure or uneasiness it may occasion. I believe it will not be very necessary to employ many words in explaining this distinction. Every one of himself will readily perceive the difference betwixt feeling and thinking. The common degrees of these are easily distinguished; tho' it is not impossible but in particular instances they may very nearly approach to each other. Thus in sleep, in a fever, in madness, or in any very violent emotions of soul, our ideas may approach to our impressions: As on the other hand it sometimes happens, that our impressions are so faint and low, that we cannot distinguish them from our ideas. But notwithstanding this near resemblance in a few instances, they are in general so very different, that no-one can make a scruple to rank them under distinct heads, and assign to each a peculiar name to mark the difference.[1]

---

1 I here make use of these terms, *impression* and idea, in a sense different from what is usual, and I hope this liberty will be allowed me. Perhaps I rather restore the word, idea, to its original sense, from which Mr. *Locke* had perverted it, in making it stand for all our perceptions. By the term of impression I would not be understood to express the manner, in which our lively perceptions are produced in the soul, but merely the perceptions themselves; for which there is no particular name either in the *English* or any other language, that I know of.

There is another division of our perceptions, which it will be convenient to observe, and which extends itself both to our impressions and ideas. This division is into Simple and Complex. Simple perceptions or impressions and ideas are such as admit of no distinction nor separation. The complex are the contrary to these, and may be distinguished into parts. Tho' a particular colour, taste, and smell are qualities all united together in this apple, 'tis easy to perceive they are not the same, but are at least distinguishable from each other.

Having by these divisions given an order and arrangement to our objects, we may now apply ourselves to consider with the more accuracy their qualities and relations. The first circumstance, that strikes my eye, is the great resemblance betwixt our impressions and ideas in every other particular, except their degree of force and vivacity. The one seem to be in a manner the reflexion of the other; so that all the perceptions of the mind are double, and appear both as impressions and ideas. When I shut my eyes and think of my chamber, the ideas I form are exact representations of the impressions I felt; nor is there any circumstance of the one, which is not to be found in the other. In running over my other perceptions, I find still the same resemblance and representation. Ideas and impressions appear always to correspond to each other. This circumstance seems to me remarkable, and engages my attention for a moment.

Upon a more accurate survey I find I have been carried away too far by the first appearance, and that I must make use of the distinction of perceptions into *simple and complex*, to limit this general decision, *that all our ideas and impressions are resembling*. I observe, that many of our complex ideas never had impressions, that corresponded to them, and that many of our complex impressions never are exactly copied in ideas. I can imagine to myself such a city as the *New Jerusalem*, whose pavement is gold and walls are rubies, tho' I never saw any such. I have seen *Paris*; but shall I affirm I can form such an idea of that city, as will perfectly represent all its streets and houses in their real and just proportions?

I perceive, therefore, that tho' there is in general a great resemblance betwixt our *complex* impressions and ideas, yet the rule is not universally true, that they are exact copies of each other. We may next consider how the case stands with our *simple* perceptions. After the most accurate examination, of which I am capable, I venture to affirm, that the rule here holds without any exception, and that every simple idea has a simple impression, which resembles it; and every simple impression a correspondent idea. That idea of red, which we form in the dark, and that impression, which strikes our eyes in sun-shine, differ only in degree, not in nature. That the case is the same with all our simple impressions and ideas, 'tis impossible to prove by a particular enumeration of them. Every one may satisfy himself in this point by running over as many as he pleases. But if any one should deny this universal resemblance, I know no way of convincing him, but by desiring him to shew a simple impression, that has not a correspondent idea, or a simple idea, that has not a correspondent impression. If he does not answer this challenge, as 'tis certain he cannot, we may from his silence and our own observation establish our conclusion.

Thus we find, that all simple ideas and impressions resemble each other; and as the complex are formed from them, we may affirm in general, that these two species of perception are exactly correspondent. Having discover'd this relation, which requires no farther examination, I am curious to find some other of their qualities. Let us consider how they stand with regard to their existence, and which of the impressions and ideas are causes and which effects.

The *full* examination of this question is the subject of the present treatise; and therefore we shall here content ourselves with establishing one general proposition, *That all our simple ideas in their first appearance are deriv'd from simple impressions, which are correspondent to them, and which they exactly represent.*

In seeking for phænomena to prove this proposition, I find only those of two kinds; but in each kind the phænomena are obvious, numerous, and conclusive. I first make myself certain, by a new review, of what I have already asserted, that every simple impression is attended with a correspondent idea, and every simple idea with a correspondent impression. From this constant conjunction of resembling perceptions I immediately conclude, that there is a great connexion betwixt our correspondent impressions and ideas, and that the existence of the one has a considerable influence upon that of the other. Such a constant conjunction, in such an infinite number of instances, can never arise from chance; but clearly proves a dependence of the impressions on the ideas, or of the ideas on the impressions. That I may know on which side this dependence lies, I consider the order of their *first appearance*; and find by constant experience, that the simple impressions always take the precedence of their correspondent ideas, but never appear in the contrary order. To give a child an idea of scarlet or orange, of sweet or bitter, I present the objects, or in other words, convey to him these impressions; but proceed not so absurdly, as to endeavour to produce the impressions by exciting the ideas. Our ideas upon their appearance produce not their correspondent impressions, nor do we perceive any colour, or feel any sensation merely upon thinking of them. On the other hand we find, that any impression either of the mind or body is constantly followed by an idea, which resembles it, and is only different in the degrees of force and liveliness. The constant conjunction of our resembling perceptions, is a convincing proof, that the one are the causes of the other; and this priority of the impressions is an equal proof, that our impressions are the causes of our ideas, not our ideas of our impressions.

To confirm this I consider another plain and convincing phænomenon; which is, that where-ever by any accident the faculties, which give rise to any impressions, are obstructed in their operations, as when one is born blind or deaf; not only the impressions are lost, but also their correspondent ideas; so that there never appear in the mind the least traces of either of them. Nor is this only true, where the organs of sensation are entirely destroy'd, but likewise where they have never been put in action to produce a particular impression. We cannot form to ourselves a just idea of the taste of a pine-apple, without having actually tasted it.

There is however one contradictory phænomenon, which may prove, that 'tis not absolutely impossible for ideas to go before their correspondent impressions. I believe it will readily be allow'd, that the several distinct ideas of colours, which enter by the eyes, or those of sounds, which are convey'd by the hearing, are really different from each other, tho' at the same time resembling. Now if this be true of different colours, it must be no less so of the different shades of the same colour, that each of them produces a distinct idea, independent of the rest. For if this shou'd be deny'd, 'tis possible, by the continual gradation of shades, to run a colour insensibly into what is most remote from it; and if you will not allow any of the means to be different, you cannot without absurdity deny the extremes to be the same. Suppose therefore a person to have enjoyed his sight for thirty years, and to have become perfectly well acquainted with colours of all kinds, excepting one particular shade of blue, for instance, which it never has been his fortune to meet with. Let all the different shades of that colour, except that single one, be plac'd before him, descending gradually from the deepest to the lightest; 'tis plain, that he will perceive a blank, where that shade is wanting, and will be sensible, that there is a greater distance in that place betwixt the contiguous colours, than in any other. Now I ask, whether 'tis possible for him, from his own imagination, to supply this deficiency, and raise up to himself the idea of that particular shade, tho' it had never been conveyed to him by his senses? I believe there are few but will be of opinion that he can; and this may serve as a proof, that the simple ideas are not always derived from the correspondent impressions; tho' the instance is so particular and singular, that 'tis scarce worth our observing, and does not merit that for it alone we should alter our general maxim.

But besides this exception, it may not be amiss to remark on this head, that the principle of the priority of impressions to ideas must be understood with another limitation, *viz.* that as our ideas are images of our impressions, so we can form secondary ideas, which are images of the primary; as appears from this very reasoning concerning them. This is not, properly speaking, an exception to the rule so much as an explanation of it. Ideas produce the images of themselves in new ideas; but as the first ideas are supposed to be derived from impressions, it still remains true, that all our simple ideas proceed either mediately or immediately, from their correspondent impressions.

This then is the first principle I establish in the science of human nature; nor ought we to despise it because of the simplicity of its appearance. For 'tis remarkable, that the present question concerning the precedency of our impressions or ideas, is the same with what has made so much noise in other terms, when it has been disputed whether there be any *innate ideas*, or whether all ideas be derived from sensation and reflexion. We may observe, that in order to prove the ideas of extension and colour not to be innate, philosophers do nothing but shew, that they are conveyed by our senses. To prove the ideas of passion and desire not to be innate, they observe that we have a preceding experience of these emotions in ourselves. Now if we carefully examine these arguments, we shall find that they prove nothing but that ideas are preceded by other more lively perceptions, from which they are derived, and which they represent. I hope this clear stating of the question will remove all disputes concerning it, and will render this principle of more use in our reasonings, than it seems hitherto to have been.

SECTION II *Division of the subject*
Since it appears, that our simple impressions are prior to their correspondent ideas, and that the exceptions are very rare, method seems to require we should examine our impressions, before we consider our ideas. Impressions may be divided into two kinds, those of Sensation and those of Reflexion. The first kind arises in the soul originally, from unknown causes. The second is derived in a great measure from our ideas, and that in the following order. An impression first strikes upon the senses, and makes us perceive heat or cold, thirst or hunger, pleasure or pain of some kind or other. Of this impression there is a copy taken by the mind, which remains after the impression ceases; and this we call an idea. This idea of pleasure or pain, when it returns upon the soul, produces the new impressions of desire and aversion, hope and fear, which may properly be called impressions of reflexion, because derived from it. These again are copied by the memory and imagination, and become ideas; which perhaps in their turn give rise to other impressions and ideas. So that the impressions of reflexion are only antecedent to their correspondent ideas; but posterior to those of sensation, and deriv'd from them. The examination of our sensations belongs more to anatomists and natural philosophers than to moral; and therefore shall not at present be enter'd upon. And as the impressions of reflexion, *viz.* passions, desires, and emotions, which principally deserve our attention, arise mostly from ideas, 'twill be necessary to reverse that method, which at first sight seems most natural; and in order to explain the nature and principles of the human mind, give a particular account of ideas, before we proceed to impressions. For this reason I have here chosen to begin with ideas.

SECTION III *Of the ideas of the memory and imagination*
We find by experience, that when any impression has been present with the mind, it again makes its appearance there as an idea; and this it may do after two different ways: either when in its new appearance it retains a considerable degree of its first vivacity, and is somewhat intermediate betwixt an impression and an idea; or when it intirely loses that vivacity, and is a perfect idea. The faculty, by which we repeat our impressions in the first manner, is called the Memory, and the other the Imagination. 'Tis evident at first sight, that the ideas of the memory are much more lively and strong than those of the imagination, and that the former faculty

paints its objects in more distinct colours, than any which are employ'd by the latter. When we remember any past event, the idea of it flows in upon the mind in a forcible manner; whereas in the imagination the perception is faint and languid, and cannot without difficulty be preserv'd by the mind steddy and uniform for any considerable time. Here then is a sensible difference betwixt one species of ideas and another. But of this more fully hereafter.

There is another difference betwixt these two kinds of ideas, which is no less evident, namely that tho' neither the ideas of the memory nor imagination, neither the lively nor faint ideas can make their appearance in the mind, unless their correspondent impressions have gone before to prepare the way for them, yet the imagination is not restrain'd to the same order and form with the original impressions; while the memory is in a manner ty'd down in that respect, without any power of variation.

'Tis evident, that the memory preserves the original form, in which its objects were presented, and that where-ever we depart from it in recollecting any thing, it proceeds from some defect or imperfection in that faculty. An historian may, perhaps, for the more convenient carrying on of his narration, relate an event before another, to which it was in fact posterior; but then he takes notice of this disorder, if he be exact; and by that means replaces the idea in its due position. 'Tis the same case in our recollection of those places and persons, with which we were formerly acquainted. The chief exercise of the memory is not to preserve the simple ideas, but their order and position. In short, this principle is supported by such a number of common and vulgar phænomena, that we may spare ourselves the trouble of insisting on it any farther.

The same evidence follows us in our second principle, *of the liberty of the imagination to transpose and change its ideas*. The fables we meet with in poems and romances put this entirely out of question. Nature there is totally confounded, and nothing mentioned but winged horses, fiery dragons, and monstrous giants. Nor will this liberty of the fancy appear strange, when we consider, that all our ideas are copy'd from our impressions, and that there are not any two impressions which are perfectly inseparable. Not to mention, that this is an evident consequence of the division of ideas into simple and complex. Where-ever the imagination perceives a difference among ideas, it can easily produce a separation.

SECTION IV *Of the connexion or association of ideas*

As all simple ideas may be separated by the imagination, and may be united again in what form it pleases, nothing wou'd be more unaccountable than the operation of that faculty, were it not guided by some universal principles, which render it, in some measure, uniform with itself in all times and places. Were ideas entirely loose and unconnected, chance alone wou'd join them; and 'tis impossible the same simple ideas should fall regularly into complex ones (as they commonly do) without some bond of union among them, some associating quality, by which one idea naturally introduces another. This uniting principle among ideas is not to be consider'd as an inseparable connexion; for that has been already excluded from the imagination: nor yet are we to conclude, that without it the mind cannot join two ideas; for nothing is more free than that faculty: but we are only to regard it as a gentle force, which commonly prevails, and is the cause why, among other things, languages so nearly correspond to each other; nature in a manner pointing out to every one those simple ideas, which are most proper to be united into a complex one. The qualities, from which this association arises, and by which the mind is after this manner convey'd from one idea to another, are three, *viz.* Resemblance, Contiguity in time or place, and Cause and Effect.

I believe it will not be very necessary to prove, that these qualities produce an association among ideas, and upon the appearance of one idea naturally introduce another. 'Tis plain, that in the course of our thinking, and in the constant revolution of our ideas, our imagination runs easily from one idea to any other that *resembles* it, and that this quality alone is to the fancy a sufficient bond and association. 'Tis likewise evident, that as the senses, in changing their objects, are necessitated to change them regularly, and take them as they lie *contiguous* to each other, the imagination must by long custom acquire the same method of thinking, and run along the parts of space and time in conceiving its objects. As to the connexion, that is made by the relation of *cause and effect*, we shall have occasion afterwards to examine it to the bottom, and therefore shall not at present insist upon it. 'Tis sufficient to observe, that there is no relation, which produces a stronger connexion in the fancy, and makes one idea more readily recall another, than the relation of cause and effect betwixt their objects.

That we may understand the full extent of these relations, we must consider, that two objects are connected together in the imagination, not only when the one is immediately resembling, contiguous to, or the cause of the other, but also when there is interposed betwixt them a third object, which bears to both of them any of these relations. This may be carried on to a great length; tho' at the same time we may observe, that each remove considerably weakens the relation. Cousins in the fourth degree are connected by *causation*, if I may be allowed to use that term; but not so closely as brothers, much less as child and parent. In general we may observe, that all the relations of blood depend upon cause and effect, and are esteemed near or remote, according to the number of connecting causes interpos'd betwixt the persons.

Of the three relations above-mention'd this of causation is the most extensive. Two objects may be consider'd as plac'd in this relation, as well when one is the cause of any of the actions or motions of the other, as when the former is the cause of the existence of the latter. For as that action or motion is nothing but the object itself, consider'd in a certain light, and as the object continues the same in all its different situations, 'tis easy to imagine how such an influence of objects upon one another may connect them in the imagination.

We may carry this farther, and remark, not only that two objects are connected by the relation of cause and effect, when the one produces a motion or any action in the other, but also when it has a power of producing it. And this we may observe to be the source of all the relations of interest and duty, by which men influence each other in society, and are plac'd in the ties of government and subordination. A master is such-a-one as by his situation, arising either from force or agreement, has a power of directing in certain particulars the actions of another, whom we call servant. A judge is one, who in all disputed cases can fix by his opinion the possession or property of any thing betwixt any members of the society. When a person is possess'd of any power, there is no more required to convert it into action, but the exertion of the will; and *that* in every case is consider'd as possible, and in many as probable; especially in the case of authority, where the obedience of the subject is a pleasure and advantage to the superior.

These are therefore the principles of union or cohesion among our simple ideas, and in the imagination supply the place of that inseparable connexion, by which they are united in our memory. Here is a kind of Attraction, which in the mental world will be found to have as extraordinary effects as in the natural, and to shew itself in as many and as various forms. Its effects are every where conspicuous; but as to its causes, they are mostly unknown, and must be resolv'd into *original* qualities of human nature, which I pretend not to explain. Nothing is more requisite for a true philosopher, than to restrain the intemperate desire of searching into causes, and having establish'd any doctrine upon a sufficient number of experiments, rest contented with that, when he sees a farther examination would lead him into obscure and uncertain speculations. In that case his enquiry wou'd be much better employ'd in examining the effects than the causes of his principle.

Source: David Hume, *A Treatise of Human Nature*, ed. L. A. Selby-Bigge, 2nd edn by P. H. Nidditch, Oxford 1975, Book 1, part 1; sections 1–4, pp. 1–13

FOUR

THOMAS REID
Mind and its Operations

In the following set of extracts we find the basis of the
philosophy of common sense, as expounded by the leading
figure of the Scottish school of common sense philosophy.
A central feature of that philosophy is the contrast between
body and mind. Philosophers have commonly tried to give
an account of mind by assuming that body and mind are
similar in important ways, and then arguing that, because
bodies have certain properties, mind also must have those
or at least very similar properties. This kind of argument
is called an 'argument from analogy', and Reid judges it a
hopelessly inappropriate form of argument in this kind of
case. His reason for this judgment is that an argument from
analogy permits us to reach a conclusion that has a serious
degree of probability only if the things we are arguing about
are sufficiently similar. It is Reid's contention that body and
mind are as different from each other as any two things
can be, and we have therefore to find another means of
investigating mind.

A.B.

Essays on the Intellectual Powers of Man

ESSAY I *Preliminary*

CHAPTER I *Explication of words*

There is no greater impediment to the advancement of knowledge than the ambiguity of words. To this chiefly it is owing that we find sects and parties in most branches of science; and disputes which are carried on from age to age, without being brought to an issue.

Sophistry has been more effectually excluded from mathematics and natural philosophy than from other sciences. In mathematics it had no place from the beginning; mathematicians having had the wisdom to define accurately the terms they use, and to lay down, as axioms, the first principles on which their reasoning is grounded. Accordingly, we find no parties among mathematicians, and hardly any disputes.

In natural philosophy, there was no less sophistry, no less dispute and uncertainty, than in other sciences, until, about a century and a half ago, this science began to be built upon the foundation of clear definitions and self-evident axioms. Since that time, the science, as if watered with the dew of Heaven, hath grown apace; disputes have ceased, truth hath prevailed, and the science hath received greater increase in two centuries than in two thousand years before.

It were to be wished that this method, which hath been so successful in those branches of science, were attempted in others; for definitions and axioms are the foundations of all science. But that definitions may not be sought where no definition can be given, nor logical definitions be attempted where the subject does not admit of them, it may be proper to lay down some general principles concerning definition, for the sake of those who are less conversant in this branch of logic.

When one undertakes to explain any art or science, he will have occasion to use many words that are common to all who use the same language, and some that are peculiar to that art or science. Words of the last kind are called *terms of the art*, and ought to be distinctly explained, that their meaning may be understood.

A definition is nothing else but an explication of the meaning of a word, by words whose meaning is already known. Hence it is evident that every word cannot be defined; for the definition must consist of words; and there could be no definition, if there were not words previously understood without definition. Common words, therefore, ought to be used in their common acceptation; and, when they have different acceptations in common language, these, when it is necessary, ought to be distinguished. But they require no definition. It is sufficient to define words that are uncommon, or that are used in an uncommon meaning.

It may farther be observed, that there are many words, which, though they may need explication, cannot be logically defined. A logical definition – that is, a strict and proper definition – must express the kind [genus] of the thing defined, and the specific difference by which the species defined is distinguished from every other species belonging to that kind. It is natural to the mind of man to class things under various kinds, and again to subdivide every kind into its various species. A species may often be subdivided into subordinate species, and then it is considered as a kind.

From what has been said of logical definition, it is evident, that no word can be logically defined which does not denote a species; because such things only can have a specific difference; and a specific difference is essential to a logical definition. On this account there can be no logical definition of individual things, such as London or Paris. Individuals are distinguished either by proper names, or by accidental circumstances of time or place; but they have no specific difference; and, therefore, though they may be known by proper names, or may be described by circumstances or relations, they cannot be defined. It is no less evident that the most general words cannot be logically defined, because there is not a more general term, of which they are a species.

Nay, we cannot define every species of things, because it happens sometimes that we have not words to express the specific difference. Thus, a scarlet colour is, no doubt, a species of colour; but how shall we express the specific difference by which scarlet is distinguished from green or blue? The difference of them is immediately perceived by the eye; but we have not words to express it. These things we are taught by logic.

Without having recourse to the principles of logic, we may easily be satisfied that words cannot be defined, which signify things perfectly simple, and void of all composition. This observation, I think, was first made by Des Cartes, and afterwards more fully illustrated by Locke. And, however obvious it appears to be, many instances may be given of great philosophers who have perplexed and darkened the subjects they have treated, by not knowing, or not attending to it.

When men attempt to define things which cannot be defined, their definitions will always be either obscure or false. It was one of the capital defects of Aristotle's philosophy, that he pretended to define the simplest things, which neither can be, nor need to be defined – such as *time* and *motion*. Among modern philosophers, I know none that has abused definition so much as Carolus [Christianus] Wolfius, the famous German philosopher, who, in a work on the human mind, called 'Psychologia Empirica,' consisting of many hundred propositions, fortified by demonstrations, with a proportional accompaniment of definitions, corollaries, and scholia, has given so many definitions of things which cannot be defined, and so many demonstrations of things self-evident, that the greatest part of the work consists of tautology, and ringing changes upon words.

There is no subject in which there is more frequent occasion to use words that cannot be logically defined, than in treating of the powers and operations of the mind. The simplest operations of our minds must all be expressed by words of this kind. No man can explain, by a logical definition, what it is to *think*, to *apprehend*, to *believe*, to *will*, to *desire*. Every man who understands the language, has some notion of the meaning of those words; and every man who is capable of reflection may, by attending to the operations of his own mind, which are signified by them, form a clear and distinct notion of them; but they cannot be logically defined.

Since, therefore, it is often impossible to define words which we must use on this subject, we must as much as possible use common words, in their common acceptation, pointing out their various senses where they are ambiguous; and, when we are obliged to use words less common, we must endeavour to explain them as well as we can, without affecting to give logical definitions, when the nature of the thing does not allow it.

The following observations on the meaning of certain words are intended to supply, as far as we can, the want of definitions, by preventing ambiguity or obscurity in the use of them.

1. By the *mind* of a man, we understand that in him which thinks, remembers, reasons, wills. The essence both of body and of mind is unknown to us. We know certain properties of the first, and certain operations of the last, and by these only we can define or describe them. We define body to be that which is extended, solid, moveable, divisible. In like manner, we define

mind to be that which thinks. We are conscious that we think, and that we have a variety of thoughts of different kinds – such as seeing, hearing, remembering, deliberating, resolving, loving, hating, and many other kinds of thought – all which we are taught by nature to attribute to one internal principle; and this principle of thought we call the *mind* or *soul* of a man.

2. By the *operations* of the mind, we understand every mode of thinking of which we are conscious.

It deserves our notice, that the various modes of thinking have always, and in all languages, as far as we know, been called by the name of operations of the mind, or by names of the same import. To body we ascribe various properties, but not operations, properly so called: it is extended, divisible, moveable, inert; it continues in any state in which it is put; every change of its state is the effect of some force impressed upon it, and is exactly proportional to the force impressed, and in the precise direction of that force. These are the general properties of matter, and these are not operations; on the contrary, they all imply its being a dead, inactive thing, which moves only as it is moved, and acts only by being acted upon.

But the mind is, from its very nature, a living and active being. Everything we know of it implies life and active energy; and the reason why all its modes of thinking are called its operations, is, that in all, or in most of them, it is not merely passive, as body is, but is really and properly active.

In all ages, and in all languages, ancient and modern, the various modes of thinking have been expressed by words of active signification, such as *seeing*, *hearing*, *reasoning*, *willing*, and the like. It seems, therefore, to be the natural judgment of mankind, that the mind is active in its various ways of thinking: and, for this reason, they are called its operations, and are expressed by active verbs.

It may be made a question, What regard is to be paid to this natural judgment? May it not be a vulgar error? Philosophers who think so have, no doubt, a right to be heard. But, until it is proved that the mind is not active in thinking, but merely passive, the common language with regard to its operations ought to be used, and ought not to give place to a phraseology invented by philosophers, which implies its being merely passive.

3. The words *power* and *faculty*, which are often used in speaking of the mind, need little explication. Every operation supposes a power in the being that operates; for to suppose anything to operate, which has no power to operate, is manifestly absurd. But, on the other hand, there is no absurdity in supposing a being to have power to operate, when it does not operate. Thus

I may have power to walk, when I sit; or to speak, when I am silent. Every operation, therefore, implies power; but the power does not imply the operation.

The *faculties* of the mind, and its *powers*, are often used as synonymous expressions. But, as most synonymes have some minute distinction that deserves notice, I apprehend that the word *faculty* is most properly applied to those powers of the mind which are original and natural, and which make a part of the constitution of the mind. There are other powers, which are acquired by use, exercise, or study, which are not called faculties, but *habits*. There must be something in the constitution of the mind necessary to our being able to acquire habits – and this is commonly called *capacity*.

4. We frequently meet with a distinction in writers upon this subject, between things *in the mind*, and things *external* to the mind. The powers, faculties, and operations of the mind, are things in the mind. Everything is said to be in the mind, of which the mind is the *subject*. It is self-evident that there are some things which cannot exist without a subject to which they belong, and of which they are attributes. Thus, colour must be in something coloured; figure in something figured; thought can only be in something that thinks; wisdom and virtue cannot exist but in some being that is wise and virtuous. When, therefore, we speak of things in the mind, we understand by this, things of which the mind is the subject. Excepting the mind itself, and things in the mind, all other things are said to be external. It ought therefore to be remembered, that this distinction between things in the mind and things external, is not meant to signify the place of the things we speak of, but their subject.

There is a figurative sense in which things are said to be in the mind, which it is sufficient barely to mention. We say such a thing was not in my mind; meaning no more than that I had not the least thought of it. By a figure, we put the thing for the thought of it. In this sense external things are in the mind as often as they are the objects of our thought.

5. *Thinking* is a very general word, which includes all the operations of our minds, and is so well understood as to need no definition.

To *perceive*, to *remember*, to be *conscious*, and to *conceive* or *imagine*, are words common to philosophers and to the vulgar. They signify different operations of the mind, which are distinguished in all languages, and by all men that think. I shall endeavour to use them in their most common and proper

THOMAS REID – *Mind and its Operations*

acceptation, and I think they are hardly capable of strict definition. But, as some philosophers, in treating of the mind, have taken the liberty to use them very improperly, so as to corrupt the English language, and to confound things which the common understanding of mankind hath always led them to distinguish, I shall make some observations on the meaning of them, that may prevent ambiguity or confusion in the use of them.

6. *First*, We are never said to *perceive* things, of the existence of which we have not a full conviction. I may *conceive* or *imagine* a mountain of gold, or a winged horse; but no man says that he perceives such a creature of imagination. Thus *perception* is distinguished from *conception* or imagination. *Secondly*, Perception is applied only to external objects, not to those that are in the mind itself. When I am pained, I do not say that I perceive pain, but that I feel it, or that I am conscious of it. Thus, *perception* is distinguished from *consciousness*. *Thirdly*, The immediate object of perception must be something present, and not what is past. We may remember what is past, but do not perceive it. I may say, I perceive such a person has had the small-pox; but this phrase is figurative, although the figure is so familiar that it is not observed. The meaning of it is, that I perceive the pits in his face, which are certain signs of his having had the small pox. We say we perceive the thing signified, when we only perceive the sign. But when the word *perception* is used properly, and without any figure, it is never applied to things past. And thus it is distinguished from *remembrance*.

In a word, perception is most properly applied to the evidence which we have of external objects by our senses. But, as this is a very clear and cogent kind of evidence, the word is often applied by analogy to the evidence of reason or of testimony, when it is clear and cogent. The perception of external objects by our senses, is an operation of the mind of a peculiar nature, and ought to have a name appropriated to it. It has so in all languages. And, in English, I know of no word more proper to express this act of the mind than perception. Seeing, hearing, smelling, tasting and touching or feeling, are words that express the operations, proper to each sense; perceiving expresses that which is common to them all.

The observations made on this word would have been unnecessary, if it had not been so much abused in philosophical writings upon the mind; for, in other writings, it has no obscurity. Although this abuse is not chargeable on Mr Hume only, yet I think he has carried it to the highest pitch. The first sentence of his 'Treatise of Human Nature' runs thus: – 'All the perceptions of the human mind resolve themselves into two distinct heads, which I shall call impressions and ideas.' He adds, a little after, that, under the name of impressions, he comprehends all our sensations, passions, and emotions. Here we learn that our passions and emotions are perceptions. I believe, no English writer before him ever gave the name of a perception to any passion or emotion. When a man is angry, we must say that he has the perception of anger. When he is in love, that he has the perception of love. He speaks often of the perceptions of memory, and of the perceptions of imagination; and he might as well speak of the hearing of sight, or the smelling of touch; for, surely, hearing is not more different from sight, or smelling from touch, than perceiving is from remembering or imagining.

7. *Consciousness* is a word used by philosophers, to signify that immediate knowledge which we have of our present thoughts and purposes, and, in general, of all the present operations of our minds. Whence we may observe, that consciousness is only of things present. To apply consciousness to things past, which sometimes is done in popular discourse, is to confound consciousness with memory; and all such confusion of words ought to be avoided in philosophical discourse. It is likewise to be observed, that consciousness is only of things in the mind, and not of external things. It is improper to say, I am conscious of the table which is before me. I perceive it, I see it; but do not say I am conscious of it. As that consciousness by which we have a knowledge of the operations of our own minds, is a different power from that by which we perceive external objects, and as these different powers have different names in our language, and, I believe, in all languages, a philosopher ought carefully to preserve this distinction, and never to confound things so different in their nature.

8. *Conceiving*, *imagining*, and *apprehending*, are commonly used as synonymous in our language, and signify the same thing which the logicians call simple apprehension. This is an operation of the mind different from all those we have mentioned. Whatever we perceive, whatever we remember, whatever we are conscious of, we have a full persuasion or conviction of its existence. But we may conceive or imagine what has no existence, and what we firmly believe to have no existence. What never had an existence cannot be remembered; what has no existence *at present* cannot be the object of perception or of consciousness; but what never had, nor has any existence, may be conceived. Every man knows

that it is as easy to conceive a winged horse, or a centaur, as it is to conceive a horse or a man. Let it be observed, therefore, that to *conceive*, to *imagine*, to *apprehend*, when taken in the proper sense, signify an act of the mind which implies no belief or judgment at all. It is an act of the mind by which nothing is affirmed or denied, and which, therefore, can neither be true nor false.

But there is another and a very different meaning of those words, so common and so well authorized in language that it cannot easily be avoided; and on that account we ought to be the more on our guard, that we be not misled by the ambiguity. Politeness and good-breeding lead men, on most occasions, to express their opinions with modesty, especially when they differ from others whom they ought to respect. Therefore, when we would express our opinion modestly, instead of saying, 'This is my opinion,' or, 'This is my judgment,' which has the air of dogmaticalness, we say, 'I conceive it to be thus – I imagine, or apprehend it to be thus;' which is understood as a modest declaration of our judgment. In like manner, when anything is said which we take to be impossible, we say, 'We cannot conceive it;' meaning that we cannot believe it.

Thus we see that the words *conceive, imagine, apprehend*, have two meanings, and are used to express two operations of the mind, which ought never to be confounded. Sometimes they express simple apprehension, which implies no judgment at all; sometimes they express judgment or opinion. This ambiguity ought to be attended to, that we may not impose upon ourselves or others in the use of them. The ambiguity is indeed remedied, in a great measure, by their construction. When they are used to express simple apprehension, they are followed by a noun in the *accusative case*, which signifies the object conceived; but, when they are used to express opinion or judgment, they are commonly followed by a verb, in the *infinitive mood*. 'I conceive an Egyptian pyramid.' This implies no judgment. 'I conceive the Egyptian pyramids to be the most ancient monuments of human art.' This implies judgment. When the words are used in the last sense, the thing conceived must be a proposition, because judgment cannot be expressed but by a proposition. When they are used in the first sense, the thing conceived may be no proposition, but a simple term only – as a pyramid, an obelisk. Yet it may be observed, that even a proposition may be simply apprehended, without forming any judgment of its truth or falsehood: for it is one thing to conceive the meaning of a proposition; it is another thing to judge it to be true or false.

Although the distinction between simple apprehension, and every degree of assent or judgment, be perfectly evident to every man who reflects attentively on what passes in his own mind – although it is very necessary, in treating of the powers of the mind, to attend carefully to this distinction – yet, in the affairs of common life, it is seldom necessary to observe it accurately. On this account we shall find, in all common languages, the words which express one of those operations frequently applied to the other. To think, to suppose, to imagine, to conceive, to apprehend, are the words we use to express simple apprehension; but they are all frequently used to express judgment. Their ambiguity seldom occasions any inconvenience in the common affairs of life, for which language is framed. But it has perplexed philosophers, in treating of the operations of the mind, and will always perplex them, if they do not attend accurately to the different meanings which are put upon those words on different occasions.

9. Most of the operations of the mind, from their very nature, must have objects to which they are directed, and about which they are employed. He that perceives, must perceive something; and that which he perceives is called the object of his perception. To perceive, without having any object of perception, is impossible. The mind that perceives, the object perceived, and the *operation* of perceiving that object, are distinct things, and are distinguished in the structure of all languages. In this sentence, 'I see, or perceive the moon,' *I* is the person or *mind*, the active verb, *see* denotes the operation of that mind, and the *moon* denotes the object. What we have said of perceiving, is equally applicable to most operations of the mind. Such operations are, in all languages, expressed by active transitive verbs; and we know that, in all languages, such verbs require a thing or person, which is the agent, and a noun following in an oblique case, which is the object. Whence it is evident, that all mankind, both those who have contrived language, and those who use it with understanding, have distinguished these three things as different – to wit, the operations of the mind, which are expressed by active verbs; the mind itself, which is the nominative to those verbs; and the object, which is, in the oblique case, governed by them.

It would have been unnecessary to explain so obvious a distinction, if some systems of philosophy had not confounded it. Mr Hume's system, in particular, confounds all distinction between the operations of the mind and their objects. When he speaks of the ideas of memory, the ideas of imagination, and the ideas of sense, it is often impossible, from the tenor of his discourse, to know whether, by those ideas, he means the operations of the mind, or the objects about which they are employed. And, indeed, according to his system, there is no distinction between the one and the other.

A philosopher is, no doubt, entitled to examine even those distinctions that are to be found in the structure of all languages; and, if he is able to shew that there is no foundation for them in the nature of the things distinguished – if he can point out some prejudice common to mankind which has led them to distinguish things that are not really different – in that case, such a distinction may be imputed to a vulgar error, which ought to be corrected in philosophy. But when, in his first setting out, he takes it for granted, without proof, that distinctions found in the structure of all languages, have no foundation in nature, this, surely, is too fastidious a way of treating the common sense of mankind. When we come to be instructed by philosophers, we must bring the old light of common sense along with us, and by it judge of the new light which the philosopher communicates to us. But when we are required to put out the old light altogether, that we may follow the new, we have reason to be on our guard. There may be distinctions that have a real foundation, and which may be necessary in philosophy, which are not made in common language, because not necessary in the common business of life. But I believe no instance will be found of a distinction made in all languages, which has not a just foundation in nature.

10. The word *idea* occurs so frequently in modern philosophical writings upon the mind, and is so ambiguous in its meaning, that it is necessary to make some observations upon it. There are chiefly two meanings of this word in modern authors – a popular and a philosophical.

First, In popular language, *idea* signifies the same thing as conception, apprehension, notion. To have an idea of anything, is to conceive it. To have a distinct idea, is to conceive it distinctly. To have no idea of it, is not to conceive it at all. It was before observed, that conceiving or apprehending has always been considered by all men as an act or operation of the mind, and, on that account, has been expressed in all languages by an active verb. When, therefore, we use the phrase of having ideas, in the popular sense, we ought to attend to this, that it signifies precisely the same thing which we commonly express by the active verbs, conceiving or apprehending.

When the word idea is taken in this popular sense, no man can possibly doubt whether he has ideas. For he that doubts must think, and to think is to have ideas.

Sometimes, in popular language, a man's ideas signify his opinions. The ideas of Aristotle, or of Epicurus, signify the opinions of these philosophers. What was formerly said of the words *imagine, conceive, apprehend*, that they are sometimes used to express judgment, is no less true of the word idea. This signification of the word seems indeed more common in the French language than in English. But it is found in this sense in good English authors, and even in Mr Locke. Thus we see, that having *ideas*, taken in the popular sense, has precisely, the same meaning with conceiving imagining, apprehending, and has likewise the same ambiguity. It may, therefore, be doubted, whether the introduction of this word into popular discourse, to signify the operation of conceiving, or apprehending, was at all necessary. For, *first*, We have, as has been shewn, several words which are either originally English, or have been long naturalized, that express the same thing; why, therefore, should we adopt a Greek word, in place of these, any more than a French or a German word? Besides, the words of our own language are less ambiguous. For the word idea has, for many ages, been used by philosophers as a term of art; and in the different systems of philosophers means very different things.

Secondly, According to the philosophical meaning of the word idea, it does not signify that act of the mind which we call thought or conception, but some object of thought. Ideas, according to Mr Locke, (whose very frequent use of this word has probably been the occasion of its being adopted into common language,) 'are nothing but the immediate objects of the mind in thinking.' But of those objects of thought called ideas, different sects of philosophers have given a very different account. Bruckerus, a learned German, wrote a whole book, giving the history of ideas.

The most ancient system we have concerning ideas, is that which is explained in several dialogues of Plato, and which many ancient, as well as modern writers, have ascribed to Plato as the inventor. But it is certain that Plato had his doctrine upon this subject, as well as the name *idea*, from the school of Pythagoras. We have still extant, a tract of Timæus, the Locrian, a Pythagorean philosopher, concerning the soul of the world, in which we find the substance of Plato's doctrine concerning ideas. They were held to be eternal, uncreated, and immutable forms, or models, according to which the Deity made every species of things that exists, of an eternal matter. Those philosophers held, that there are three first principles of all things: *First*, An eternal matter, of which all things were made; *Secondly*, Eternal and immaterial forms, or ideas, according to which they were made; and, *Thirdly*, An efficient cause, the Deity who made them. The mind of man, in order to its being fitted for the contemplation of these eternal ideas, must undergo a certain purification, and be weaned from sensible things. The eternal ideas are the only object of science; because the objects of sense, being in a perpetual flux, there can be no real knowledge with regard to them.

The philosophers of the Alexandrian school, commonly called *the latter Platonists*, made some change upon the system of the ancient Platonists with respect to the eternal ideas. They held them not to be a principle distinct from the Deity, but to be the conceptions of things in the divine understanding; the natures and essences of all things being perfectly known to him from eternity.

It ought to be observed that the Pythagoreans, and the Platonists, whether elder or latter, made the eternal ideas to be objects of science only, and of abstract contemplation, not the objects of sense. And in this, the ancient system of eternal ideas differs from the modern one of Father Malebranche. He held, in common with other modern philosophers, that no external thing is perceived by us immediately, but only by ideas. But he thought that the ideas, by which we perceive an external world, are the ideas of the Deity himself, in whose mind the ideas of all things, past, present, and future, must have been from eternity; for the Deity being intimately present to our minds at all times, may discover to us as much of his ideas as he sees proper, according to certain established laws of nature; and in his ideas, as in a mirror, we perceive whatever we do perceive of the external world.

Thus we have three systems, which maintain that the ideas which are the immediate objects of human knowledge, are eternal and immutable, and existed before the things which they represent. There are other systems, according to which the ideas which are the immediate objects of all our thoughts, are posterior to the things which they represent, and derived from them. We shall give some account of these; but, as they have gradually sprung out of the ancient Peripatetic system, it is necessary to begin with some account of it.

Aristotle taught that all the objects of our thoughts enter at first by the senses; and, since the sense cannot receive external material objects themselves, it receives their species – that is, their images or forms, without the matter; as wax receives the form of the seal without any of the matter of it. These images or forms, impressed upon the senses, are called *sensible species*, and are the objects only of the sensitive part of the mind; but, by various internal powers, they are retained, refined, and spiritualized, so as to become objects of memory and imagination, and, at last, of pure intellection. When they are objects of memory and of imagination, they get the name of *phantasms*. When, by farther refinement, and being stripped of their particularities, they become objects of science, they are called *intelligible species:* so that every immediate object, whether of sense, of memory, of imagination, or of reasoning, must be some phantasm or species in the mind itself.

The followers of Aristotle, especially the schoolmen, made great additions to this theory, which the author himself mentions very briefly, and with an appearance of reserve. They entered into large disquisitions with regard to the sensible species: what kind of things they are; how they are sent forth by the object, and enter by the organs of the senses; how they are preserved and refined by various agents, called internal senses, concerning the number and offices of which they had many controversies. But we shall not enter into a detail of these matters.

The reason of giving this brief account of the theory of the Peripatetics, with regard to the immediate objects of our thoughts, is, because the doctrine of modern philosophers concerning ideas is built upon it. Mr Locke, who uses this word so very frequently, tells us, that he means the same thing by it as is commonly meant by *species* or *phantasm*.Gassendi, from whom Locke borrowed more than from any other author, says the same. The words *species* and *phantasm*, are terms of art in the Peripatetic system, and the meaning of them is to be learned from it.

The theory of Democritus and Epicurus, on this subject, was not very unlike to that of the Peripatetics. They held that all bodies continually send forth slender films or spectres from their surface, of such extreme subtilty that they easily penetrate our gross bodies, or enter by the organs of sense, and stamp their image upon the mind. The sensible species of Aristotle were mere forms without matter. The spectres of Epicurus were composed of a very subtile matter.

Modern philosophers, as well as the Peripatetics and Epicureans of old, have conceived that external objects cannot be the immediate objects of our thought; that there must be some image of them in the mind itself, in which, as in a mirror, they are seen. And the name *idea*, in the philosophical sense of it, is given to those internal and immediate objects of our thoughts. The external thing is the remote or mediate object; but the idea, or image of that object in the mind, is the immediate object, without which we could have no perception, no remembrance, no conception of the mediate object.

When, therefore, in common language, we speak of having an idea of anything, we mean no more by that expression, but thinking of it. The vulgar allows that this expression implies a mind that thinks, an act of that mind which we call thinking, and an object about which we think. But, besides these three, the philosopher conceives that there is a fourth – to wit, the *idea*, which is the immediate object. The idea is in the mind itself, and can have no existence but in a mind that thinks; but the remote or mediate object may be something external, as the sun or moon; it may be something past or future; it may be something which never existed. This is the philosophical meaning of the word *idea;* and we may observe that this meaning of that word is built upon a philosophical opinion: for, if philosophers had not believed that there are such immediate objects of all our thoughts in the mind, they would never have used the word idea to express them.

I shall only add, on this article, that, although I may have occasion to use the word idea in this philosophical sense in explaining the opinions of others, I shall have no occasion to use it in expressing my own, because I believe *ideas*, taken in this sense, to be a mere fiction of philosophers. And, in the popular meaning of the word, there is the less occasion to use it, because the English words *thought, notion, apprehension*, answer the purpose as well as the Greek word *idea;* with this advantage, that they are less ambiguous. There is, indeed, a meaning of the word idea, which I think most agreeable to its use in ancient philosophy, and which I would willingly adopt, if use, the arbiter of language, did permit. But this will come to be explained afterwards.

11. The word *impression* is used by Mr Hume, in speaking of the operations of the mind, almost as often as the word *idea* is by Mr Locke. What the latter calls ideas, the former divides into two classes; one of which he calls impressions, the other ideas. I shall make some observations upon Mr Hume's explication of *that* word, and then consider the proper meaning of it in the English language.

'We may divide,' (says Mr Hume, 'Essays,' vol. II., p. 18,) 'all the perceptions of the human mind into two classes or species, which are distinguished by their different degrees of force and vivacity. The less lively and forcible are commonly denominated Thoughts or Ideas. The other species want a name in our language, and in most others; [I suppose because it was not requisite for any but philosophical purposes to rank them under a general term or appellation.] Let us, therefore, use a little freedom, and call them Impressions; [employing that word in a sense somewhat different from the usual.] By the term *impression*, then, I mean all our more lively perceptions, when we hear, or see, or feel, or love, or hate, or desire, or will. [And impressions are distinguished from] ideas [which] are the less lively perceptions, of which we are conscious, when we reflect on any of those sensations or movements above mentioned.'

This is the explication Mr Hume hath given in his 'Essays' of the term *impressions*, when applied to the mind; and his explication of it, in his 'Treatise of Human Nature,' is to the same purpose. [Vol. I, p. 11.]

Disputes about words belong rather to grammarians than to philosophers; but philosophers ought not to escape censure when they corrupt a language, by using words in a way which the purity of the language will not admit. I find fault with Mr Hume's phraseology in the words I have quoted –

First, Because he gives the name of perceptions to every operation of the mind. Love is a perception, hatred a perception; desire is a perception, will is a perception; and, by the same rule, a doubt, a question, a command, is a perception. This is an intolerable abuse of language, which no philosopher has authority to introduce.

Secondly, When Mr Hume says, *that we may divide all the perceptions of the human mind into two classes or species, which are distinguished by their degrees of force and vivacity*, the manner of expression is loose and unphilosophical. To differ in species is one thing; to differ in degree is another. Things which differ in degree only must be of the same species. It is a maxim of common sense, admitted by all men, that *greater* and *less* do not make a change of species. The same man may differ in the degree of his force and vivacity, in the morning and at night, in health and in sickness; but this is so far from making him a different species, that it does not so much as make him a different individual. To say, therefore, that two different classes, or species of perceptions, are distinguished by the degrees of their force and vivacity, is to confound a difference of *degree* with a difference of *species*, which every man of understanding knows how to distinguish.

Thirdly, We may observe, that this author, having given the general name of perception to all the operations of the mind, and distinguished them into two classes or species, which differ only in degree of force and vivacity, tells us, that he gives the name of impressions to all our more lively perceptions – to wit, when we hear, or see, or feel, or love, or hate, or desire, or will. There is great confusion in this account of the meaning of the word *impression*. When I see, this is an *impression*. But why has not the author told us whether he gives the name of *impression* to the object seen, or to that act of my mind by which I see it? When I see the full moon, the full moon is one thing, my perceiving it is another thing. Which of these two things does he call an impression? We are left to guess this; nor does all that this author writes about impressions clear this point. Everything he says tends to darken it, and to lead us to think that the full moon which I see, and my seeing it, are not two things, but one and the same thing.

The same observation may be applied to every other instance the author gives to illustrate the meaning of the word *impression*. 'When we hear, when we feel, when we love, when we hate, when we desire, when we will.' In all these acts of the mind there must be an *object*, which is heard, or felt, or loved, or hated, or desired, or willed. Thus, for instance, I love my country. This, says Mr Hume, is an *impression*. But what is the *impression*? Is it my country, or is it the affection I bear to it? I ask the philosopher this question; but I find no answer to it. And when I read all that he has *written* on this subject, I find this word *impression* sometimes used to signify an operation of the mind, sometimes the object of the operation; but, for the most part, it is a vague and indetermined word that signifies both.

I know not whether it may be considered as an apology for such abuse of words, in an author who understood the language so well, and used it with so great propriety in writing on other subjects, that Mr Hume's system, with regard to the mind, required a language of a different structure from the common: or, if expressed in plain English, would have been too shocking to the common sense of mankind. To give an instance or two of this. If a man receives a present on which he puts a high value, if he see and handle it, and put it in his pocket, this, says Mr Hume, is an *impression*. If the man only dream that he received such a present, this is an *idea*. Wherein lies the difference between this impression and this idea – between the dream and the reality? They are different classes or species, says Mr Hume: so far all men will agree with him. But he adds, that they are distinguished only by different degrees of force and vivacity. Here he insinuates a tenet of his own, in contradiction to the commonsense of mankind. Common sense convinces every man, that a lively dream is no nearer to a reality than a faint one; and that, if a man should dream that he had all the wealth of Crœsus, it would not put one farthing in his pocket. It is impossible to fabricate arguments against such undeniable principles, without confounding the meaning of words.

In like manner, if a man would persuade me that the moon which I see, and my seeing it, are not two things, but one and the same thing, he will answer his purpose less by arguing this point in plain English, than by confounding the two under one name – such as that of an *impression*. For such is the power of words, that, if we can be brought to the habit of calling two things that are connected *by the same name*, we are the more easily led to believe them to be one and the same thing.

Let us next consider the proper meaning of the word *impression* in English, that we may see how far it is fit to express either the operations of the mind or their objects.

When a figure is stamped upon a body by pressure, that figure is called an *impression*, as the impression of a seal on wax, of printing-types, or of a copperplate on paper. This seems now to be the literal sense of the word; the effect borrowing its name from the cause. But, by metaphor or analogy, like most other words, its meaning is extended, so as to signify any change produced in a body by the operation of some external cause. A blow of the hand makes no impression on a stone wall; but a battery of cannon may. The moon raises a tide in the ocean, but makes no impression on rivers and lakes.

When we speak of making an impression on the mind, the word is carried still farther from its literal meaning; use, however, which is the arbiter of language, authorizes this application of it – as when we say that admonition and reproof make little impression on those who are confirmed in bad habits. The same discourse delivered in one way makes a strong impression on the hearers; delivered in another way, it makes no impression at all.

It may be observed that, in such examples, an impression made on the mind always implies some change of purpose or will; some new habit produced, or some former habit weakened; some passion raised or allayed. When such changes are produced by persuasion, example, or any external cause, we say that such causes make an impression upon the mind; but, when things are seen, or heard, or apprehended, without producing any passion or emotion, we say that they make no impression.

In the most extensive sense, an impression is a change produced in some passive subject by the operation of an external cause. If we suppose an active being to produce any change in itself by its own active power, this is never called an impression. It is the act or operation of the being itself, not an impression upon it. From this it appears, that to give the name of an impression to any effect produced in the mind, is to suppose that the mind does not act at all in the production of that effect. If seeing, hearing, desiring, willing, be operations of the mind, they cannot be impressions. If they be impressions, they cannot be operations of the mind. In the structure of all languages, they are considered as acts or operations of the mind itself, and the names given them imply this. To call them impressions, therefore, is to trespass against the structure, not of a particular language only, but of all languages.

If the word *impression* be an improper word to signify the operations of the mind, it is at least as improper to signify their objects; for would any man be thought to speak with propriety, who should say that the sun is an impression, that the earth and the sea are impressions?

It is commonly believed, and taken for granted, that every language, if it be sufficiently copious in words, is equally fit to express all opinions, whether they be true or false. I apprehend, however, that there is an exception to this general rule, which deserves our notice. There are certain common opinions of mankind, upon which the structure and grammar of all languages are founded. While these opinions are common to all men, there will be a great similarity in all languages that are to be found on the face of the earth. Such a similarity there really is; for we find in all languages the same parts of speech, the distinction of nouns and verbs, the distinction of nouns into adjective and substantive, of verbs into active and passive. In verbs we find like tenses, moods, persons, and numbers. There are general rules of grammar, the same in all languages. This similarity of structure in all languages, shews an uniformity among men in those opinions upon which the structure of language is founded.

If, for instance, we should suppose that there was a nation who believed that the things which we call attributes might exist without a subject, there would be in their language no distinction between adjectives and substantives, nor would it be a rule with them that an adjective has no meaning, unless when joined to a substantive. If there was any nation who did not distinguish between acting and being acted upon, there would in their language be no distinction between active and passive verbs; nor would it be a rule that the active verb must have an agent in the nominative case, but that, in the passive verb, the agent must be in an oblique case.

The structure of all languages is grounded upon common notions, which Mr Hume's philosophy opposes, and endeavours to overturn. This, no doubt, led him to warp the common language into a conformity with his principles; but we ought not to imitate him in this, until we are satisfied that his principles are built on a solid foundation.

12. *Sensation* is a name given by philosophers to an act-of-mind, which may be distinguished from all others by this, that it hath no object distinct from the act itself. Pain of every kind is an uneasy sensation. When I am pained, I cannot say that the pain I feel is one thing, and that my feeling it is another thing. They are one and the same thing, and cannot be disjoined, even in imagination. Pain, when it is not felt, has no existence. It can be neither greater nor less in degree or duration, nor anything else in kind than it is felt to be. It cannot exist by itself, nor in any subject but in a sentient being. No quality of an inanimate insentient being can have the least resemblance to it.

What we have said of pain may be applied to every other sensation. Some of them are agreeable, others uneasy, in various degrees. These being objects of desire or aversion, have some attention given to them; but many are indifferent, and so little attended to that they have no name in any language.

Most operations of the mind that have names in common language, are complex in their nature, and made up of various ingredients, or more simple acts; which, though conjoined in our constitution, must be disjoined by abstraction, in order to our having a distinct and scientific notion of the complex operation. In such operations, sensation, for the most part, makes an ingredient. Those who do not attend to the complex nature of such operations, are apt to resolve them into some one of the simple acts of which they are compounded, overlooking the others. And from this cause many disputes have been raised, and many errors have been occasioned with regard to the nature of such operations.

The perception of external objects is accompanied with some sensation corresponding to the object perceived, and such sensations have, in many cases, in all languages, the same name with the external object which they always accompany. The difficulty of disjoining, by abstraction, things thus constantly conjoined in the course of nature, and things which have one and the same name in all languages, has likewise been frequently an occasion of errors in the philosophy of the mind. To avoid such errors, nothing is of more importance than to have a distinct notion of that simple act of the mind which we call *sensation*, and which we have endeavoured to describe. By this means, we shall find it more easy to distinguish it from every external object that it accompanies, and from every other act of the mind that may be conjoined with it. For this purpose, it is likewise of importance that the name of *sensation* should, in philosophical writings, be appropriated to signify this simple act of the mind, without including anything more in its signification, or being applied to other purposes.

I shall add an observation concerning the word *feeling*. This word has two meanings. *First*, it signifies the perceptions we have of external objects, by the sense of touch. When we speak of feeling a body to be hard or soft, rough or smooth, hot or cold, to feel these things is to perceive them by touch. They are external things, and that act of the mind by which we feel them is easily distinguished from the objects felt. *Secondly*, the word *feeling* is used to signify the same thing as *sensation*, which we have just now explained; and, in this sense, it has no object; the feeling and the thing felt are one and the same.

Perhaps betwixt feeling, taken in this last sense, and sensation, there may be this small difference, that sensation is most commonly used to signify those feelings which we have by our external senses and bodily appetites, and all our bodily pains and pleasures. But there are *feelings* of a nobler nature accompanying our affections, our moral judgments, and our determinations in matters of taste, to which the word *sensation* is less properly applied.

I have premised these observations on the meaning of certain words that frequently occur in treating of this subject, for two reasons: *First*, That I may be the better understood when I use them; and, *Secondly*, That those who would make any progress in this branch of science, may accustom themselves to attend very carefully to the meaning of words that are used in it. They may be assured of this, that the ambiguity of words, and the vague and improper application of them, have thrown more darkness upon this subject than the subtilty and intricacy of things.

When we use common words, we ought to use them in the sense in which they are most commonly used by the best and purest writers in the language; and, when we have occasion to enlarge or restrict the meaning of a common word, or give it more precision than it has in common language, the reader ought to have a warning of this, otherwise we shall impose upon ourselves and upon him.

A very respectable writer has given a good example of this kind, by explaining, in an Appendix to his 'Elements of Criticism,' the terms he has occasion to use. In that Appendix, most of the words are explained on which I have been making observations; and the explication I have given, I think, agrees, for the most part, with his.

Other words that need explication, shall be explained as they occur.

CHAPTER II *Principles taken for granted*

As there are words common to philosophers and to the vulgar, which need no explication, so there are principles common to both, which need no proof, and which do not admit of direct proof.

One who applies to any branch of science, must be come to years of understanding, and, consequently, must have exercised his reason, and the other powers of his mind, in various ways. He must have formed various opinions and principles, by which he conducts himself in the affairs of life. Of those principles, some are common to all men, being evident in themselves, and so necessary in the conduct of life that a man cannot live and act according to the rules of common prudence without them.

All men that have common understanding, agree in such principles; and consider a man as lunatic or destitute of common sense, who denies or calls them in question. Thus, if any man were found of so strange a turn as not to believe his own eyes, to put no trust in his senses, nor have the least regard to their testimony, would any man think it worth while to reason gravely with such a person, and, by argument, to convince him of his error? Surely no wise man would. For, before men can reason together, they must agree in first principles; and it is impossible to reason with a man who has no principles in common with you.

There are, therefore, common principles, which are the foundation of all reasoning and of all science. Such common principles seldom admit of direct proof, nor do they need it. Men need not to be taught them; for they are such as all men of common understanding know; or such, at least, as they give a ready assent to, as soon as they are proposed and understood.

Such principles, when we have occasion to use them in science, are called *axioms*. And, although it be not absolutely necessary, yet it may be of great use, to point out the principles or axioms on which a science is grounded.

Thus, mathematicians, before they prove any of the propositions of mathematics, lay down certain axioms, or common principles, upon which they build their reasonings. And although those axioms be truths which every man knew before – such as, That the whole is greater than a part, That equal quantities added to equal quantities make equal sums; yet, when we see nothing assumed in the proof of mathematical propositions, but such self-evident axioms, the propositions appear more certain, and leave no room for doubt or dispute.

In all other sciences, as well as in mathematics, it will be found that there are a few common principles, upon which all the reasonings in that science are grounded, and into which they may be resolved. If these were pointed out and considered, we should be better able to judge what stress may be laid upon the conclusions in that science. If the principles be certain, the conclusions justly drawn from them must be certain. If the principles be only probable, the conclusions can only be probable. If the principles be false, dubious, or obscure, the superstructure that is built upon them must partake of the weakness of the foundation.

Sir Isaac Newton, the greatest of natural philosophers, has given an example well worthy of imitation, by laying down the common principles or axioms, on which the reasonings in natural philosophy are built. Before this was done, the reasonings of philosophers in that science were as vague and uncertain as they are in most others. Nothing was fixed; all was dispute and controversy; but, by this happy expedient, a solid foundation is laid in that science, and a noble superstructure is raised upon it, about which there is now no more dispute or controversy among men of knowledge, than there is about the conclusions of mathematics.

It may, however, be observed, that the first principles of natural philosophy are of a quite different nature from mathematical axioms: they have not the same kind of evidence, nor are they necessary truths, as mathematical axioms are. They are such as these: That similar effects proceed from the same or similar causes; That we ought to admit of no other causes of natural effects, but such as are true, and sufficient to account for the effects. These are principles which, though they have not the same kind of evidence that mathematical axioms have; yet have such evidence that every man of common understanding readily assents to them, and finds it absolutely necessary to conduct his actions and opinions by them, in the ordinary affairs of life.

Though it has not been usual, yet I conceive it may be useful, to point out some of those things which I shall take for granted, as first principles, in treating of the mind and its faculties. There is the more occasion for this; because very ingenious men, such as Des Cartes, Malebranche, Arnauld, Locke, and many others, have lost much labour, by not distinguishing things which require proof, from things which, though they may admit of illustration, yet, being self-evident, do not admit of proof. When men attempt to deduce such self-evident principles from others more evident, they alway fall into inconclusive reasoning: and the consequence of this has been, that others, such as Berkeley and Hume, finding the arguments brought to prove such first principles to be weak and inconclusive, have been tempted first to doubt of them, and afterwards to deny them.

It is so irksome to reason with those who deny first principles, that wise men commonly decline it. Yet it is not impossible, that what is only a vulgar prejudice may be mistaken for a first principle. Nor is it impossible that what is really a first principle may, by the enchantment of words, have such a mist thrown about it, as to hide its evidence, and to make a man of candour doubt of it. Such cases happen more frequently, perhaps, in this science than in any other; but they are not altogether without remedy. There are ways by which the evidence of first principles may be made more apparent when they are brought into dispute; but they require to be handled in a way peculiar to themselves. Their evidence is not demonstrative, but intuitive. They require not proof, but to be placed in a proper point of view. This will be shewn more fully in its proper place, and applied to those very principles which we now assume. In the meantime, when they are proposed as first principles, the reader is put on his guard, and warned to consider whether they have a just claim to that character.

1. *First*, then, I shall take it for granted, that I *think*, that I *remember*, that I *reason*, and, in general, that I really perform all those operations of mind of which I am conscious.

The operations of our minds are attended with consciousness; and this consciousness is the evidence, the only evidence, which we have or can have of their existence. If a man should take it into his head to think or to say that his consciousness may deceive him, and to require proof that it cannot, I know of no proof that can be given him; he must be left to himself, as a man that denies first principles, without which there can be no reasoning. Every man finds himself under a necessity of believing what consciousness testifies, and everything that hath this testimony is to be taken as a first principle.

2. As by consciousness we know certainly the existence of our present thoughts and passions; so we know the past by remembrance. And, when they are recent, and the remembrance of them fresh, the knowledge of them, from such distinct remembrance, is, in its certainty and evidence, next to that of consciousness.

3. But it is to be observed that we are conscious of many things to which we give little or no *attention*. We can hardly attend to several things at the same time; and our attention is commonly employed about that which is the object of our thought, and rarely about the thought itself. Thus, when a man is angry, his attention is turned to the injury done him, or the injurious person; and he gives very little attention to the passion of anger, although he is conscious of it. It is in our power, however, when we come to the years of understanding, to give attention to our own thoughts and passions, and the various operations of our minds. And, when we make these the objects of our attention, either while they are present or when they are recent and fresh in our memory, this act of mind is called *reflection*.

We take it for granted, therefore, that, by attentive reflection, a man may have a clear and certain knowledge of the operations of his own mind; a knowledge no less clear and certain than that which he has of an external object when it is set before his eyes.

This reflection is a kind of intuition, it gives a like conviction with regard to internal objects, or things in the mind, as the faculty of seeing gives with regard to objects of sight. A man must, therefore, be convinced beyond possibility of doubt, of everything with regard to the operations of his own mind, which he clearly and distinctly discerns by attentive reflection.

4. I take it for granted that all the thoughts I am conscious of, or remember, are the thoughts of one and the same thinking principle, which I call *myself*, or my *mind*. Every man has an immediate and irresistible conviction, not only of his present existence, but of his continued existence and identity, as far back as he can remember. If any man should think fit to demand a proof that the thoughts he is successively conscious of, belong to one and the same thinking principle – if he should demand a proof that he is the same person to-day as he was yesterday, or a year ago – I know no proof that can be given him: he must be left to himself, either as a man that is lunatic, or as one who denies first principles, and is not to be reasoned with.

Every man of a sound mind, finds himself under a necessity of believing his own identity, and continued existence. The conviction of this is immediate and irresistible; and if he should lose this conviction, it would be a certain proof of insanity, which is not to be remedied by reasoning.

5. I take it for granted, that there are some things which cannot exist by themselves, but must be in something else to which they belong, as qualities, or attributes.

Thus, motion cannot exist, but in something that is moved. And to suppose that there can be motion while everything is at rest, is a gross and palpable absurdity. In like manner, hardness and softness, sweetness and bitterness, are things which cannot exist by themselves; they are qualities of something which is hard or soft, sweet or bitter. That thing, whatever it be, of which they are qualities, is called their subject; and such qualities necessarily suppose a subject.

Things which may exist by themselves, and do not necessarily suppose the existence of anything else, are called substances; and, with relation to the qualities or attributes that belong to them, they are called the subjects of such qualities or attributes.

All the things which we immediately perceive by our senses, and all the things we are conscious of, are things which must be in something else, as their subject. Thus, by my senses, I perceive figure, colour, hardness, softness, motion, resistance, and such like things. But these are qualities, and must necessarily be in something that is figured, coloured, hard or soft, that moves, or resists. It is not to these qualities, but to that which is the subject of them, that we give the name of body. If any man should think fit to deny that these things are qualities, or that they require any subject, I leave him to enjoy his opinion as a man who denies first principles, and is not fit to be reasoned with. If he has common understanding, he will find that he cannot converse half an hour without saying things which imply the contrary of what he professes to believe.

In like manner, the things I am conscious of, such as thought, reasoning, desire, necessarily suppose something that thinks, that reasons, that desires. We do not give the name of mind to thought, reason, or desire; but to that being which thinks, which reasons, and which desires.

That every act or operation, therefore, supposes an agent, that every quality supposes a subject, are things which I do not attempt to prove, but take for granted. Every man of common understanding discerns this immediately, and cannot entertain the least doubt of it. In all languages, we find certain words which, by grammarians, are called adjectives. Such words denote attributes, and every adjective must have a substantive to which it belongs – that is, every attribute must have a subject. In all languages, we find active verbs which denote some action or operation; and it is a fundamental rule in the grammar of all languages, that such a verb supposes a person – that is, in other words, that every action must have an agent. We take it, therefore, as a first principle, that goodness, wisdom, and virtue, can only be in some being that is good, wise, and virtuous; that thinking supposes a being that thinks; and that every operation we are conscious of supposes an agent that operates, which we call mind.

6. I take it for granted, that, in most operations of the mind, there must be an object distinct from the operation itself. I cannot see, without seeing something. To see without having any object of sight is absurd. I cannot remember, without remembering something. The thing remembered is past, while the remembrance of it is present; and, therefore, the operation and the object of it must be distinct things. The operations of our mind are denoted, in all languages, by active transitive verbs, which, from their construction in grammar, require not only a person or agent, but likewise an object of the operation. Thus, the verb know, denotes an operation of mind. From the general structure of language, this verb requires a person – I know, you know, or he knows; but it requires no less a noun in the accusative case, denoting the thing known; for he that knows must know something; and, to know, without having any object of knowledge, is an absurdity too gross to admit of reasoning.

7. We ought likewise to take for granted, as first principles, things wherein we find an universal agreement, among the learned and the unlearned, in the different nations and ages of the world. A consent of ages and nations, of the learned and vulgar, ought, at least, to have great authority, unless we can shew some prejudice as universal as that consent is, which might be the cause of it. Truth is one, but error is infinite. There are many truths so obvious to the human faculties, that it may be expected that men should universally agree in them. And this is actually found to be the case with regard to many truths, against which we find no dissent, unless perhaps that of a few sceptical philosophers, who may justly be suspected, in such cases, to differ from the rest of mankind, through pride, obstinacy, or some favourite passion. Where there is such universal consent in things not deep nor intricate, but which lie, as it were, on the surface, there is the greatest presumption that can be, that it is the natural result of the human faculties; and it must have great authority with every sober mind that loves truth. *Major enim pars eo fere deferri solet quo a natura deducitur.* – Cic. de Off. I. 41.

Perhaps it may be thought that it is impossible to collect the opinions of all men upon any point whatsoever; and, therefore, that this maxim can be of no use. But there are many cases wherein it is otherwise. Who can doubt, for instance, whether mankind have, in all ages, believed the existence of a material world, and that those things which they see and handle are real, and not mere illusions and apparitions? Who can doubt whether mankind have universally believed that everything that begins to exist, and every change that happens in nature, must have a cause? Who can doubt whether mankind have been universally persuaded that there is a right and a wrong in human conduct? – some things which, in certain circumstances, they ought to do, and other things which they ought not to do? The universality of these opinions, and of many such that might be named, is sufficiently evident, from the whole tenor of men's conduct, as far as our acquaintance reaches, and from the records of history, in all ages and nations, that are transmitted to us.

There are other opinions that appear to be universal, from what is common in the structure of all languages, ancient and modern, polished and barbarous. Language is the express image and picture of human thoughts; and, from the picture, we may often draw very certain conclusions with regard to the original. We find in all languages the same parts of speech – nouns substantive and adjective, verbs active and passive, varied according to the tenses of past, present, and future; we find adverbs, prepositions, and conjunctions. There are general rules of syntax common to all languages. This uniformity in the structure of language shews a certain degree of uniformity in those notions upon which the structure of language is grounded.

We find, in the structure of all languages, the distinction of acting and being acted upon, the distinction of action and agent, of quality and subject, and many others of the like kind; which shews that these distinctions are founded in the universal sense of mankind. We shall have frequent occasion to argue from the sense of mankind expressed in the structure of language; and therefore it was proper here to take notice of the force of arguments drawn from this topic.

8. I need hardly say that I shall also take for granted such facts as are attested to the conviction of all sober and reasonable men, either by our senses, by memory, or by human testimony. Although some writers on this subject have disputed the authority of the senses, of memory, and of every human faculty, yet we find that such persons, in the conduct of life, in pursuing their ends, or in avoiding dangers, pay the same regard to the authority of their senses and other faculties, as the rest of mankind. By this they give us just ground to doubt of their candour in their professions of scepticism.

This, indeed, has always been the fate of the few that have professed scepticism, that, when they have done what they can to discredit their senses, they find themselves, after all, under a necessity of trusting to them. Mr Hume has been so candid as to acknowledge this; and it is no less true of those who have not shewn the same candour; for I never heard that any sceptic run his head against a post, or stepped into a kennel, because he did not believe his eyes.

Upon the whole, I acknowledge that we ought to be cautious that we do not adopt opinions as first principles which are not entitled to that character. But there is surely the least danger of men's being imposed upon in this way, when such principles openly lay claim to the character, and are thereby fairly exposed to the examination of those who may dispute their authority. We do not pretend that those things that are laid down as first principles may not be examined, and that we ought not to have our ears open to what may be pleaded against their being admitted as such. Let us deal with them as an upright judge does with a witness who has a fair character. He pays a regard to the testimony of such a witness while his character is unimpeached; but, if it can be shewn that he is suborned, or that he is influenced by malice or partial favour, his testimony loses all its credit, and is justly rejected.

.   .   .

CHAPTER V *Of the proper means of knowing the operations of the mind*

Since we ought to pay no regard to hypotheses, and to be very suspicious of analogical reasoning, it may be asked, From what source must the knowledge of the mind and its faculties be drawn?

I answer, the chief and proper source of this branch of knowledge is accurate reflection upon the operations of our own minds. Of this source we shall speak more fully, after making some remarks upon two others that may be subservient to it. The first of them is attention to the structure of language.

The language of mankind is expressive of their thoughts, and of the various operations of their minds. The various operations of the understanding, will, and passions, which are common to mankind, have various forms of speech corresponding to them in all languages, which are the signs of them, and by which they are expressed: And a due attention to the signs may, in many cases, give considerable light to the things signified by them.

There are in all languages modes of speech, by which men signify their judgment, or give their testimony; by which they accept or refuse; by which they ask information or advice; by which they command, or threaten, or supplicate; by which they plight their faith in promises or contracts. If such operations were not common to mankind, we should not find in all languages forms of speech, by which they are expressed.

All languages, indeed, have their imperfections – they can never be adequate to all the varieties of human thought; and therefore things may be really distinct in their nature, and capable of being distinguished by the human mind, which are not distinguished in common language. We can only expect, in the structure of languages, those distinctions which all mankind in the common business of life have occasion to make.

There may be peculiarities in a particular language, of the causes of which we are ignorant, and from which, therefore, we can draw no conclusion. But whatever we find common to all languages, must have a common cause; must be owing to some common notion or sentiment of the human mind.

We gave some examples of this before, and shall here add another. All languages have a plural number in many of their nouns; from which we may infer that all men have notions, not of individual things only, but of attributes, or things which are common to many individuals; for no individual can have a plural number.

Another source of information in this subject, is a due attention to the course of human actions and conduct. The actions of men are effects; their sentiments, their passions, and their affections, are the causes of those effects; and we may, in many cases, form a judgment of the cause from the effect.

The behaviour of parents towards their children gives sufficient evidence even to those who never had children, that the parental affection is common to mankind. It is easy to see, from the general conduct of men, what are the natural objects of their esteem, their admiration, their love, their approbation, their resentment, and of all their other original dispositions. It is obvious, from the conduct of men in all ages, that man is by his nature a social animal; that he delights to associate with his species; to converse, and to exchange good offices with them.

Not only the actions, but even the opinions of men may sometimes give light into the frame of the human mind. The opinions of men may be considered as the effects of their intellectual powers, as their actions are the effects of their active principles. Even the prejudices and errors of mankind, when they are general, must have some cause no less general; the discovery of which will throw some light upon the frame of the human understanding.

I conceive this to be the principal use of the history of philosophy. When we trace the history of the various philosophical opinions that have sprung up among thinking men, we are led into a labyrinth of fanciful opinions, contradictions, and absurdities, intermixed with some truths; yet we may sometimes find a clue to lead us through the several windings of this labyrinth. We may find that point of view which presented things to the author of the system, in the light in which they appeared to him. This will often give a consistency to things seemingly contradictory, and some degree of probability to those that appeared most fanciful.

The history of philosophy, considered as a map of the intellectual operations of men of genius, must always be entertaining, and may sometimes give us views of the human understanding, which could not easily be had any other way.

I return to what I mentioned as the main source of information on this subject – attentive reflection upon the operations of our own minds.

All the notions we have of mind and of its operations, are, by Mr Locke, called *ideas of reflection*. A man may have as distinct notions of remembrance, of judgment, of will, of desire, as he has of any object whatever. Such notions, as Mr Locke justly observes, are got by the power of reflection. But what is this power of reflection? 'It is,' says the same author, 'that power by which the mind turns its view inward, and observes its own actions and operations.' He observes elsewhere, 'That the understanding, like the eye, whilst it makes us see and perceive all other things, takes no notice of itself; and that it requires art and pains to set it at a distance, and make it its own object.' Cicero hath expressed this sentiment most beautifully. Tusc. I. 28.

This power of the understanding to make its own operations its object, to attend to them, and examine them on all sides, is the power of reflection, by which alone we can have any distinct notion of the powers of our own or of other minds.

This reflection ought to be distinguished from consciousness, with which it is too often confounded, even by Mr Locke. All men are conscious of the operations of their own minds, at all times, while they are awake; but there are few who reflect upon them, or make them objects of thought.

From infancy, till we come to the years of understanding, we are employed solely about external objects. And, although the mind is conscious of its operations, it does not attend to them; its attention is turned solely to the external objects, about which those operations are employed. Thus, when a man is angry, he is conscious of his passion; but his attention is turned to the person who offended him, and the circumstances of the offence, while the passion of anger is not in the least the object of his attention.

I conceive this is sufficient to shew the difference between consciousness of the operations of our minds, and reflection upon them; and to shew that we may have the former without any degree of the latter. The difference between consciousness and reflection, is like the difference between a superficial view of an object which presents itself to the eye while we are engaged about something else, and that attentive examination which we give to an object when we are wholly employed in surveying it. Attention is a voluntary act; it requires an active exertion to begin and to continue it, and it may be continued as long as we will; but consciousness is involuntary and of no continuance, changing with every thought.

The power of reflection upon the operations of their own minds, does not appear at all in children. Men must be come to some ripeness of understanding before they are capable of it. Of all the powers of the human mind, it seems to be the last that unfolds itself. Most men seem incapable of acquiring it in any considerable degree. Like all our other powers, it is greatly improved by exercise; and until a man has got the habit of attending to the operations of his own mind, he can never have clear and distinct notions of them, nor form any steady judgment concerning them. His opinions must be borrowed from others, his notions confused and indistinct, and he may easily be led to swallow very gross absurdities. To acquire this habit, is a work of time and labour, even in those who begin it early, and whose natural talents are tolerably fitted for it; but the difficulty will be daily diminishing, and the advantage of it is great. They will, thereby, be enabled to think with precision and accuracy on every subject, especially on those subjects that are more abstract. They will be able to judge for themselves in many important points, wherein others must blindly follow a leader.

CHAPTER VI *Of the difficulty of attending to the operations of our own minds*

The difficulty of attending to our mental operations, ought to be well understood, and justly estimated, by those who would make any progress in this science; that they may neither, on the one hand, expect success without pains and application of thought; nor, on the other, be discouraged, by conceiving that the obstacles that lie in the way are insuperable, and that there is no certainty to be attained in it. I shall, therefore, endeavour to point out the causes of this difficulty, and the effects that have arisen from it, that we may be able to form a true judgment of both.

1. The number and quick succession of the operations of the mind, make it difficult to give due attention to them. It is well known that, if a great number of objects be presented in quick succession, even to the eye, they are confounded in the memory and imagination. We retain a confused notion of the whole, and a more confused one of the several parts, especially if they are objects to which we have never before given particular attention. No succession can be more quick than that of thought. The mind is busy while we are awake, continually passing from one thought and one operation to another. The scene is constantly shifting. Every man will be sensible of this, who tries but for one minute to keep the same thought in his imagination, without addition or variation. He will find it impossible to keep the scene of his imagination fixed. Other objects will intrude, without being called, and all he can do is to reject these intruders as quickly as possible, and return to his principal object.

2. In this exercise, we go contrary to habits which have been early acquired, and confirmed by long unvaried practice. From infancy, we are accustomed to attend to objects of sense, and to them only; and, when sensible objects have got such strong hold of the attention by confirmed habit, it is not easy to dispossess them. When we grow up, a variety of external objects solicits our attention, excites our curiosity, engages our affections, or touches our passions; and the constant round of employment, about external objects, draws off the mind from attending to itself; so that nothing is more just than the observation of Mr Locke, before mentioned, 'That the understanding, like the eye, while it surveys all the objects around it, commonly takes no notice of itself.'

3. The operations of the mind, from their very nature, lead the mind to give its attention to some other object. Our sensations, as will be shewn afterwards, are natural signs, and turn our attention to the things signified by them; so much that most of them, and those the most frequent and familiar, have no name in any language. In perception, memory, judgment, imagination, and reasoning, there is an object distinct from the operation itself;

and while we are led by a strong impulse to attend to the object, the operation escapes our notice. Our passions, affections, and all our active powers, have, in like manner, their objects which engross our attention, and divert it from the passion itself.

4. To this we may add a just observation made by Mr Hume, That, when the mind is agitated by any passion, as soon as we turn our attention from the object to the passion itself, the passion subsides or vanishes, and, by that means, escapes our inquiry. This, indeed, is common to almost every operation of the mind. When it is exerted, we are conscious of it; but then we do not attend to the operation, but to its object. When the mind is drawn off from the object to attend to its own operation, that operation ceases, and escapes our notice.

5. As it is not sufficient to the discovery of mathematical truths, that a man be able to attend to mathematical figures, as it is necessary that he should have the ability to distinguish accurately things that differ, and to discern clearly the various relations of the quantities he compares – an ability which, though much greater in those who have the force of genius than in others, yet, even in them, requires exercise and habit to bring it to maturity – so, in order to discover the truth in what relates to the operations of the mind, it is not enough that a man be able to give attention to them: he must have the ability to distinguish accurately their minute differences; to resolve and analyse complex operations into their simple ingredients; to unfold the ambiguity of words, which in this science is greater than in any other, and to give them the same accuracy and precision that mathematical terms have; for, indeed, the same precision in the use of words, the same cool attention to the minute differences of things, the same talent for abstraction and analysing, which fit a man for the study of mathematics, are no less necessary in this. But there is this great difference between the two sciences – that the objects of mathematics being things external to the mind, it is much more easy to attend to them, and fix them steadily in the imagination.

The difficulty attending our inquiries into the powers of the mind, serves to account for some events respecting this branch of philosophy, which deserve to be mentioned.

While most branches of science have, either in ancient or in modern times, been highly cultivated, and brought to a considerable degree of perfection, this remains, to this day, in a very low state, and, as it were, in its infancy.

Every science invented by men must have its beginning and its progress; and, from various causes, it may happen that one science shall be brought to a great degree of maturity, while another is yet in its infancy. The maturity of a science may be judged of by this – When it contains a system of principles, and conclusions drawn from them, which are so firmly established that, among thinking and intelligent men, there remains no doubt or dispute about them; so that those who come after may raise the superstructure higher, but shall never be able to overturn what is already built, in order to begin on a new foundation.

Geometry seems to have been in its infancy about the time of Thales and Pythagoras; because many of the elementary propositions, on which the whole science is built, are ascribed to them as the inventors. Euclid's 'Elements,' which were written some ages after Pythagoras, exhibit a system of geometry which deserves the name of a science; and, though great additions have been made by Apollonius, Archimedes, Pappus, and others among the ancients, and still greater by the moderns; yet what was laid down in Euclid's 'Elements' was never set aside. It remains as the firm foundation of all future superstructures in that science.

Natural philosophy remained in its infant state near two thousand years after geometry had attained to its manly form: for natural philosophy seems not to have been built on a stable foundation, nor carried to any degree of maturity, till the last century. The system of Des Cartes, which was all hypothesis, prevailed in the most enlightened part of Europe till towards the end of last century. Sir Isaac Newton has the merit of giving the form of a science to this branch of philosophy; and it need not appear surprising, if the philosophy of the human mind should be a century or two later in being brought to maturity.

It has received great accessions from the labours of several modern authors; and perhaps wants little more to entitle it to the name of a science, but to be purged of certain hypotheses, which have imposed on some of the most acute writers on this subject, and led them into downright scepticism.

What the ancients have delivered to us concerning the mind and its operations, is almost entirely drawn, not from accurate reflection, but from some conceived analogy between body and mind. And, although the modern authors I formerly named have given more attention to the operations of their own minds, and by that means have made important discoveries, yet, by retaining some of the ancient analogical notions, their discoveries have been less useful than they might have been, and have led to scepticism.

It may happen in science, as in building, that an error in the foundation shall weaken the whole; and the farther the building is carried on, this weakness shall become the more apparent and the more threatening. Something of this kind seems to have happened in our systems concerning the mind. The accession they have received by modern discoveries, though very important in itself, has thrown darkness and obscurity upon the whole, and has led men rather to scepticism than to knowledge. This must be owing to some fundamental errors that have not been observed; and when these are corrected, it is to be hoped that the improvements that have been made will have their due effect.

The last effect I observe of the difficulty of inquiries into the powers of the mind, is, that there is no other part of human knowledge in which ingenious authors have been so apt to run into strange paradoxes, and even into gross absurdities.

When we find philosophers maintaining that there is no heat in the fire, nor colour in the rainbow; when we find the gravest philosophers, from Des Cartes down to Bishop Berkeley, mustering up arguments to prove the existence of a material world, and unable to find any that will bear examination; when we find Bishop Berkeley and Mr Hume, the acutest metaphysicians of the age, maintaining that there is no such thing as matter in the universe – that sun, moon, and stars, the earth which we inhabit, our own bodies, and those of our friends, are only ideas in our minds, and have no existence but in thought; when we find the last maintaining that there is neither body nor mind – nothing in nature but ideas and impressions, without any substance on which they are impressed – that there is no certainty, nor indeed probability, even in mathematical axioms: I say, when we consider such extravagancies of many of the most acute writers on this subject, we may be apt to think the whole to be only a dream of fanciful men, who have entangled themselves in cobwebs spun out of their own brain. But we ought to consider that the more closely and ingeniously men reason from false principles, the more absurdities they will be led into; and when such absurdities help to bring to light the false principles from which they are drawn, they may be the more easily forgiven.

CHAPTER VII *Division of the powers of the mind*

The powers of the mind are so many, so various, and so connected and complicated in most of its operations, that there never has been any division of them proposed which is not liable to considerable objections. We shall, therefore, take that general division which is the most common, into the powers of *understanding* and those of *will*. Under the will we comprehend our active powers, and all that lead to action, or influence the mind to act – such as appetites, passions, affections. The understanding comprehends our contemplative powers; by which we perceive objects; by which we conceive or remember them; by which we analyse or compound them; and by which we judge and reason concerning them.

Although this general division may be of use in order to our proceeding more methodically in our subject, we are not to understand it as if, in those operations which are ascribed to the understanding, there were no exertion of will or activity, or as if the understanding were not employed in the operations ascribed to the will; for I conceive there is no operation of the understanding wherein the mind is not active in some degree. We have some command over our thoughts, and can attend to this or to that, of many objects which present themselves to our senses, to our memory, or to our imagination. We can survey an object on this side or that, superficially or accurately, for a longer or a shorter time; so that our contemplative powers are under the guidance and direction of the active; and the former never pursue their object without being led and directed, urged or restrained by the latter: and because the understanding is always more or less directed by the will, mankind have ascribed some degree of activity to the mind in its intellectual operations, as well as in those which belong to the will, and have expressed them by active verbs, such as seeing, hearing, judging, reasoning, and the like.

And as the mind exerts some degree of activity even in the operations of understanding, so it is certain that there can be no act of will which is not accompanied with some act of understanding. The will must have an object, and that object must be apprehended or conceived in the understanding. It is, therefore, to be remembered, that, in most, if not all operations of the mind, both faculties concur; and we range the operation under that faculty which hath the largest share in it.

The intellectual powers are commonly divided into simple apprehension, judgment, and reasoning. As this division has in its favour the authority of antiquity, and of a very general reception, it would be improper to set it aside without giving any reason: I shall, therefore, explain it briefly, and give the reasons why I choose to follow another.

It may be observed that, without apprehension of the objects concerning which we judge, there can be no judgment; as little can there be reasoning without both apprehension and judgment: these three operations, therefore, are not independent of each other. The second includes the first, and the third includes both the first and second; but the first may be exercised without either of the other two. It is on that account called *simple apprehension;* that is, apprehension unaccompanied with any judgment about the object apprehended. This simple apprehension of an object is, in common language, called *having a notion, or having a conception* of the object, and by late authors is called *having an idea of it.* In speaking, it is expressed by a word, or by a part of a proposition, without that composition and structure which makes a complete sentence; as *a man, a man of fortune.* Such words, taken by themselves, signify simple apprehensions. They neither affirm nor deny; they imply no judgment or opinion of the thing signified by them; and, therefore, cannot be said to be either true or false.

The second operation in this division is *judgment*; in which, say the philosophers, there must be two objects of thought compared, and some agreement or disagreement, or, in general, some relation discerned between them; in consequence of which, there is an opinion or belief of that relation which we discern. This operation is expressed in speech by a proposition, in which some relation between the things compared is affirmed or denied: as when we say, *All men are fallible.*

Truth and falsehood are qualities which belong to judgment only; or to propositions by which judgment is expressed. Every judgment, every opinion, and every proposition, is either true or false. But words which neither affirm nor deny anything, can have neither of those qualities; and the same may be said of simple apprehensions, which are signified by such words.

The third operation is *reasoning*; in which, from two or more judgments, we draw a conclusion.

This division of our intellectual powers corresponds perfectly with the account commonly given by philosophers, of the successive steps by which the mind proceeds in the acquisition of its knowledge; which are these three: *First,* By the senses, or by other means, it is furnished with various simple apprehensions, notions, or ideas. These are the materials which nature gives it to work upon; and from the simple ideas it is furnished with by nature, it forms various others more complex. *Secondly,* By comparing its ideas, and by perceiving their agreements and disagreements, it forms its judgments. And, *Lastly,* From two or more judgments, it deduces conclusions of reasoning.

Now, if all our knowledge is got by a procedure of this kind, certainly the threefold division of the powers of understanding, into simple apprehension, judgment, and reasoning, is the most natural and the most proper that can be devised. This theory and that division are so closely connected that it is difficult to judge which of them has given rise to the other; and they must stand or fall together. But, if all our knowledge is not got by a process of this kind – if there are other avenues of knowledge besides the comparing our ideas, and perceiving their agreements and disagreements – it is probable that there may be operations of the understanding which cannot be properly reduced under any of the three that have been explained.

Let us consider some of the most familiar operations of our minds, and see to which of the three they belong. I begin with consciousness. I know that I think, and this of all knowledge is the most certain. Is that operation of my mind which gives me this certain knowledge, to be called simple apprehension? No, surely. Simple apprehension neither affirms nor denies. It will not be said that it is by reasoning that I know that I think. It remains, therefore, that it must be by judgment – that is, according to the account given of judgment, by comparing two ideas, and perceiving the agreement between them. But what are the ideas compared? They must be the idea of myself, and the idea of thought, for they are the terms of the proposition *I think*. According to this account, then, first, I have the idea of myself and the idea of thought; then, by comparing these two ideas, I perceive that I think.

Let any man who is capable of reflection judge for himself, whether it is by an operation of this kind that he comes to be convinced that he thinks? To me it appears evident, that the conviction I have that I think, is not got in this way; and, therefore, I conclude, either that consciousness is not judgment, or that judgment is not rightly defined to be the perception of some agreement or disagreement between two ideas.

The perception of an object by my senses is another operation of the understanding. I would know whether it be simple apprehension, or judgment, or reasoning. It is not simple apprehension, because I am persuaded of the existence of the object as much as I could be by demonstration. It is not judgment, if by judgment be meant the comparing ideas, and perceiving their agreements or disagreements. It is not reasoning, because those who cannot reason can perceive.

I find the same difficulty in classing memory under any of the operations mentioned.

There is not a more fruitful source of error in this branch of philosophy, than divisions of things which are taken to be complete when they are not really so. To make a perfect division of any class of things, a man ought to have the whole under his view at once. But the greatest capacity very often is not sufficient for this. Something is left out which did not come under the philosopher's view when he made his division: and to suit this to the division, it must be made what nature never made it. This has been so common a fault of philosophers, that one who would avoid error ought to be suspicious of divisions, though long received, and of great authority, especially when they are grounded on a theory that may be called in question. In a subject imperfectly known, we ought not to pretend to perfect divisions, but to leave room for such additions or alterations as a more perfect view of the subject may afterwards suggest.

I shall not, therefore, attempt a complete enumeration of the powers of the human understanding. I shall only mention those which I propose to explain; and they are the following:—

1st, The powers we have by means of our external senses. *2dly*, Memory. *3dly*, Conception. *4thly*, The powers of resolving and analysing complex subjects, and compounding those that are more simple. *5thly*, Judging. *6thly*, Reasoning. *7thly*, Taste. *8thly*, Moral Perception; and, *last* of all, Consciousness.

CHAPTER VIII *Of social operations of mind*

There is another division of the powers of the mind, which, though it has been, ought not to be overlooked by writers on this subject, because it has a real foundation in nature. Some operations of our minds, from their very nature, are *social*, others are *solitary*.

By the first, I understand such operations as necessarily suppose an intercourse with some other intelligent being. A man may understand and will; he may apprehend, and judge, and reason, though he should know of no intelligent being in the universe besides himself. But, when he asks information, or receives it; when he bears testimony, or receives the testimony of another; when he asks a favour, or accepts one; when he gives a command to his servant, or receives one from a superior; when he plights his faith in a promise or contract – these are acts of social intercourse between intelligent beings, and can have no place in solitude. They suppose understanding and will; but they suppose something more, which is neither understanding nor will; that is, society with other intelligent beings. They may be called intellectual, because they can only be in intellectual beings; but they are neither simple apprehension, nor judgment, nor reasoning, nor are they any combination of these operations.

To ask a question, is as simple an operation as to judge or to reason; yet it is neither judgment nor reasoning, nor simple apprehension, nor is it any composition of these. Testimony is neither simple apprehension, nor judgment, nor reasoning. The same may be said of a promise, or of a contract. These acts of mind are perfectly understood by every man of common understanding; but, when philosophers attempt to bring them within the pale of their divisions, by analysing them, they find inexplicable mysteries, and even contradictions, in them. One may see an instance of this, of many that might be mentioned, in Mr Hume's 'Enquiry concerning the Principles of Morals,' § 3, part 2, note, near the end.

The attempts of philosophers to reduce the social operations under the common philosophical divisions, resemble very much the attempts of some philosophers to reduce all our social affections to certain modifications of self-love. The Author of our being intended us to be social beings, and has, for that end, given us social intellectual powers, as well as social affections. Both are original parts of our constitution, and the exertions of both no less natural than the exertions of those powers that are solitary and selfish.

Our social intellectual operations, as well as our social affections, appear very early in life, before we are capable of reasoning; yet both suppose a conviction of the existence of other intelligent beings. When a child asks a question of his nurse, this act of his mind supposes not only a desire to know what he asks; it supposes, likewise, a conviction that the nurse is an intelligent being, to whom he can communicate his thoughts, and who can communicate her thoughts to him. How he came by this conviction so early, is a question of some importance in the knowledge of the human mind, and, therefore, worthy of the consideration of philosophers. But they seem to have given no attention, either to this early conviction, or to those operations of mind which suppose it. Of this we shall have occasion to treat afterwards.

All languages are fitted to express the social as well as the solitary operations of the mind. It may indeed be affirmed, that, to express the former, is the primary and direct intention of language. A man who had no intercourse with any other intelligent being, would never think of language. He would be as mute as the beasts of the field, even more so, because they have some degree of social intercourse with one another, and some of them with man. When language is once learned, it may be useful even in our solitary meditations; and by clothing our thoughts with words, we may have a firmer hold of them. But this was not its first intention; and the structure of every language shews that it is not intended solely for this purpose.

In every language, a question, a command, a promise, which are social acts, can be expressed as easily and as properly as judgment, which is a solitary act. The expression of the last has been honoured with a particular name; it is called a proposition; it has been an object of great attention to philosophers; it has been analysed into its very elements of subject predicate, and copula. All the various modifications of these, and of propositions which are compounded of them, have been anxiously examined in many voluminous tracts. The expression of a question, of a command, or of a promise, is as capable of being analysed as a proposition is; but we do not find that this has been attempted; we have not so much as given them a name different from the operations which they express.

Why have speculative men laboured so anxiously to analyse our solitary operations, and given so little attention to the social? I know no other reason but this, that, in the divisions that have been made of the mind's operations, the social have been omitted, and thereby thrown behind the curtain.

In all languages, the second person of verbs, the pronoun of the second person, and the vocative case in nouns, are appropriated to the expression of social operations of mind, and could never have had place in language but for this purpose: nor is it a good argument against this observation, that, by a rhetorical figure, we sometimes address persons that are absent, or even inanimated beings, in the second person. For it ought to be remembered, that all figurative ways of using words or phrases suppose a natural and literal meaning of them.

Source: Thomas Reid, *Essays on the Intellectual Powers of Man*, essay 1, chapters 1, 2, 5-8, in *The Works of Thomas Reid*, ed. William Hamilton, 6th edn, Edinburgh 1863, vol. 1, pp. 219-34, 238-45

PART III
ETHICS

FIVE

FRANCIS HUTCHESON
Morality and the Moral Sense

Hutcheson wrote his moral philosophy within the context of lively debate on the egoistic philosophy of Thomas Hobbes. Hobbes argued, in his *Leviathan*, that all human acts are motivated directly or indirectly by the desire to survive. Put in other terms, we are motivated by self-love or self-interest and by nothing else. Motives that seem not to be reducible to self-interest are shown by Hobbes to be reducible, after all, to that single motive. Granted that the only interest which really interests us is our own, the question of how we ought to behave reduces therefore to the question of how best to serve our own interests. It is in terms such as these that we have to understand the concept of the moral good.

Against this position Hutcheson mounts a challenge, in which he displays at least as much psychological insight as his formidable opponent. His starting point is the distinction between moral good and evil on the one hand and natural good and evil on the other. That there is such a distinction is not at issue. Health, strength and sagacity are unquestionably good, but that they are goods of a different sort from honesty, generosity and kindness is evident from our reaction to their possessors, for while we feel love for and approve of those who are honest, generous and kind, we may have no such feeling towards those who are healthy, strong and sagacious. On the contrary we may even hate them. And we dislike those who are morally evil, though we might love those who suffer from natural evils such as pain, poverty and sickness. Hutcheson starts, therefore, with what he regards as incontrovertible facts about human nature: anyone who attempts to develop a theory of virtue or moral goodness has to respect these fundamental facts.

This starting point gives Hutcheson an opening against Hobbes, for if we take our feelings as sources of insight we can ask whether Hobbes's account of the role of self-interest in our lives squares with the facts. It is plain to Hutcheson that it does not. We need only consider the difference in our reaction to two people of whom one has helped us from the motive of benevolence and the other from the motive of self-interest. We have a distinct 'perception of moral excellence' in the presence of the benevolent (and therefore virtuous) act. But perception of any kind implies a sensory power, as for example visual perception implies a sense of sight. If, then, we are able to perceive moral qualities, we must have a moral sense. A crucial feature of sense, and therefore of the moral sense also, is the absence of will. With eyes wide open, and a stick right in front of me, I come to see the stick. The explanation of how this perception occurs must be given purely in terms of natural, and not of free, causation. If the stick is right in front of me I do not see it voluntarily; on the contrary I cannot help seeing it. This holds also of the moral sense. Will does not enter into the moral perceptual act. Faced with an act of generosity I cannot help perceiving its excellence; faced with an act of treachery I cannot help perceiving its wickedness. Nature operates at a further level also, that so far as I perceive the moral excellence of an act I approve of the act, and do so by nature; the approval wells up unbidden. And so far as I perceive evil in the act I disapprove of the act, and do so by nature; the disapproval, again, wells up.

This doctrine is as far removed from Hobbes's theory as any could be. Central parts of it were duly adopted by Hutcheson's pupil Adam Smith, and by David Hume.

A.B.

Concerning Moral Good and Evil

Introduction

The word *moral goodness* in this treatise, denotes our idea of some quality apprehended in actions, which procures approbation, attended with a desire of the agent's happiness. *Moral evil* denotes our idea of a contrary quality, which excites condemnation or dislike. Approbation and condemnation are probably simple ideas, which cannot be further explained. We must be contented with these imperfect descriptions, until we discover whether we really have such ideas, and what general foundation there is in nature for this difference of actions, as morally good or evil.

These descriptions seem to contain an universally acknowledged difference of moral good and evil, from natural. All men who speak of moral good, acknowledge that it procures approbation and good will toward those we apprehend possessed of it, whereas natural good does not. In this matter men must consult their own beliefs. How differently are they affected toward those they suppose possessed of honesty, faith, generosity, kindness; and those who are possessed of the natural goods, such as houses, lands, gardens, vineyards, health, strength, sagacity? We shall find that we necessarily love and approve the possessors of the former; but the possession of the latter procures no approbation or good-will at all toward the possessor, but often contrary affections of envy and hatred. In the same manner, whatever quality we apprehend to be morally evil, raises our dislike toward the person in whom we observe it, such as treachery, cruelty, ingratitude; whereas we heartily love, esteem, and pity many who are exposed to natural evils, such as pain, poverty, hunger, sickness, death.

Now the first question on this subject is, 'Whence arise these different ideas of actions?'

Because we shall afterwards frequently use the words interest, advantage, natural good, it is necessary here to fix their ideas. The pleasure in our sensible perceptions of any kind, gives us our first idea of natural good or happiness; and then all objects which are apt to excite this pleasure are called immediately good. Those objects which may procure others immediately pleasant, are called advantageous: and we pursue both kinds from a view of interest, or from self-love.

Our sense of pleasure is antecedent to advantage or interest, and is the foundation of it. We do not perceive pleasure in objects, because it is our interest to do so; but objects or actions are advantageous, and are pursued or undertaken from interest, because we receive pleasure from them. Our perception of pleasure is necessary, and nothing is advantageous or naturally good to us, but what is apt to raise pleasure mediately, or immediately. Such objects as we know either from experience of sense, or reason, to be immediately or mediately advantageous, or apt to minister pleasure, we are said to pursue from self-interest, when our intention is only to enjoy this pleasure, which they have the power of exciting. Thus meats, drink, harmony, fine prospects, painting, statues, are perceived by our senses to be immediately good; and our reason shews riches and power to be mediately so, that is, apt to furnish us with objects of immediate pleasure: and both kinds of these natural goods are pursued from interest, or self-love.

Now the greatest part of our later moralists establish it as undeniable, 'That all moral qualities have necessarily some relation to the law of a superior, of sufficient power to make us happy or miserable'; and since all laws operate only by sanctions of rewards, or punishments, which determine us to obedience by motives of self-interest, they suppose, that it is thus that laws do constitute 'some actions mediately good, or advantageous, and others the same way disadvantageous.' They say indeed, 'That a benevolent legislator constitutes no actions advantageous to the agent by law, but such as in their own nature tend to the natural good of the whole, or, at least, are not inconsistent with it; and that therefore we approve the virtue of others, because it has some small tendency to our happiness, either from its own nature, or from this general consideration, that obedience to a benevolent legislator is in general advantageous to the whole, and to us in particular; and that for the contrary reasons alone, we disapprove the vice of others, that is, the prohibited action, as tending to our particular detriment in some degree.' And then they maintain, 'That we are determined to obedience to laws, or deterred from disobedience, merely by motives of self-interest, to obtain either the natural good arising from the commanded action, or the rewards promised by the sanction; or to avoid the natural evil consequences of disobedience, or at least the penalties of the law.'

Some other moralists suppose 'an immediate natural good in the actions called virtuous; that is, that we are determined to perceive some beauty in the actions of others, and to love the agent, even without reflecting upon any advantage which can any way redound to us from the action; that we have also a secret sense of pleasure arising from reflection upon such of our own actions as we call virtuous, even when we expect no other advantage from them.' But they alledge at the same time, 'That we are excited to perform these actions, even as we pursue, or purchase pictures, statues, landskips, from self-interest, to obtain this pleasure which arises from reflection upon the action, or some other future advantage.' The design of the following sections is to inquire into this matter; and perhaps the reasons to be offered may prove,

I 'That some actions have to men an immediate goodness; or, that by a superior sense, which I call a moral one, we approve the actions of others, and perceive them to be their perfection and dignity, and are determined to love the agent; a like perception we have in reflecting on such actions of our own, without any view of natural advantage from them.'

II It may perhaps also appear, 'That the affection, desire, or intention, which gains approbation to the actions flowing from it, is not an intention to obtain even this pleasant self-approbation; much less the future rewards from sanctions of laws, or any other natural good, which may be the consequence of the virtuous action; but an intirely different principle of action from self-love, or desire of private good.'

SECTION I *Of the moral Sense, by which we Perceive Virtue and Vice, and Approve or Disapprove them in Others*

I That the perceptions of moral good and evil, are perfectly different from those of natural good or advantage, every one must convince himself, by reflecting upon the different manner in which he finds himself affected when these objects occur to him. Had we no sense of good distinct from the advantage or interest arising from the external senses, and the perceptions of beauty and harmony; the sensations and affections toward a fruitful field, or commodious habitation, would be much the same with what we have toward a generous friend, or any noble character; for both are or may be advantageous to us: and we should no more admire any action, or love any person in a distant country, or age, whose influence could not extend to us, than we love the mountains of Peru, while we are unconcerned in the Spanish trade. We should have the same sentiments and affections toward inanimate beings, which we have toward rational agents, which yet every one knows to be false. Upon comparison, we say, 'Why should we approve or love inanimate beings? They have no intention of good to us, or to any other person; their nature makes them fit for our uses, which they neither know nor study to serve. But it is not so with rational agents; they study the interest, and desire the happiness of other beings with whom they converse.'

We are all then conscious of the difference between that approbation or perception of moral excellence, which benevolence excites toward the person in whom we observe it, and that opinion of natural goodness, which only raises desire of possession toward the good object. Now 'what should make this difference, if all approbation, or sense of good be from prospect of advantage? Do not inanimate objects promote our advantage as well as benevolent persons, who do us offices of kindness and friendship? Should we not then have the same endearing approbation of both? or only the same cold opinion of advantage in both?' The reason why it is not so, must be this, 'That we have a distinct perception of beauty or excellence in the kind affections of rational agents; whence we are determined to admire and love such characters and persons.'

Suppose we reap the same advantage from two men, one of whom serves us from an ultimate desire of our happiness, or good-will toward us; the other from views of self-interest, or by constraint; both are in this case equally beneficial or advantageous to us, and yet we shall have quite different sentiments of them. We must then certainly have other perceptions of moral actions, than those of advantage; and that power of receiving these perceptions may be called a moral sense, since the definition agrees to it, viz. a determination of the mind, to receive any idea from the presence of an object which occurs to us, independent on our will.

This perhaps will be equally evident from our ideas of evil, done to us designedly by a rational agent. Our senses of natural good and evil would make us receive, with equal serenity and composure, an assault, a buffet, an affront from a neighbour, a cheat from a partner, or trustee, as we would an equal damage from the fall of a beam, a tile, or a tempest; and we should have the same affections and sentiments on both occasions. Villainy, treachery, cruelty, would be as meekly resented as a blast, or mildew, or an overflowing stream. But I fancy every one is very differently affected on these occasions, tho' there may be equal natural evil in both. Nay, actions no way detrimental may occasion the strongest anger and indignation, if they evidence only impotent hatred or contempt. And, on the other hand, the intervention of moral ideas may prevent our condemnation of the agent, or bad moral apprehension of that action which causes to us the greatest natural evil. Thus the opinion of justice in any sentence, will prevent all ideas of moral evil in the execution, or hatred toward the magistrate, who is the immediate cause of our greatest sufferings.

II In our sentiments of action which affect ourselves, there is indeed a mixture of the ideas of natural and moral good, which require some attention to separate them. But when we reflect upon the actions which affect other persons only, we may observe the moral ideas unmix'd with those of natural good or evil. For let it be here observ'd, that those senses by which we perceive pleasure in natural objects, whence they are constituted advantageous, could never raise in us any desire of public good, but only of what was good to ourselves in particular. Nor could they ever make us approve an action merely because of its promoting the happiness of others. And yet, as soon as any action is represented to us as flowing from love, humanity, gratitude, compassion, a study of the good of others, and an ultimate desire of their happiness, although it were in the most distant part of the world, or in some past age, we feel joy within us, admire the lovely action, and praise its author. And on the contrary, every action represented as flowing from ill will, desire of the misery of others without view to any prevalent good to the public, or ingratitude, raises abhorrence and aversion.

It is true indeed, that the actions we approve in others, are generally imagined to tend to the natural good of mankind, or of some parts of it. But whence this secret chain between each person and mankind? How is my interest connected with the most distant parts of it? And yet I must admire actions which shew good-will toward them, and love the author. Whence this love, compassion, indignation and hatred toward even feigned characters, in the most distant ages, and nations, according as they appear kind, faithful, compassionate, or of the opposite dispositions, toward their imaginary contemporaries? If there is no moral sense, which makes benevolent actions appear beautiful; if all approbation be from the interest of the approver,

What's Hecuba to us, or we to Hecuba?

III Some refin'd explainers of self-love may tell us, 'That we approve or condemn characters, according as we apprehend we should have been supported, or injur'd by them, had we liv'd in their days.' But how obvious is the answer, if we only observe, that had we no sense of moral good in humanity, mercy, faithfulness, why should not self-love, and our sense of natural good engage us always to the victorious side, and make us admire and love the successful tyrant, or traitor? Why do not we love Sinon or Pyrrhus, in the Aeneid? for, had we been Greeks, these two would have been very advantageous characters. Why are we affected with the fortunes of Priamus, Polites, Choroebus or Aeneas? Would not the parsimony of a miser be as advantageous to his heir, as the generosity of a worthy man is to his friend? And cannot we as easily imagine ourselves heirs to misers, as the favourites of heroes? Why don't we then approve both alike? It is plain we have some secret sense which determines our approbation without regard to self-interest; otherwise we should always favour the fortunate side without regard to virtue, and suppose ourselves engaged with that party.

As Mr Hobbes explains all the sensations of pity by our fear of the like evils, when by imagination we place ourselves in the case of the sufferers; so others explain all approbation and condemnation of actions in distant ages or nations, by a like effort of imagination: we place ourselves in the case of others, and then discern an imaginary private advantage or disadvantage in these actions. But as his account of pity will never explain how the sensation increases, according to the apprehended worth of the sufferer, or according to the affection we formerly had to him; since the sufferings of any stranger may suggest the same possibility of our suffering the like: so this explication will never account for our high approbation of brave unsuccessful attempts, which we see prove detrimental both to the agent, and to those for whose service they were intended; here there is no private advantage to be imagined. Nor will it account for our abhorrence of such injuries as we are capable of suffering. Sure, when a man abhors the attempt of the young Tarquin, he does not imagine that he has chang'd his sex like Caeneus. And then, when one corrects his imagination, by remembering his own situation, and circumstances, we find the moral approbation and condemnation continues as lively as it was before, tho' the imagination of advantage is gone.

Suppose any great destruction occasion'd by mere accident, without any design, or negligence of the person who casually was the author of it: this action might have been as disadvantageous to us as design'd cruelty, or malice; but who will say he has the same idea of both actions, or sentiments of the agents? thus also an easy, indolent simplicity, which exposes a man of wealth as a prey to others, may be as advantageous a disposition as the most prudent generosity, to those he converses with; and yet our sentiments of this latter temper are far nobler than of the former. 'Whence then this difference?'

And farther, let us make a supposition, which perhaps is not far from matter of fact, to try if we cannot approve even disadvantageous actions, and perceive moral good in them. A few ingenious artisans, persecuted in their own country, flee to ours for protection; they instruct us in manufactures which support millions of poor, increase the wealth of almost every person in the state, and make us formidable to our neighbours. In a nation not far distant from us, some resolute burgomasters, full of love to their country, and compassion toward their fellow-citizens, oppress'd in body and soul by a tyrant and inquisition, with indefatigable diligence, public spirit, and courage, support a tedious perilous war against the tyrant, and form an industrious republic, which rivals us in trade, and almost in power. All the world sees whether the former or the latter have been more advantageous to us: and yet let every man consult his own breast, which of the two characters he has the most agreeable idea of? whether of the useful refugee, or the public-spirited burgomaster, by whose love to his own country, we have often suffered in our interests? And I am confident he will find some other foundation of esteem than advantage, and will see a just reason, why the memory of our artisans is so obscure among us, and yet that of our rivals is immortal.

IV Some moralists, who will rather twist self-love into a thousand shapes, than allow any other principle of approbation than interest, may tell us, 'That whatever profits one part without detriment to another, profits the whole, and then some small share will redound to each individual; that those actions which tend to the good of the whole, if universally performed, would most effectually secure to each individual his own happiness; and that consequently, we may approve such actions, from the opinion of their tending ultimately to our own advantage.'

We need not trouble these gentlemen to shew by their nice train of consequences, and influences of actions by way of precedent in particular instances, that we in this age reap any advantage from Orestes's killing the treacherous Aegysthus, or from the actions of Codrus or Decius. Allow their reasonings to be perfectly good, they only prove, that after long reflection and reasoning, we may find out some ground to judge certain actions advantageous to us, which every man admires as soon as he hears of them; and that too under a quite different conception.

Should any of our travellers find some old Grecian treasure, the miser who hid it, certainly performed an action more to the traveller's advantage, than Codrus or Orestes; for he must have but a small share of benefit from their actions, whose influence is so dispersed, and lost in various ages and nations: surely then this miser must appear to the traveller a prodigious hero in virtue! For self interest will recommend men to us only according to the good they do to ourselves, and not give us high ideas of public good, but in proportion to our share of it. But must a man have the reflection of Cumberland or Puffendorf, to admire generosity, faith, humanity, gratitude? Or reason so nicely to apprehend the evil in cruelty, treachery, ingratitude? Do not the former excite our admiration, and love, and study of imitation, wherever we see them, almost at full view, without any such reflection, and the latter, our contempt, and abhorrence? Unhappy would it be for mankind, if a sense of virtue was of as narrow an extent, as a capacity for such metaphysics.

V This moral sense, either of our own actions, or of those of others, has this in common with our other senses, that however our desire of virtue may be counterbalanced by interest, our sentiment or perception of its beauty cannot; as it certainly might be, if the only ground of our approbation were views of advantage. Let us consider this both as to our own actions, and those of others.

A covetous man shall dislike any branch of trade, how useful soever it may be to the public, if there is no gain for himself in it; here is an aversion from interest. Propose a sufficient premium, and he shall be the first who sets about it, with full satisfaction in his own conduct. Now is it the same way with our sense of moral actions? Should any one advise us to wrong a minor, or orphan, or to do an ungrateful action, toward a benefactor; we at first view abhor it: assure us that it will be very advantageous to us, propose even a reward; our sense of the action is not alter'd. It is true, these motives may make us undertake it; but they have no more influence upon us to make us approve it, than a physician's advice has to make a nauseous potion pleasant to the taste, when we perhaps force ourselves to take it for the recovery of health.

Had we no notion of actions, beside our opinion of their advantage or disadvantage, could we ever choose an action as advantageous, which we are conscious is still evil? as it too often happens in human affairs. Where would be the need of such high bribes to prevail with men to abandon the interests of a ruin'd party, or of tortures to force out the secrets of their friends? Is it so hard to convince men's understandings, if that be the only faculty we have to do with, that it is probably more advantageous to secure present gain, and avoid present evils, by joining with the prevalent party, than to wait for the remote possibility of future good, upon a revolution often improbable, and sometimes unexpected? And when men are over-persuaded by advantage, do they always approve their own conduct? Nay, how often is their remaining life odious, and shameful, in their own sense of it, as well as in that of others, to whom the base action was profitable?

If any one becomes satisfy'd with his own conduct in such a case, upon what ground is it? How does he please himself, or vindicate his actions to others? Never by reflecting upon his private advantage, or alledging this to others as a vindication; but by gradually warping into the moral principles of his new party; for no party is without them. And thus men become pleas'd with their actions under some appearance of moral good, distinct from advantage.

It may perhaps be alledged, 'That in those actions of our own which we call good, there is this constant advantage, superior to all others, which is the ground of our approbation, and the motive to them from self-love, viz. That we suppose the Deity will reward them.' This will be more fully considered hereafter: at present it is enough to observe, that many have high notions of honour, faith, generosity, justice, who have scarce any suppositions of piety, or thoughts of future rewards; and abhor any thing which is treacherous, cruel, or unfit, without any regard to future punishments.

But farther, tho' these rewards and punishments, may make my own actions appear advantageous to me, yet they would never make me approve, and love another person for the like actions, whose merit would not be imputed to me. Those actions are advantageous indeed to the agent; but his advantage is not my advantage: and self-love could never recommend to me actions as advantageous to others, or make me like the authors of them on that account.

This is the second thing to be considered, 'Whether our sense of the moral good or evil in the actions of others, can be overbalanc'd, or bribed by views of interest.' Now I may indeed easily be capable of wishing, that another would do an action I abhor as morally evil, if it were very advantageous to me: interest in that case may overbalance my desire of virtue in another: but no interest to myself, will make me approve an action as morally good, which without that interest to myself, would have appeared morally evil; if upon computing its whole effects, it appears to produce as great a moment of good in the whole, when it is not beneficial to me, as it did before, when it was. In our sense of moral good or evil, our own private advantage or loss is of no more moment, than the advantage or loss of a third person, to make an action appear good or evil. This sense therefore cannot be over-balanced by interest. How ridiculous an attempt would it be, to engage a man by rewards or threatnings into a good opinion of an action, which was contrary to his moral notions? We may produce dissimulation by such means, and that is all.

.   .   .

VII If what is said makes it appear, that we have some other amiable idea of actions than that of advantageous to ourselves, we may conclude, 'that this perception of moral good is not derived from custom, education, example, or study.' These give us no new ideas: they might make us see private advantage in actions whose usefulness did not at first appear; or give us opinions of some tendency of actions to our detriment, by some nice deductions of reason, or by a rash prejudice, when upon the first view of the action we should have observed no such thing: but they never could have made us apprehend actions as amiable or odious, without any consideration of our own advantage.

VIII It remains then, 'That as the Author of nature has determined us to receive, by our external senses, pleasant or disagreeable ideas of objects, according as they are useful or hurtful to our bodies; and to receive from uniform objects the pleasures of beauty and harmony, to excite us to the pursuit of knowledge, and to reward us for it; or to be an argument to us of his goodness, as the uniformity itself proves his existence, whether we had a sense of beauty in uniformity or not; in the same manner he has given us a *moral sense*, to direct our actions, and to give us still nobler pleasures: so that while we are only intending the good of others, we undesignedly promote our own greatest private good.'

We are not to imagine, that this moral sense, more than the other senses, supposes any innate ideas, knowledge, or practical proposition; we mean by it only 'a determination of our minds to receive the simple ideas of approbation or condemnation, from actions observed, antecedent to any opinions of advantage or loss to redound to ourselves from them;' even as we are pleased with a regular form, or an harmonious composition, without having any knowledge of Mathematics, or seeing any advantage in that form or composition, different from the immediate pleasure.

That we may discern more distinctly the difference between

moral perceptions and others, let us consider, when we taste a pleasant fruit, we are conscious of pleasure; when another tastes it, we only conclude or form an opinion that he enjoys pleasure; and, abstracting from some previous good-will or anger, his enjoying this pleasure is to us a matter wholly indifferent, raising no new sentiment or affection. But when we are under the influence of a virtuous temper, and thereby engaged in virtuous actions, we are not always conscious of any pleasure, nor are we only pursuing private pleasures, as will appear hereafter: 'tis only by reflex acts upon our temper and conduct, that virtue never fails to give pleasure. When also we judge the temper of another to be virtuous, we do not necessarily imagine him then to enjoy pleasure, though we know reflection will give it to him: and farther, our apprehension of his virtuous temper raises sentiments of approbation, esteem or admiration, and the affection of good-will toward him. The quality approved by our moral sense is conceived to reside in the person approved, and to be a perfection and dignity in him: approbation of another's virtue is not conceived as making the approver happy, or virtuous, or worthy, though it is attended with some small pleasure. Virtue is then called amiable or lovely, from its raising good-will or love in spectators toward the agent; and not from the agent's perceiving the virtuous temper to be advantageous to him, or desiring to obtain it under that view. A virtuous temper is called good or beatific, not that it is always attended with pleasure in the agent; much less that some small pleasure attends the contemplation of it in the approver: but from this, that every spectator is persuaded that the reflex acts of the virtuous agent upon his own temper will give him the highest pleasures. The admired quality is conceived as the perfection of the agent, and such a one as is distinct from the pleasure either in the agent or the approver; though it is a sure source of pleasure to the agent. The perception of the approver, though attended with pleasure, plainly represents something quite distinct from this pleasure; even as the perception of external forms is attended with pleasure, and yet represents something distinct from this pleasure. This may prevent many cavils upon this subject.

SECTION II *Concerning the Immediate Motive to Virtuous Actions*

The motives of human actions, or their immediate causes, would be best understood after considering the passions and affections; but here we shall only consider the springs of the actions which we call virtuous, as far as it is necessary to settle the general foundation of the moral sense.

I Every action, which we apprehend as either morally good or evil, is always supposed to flow from some affection toward sensitive natures; and whatever we call virtue or vice, is either some such affection, or some action consequent upon it. Or it may perhaps be enough to make an action or omission, appear vitious, if it argues the want of such affection toward rational agents, as we expect in characters counted morally good. All the actions counted religious in any country, are supposed, by those who count them so, to flow from some affections toward the Deity; and whatever we call social virtue, we still suppose to flow from affections toward our fellow-creatures: for in this all seem to agree, 'That external motions, when accompanied with no affections toward God or man, or evidencing no want of the expected affections toward either, can have no moral good or evil in them.'

Ask, for instance, the most abstemious hermit, if temperance of itself would be morally good, supposing it shewed no obedience toward the Deity, made us no fitter for devotion, or the service of mankind, or the search after truth, than luxury; and he will easily grant, that it would be no moral good, though still it might be naturally good or advantageous to health: and mere courage, or contempt of danger, if we conceive it to have no regard to the defence of the innocent, or repairing of wrongs or self-interest, would only entitle its possessor to bedlam. When such sort of courage is sometimes admired, it is upon some secret apprehension of a good intention in the use of it, or as a natural ability capable of an useful application. Prudence, if it was only employed in promoting private interest, is never imagined to be a virtue: and justice, or observing a strict equality, if it has no regard to the good of mankind, the preservation of rights, and securing peace, is a quality properer for its ordinary gestamen, a beam and scales, than for a rational agent. So that these four qualities, commonly called *cardinal virtues*, obtain that name, because they are dispositions universally necessary to promote public good, and denote affections toward rational agents; otherwise there would appear no virtue in them.

II Now, if it can be made appear, that none of these affections which we approve as virtuous, are either self-love, or desire of private interest; since all virtue is either some such affections, or actions consequent upon them; it must necessarily follow, 'That virtue springs from some other affection than self-love, or desire of private advantage. And where self-interest excites to the same action, the approbation is given only to the disinterested principle.'

The affections which are of most importance in morals, are commonly included under the names *love* and *hatred*. Now in discoursing of love, we need not be cautioned not to include that love between the sexes, which, when no other affections accompany it, is only desire of pleasure, and is never counted a virtue. Love toward rational agents, is subdivided into love of complacence or esteem, and love of benevolence: and hatred is subdivided into hatred of displicence or contempt, and hatred of malice. Complacence denotes approbation of any person by our moral sense; and is rather a perception than an affection; though the affection of good-will is ordinarily subsequent to it. Benevolence is the desire of the happiness of another. Their opposites are called dislike and malice. Concerning each of these separately we shall consider, 'Whether they can be influenced by motives of self-interest.'

Complacence, esteem, or good liking, at first view appears to be disinterested, and so displicence or dislike; and are intirely excited by some moral qualities, good or evil, apprehended to be in the objects; which qualities the very frame of our nature determines us to approve or disapprove, according to the moral sense above explained. Propose to a man all the rewards in the world, or threaten all the punishments, to engage him to esteem and complacence toward a ,person intirely unknown, or if known, apprehended to be cruél, treacherous, ungrateful; you may procure external obsequiousness, or good offices, or dissimulation; but real esteem no price can purchase. And the same is obvious as to contempt, which no motive of advantage can prevent. On the contrary, represent a character as generous, kind, faithful, humane, though in the most distant parts of the world, and we cannot avoid esteem and complacence. A bribe may possibly make us attempt to ruin such a man, or some strong motive of advantage may excite us to oppose his interest; but it can never make us disapprove him, while we retain the same opinion of his temper and intentions. Nay, when we consult our own hearts, we shall find, that we can scarce ever persuade ourselves to attempt any mischief against such persons, from any motive of advantage; nor execute it without the strongest reluctance and remorse, until we have blinded ourselves into a false opinion about his temper.

III As to the love of benevolence, the very name excludes

self-interest. We never call that man benevolent, who is in fact useful to others, but at the same time only intends his own interest, without any ultimate desire of the good of others. If there be any real good-will or kindness at all, it must be disinterested; for the most useful action imaginable loses all appearance of benevolence, as soon as we discern that it only flowed from self-love, or interest. Thus, never were any human actions more advantageous, than the inventions of fire, and iron; but if these were casual, or if the inventor only intended his own interest in them, there is nothing which can be called benevolent in them. Where-ever then benevolence is supposed, there it is imagined disinterested, and designed for the good of others. To raise benevolence, no more is required than calmly to consider any sensitive nature not pernicious to others. Gratitude arises from benefits conferred from good-will on ourselves, or those we love; complacence is a perception of the moral sense. Gratitude includes some complacence, and complacence still raises a stronger good-will than that we have toward indifferent characters, where there is no opposition of interests.

But it must be here observed, that as all men have self-love, as well as benevolence, these two principles may jointly excite a man to the same action; and then they are to be considered as two forces impelling the same body to motion; sometimes they conspire, sometimes are indifferent to each other, and sometimes are in some degree opposite. Thus, if a man have such strong benevolence, as would have produced an action without any views of self-interest; that such a man has also in view private advantage, along with public good, as the effect of his action does no way diminish the benevolence of the action. When he would not have produced so much public good, had it not been for prospect of self-interest, then the effect of self-love is to be deducted, and his benevolence is proportioned to the remainder of good, which pure benevolence would have produced. When a man's benevolence is hurtful to himself, then self-love is opposite to benevolence, and the benevolence is proportioned to the sum of the good produced, added to the resistance of self-love surmounted by it. In most cases it is impossible for men to know how far their fellows are influenced by the one or other of these principles; but yet the general truth is sufficiently certain, that this is the way in which the benevolence of actions is to be computed.

IV There are two ways in which some may deduce benevolence from self-love, the one supposing that 'we voluntarily bring this affection upon ourselves, whenever we have an opinion that it will be for our interest to have this affection, either as it may be immediately pleasant, or may afford pleasant reflection afterwards by our moral sense, or as it may tend to procure some external reward from God or man.' The other scheme alledges no such power in us of raising desire or affection of any kind by our choice or volition; but 'supposes our minds determined by the frame of their nature to desire whatever is apprehended as the means of any private happiness; and that the observation of the happiness of other persons, in many cases is made the necessary occasion of pleasure to the observer, as their misery is the occasion of his uneasiness; and in consequence of this connexion, as soon as we have observed it, we begin to desire happiness of others as the means of obtaining this happiness to ourselves, which we expect from the contemplation of others in a happy state. They alledge it to be impossible to desire either the happiness of another, or any event whatsoever, without conceiving it as the means of some happiness or pleasure to ourselves; but own at the same time, that desire is not raised in us directly by any volition, but arises necessarily upon our apprehending any object or event to be conducive to our happiness.'

That the former scheme is not just, may appear from this general consideration, that 'neither benevolence nor any other affection or desire can be directly raised by volition.' If they could, then we could be bribed into any affection whatsoever toward any object, even the most improper; we might raise jealousy, fear, anger, love, toward any sort of persons indifferently by an hire, even as we engage men to external actions, or to the dissimulation of passions; but this every person will by his own reflection find to be impossible. The prospect of any advantage to arise to us from having any affection, may indeed turn our attention to those qualities in the object, which are naturally constituted the necessary causes or occasions of the advantageous affection; and if we find such qualities in the object, the affection will certainly arise. Thus indirectly the prospect of advantage may tend to raise any affection; but if these qualities be not found or apprehended in the object, no volition of ours, nor desire, will ever raise any affection in us.

But more particularly, that desire of the good of others, which we approve as virtuous, cannot be alledged to be voluntarily raised from prospect of any pleasure accompanying the affection itself: for it is plain that our benevolence is not always accompanied with pleasure; nay, 'tis often attended with pain, when the object is in distress. Desire in general is rather uneasy than pleasant. 'Tis true, indeed, all the passions and affections justify themselves; while they continue, (as Malebranch expresses it) we generally approve our being thus affected on this occasion, as an innocent disposition, or a just one, and condemn a person who would be otherwise affected on the like occasion. So the sorrowful, the angry, the jealous, the compassionate, approve their several passions on the apprehended occasion; but we should not therefore conclude that sorrow, anger, jealousy, or pity are pleasant, or chosen for their concomitant pleasure. The case is plainly thus: the frame of our nature on the occasions which move these passions, determines us to be thus affected, and to approve our affection at least as innocent. Uneasiness generally attends our desires of any kind; and this sensation tends to fix our attention, and to continue the desire. But the desire does not terminate upon the removal of the pain accompanying the desire, but upon some other event: the concomitant pain is what we seldom reflect upon, unless when it is very violent. Nor does any desire or affection terminate upon the pleasure which may accompany the affection; much less is it raised by an act of our will, with a view to obtain this pleasure.

The same reflection will shew, that we do not by an act of our will raise in ourselves that benevolence which we approve as virtuous, with a view to obtain future pleasures of self-approbation by our moral sense. Could we raise affections in this manner, we should be engaged to any affection by the prospect of an interest equivalent to this of self-approbation, such as wealth or sensual pleasure, which with many tempers are more powerful; and yet we universally own, that that disposition to do good offices to others, which is raised by these motives, is not virtuous: how can we then imagine, that the virtuous benevolence is brought upon us by a motive equally selfish?

But what will most effectually convince us of the truth on this point, is reflection upon our own hearts, whether we have not a desire of the good of others, generally without any consideration or intention of obtaining these pleasant reflections on our own virtue; nay, often this desire is strongest where we least imagine virtue, in natural affection toward offspring, and in gratitude to a great benefactor; the absence of which is indeed the greatest vice, but the affections themselves are not esteemed in any considerable degree virtuous. The same reflection will also convince us, that these desires or affections are not produced by choice, with a view to obtain this private good.

In like manner, if no volition of ours can directly raise affections from the former prospects of interest, no more can any volition raise them from prospects of eternal rewards, or to avoid eternal punishments. The former motives differ from these only as smaller from greater, shorter from more durable. If affections could be directly raised by volition, the same consideration would make us angry at the most innocent or virtuous character, and jealous of the most faithful and affectionate, or sorrowful for the prosperity of a friend; which we all find to be impossible. The prospect of a future state, may, no doubt, have a greater indirect influence, by turning our attention to the qualities in the objects naturally apt to raise the required affection, than any other consideration.

'Tis indeed probably true in fact, that those who are engaged by prospect of future rewards to do good offices to mankind, have generally the virtuous benevolence jointly exciting them to action; because, as it may appear hereafter, benevolence is natural to mankind, and still operates where there is no opposition of apparent interest, or where any contrary apparent interest is overbalanced by a greater interest. Men, conscious of this, do generally approve good offices, to which motives of a future state partly excited the agent. But that the approbation is founded upon the apprehension of a disinterested desire partly exciting the agent, is plain from this, that not only obedience to an evil deity in doing mischief, or even in performing trifling ceremonies, only from hope of reward, or prospect of avoiding punishment, but even obedience to a good Deity only from the same motives, without any love or gratitude towards him, and with a perfect indifference about the happiness or misery of mankind, abstracting from this private interest, would meet with no approbation. We plainly see that a change of external circumstances of interest under an evil Deity, without any change in the disposition of the agent, would lead him into every cruelty and inhumanity.

Gratitude toward the Deity is indeed disinterested, as it will appear hereafter. This affection therefore may obtain our approbation, where it excites to action, though there were no other benevolence exciting the agent. But this case scarce occurs among men. But where the sanction of the law is the only motive of action, we could expect no more benevolence, nor no other affection, than those in one forced by the law to be curator to a person for whom he has not the least regard. The agent would so manage as to save himself harmless if he could, but would be under no concern about the success of his attempts, or the happiness of the person whom he served, provided he performed the task required by law; nor would any spectator approve this conduct.

V The other scheme is more plausible: that benevolence is not raised by any volition upon prospect of advantage; but that we desire the happiness of others, as conceiving it necessary to procure some pleasant sensations which we expect to feel upon seeing others happy; and that for like reason we have aversion to their misery. This connection between the happiness of others and our pleasure, say they, is chiefly felt among friends, parents and children, and eminently virtuous characters. But this benevolence flows as directly from self-love as any other desire.

To shew that this scheme is not true in fact, let us consider, that if in our benevolence we only desired the happiness of others as the means of this pleasure to ourselves, whence is it that no man approves the desire of the happiness of others as a means of procuring wealth or sensual pleasure to ourselves? If a person had wagered concerning the future happiness of a man of such veracity, that he would sincerely confess whether he were happy or not; would this wagerer's desire of the happiness of another, in order to win the wager, be approved as virtuous? If not, wherein does this desire differ from the former? except that in one case there is one pleasant sensation expected, and in the other case other sensations; for by increasing or diminishing the sum wagered, the interest in this case may be made either greater or less than that in the other.

Reflecting on our own minds again will best discover the truth. Many have never thought upon this connection: nor do we ordinarily intend the obtaining of any such pleasure when we do generous offices. We all often feel delight upon seeing others happy, but during our pursuit of their happiness we have no intention of obtaining this delight. We often feel the pain of compassion; but were our sole ultimate intention or desire the freeing ourselves from this pain, would the Deity offer to us either wholly to blot out all memory of the person in distress, to take away this connection, so that we should be easy during the misery of our friend on the one hand, or on the other would relieve him from his misery, we should be as ready to choose the former way as the latter; since either of them would free us from our pain, which upon this scheme is the sole end proposed by the compassionate person. — Don't we find in ourselves that our desire does not terminate upon the removal of our own pain? Were this our sole intention, we would run away, shut our eyes, or divert our thoughts from the miserable object, as the readiest way of removing our pain: this we seldom do, nay, we croud about such objects, and voluntarily expose ourselves to this pain, unless calm reflection upon our inability to relieve the miserable, countermand our inclination, or some selfish affection, as fear of danger, over-power it.

To make this yet clearer, suppose that the Deity should declare to a good man that he should be suddenly annihilated, but at the instant of his exit it should be left to his choice whether his friend, his children, or his country should be made happy or miserable for the future, when he himself could have no sense of either pleasure or pain from their state. Pray would he be any more indifferent about their state now, that he neither hoped or feared any thing to himself from it, than he was in any prior period of his life? Nay, is it not a pretty common opinion among us, that after our decease we know nothing of what befalls those who survive us? How comes it then that we do not lose, at the approach of death, all concern for our families, friends, or country? Can there be any instance given of our desiring any thing only as the means of private good, as violently when we know that we shall not enjoy this good many minutes, as if we expected the possession of this good for many years? Is this the way we compute the value of annuities?

How the disinterested desire of the good of others should seem inconceivable, 'tis hard to account: perhaps 'tis owing to the attempts of some great men to give definitions of simple ideas. — Desire, say they, is uneasiness, or uneasy sensation upon the absence of any good. — Whereas desire is as distinct from uneasiness, as volition is from sensation. Don't they themselves often speak of our desiring to remove uneasiness? Desire then is different from uneasiness, however a sense of uneasiness accompanies it, as extension does the idea of colour, which yet is a very distinct idea. Now wherein lies the impossibility of desiring the happiness of another without conceiving it as the means of obtaining any thing farther, even as we desire our own happiness without farther view? If any alledge, that we desire our own happiness as the means of removing the uneasiness we feel in the absence of happiness, then at least the desire of removing our own uneasiness is an ultimate desire: and why may we not have other ultimate desires?

'But can any being be concerned about the absence of an event which gives it no uneasiness?' Perhaps superior natures desire without uneasy sensation. But what if we cannot? We may be uneasy while a desired event is in suspense, and yet not desire this event only as the means of removing this uneasiness: nay, if we did not desire the event without view to this uneasiness, we should never have brought the uneasiness upon ourselves by desiring it. So likewise we may feel delight upon the existence of a desired event, when yet we did not desire the event only as the means of obtaining this delight; even as we often receive delight from events which we had an aversion to.

VI If any one should ask, since none of these motives of self-interest excite our benevolence, but we are in virtuous actions intending solely the good of others, to what purpose serves our moral sense, our sense of pleasure from the happiness of others? To what purpose serves the wise order of nature, by which virtue is even made generally advantageous in this life? To what end are eternal rewards appointed and revealed? The answer to these questions was given partly already: all these motives may make us desire to have benevolent affections, and consequently turn our attention to those qualities in objects which excite them; they may overbalance all apparent contrary motives, and all temptations to vice. But farther, I hope it will be still thought an end worthy of the Deity, to make the virtuous happy, by a wise constitution of nature, whether the virtuous were in every action intending to obtain this happiness or not. Beneficent actions tend to the public good; it is therefore good and kind to give all possible additional motives to them; and to excite men, who have some weak degrees of good affection, to promote the public good more vigorously by motives of self-interest; or even to excite those who have no virtue at all to external acts of beneficence, and to restrain them from vice.

From the whole it may appear, that there is in human nature a disinterested ultimate desire of the happiness of others; and that our moral sense determines us to approve only such actions as virtuous, which are apprehended to proceed partly at least from such desire.

VII As to malice, human nature seems scarce capable of malicious disinterested hatred, or a sedate ultimate desire of the misery of others, when we imagine them no way pernicious to us, or opposite to our interest: and for that hatred which makes us oppose those whose interests are opposite to ours, it is only the effect of self-love, and not of disinterested malice. A sudden passion may give us wrong representations of our fellow-creatures, and for a little time represent them as absolutely evil; and during this imagination perhaps we may give some evidences of disinterested malice: but as soon as we reflect upon human nature, and form just conceptions, this unnatural passion is allayed, and only self-love remains, which may make us, from self-interest, oppose our adversaries.

Every one at present rejoices in the destruction of our pirates; and yet let us suppose a band of such villains cast in upon some desolate island, and that we were assured some fate would confine them there perpetually, so that they should disturb mankind no more: now let us calmly reflect, that these persons are capable of knowledge and counsel, may be happy and joyful, or may be involved in misery, sorrow, and pain; that they may return to a state of love, humanity, kindness, and become friends, citizens, husbands, parents, with all the sweet sentiments which accompany these relations: then let us ask ourselves, when self-love, or regard to the safety of better men, no longer makes us desire their destruction, and when we cease to look upon them under the ideas suggested by fresh resentment of injuries done to us or our friends, as utterly incapable of any good moral quality; whether we would wish them the fate of Cadmus's army, by plunging their swords in each others breast, or a worse fate by the most exquisite tortures; or rather, that they should recover the ordinary affections of men, become kind, compassionate, and friendly; contrive laws, constitutions, governments, properties; and form an honest happy society with marriages, and

> Relations dear, and all the charities
> Of father, son, and brother——?[1]

I fancy the latter would be the wish of every mortal, notwithstanding our present just abhorrence of them from self-interest, or public love, and desire of promoting the interest of our friends who are exposed to their fury. Now this plainly evidences, that we scarce ever have any sedate malice against any person, or ultimate desire of his misery. Our calm ill-will is only from opposition of interest; or if we can entertain sedate malice, it must be toward a character apprehended necessarily and unalterably evil in a moral sense; such as a sudden passion sometimes represents our enemies to us; yet perhaps no such being occurs to us among the works of a good Deity.

.   .   .

X Having removed these false springs of virtuous actions, let us next establish the true one, viz. some determination of our

---

1 Milton, *Paradise Lost* Bk 4, verses 756–7.

nature to study the good of others; or some instinct, antecedent to all reason from interest, which influences us to the love of others; even as the moral sense, above explained, determines us to approve the actions which flow from this love in ourselves or others. This disinterested affection, may appear strange to men impressed with notions of self-love as the sole spring of action, from the pulpit, the schools, the systems, and conversations regulated by them: but let us consider it in its strongest and simplest kinds; and when we see the possibility of it in these instances, we may easily discover its universal extent.

An honest farmer will tell you, that he studies the preservation and happiness of his children, and loves them without any design of good to himself. But say some of our philosophers 'The happiness of their children gives parents pleasure, and their misery gives them pain; and therefore to obtain the former, and avoid the latter, they study, from self-love, the good of their children.' Suppose several merchants joined in partnership of their whole effects; one of them is employed abroad in managing the flock of the company; his prosperity occasions gain to all, and his losses give them pain for their share in the loss: is this then the same kind of affection with that of parents to their children? Is there the same tender, personal regard? I fancy no parent will say so. In this case of merchants there is a plain conjunction of interest; but whence the conjunction of interest between the parent and child? Do the child's sensations give pleasure or pain to the parent? Is the parent hungry, thirsty, sick, when his children are so? No; but his naturally implanted desire of their good, and aversion to their misery, makes him be affected with joy or sorrow from their pleasures or pains. This desire then is antecedent to the conjunction of interest, and the cause of it, not the effect: it then must be disinterested. 'No; say others, children are parts of ourselves, and in loving them we but love ourselves in them.' A very good answer! Let us carry it as far as it will go. How are they parts of ourselves? Not as a leg or an arm: we are not conscious of their sensations. 'But their bodys were formed from parts of ours.' So is a fly, or a maggot, which may breed in any discharged blood or humour: very dear insects surely! there must be something else then which makes children parts of ourselves; and what is this but that affection, which nature determines us to have toward them? This love makes them parts of ourselves, and therefore does not flow from their being so before. This is indeed a good metaphor; and where-ever we find a determination among several rational agents to mutual love, let each individual be looked upon as a part of a great whole, or system, and concern himself in the public good of it.

Another author thinks all this easily deducible from self-love. 'Children are not only made of our bodies, but resemble us in body and mind; they are rational agents as we are, and we only love our own likeness in them.' Very good all this. What is likeness? 'Tis not individual sameness; 'tis only being included under one general or specifical idea. Thus there is likeness between us and other mens children, thus any man is like any other, in some respects; a man is also like an angel, and in some respects like a brute. Is there then a natural disposition in every man to love his like, to wish well not only to his individual self, but to any other like rational or sensitive being? and this disposition strongest, where there is the greatest likeness in the more noble qualities? If all this is called by the name of self-love; be it so: the highest mystic needs no more disinterested principle; 'tis not confined to the individual, but terminates ultimately on the good of others, and may extend to all; since each one some way resembles each other. Nothing can be better than this self-love, nothing more generous.

If any allege that 'parents always derive pleasure, often honour, and sometimes wealth, from the wisdom and prosperity of their children, and hence all parental solicitude arises;' let us recollect what we said above; all these motives cease upon approach of death, and yet the affection is as strong then as ever. Let parents examine their own hearts, and see if these views are the only springs of their affection, and that toward the most infirm, from whom there is least hope.

But a later author observes,[1] 'That natural affection in parents is weak, till the children begin to give evidences of knowledge and affections.' Mothers say they feel it strong from the very first: and yet I could wish, for the destruction of his hypothesis, that what he alledges was true; as I fancy it is in some measure, tho' we may find in some parents an affection toward idiots. The observing of understanding and affections in children, which make them appear moral agents, can increase love toward them without prospect of interest; for I hope, this increase of love is not from prospect of advantage from the knowledge or affection of children, for whom parents are still toiling, and never intend to be refunded their expences, or recompensed for their labour, but in cases of extreme necessity. If then the observing a moral capacity can be

[1] See [Bernard Mandeville], *The fable of the Bees*.

the occasion of increasing love without self-interest, even from the frame of our nature: pray, may not this be a foundation of weaker degrees of love, where there is no preceding tie of parentage, and extend it to all mankind?

Source: Francis Hutcheson, *An Inquiry into the Original of our Ideas of Beauty and Virtue*, printed from 4th edn of 1738, Glasgow 1772, Treatise I, Introduction, sections 1, 2

SIX

DAVID HUME
Morality and Benevolence

Hume starts his investigation into the general principles of morality by consideration of a basic fact of human nature, namely that everyone makes moral distinctions: 'let a man's insensibility be ever so great, he must often be touched with the images of Right and Wrong; and let his prejudices be ever so obstinate, he must observe, that others are susceptible of like impressions'. The universality of this susceptibility raises a question regarding the identity of the faculty or faculties in which our moral judgments are grounded. Since the susceptibility is universal among human beings, the faculty or faculties grounding it must likewise be universal. What are these faculties? Two candidates in particular are commonly invoked as the faculty at issue. One of them is reason and the other is sentiment or feeling.

If moral judgments are founded upon reason then they are reached, or at least are reachable, by a chain of argument, and they would be the same for every rational intelligent being, whether human or otherwise. If on the other hand they are founded upon sentiment or feeling then they are 'founded entirely upon the particular fabric and constitution of the human species' and in that case we cannot say that morality would be the same for human and for non-human beings. There is no suggestion in this that a morality founded upon sentiment may be valid for one person and not for another. Some sentiments, such as hate, spite and envy, can surely be ruled out at the start as possible sentimental bases for morality.

There are, as Hume acknowledges, grounds for holding that morality is based upon reason. Principally there is the fact that people do in fact argue about morality, for example in tackling the question of whether someone's behaviour is just or unjust. And if it is appropriate to produce arguments in support of a moral belief then surely there is at least something essentially rational about morality. To which it might be added that one moral judgment can contradict another, and one can imply another, and these relations between moral judgments are of a logical kind. How then can morality not be rational?

Yet morality surely is something we feel as well as argue about; we approve of virtue and disapprove of vice, and approval and disapproval are sentiments or feelings. This link between morality and sentiment enters into the essence of morality. Morality is essentially practical in that we are moved to act by moral considerations. But reason, however helpful it is in bringing us to moral conclusions, can never of itself move us to act. It is our sentiments or feelings that move us. Morality is therefore surely grounded on sentiment.

Hume respects both sides of the argument and develops a moral philosophy in which both components or features of our nature, the rational and the sentimental, are displayed as playing a role in our moral judgments. Hume states the relation in a famous phrase: 'reason is, and ought only to be the slave of the passions, and can never pretend to any other office than to serve and obey them' (*A Treatise of Human Nature*, Book 2, part 3, section 3).

He places great emphasis in his moral philosophy on the concept of utility. All acts which we praise morally are judged by us to be useful. But useful for what? The answer is: useful as conducive to the happiness of mankind. Those who have a love or affection for mankind, and therefore seek its happiness, are benevolent. Benevolence, or common humanity, is the sentimental basis of morality, and the role of reason in morality is to direct us to the best means of achieving what benevolence seeks. Given the role of benevolence in Hume's system, it is not surprising that when in the *Enquiry concerning the Principles of Morals* he applies his 'experimental method of reasoning' to the moral side of human nature, he begins with a study of benevolence.

A.B.

An Enquiry concerning the Principles of Morals

SECTION I *Of the General Principles of Morals*

Disputes with men, pertinaciously obstinate in their principles, are, of all others, the most irksome; except, perhaps, those with persons, entirely disingenuous, who really do not believe the opinions they defend, but engage in the controversy, from affectation, from a spirit of opposition, or from a desire of showing wit and ingenuity, superior to the rest of mankind. The same blind adherence to their own arguments is to be expected in both; the same contempt of their antagonists; and the same passionate vehemence, in inforcing sophistry and falsehood. And as reasoning is not the source, whence either disputant derives his tenets; it is in vain to expect, that any logic, which speaks not to the affections, will ever engage him to embrace sounder principles.

Those who have denied the reality of moral distinctions, may be ranked among the disingenuous disputants; nor is it conceivable, that any human creature could ever seriously believe, that all characters and actions were alike entitled to the affection and regard of everyone. The difference, which nature has placed between one man and another, is so wide, and this difference is still so much farther widened, by education, example, and habit, that, where the opposite extremes come at once under our apprehension, there is no scepticism so scrupulous, and scarce any assurance so determined, as absolutely to deny all distinction between them. Let a man's insensibility be ever so great, he must often be touched with the images of Right and Wrong; and let his prejudices be ever so obstinate, he must observe, that others are susceptible of like impressions. The only way, therefore, of converting an antagonist of this kind, is to leave him to himself. For, finding that nobody keeps up the controversy with him, it is probable he will, at last, of himself, from mere weariness, come over to the side of common sense and reason.

There has been a controversy started of late, much better worth examination, concerning the general foundation of Morals; whether they be derived from Reason, or from Sentiment; whether we attain the knowledge of them by a chain of argument and induction, or by an immediate feeling and finer internal sense; whether, like all sound judgement of truth and falsehood, they should be the same to every rational intelligent being; or whether, like the perception of beauty and deformity, they be founded entirely on the particular fabric and constitution of the human species.

The ancient philosophers, though they often affirm, that virtue is nothing but conformity to reason, yet, in general, seem to consider morals as deriving their existence from taste and sentiment. On the other hand, our modern enquirers, though they also talk much of the beauty of virtue, and deformity of vice, yet have commonly endeavoured to account for these distinctions by metaphysical reasonings, and by deductions from the most abstract principles of the understanding. Such confusion reigned in these subjects, that an opposition of the greatest consequence could prevail between one system and another, and even in the parts of almost each individual system; and yet nobody, till very lately, was ever sensible of it. The elegant Lord Shaftesbury, who first gave occasion to remark this distinction, and who, in general, adhered to the principles of the ancients, is not, himself, entirely free from the same confusion.

It must be acknowledged, that both sides of the question are susceptible of specious arguments. Moral distinctions, it may be said, are discernible by pure *reason*: else, whence the many disputes that reign in common life, as well as in philosophy, with regard to this subject: the long chain of proofs often produced on both sides; the examples cited, the authorities appealed to, the analogies employed, the fallacies detected, the inferences drawn, and the several conclusions adjusted to their proper principles. Truth is disputable; not taste: what exists in the nature of things is the standard of our judgement; what each man feels within himself is the standard of sentiment. Propositions in geometry may be proved, systems in physics may be controverted; but the harmony of verse, the tenderness of passion, the brilliancy of wit, must give immediate pleasure. No man reasons concerning another's beauty; but frequently concerning the justice or injustice of his actions. In every criminal trial the first object of the prisoner is to disprove the facts alleged, and deny the actions imputed to him: the second to prove, that, even if these actions were real, they might be justified, as innocent and lawful. It is confessedly by deductions of the understanding, that the first point is ascertained: how can we suppose that a different faculty of the mind is employed in fixing the other?

On the other hand, those who would resolve all moral determinations into *sentiment*, may endeavour to show, that it is impossible for reason ever to draw conclusions of this nature. To virtue, say they, it belongs to be *amiable*, and vice *odious*. This forms their very nature or essence. But can reason or argumentation distribute these different epithets to any subjects, and pronounce beforehand, that this must produce love, and that hatred? Or what other reason can we ever assign for these affections, but the original fabric and formation of the human mind, which is naturally adapted to receive them?

The end of all moral speculations is to teach us our duty; and, by proper representations of the deformity of vice and beauty of virtue, beget correspondent habits, and engage us to avoid the one, and embrace the other. But is this ever to be expected from inferences and conclusions of the understanding, which of themselves have no hold of the affections or set in motion the active powers of men? They discover truths: but where the truths which they discover are indifferent, and beget no desire or aversion, they can have no influence on conduct and behaviour. What is honourable, what is fair, what is becoming, what is noble, what is generous, takes possession of the heart, and animates us to embrace and maintain it. What is intelligible, what is evident, what is probable, what is true, procures only the cool assent of the understanding; and gratifying a speculative curiosity, puts an end to our researches.

Extinguish all the warm feelings and prepossessions in favour of virtue, and all disgust or aversion to vice: render men totally indifferent towards these distinctions; and morality is no longer a practical study, nor has any tendency to regulate our lives and actions.

These arguments on each side (and many more might be produced) are so plausible, that I am apt to suspect, they may, the one as well as the other, be solid and satisfactory, and that *reason* and *sentiment* concur in almost all moral determinations and conclusions. The final sentence, it is probable, which pronounces characters and actions amiable or odious, praise-worthy or blameable; that which stamps on them the mark of honour or infamy, approbation or censure; that which renders morality an active principle and constitutes virtue our happiness, and vice our misery: it is probable, I say, that this final sentence depends on some internal sense or feeling, which nature has made universal in the whole species. For what else can have an influence of this nature? But in order to pave the way for such a sentiment, and give a proper discernment of its object, it is often necessary, we find, that much reasoning should precede, that nice distinctions be made, just conclusions drawn, distant comparisons formed, complicated relations examined, and general facts fixed and ascertained. Some species of beauty, especially the natural kinds, on their first appearance, command our affection and approbation; and where they fail of this effect, it is impossible for any reasoning to redress their influence, or adapt them better to our taste and sentiment. But in many orders of beauty, particularly those of the finer arts, it is requisite to employ much reasoning, in order to feel the proper sentiment; and a false relish may frequently be corrected by argument and reflection. There are just grounds to conclude, that moral beauty partakes much of this latter species, and demands the assistance of our intellectual faculties, in order to give it a suitable influence on the human mind.

But though this question, concerning the general principles of morals, be curious and important, it is needless for us, at present, to employ farther care in our researches concerning it. For if we can be so happy, in the course of this enquiry, as to discover the true origin of morals, it will then easily appear how far either sentiment or reason enters into all determinations of this nature. In order to attain this purpose, we shall endeavour to follow a very simple method: we shall analyse that complication of mental qualities, which form what, in common life, we call Personal Merit: we shall consider every attribute of the mind, which renders a man an object either of esteem and affection, or of hatred and contempt; every habit or sentiment or faculty, which, if ascribed to any person, implies either praise or blame, and may enter into any panegyric or satire of his character and manners. The quick sensibility, which, on this head, is so universal among mankind, gives a philosopher sufficient assurance, that he can never be considerably mistaken in framing the catalogue, or incur any danger of misplacing the objects of his contemplation: he needs only enter into his own breast for a moment, and consider whether or not he should desire to have this or that quality ascribed to him, and whether such or such an imputation would proceed from a friend or an enemy. The very nature of language guides us almost infallibly in forming a judgement of this nature; and as every tongue possesses one set of words which are taken in a good sense, and another in the opposite, the least acquaintance with the idiom suffices, without any reasoning, to direct us in collecting and arranging the estimable or blameable qualities of men. The only object of reasoning is to discover the circumstances on both sides, which are common to these qualities; to observe that particular in which the estimable qualities agree on the one hand, and the blameable on the other; and thence to reach the foundation of ethics, and find those universal principles, from which all censure or approbation is ultimately derived. As this is a question of fact, not of abstract science, we can only expect success, by following the experimental method, and deducing general maxims from a comparison of particular instances. The other scientific method, where a general abstract principle is first established, and is afterwards branched out into a variety of inferences and conclusions, may be more perfect in itself, but suits less the imperfection of human nature, and is a common source of illusion and mistake in this as well as in other subjects. Men are not cured of their passion for hypotheses and systems in natural philosophy, and will hearken to no arguments but those which are derived from experience. It is full time they should attempt a like reformation in all moral disquisitions; and reject every system of ethics, however subtle or ingenious, which is not founded on fact and observation.

We shall begin our enquiry on this head by the consideration of the social virtues, Benevolence and Justice. The explication of them will probably give us an opening by which the others may be accounted for.

SECTION II *Of Benevolence*

PART I

It may be esteemed, perhaps, a superfluous task to prove, that the benevolent or softer affections are estimable; and wherever they appear, engage the approbation and good-will of mankind. The epithets *sociable, good-natured, humane, merciful, grateful, friendly, generous, beneficent*, or their equivalents, are known in all languages, and universally express the highest merit, which *human nature* is capable of attaining. Where these amiable qualities are attended with birth and power and eminent abilities, and display themselves in the good government or useful instruction of mankind, they seem even to raise the possessors of them above the rank of *human nature*, and make them approach in some measure to the divine. Exalted capacity, undaunted courage, prosperous success; these may only expose a hero or politician to the envy and ill-will of the public: but as soon as the praises are added of humane and beneficent; when instances are displayed of lenity, tenderness or friendship; envy itself is silent, or joins the general voice of approbation and applause.

When Pericles, the great Athenian statesman and general, was on his death-bed, his surrounding friends, deeming him now insensible, began to indulge their sorrow for their expiring patron, by enumerating his great qualities and successes, his conquests and victories, the unusual length of his administration, and his nine trophies erected over the enemies of the republic. *You forget*, cries the dying hero, who had heard all, *you forget the most eminent of my praises, while you dwell so much on those vulgar advantages, in which fortune had a principal share. You have not observed that no citizen has ever yet worne mourning on my account.*[1]

In men of more ordinary talents and capacity, the social virtues become, if possible, still more essentially requisite; there being nothing eminent, in that case, to compensate for the want of them, or preserve the person from our severest hatred, as well as contempt. A high ambition, an elevated courage, is apt, says Cicero, in less perfect characters, to degenerate into a turbulent ferocity. The more social and softer virtues are there chiefly to be regarded. These are always good and amiable.[2]

The principal advantage, which Juvenal discovers in the extensive capacity of the human species, is that it renders our benevolence also more extensive, and gives us larger opportunities of spreading our kindly influence than what are indulged to the inferior creation.[3] It must, indeed, be confessed, that by doing good only, can a man truly enjoy the advantages of being eminent. His exalted station, of itself but the more exposes him to danger and tempest. His sole prerogative is to afford shelter to inferiors, who repose themselves under his cover and protection.

But I forget, that it is not my present business to recommend generosity and benevolence, or to paint, in their true colours, all the genuine charms of the social virtues. These, indeed, sufficiently engage every heart, on the first apprehension of them; and it is difficult to abstain from some sally of panegyric, as often as they occur in discourse or reasoning. But our object here being more the speculative, than the practical part of morals, it will suffice to remark, (what will readily, I believe, be allowed) that no qualities are more intitled to the general good-will and approbation of mankind than beneficence and humanity, friendship and gratitude, natural affection and public spirit, or

1 Plut. in Pericle.
2 Cic. de Officiis, lib. 1.
3 Sat. xv. 139 and seq.

whatever proceeds from a tender sympathy with others, and a generous concern for our kind and species. These wherever they appear, seem to transfuse themselves, in a manner, into each beholder, and to call forth, in their own behalf, the same favourable and affectionate sentiments, which they exert on all around.

PART II

We may observe that, in displaying the praises of any humane, beneficent man, there is one circumstance which never fails to be amply insisted on, namely, the happiness and satisfaction, derived to society from his intercourse and good offices. To his parents, we are apt to say, he endears himself by his pious attachment and duteous care still more than by the connexions of nature. His children never feel his authority, but when employed for their advantage. With him, the ties of love are consolidated by beneficence and friendship. The ties of friendship approach, in a fond observance of each obliging office, to those of love and inclination. His domestics and dependants have in him a sure resource; and no longer dread the power of fortune, but so far as she exercises it over him. From him the hungry receive food, the naked clothing, the ignorant and slothful skill and industry. Like the sun, an inferior minister of providence he cheers, invigorates, and sustains the surrounding world.

If confined to private life, the sphere of his activity is narrower; but his influence is all benign and gentle. If exalted into a higher station, mankind and posterity reap the fruit of his labours.

As these topics of praise never fail to be employed, and with success, where we would inspire esteem for any one; may it not thence be concluded, that the utility, resulting from the social virtues, forms, at least, a *part* of their merit, and is one source of that approbation and regard so universally paid to them?

When we recommend even an animal or a plant as *useful* and *beneficial*, we give it an applause and recommendation suited to its nature. As, on the other hand, reflection on the baneful influence of any of these inferior beings always inspires us with the sentiment of aversion. The eye is pleased with the prospect of corn-fields and loaded vineyards; horses grazing, and flocks pasturing: but flies the view of briars and brambles, affording shelter to wolves and serpents.

A machine, a piece of furniture, a vestment, a house well contrived for use and conveniency, is so far beautiful, and is contemplated with pleasure and approbation. An experienced eye is here sensible to many excellencies, which escape persons ignorant and uninstructed.

Can anything stronger be said in praise of a profession, such as merchandize or manufacture, than to observe the advantages which it procures to society; and is not a monk and inquisitor enraged when we treat his order as useless or pernicious to mankind?

The historian exults in displaying the benefit arising from his labours. The writer of romance alleviates or denies the bad consequences ascribed to his manner of composition.

In general, what praise is implied in the simple epithet *useful*! What reproach in the contrary!

Your Gods, says Cicero,[1] in opposition to the Epicureans, cannot justly claim any worship or adoration, with whatever imaginary perfections you may suppose them endowed. They are totally useless and inactive. Even the Egyptians, whom you so much ridicule, never consecrated any animal but on account of its utility.

The sceptics assert,[2] though absurdly, that the origin of all religious worship was derived from the utility of inanimate objects, as the sun and moon, to the support and well-being of mankind. This is also the common reason assigned by historians, for the deification of eminent heroes and legislators.[3]

To plant a tree, to cultivate a field, to beget children; meritorious acts, according to the religion of Zoroaster.

In all determinations of morality, this circumstance of public utility is ever principally in view; and wherever disputes arise, either in philosophy or common life, concerning the bounds of duty, the question cannot, by any means, be decided with greater certainty, than by ascertaining, on any side, the true interests of mankind. If any false opinion, embraced from appearances, has been found to prevail; as soon as farther experience and sounder reasoning have given us juster notions of human affairs, we retract our first sentiment, and adjust anew the boundaries of moral good and evil.

Giving alms to common beggars is naturally praised; because it seems to carry relief to the distressed and indigent: but when we observe the encouragement thence arising to idleness and

1 De Nat. Deor. lib. i.
2 Sext. Emp. adversus Math. lib. viii.
3 Diod. Sic. passim.

debauchery, we regard that species of charity rather as a weakness than a virtue.

Tyrannicide, or the assassination of usurpers and oppressive princes, was highly extolled in ancient times; because it both freed mankind from many of these monsters, and seemed to keep the others in awe, whom the sword or poinard could not reach. But history and experience having since convinced us, that this practice increases the jealousy and cruelty of princes, a Timoleon and a Brutus, though treated with indulgence on account of the prejudices of their times, are now considered as very improper models for imitation.

Liberality in princes is regarded as a mark of beneficence, but when it occurs, that the homely bread of the honest and industrious is often thereby converted into delicious cates for the idle and the prodigal, we soon retract our heedless praises. The regrets of a prince, for having lost a day, were noble and generous: but had he intended to have spent it in acts of generosity to his greedy courtiers, it was better lost than misemployed after that manner.

Luxury, or a refinement on the pleasures and conveniences of life, had not long been supposed the source of every corruption in government, and the immediate cause of faction, sedition, civil wars, and the total loss of liberty. It was, therefore, universally regarded as a vice, and was an object of declamation to all satirists, and severe moralists. Those, who prove, or attempt to prove, that such refinements rather tend to the increase of industry, civility, and arts regulate anew our *moral* as well as *political* sentiments, and represent, as laudable or innocent, what had formerly been regarded as pernicious and blameable.

Upon the whole, then, it seems undeniable, *that* nothing can bestow more merit on any human creature than the sentiment of benevolence in an eminent degree; and *that a part*, at least, of its merit arises from its tendency to promote the interests of our species, and bestow happiness on human society. We carry our view into the salutary consequences of such a character and disposition; and whatever has so benign an influence, and forwards so desirable an end, is beheld with complacency and pleasure. The social virtues are never regarded without their beneficial tendencies, nor viewed as barren and unfruitful. The happiness of mankind, the order of society, the harmony of families, the mutual support of friends, are always considered as the result of their gentle dominion over the breasts of men.

How considerable a *part* of their merit we ought to ascribe to their utility, will better appear from future disquisitions; as well as the reason, why this circumstance has such a command over our esteem and approbation.

Source: David Hume, *An Enquiry concerning the Principles of Morals*, sections 1, 2, in *Enquiries concerning Human Understanding and concerning the Principles of Morals*, ed. L. A. Selby-Bigge, 3rd edn by P. H. Nidditch, Oxford 1975, pp. 169–82

SEVEN

ADAM SMITH
Sympathy, Propriety and Merit

Smith holds that there are two fundamental types of moral judgment: one concerning the propriety of our acts, that is, concerning their rightness or wrongness; and the other concerning the merit or demerit of our acts, that is, concerning their praiseworthiness or blameworthiness. The whole of the *Theory of Moral Sentiments* deals with these two types of judgment, and since the concept of sympathy is fundamental to the analysis of both types of judgment Smith starts by investigating that concept.

'Sympathy' is a technical term in Smith's philosophy and has to be dealt with on that basis. In particular, we often speak of people acting from the motive of sympathy, meaning that they are acting compassionately, and this is simply not what the term means when it is being used in its technical sense. In the technical sense, to sympathise with someone is to have a feeling which one knows or supposes another person to have, and to acquire the feeling by imagining oneself in the very same circumstances that we know the other person to be in. This is not to say that the other person must in fact have the feeling. For example, Smith discusses sympathy produced by a person who has lost his reason; that person is apparently himself very happy, yet we are distressed at the thought of ourselves being in those very same circumstances. But the standard case of sympathy is that in which one person has the same feeling that he takes another to have, and has it because he has imaginatively put himself into the shoes of the other.

It is clear that sympathy may not involve a painful feeling. We can enter sympathetically into the supposed joy of another no less than into his supposed sorrow. Since the fellow-feeling associated with Smithian sympathy need not be a feeling of pity or compassion, the term 'sympathy' as employed by Smith, does not have its customary sense.

The term is deployed crucially, as I stated earlier, in the

analysis of two types of judgment, concerning propriety and merit. Our response to the sight of someone speaking angrily to another might be to sympathise fully with the anger, in the sense that, on imagining ourselves in the same situation as the angry person, we realise we also would have been angry. We think his anger proper, or appropriate, and therefore approve of it. If we are not in sympathy with it we say it is improper or inappropriate.

What of the person who is the object of the anger? One response he might make is to be resentful. If we sympathise with that response then we say that what provoked it lacks merit and deserves punishment. Suppose however we see a person perform a kindly act, and sympathise with the recipient's feeling of gratitude. In that case we judge the act to have been meritorious and to deserve a reward.

It is on the basis of these concepts of propriety and merit, that Smith constructs a wide-ranging and psychologically deep system of moral philosophy. The whole edifice rests on the concept of sympathy. Sympathy is not being treated as *a*, even less as *the*, moral motive. Instead it is treated as an element in the analysis of moral judgment. In due course the fact that Smith's economic theory in his *Wealth of Nations* was based on an assumption that people will act from the motive of self-interest was seen as in conflict with the doctrine of sympathy in the *Theory of Moral Sentiments*. But since Smith does not present sympathy as a moral motive, there is no such conflict. (For more on this see excerpt 22.)

A.B.

PART I
Of the Propriety of Action
SECTION I *Of the Sense of Propriety*

CHAPTER I *Of sympathy*

How selfish soever man may be supposed, there are evidently some principles in his nature, which interest him in the fortune of others, and render their happiness necessary to him, though he derives nothing from it except the pleasure of seeing it. Of this kind is pity or compassion, the emotion which we feel for the misery of others, when we either see it, or are made to conceive it in a very lively manner. That we often derive sorrow from the sorrow of others, is a matter of fact too obvious to require any instances to prove it; for this sentiment, like all the other original passions of human nature, is by no means confined to the virtuous and humane, though they perhaps may feel it with the most exquisite sensibility. The greatest ruffian, the most hardened violator of the laws of society, is not altogether without it.

As we have no immediate experience of what other men feel, we can form no idea of the manner in which they are affected, but by conceiving what we ourselves should feel in the like situation. Though our brother is upon the rack, as long as we ourselves are at our ease, our senses will never inform us of what he suffers. They never did, and never can, carry us beyond our own person, and it is by the imagination only that we can form any conception of what are his sensations. Neither can that faculty help us to this any other way, than by representing to us what would be our own, if we were in his case. It is the impressions of our own senses only, not those of his, which our imaginations copy. By the imagination we place ourselves in his situation, we conceive ourselves enduring all the same torments, we enter as it were into his body, and become in some measure the same person with him, and thence form some idea of his sensations, and even feel something which, though weaker in degree, is not altogether unlike them. His agonies, when they are thus brought home to ourselves, when we have thus adopted and made them our own, begin at last to affect us, and we then tremble and shudder at the thought of what he feels. For as to be in pain or distress of any kind excites the most excessive sorrow, so to conceive or to imagine that we are in it, excites some degree of the same emotion, in proportion to the vivacity or dulness of the conception.

That this is the source of our fellow-feeling for the misery of others, that it is by changing places in fancy with the sufferer, that we come either to conceive or to be affected by what he feels, may be demonstrated by many obvious observations, if it should not be thought sufficiently evident of itself. When we see a stroke aimed and just ready to fall upon the leg or arm of another person, we naturally shrink and draw back our own leg or our own arm; and when it does fall, we feel it in some measure, and are hurt by it as well as the sufferer. The mob, when they are gazing at a dancer on the slack rope, naturally writhe and twist and balance their own bodies, as they see him do, and as they feel that they themselves must do if in his situation. Persons of delicate fibres and a weak constitution of body complain, that in looking on the sores and ulcers which are exposed by beggars in the streets, they are apt to feel an itching or uneasy sensation in the correspondent part of their own bodies. The horror which they conceive at the misery of those wretches affects that particular part in themselves more than any other; because that horror arises from conceiving what they themselves would suffer, if they really were the wretches whom they are looking upon, and if that particular part in themselves was actually affected in the same miserable manner. The very force of this conception is sufficient, in their feeble frames, to produce that itching or uneasy sensation complained of. Men of the most robust make, observe that in looking upon sore eyes they often feel a very sensible soreness in their own, which proceeds from the same reason; that organ being in the strongest man more delicate, than any other part of the body is in the weakest.

Neither is it those circumstances only, which create pain or sorrow, that call forth our fellow-feeling. Whatever is the passion which arises from any object in the person principally concerned, an analogous emotion springs up, at the thought of his situation, in the breast of every attentive spectator. Our joy for the deliverance of those heroes of tragedy or romance who interest us, is as sincere as our grief for their distress, and our fellow-feeling with their misery is not more real than that with their happiness. We enter into their gratitude towards those faithful friends who did not desert them in their difficulties; and we heartily go along with their resentment against those perfidious traitors who injured, abandoned, or deceived them. In every passion of which the mind of man is susceptible, the emotions of the by-stander always correspond to what, by bringing the case home to himself, he imagines should be the sentiments of the sufferer.

Pity and compassion are words appropriated to signify our fellow-feeling with the sorrow of others. Sympathy, though its meaning was, perhaps, originally the same, may now, however, without much impropriety, be made use of to denote our fellow-feeling with any passion whatever.

Upon some occasions sympathy may seem to arise merely from the view of a certain emotion in another person. The passions, upon some occasions, may seem to be transfused from one man to another, instantaneously, and antecedent to any knowledge of what excited them in the person principally concerned. Grief and joy, for example, strongly expressed in the look and gestures of any one, at once affect the spectator with some degree of a like painful or agreeable emotion. A smiling face is, to every body that sees it, a cheerful object; as a sorrowful countenance, on the other hand, is a melancholy one.

This, however, does not hold universally, or with regard to every passion. There are some passions of which the expressions excite no sort of sympathy, but before we are acquainted with what gave occasion to them, serve rather to disgust and provoke us against them. The furious behaviour of an angry man is more likely to exasperate us against himself than against his enemies. As we are unacquainted with his provocation, we cannot bring his case home to ourselves, nor conceive any thing like the passions which it excites. But we plainly see what is the situation of those with whom he is angry, and to what violence they may be exposed from so enraged an adversary. We readily, therefore, sympathize with their fear or resentment, and are immediately disposed to take part against the man from whom they appear to be in so much danger.

If the very appearances of grief and joy inspire us with some degree of the like emotions, it is because they suggest to us the general idea of some good or bad fortune that has befallen the person in whom we observe them: and in these passions this is sufficient to have some little influence upon us. The effects of grief and joy terminate in the person who feels those emotions, of which the expressions do not, like those of resentment, suggest to us the idea of any other person for whom we are concerned, and whose interests are opposite to his. The general idea of good or bad fortune, therefore, creates some concern for the person who has met with it, but the general idea of provocation excites no sympathy with the anger of the man who has received it. Nature, it seems, teaches us to be more averse to enter into this passion, and, till informed of its cause, to be disposed rather to take part against it.

Even our sympathy with the grief or joy of another, before we are informed of the cause of either, is always extremely imperfect. General lamentations, which express nothing but the anguish of the sufferer, create rather a curiosity to inquire into his situation, along with some disposition to sympathize with him, than any actual sympathy that is very sensible. The first question which we ask is, What has befallen you? Till this be answered, though we are uneasy both from the vague idea of his misfortune, and still more from torturing ourselves with conjectures about what it may be, yet our fellow-feeling is not very considerable.

Sympathy, therefore, does not arise so much from the view of the passion, as from that of the situation which excites it. We sometimes feel for another, a passion of which he himself seems to be altogether incapable; because, when we put ourselves in his case, that passion arises in our breast from the imagination, though it does not in his from the reality. We blush for the impudence and rudeness of another, though he himself appears to have no sense of the impropriety of his own behaviour; because we cannot help feeling with what confusion we ourselves should be covered, had we behaved in so absurd a manner.

Of all the calamities to which the condition of mortality exposes mankind, the loss of reason appears, to those who have the least spark of humanity, by far the most dreadful, and they behold that last stage of human wretchedness with deeper commiseration than any other. But the poor wretch, who is in it, laughs and sings perhaps, and is altogether insensible of his own misery. The anguish which humanity feels, therefore, at the sight of such an object, cannot be the reflection of any sentiment of the sufferer. The compassion of the spectator must arise altogether from the consideration of what he himself would feel if he was reduced to the same unhappy situation, and, what perhaps is impossible, was at the same time able to regard it with his present reason and judgment.

What are the pangs of a mother, when she hears the moanings of her infant that during the agony of disease cannot express what it feels? In her idea of what it suffers, she joins, to its real helplessness, her own consciousness of that helplessness, and her own terrors for the unknown consequences of its disorder; and out of all these, forms, for her own sorrow, the most complete image of misery and distress. The infant, however, feels only the uneasiness of the present instant, which can never be great. With regard to the future, it is perfectly secure, and in its thoughtlessness and want of foresight, possesses an antidote against fear and anxiety, the great tormentors of the human breast, from which reason and philosophy will, in vain, attempt to defend it, when it grows up to a man.

We sympathize even with the dead, and overlooking what is of real importance in their situation, that awful futurity which awaits them, we are chiefly affected by those circumstances which strike our senses, but can have no influence upon their happiness. It is miserable, we think, to be deprived of the light of the sun; to be shut out from life and conversation; to be laid in the cold grave, a prey to corruption and the reptiles of the earth; to be no more thought of in this world, but to be obliterated, in a little time, from the affections, and almost from the memory, of their dearest friends and relations. Surely, we imagine, we can never feel too much for those who have suffered so dreadful a calamity. The tribute of our fellow-feeling seems doubly due to them now, when they are in danger of being forgot by every body; and, by the vain honours which we pay to their memory, we endeavour, for our own misery, artificially to keep alive our melancholy remembrance of their misfortune. That our sympathy can afford them no consolation seems to be an addition to their calamity; and to think that all we can do is unavailing, and that, what alleviates all other distress, the regret, the love, and the lamentations of their friends, can yield no comfort to them, serves only to exasperate our sense of their misery. The happiness of the dead, however, most assuredly, is affected by none of these circumstances; nor is it the thought of these things which can ever disturb the profound security of their repose. The idea of that dreary and endless melancholy, which the fancy naturally ascribes to their condition, arises altogether from our joining to the change which has been produced upon them, our own consciousness of that change, from our putting ourselves in their situation, and from our lodging, if I may be allowed to say so, our own living souls in their inanimated bodies, and thence conceiving what would be our emotions in this case. It is from this very illusion of the imagination, that the foresight of our own dissolution is so terrible to us, and that the idea of those circumstances, which undoubtedly can give us no pain when we are dead, makes us miserable while we are alive. And from thence arises one of the most important principles in human nature, the dread of death, the great poison to the happiness, but the great restraint upon the injustice of mankind, which, while it afflicts and mortifies the individual, guards and protects the society.

CHAPTER II *Of the pleasure of mutual sympathy*
But whatever may be the cause of sympathy, or however it may be excited, nothing pleases us more than to observe in other men a fellow-feeling with all the emotions of our own breast; nor are we ever so much shocked as by the appearance of the contrary. Those who are fond of deducing all our sentiments from certain refinements of self-love, think themselves at no loss to account, according to their own principles, both for this pleasure and this pain. Man, say they, conscious of his own weakness, and of the need which he has for the assistance of others, rejoices whenever he observes that they adopt his own passions, because he is then assured of that assistance; and grieves whenever he observes the contrary, because he is then assured of their opposition. But both the pleasure and the pain are always felt so instantaneously, and often upon such frivolous occasions, that it seems evident that neither of them can be derived from any such self-interested consideration. A man is mortified when, after having endeavoured to divert the company, he looks round and sees that nobody laughs at his jests but himself. On the contrary, the mirth of the company is highly agreeable to him, and he regards this correspondence of their sentiments with his own as the greatest applause.

Neither does his pleasure seem to arise altogether from the additional vivacity which his mirth may receive from sympathy with theirs, nor his pain from the disappointment he meets with when he misses this pleasure; though both the one and the other, no doubt, do in some measure. When we have read a book or poem so often that we can no longer find any amusement in reading it by ourselves, we can still take pleasure in reading it to a companion. To him it has all the graces of novelty; we enter into the surprise and admiration which it naturally excites in him, but which it is no longer capable of exciting in us; we consider all the ideas which it presents rather in the light in which they appear to him, than in that in which they appear to ourselves, and we are amused by sympathy with his amusement which thus enlivens our own. On the contrary, we should be vexed if he did not seem to be entertained with it, and we could no longer take any pleasure in reading it to him. It is the same case here. The mirth of the company, no doubt, enlivens our own mirth, and their silence, no doubt, disappoints us. But though this may contribute both to the pleasure which we derive from the one, and to the pain which we feel from the other, it is by no means the sole cause of either; and this correspondence of the sentiments of others with our own appears to be a cause of pleasure, and the want of it a cause of pain, which cannot be accounted for in this manner. The sympathy, which my friends express with my joy, might, indeed, give me pleasure by enlivening that joy: but that which they express with my grief could give me none, if it served only to enliven that grief. Sympathy, however, enlivens joy and alleviates grief. It enlivens joy by presenting another source of satisfaction; and it alleviates grief by insinuating into the heart almost the only agreeable sensation which it is at that time capable of receiving.

It is to be observed accordingly, that we are still more anxious to communicate to our friends our disagreeable than our agreeable passions, that we derive still more satisfaction from their sympathy with the former than from that with the latter, and that we are still more shocked by the want of it.

How are the unfortunate relieved when they have found out a person to whom they can communicate the cause of their sorrow? Upon his sympathy they seem to disburthen themselves of a part of their distress: he is not improperly said to share it with them. He not only feels a sorrow of the same kind with that which they feel, but as if he had derived a part of it to himself, what he feels seems to alleviate the weight of what they feel. Yet by relating their misfortunes they in some measure renew their grief. They awaken in their memory the remembrance of those circumstances which occasioned their affliction. Their tears accordingly flow faster than before, and they are apt to abandon themselves to all the weakness of sorrow. They take pleasure, however, in all this, and, it is evident, are sensibly relieved by it; because the sweetness of his sympathy more than compensates the bitterness of that sorrow, which, in order to excite this sympathy, they had thus enlivened and renewed. The cruelest insult, on the contrary, which can be offered to the unfortunate, is to appear to make light of their calamities. To seem not to be affected with the joy of our companions is but want of politeness; but not to wear a serious countenance when they tell us their afflictions, is real and gross inhumanity.

Love is an agreeable; resentment, a disagreeable passion; and accordingly we are not half so anxious that our friends should adopt our friendships, as that they should enter into our resentments. We can forgive them though they seem to be little affected with the favours which we may have received, but lose all patience if they seem indifferent about the injuries which may have been done to us: nor are we half so angry with them for not entering into our gratitude, as for not sympathizing with our resentment. They can easily avoid being friends to our friends, but can hardly avoid being enemies to those with whom we are at variance. We seldom resent their being at enmity with the first, though upon that account we may sometimes affect to make an awkward quarrel with them; but we quarrel with them in good earnest if they live in friendship with the last. The agreeable passions of love and joy can satisfy and support the heart without any auxiliary pleasure. The bitter and painful emotions of grief and resentment more strongly require the healing consolation of sympathy.

As the person who is principally interested in any event is pleased with our sympathy, and hurt by the want of it, so we, too, seem to be pleased when we are able to sympathize with him, and to be hurt when we are unable to do so. We run not only to congratulate the successful, but to condole with the afflicted; and the pleasure which we find in the conversation of one whom in all the passions of his heart we can entirely sympathize with, seems to do more than compensate the painfulness of that sorrow with which the view of his situation affects us. On the contrary, it is always disagreeable to feel that we cannot sympathize with him, and instead of being pleased with this exemption from sympathetic pain, it hurts us to find that we cannot share his uneasiness. If we hear a person loudly lamenting his misfortunes, which, however, upon bringing the case home to ourselves, we feel, can produce no such violent effect upon us, we are shocked at his grief; and, because we cannot enter into it, call it pusillanimity and weakness. It gives us the spleen, on the other hand, to see another too happy or too much elevated, as we call it, with any little piece of good fortune. We are disobliged even with his joy; and, because we cannot go along with it, call it levity and folly. We are even put out of humour if our companion laughs louder or longer at a joke than we think it deserves; that is, than we feel that we ourselves could laugh at it.

CHAPTER III *Of the manner in which we judge of the propriety or impropriety of the affections of other men, by their concord or dissonance with our own*
When the original passions of the person principally concerned are in perfect concord with the sympathetic emotions of the spectator,

they necessarily appear to this last just and proper, and suitable to their objects; and, on the contrary, when, upon bringing the case home to himself, he finds that they do not coincide with what he feels, they necessarily appear to him unjust and improper, and unsuitable to the causes which excite them. To approve of the passions of another, therefore, as suitable to their objects, is the same thing as to observe that we entirely sympathize with them; and not to approve of them as such, is the same thing as to observe that we do not entirely sympathize with them. The man who resents the injuries that have been done to me, and observes that I resent them precisely as he does, necessarily approves of my resentment. The man whose sympathy keeps time to my grief, cannot but admit the reasonableness of my sorrow. He who admires the same poem, or the same picture, and admires them exactly as I do, must surely allow the justness of my admiration. He who laughs at the same joke, and laughs along with me, cannot well deny the propriety of my laughter. On the contrary, the person who, upon these different occasions, either feels no such emotion as that which I feel, or feels none that bears any proportion to mine, cannot avoid disapproving my sentiments on account of their dissonance with his own. If my animosity goes beyond what the indignation of my friend can correspond to; if my grief exceeds what his most tender compassion can go along with; if my admiration is either too high or too low to tally with his own; if I laugh loud and heartily when he only smiles, or, on the contrary, only smile when he laughs loud and heartily; in all these cases, as soon as he comes from considering the object, to observe how I am affected by it, according as there is more or less disproportion between his sentiments and mine, I must incur a greater or less degree of his disapprobation: and upon all occasions his own sentiments are the standards and measures by which he judges of mine.

To approve of another man's opinions is to adopt those opinions, and to adopt them is to approve of them. If the same arguments which convince you convince me likewise, I necessarily approve of your conviction; and if they do not, I necessarily disapprove of it: neither can I possibly conceive that I should do the one without the other. To approve or disapprove, therefore, of the opinions of others is acknowledged, by every body, to mean no more than to observe their agreement or disagreement with our own. But this is equally the case with regard to our approbation or disapprobation of the sentiments or passions of others.

There are, indeed, some cases in which we seem to approve without any sympathy or correspondence of sentiments, and in which, consequently, the sentiment of approbation would seem to be different from the perception of this coincidence. A little attention, however, will convince us that even in these cases our approbation is ultimately founded upon a sympathy or correspondence of this kind. I shall give an instance in things of a very frivolous nature, because in them the judgments of mankind are less apt to be perverted by wrong systems. We may often approve of a jest, and think the laughter of the company quite just and proper, though we ourselves do not laugh, because, perhaps, we are in a grave humour, or happen to have our attention engaged with other objects. We have learned, however, from experience, what sort of pleasantry is upon most occasions capable of making us laugh, and we observe that this is one of that kind. We approve, therefore, of the laughter of the company, and feel that it is natural and suitable to its object; because, though in our present mood we cannot easily enter into it, we are sensible that upon most occasions we should very heartily join in it.

The same thing often happens with regard to all the other passions. A stranger passes by us in the street with all the marks of the deepest affliction; and we are immediately told that he has just received the news of the death of his father. It is impossible that, in this case, we should not approve of his grief. Yet it may often happen, without any defect of humanity on our part, that, so far from entering into the violence of his sorrow, we should scarce conceive the first movements of concern upon his account. Both he and his father, perhaps, are entirely unknown to us, or we happen to be employed about other things, and do not take time to picture out in our imagination the different circumstances of distress which must occur to him. We have learned, however, from experience, that such a misfortune naturally excites such a degree of sorrow, and we know that if we took time to consider his situation, fully and in all its parts, we should, without doubt, most sincerely sympathize with him. It is upon the consciousness of this conditional sympathy, that our approbation of his sorrow is founded, even in those cases in which that sympathy does not actually take place; and the general rules derived from our preceding experience of what our sentiments would commonly correspond with, correct upon this, as upon many other occasions, the impropriety of our present emotions.

The sentiment or affection of the heart from which any action proceeds, and upon which its whole virtue or vice must ultimately depend, may be considered under two different aspects, or in two different relations; first, in relation to the cause which excites it, or the motive which gives occasion to it; and secondly, in relation to the end which it proposes, or the effect which it tends to produce.

In the suitableness or unsuitableness, in the proportion or disproportion which the affection seems to bear to the cause or object which excites it, consists the propriety or impropriety, the decency or ungracefulness of the consequent action.

In the beneficial or hurtful nature of the effects which the affection aims at, or tends to produce, consists the merit or demerit of the action, the qualities by which it is entitled to reward, or is deserving of punishment.

Philosophers have, of late years, considered chiefly the tendency of affections, and have given little attention to the relation which they stand in to the cause which excites them. In common life, however, when we judge of any person's conduct, and of the sentiments which directed it, we constantly consider them under both these aspects. When we blame in another man the excesses of love, of grief, of resentment, we not only consider the ruinous effects which they tend to produce, but the little occasion which was given for them. The merit of his favourite, we say, is not so great, his misfortune is not so dreadful, his provocation is not so extraordinary, as to justify so violent a passion. We should have indulged, we say; perhaps, have approved of the violence of his emotion, had the cause been in any respect proportioned to it.

When we judge in this manner of any affection, as proportioned or disproportioned to the cause which excites it, it is scarce possible that we should make use of any other rule or canon but the correspondent affection in ourselves. If, upon bringing the case home to our own breast, we find that the sentiments which it gives occasion to, coincide and tally with our own, we necessarily approve of them as proportioned and suitable to their objects; if otherwise, we necessarily disapprove of them, as extravagant and out of proportion.

Every faculty in one man is the measure by which he judges of the like faculty in another. I judge of your sight by my sight, of your ear by my ear, of your reason by my reason, of your resentment by my resentment, of your love by my love. I neither have, nor can have, any other way of judging about them.

CHAPTER IV *The same subject continued*
We may judge of the propriety or impropriety of the sentiments of

another person by their correspondence or disagreement with our own, upon two different occasions; either, first, when the objects which excite them are considered without any peculiar relation, either to ourselves or to the person whose sentiments we judge of; or, secondly, when they are considered as peculiarly affecting one or other of us.

1. With regard to those objects which are considered without any peculiar relation either to ourselves or to the person whose sentiments we judge of; wherever his sentiments entirely correspond with our own, we ascribe to him the qualities of taste and good judgment. The beauty of a plain, the greatness of a mountain, the ornaments of a building, the expression of a picture, the composition of a discourse, the conduct of a third person, the proportions of different quantities and numbers, the various appearances which the great machine of the universe is perpetually exhibiting, with the secret wheels and springs which produce them; all the general subjects of science and taste, are what we and our companion regard as having no peculiar relation to either of us. We both look at them from the same point of view, and we have no occasion for sympathy, or for that imaginary change of situations from which it arises, in order to produce, with regard to these, the most perfect harmony of sentiments and affections. If, notwithstanding, we are often differently affected, it arises either from the different degrees of attention, which our different habits of life allow us to give easily to the several parts of those complex objects, or from the different degrees of natural acuteness in the faculty of the mind to which they are addressed.

When the sentiments of our companion coincide with our own in things of this kind, which are obvious and easy, and in which, perhaps, we never found a single person who differed from us, though we, no doubt, must approve of them, yet he seems to deserve no praise or admiration on account of them. But when they not only coincide with our own, but lead and direct our own; when in forming them he appears to have attended to many things which we had overlooked, and to have adjusted them to all the various circumstances of their objects; we not only approve of them, but wonder and are surprised at their uncommon and unexpected acuteness and comprehensiveness, and he appears to deserve a very high degree of admiration and applause. For approbation heightened by wonder and surprise, constitutes the sentiment which is properly called admiration, and of which applause is the natural expression. The decision of the man who judges that exquisite beauty is preferable to the grossest deformity, or that twice two are equal to four, must certainly be approved of by all the world, but will not, surely, be much admired. It is the acute and delicate discernment of the man of taste, who distinguishes the minute, and scarce perceptible differences of beauty and deformity; it is the comprehensive accuracy of the experienced mathematician, who unravels, with ease, the most intricate and perplexed proportions; it is the great leader in science and taste, the man who directs and conducts our own sentiments, the extent and superior justness of whose talents astonish us with wonder and surprise, who excites our admiration, and seems to deserve our applause: and upon this foundation is grounded the greater part of the praise which is bestowed upon what are called the intellectual virtues.

The utility of those qualities, it may be thought, is what first recommends them to us; and, no doubt, the consideration of this, when we come to attend to it, gives them a new value. Originally, however, we approve of another man's judgment, not as something useful, but as right, as accurate, as agreeable to truth and reality: and it is evident we attribute those qualities to it for no other reason but because we find that it agrees with our own. Taste, in the same manner, is originally approved of, not as useful, but as just, as delicate, and as precisely suited to its object. The idea of the utility of all qualities of this kind, is plainly an after-thought, and not what first recommends them to our approbation.

2. With regard to those objects, which affect in a particular manner either ourselves or the person whose sentiments we judge of, it is at once more difficult to preserve this harmony and correspondence, and at the same time, vastly more important. My companion does not naturally look upon the misfortune that has befallen me, or the injury that has been done me, from the same point of view in which I consider them. They affect me much more nearly. We do not view them from the same station, as we do a picture, or a poem, or a system of philosophy, and are, therefore, apt to be very differently affected by them. But I can much more easily overlook the want of this correspondence of sentiments with regard to such indifferent objects as concern neither me nor my companion, than with regard to what interests me so much as the misfortune that has befallen me, or the injury

that has been done me. Though you despise that picture, or that poem, or even that system of philosophy, which I admire, there is little danger of our quarrelling upon that account. Neither of us can reasonably be much interested about them. They ought all of them to be matters of great indifference to us both; so that, though our opinions may be opposite, our affections may still be very nearly the same. But it is quite otherwise with regard to those objects by which either you or I are particularly affected. Though your judgments in matters of speculation, though your sentiments in matters of taste, are quite opposite to mine, I can easily overlook this opposition; and if I have any degree of temper, I may still find some entertainment in your conversation, even upon those very subjects. But if you have either no fellow-feeling for the misfortunes I have met with, or none that bears any proportion to the grief which distracts me; or if you have either no indignation at the injuries I have suffered, or none that bears any proportion to the resentment which transports me, we can no longer converse upon these subjects. We become intolerable to one another. I can neither support your company, nor you mine. You are confounded at my violence and passion, and I am enraged at your cold insensibility and want of feeling.

In all such cases, that there may be some correspondence of sentiments between the spectator and the person principally concerned, the spectator must, first of all, endeavour, as much as he can, to put himself in the situation of the other, and to bring home to himself every little circumstance of distress which can possibly occur to the sufferer. He must adopt the whole case of his companion with all its minutest incidents; and strive to render as perfect as possible, that imaginary change of situation upon which his sympathy is founded.

After all this, however, the emotions of the spectator will still be very apt to fall short of the violence of what is felt by the sufferer. Mankind, though naturally sympathetic, never conceive, for what has befallen another, that degree of passion which naturally animates the person principally concerned. That imaginary change of situation, upon which their sympathy is founded, is but momentary. The thought of their own safety, the thought that they themselves are not really the sufferers, continually intrudes itself upon them; and although it does not hinder them from conceiving a passion somewhat analogous to what is felt by the sufferer, hinders them from conceiving any thing that approaches to the same degree of violence. The person principally concerned is sensible of this, and at the same time passionately desires a more complete sympathy. He longs for that relief which nothing can afford him but the entire concord of the affections of the spectators with his own. To see the emotions of their hearts, in every respect, beat time to his own, in the violent and disagreeable passions, constitutes his sole consolation. But he can only hope to obtain this by lowering his passion to that pitch, in which the spectators are capable of going along with him. He must flatten, if I may be allowed to say so, the sharpness of its natural tone, in order to reduce it to harmony and concord with the emotions of those who are about him. What they feel, will, indeed, always be, in some respects, different from what he feels, and compassion can never be exactly the same with original sorrow; because the secret consciousness that the change of situations, from which the sympathetic sentiment arises, is but imaginary, not only lowers it in degree, but, in some measure, varies it in kind, and gives it a quite different modification. These two sentiments, however, may, it is evident, have such a correspondence with one another, as is sufficient for the harmony of society. Though they will never be unisons, they may be concords, and this is all that is wanted or required.

In order to produce this concord, as nature teaches the spectators to assume the circumstances of the person principally concerned, so she teaches this last in some measure to assume those of the spectators. As they are continually placing themselves in his situation, and thence conceiving emotions similar to what he feels; so he is as constantly placing himself in theirs, and thence conceiving some degree of that coolness about his own fortune, with which he is sensible that they will view it. As they are constantly considering what they themselves would feel, if they actually were the sufferers, so he is as constantly led to imagine in what manner he would be affected if he was only one of the spectators of his own situation. As their sympathy makes them look at it, in some measure, with his eyes, so his sympathy makes him look at it, in some measure, with theirs, especially when in their presence and acting under their observation: and as the reflected passion, which he thus conceives, is much weaker than the original one, it necessarily abates the violence of what he felt before he came into their presence, before he began to recollect in what manner they would be affected by it, and to view his situation in this candid and impartial light.

The mind, therefore, is rarely so disturbed, but that the company of a friend will restore it to some degree of tranquillity and sedateness. The breast is, in some measure, calmed and composed the moment we come into his presence. We are immediately put in mind of the light in which he will view our situation, and we begin to view it ourselves in the same light; for the effect of sympathy is instantaneous. We expect less sympathy from a common acquaintance than from a friend: we cannot open to the former all those little circumstances which we can unfold to the latter: we assume, therefore, more tranquillity before him, and endeavour to fix our thoughts upon those general outlines of our situation which he is willing to consider. We expect still less sympathy from an assembly of strangers, and we assume, therefore, still more tranquillity before them, and always endeavour to bring down our passion to that pitch, which the particular company we are in may be expected to go along with. Nor is this only an assumed appearance: for if we are at all masters of ourselves, the presence of a mere acquaintance will really compose us, still more than that of a friend; and that of an assembly of strangers still more than that of an acquaintance.

Society and conversation, therefore, are the most powerful remedies for restoring the mind to its tranquillity, if, at any time, it has unfortunately lost it; as well as the best preservatives of that equal and happy temper, which is so necessary to self-satisfaction and enjoyment. Men of retirement and speculation, who are apt to sit brooding at home over either grief or resentment, though they may often have more humanity, more generosity, and a nicer sense of honour, yet seldom possess that equality of temper which is so common among men of the world.

CHAPTER V *Of the amiable and respectable virtues*

Upon these two different efforts, upon that of the spectator to enter into the sentiments of the person principally concerned, and upon that of the person principally concerned, to bring down his emotions to what the spectator can go along with, are founded two different sets of virtues. The soft, the gentle, the amiable virtues, the virtues of candid condescension and indulgent humanity, are founded upon the one: the great, the awful and respectable, the virtues of self-denial, of self-government, of that command of the passions which subjects all the movements of our nature to what our own dignity and honour, and the propriety of our own conduct require, take their origin from the other.

How amiable does he appear to be, whose sympathetic heart seems to re-echo all the sentiments of those with whom he converses, who grieves for their calamities, who resents their injuries, and who rejoices at their good fortune! When we bring home to ourselves the situation of his companions, we enter into their gratitude, and feel what consolation they must derive from the tender sympathy of so affectionate a friend. And for a contrary reason, how disagreeable does he appear to be, whose hard and obdurate heart feels for himself only, but is altogether insensible to the happiness or misery of others! We enter, in this case too, into the pain which his presence must give to every mortal with whom he converses, to those especially with whom we are most apt to sympathize, the unfortunate and the injured.

On the other hand, what noble propriety and grace do we feel in the conduct of those who, in their own case, exert that recollection and self-command which constitute the dignity of every passion, and which bring it down to what others can enter into! We are disgusted with that clamorous grief, which, without any delicacy, calls upon our compassion with sighs and tears and importunate lamentations. But we reverence that reserved, that silent and majestic sorrow, which discovers itself only in the swelling of the eyes, in the quivering of the lips and cheeks, and in the distant, but affecting, coldness of the whole behaviour. It imposes the like silence upon us. We regard it with respectful attention, and watch with anxious concern over our whole behaviour, lest by any impropriety we should disturb that concerted tranquillity, which it requires so great an effort to support.

The insolence and brutality of anger, in the same manner, when we indulge its fury without check or restraint, is, of all objects, the most detestable. But we admire that noble and generous resentment which governs its pursuit of the greatest injuries, not by the rage which they are apt to excite in the breast of the sufferer, but by the indignation which they naturally call forth in that of the impartial spectator; which allows no word, no gesture, to escape it beyond what this more equitable sentiment would dictate; which never, even in thought, attempts any greater vengeance, nor desires to inflict any greater punishment, than what every indifferent person would rejoice to see executed.

And hence it is, that to feel much for others and little for ourselves, that to restrain our selfish, and to indulge our benevolent affections, constitutes the perfection of human nature; and can alone produce among mankind that harmony of sentiments and passions in which consists their whole grace and propriety. As to love our neighbour as we love ourselves is the great law of Christianity, so it is the great precept of nature to love ourselves only as we love our neighbour, or what comes to the same thing, as our neighbour is capable of loving us.

As taste and good judgment, when they are considered as qualities which deserve praise and admiration, are supposed to imply a delicacy of sentiment and an acuteness of understanding not commonly to be met with; so the virtues of sensibility and self-command are not apprehended to consist in the ordinary, but in the uncommon degrees of those qualities. The amiable virtue of humanity requires, surely, a sensibility, much beyond what is possessed by the rude vulgar of mankind. The great and exalted virtue of magnanimity undoubtedly demands much more than that degree of self-command, which the weakest of mortals is capable of exerting. As in the common degree of the intellectual qualities, there is no abilities; so in the common degree of the moral, there is no virtue. Virtue is excellence, something uncommonly great and beautiful, which rises far above what is vulgar and ordinary. The amiable virtues consist in that degree of sensibility which surprises by its exquisite and unexpected delicacy and tenderness. The awful and respectable, in that degree of self-command which astonishes by its amazing superiority over the most ungovernable passions of human nature.

There is, in this respect, a considerable difference between virtue and mere propriety; between those qualities and actions which deserve to be admired and celebrated, and those which simply deserve to be approved of. Upon many occasions, to act with the most perfect propriety, requires no more than that common and ordinary degree of sensibility or self-command which the most worthless of mankind are possest of, and sometimes even that degree is not necessary. Thus, to give a very low instance, to eat when we are hungry, is certainly, upon ordinary occasions, perfectly right and proper, and cannot miss being approved of as such by every body. Nothing, however, could be more absurd than to say it was virtuous.

On the contrary, there may frequently be a considerable degree of virtue in those actions which fall short of the most perfect propriety; because they may still approach nearer to perfection than could well be expected upon occasions in which it was so extremely difficult to attain it: and this is very often the case upon those occasions which require the greatest exertions of self-command. There are some situations which bear so hard upon human nature, that the greatest degree of self-government, which can belong to so imperfect a creature as man, is not able to stifle, altogether, the voice of human weakness, or reduce the violence of the passions to that pitch of moderation, in which the impartial spectator can entirely enter into them. Though in those cases, therefore, the behaviour of the sufferer fall short of the most perfect propriety, it may still deserve some applause, and even in a certain sense, may be denominated virtuous. It may still manifest an effort of generosity and magnanimity of which the greater part of men are incapable; and though it fails of absolute perfection, it may be a much nearer approximation towards perfection, than what, upon such trying occasions, is commonly either to be found or to be expected.

In cases of this kind, when we are determining the degree of blame or applause which seems due to any action, we very frequently make use of two different standards. The first is the idea of complete propriety and perfection, which, in those difficult situations, no human conduct ever did, or ever can come up to; and in comparison with which the actions of all men must for ever appear blameable and imperfect. The second is the idea of that degree of proximity or distance from this complete perfection, which the actions of the greater part of men commonly arrive at. Whatever goes beyond this degree, how far soever it may be removed from absolute perfection, seems to deserve applause; and whatever falls short of it, to deserve blame.

It is in the same manner that we judge of the productions of all the arts which address themselves to the imagination. When a critic examines the work of any of the great masters in poetry or painting, he may sometimes examine it by an idea of perfection, in his own mind, which neither that nor any other human work will ever come up to; and as long as he compares it with this standard, he can see nothing in it but faults and imperfections. But when he comes to consider the rank which it ought to hold among other works of the same kind, he necessarily compares it with a very different standard, the common degree of excellence which is usually attained in this particular art; and when he judges of it by this new measure, it may often appear to deserve the highest applause, upon account of its approaching much nearer to perfection than the greater part of those works which can be brought into competition with it.

PART II
Of Merit and Demerit; or,
of the Objects of Reward and Punishment

SECTION I *Of the Sense of Merit and Demerit*

Introduction
There is another set of qualities ascribed to the actions and
conduct of mankind, distinct from their propriety or impropriety,
their decency or ungracefulness, and which are the objects of a
distinct species of approbation and disapprobation. These are
Merit and Demerit, the qualities of deserving reward, and of
deserving punishment.

It has already been observed, that the sentiment or affection
of the heart, from which any action proceeds, and upon which
its whole virtue or vice depends, may be considered under two
different aspects, or in two different relations: first, in relation to
the cause or object which excites it; and, secondly, in relation to the
end which it proposes, or to the effect which it tends to produce:
that upon the suitableness or unsuitableness, upon the proportion
or disproportion, which the affection seems to bear to the cause
or object which excites it, depends the propriety or impropriety,
the decency or ungracefulness of the consequent action; and that
upon the beneficial or hurtful effects which the affection proposes
or tends to produce, depends the merit or demerit, the good or ill
desert of the action to which it gives occasion. Wherein consists
our sense of the propriety or impropriety of actions, has been
explained in the former part of this discourse. We come now to
consider, wherein consists that of their good or ill desert.

CHAPTER I *That whatever appears to be the proper object of
gratitude, appears to deserve reward; and that, in the same
manner, whatever appears to be the proper object of resentment,
appears to deserve punishment*
To us, therefore, that action must appear to deserve reward,
which appears to be the proper and approved object of that
sentiment, which most immediately and directly prompts us to
reward, or to do good to another. And in the same manner, that
action must appear to deserve punishment, which appears to be

the proper and approved object of that sentiment which most immediately and directly prompts us to punish, or to inflict evil upon another.

The sentiment which most immediately and directly prompts us to reward, is gratitude; that which most immediately and directly prompts us to punish, is resentment.

To us, therefore, that action must appear to deserve reward, which appears to be the proper and approved object of gratitude; as, on the other hand, that action must appear to deserve punishment, which appears to be the proper and approved object of resentment.

To reward, is to recompense, to remunerate, to return good for good received. To punish, too, is to recompense, to remunerate, though in a different manner; it is to return evil for evil that has been done.

There are some other passions, besides gratitude and resentment, which interest us in the happiness or misery of others; but there are none which so directly excite us to be the instruments of either. The love and esteem which grow upon acquaintance and habitual approbation, necessarily lead us to be pleased with the good fortune of the man who is the object of such agreeable emotions, and consequently, to be willing to lend a hand to promote it. Our love, however, is fully satisfied, though his good fortune should be brought about without our assistance. All that this passion desires is to see him happy, without regarding who was the author of his prosperity. But gratitude is not to be satisfied in this manner. If the person to whom we owe many obligations, is made happy without our assistance, though it pleases our love, it does not content our gratitude. Till we have recompensed him, till we ourselves have been instrumental in promoting his happiness, we feel ourselves still loaded with that debt which his past services have laid upon us.

The hatred and dislike, in the same manner, which grow upon habitual disapprobation, would often lead us to take a malicious pleasure in the misfortune of the man whose conduct and character excite so painful a passion. But though dislike and hatred harden us against all sympathy, and sometimes dispose us even to rejoice at the distress of another, yet, if there is no resentment in the case, if neither we nor our friends have received any great personal provocation, these passions would not naturally lead us to wish to be instrumental in bringing it about. Though we could fear no punishment in consequence of our having had some hand in it, we would rather that it should happen by other means. To one under the dominion of violent hatred it would be agreeable, perhaps, to hear, that the person whom he abhorred and detested was killed by some accident. But if he had the least spark of justice, which, though this passion is not very favourable to virtue, he might still have, it would hurt him excessively to have been himself, even without design, the occasion of this misfortune. Much more would the very thought of voluntarily contributing to it shock him beyond all measure. He would reject with horror even the imagination of so execrable a design; and if he could imagine himself capable of such an enormity, he would begin to regard himself in the same odious light in which he had considered the person who was the object of his dislike. But it is quite otherwise with resentment: if the person who had done us some great injury, who had murdered our father or our brother, for example, should soon afterwards die of a fever, or even be brought to the scaffold upon account of some other crime, though it might sooth our hatred, it would not fully gratify our resentment. Resentment would prompt us to desire, not only that he should be punished, but that he should be punished by our means, and upon account of that particular injury which he has done to us. Resentment cannot be fully gratified, unless the offender is not only made to grieve in his turn, but to grieve for that particular wrong which we have suffered from him. He must be made to repent and be sorry for this very action, that others, through fear of the like punishment, may be terrified from being guilty of the like offence. The natural gratification of this passion tends, of its own accord, to produce all the political ends of punishment; the correction of the criminal, and the example to the public.

Gratitude and resentment, therefore, are the sentiments which most immediately and directly prompt to reward and to punish. To us, therefore, he must appear to deserve reward, who appears to be the proper and approved object of gratitude; and he to deserve punishment, who appears to be that of resentment.

CHAPTER II *Of the proper objects of gratitude and resentment*
To be the proper and approved object either of gratitude or resentment, can mean nothing but to be the object of that gratitude, and of that resentment, which naturally seems proper, and is approved of.

But these, as well as all the other passions of human nature, seem proper and are approved of, when the heart of every impartial spectator entirely sympathizes with them, when every indifferent by-stander entirely enters into, and goes along with them.

He, therefore, appears to deserve reward, who, to some person or persons, is the natural object of a gratitude which every human heart is disposed to beat time to, and thereby applaud: and he, on the other hand, appears to deserve punishment, who in the same manner is to some person or persons the natural object of a resentment which the breast of every reasonable man is ready to adopt and sympathize with. To us, surely, that action must appear to deserve reward, which every body who knows of it would wish to reward, and therefore delights to see rewarded: and that action must as surely appear to deserve punishment, which every body who hears of it is angry with, and upon that account rejoices to see punished.

1. As we sympathize with the joy of our companions when in prosperity, so we join with them in the complacency and satisfaction with which they naturally regard whatever is the cause of their good fortune. We enter into the love and affection which they conceive for it, and begin to love it too. We should be sorry for their sakes if it was destroyed, or even if it was placed at too great a distance from them, and out of the reach of their care and protection, though they should lose nothing by its absence except the pleasure of seeing it. If it is a man who has thus been the fortunate instrument of the happiness of his brethren, this is still more peculiarly the case. When we see one man assisted, protected, relieved by another, our sympathy with the joy of the person who receives the benefit serves only to animate our fellow-feeling with his gratitude towards him who bestows it. When we look upon the person who is the cause of his pleasure with the eyes with which we imagine he must look upon him, his benefactor seems to stand before us in the most engaging and amiable light. We readily therefore sympathize with the grateful affection which he conceives for a person to whom he has been so much obliged; and consequently applaud the returns which he is disposed to make for the good offices conferred upon him. As we entirely enter into the affection from which these returns proceed, they necessarily seem every way proper and suitable to their object.

2. In the same manner, as we sympathize with the sorrow of our fellow-creature whenever we see his distress, so we likewise enter into his abhorrence and aversion for whatever has given occasion to it. Our heart, as it adopts and beats time to his grief, so is it likewise animated with that spirit by which he endeavours

to drive away or destroy the cause of it. The indolent and passive
fellow-feeling, by which we accompany him in his sufferings,
readily gives way to that more vigorous and active sentiment
by which we go along with him in the effort he makes, either to
repel them, or to gratify his aversion to what has given occasion
to them. This is still more peculiarly the case, when it is man who
has caused them. When we see one man oppressed or injured
by another, the sympathy which we feel with the distress of the
sufferer seems to serve only to animate our fellow-feeling with
his resentment against the offender. We are rejoiced to see him
attack his adversary in his turn, and are eager and ready to assist
him whenever he exerts himself for defence, or even for vengeance
within a certain degree. If the injured should perish in the quarrel,
we not only sympathize with the real resentment of his friends and
relations, but with the imaginary resentment which in fancy we
lend to the dead, who is no longer capable of feeling that or any
other human sentiment. But as we put ourselves in his situation,
as we enter, as it were, into his body, and in our imaginations, in
some measure, animate anew the deformed and mangled carcass
of the slain, when we bring home in this manner his case to our
own bosoms, we feel upon this, as upon many other occasions,
an emotion which the person principally concerned is incapable
of feeling, and which yet we feel by an illusive sympathy with
him. The sympathetic tears which we shed for that immense
and irretrievable loss, which in our fancy he appears to have
sustained, seem to be but a small part of the duty which we
owe him. The injury which he has suffered demands, we think,
a principal part of our attention. We feel that resentment which
we imagine he ought to feel, and which he would feel, if in
his cold and lifeless body there remained any consciousness of
what passes upon earth. His blood, we think, calls aloud for
vengeance. The very ashes of the dead seem to be disturbed at
the thought that his injuries are to pass unrevenged. The horrors
which are supposed to haunt the bed of the murderer, the ghosts
which, superstition imagines, rise from their graves to demand
vengeance upon those who brought them to an untimely end, all
take their origin from this natural sympathy with the imaginary
resentment of the slain. And with regard, at least, to this most
dreadful of all crimes, Nature, antecedent to all reflections upon
the utility of punishment, has in this manner stamped upon the
human heart, in the strongest and most indelible characters,
an immediate and instinctive approbation of the sacred and
necessary law of retaliation.

CHAPTER III *That where there is no approbation of the conduct of the person who confers the benefit, there is little sympathy with the gratitude of him who receives it: and that, on the contrary, where there is no disapprobation of the motives of the person who does the mischief, there is no sort of sympathy with the resentment of him who suffers it*

It is to be observed, however, that, how beneficial soever on the one hand, or how hurtful soever on the other, the actions or intentions of the person who acts may have been to the person who is, if I may say so, acted upon, yet if in the one case there appears to have been no propriety in the motives of the agent, if we cannot enter into the affections which influenced his conduct, we have little sympathy with the gratitude of the person who receives the benefit: or if, in the other case, there appears to have been no impropriety in the motives of the agent, if, on the contrary, the affections which influenced his conduct are such as we must necessarily enter into, we can have no sort of sympathy with the resentment of the person who suffers. Little gratitude seems due in the one case, and all sort of resentment seems unjust in the other. The one action seems to merit little reward, the other to deserve no punishment.

1. First, I say, That wherever we cannot sympathize with the affections of the agent, wherever there seems to be no propriety in the motives which influenced his conduct, we are less disposed to enter into the gratitude of the person who received the benefit of his actions. A very small return seems due to that foolish and profuse generosity which confers the greatest benefits from the most trivial motives, and gives an estate to a man merely because his name and sirname happen to be the same with those of the giver. Such services do not seem to demand any proportionable recompense. Our contempt for the folly of the agent hinders us from thoroughly entering into the gratitude of the person to whom the good office has been done. His benefactor seems unworthy of it. As when we place ourselves in the situation of the person obliged, we feel that we could conceive no great reverence for such a benefactor, we easily absolve him from a great deal of that submissive veneration and esteem which we should think due to a more respectable character; and provided he always treats his weak friend with kindness and humanity, we are willing to excuse him from many attentions and regards which we should demand to a worthier patron. Those Princes,

who have heaped, with the greatest profusion, wealth, power, and honours, upon their favourites, have seldom excited that degree of attachment to their persons which has often been experienced by those who were more frugal of their favours. The well-natured, but injudicious prodigality of James the First of Great Britain seems to have attached nobody to his person; and that Prince, notwithstanding his social and harmless disposition, appears to have lived and died without a friend. The whole gentry and nobility of England exposed their lives and fortunes in the cause of his more frugal and distinguishing son, notwithstanding the coldness and distant severity of his ordinary deportment.

2. Secondly, I say, That wherever the conduct of the agent appears to have been entirely directed by motives and affections which we thoroughly enter into and approve of, we can have no sort of sympathy with the resentment of the sufferer, how great soever the mischief which may have been done to him. When two people quarrel, if we take part with, and entirely adopt the resentment of one of them, it is impossible that we should enter into that of the other. Our sympathy with the person whose motives we go along with, and whom therefore we look upon as in the right, cannot but harden us against all fellow-feeling with the other, whom we necessarily regard as in the wrong. Whatever this last, therefore, may have suffered, while it is no more than what we ourselves should have wished him to suffer, while it is no more than what our own sympathetic indignation would have prompted us to inflict upon him, it cannot either displease or provoke us. When an inhuman murderer is brought to the scaffold, though we have some compassion for his misery, we can have no sort of fellow-feeling with his resentment, if he should be so absurd as to express any against either his prosecutor or his judge. The natural tendency of their just indignation against so vile a criminal is indeed the most fatal and ruinous to him. But it is impossible that we should be displeased with the tendency of a sentiment, which, when we bring the case home to ourselves, we feel that we cannot avoid adopting.

Source: Adam Smith, *The Theory of Moral Sentiments*, ed. D. D. Raphael and A. L. Macfie, Oxford 1976, pp. 9–26, 67–73

EIGHT

HUGH BLAIR
On the Proper Estimate of Human Life

As minister of St Giles, the High Kirk of Edinburgh, and therefore occupying the most prominent pulpit in Scotland, Hugh Blair was well placed to promote his account of the relations between ourselves and our maker. And he promoted it brilliantly. The theological content of his sermons is not at all of the heavily metaphysical sort, but leans instead to the pastoral side of things, emphasising practical rather than theoretical considerations, how best to live this life rather than what to believe about the next. Sermon 22 demonstrates Blair's lightness of theological touch and at the same time provides support for R.B. Sher's description of him as 'the greatest Moderate preacher of Christian Stoicism'.

There is a long tradition of Christian Stoicism among Scottish thinkers. I have in mind men such as Florence Wilson from Moray (died 1550s), whose chief work, a dialogue on tranquillity of mind, *De animi tranquillitate dialogus* (Lyons 1543), was reissued by Principal William Wishart for the benefit of Edinburgh students c.1740. It is significant that 'On tranquillity of mind' is also the title of one of Blair's sermons.

In many sermons he places particular emphasis on the concept of self-control or self-rule. The nub of his position as expressed in 'On the proper estimate of human life' is this: 'if we cannot control fortune, [let us] study at least to control ourselves'. That study must consist in part in the investigation of our place in the universe, so that we may gain insight into the extent to which there is a principle of justice governing everything. If we have lived a good life we can look forward to a divinely ordained happiness. But Blair is no despiser of happiness in this life and in this sermon he has a good deal of advice, based on a close study of human psychology, regarding how best we are to achieve happiness during this, the pilgrim stage of our existence.

His message, typically stoic, is that happiness cannot be achieved except within the framework of a virtuously lived life, though even within such a framework we are still at the mercy of fortune – virtue gives us at best some, but never perfect, protection against the slings and arrows.

The motto of the text, 'Vanity of vanities, saith the preacher, all is vanity', is kept busy throughout the sermon, for Blair's question is how best to prevent vanity taking over our whole life. It quickly becomes plain that the vanity Blair has it in mind to counter is the vanity of what the great nineteenth-century Danish theologian Søren Kierkegaard was to call the 'aesthetic life', the life lived at the level of feeling, where we have a sense of freedom because we act on a whim, consulting only our feelings when deciding what to do. And just as Kierkegaard denounces the freedom of such a life as a sham, being in truth a form of slavery, slavery to passion, so Blair denounces a life dedicated to worldly pleasure as a vanity, being in reality a life able to deliver up pain, not pleasure.

In an important twist to his story (again mirroring Kierkegaard), Blair argues that not only does the search for worldly pleasure end in disappointment; it is really as well for us that it should do so. For it is through the failure of the search that we come, if ever we do, to a realisation of the essential vanity of the life we have been living, and thereafter move to the next stage, in which we realise that happiness is to be sought from God and virtue. There are many who regard our sufferings as the basis of an argument for the non-existence of God, for if there were a God then since he would be good he would not permit us to suffer. Blair on the other hand sees our sufferings as providing a context within which we can discover that the goal set by our true nature is best realised by the adoption of a life-plan whose overarching principle is religious. This sermon constitutes a luminously clear definition of the gentle humanism of the moderate party in the Kirk.

A.B.

On the Proper Estimate of Human Life

Ecclesiastes, xii. 8
Vanity of vanities, saith the preacher, all is vanity.

No serious maxim has been more generally adopted than that of the text. In every age, the vanity of human life has been the theme of declamation, and the subject of complaint. It is a conclusion in which men of all characters and ranks, the high and the low, the young and the old, the religious and the worldly, have more frequently concurred than in any other. But how just soever the conclusion may be, the premises which lead to it are often false. For it is prompted by various motives, and derived from very different views of things. Sometimes the language of the text is assumed by a sceptic, who cavils at Providence, and censures the constitution of the world. Sometimes it is the complaint of a peevish man, who is discontented with his station, and ruffled by the disappointment of unreasonable hopes. Sometimes it is the style of the licentious, when groaning under miseries in which their vices have involved them. Invectives against the vanity of the world, which come from any of these quarters, deserve no regard; as they are the dictates of impiety, of spleen, or of folly. The only case in which the sentiment of the text claims our attention is, when uttered, not as an aspersion on Providence, or a reflection on human affairs in general; not as the language of private discontent, or the result of guilty sufferings; but as the sober conclusion of a wise and good man, concerning the imperfection of that happiness which rests solely on worldly pleasures. These, in their fairest form, are not what they seem to be. They never bestow that complete satisfaction which they promise; and therefore he who looks to nothing beyond them, shall have frequent cause to deplore their vanity.

Nothing is of higher importance to us, as men and as Christians, than to form a proper estimate of human life, without either loading it with imaginary evils, or expecting from it greater advantages than it is able to yield. It shall be my business, therefore, in this discourse, to distinguish a just and religious sense of the vanity of the world from the unreasonable complaints of it which we often hear. I shall endeavour, I. To show in what sense it is true that all earthly pleasures are vanity. II. To inquire how this vanity of the world can be reconciled with the perfections of its great Author. III. To examine whether there are not some real and solid enjoyments in human life, which fall not under this general charge of vanity. And, IV. To point out the proper improvement to be made of such a state as the life of man shall appear on the whole to be.

I I am to show in what sense it is true that all human pleasures are vanity. This is a topic which might be embellished with the pomp of much description. But I shall studiously avoid exaggeration, and only point out a threefold vanity in human life, which every impartial observer cannot but admit; disappointment in pursuit, dissatisfaction in enjoyment, uncertainty in possession.

First, Disappointment in pursuit. When we look around us on the world, we every where behold a busy multitude, intent on the prosecution of various designs which their wants or desires have suggested. We behold them employing every method which ingenuity can devise; some the patience of industry, some the boldness of enterprise, others the dexterity of stratagem, in order to compass their ends. Of this incessant stir and activity what is the fruit? In comparison of the crowd who have toiled in vain, how small is the number of the successful! Or rather, where is the man who will declare, that in every point he has completed his plan, and attained his utmost wish? No extent of human abilities has been able to discover a path, which, in any line of life, leads unerringly to success. *The race is not always to the swift, nor the battle to the strong, nor riches to men of understanding*. We may form our plans with the most profound sagacity, and with the most vigilant caution may guard against dangers on every side. But some unforeseen occurrence comes across, which baffles our wisdom, and lays our labours in the dust.

Were such disappointments confined to those who aspire at engrossing the higher departments of life, the misfortune would be less. The humiliation of the mighty, and the fall of ambition from its towering height, little concern the bulk of mankind. These are objects on which, as on distant meteors, they gaze from afar, without drawing personal instruction from events so much above them. But, alas! when we descend into the regions of private life, we find disappointment and blasted hope equally prevalent there. Neither the moderation of our views, nor the justice of our pretensions, can ensure success. But *time and chance happen to all*. Against the stream of events, both the worthy and the undeserving are obliged to struggle; and both are frequently overborne alike by the current.

Besides disappointment in pursuit, dissatisfaction in enjoyment is a further vanity to which the human state is subject. This is the severest of all mortifications; after having been successful in the pursuit, to be baffled in the enjoyment itself. Yet this is found to be an evil still more general than the former. Some may be so fortunate as to attain what they have pursued; but none are rendered completely happy by what they have attained. Disappointed hope is misery; and yet successful hope is only imperfect bliss. Look through all the ranks of mankind. Examine the condition of those who appear most prosperous, and you will find that they are never just what they desire to be. If retired, they languish for action; if busy, they complain of fatigue. If in middle life, they are impatient for distinction; if in high stations, they sigh after freedom and ease. Something is still wanting to that plenitude of satisfaction which they expected to acquire. Together with every wish that is gratified, a new demand arises. One void opens in the heart as another is filled. On wishes, wishes grow; and, to the end, it is rather the expectation of what they have not, than the enjoyment of what they have, which occupies and interests the most successful.

This dissatisfaction in the midst of human pleasure springs partly from the nature of our enjoyments themselves, and partly from circumstances which corrupt them. No worldly enjoyments are adequate to the high desires and powers of an immortal spirit. Fancy paints them at a distance with splendid colours; but possession unveils the fallacy. The eagerness of passion bestows upon them at first a brisk and lively relish. But it is their fate always to pall by familiarity, and sometimes to pass from satiety into disgust. Happy would the poor man think himself, if he could enter on all the treasures of the rich; and happy for a short while he might be; but, before he had long contemplated and admired his state, his possessions would seem to lessen, and his cares would grow.

Add to the unsatisfying nature of our pleasures the attending circumstances which never fail to corrupt them. For such as they are, they are at no time possessed unmixed. To human lips it is not given to taste the cup of pure joy. When external circumstances show fairest to the world, the envied man groans in private under his own burden. Some vexation disquiets; some passion corrodes him; some distress, either felt or feared, gnaws, like a worm, the root of his felicity. When there is nothing from without to disturb the prosperous, a secret poison operates within. For worldly happiness ever tends to destroy itself, by corrupting the heart. It fosters the loose and the violent passions. It engenders noxious habits; and taints the mind with a false delicacy, which makes it feel a thousand unreal evils.

But put the case in the most favourable light. Lay aside from human pleasures both disappointment in pursuit, and deceitfulness in enjoyment; suppose them to be fully attainable, and completely satisfactory; still there remains to be considered the vanity of uncertain possession and short duration. Were there in worldly things any fixed point of security which we could gain, the mind would then have some basis on which to rest. But our condition is such, that every thing wavers and totters around us. *Boast not thyself of to-morrow, for thou knowest not what a day may bring forth.* It is much if, during its course, thou hearest not of somewhat to disquiet or alarm thee. For life never proceeds long in an uniform train. It is continually varied by unexpected events. The seeds of alteration are every where sown; and the sunshine of prosperity commonly accelerates their growth. If your enjoyments be numerous, you lie more open on different sides to be wounded. If you have possessed them long, you have greater cause to dread an approaching change. By slow degrees prosperity rises; but rapid is the progress of evil. It requires no preparation to bring it forward. The edifice which it cost much time and labour to erect, one inauspicious event, one sudden blow, can level with the dust. Even supposing the accidents of life to leave us untouched, human bliss must still be transitory; for man changes of himself. No course of enjoyment can delight us long. What amused our youth, loses its charm in maturer age. As years advance, our powers are blunted and our pleasurable feelings decline. The silent lapse of time is ever carrying somewhat from us, till at length the period comes when all must be swept away. The prospect of this termination of our labours and pursuits is sufficient to mark our stage with vanity. *Our days are a hand-breadth, and our age is as nothing.* Within that little space is all our enterprise bounded. We crowd it with toils and care, with contention and strife. We project great designs, entertain high hopes, and then leave our plans unfinished, and sink into oblivion.

Thus much let it suffice to have said concerning the vanity of the world. That too much has not been said, must appear to every one who considers how generally mankind lean to the opposite side; and how often, by undue attachment to the present state, they both feed the most sinful passions, and *pierce themselves through with many sorrows*. Let us proceed to inquire,

II How this vanity of the world can be reconciled with the perfections of its divine Author. This inquiry involves that great difficulty which has perplexed the thoughtful and serious in every age. If God be good, whence the evil that fills the earth? In answer to this interesting question, let us observe,

In the first place, that the present condition of man was not his original or primary state. We are informed by divine revelation, that it is the consequence of his voluntary apostacy from God and a state of innocence. By this his nature was corrupted; his powers were enfeebled, and vanity and vexation introduced into his life. All nature became involved in the condemnation of man. The earth was cursed upon his account, and the whole creation made to *groan and travail in pain.*

How mysterious soever the account of this fall may appear to us, many circumstances concur to authenticate the fact, and to show that human nature and the human state have undergone an unhappy change. The belief of this has obtained in almost all nations and religions. It can be traced through all the fables of antiquity. An obscure tradition appears to have pervaded the whole earth, that man is not now what he was at first; but that, in consequence of some transgression against his great Lord, a state of degradation and exile succeeded to a condition that was more flourishing and happy. As our nature carries plain marks of perversion and disorder, so the world which we inhabit bears the symptoms of having been convulsed in all its frame. Naturalists point out to us every where the traces of some violent change which it has suffered. Islands torn from the continent, burning mountains, shattered precipices, uninhabitable wastes, give it all the appearance of a mighty ruin. The physical and moral state of man in this world mutually sympathize and correspond. They indicate not a regular and orderly structure, either of matter or of mind, but the remains of somewhat that was once more fair and magnificent. – Let us observe,

In the second place, that as this was not the original, so it is not intended to be the final state of man. Though, in consequence of the abuse of the human powers, sin and vanity were introduced into this region of the universe, it was not the purpose of the Creator that they should be permitted to reign for ever. He hath made ample provision for the recovery of the penitent and faithful part of his subjects, by the merciful undertaking of that great restorer of the world, our Lord Jesus Christ. By him *life and immortality were* both purchased and *brought to life. The new heavens and the new earth* are discovered, *wherein dwelleth righteousness*; where, through the divine grace, human nature shall regain its original honours, and man shall return to be what once he was in paradise. Through those high discoveries of the gospel, this life appears to good men only in the light of an intermediate and preparatory state. Its vanity and misery, in a manner, disappear. They have every reason to submit, without complaint, to its laws, and to wait in patience till the appointed time come for *the restitution of all things*. – Let us take notice,

In the third place, that a future state being made known, we can account, in a satisfying manner, for the present distress of human life, without the smallest impeachment of divine goodness. The sufferings we here undergo, are converted into discipline and improvement. Through the blessing of Heaven, good is extracted from apparent evil; and the very misery which originated from sin, is rendered the means of correcting sinful passions, and preparing us for felicity. There is much reason to believe that creatures as imperfect as we are, require some such preliminary state of experience, before they can recover the perfection of their nature. It is in the midst of disappointments and trials that we learn the insufficiency of temporal things to happiness, and are taught to seek it from God and virtue. By these the violence of our passions is tamed, and our minds are formed to sobriety and reflection. In the varieties of life occasioned by the vicissitude of worldly fortune, we are inured to habits both of the active and the suffering virtues. How much soever we complain of the vanity of the world, facts plainly show that if its vanity were less, it could not answer the purpose of salutary discipline. Unsatisfactory as it is, its pleasures are still too apt to corrupt our hearts. How fatal, then, must the consequences have been, had it yielded us more complete enjoyment! If, with all its troubles, we are in danger of being too much attached to it, how entirely would it have seduced our affections, if no troubles had been mingled with its pleasures!

These observations serve, in a great measure, to obviate the difficulties which arise from the apparent vanity of the human state, by showing how, upon the Christian system, that vanity may be reconciled with the infinite goodness of the Sovereign of the universe. The present condition of man is not that for which he was originally designed; it is not to be his final state; and during his passage through the world, the distresses which he undergoes are rendered medicinal and improving. After having taken this view of things, the cloud, which in the preceding part of the discourse appeared to sit so thick upon human life, begins to be dissipated. We now perceive that man is not abandoned by his Creator. We discern great and good designs going on in his behalf. We are allowed to entertain better hopes; and are encouraged to inquire, as was proposed, for the

IIId Head of discourse – Whether there be not, in the present condition of human life, some real and solid enjoyments which come not under the general charge of *vanity of vanities*. The doctrine of the text is to be considered as chiefly addressed to worldly men. Them Solomon means to teach, that all expectations of bliss, which rest solely on earthly possessions and pleasures, shall end in disappointment. But surely he did not intend to assert, that there is no material difference in the pursuits of men, or that no real happiness of any kind could now be attained by the virtuous. For, besides the unanswerable objection which this would form against the divine administration, it would directly contradict what he elsewhere asserts, that while *God giveth sore travail to the sinner, he giveth to the man that is good in his sight, wisdom, and knowledge, and joy.*[1] It may, it must indeed be admitted, that unmixed and complete happiness is unknown on earth. No regulation of conduct can altogether prevent passions from disturbing our peace, and misfortunes from wounding our heart. But after this concession is made, will it follow that there is no object on earth which deserves our pursuit, or that all enjoyment becomes contemptible, which is not perfect? Let us survey our state with an impartial eye, and be just to the various gifts of Heaven. How vain soever this life, considered in itself, may be, the comforts and hopes of religion are sufficient to give solidity to the enjoyments of the righteous. In the exercise of good affections, and the testimony of an approving conscience; in the sense of peace and reconciliation with God through the great Redeemer of mankind; in the firm confidence of being conducted through all the trials of life by infinite wisdom and goodness; and in the joyful prospect of arriving in the end at immortal felicity; they possess a happiness, which, descending from a purer and more perfect region than this world, partakes not of its vanity.

Besides the enjoyments peculiar to religion, there are other pleasures of our present state, which, though of an inferior order, must not be overlooked in the estimate of human life. It is necessary to call attention to these, in order to check that repining and unthankful spirit to which man is always too prone.

1 Eccles. ii. 26.

Some degree of importance must be allowed to the comforts of health, to the innocent gratifications of sense, and to the entertainment afforded us by all the beautiful scenes of nature; some to the pursuits and amusements of social life; and more to the internal enjoyments of thought and reflection, and to the pleasures of affectionate intercourse with those whom we love. These comforts are often held in too low estimation, merely because they are ordinary and common; although that be the circumstance which ought, in reason, to enhance their value. They lie open, in some degree, to all; extend through every rank of life, and fill up agreeably many of those spaces in our present existence which are not occupied with higher objects, or with serious cares.

We are in several respects unjust to Providence in the computation of our pleasures and our pains. We number the hours which are spent in distress or sorrow; but we forget those which have passed away, if not in high enjoyment, yet in the midst of those gentle satisfactions and placid emotions which make life glide smoothly along. We complain of the frequent disappointments which we suffer in our pursuits. But we recollect not, that it is in pursuit, more than in attainment, that our pleasure now consists. In the present state of human nature, man derives more enjoyment from the exertion of his active powers in the midst of toils and efforts, than he could receive from a still and uniform possession of the object which he strives to gain. The solace of the mind under all its labours is hope; and there are few situations which entirely exclude it. Forms of expected bliss are often gleaming upon us through a cloud, to revive and exhilarate the most distressed. If pains be scattered through all the conditions of life, so also are pleasures. Happiness, as far as life affords it, can be engrossed by no rank of men to the exclusion of the rest; on the contrary, it is often found where, at first view, it would have been least expected. When the human condition appears most depressed, the feelings of men, through the gracious appointment of Providence, adjust themselves wonderfully to their state, and enable them to extract satisfaction from sources that are totally unknown to others. Were the great body of men fairly to compute the hours which they pass in ease, and even with some degree of pleasure, they would be found far to exceed the number of those which are spent in absolute pain either of body or mind. But in order to make a still more accurate estimation of the degree of satisfaction which, in the midst of earthly vanity, man is permitted to enjoy, the three following observations claim our attention:

The first is, that many of the evils which occasion our complaints of the world are wholly imaginary. They derive their existence from fancy and humour, and childish subjection to the opinion of others. The distress which they produce, I admit, is real; but its reality arises not from the nature of things, but from that disorder of imagination which a small measure of reflection might rectify. In proof of this, we may observe, that the persons who live most simply, and follow the dictates of plain unadulterated nature, are most exempted from this class of evils. It is among the higher ranks of mankind that they chiefly abound; where fantastic refinements, sickly delicacy, and eager emulation, open a thousand sources of vexation peculiar to themselves. Life cannot but prove vain to them who affect a disrelish of every pleasure that is not both exquisite and new; who measure enjoyment, not by their own feelings, but by the standard of fashion; who think themselves miserable, if others do not admire their state. It is not from wants or sorrows that their complaints arise; but, though it may appear a paradox, from too much freedom from sorrow and want; from the languor of vacant life, and the irritation occasioned by those stagnating humours which ease and indulgence have bred within them. In their case, therefore, it is not the vanity of the world, but the vanity of their minds, which is to be accused. Fancy has raised up the spectres which haunt them. Fancy has formed the cloud which hangs over their life. Did they allow the light of reason to break forth, the spectres would vanish, and the cloud be dispelled.

The second observation on this head is, that of those evils which may be called real, because they owe not their existence to fancy, nor can be removed by rectifying opinion, a great proportion is brought upon us by our own misconduct. Diseases, poverty, disappointment, and shame are far from being, in every instance, the unavoidable doom of men. They are much more frequently the offspring of their own misguided choice. Intemperance engenders disease, sloth produces poverty, pride creates disappointments, and dishonesty exposes to shame. The ungoverned passions of men betray them into a thousand follies; their follies into crimes, and their crimes into misfortunes. Yet nothing is more common than for such as have been the authors of their own misery, to make loud complaints of the hard fate of man, and to take revenge upon the human condition by arraigning its supposed vanity. *The foolishness of man first perverteth his way, and then his heart fretteth against the Lord.*

I do not, however, maintain that it is within our power to be altogether free of those self-procured evils; for perfection of any kind is beyond the reach of man. Where is the wisdom that never errs? where the just man that offendeth not? Nevertheless, much is here left to ourselves; and, imperfect as we are, the consequences of right or of wrong conduct make a wide difference in the happiness of men. Experience every day shows that a sound, a well-governed, and virtuous mind contributes greatly to smooth the path of life; and that *wisdom excelleth folly as far as light excelleth darkness. The way of the wicked is as darkness; they know not at what they stumble. But the righteousness of the perfect shall direct his ways; and he that walketh uprightly walketh surely.* The tendency of the one is towards a plain and safe region; the course of the other leads him amidst snares and precipices. The one occasionally may, the other unavoidably must, incur much trouble. Let us not then confound, under one general charge, those evils of the world which belong to the lot of humanity, and those which, through divine assistance, a wise and good man may in a great measure escape.

The third observation which I make, respects those evils which are both real and unavoidable; from which neither wisdom nor goodness can procure our exemption. Under these this comfort remains, that if they cannot be prevented, there are means, however, by which they may be much alleviated. Religion is the great principle which acts, under such circumstances, as the corrective of human vanity. It inspires fortitude, supports patience, and by its prospects and promises, darts a cheering ray into the darkest shade of human life. If it cannot secure the virtuous from disappointment in their pursuits, it forms them to such a temper as renders their disappointments more light and easy than those of other men. If it does not banish dissatisfaction from their worldly pleasures, it confers spiritual pleasures in their stead. If it ensures them not the possession of what they love, it furnishes comfort under the loss. As far as it establishes a contented frame of mind, it supplies the want of all that worldly men covet to possess. Compare the behaviour of the sensual and corrupted with that of the upright and holy, when both are feeling the effects of human vanity, and the difference of their situation will be manifest. Among the former you are likely to find a querulous and dejected, among the latter a composed and manly spirit. The lamentations of the one excite a mixture of pity and contempt; while the dignity which the other maintains in distress, commands respect. The sufferings of the former settle into a peevish and fretful disposition; those of the latter soften the temper, and improve the heart. These consequences extend so far as to give ground for asserting, that a good man enjoys more happiness in the course of a seemingly unprosperous life, than a bad man does in the midst of affluence and luxury. What a conspicuous proof of this is afforded by the apostle Paul, who from the very depth of affliction could send forth such a triumphant voice as proclaims the complete victory which he had gained over the evils of life! *Troubled on every side, yet not distressed; perplexed, but not in despair; persecuted, but not forsaken; cast down, but not destroyed. For though our outward man perish, our inward man is renewed day by day.*[1] Such, though perhaps in an inferior degree, will be the influence of a genuine religious principle upon all true Christians. It begins to perform that office to them here, which hereafter it will more completely discharge, of *wiping away the tears from their eyes.*

Such, upon the whole, is the estimate which we are to form of human life. Much vanity will always belong to it; though the degree of its vanity will depend, in a great measure, on our own character and conduct. To the vicious, it presents nothing but a continued scene of disappointment and dissatisfaction. To the good, it is a mixed state of things; where many real comforts may be enjoyed; where many resources under trouble may be obtained; but where trouble, in one form or other, is to be expected as the lot of man. From this view of human life,

The first practical conclusion which we are to draw is, that it highly concerns us not to be unreasonable in our expectations of worldly felicity. Let us always remember where we are; from what causes the human state has become subject to depression; and upon what account it must remain under its present law. Such is the infatuation of self-love, that though in the general doctrine of the vanity of the world all men agree, yet almost every one flatters himself that his own case is to be an exception from the common rule. He rests on expectations which he thinks cannot fail him; and though the present be not altogether according to his wish, yet with the confidence of certain hope he anticipates futurity. Hence the anguish of disappointment fills the world; and evils, which are of themselves sufficiently severe, oppress with double force the unprepared and unsuspecting mind. Nothing, therefore, is of greater consequence to our peace, than to have always before our eyes such views of the world as shall prevent our expecting more from it than it is destined to afford. We destroy our joys

[1] 2 Cor. iv. 8, 9. 16.

by devouring them beforehand with too eager expectation. We ruin the happiness of life when we attempt to raise it too high. A tolerable and comfortable state is all that we can propose to ourselves on earth. Peace and contentment, not bliss nor transport, is the full portion of man. Perfect joy is reserved for heaven.

But while we repress too sanguine hopes formed upon human life, let us, in the second place, guard against the other extreme, of repining and discontent. Enough has already been said to show, that, notwithstanding the vanity of the world, a considerable degree of comfort is attainable in the present state. Let the recollection of this serve to reconcile us to our condition, and to check the arrogance of complaints and murmurs. – What art thou, O son of man! who, having sprung but yesterday out of the dust, darest to lift up thy voice against thy Maker, and to arraign his providence, because all things are not ordered according to thy wish? What title hast thou to find fault with the order of the universe, whose lot is so much beyond what thy virtue or merit gave thee ground to claim? Is it nothing to thee to have been introduced into this magnificent world; to have been admitted as a spectator of the divine wisdom and works; and to have had access to all the comforts which Nature, with a bountiful hand, has poured forth round thee? Are all the hours forgotten which thou hast passed in ease, in complacency, or joy? Is it a small favour in thy eyes that the hand of divine mercy has been stretched forth to aid thee, and, if thou reject not its proffered assistance, is ready to conduct thee into a happier state of existence? When thou comparest thy condition with thy desert, blush, and be ashamed of thy complaints. Be silent, be grateful, and adore. Receive with thankfulness the blessings which are allowed thee. Revere that government which at present refuses thee more. Rest in this conclusion, that though there be evils in the world, its Creator is wise and good, and has been bountiful to thee.

In the third place, the view which we have taken of human life should naturally direct us to such pursuits as may have most influence for correcting its vanity. There are two great lines of conduct which offer themselves to our choice. The one leads towards the goods of the mind; the other towards those of fortune. The former, which is adopted only by the few, engages us chiefly in forming our principles, regulating our dispositions, improving all our inward powers. The latter, which in every age has been followed by the multitude, points at no other end but attaining the conveniences and pleasures of external life. It is obvious that, in this last pursuit, the vanity of the world will encounter us at every step. For this is the region in which it reigns, and where it chiefly displays its power. At the same time, to lay the world totally out of view, is a vain attempt. The numberless ties by which we are connected with external things, put it out of our power to behold them with indifference. But though we cannot wrap ourselves up entirely in the care of the mind, yet the more we make its welfare our chief object, the nearer shall we approach to that happy independence on the world, which places us beyond the reach of suffering from its vanity.

That discipline, therefore, which corrects the eagerness of worldly passions, which fortifies the heart with virtuous principles, which enlightens the mind with useful knowledge, and furnishes to it matter of enjoyment from within itself, is of more consequence to real felicity than all the provision which we can make of the goods of fortune. To this let us bend our chief attention. Let us *keep the heart with all diligence, seeing out of it are the issues of life*. Let us account our minds the most important province which is committed to our care; and if we cannot rule fortune, study at least to rule ourselves. Let us propose for our object, not worldly success, which it depends not on us to obtain; but that upright and honourable discharge of our duty, in every conjuncture, which, through the divine assistance, is always within our power. Let our happiness be sought where our proper praise is found; and that be accounted our only real evil, which is the evil of our nature; not that, which is either the appointment of Providence, or which arises from the evil of others.

But, in order to carry on with success this rational and manly plan of conduct, it is necessary, in the last place, that to moral we join religious discipline. Under the present imperfection of our minds, and amidst the frequent shocks which we receive from human evils, much do we stand in need of every assistance for supporting our constancy. Of all assistance to which we can have recourse, none is so powerful as what may be derived from the principles of the Christian faith. He who builds on any other foundation, will find in the day of trial that he had built his house on the sand. Man is formed by his nature to look up to a superior Being, and to lean upon a strength that is greater than his own. All the considerations which we can offer for confirming his mind, presuppose this resource, and derive from it their principal efficacy.

Never, then, let us lose sight of those great objects which religion brings under our view, if we hope to stand firm and erect amidst the dangers and distresses of our present state. Let us cultivate all that connexion with the great Father of spirits which our condition admits; by piety and prayer; by dependence on his aid, and trust in his promises; by a devout sense of his presence, and a continual endeavour to acquire his grace and favour. Let us, with humble faith and reverence, commit ourselves to the blessed Redeemer of the world; encouraged by the discoveries which he has made to us of the divine mercy, and by the hopes which he has afforded us of being raised to a nobler and happier station in the kingdom of God. So shall virtue, grounded upon piety, attain its full strength. Inspired with a religious spirit, and guided by rational principles, we shall be enabled to hold a steady course through this mixed region of pleasure and pain, of hope and fears; until the period arrive when that cloud, which the present vanity of the world throws over human affairs, shall entirely disappear, and eternal light be diffused over all the works and ways of God.

Source: Hugh Blair, *Sermons*, Edinburgh 1824, vol. 1, sermon 22, pp. 298–315

PART IV

AESTHETICS

NINE

FRANCIS HUTCHESON
A Sense of Beauty

Central to Hutcheson's aesthetics is the idea that, as well as the five senses of sight, hearing and so on, we have also a sense of beauty. 'Sense' is a technical term in Hutcheson's vocabulary: it is 'a determination of the mind to receive any idea from the presence of an object which occurs to us independent of our will'. When I open my eyes I have certain visual sensations, of colours and shapes, and the fact that I have them is not something subject to my will; it happens by nature and not by will. In addition the formation of the idea is immediate; it is not mediated by any reasoning process. Hence in speaking of a 'sense of beauty' Hutcheson signals, first, the doctrine that our forming the idea of the beauty of a thing when we perceive the thing is due to a natural necessity, and secondly, the doctrine that the formation of the idea of the beauty of the thing is immediate.

Beauty is a perception of the mind. Hutcheson adds: 'were there no mind with a sense of beauty to contemplate objects, I see not how they could be called beautiful'. It becomes clear that the teaching here is not merely that things would not be *called* beautiful, but that there would be no beauty in the universe if there were no percipient beings to make the aesthetic judgment.

What are the qualities that prompt us to judge something beautiful? They are covered by Hutcheson's phrase 'uniformity amidst diversity'. The things we judge beautiful exhibit a uniformity or unity, but a diversity or variety also. Variety is essential, for in the absence of much variety a thing is simply dull and uninteresting. Uniformity also is needed, for a thing with insufficient unity, as for example a set of random marks on paper, will also give no pleasure.

It is not to be denied that some of Hutcheson's comments in this area strike us now as odd, comments regarding, for example, the relative aesthetic value of different geometric figures. But there are none the less many valuable insights to be found in Hutcheson's writings on beauty. His discussion of the nature of the aesthetic sense and his ideas on the relation between beauty and pleasure, were seminal in the history of aesthetics.

A.B.

Of Beauty, Order, Harmony, Design

SECTION I *Concerning some Powers of Perception, distinct from what is generally understood by Sensation*

To make the following observations understood, it may be necessary to premise some definitions, and observations, either universally acknowledged, or sufficiently proved by many writers both ancient and modern, concerning our perceptions called sensations, and the actions of the mind consequent upon them.

I Those ideas which are rais'd in the mind upon the presence of external objects, and their acting upon our bodies, are called sensations. We find that the mind in such cases is passive, and has not power directly to prevent the perception or idea, or to vary it at its reception, as long as we continue our bodies in a state fit to be acted upon by the external object.

II When two perceptions are intirely different from each other, or agree in nothing but the general idea of sensation, we call the powers of receiving those different perceptions, different senses. Thus seeing and hearing denote the different powers of receiving the ideas of colours and sounds. And although colours have great differences among themselves, as also have sounds; yet there is a greater agreement among the most opposite colours, than between any colour and a sound: hence we call all colours perceptions of the same sense. All the several senses seem to have their distinct organs, except feeling, which is in some degree diffused over the whole body.

III The mind has a power of compounding ideas, which were received separately; of comparing objects by means of the ideas, and of observing their relations and proportions; of enlarging and diminishing its ideas at pleasure, or in any certain ratio, or degree; and of considering separately each of the simple ideas, which might perhaps have been impressed jointly in the sensation. This last operation we commonly call abstraction.

IV The ideas of corporeal substances are compounded of the various simple ideas jointly impressed, when they presented themselves to our senses. We define substances only by enumerating these sensible ideas. And such definitions may raise a clear enough idea of the substance in the mind of one who never immediately perceiv'd the substance; provided he has separately received by his senses all the simple ideas which are in the composition of the complex one of the substance defined: but if there be any simple ideas which he has not received, or if he wants any of the senses necessary for the perception of them, no definition can raise any simple idea which has not been before perceiv'd by the senses.

V Hence it follows, 'That when instruction, education, or prejudice of any kind, raise any desire or aversion toward an object, this desire or aversion must be founded upon an opinion of some perfection, or of some deficiency in those qualities, for perception of which we have the proper senses.' Thus, if beauty be defin'd by one who has not the sense of sight, the desire must be rais'd by some apprehended regularity of figure, sweetness of voice, smoothness, or softness, or some other quality perceivable by the other senses, without relation to the ideas of colour.

VI Many of our sensitive perceptions are pleasant and many painful, immediately, and that without any knowledge of the cause of this pleasure or pain, or how the objects excite it, or are the occasions of it; or without seeing to what farther advantage or detriment the use of such objects might tend: nor would the most accurate knowledge of these things vary either the pleasure or pain of the perception, however it might give a rational pleasure distinct from the sensible; or might raise a distinct joy, from a prospect of farther advantage in the object, or aversion, from an apprehension of evil.

VII The simple ideas raised in different persons by the same object, are probably some way different, when they disagree in their approbation or dislike; and in the same person, when his fancy at one time differs from what it was at another. This will appear from reflecting on those objects, to which we have now an aversion, tho' they were formerly agreeable: and we shall generally find that there is some accidental conjunction of a disagreeable idea, which always recurs with the object; as in those wines to which men acquire an aversion, after they have taken them in an emetic preparation, we are conscious that the idea is alter'd from what it was when that wine was agreeable, by the conjunction of the ideas of loathing and sickness of stomach. The like change of idea may be insensibly made by the change of our bodies as we advance in years, or when we are accustomed to any object, which may occasion an indifference toward meats we were fond of in our childhood; and may make some objects cease to raise the disagreeable ideas, which they excited upon our first use of them. Many of our simple perceptions are disagreeable only through the too great intenseness of the quality: thus moderate light is agreeable, very strong light may be painful; moderate bitter may be pleasant, a higher degree may be offensive. A change in our organs will necessarily occasion a change in the intenseness of the perception at least; nay, sometimes will occasion a quite contrary perception: thus a warm hand shall feel that water cold, which a cold hand shall feel warm.

We shall not find it perhaps so easy to account for the diversity of fancy about more complex ideas of objects, including many ideas of different senses at once; as some perceptions of those called primary qualities, and some secondary, as explained by Mr. Locke: for instance, in the different fancies about architecture, gardening, dress. Of the two former we shall offer something in sect. VI. As to dress, we may generally account for the diversity of fancies from a like conjunction of ideas: thus, if either from any thing in nature, or from the opinion of our country or acquaintance, the fancying of glaring colours be looked upon as an evidence of levity, or of any other evil quality of mind; or if any colour or fashion be commonly used by rustics, or by men of any disagreeable profession, employment, or temper; these additional ideas may recur constantly with that of the colour or fashion, and cause a constant dislike to them in those who join the additional ideas, although the colour or form be no way disagreeable of themselves, and actually do please others who join no such ideas to them. But there appears no ground to believe such a diversity in human minds, as that the same simple idea or perception should give pleasure to one and pain to another, or to the same person at different times; not to say that it seems a contradiction, that the same simple idea should do so.

VIII The only pleasure of sense, which many philosophers seem to consider, is that which accompanies the simple ideas of sensation: but there are far greater pleasures in those complex ideas of objects, which obtain the names of beautiful, regular, harmonious. Thus every one acknowledges he is more delighted with a fine face, a just picture, than with the view of any one colour, were it as strong and lively as possible; and more pleased with a prospect of the sun arising among settled clouds, and colouring their edges, with a starry hemisphere, a fine landskip, a regular building, than with a clear blue sky, a smooth sea, or a large open plain, not diversified by woods, hills, waters, buildings: and yet even these latter appearances are not quite simple. So in music the pleasure of fine composition is incomparably greater than that of any one note, how sweet, full, or swelling soever.

IX Let it be observed, that in the following papers, the word *beauty* is taken for the idea raised in us, and a sense of beauty for our power of receiving this idea. Harmony also denotes our pleasant ideas arising from composition of sounds, and a good ear (as it is generally taken) a power of perceiving this pleasure. In the following sections, an attempt is made to discover 'what is the immediate occasion of these pleasant ideas, or what real quality in the objects ordinarily excites them.'

X It is of no consequence whether we call these ideas of beauty and harmony, perceptions of the external senses of seeing and hearing, or not. I should rather choose to call our power of perceiving these ideas, an internal sense, were it only for the convenience of distinguishing them from other sensations of seeing and hearing, which men may have without perception of beauty and harmony. It is plain from experience, that many men have, in the common meaning, the senses of seeing and hearing perfect enough; they perceive all the simple ideas separately, and have their pleasures; they distinguish them from each other, such as one colour from another, either quite different, or the stronger or fainter of the same colour, when they are placed beside each other, although they may often confound their names when they occur apart from each other, as some do the names of green and blue: they can tell in separate notes the higher, lower, sharper or flatter, when separately sounded; in figures they discern the length, breadth, wideness of each line, surface, angle; and may be as capable of hearing and seeing at great distances as any men whatsoever: and yet perhaps they shall find no pleasure in musical compositions, in painting, architecture, natural landskip; or but a very weak one in comparison of what others enjoy from the same objects. This greater capacity of receiving such pleasant ideas we commonly call a fine genius or taste: in music we seem universally to acknowledge something like a distinct sense from the external one of hearing, and call it a good ear; and the like distinction we should probably acknowledge in other objects, had we also got distinct names to denote these powers of perception by.

XI We generally imagine the brute animals endowed with the same sort of powers of perception as our external selves, and having sometimes greater acuteness in them: but we conceive few or none of them with any of these sublimer powers of perception here called internal senses; or at least if some of them have them, it is in a degree much inferior to ours.

There will appear another reason perhaps hereafter for calling this power of perceiving the ideas of beauty, an internal sense, from this, that in some other affairs, where our external senses are not much concerned, we discern a sort of beauty, very like, in many respects, to that observed in sensible objects, and accompanied with like pleasure: such is that beauty perceived in theorems, or universal truths, in general causes, and in some extensive principles of action.

XII Let one consider, first, That it is probable a being may have the full power of external sensation, which we enjoy, so as to perceive each colour, line, surface, as we do; yet, without the power of comparing, or of discerning the similitudes or proportions: again, it might discern these also, and yet have no pleasure or delight accompanying these perceptions. The bare idea of the form is something separable from pleasure, as may appear from the different tastes of men about the beauty of forms, where we do not imagine that they differ in any ideas, either of the primary or secondary qualities. Similitude, proportion, analogy, or equality of proportion, are objects of the understanding, and must be actually known before we know the natural causes of our pleasure. But pleasure perhaps is not necessarily connected with the perception of them: and may be felt where the proportion is not known or attended to: and may not be felt where the proportion is observed. Since then there are such different powers of perception, where what are commonly called the external senses are the same; since the most accurate knowledge of what the external senses discover, may often not give the pleasure of beauty or harmony, which yet one of a good taste will enjoy at once without much knowledge; we may justly use another name for these higher and more delightful perceptions of beauty and harmony, and call the power of receiving such impressions, an internal sense: the difference of the perceptions seems sufficient to vindicate the use of a different name, especially when we are told in what meaning the word is applied.

This superior power of perception is justly called a sense, because of its affinity to the other senses in this, that the pleasure is different from any knowledge of principles, proportions, causes, or of the usefulness of the object; we are struck at the first with the beauty: nor does the most accurate knowledge increase this pleasure of beauty, however it may superadd a distinct rational pleasure from prospects of advantage, or may bring along that peculiar kind of pleasure, which attends the increase of knowledge.

XIII And farther, the ideas of beauty and harmony, like other sensible ideas, are necessarily pleasant to us, as well as immediately so; neither can any resolution of our own, nor any prospect of advantage or disadvantage, vary the beauty or deformity of an object: for as in the external sensations, no view of interest will make an object grateful, nor view of detriment, distinct from immediate pain in the perception, make it disagreeable to the sense; so propose the whole world as a reward, or threaten the greatest evil, to make us approve a deformed object, or disapprove a beautiful one; dissimulation may be procured by rewards or threatnings, or we may in external conduct abstain from any pursuit of the beautiful, and pursue the deform'd; but our sentiments of the forms, and our perceptions, would continue invariably the same.

XIV Hence it plainly appears, 'that some objects are immediately the occasions of this pleasure of beauty, and that we have senses fitted for perceiving it; and that it is distinct from that joy which arises upon prospect of advantage.' Nay, do not we often see convenience and use neglected to obtain beauty, without any other prospect of advantage in the beautiful form, than the suggesting the pleasant ideas of beauty? Now this shews us, that however we may pursue beautiful objects from self-love, with a view to obtain the pleasures of beauty, as in architecture, gardening, and many other affairs yet there must be a sense of beauty, antecedent to prospects even of this advantage, without which sense these objects would not be thus advantageous, nor excite in us this pleasure which constitutes them advantageous. Our sense of beauty from objects, by which they are constituted good to us, is very distinct from our desire of them when they are thus constituted: our desire of beauty may be counter-balanced by rewards or threatnings, but never our sense of it; even as fear of death may make us desire a bitter potion, or neglect those meats which the sense of taste would recommend as pleasant; but cannot make that potion agreeable to the sense, or meat disagreeable to it, which was not so antecedently to this prospect. The same holds true of the sense of beauty and harmony; that the pursuit of such objects is frequently neglected, from prospects of advantage, aversion to labour, or any other motive of interest, does not prove that we have no sense of beauty, but only that our desire of it may be counterbalanced by a stronger desire.

XV Had we no such sense of beauty and harmony, houses, gardens, dress, equipage, might have been recommended to us as convenient, fruitful, warm, easy; but never as beautiful: and yet nothing is more certain, than that all these objects are recommended under quite different views on many occasions: it is true, what chiefly pleases in the countenance, are the indications of moral dispositions; and yet were we by the longest acquaintance fully convinced of the best moral dispositions in any person, with that countenance we now think deform'd, this would never hinder our immediate dislike of the form, or our liking other forms more: and custom, education, or example, could never give us perceptions distinct from those of the senses which we had the use of before, or recommend objects under another conception than grateful to them. But of the influence of custom, education, example, upon the sense of beauty, we shall treat below.

XVI Beauty, in corporeal forms, is either original or comparative; or, if any like the terms better, absolute, or relative: only let it be observed, that by absolute or original beauty, is not understood any quality supposed to be in the object, which should of itself be beautiful, without relation to any mind which perceives it: for beauty, like other names of sensible ideas, properly denotes the perception of some mind; so cold, hot, sweet, bitter, denote the sensations in our minds, to which perhaps there is no resemblance in the objects, which excite these ideas in us, however we generally imagine otherwise. The ideas of beauty and harmony being excited upon our perception of some primary quality, and having relation to figure and time, may indeed have a nearer resemblance to objects, than these sensations, which seem not so much any pictures of objects, as modifications of the perceiving mind; and yet were there no mind with a sense of beauty to contemplate objects, I see not how they could be called beautiful. We therefore by absolute beauty understand only that beauty which we perceive in objects without comparison to any thing external, of which the object is supposed an imitation, or picture; such as that beauty perceived from the works of nature, artificial forms, figures. Comparative or relative beauty is that which we perceive in objects, commonly considered as imitations or resemblances of something else.[1] These two kinds of beauty employ the three following sections.

---

1 This division of beauty is taken from the different foundations of pleasure to our sense of it, rather than from the objects themselves: for most of the following instances of relative beauty have also absolute beauty; and many of the instances of absolute beauty, have also relative beauty in some respect or other. But we may distinctly consider these two fountains of pleasure, uniformity in the object itself, and resemblance to some original.

SECTION II *Of Original or Absolute Beauty*

I Since it is certain that we have ideas of beauty and harmony, let us examine what quality in objects excites these ideas, or is the occasion of them. And let it be here observed, that our inquiry is only about the qualities which are beautiful to men; or about the foundation of their sense of beauty: for, as was above hinted, beauty has always relation to the sense of some mind; and when we afterwards shew how generally the objects which occur to us are beautiful, we mean, that such objects are agreeable to the sense of men: for there are many objects which seem no way beautiful to men, and yet other animals seem delighted with them; they may have senses otherwise constituted than those of men, and may have the ideas of beauty excited by objects of a quite different form. We see animals fitted for every place; and what to men appears rude and shapeless, or loathsome, may be to them a paradise.

II That we may more distinctly discover the general foundation or occasion of the ideas of beauty among men, it will be necessary to consider it first in its simpler kinds, such as occurs to us in regular figures; and we may perhaps find that the same foundation extends to all the more complex species of it.

III The figures which excite in us the ideas of beauty, seem to be those in which there is uniformity amidst variety. There are many conceptions of objects which are agreeable upon other accounts, such as grandeur, novelty, sanctity, and some others, which shall be mentioned hereafter. But what we call beautiful in objects, to speak in the mathematical style, seems to be in a compound ratio of uniformity and variety: so that where the uniformity of bodies is equal, the beauty is as the variety; and where the variety is equal, the beauty is as the uniformity. This may seem probable, and hold pretty generally.

First, the variety increases the beauty in equal uniformity. The beauty of an equilateral triangle is less than that of the square; which is less than that of a pentagon; and this again is sur-pass'd by the hexagon. When indeed the number of sides is much increased, the proportion of them to the radius, or diameter of the figure, or of the circle, to which regular polygons have an obvious relation, is so much lost to our observation, that the beauty does not always increase with the number of sides; and the want of parallelism in the sides of heptagons, and other figures of odd numbers, may also diminish their beauty. So in solids, the icosahedron surpasses the dodecahedron, and this the octahedron, which is still more beautiful than the cube; and this again surpasses the regular pyramid: the obvious ground of this, is greater variety with equal uniformity.

The greater uniformity increases the beauty amidst equal variety, in these instances: an equilateral triangle, or even isosceles, surpasses the scalenum: a square surpasses the rhombus or lozenge, and this again the rhomboides, which is still more beautiful than the trapezium, or any figure with irregular curve sides. So the regular solids surpass all other solids of equal number of plain surfaces: and the same is observable not only in the five perfectly regular solids, but in all those which have any considerable uniformity, as cylinders, prisms, pyramids, obelisks; which please every eye more than any rude figures, where there is no unity or resemblance among the parts.

Instances of the compound ratio we have in comparing circles or spheres, with ellipses or spheroids not very eccentric; and in comparing the compound solids, the exoctahedron, and icosidodecahedron, with the perfectly regular ones of which they are compounded: and we shall find, that the want of that most perfect uniformity observable in the latter, is compensated by the greater variety in the former, so that the beauty is nearly equal.

IV These observations would probably hold true for the most part, and might be confirmed by the judgment of children in the simpler figures, where the variety is not too great for their comprehension. And however uncertain some of the particular aforesaid influences may seem, yet this is perpetually to be observed, that children are fond of all regular figures in their little diversions, altho' they be no more convenient, or useful for them, than the figures of our common pebbles: we see how early they discover a taste or sense of beauty, in desiring to see buildings, regular gardens, or even representations of them in pictures of any kind.

V The same foundation we have for our sense of beauty, in the works of nature. In every part of the world which we call beautiful, there is a surprising uniformity amidst an almost infinite variety. Many parts of the universe seem not at all designed for the use of man; nay, it is but a very small spot with which we have any acquaintance. The figures and motions of the great bodies are not obvious to our senses, but found out by reasoning and reflection, upon many long observations: and yet as far as we can by sense discover, or by reasoning enlarge our knowledge, and extend our imagination, we generally find their structure, order, and motion, agreeable to our sense of beauty. Every particular object in nature does not indeed appear beautiful to us; but there is a great profusion of beauty over most of the objects which occur either to our senses, or reasonings upon observation: for, not to mention the apparent situation of the heavenly bodies in the circumference of a great sphere, which is wholly occasioned by the imperfection of our sight in discerning distances; the forms of all the great bodies in the universe are nearly spherical; the orbits of their revolutions generally elliptic, and without great eccentricity, in those which continually occur to our observation: now these are figures of great uniformity, and therefore pleasing to us.

Further, to pass by the less obvious uniformity in the proportion of their quantities of matter, distances, times, of revolving, to each other; what can exhibit a greater instance of uniformity, amidst variety, than the constant tenor of revolutions in nearly equal times, in each planet, around its axis, and the central fire or sun, thro' all the ages of which we have any records, and in nearly the same orbit? Thus after certain periods, all the same appearances are again renew'd; the alternate successions of light and shade, or day and night, constantly pursuing each other around each planet, with an agreeable and regular diversity in the times they possess the several hemispheres, in the summer, harvest, winter, and spring; and the various phases, aspects, and situations, of the planets to each other, their conjunctions and oppositions, in which they suddenly darken each other with their conic shades in eclipses, are repeated to us at their fixed periods with invariable constancy: These are the beautys which charm the astronomer, and make his tedious calculations pleasant.

Molliter austerum studio fallente laborem [Where the excitement pleasantly beguiles the hard toil].

VI Again, as to the dry part of the surface of our globe, a great part of which is covered with a very pleasant inoffensive colour, how beautifully is it diversified with various degrees of light and shade, according to the different situations of the parts of its surface, in mountains, valleys, hills, and open plains, which are variously inclined toward the great luminary!

VII If we descend to the minuter works of nature, what great uniformity among all the species of plants and vegetables in the manner of their growth and propagation! how near the resemblance among all the plants of the same species, whose numbers surpass our imagination! And this uniformity is not only observable in the form in gross; (nay, in this it is not so very exact in all instances) but in the structure of their minuter parts, even of those which no eye unassisted with glasses can discern. In the almost infinite multitude of leaves, fruit, seed, flowers of any one species, we often see a very great uniformity in the structure and situation of the smallest fibres. This is the beauty which charms an ingenious botanist. Nay, what great uniformity and regularity of figure is found in each particular plant, leaf, or flower! In all trees and most of the smaller plants, the stalks or trunks are either cylinders nearly, or regular prisms; the branches similar to their several trunks, arising at nearly regular distances, when no accidents retard their natural growth: in one species the branches arise in pairs on the opposite sides; the perpendicular plain of direction of the immediately superior pair, intersecting the plain of direction of the inferior, nearly at right angles: in another species, the branches spring singly and alternately, all around in nearly equal distances: and the branches in other species sprout all in knots around the trunk, one for each year. And in each species, all the branches in the first shoots preserve the same angles with their trunk; and they again sprout out into smaller branches exactly after the manner of their trunks. Nor ought we to pass over that great unity of colours which we often see in all the flowers of the same plant or tree, and often of a whole species; and their exact agreement in many shaded transitions into opposite colours, in which all the flowers of the same plant generally agree, nay, often all the flowers of a species.

VIII Again, as to the beauty of animals, either in their inward structure, which we come to the knowledge of by experiment and long observation, or their outward form, we shall find surprizing uniformity among all the species which are known to us, in the structure of those parts, upon which life depends more immediately. And how amazing is the unity of mechanism, when we shall find an almost infinite diversity of motions, all their actions in walking, running, flying, swimming; all their serious efforts for self-preservation, all their freakish contortions when they are gay and sportful, in all their various limbs, perform'd by one simple contrivance of a contracting muscle, applied with inconceivable diversities to answer all these ends! various engines might have obtained the same ends; but then there had been less uniformity, and the beauty of our animal systems, and of particular animals, had been much less, when this surprizing unity of mechanism had been removed from them.

IX Among animals of the same species, the unity is very obvious, and this resemblance is the very ground of our ranking them in such classes or species, notwithstanding the great diversities in bulk, colour, shape, which are observed even in those called of the same species. And then in each individual, how universal is that beauty which arises from the exact resemblance of all the external double members to each other, which seems the universal intention of nature, when no accident prevents it! We see the want of this resemblance never fails to pass for an imperfection, and want of beauty, tho' no other inconvenience ensues; as when the eyes are not exactly like, or one arm or leg is a little shorter or smaller than its fellow.

As to the most powerful beauty in countenances, airs, gestures, motion, we shall shew in the second treatise, that it arises from some imagined indication of morally good dispositions of mind. In motion there is also a natural beauty, when at fixed periods like gestures and steps are regularly repeated, suiting the time and air of music, which is observed in regular dancing.

X There is a farther beauty in animals, arising from a certain proportion of the various parts to each other, which still pleases the sense of spectators, though they cannot calculate it with the accuracy of a statuary. The statuary knows what proportion of each part of the face to the whole face is most agreeable, and can tell us the same of the proportion of the face to the body, or any parts of it; and between the diameters and lengths of each limb: When this proportion of the head to the body is remarkably altered, we shall have a giant or a dwarf. And hence it is, that either the one or the other may be represented to us even in miniature, without relation to any external object, by observing how the body surpasses the proportion it should have to the head in giants, and falls below it in dwarfs. There is a farther beauty arising from that figure, which is a natural indication of strength; but this may be passed over, because probably it may be alledged, that our approbation of this shape flows from an opinion of advantage, and not from the form itself.

The beauty arising from mechanism, apparently adapted to the necessities and advantages of any animal; which pleases us, even tho' there be no advantage to ourselves ensuing from it; will be consider'd under the head of relative beauty, or design.

XI The peculiar beauty of fowls can scarce be omitted, which arises from the great variety of feathers, a curious sort of machines adapted to many admirable uses, which retain a considerable resemblance in their structure among all the species; frequently a perfect uniformity in those of the same species in the corresponding parts, and in the two sides of each individual; besides all the beauty of lively colours and gradual shades, not only in the external appearance of the fowl, resulting from an artful combination of shaded feathers, but often visible even in one feather separately.

XII If our reasonings about the nature of fluids be just, the vast stores of water will give us an instance of uniformity in nature above imagination, when we reflect upon the almost infinite multitude of small, polished, smooth spheres, which must be supposed formed in all the parts of this globe. The same uniformity there is probably among the parts of other fluids as well as water; and the like must be observed in several other natural bodies, as salts, sulphurs, and such like; whose uniform properties do probably depend upon an uniformity in the figures of their parts.

XIII Under original beauty we may include harmony, or beauty of sound, if that expression can be allowed, because harmony is not usually conceiv'd as an imitation of any thing else. Harmony often raises pleasure in those who know not what is the occasion of it: and yet the foundation of this pleasure is known to be a sort of uniformity. When the several vibrations of one note regularly coincide with the vibrations of another, they make an agreeable composition; and such notes are called concords. Thus the vibrations of any one note coincide in time with two vibrations of its octave; and two vibrations of any note coincide with three of its fifth; and so on in the rest of the concords. Now no composition can be harmonious, in which the notes are not, for the most part, disposed according to these natural proportions. Besides which, a due regard must be had to the key, which governs the whole, and to the time and humour, in which the composition is begun: a frequent and inartificial change of any of which will produce the greatest and most unnatural discord. This will appear, by observing the dissonance which would arise from tacking parts of different tunes together as one, altho' both were separately agreeable. A like uniformity is also observable among the bases, tenors, trebles of the same tune.

There is indeed observable, in the best compositions, a mysterious effect of discords: they often give as great pleasure as continued harmony; whether by refreshing the ear with variety, or by awakening the attention, and enlivening the relish for the succeeding harmony of concords, as shades enliven and beautify pictures, or by some other means not yet known: certain it is, however, that they have their place, and some good effect on our best compositions. Some other powers of music may be considered hereafter.

XIV But in all these instances of beauty let it be observed, That the pleasure is communicated to those who never reflected on this general foundation; and that all here alledged is this, 'That the pleasant sensation arises only from objects, in which there is uniformity amidst variety:' we may have the sensation without knowing what is the occasion of it; as a man's taste may suggest ideas of sweets, acids, bitters, tho' he be ignorant of the forms of the small bodies, or their motions, which excite these perceptions in him.

SECTION III *Of the Beauty of Theorems*

I The beauty of theorems, or universal truths demonstrated, deserves a distinct consideration, being of a nature pretty different from the former kinds of beauty; and yet there is none in which we shall see such an amazing variety with uniformity: and hence arises a very great pleasure distinct from prospects of any further advantage.

II For in one theorem we may find included, with the most exact agreement, an infinite multitude of particular truths; nay, often a multitude of infinites: so that altho' the necessity of forming abstract ideas, and universal theorems, arises perhaps from the limitation of our minds, which cannot admit an infinite multitude of singular ideas or judgments at once, yet this power gives us an evidence of the largeness of the human capacity above our imagination. Thus, for instance, the 47th proposition of the first book of Euclid's Elements contains an infinite multitude of truths, concerning the infinite possible sizes of right-angled triangles, as you make the area greater or less; and in each of these sizes, you may find an infinite multitude of dissimilar triangles, as you vary the proportion of the base [to] the perpendicular; all which infinites agree in the general theorem. In algebraic, and fluxional calculations, we shall find a like variety of particular truths included in general theorems; not only in general equations applicable to all kinds of quantity, but in more particular investigations of areas and tangents: in which one manner of operation shall discover theorems applicable to many orders or species of curves to the infinite sizes of each species, and to the infinite points of the innumerable individuals of each size.

III That we may the better discern this agreement, or unity of an infinity of objects, in the general theorem, to be the foundation of the beauty or pleasure attending their discovery, let us compare our satisfaction in such discoveries, with the uneasy state of mind when we can only measure lines, or surfaces, by a scale, or are making experiments which we can reduce to no general canon, but are only heaping up a multitude of particular incoherent observations. Now each of these trials discovers a new truth, but with no pleasure or beauty, notwithstanding the variety, till we can discover some sort of unity, or reduce them to some general canon.

IV Again, let us take a metaphysical axiom, such as this, Every whole is greater than its part; and we shall find no beauty in the contemplation. For though this proposition contains many infinities of particular truths; yet the unity is inconsiderable, since they all agree only in a vague, undetermined conception of whole and part, and in an indefinite excess of the former above the latter, which is sometimes great and sometimes small. So, should we hear that the cylinder is greater than the inscribed sphere, and this again greater than the cone of the same altitude, and diameter of the base, we shall find no pleasure in this knowledge of a general relation of greater and less, without any precise difference or proportion. But when we see the universal exact agreement of all possible sizes of such systems of solids, that they preserve to each other the constant ratio of 3, 2, 1: how beautiful is the theorem, and how are we ravished with its first discovery!

We may likewise observe, that easy or obvious propositions, even where the unity is sufficiently distinct and determinate, do not please us so much as those, which being less obvious, give us some surprize in the discovery: thus we find little pleasure in discovering, That a line bisecting the vertical angle of an isosceles triangle, bisects the base, or the reverse; or that equilateral triangles are equiangular. These truths we almost know intuitively, without demonstration: they are like common goods, or those which men have long possessed, which do not give such sensible joys as much smaller new additions may give us. But let none hence imagine, that the sole pleasure of theorems is from surprize; for the same novelty of a single experiment does not please us much: nor ought we to conclude from the greater pleasure accompanying a new, or unexpected advantage, that surprize, or novelty, is the only pleasure of life, or the only ground of delight in truth. Another kind of surprize in certain theorems increases our pleasure above that we have in theorems of greater extent; when we discover a general truth, which upon some confused notion we had reputed false: as that asymptotes always approaching should never meet the curve. This is like the joy of unexpected advantage where we dreaded evil. But still the unity of many particulars in the general theorem is necessary to give pleasure in any theorem.

V There is another beauty in propositions, when one theorem contains a great multitude of corollaries easily deducible from it. Thus there are some leading, or fundamental properties upon which a long series of theorems can be naturally built: such a theorem is the 35th of the 1st book of Euclid, from which the whole art of measuring right-lined areas is deduced, by resolution into triangles, which are the halfs of so many parallelograms; and these are each respectively equal to so many rectangles of the base into the perpendicular altitude: the 47th of the 1st book is another of like beauty, and so are many others, in higher parts of geometry. In the search of nature there is the like beauty in the knowledge of some great principles, or universal forces, from which innumerable effects do flow. Such is gravitation, in Sir Isaac Newton's scheme. What is the aim of our ingenious geometers? A continual inlargement of theorems, or making them extensive, shewing how what was formerly known of one figure extends to many others, to figures very unlike the former in appearance.

It is easy to see how men are charmed with the beauty of such knowledge, besides its usefulness; and how this sets them upon deducing the properties of each figure from one genesis, and demonstrating the mechanic forces from one theorem of the composition of motion; even after they have sufficient knowledge and certainty in all these truths from distinct independent demonstrations. And this pleasure we enjoy even when we have no prospect of obtaining any other advantage from such manner of deduction, than the immediate pleasure of contemplating the beauty: nor could love of fame excite us to such regular methods of deduction, were we not conscious that mankind are pleased with them immediately, by this internal sense of their beauty.

It is no less easy to see into what absurd attempts men have been led by this sense of beauty, and an affectation of obtaining it in the other sciences as well as the mathematics. It was this probably which set Descartes on that hopeful project of deducing all human knowledge from one proposition, viz, 'Cogito, ergo sum;' while others pleaded that 'Impossibile est idem simul esse et non esse,' ['It is impossible for the same thing to be and not to be'] had much fairer pretensions to the style and title of 'Principium humanae cognitionis absolute primum.' ['the absolutely first principle of human knowledge'] Mr. Leibnitz had an equal affection for his favourite principle of a sufficient reason for every thing in nature, and boasts of the wonders he had wrought in the intellectual world by its assistance. If we look into particular sciences, we see the inconveniences of this love of uniformity. How awkwardly does Puffendorf deduce the several duties of men to God, themselves, and their neighbours, from his single fundamental principle of sociableness to the whole race of mankind? This observation is a strong proof, that men perceive the beauty of uniformity in the sciences, since they are led into unnatural deductions by pursuing it too far.

VI This delight which accompanies sciences, or universal theorems, may really be called a kind of sensation; since it necessarily accompanies the discovery of any proposition, and is distinct from bare knowledge itself, being most violent at first, whereas the knowledge is uniformly the same. And however knowledge inlarges the mind, and makes us more capable of comprehensive views and projects in some kinds of business, whence advantage may also arise to us; yet we may leave it in the breast of every student to determine, whether he has not often felt this pleasure without any such prospect of advantage from the discovery of his theorem. All which can thence be inferred is only this, that as in our external senses, so in our internal ones, the pleasant sensations generally arise from those objects which calm reason would have recommended, had we understood their use, and which might have engaged our pursuits from self-interest.

VII As to the works of art, were we to run through the various artificial contrivances or structures, we should constantly find the foundation of the beauty which appears in them, to be some kind of uniformity, or unity of proportion among the parts, and of each part to the whole. As there is a great diversity of proportions possible, and different kinds of uniformity, so there is room enough for that diversity of fancys observable in architecture, gardening, and such-like arts in different nations; they too may have uniformity, though the parts in one may differ from those in another. The Chinese or Persian buildings are not like the Grecian and Roman, and yet the former has its uniformity of the various parts to each other, and to the whole, as well as the latter. In that kind of architecture which the Europeans call regular, the uniformity of parts is very obvious, the several parts are regular figures, and either equal or similar at least in the same range; the pedestals are parallelopipedons, or square prisms; the pillars, cylinders nearly; the arches circular, and all those in the same row equal; there is the same proportion every where observed in the same range between the diameters of pillars and their heights, their capitals, the diameters of arches, the heights of the pedestals, the projections of the cornice, and all the ornaments in each of our five orders. And tho' other countrys do not follow the Grecian or Roman proportions; yet there is even among them a proportion retained, a uniformity, and resemblance of corresponding figures; and every deviation in one part from the proportion which is observed in the rest of the building, is displeasing to every eye, and destroys or diminishes at least the beauty of the whole.

VIII The same might be observed thro' all other works of art, even to the meanest utensil; the beauty of every one of which we shall always find to have the same foundation of uniformity amidst variety, without which they appear mean, irregular, and deformed.

SECTION IV *Of Relative or Comparative Beauty*

If the preceding thoughts concerning the foundation of absolute beauty be just, we may easily understand wherein relative beauty consists. All beauty is relative to the sense of some mind perceiving it; but what we call relative is that which is apprehended in any object, commonly considered as an imitation of some original: and this beauty is founded on a conformity, or a kind of unity between the original and the copy. The original may be either some object in nature, or some established idea; for if there be any known idea as a standard, and rules to fix this image or idea by, we may make a beautiful imitation. Thus a statuary, painter, or poet, may please us with an Hercules, if his piece retains that grandeur, and those marks of strength and courage, which we imagine in that hero.

And farther, to obtain comparative beauty alone, it is not necessary that there be any beauty in the original; the imitation of absolute beauty may indeed in the whole make a more lovely piece, and yet an exact imitation shall still be beautiful, though the original were entirely void of it: thus the deformitys of old age in a picture, the rudest rocks or mountains in a landskip, if well represented, shall have abundant beauty, though perhaps not so great as if the original were absolutely beautiful, and as well represented: nay, perhaps the novelty may make us prefer the representation of irregularity.

II The same observation holds true in the descriptions of the poet, either of natural objects or persons: and this relative beauty is what they should principally endeavour to obtain, as the peculiar beauty of their works. By the *moratae fabulae*, or the ἤθη of Aristotle, we are not to understand virtuous manners but a just representation of manners or characters as they are in nature;

and that the actions and sentiments be suited to the characters of the persons to whom they are ascribed in epic and dramatic poetry. Perhaps very good reasons may be suggested from the nature of our passions, to prove that a poet should not draw his characters perfectly virtuous; these characters indeed, abstractly considered, might give more pleasure, and have more beauty than the imperfect ones which occur in life with a mixture of good and evil; but it may suffice at present to suggest against this choice, that we have more lively ideas of imperfect men with all their passions, than of morally perfect heroes, such as really never occur to our observation; and of which consequently we cannot judge exactly as to their agreement with the copy. And farther, through consciousness of our own state, we are more nearly touched and affected by the imperfect characters; since in them we see represented, in the persons of others, the contrasts of inclinations, and the struggles between the passions of self-love and those of honour and virtue, which we often feel in our own breasts. This is the perfection of beauty for which Homer is justly admired, as well as for the variety of his characters.

III Many other beautys of poetry may be reduced under this class of relative beauty: the probability is absolutely necessary to make us imagine resemblance; it is by resemblance that the similitudes, metaphors and allegories are made beautiful, whether either the subject or the thing compared to it have beauty or not; the beauty indeed is greater, when both have some original beauty or dignity as well as resemblance: and this is the foundation of the rule of studying decency in metaphors and similes as well as likeness. The measures and cadence are instances of harmony, and come under the head of absolute beauty.

IV We may here observe a strange proneness in our minds to make perpetual comparisons of all things which occur to our observation, even of those which are very different from each other. There are certain resemblances in the motions of all animals upon like passions, which easily found a comparison; but this does not serve to entertain our fancy: inanimate objects have often such positions as resemble those of the human body in various circumstances; these airs or gestures of the body are indications of certain dispositions in the mind, so that our very passions and affections, as well as other circumstances, obtain a resemblance to natural inanimate objects. Thus a tempest at sea is often an emblem of wrath; a plant or tree drooping under the rain, of a person in sorrow; a poppy bending its stalk, or a flower withering when cut by the plow, resembles the death of a blooming hero; an aged oak in the mountains shall represent an old empire, a flame seizing a wood shall represent a war. In short, every thing in nature, by our strange inclination to resemblance, shall be brought to represent other things, even the most remote, especially the passions and circumstances of human nature in which we are more nearly concerned; and to confirm this, and furnish instances of it, one need only look into Homer or Virgil. A fruitful fancy would find in a grove or a wood, an emblem of every character in a commonwealth, and every turn of temper, or station in life.

V Concerning that kind of comparative beauty which has a necessary relation to some established idea, we may observe, that some works of art acquire a distinct beauty by their correspondence to some universally supposed intention in the artificer, or the persons who employed him: and to obtain this beauty, sometimes they do not form their works so as to attain the highest perfection of original beauty separately considered; because a composition of this relative beauty, along with some degree of the original kind, may give more pleasure, than a more perfect original beauty separately. Thus we see, that strict regularity in laying out of gardens in parterres, vistas, parallel walks, is often neglected, to obtain an imitation of nature even in some of its wildnesses. And we are more pleased with this imitation, especially when the scene is large and spacious, than with the more confined exactness of regular works. So likewise in the monuments erected in honour of deceased heroes, altho' a cylinder, or prism or regular solid, may have more original beauty than a very acute pyramid or obelisk, yet the latter pleases more, by answering better the supposed intentions of stability, and being conspicuous. For the same reason cubes, or square prisms, are generally chosen for the pedestals of statues, and not any of the more beautiful solids, which do not seem so secure from rolling. This may be the reason too, why columns or pillars look best when made a little taper from the middle or a third from the bottom, that they may not seem top-heavy, and in danger of falling.

VI The like reason may influence artists, in many other instances, to depart from the rules of original beauty, as above laid down. And yet this is no argument against our sense of beauty being founded, as was above explained, on uniformity amidst variety, but only an evidence, that our sense of beauty of the original kind may be varied and over-balanced by another kind of beauty.

VII This beauty arising from correspondence to intention, would open to curious observers a new scene of beauty in the works of nature, by considering how the mechanism of the various parts known to us, seems adapted to the perfection of that part, and yet in subordination to the good of some system or whole. We generally suppose the good of the greatest whole, or of all beings, to have been the intention of the Author of nature; and cannot avoid being pleased when we see any part of this design executed in the systems we are acquainted with. The observations already made on this subject are in every one's hand, in the treatises of our late improvers of mechanical philosophy. We shall only observe here, that every one has a certain pleasure in seeing any design well executed by curious mechanism, even when his own advantage is no way concerned; and also in discovering the design to which any complex machine is adapted, when he has perhaps had a general knowledge of the machine before, without seeing its correspondence or aptness to execute any design.

Source: Francis Hutcheson, *An Inquiry into the Original of our Ideas of Beauty and Virtue*, printed from 4th edn of 1738; Glasgow 1772, Treatise I, sections 1–4

TEN

FRANCIS HUTCHESON
Laughter and Self-love

The *Reflections*, published pseudonymously in the *Dublin Journal* 1725-6, is a rather rare work in philosophical literature, for though it is common enough for philosophers to comment briefly on laughter, few have investigated the topic. The concept of a human being as *animal risibile* – the animal that can laugh, that is, is able not merely to make laughter noises but to see things as funny – was commonly invoked during the Middle Ages, but it was not until Hutcheson's *Reflections* that the philosophical significance of that concept was spelled out.

He begins by quoting the *Poetics* of Aristotle and *The Leviathan* of Thomas Hobbes, and each of those quotations animates, though in very different ways, the whole of the *Reflections*. Aristotle states that ridicule (this being a form of laughter) is directed to 'some mistake, or some turpitude, without grievous pain, and not very pernicious or destructive'. Hobbes defines laughter as 'nothing else but sudden glory, arising from some sudden conception or eminency in ourselves, by comparison with the infirmity of others, or with our own formerly'. Hutcheson's reply to these two positions is, first, that while Aristotle correctly describes the proper object of our ridicule, ridiculing a person is not the only way of laughing at him. And much of the *Reflections* thereafter is taken up with a description of kinds of laughter which are not ridicule. Secondly, Hutcheson notes that Hobbes's definition of laughter has to be seen in the context of the Hobbesian account of human beings as essentially driven by self-love. Laughter, considered as 'sudden glory, arising from some sudden conception of some eminency in ourselves', is an exercise in self-esteem, which is itself a form of self-love. Hutcheson demonstrates, against Hobbes, that in many cases we do not derive a sense of 'eminency' in ourselves from a consideration of what it is that we are laughing at, but on the contrary there are cases in which our laughter exhibits a certain esteem for the object of our laughter. Indeed for Hutcheson there are many contexts in which we would strongly disapprove of laughter grounded on self-love. Since Hobbes's entire moral teaching is based on his theory that all human motivation is a set of variations on the theme of self-love, Hutcheson's investigation of laughter turns out to have very large implications for moral philosophy.

That the *Reflections* are no less a contribution to moral philosophy than to aesthetics is particularly noticeable in the third letter, where there are valuable insights concerning the morally acceptable deployment of ridicule in literary works and in conversation. Hutcheson tells us that 'the enormous crime or grievous calamity of another is not itself a subject which can be naturally turned into ridicule: the former raises horror in us, and hatred, and the latter pity . . . some fantastic circumstances accompanying a crime may raise laughter; but a piece of cruel barbarity, or treacherous villainy, of itself, must raise very contrary passions'. Insights of this kind were later to find their way into *The Theory of Moral Sentiments* by Hutcheson's pupil Adam Smith.

A.B.

Reflections upon Laughter

Rapias in jus malis ridentem alienis[1]

To Hibernicus

There is scarce any thing that concerns human nature, which
does not deserve to be inquired into: I send you some thoughts
upon a very common subject, Laughter, which you may publish,
if you think they can be of any use to help us to understand what
so often happens in our own minds, and to know the use for which
it is designed in the constitution of our nature.

Aristotle, in his *Art of Poetry*, has very justly explained the
nature of one species of Laughter, viz. the Ridiculing of Persons;
the occasion or object of which he tells us, is 'Αμαρτημα τι και
αισχος ανωδυνον και ου φθαρτικον,' 'Some mistake, or some
turpitude, without grievous pain, and not very pernicious or
destructive.' But this he never intended as a general account
of all sorts of Laughter.

But Mr. Hobbes, who very much owes his character of a
Philosopher to his assuming positive solemn airs, which he uses
most when he is going to assert some palpable absurdity, or
some ill-natured nonsense, assures us, that 'Laughter is nothing
else but sudden glory, arising from some sudden conception of
some eminency in ourselves, by comparison with the infirmity
of others, or with our own formerly: for men laugh at the follies
of themselves past, when they come suddenly to rememberance,
except they bring with them any present dishonour.'

This notion the authors of the Spectator, No 47, have adopted
from Mr. Hobbes. That bold author having carried on his
inquiries, in a singular manner, without regard to authorities;
and having fallen into a way of speaking, which was much more
intelligible than that of the Schoolmen, soon became agreeable to
many free wits of his age. His grand view was to deduce all human
actions from Self-Love: by some bad fortune he has over-looked
every thing which is generous or kind in mankind; and represents
men in that light in which a thorow knave or coward beholds them,

---

1 ['When you drag him into court he will laugh at your
expense', Horace, *Satires*, Book II, Satire iii, v. 72,
trans. H. R. Fairclough]

suspecting all friendship, love, or social affection, of hypocrisy, or selfish design or fear.

The learned world has often been told that Puffendorf had strongly imbibed Hobbes's first principles, although he draws much better consequences from them; and this last author, as he is certainly much preferable to the generality of the Schoolmen, in distinct intelligible reasoning, has been made the grand instructor in morals to all who have of late given themselves to that study: hence it is that the old notions of natural affections, and kind instincts, the sensus communis, the decorum, and honestum, are almost banished out of our books of morals; we must never hear of them in any of our lectures for fear of innate ideas: all must be interest, and some selfish view; Laughter itself must be a joy from the same spring.

If Mr. Hobbes's notion be just, then, first, there can be no Laughter on any occasion where we make no comparison of ourselves to others, or of our present state to a worse state, or where we do not observe some superiority of ourselves above some other thing: and again, it must follow, that every sudden appearance of superiority over another must excite Laughter, when we attend to it. If both these conclusions be false, the notion from whence they are drawn must be so too.

First then, that Laughter often arises without any imagined superiority of ourselves, may appear from one great fund of pleasantry, the Parody, and Burlesque Allusion; which move Laughter in those who may have the highest veneration for the writing alluded to, and also admire the wit of the person who makes the allusion. Thus many a profound admirer of the machinery in Homer and Virgil has laughed heartily at the interposition of Pallas, in Hudibras, to save the bold Talgol from the knight's pistol, presented to the outside of his skull:

> *But Pallas came in shape of rust,*
> *And 'twixt the spring and hammer thrust*
> *Her Gorgon shield, which made the cock*
> *Stand stiff, as 'twere transform'd to stock.*

And few, who read this, imagine themselves superior either to Homer or Butler; we indeed generally imagine ourselves superior in sense to the valorous knights, but not in this point, of firing rusty pistols. And pray, would any mortal have laughed, had the poet told, in a simple unadorned manner, that his knight attempted to shoot Talgol, but his pistol was so rusty that it would not give fire? and yet this would have given us the same ground of sudden glory from our superiority over the doughty knight.

Again, to what do we compare ourselves, or imagine ourselves superior, when we laugh at this fantastical imitation of the poetical imagery, and similitudes of the morning?

> *The sun, long since, had in the lap*
> *Of Thetis taken out his nap;*
> *And, like a lobster boil'd, the morn*
> *From black to red began to turn.*

Many an orthodox Scotch Presbyterian, which sect few accuse of disregard for the holy scriptures, has been put to it to preserve his gravity, upon hearing the application of Scripture made by his countryman Dr. Pitcairn, as he observed a croud in the streets about a mason, who had fallen along with his scaffold, and was over-whelmed with the ruins of the chimney which he had been building, and which fell immediately after the fall of the poor mason; 'Blessed are the dead which die in the Lord, for they rest from their labours, and their works follow them.' And yet few imagine themselves superior either to the apostle or the doctor. Their superiority to the poor mason, I am sure, could never have raised such Laughter, for this occurred to them before the doctor's consolation. In this case no opinion of superiority could have occasioned the Laughter, unless we say, that people imagined themselves superior to the doctor in religion: but an imagined superiority to a doctor in religion, is not a matter so rare as to raise sudden joy; and with people who value religion, the impiety of another is no matter of Laughter.

It is said, 'That when men of wit make us laugh, it is by representing some oddness or infirmity in themselves, or others.' Thus allusions made on trifling occasions, to the most solemn figured speeches of great writers, contain such an obvious impropriety, that we imagine ourselves incapable of such mistakes as the alluder seemingly falls into; so that in this case too, there is an imagined superiority. But in answer to this, we may observe, that we often laugh at such allusions, when we are conscious, that the person who raises the laugh knows abundantly the justest propriety of speaking, and knows, at present, the oddness and impropriety of his own allusion as well as any in company; nay, laughs at it himself: we often admire his wit in such allusions, and study to imitate him in it, as far as we can. Now, what sudden sense of glory, or joy in our superiority, can arise from observing a quality in another, which we study to imitate, I cannot imagine. I doubt, if men compared themselves with the alluder, whom they study to imitate, they would rather often grow grave or sorrowful.

Nay, farther, this is so far from truth, that imagined superiority moves our Laughter, that one would imagine from some instances the very contrary: for if Laughter arose from our imagined superiority, then, the more that any object appeared inferior to us, the greater would be the jest; and the nearer any one came to an equality with us, or resemblance of our actions, the less we should be moved with Laughter. But we see, on the contrary, that some ingenuity in dogs and monkeys, which comes near to some of our own arts, very often make us merry; whereas their duller actions, in which they are much below us, are no matter of jest at all. Whence the author in the Spectator drew his observation, 'That the actions of beasts, which move our Laughter, bear a resemblance to a human blunder,' I confess I cannot guess; I fear the very contrary is true, that their imitation of our grave wise actions, would be fittest to raise mirth in the observer.

The second part of the argument, that opinion of superiority suddenly incited in us does not move Laughter, seems the most obvious thing imaginable. If we observe an object in pain while we are at ease, we are in greater danger of weeping than laughing: and yet here is occasion for Hobbes's sudden joy. It must be a very merry state in which a fine gentleman is, when well dressed, in his coach, he passes our streets, where he will see so many ragged beggars, and porters and chairmen sweating at their labour, on every side of him. It is a great pity that we had not an infirmary or lazar-house to retire to in cloudy weather, to get an afternoon of Laughter at these inferior objects: Strange! that none of our Hobbists banish all Canary birds and squirrels, and lap-dogs and pugs, and cats out of their houses, and substitute in their places asses, and owls, and snails, and oysters, to be merry upon. From these they might have higher joys of superiority, than from those with whom we now please ourselves. Pride, or an high opinion of ourselves, must be entirely inconsistent with gravity; emptiness must always make men solemn in their behaviour; and conscious virtue and great abilities must always be upon the sneer. An orthodox believer, who is very sure that he is in the true way to salvation, must always be merry upon heretics, to whom he is so much superior in his own opinion; and no other passion but mirth should arise upon hearing of their heterodoxy. In general, all men of true sense, and reflection, and integrity, of great capacity for business, and penetration into the tempers and interests of men,

must be the merriest little grigs imaginable; Democritus must be
the sole leader of all the philosophers; and perpetual Laughter
must succeed into the place of the long beard,

> —*To be the grace*
> *Both of our wisdom and our face.*

It is pretty strange, that the authors whom we mentioned
above, have never distinguished between the words Laughter and
Ridicule: this last is but one particular species of the former, when
we are laughing at the follies of others; and in this species there
may be some pretence to allege that some imagined superiority
may occasion it; but then there are innumerable instances of
Laughter, where no person is ridiculed; nor does he who laughs
compare himself to any thing whatsoever. Thus how often do
we laugh at some out-of-the-way description of natural objects,
to which we never compare our state at all. I fancy few have ever
read the City Shower without a strong disposition to Laughter;
and instead of imagining any superiority, are very sensible of a
turn of wit in the author which they despair of imitating: thus
what relation to our affairs has that simile in Hudibras,

> *Instead of trumpet and of drum,*
> *Which makes the warrior's stomach come,*
> *And whets mens valour sharp, like beer*
> *By thunder turn'd to vinegar.*

The Laughter is not here raised against either valour or martial
music, but merely by the wild resemblance of a mean event.

And then farther, even in ridicule itself there must be something
else than bare opinion to raise it, as may appear from this, that if
any one would relate in the simplest manner these very weaknesses
of others, their extravagant passions, their absurd opinions, upon
which the man of wit would rally, should we hear the best vouchers
of all the facts alleged, we shall not be disposed to Laughter by bare
narration; or should one do a real important injury to another, by
taking advantage of his weakness, or by some pernicious fraud
let us see another's simplicity, this is no matter of Laughter:
and yet these important cheats do really discover our superiority
over the person cheated, more than the trifling impostures of our
humourists. The opinion of our superiority may raise a sedate joy
in our minds, very different from Laughter; but such a thought
seldom arises in our minds in the hurry of a chearful conversation
among friends, where there is often an high mutual esteem. But
we go to our closets often to spin out some fine conjecture about
the principles of our actions, which no mortal is conscious of in

himself during the action; thus the same authors above-mentioned tell us, that the desire which we have to see tragical representations is, because of the secret pleasure we find in thinking ourselves secure from such evils; we know from what sect this notion was derived.

> *Quibus ipse malis liber es, quia cernere suave.* [1]

This pleasure must indeed be a secret one, so very secret, that many a kind compassionate heart was never conscious of it, but felt itself in a continual state of horror and sorrow; our desiring such sights flows from a kind instinct of nature, a secret bond between us and our fellow-creatures.

> *Naturae imperio gemimus cum funus adultae*
> *Virginis occurrit, vel terra clauditur infans.*
> *— Quis enim bonus —*
> *Ulla aliena fibi credat mala.* [2]

To the Author of the Dublin Journal

> *Humano capiti cervicem pictor equinam*
> *Jungere si velit, et varias inducere plumas*
> *Undique conlatis membris, ut turpiter atrum*
> *Desinat in piscem mulier formosa superne,*
> *Spectatum admissi risum teneatis amici?* [3]

SIR,

In my former letter, I attempted to shew that Mr. Hobbes's account of Laughter was not just. I shall now endeavour to discover some other ground of that sensation, action, passion, or affection, I know not which of them a philosopher would call it.

1 ['For to discern the bad things from which you are free is pleasant.' Lucretius, *De Rerum*, Book I, line 4.]
2 ['At nature's command we lament when the funeral of full-grown maiden occurs, or when the earth closes over an infant . . . For what good man . . . believes that any ills are distant from him,' Juvenal, *Satires* XV 138.]
3 ['If a painter chose to join a human head to the neck of a horse, and to spread feathers of many a hue over limbs picked up now here, now there, so that what at top is a lovely woman ends below in a black and ugly fish, would you, my friend, if favoured with a private view, refrain from laughing?' Horace, *De Arte Poetica* 1, trans. H. R. Fairclough.]

The ingenious Mr. Addison, in his treatise of the pleasures of the imagination, has justly observed many sublimer sensations than those commonly mentioned among philosophers: he observes particularly, that we receive sensations of pleasure from those objects which are great, new, or beautiful; and on the contrary, that objects which are more narrow and confined, or deformed and irregular, give us disagreeable ideas. It is unquestionable, that we have a great number of perceptions, which one can scarcely reduce to any of the five senses, as they are commonly explained; such as either the ideas of grandeur, dignity, decency, beauty, harmony; or, on the other hand, of meanness, baseness, indecency, deformity; and that we apply these ideas not only to material objects, but to characters, abilities, actions.

It may be farther observed, that by some strange associations of ideas made in our infancy, we have frequently some of these ideas recurring along with a great many objects, with which they have no other connection than what custom and education, or frequent allusions, give them, or at most, some very distant resemblance. The very affections of our minds are ascribed to inanimate objects; and some animals, perfect enough in their own kind, are made constant emblems of some vices or meanness: whereas other kinds are made emblems of the contrary qualities. For instances of these associations, partly from nature, partly from custom, we may take the following ones; sanctity in our churches, magnificence in public buildings, affection between the oak and ivy, the elm and vine; hospitality in a shade, a pleasant sensation of grandeur in the sky, the sea, and mountains, distinct from a bare apprehension or image of their extension; solemnity and horror in shady woods. An ass is the common emblem of stupidity and sloth, a swine of selfish luxury; an eagle of a great genius; a lion of intrepidity; an ant or bee of low industry, and prudent œconomy. Some inanimate objects have in like manner some accessary ideas of meanness, either for some natural reason, or oftner by mere chance and custom.

Now, the same ingenious author observes, in the Spectator, Vol. I. No 62, that what we call a great genius, such as becomes a heroic poet, gives us pleasure by filling the mind with great conceptions; and therefore they bring most of their similitudes and metaphors from objects of dignity and grandeur, where the resemblance is generally very obvious. This is not usually called wit, but something nobler. What we call grave wit, consists in bringing such resembling ideas together, as one could scarce have imagined had so exact a relation to each other; or when the resemblance is carried on through many more particulars than we could have at first expected: and this therefore gives the pleasure of surprize. In this serious wit, though we are not solicitous about the grandeur of the images, we must still beware of bringing in ideas of baseness or deformity, unless we are studying to represent an object as base and deformed. Now this sort of wit is seldom apt to move Laughter, more than heroic poetry.

That then which seems generally the cause of Laughter, is 'the bringing together of images which have contrary additional ideas, as well as some resemblance in the principal idea: this contrast between ideas of grandeur, dignity, sanctity, perfection, and ideas of meanness, baseness, profanity, seems to be the very spirit of burlesque; and the greatest part of our raillery and jest is founded upon it.'

We also find ourselves moved to Laughter by an overstraining of wit, by bringing resemblances from subjects of a quite different kind from the subject to which they are compared. 'When we see, instead of the easiness, and natural resemblance, which constitutes true wit, a forced straining of a likeness, our Laughter is apt to arise; as also, when the only resemblance is not in the idea, but in the sound of the words.' And this is the matter of Laughter in the pun.

Let us see if this thought may not be confirmed in many instances. If any writing has obtained an high character for grandeur, sanctity, inspiration, or sublimity of thoughts, and boldness of images; the application of any known sentence of such writings to low, vulgar, or base subjects, never fails to divert the audience, and set them a-laughing. This fund of Laughter the ancients had by allusions to Homer: of this the lives of some of the philosophers in Diogenes Laertius supply abundance of instances. Our late burlesque writers derive a great part of their pleasantry from their introducing, on the most trifling occasions, allusions to some of the bold schemes, or figures, or sentences, of the great poets, upon the most solemn subjects. Hudibras and Don Quixote will supply one with instances of this in almost every page. It were to be wished that the boldness of our age had never carried their ludicrous allusions to yet more venerable writings. We know that allusions to the phrases of holy writ have obtained to some gentlemen a character of wit, and often furnished Laughter to their hearers, when their imaginations have been too barren to give any other entertainment. But I appeal to the religious themselves, if these allusions are not apt to move

Laughter, unless a more strong affection of the mind, a religious horror at the profanity of such allusions, prevents their allowing themselves the liberty of laughing at them. Now in this affair I fancy any one will acknowledge that an opinion of superiority is not at all the occasion of the Laughter.

Again, any little accident to which we have joined the idea of meanness, befalling a person of great gravity, ability, dignity, is a matter of Laughter, for the very same reason; thus the strange contortions of the body in a fall, the dirtying of a decent dress, the natural functions which we study to conceal from sight, are matter of Laughter, when they occur to observation in persons of whom we have high ideas: nay, the very human form has the ideas of dignity so generally joined with it, that even in ordinary persons such mean accidents are matter of jest; but still the jest is increased by the dignity, gravity, or modesty of the person; which shews that it is this contrast, or opposition of ideas of dignity and meanness, which is the occasion of Laughter.

We generally imagine in mankind some degree of wisdom above other animals, and have high ideas of them on this account. If then along with our notion of wisdom in our fellows, there occurs any instance of gross inadvertence, or great mistake; this is a great cause of Laughter. Our countrymen are very subject to little trips of this kind, and furnish often some diversion to their neighbours, not only by mistakes in their speech, but in actions. Yet even this kind of Laughter cannot well be said to arise from our sense of superiority. This alone may give a sedate joy, but not be a matter of Laughter; since we shall find the same kind of Laughter arising in us, where this opinion of superiority does not attend it: for if the most ingenious person in the world, whom the whole company esteems, should through inadvertent hearing, or any other mistake, answer quite from the purpose, the whole audience may laugh heartily, without the least abatement of their good opinion. Thus we know some very ingenious men have not in the least suffered in their characters by an extemporary pun, which raises the laugh very readily; whereas a premeditated pun, which diminishes our opinion of a writer, will seldom raise any Laughter.

Again, the more violent passions, as fear, anger, sorrow, compassion, are generally looked upon as something great and solemn; the beholding of these passions in another strikes a man with gravity: now if these passions are artfully, or accidentally, raised upon a small, or a fictitious occasion, they move the Laughter of those who imagine the occasions to be small and contemptible, or who are conscious of the fraud: this is the occasion of the laugh in biting, as they call such deceptions.

According to this scheme, there must necessarily arise a great diversity in mens sentiments of the ridiculous in actions or characters, according as their ideas of dignity and wisdom are various. A truly wise man, who places the dignity of human nature in good affections and suitable actions, may be apt to laugh at those who employ their most solemn and strong affections about what, to the wise man, appears perhaps very useless or mean. The same solemnity of behaviour and keenness of passion, about a place or ceremony, which ordinary people only employ about the absolute necessaries of life, may make them laugh at their betters. When a gentleman of pleasure, who thinks that good fellowship and gallantry are the only valuable enjoyments of life, observes men, with great solemnity and earnestness, heaping up money, without using it, or incumbering themselves with purchases and mortgages, which the gay gentleman, with his paternal revenues, thinks very silly affairs, he may make himself very merry upon them: and the frugal man, in his turn, makes the same jest of the man of pleasure. The successful gamester, whom no disaster forces to lay aside the trifling ideas of an amusement in his play, may laugh to see the serious looks and passions of the gravest business arising in the loser, amidst the ideas of a recreation. There is indeed in these last cases an opinion of superiority in the Laughter; but this is not the proper occasion of his Laughter; otherwise I see not how we should ever meet with a composed countenance any where: men have their different relishes of life, most people prefer their own taste to that of others; but this moves no Laughter, unless, in representing the pursuits of others, they do join together some whimsical image of opposite ideas.

In the more polite nations, there are certain modes of dress, behaviour, ceremony, generally received by all the better sort, as they are commonly called: to these modes, ideas of decency, grandeur, and dignity are generally joined; hence men are fond of imitating the mode: and if in any polite assembly, a contrary dress, behaviour, or ceremony appear, to which we have joined in our country the contrary ideas of meanness, rusticity, sullenness, a laugh does ordinarily arise, or a disposition to it, in those who have not the thorough good breeding, or reflection to restrain themselves, or break through these customary associations.

And hence we may see, that what is counted ridiculous in one age or nation, may not be so in another. We are apt to laugh at Homer, when he compares Ajax unwillingly retreating, to an ass driven out of a corn-field; or when he compares him to a boar: or Ulysses tossing all night without sleep through anxiety, to a pudding frying on the coals. Those three similes have got low mean ideas joined to them with us, which it is very probable they had not in Greece in Homer's days; nay, as to one of them, the boar, it is well known that in some countries of Europe, where they have wild boars for hunting, even in our times, they have not these low sordid ideas joined to that animal, which we have in these kingdoms, who never see them but in their dirty sties, or on dunghills. This may teach us how impertinent a great many jests are, which are made upon the style of some other ancient writings, in ages where manners were very different from ours, though perhaps fully as rational, and every way as human and just.

To the Author of the Dublin Journal

— Ridiculum acri
Fortius et melius magnas plerumque secat res.[1]

SIR,
To treat this subject of Laughter gravely, may subject the author to a censure, like to that which Longinus makes upon a prior treatise of the Sublime, because wrote in a manner very unsuitable to the subject. But yet it may be worth our pains to consider the effects of Laughter, and the ends for which it was implanted in our nature, that thence we may know the proper use of it: which may be done in the following observations.

First, we may observe, that Laughter, like many other dispositions of our mind, is necessarily pleasant to us, when it begins in the natural manner, from some perception in the mind of something ludicrous, and does not take its rise unnaturally from external motions in the body. Every one is conscious that a state of Laughter is an easy and agreeable state, that the recurring or suggestion of ludicrous images tends to dispel fretfulness, anxiety, or sorrow, and to reduce the mind to an easy, happy state; as on the other hand, an easy and happy state is that in which we are most lively and acute in perceiving the ludicrous in objects: any thing, that gives us pleasure, puts us also in a fitness for Laughter, when something ridiculous occurs; and ridiculous

1 ['A jest often cuts great matters more forcefully and better than severity.' Horace, *Satires*, Book 1, Satire 10, verses 14–15.]

objects, occurring to a soured temper, will be apt to recover it
to easiness. The implanting then a sense of the ridiculous, in
our nature, was giving us an avenue to pleasure, and an easy
remedy for discontent and sorrow.

Again, Laughter, like other affections, is very contagious; our
whole frame is so sociable, that one merry countenance may
diffuse cheerfulness to many; nor are they all fools who are apt
to laugh before they know the jest, however curiosity in wise men
may restrain it, that their attention may be kept awake.

We are disposed by Laughter to a good opinion of the person
who raises it, if neither ourselves nor our friends are made the butt.
Laughter is none of the smallest bonds of common friendships,
though it be of less consequence in great heroic friendships.

If an object, action, or event, be truly great in every respect, it
will have no natural relation or resemblance to any thing mean
or base; and consequently, no mean idea can be joined to it
with any natural resemblance. If we make some forced remote
jests upon such subjects, they can never be pleasing to a man
of sense and reflection, but raise contempt of the ridiculer, as
void of just sense of those things which are truly great. As to
any great and truly sublime sentiments, we may perhaps find
that, by a playing upon words, they may be applied to a trifling
or mean action, or object; but this application will not diminish
our high idea of the great sentiment. He must be of a poor trifling
temper who would lose his relish of the grandeur and beauty of
that noble sentence of holy writ, mentioned in a former paper,
from the doctor's application of it. Virgil Travesty may often
come into an ingenious man's head, when he reads the original,
and make him uneasy with impertinent interruptions; but will
never diminish his admiration of Virgil. Who dislikes that line in
Homer, by which Diogenes the Cynic answered a neighbour at
an execution, who was inquiring into the cause of the criminal's
condemnation? which has been the counterfeiting of the ancient
purple.

Ἔλλαβε πορφύρεος και μοιρα κραταιη.[1]

Let any of our wits try their mettle in ridiculing the opinion of
a good and wise mind governing the whole universe; let them
try to ridicule integrity and honesty, gratitude, generosity, or the
love of one's country, accompanied with wisdom. All their art

1 ['and down over his eyes came dark death and mighty
fate', Homer, *Iliad*, V 83, trans. A. T. Murray.]

will never diminish the admiration which we must have for such dispositions, where-ever we observe them pure and unmixed with any low views, or any folly in the exercise of them.

When in any object there is a mixture of what is truly great, along with something weak or mean, ridicule may, with a weak mind which cannot separate the great from the mean, bring the whole into disesteem, or make the whole appear weak or contemptible: but with a person of just discernment and reflection it will have no other effect, but to separate what is great from what is not so.

When any object either good or evil is aggravated and increased by the violence of our passions, or an enthusiastic admiration, or fear, the application of ridicule is the readiest way to bring down our high imaginations to a conformity to the real moment or importance of the affair. Ridicule gives our minds as it were a bend to the contrary side; so that upon reflection they may be more capable of settling in a just conformity to nature.

Laughter is received in a different manner by the person ridiculed, according as he who uses the ridicule evidences good-nature, friendship, and esteem of the person whom he laughs at; or the contrary.

The enormous crime or grievous calamity of another, is not of itself a subject which can be naturally turned into ridicule: the former raises horror in us, and hatred; and the latter pity. When Laughter arises on such occasions, it is not excited by the guilt or the misery. To observe the contortions of the human body in the air, upon the blowing up of an enemy's ship, may raise Laughter in those who do not reflect on the agony and distress of the sufferers; but the reflecting on this distress could never move Laughter of itself. So some fantastic circumstances accompanying a crime may raise Laughter; but a piece of cruel barbarity, or treacherous villainy, of itself, must raise very contrary passions. A jest is not ordinary in an impeachment of a criminal, or an invective oration: it rather diminishes than increases the abhorrence in the audience, and may justly raise contempt of the orator for an unnatural affectation of wit. Jesting is still more unnatural in discourses designed to move compassion toward the distressed. A forced unnatural ridicule, on either of these occasions, must be apt to raise, in the guilty or the miserable, hatred against the Laughter; since it must be supposed to flow from hatred in him toward the object of his ridicule, or from want of all compassion. The guilty will take Laughter to be a triumph over him as contemptible; the miserable will interpret it as hardness of heart, and insensibility of the calamities of another.

This is the natural effect of joining to either of these objects mean ludicrous ideas.

If smaller faults, such as are not inconsistent with a character in the main amiable, be set in a ridiculous light, the guilty are apt to be made sensible of their folly, more than by a bare grave admonition. In many of our faults, occasioned by too great violence of some passion, we get such enthusiastic apprehensions of some objects, as lead us to justify our conduct: the joining of opposite ideas or images allays this enthusiasm; and, if this be done with good nature, it may be the least offensive, and most effectual, reproof.

Ridicule upon the smallest faults, when it does not appear to flow from kindness, is apt to be extremely provoking; since the applying of mean ideas to our conduct discovers contempt of us in the ridiculer, and that he designs to make us contemptible to others.

Ridicule applied to those qualities or circumstances in one of our companions, which neither he nor the ridiculer thinks dishonourable, is agreeable to every one; the butt himself is as well pleased as any in company.

Ridicule upon any small misfortune or injury, which we have received with sorrow or keen resentment, when it is applied by a third person, with appearance of good-nature, is exceeding useful to abate our concern or resentment, and to reconcile us to the person who injured us, if he does not persist in his injury.

From this consideration of the effects of Laughter, it may be easy to see for what cause, or end, a sense of the ridiculous was implanted in human nature, and how it ought to be managed.

It is plainly of considerable moment in human society. It is often a great occasion of pleasure, and enlivens our conversation exceedingly, when it is conducted by good-nature. It spreads a pleasantry of temper over multitudes at once; and one merry easy mind may by this means diffuse a like disposition over all who are in company. There is nothing of which we are more communicative than of a good jest: and many a man, who is incapable of obliging us otherwise, can oblige us by his mirth, and really insinuate himself into our kind affections, and good wishes.

But this is not all the use of Laughter. It is well known, that our passions of every kind lead us into wild enthusiastic apprehensions of their several objects. When any object seems great in comparison of ourselves, our minds are apt to run into a perfect veneration: when an object appears formidable, a weak mind will run into a panic, an unreasonable, impotent horror. Now in both these cases, by our sense of the ridiculous, we are made capable of relief from any pleasant, ingenious well-wisher, by more effectual means, than the most solemn, sedate reasoning. Nothing is so properly applied to the false grandeur, either of good or evil, as ridicule: nothing will sooner prevent our excessive admiration of mixed grandeur, or hinder our being led by that, which is, perhaps, really great in such an object, to imitate also and approve what is really mean.

I question not but the jest of Elijah upon the false deity, whom his countrymen had set up, has been very effectual to rectify their notions of the divine nature; as we find that like jests have been very seasonable in other nations. Baal, no doubt, had been represented as a great personage of unconquerable power: but how ridiculous does the image appear, when the prophet sets before them, at once, the poor ideas which must arise from such a limitation of nature as could be represented by their statues, and the high ideas of omniscience, and omnipotence, with which the people declared themselves possessed by their invocation. 'Cry aloud, either he is talking, or pursuing, or he is on a journey, or he is asleep.'

This engine of ridicule, no doubt, may be abused, and have a bad effect upon a weak mind; but with men of any reflection, there is little fear that it will ever be very pernicious. An attempt of ridicule before such men, upon a subject every way great, is sure to return upon the author of it. One might dare the boldest wit in company with men of sense, to make a jest upon a completely great action, or character. Let him try the story of Scipio and his fair captive, upon the taking of Cartagena; or the old story of Pylades and Orestes; I fancy he would sooner appear in a fool's coat himself, than he could put either of these characters in such a dress. The only danger is in objects of a mixed nature before people of little judgment, who, by jests upon the weak side, are sometimes led into neglect, or contempt, of that which is truly valuable in any character, institution, or office. And this may shew us the impertinence, and pernicious tendency of general undistinguished jests upon any character, or office, which has been too much over-rated. But, that ridicule may be abused, does not prove it useless, or unnecessary, more than a like possibility of abuse would prove all our senses and passions, impertinent or hurtful. Ridicule, like other edged tools, may do good in a wise man's hands, though fools may cut their fingers with it, or be injurious to an unwary by-stander.

The rules to avoid abuse of this kind of ridicule, are, first, 'Either never to attempt ridicule upon what is every way great, whether it be any great being, character, or sentiments:' or, if our wit must sometimes run into allusions, on low occasions, to the expressions of great sentiments, 'Let it not be in weak company, who have not a just discernment of true grandeur.' And, secondly, concerning objects of a mixed nature, partly great, and partly mean, 'Let us never turn the meanness into ridicule, without acknowledging what is truly great, and paying a just veneration to it.' In this sort of jesting we ought to be cautious of our company.

> *Discit enim citius, meminitque libentius illud,*
> *Quod quis deridet, quam quod probat et veneratur.* [1]

Another valuable purpose of ridicule is with relation to smaller vices, which are often more effectually corrected by ridicule, than by grave admonition. Men have been laughed out of faults which a sermon could not reform; nay, there are many little indecencies which are improper to be mentioned in such solemn discourses. Now ridicule, with contempt or ill-nature, is indeed always irritating and offensive; but we may, by testifying a just esteem for the good qualities of the person ridiculed, and our concern for his interests, let him see that our ridicule of his weakness flows from love to him, and then we may hope for a good effect. This then is another necessary rule, 'That along with our ridicule of smaller faults we should always join evidences of good-nature and esteem.'

As to jests upon imperfections, which one cannot amend, I cannot see of what use they can be: men of sense cannot relish such jests; foolish trifling minds may by them be led to despise the truest merit, which is not exempted from the casual misfortunes of our mortal state. If these imperfections occur along with a vitious character, against which people should be alarmed and cautioned, it is below a wise man to raise aversions to bad men from their necessary infirmities, when they have a juster handle from their vitious dispositions.

I shall conclude this essay with the words of father Malebranche, upon the last subject of Laughter, the smaller misfortunes of others. That author amidst all his visions shews sometimes as fine sense as any of his neighbours.

---

1 ['One learns more quickly and remembers more gladly
   what one derides than what one approves of and
   adores.' Horace, *Epistles* II, i. 262.]

'There is nothing more admirably contrived than those natural correspondences observable between the inclinations of mens minds and the motions of their bodies. – All this secret chain-work is a miracle, which can never sufficiently be admired or understood. Upon sense of some surprizing evil, which appears too strong for one to overcome with his own strength, he raises, suppose, a loud cry: this cry, forced out by the disposition of our machine, pierces the ears of those who are near, and makes them understand it, let them be of what nation or quality soever: for it is the cry of all nations, and all conditions, as indeed it ought to be. It raises a commotion in their brain, – and makes them run to give succour without so much as knowing it. It soon obliges their will to desire, and their understanding to contrive, provided that it was just and according to the rules of society. For an indiscrete out-cry, made upon no occasion, or out of an idle fear, produces, in the assistants, indignation or Laughter instead of pity. – That indiscreet cry naturally produces aversion, and desire of revenging the affront offered to nature, if he that made it without cause, did it wilfully: but it ought only to produce the passion of derision, mingled with some compassion, without aversion or desire of revenge, if it were a fright, that is, a false appearance of a pressing exigency, which caused the clamour. For scoff or ridicule is necessary to re-assure and correct the man as fearful; and compassion to succour him as weak. It is impossible to conceive any thing better ordered.'

 I am, Sir,
  Your very humble Servant,
   Philomeides

Source: Francis Hutcheson, *Reflections upon Laughter*, in *Reflections upon Laughter and Remarks upon the Fable of the Bees*, Glasgow 1750, pp. 15–38

ELEVEN

DAVID HUME
of the Standard of Taste

Hume's essay is a major source of light, and of dispute, in the field of aesthetics, offering perhaps the most plausible account that can be given by a 'sentimentalist', of the nature of our aesthetic judgments. His chief concern is with what used to be called the objectivity of aesthetic judgment, though it is now more common to call the quality in question 'normativity'. In brief, what entitles us to say that a given aesthetic judgment is right and that its denial is wrong? If beauty and ugliness are a matter of sentiment, and if sentiments cannot be either right or wrong, for they are simply *there*, then how can some aesthetic judgments be right and others wrong? Why are they not all equally right? Or, more precisely, why cannot people, with equal justification, think exactly what they want regarding the aesthetic status of any object? Are there perhaps aesthetic qualities residing in things, which make our aesthetic judgments right or wrong? Hume says 'no' to this question, and looks elsewhere for the grounds of normativity or objectivity. The sentimentalism which underlies his moral philosophy, and which emerges clearly in his slogan 'Reason is the slave of the passions', is equally present in his aesthetics, where again passion or sentiment is in the driving seat, and reason aids and abets it.

The starting point for worries about the normativity of judgments of aesthetic taste is the fact that there is such a wide variety of taste. There seems always to be room for dispute as to whether a poem, novel, play or painting is good or bad, and just how good or how bad. Where we find near universal agreement in matters of aesthetic taste, the agreement is basically about the meaning of terminology, and not agreement about the substantive matter of whether some term or other is appropriately applied to a particular act or object. The situation is much the same as in morality, where we might all agree that justice is a fine thing but disagree about whether a particular act or institution counts as just.

Hume asserts: 'beauty and deformity . . . are not qualities in objects, but belong entirely to the sentiment'. Why then can I not say that my sentiments are as good as yours, and yours as good as mine? Hume's reply is that we do in fact acknowledge 'a rule by which the various sentiments of men may be reconciled; at least, a decision, afforded, confirming one sentiment, and condemning another'. The reference to a rule implies that Hume will provide us with a rule that permits us to make correct aesthetic judgments, as if there is some formula whose application to a painting or statue will enable us to say that it is, or falls short of being, a good painting or statue. In fact Hume does not quite provide us with such a rule, though he does give us hints as to how we might improve our powers of aesthetic judgment.

We are all, to a greater or lesser extent, sensitive to aesthetic qualities. A good critic has a well-developed aesthetic sensibility. An important part of Hume's 'Of the standard of taste' is taken up with a description of the good critic. This description is crucial to the argument, for sound judgments of aesthetic taste are judgments made by good critics. The order of these concepts is important. Hume derives the concept of a sound aesthetic judgment from the concept of a good critic, not the concept of a good critic from that of a sound aesthetic judgment.

A good critic has five distinct features. First he has delicacy of taste, without which he would be affected only by the grosser qualities of what he is judging. Secondly, he is well practised in the exercise of his critical powers – 'Where he is not aided by practice, his verdict is attended with confusion and hesitation'. Thirdly, and relatedly, he requires a range of practice in order to make comparisons. In the absence of such practice he is likely to give more weight than he should to superficial or frivolous features of the objects judged. Fourthly, he must be free from prejudice about what he is judging. Jealousy of, or affection for, an artist or poet must not be allowed to direct the judgment of the critic. Impartiality therefore is a virtue in a critic. And finally he requires good sense, without which he will not properly understand what a painting, novel, poem or play is about in a broad sense of 'about', nor will he be well placed to detect prejudice when it is at work directing his judgment.

In answer therefore to the question: 'What makes one person's aesthetic judgment better than another's?', Hume tells us that the better judgment is made by the person with the better critical powers and, as regards those powers, Hume's approach is simply to enumerate them. Such a person, one with these powers, it is surely obvious, will make judgments we can trust.

Whether Hume succeeds in establishing that a sentimentalist is entitled to believe in a standard of taste is open to dispute; in particular he may be begging the question in the way he sets up his solution. He identifies certain virtues that the good critic possesses, but why should we call these qualities the virtues of a critic unless we think they will deliver up correct aesthetic judgments? And in that case, we must have criteria of a correct aesthetic judgment antecedent to our criteria of a good critic. Yet, as we have seen, Hume wishes to base the idea of a correct aesthetic judgment upon the idea of a good critic, and not vice versa. Whether or not Hume has a satisfactory answer to this point, his essay 'Of the standard of taste' remains one of the masterpieces of aesthetics.

Hume plainly believed that we are not glued to the level of refinement of sensibility at which we find ourselves. One purpose of the essay is to describe what we have to do to move to a higher level. In that respect the essay might be seen as contributing to that search for improvement that so characterised the Enlightenment in Scotland.

A.B.

Of the Standard of Taste

The great variety of Taste, as well as of opinion, which prevails in the world, is too obvious not to have fallen under every one's observation. Men of the most confined knowledge are able to remark a difference of taste in the narrow circle of their acquaintance, even where the persons have been educated under the same government, and have early imbibed the same prejudices. But those, who can enlarge their views to contemplate distant nations and remote ages, are still more surprized at the great inconsistence and contrariety. We are apt to call *barbarous* whatever departs widely from our own taste and apprehension: But soon find the epithet of reproach retorted on us. And the highest arrogance and self-deceit is at last startled, on observing an equal assurance on all sides, and scruples, amidst such a contest of sentiment, to pronounce positively in its own favour.

As this variety of taste is obvious to the most careless enquirer; so will it be found, on examination, to be still greater in reality than in appearance. The sentiments of men often differ with regard to beauty and deformity of all kinds, even while their general discourse is the same. There are certain terms in every language, which import blame, and others praise; and all men, who use the same tongue, must agree in their application of them. Every voice is united in applauding elegance, propriety, simplicity, spirit in writing; and in blaming fustian, affectation, coldness, and a false brilliancy: But when critics come to particulars, this seeming unanimity vanishes; and it is found, that they had affixed a very different meaning to their expressions. In all matters of opinion and science, the case is opposite: The difference among men is there oftener found to lie in generals than in particulars; and to be less in reality than in appearance. An explanation of the terms commonly ends the controversy; and the disputants are surprized to find, that they had been quarrelling, while at bottom they agreed in their judgment.

Those who found morality on sentiment, more than on reason, are inclined to comprehend ethics under the former observation, and to maintain, that, in all questions, which regard conduct and manners, the difference among men is really greater than at first sight it appears. It is indeed obvious, that writers of all nations and all ages concur in applauding justice, humanity, magnanimity, prudence, veracity; and in blaming the opposite qualities. Even poets and other authors, whose compositions are chiefly calculated to please the imagination, are yet found from Homer down to Fenelon, to inculcate the same moral precepts, and to bestow their applause and blame on the same virtues and vices. This great unanimity is usually ascribed to the influence of plain reason; which, in all these cases, maintains similar sentiments in all men, and prevents those controversies, to which the abstract sciences are so much exposed. So far as the unanimity is real, this account may be admitted as satisfactory: But we must also allow that some part of the seeming harmony in morals may be accounted for from the very nature of language. The word *virtue*, with its equivalent in every tongue, implies praise; as that of *vice* does blame: And no one, without the most obvious and grossest impropriety, could affix reproach to a term, which in general acceptation is understood in a good sense; or bestow applause, where the idiom requires disapprobation. Homer's general precepts, where he delivers any such, will never be controverted; but it is obvious, that, when he draws particular pictures of manners, and represents heroism in Achilles and prudence in Ulysses, he intermixes a much greater degree of ferocity in the former, and of cunning and fraud in the latter, than Fenelon would admit of. The sage Ulysses in the Greek poet seems to delight in lies and fictions, and often employs them without any necessity or even advantage: But his more scrupulous son, in the French epic writer, exposes himself to the most imminent perils, rather than depart from the most exact line of truth and veracity.

The admirers and followers of the Alcoran insist on the excellent moral precepts interspersed throughout that wild and absurd performance. But it is to be supposed, that the Arabic words, which correspond to the English, equity, justice, temperance, meekness, charity, were such as, from the constant use of that tongue, must always be taken in a good sense; and it would have argued the greatest ignorance, not of morals, but of language, to have mentioned them with any epithets, besides those of applause and approbation. But would we know, whether the pretended prophet had really attained a just sentiment of morals? Let us attend to his narration; and we shall soon find, that he bestows praise on such instances of treachery, inhumanity, cruelty, revenge, bigotry, as are utterly incompatible with civilized society. No steady rule of right seems there to be attended to; and every action is blamed or praised, so far only as it is beneficial or hurtful to the true believers.

The merit of delivering true general precepts in ethics is indeed very small. Whoever recommends any moral virtues, really does no more than is implied in the terms themselves. That people, who invented the word *charity*, and used it in a good sense, inculcated more clearly and much more efficaciously, the precept, *be charitable*, than any pretended legislator or prophet, who should insert such a *maxim* in his writings. Of all expressions, those, which, together with their other meaning, imply a degree either of blame or approbation, are the least liable to be perverted or mistaken.

It is natural for us to seek a *Standard of Taste;* a rule, by which the various sentiments of men may be reconciled; at least, a decision, afforded, confirming one sentiment, and condemning another.

There is a species of philosophy, which cuts off all hopes of success in such an attempt, and represents the impossibility of ever attaining any standard of taste. The difference, it is said, is very wide between judgment and sentiment. All sentiment is right; because sentiment has a reference to nothing beyond itself, and is always real, wherever a man is conscious of it. But all determinations of the understanding are not right; because they have a reference to something beyond themselves, to wit, real matter of fact; and are not always conformable to that standard. Among a thousand different opinions which different men may entertain of the same subject, there is one, and but one, that is just and true; and the only difficulty is to fix and ascertain it. On the contrary, a thousand different sentiments, excited by the same object, are all right: Because no sentiment represents what is really in the object. It only marks a certain conformity or relation between the object and the organs or faculties of the mind; and if that conformity did not really exist, the sentiment could never possibly have being. Beauty is no quality in things themselves: It exists merely in the mind which contemplates them; and each mind perceives a different beauty. One person may even perceive deformity, where another is sensible of beauty; and every individual ought to acquiesce in his own sentiment, without pretending to regulate those of others. To seek the real beauty, or real deformity, is as fruitless an enquiry, as to pretend to ascertain the real sweet or real bitter. According to the disposition of the organs, the same object may be both sweet and bitter; and the proverb has justly determined it to be fruitless to dispute concerning tastes. It is very natural, and even quite necessary, to extend this axiom to mental, as well as bodily taste; and thus common sense, which is so often at variance with philosophy, especially with the sceptical kind, is found, in one instance at least, to agree in pronouncing the same decision.

But though this axiom, by passing into a proverb, seems to have attained the sanction of common sense; there is certainly a species of common sense which opposes it, at least serves to modify and restrain it. Whoever would assert an equality of genius and elegance between Ogilby and Milton, or Bunyan and Addison, would be thought to defend no less an extravagance, than if he had maintained a mole-hill to be as high as Teneriffe, or a pond as extensive as the ocean. Though there may be found persons, who give the preference to the former authors; no one pays attention to such a taste; and we pronounce without scruple the sentiment of these pretended critics to be absurd and ridiculous. The principle of the natural equality of tastes is then totally forgot, and while we admit it on some occasions, where the objects seem near an equality, it appears an extravagant paradox, or rather a palpable absurdity, where objects so disproportioned are compared together.

It is evident that none of the rules of composition are fixed by reasonings *a priori*, or can be esteemed abstract conclusions of the understanding, from comparing those habitudes and relations of ideas, which are eternal and immutable. Their foundation is the same with that of all the practical sciences, experience; nor are they any thing but general observations, concerning what has been universally found to please in all countries and in all ages. Many of the beauties of poetry and even of eloquence are founded on falsehood and fiction, on hyperboles, metaphors, and an abuse or perversion of terms from their natural meaning. To check the sallies of the imagination, and to reduce every expression to geometrical truth and exactness, would be the most contrary to the laws of criticism; because it would produce a work, which, by universal experience, has been found the most insipid and disagreeable. But though poetry can never submit to exact truth, it must be confined by rules of art, discovered to the author either by genius or observation. If some negligent or irregular writers have pleased, they have not pleased by their transgressions of rule or order, but in spite of these transgressions: They have possessed other beauties, which were conformable to just criticism; and the force of these beauties has been able to overpower censure, and give the mind a satisfaction superior to the disgust arising from the blemishes. Ariosto pleases; but not by his monstrous and improbable fictions, by his bizarre mixture of the serious and comic styles, by the want of coherence in his stories, or by the continual interruptions of his narration. He charms by the force and clearness of his expression, by the readiness and variety of his inventions, and by his natural pictures of the passions, especially those of the gay and amorous kind: And however his faults may diminish our satisfaction, they are not able entirely to destroy it. Did our pleasure really arise from those parts of his poem, which we denominate faults, this would be no objection to criticism in general: It would only be an objection to those particular rules of criticism, which would establish such circumstances to be faults, and would represent them as universally blameable. If they are found to please, they cannot be faults; let the pleasure, which they produce, be ever so unexpected and unaccountable.

But though all the general rules of art are founded only on experience and on the observation of the common sentiments of human nature, we must not imagine, that, on every occasion, the feelings of men will be conformable to these rules. Those finer emotions of the mind are of a very tender and delicate nature, and require the concurrence of many favourable circumstances to make them play with facility and exactness, according to their general and established principles. The least exterior hindrance to such small springs, or the least internal disorder, disturbs their motion, and confounds the operation of the whole machine. When we would make an experiment of this nature, and would try the force of any beauty or deformity, we must choose with care a proper time and place, and bring the fancy to a suitable situation and disposition. A perfect serenity of mind, a recollection of thought, a due attention to the object; if any of these circumstances be wanting, our experiment will be fallacious, and we shall be unable to judge of the catholic and universal beauty. The relation, which nature has placed between the form and the sentiment, will at least be more obscure; and it will require greater accuracy to trace and discern it. We shall be able to ascertain its influence not so much from the operation of each particular beauty, as from the durable admiration, which attends those works, that have survived all the caprices of mode and fashion, all the mistakes of ignorance and envy.

The same Homer, who pleased at Athens and Rome two thousand years ago, is still admired at Paris and at London. All the changes of climate, government, religion, and language, have not been able to obscure his glory. Authority or prejudice may give a temporary vogue to a bad poet or orator; but his reputation will never be durable or general. When his compositions are examined by posterity or by foreigners, the enchantment is dissipated, and his faults appear in their true colours. On the contrary, a real genius, the longer his works endure, and the more wide they are spread, the more sincere is the admiration which he meets with. Envy and jealousy have too much place in a narrow circle; and even familiar acquaintance with his person may diminish the applause due to his performances: But when these obstructions are removed, the beauties, which are naturally fitted to excite agreeable sentiments, immediately display their energy; and while the world endures, they maintain their authority over the minds of men.

It appears then, that, amidst all the variety and caprice of taste, there are certain general principles of approbation or blame, whose influence a careful eye may trace in all operations of the mind. Some particular forms or qualities, from the original structure of the internal fabric, are calculated to please, and others to displease; and if they fail of their effect in any particular instance, it is from some apparent defect or imperfection in the organ. A man in a fever would not insist on his palate as able to decide concerning flavours; nor would one, affected with the jaundice, pretend to give a verdict with regard to colours. In each creature, there is a sound and a defective state; and the former alone can be supposed to afford us a true standard of taste and sentiment. If, in the sound state of the organ, there be an entire or a considerable uniformity of sentiment among men, we may thence derive an idea of the perfect beauty; in like manner as the appearance of objects in day-light, to the eye of a man in health, is denominated their true and real colour, even while colour is allowed to be merely a phantasm of the senses.

Many and frequent are the defects in the internal organs, which prevent or weaken the influence of those general principles, on which depends our sentiment of beauty or deformity. Though some objects, by the structure of the mind, be naturally calculated to give pleasure, it is not to be expected, that in every individual the pleasure will be equally felt. Particular incidents and situations occur, which either throw a false light on the objects, or hinder the true from conveying to the imagination the proper sentiment and perception.

One obvious cause, which many feel not the proper sentiment of beauty, is the want of that *delicacy* of imagination, which is requisite to convey a sensibility of those finer emotions. This delicacy every one pretends to: Every one talks of it; and would reduce every kind of taste or sentiment to its standard. But as our intention in this essay is to mingle some light of the understanding with the feelings of sentiment, it will be proper to give a more accurate definition of delicacy, than has hitherto been attempted. And not to draw our philosophy from too profound a source, we shall have recourse to a noted story in Don Quixote.

It is with good reason, says Sancho to the squire with the great nose, that I pretend to have a judgment in wine: This is a quality hereditary in our family. Two of my kinsmen were once called to give their opinion of a hogshead, which was supposed to be excellent, being old and of a good vintage. One of them tastes it; considers it; and after mature reflection pronounces the wine to be good, were it not for a small taste of leather, which he perceived in it. The other, after using the same precautions, gives also his verdict in favour of the wine; but with the reserve of a taste of iron, which he could easily distinguish. You cannot imagine how much they were both ridiculed for their judgment. But who laughed in the end? On emptying the hogshead, there was found at the bottom, an old key with a leathern thong tied to it.

The great resemblance between mental and bodily taste will easily teach us to apply this story. Though it be certain, that beauty and deformity, more than sweet and bitter, are not qualities in objects, but belong entirely to the sentiment, internal or external; it must be allowed, that there are certain qualities in objects, which are fitted by nature to produce those particular feelings. Now as these qualities may be found in a small degree, or may be mixed and confounded with each other, it often happens, that the taste is not affected with such minute qualities, or is not able to distinguish all the particular flavours, amidst the disorder, in which they are presented. Where the organs are so fine, as to allow nothing to escape them; and at the same time so exact as to perceive every ingredient in the composition: This we call delicacy of taste, whether we employ these terms in the literal or metaphorical sense. Here then the general rules of beauty are of use; being drawn from established models, and from the observation of what pleases or displeases, when presented singly and in a high degree. And if the same qualities, in a continued composition and in a smaller degree, affect not the organs with a sensible delight or uneasiness, we exclude the person from all pretensions to this delicacy. To produce these general rules or avowed patterns of composition is like finding the key with the leathern thong; which justified the verdict of Sancho's kinsmen, and confounded those pretended judges who had condemned them. Though the hogshead had never been emptied, the taste of the one was still equally delicate, and that of the other equally dull and languid: But it would have been more difficult to have proved the superiority of the former, to the conviction of every by-stander. In like manner, though the beauties of writing had never been methodized, or reduced to general principles; though no excellent models had ever been acknowledged; the different degrees of taste would still have subsisted, and the judgment of one man been preferable to that of another; but it would not have been so easy to silence the bad critic, who might always insist upon his particular sentiment, and refuse to submit to his antagonist. But when we show him an avowed principle of art; when we illustrate this principle by examples, whose operation, from his own particular taste, he acknowledges to be conformable to the principle; when we prove, that the same principle may be applied to the present case, where he did not perceive or feel its influence: He must conclude, upon the whole, that the fault lies in himself, and that he wants the delicacy, which is requisite to make him sensible of every beauty and every blemish, in any composition or discourse.

It is acknowledged to be the perfection of every sense or faculty, to perceive with exactness its most minute objects, and allow nothing to escape its notice and observation. The smaller the objects are, which become sensible to the eye, the finer is that organ, and the more elaborate its make and composition. A good palate is not tried by strong flavours; but by a mixture of small ingredients, where we are still sensible of each part, notwithstanding its minuteness and its confusion with the rest. In like manner, a quick and acute perception of beauty and deformity must be the perfection of our mental taste; nor can a man be satisfied with himself while he suspects, that any excellence or blemish in a discourse has passed him unobserved. In this case, the perfection of the man, and the perfection of the sense or feeling, are found to be united. A very delicate palate, on many occasions, may be a great inconvenience both to a man himself and to his friends. But a delicate taste of wit or beauty must always be a desirable quality; because it is the source of all the finest and most innocent enjoyments, of which human nature is susceptible. In this decision the sentiments of all mankind are agreed. Wherever you can ascertain a delicacy of taste, it is sure to meet with approbation; and the best way of ascertaining it is to appeal to those models and principles, which have been established by the uniform consent and experience of nations and ages.

But though there be naturally a wide difference in point of delicacy between one person and another, nothing tends further to encrease and improve this talent, than *practice* in a particular art, and the frequent survey or contemplation of a particular species of beauty. When objects of any kind are first presented to the eye or imagination, the sentiment, which attends them, is obscure and confused; and the mind is, in a great measure, incapable of pronouncing concerning their merits or defects. The taste cannot perceive the several excellencies of the performance; much less distinguish the particular character of each excellency, and ascertain its quality and degree. If it pronounce the whole in general to be beautiful or deformed, it is the utmost that can be expected; and even this judgment, a person, so unpractised, will be apt to deliver with great hesitation and reserve. But allow him to acquire experience in those objects, his feeling becomes more exact and nice: He not only perceives the beauties and defects of each part, but marks the distinguishing species of each quality, and assigns it suitable praise or blame. A clear and distinct sentiment attends him through the whole survey of the objects; and he discerns that very degree and kind of approbation or displeasure, which each part is naturally fitted to produce. The mist dissipates, which seemed formerly to hang over the object: The organ acquires greater perfection in its operations; and can pronounce, without danger of mistake, concerning the merits of every performance. In a word, the same address and dexterity, which practice gives to the execution of any work, is also acquired by the same means, in the judging of it.

So advantageous is practice to the discernment of beauty, that, before we can give judgment on any work of importance, it will even be requisite, that that very individual performance be more than once perused by us, and be surveyed in different lights with attention and deliberation. There is a flutter or hurry of thought which attends the first perusal of any piece, and which confounds the genuine sentiment of beauty. The relation of the parts is not discerned. The true characters of style are little distinguished: The several perfections and defects seem wrapped up in a species of confusion, and present themselves indistinctly to the imagination. Not to mention, that there is a species of beauty, which, as it is florid and superficial, pleases at first; but being found incompatible with a just expression either of reason or passion, soon palls upon the taste, and is then rejected with disdain, at least rated at a much lower value.

It is impossible to continue in the practice of contemplating any order of beauty, without being frequently obliged to form *comparisons* between the several species and degrees of excellence, and estimating their proportion to each other. A man, who has had no opportunity of comparing the different kinds of beauty, is indeed totally unqualified to pronounce an opinion with regard to any object presented to him. By comparison alone we fix the epithets of praise or blame, and learn how to assign the due degree of each. The coarsest daubing contains a certain lustre of colours and exactness of imitation, which are so far beauties, and would affect the mind of a peasant or Indian with the highest admiration. The most vulgar ballads are not entirely destitute of harmony or nature; and none but a person, familiarized to superior beauties, would pronounce their numbers harsh, or narration uninteresting. A great inferiority of beauty gives pain to a person conversant in the highest excellence of the kind, and is for that reason pronounced a deformity: As the most finished object, with which we are acquainted, is naturally supposed to have reached the pinnacle of perfection, and to be entitled to the highest applause. One accustomed to see, and examine, and weigh the several performances, admired in different ages and nations, can alone rate the merits of a work exhibited to his view, and assign its proper rank among the productions of genius.

But to enable a critic the more fully to execute this undertaking, he must preserve his mind free from all *prejudice*, and allow nothing to enter into his consideration, but the very object which is submitted to his examination. We may observe, that every work of art, in order to produce its due effect on the mind, must be surveyed in a certain point of view, and cannot be fully relished by persons, whose situation, real or imaginary, is not conformable to that which is required by the performance. An orator addresses himself to a particular audience, and must have a regard to their particular genius, interests, opinions, passions, and prejudices; otherwise he hopes in vain to govern their resolutions, and inflame their affections. Should they even have entertained some prepossessions against him, however unreasonable, he must not overlook this disadvantage; but, before he enters upon the subject, must endeavour to conciliate their affection, and acquire their good graces. A critic of a different age or nation, who should peruse this discourse, must have all these circumstances in his eye, and must place himself in the same situation as the audience, in order to form a true judgment of the oration. In like manner, when any work is addressed to the public, though I should have a friendship or enmity with the author, I must depart from this situation; and considering myself as a man in general, forget, if possible, my individual being and my peculiar circumstances. A person influenced by prejudice, complies not with this condition; but obstinately maintains his natural position, without placing himself in that point of view, which the performance supposes. If the work be addressed to persons of a different age or nation, he makes no allowance for their peculiar views and prejudices; but, full of the manners of his own age and country, rashly condemns what seemed admirable in the eyes of those for whom alone the discourse was calculated. If the work be executed for the public, he never sufficiently enlarges his comprehension, or forgets his interest as a friend or enemy, as a rival or commentator. By this means, his sentiments are perverted; nor have the same beauties and blemishes the same influence upon him, as if he had imposed a proper violence on his imagination, and had forgotten himself for a moment. So far his taste evidently departs from the true standard; and of consequence loses all credit and authority.

It is well known, that in all questions, submitted to the understanding, prejudice is destructive of sound judgment, and perverts all operations of the intellectual faculties: It is no less contrary to good taste; nor has it less influence to corrupt our sentiment of beauty. It belongs to *good sense* to check its influence in both cases; and in this respect, as well as in many others, reason, if not an essential part of taste, is at least requisite to the operations of this latter faculty. In all the nobler productions of genius, there is a mutual relation and correspondence of parts; nor can either the beauties or blemishes be perceived by him, whose thought is not capacious enough to comprehend all those parts, and compare them with each other, in order to perceive the consistence and uniformity of the whole. Every work of art has also a certain end or purpose, for which it is calculated; and is to be deemed more or less perfect, as it is more or less fitted to attain this end. The object of eloquence is to persuade, of history to instruct, of poetry to please by means of the passions and the imagination. These ends we must carry constantly in our view, when we peruse any performance; and we must be able to judge how far the means employed are adapted to their respective purposes. Besides, every kind of composition, even the most poetical, is nothing but a chain of propositions and reasonings; not always, indeed, the justest and most exact, but still plausible and specious, however disguised by the colouring of the imagination. The persons introduced in tragedy and epic poetry, must be represented as reasoning, and thinking, and concluding, and acting, suitably to their character and circumstances; and without judgment, as well as taste and invention, a poet can never hope to succeed in so delicate an undertaking. Not to mention, that the same excellence of faculties which contributes to the improvement of reason, the same clearness of conception, the same exactness of distinction, the same vivacity of apprehension, are essential to the operations of true taste, and are its infallible concomitants. It seldom, or never happens, that a man of sense, who has experience in any art, cannot judge of its beauty; and it is no less rare to meet with a man who has a just taste without a sound understanding.

Thus, though the principles of taste be universal, and nearly, if not entirely the same in all men; yet few are qualified to give judgment on any work of art, or establish their own sentiment as the standard of beauty. The organs of internal sensation are seldom so perfect as to allow the general principles their full play, and produce a feeling correspondent to those principles. They either labour under some defect, or are vitiated by some disorder; and by that means, excite a sentiment, which may be pronounced erroneous. When the critic has no delicacy, he judges without any distinction, and is only affected by the grosser and more palpable qualities of the object: The finer touches pass unnoticed and disregarded. Where he is not aided by practice, his verdict is attended with confusion and hesitation. Where no comparison has been employed, the most frivolous beauties, such as rather merit the name of defects, are the object of his admiration. Where he lies under the influence of prejudice, all his natural sentiments are perverted. Where good sense is wanting, he is not qualified to discern the beauties of design and reasoning, which are the highest and most excellent. Under some or other of these imperfections, the generality of men labour; and hence a true judge in the finer arts is observed, even during the most polished ages, to be so rare a character: Strong sense, united to delicate sentiment, improved by practice, perfected by comparison, and cleared of all prejudice, can alone entitle critics to this valuable character; and the joint verdict of such, wherever they are to be found, is the true standard of taste and beauty.

But where are such critics to be found? By what marks are they to be known? How distinguish them from pretenders? These questions are embarrassing; and seem to throw us back into the same uncertainty, from which, during the course of this essay, we have endeavoured to extricate ourselves.

But if we consider the matter aright, these are questions of fact, not of sentiment. Whether any particular person be endowed with good sense and a delicate imagination, free from prejudice, may often be the subject of dispute, and be liable to great discussion and enquiry: But that such a character is valuable and estimable will be agreed in by all mankind. Where these doubts occur, men can do no more than in other disputable questions, which are submitted to the understanding. They must produce the best arguments, that their invention suggests to them; they must acknowledge a true and decisive standard to exist somewhere, to wit, real existence and matter of fact; and they must have indulgence to such as differ from them in their appeals to this standard. It is sufficient for our present purpose, if we have proved, that the taste of all individuals is not upon an equal footing, and that some men in general, however difficult to be particularly pitched upon, will be acknowledged by universal sentiment to have a preference above others.

But in reality the difficulty of finding, even in particulars, the standard of taste, is not so great as it is represented. Though in speculation, we may readily avow a certain criterion in science and deny it in sentiment, the matter is found in practice to be much more hard to ascertain in the former case than in the latter. Theories of abstract philosophy, systems of profound theology, have prevailed during one age: In a successive period, these have been universally exploded: Their absurdity has been detected: Other theories and systems have supplied their place, which again gave place to their successors: And nothing has been experienced more liable to the revolutions of chance and fashion than these pretended decisions of science. The case is not the same with the beauties of eloquence and poetry. Just expressions of passion and nature are sure, after a little time, to gain public applause, which they maintain for ever. Aristotle, and Plato, and Epicurus, and Descartes, may successively yield to each other: But Terence and Virgil maintain an universal, undisputed empire over the minds of men. The abstract philosophy of Cicero has lost its credit: The vehemence of his oratory is still the object of our admiration.

Though men of delicate taste be rare, they are easily to be distinguished in society, by the soundness of their understanding and the superiority of their faculties above the rest of mankind. The ascendant, which they acquire, gives a prevalence to that lively approbation, with which they receive any productions of genius, and renders it generally predominant. Many men, when left to themselves, have but a faint and dubious perception of beauty, who yet are capable of relishing any fine stroke, which is pointed out to them. Every convert to the admiration of the real poet or orator is the cause of some new conversion. And though prejudices may prevail for a time, they never unite in celebrating any rival to the true genius, but yield at last to the force of nature and just sentiment. Thus, though a civilized nation may easily be mistaken in the choice of their admired philosopher, they never have been found long to err, in their affection for a favourite epic or tragic author.

But notwithstanding all our endeavours to fix a standard of taste, and reconcile the discordant apprehensions of men, there still remain two sources of variation, which are not sufficient indeed to confound all the boundaries of beauty and deformity, but will often serve to produce a difference in the degrees of our approbation or blame. The one is the different humours of particular men; the other, the particular manners and opinions of our age and country. The general principles of taste are uniform in human nature: Where men vary in their judgments, some defect or perversion in the faculties may commonly be remarked; proceeding either from prejudice, from want of practice, or want of delicacy; and there is just reason for approving one taste, and condemning another. But where there is such a diversity in the internal frame or external situation as is entirely blameless on both sides, and leaves no room to give one the preference above the other; in that case a certain degree of diversity in judgment is unavoidable, and we seek in vain for a standard, by which we can reconcile the contrary sentiments.

A young man, whose passions are warm, will be more sensibly touched with amorous and tender images, than a man more advanced in years, who takes pleasure in wise, philosophical reflections concerning the conduct of life and moderation of the passions. At twenty, Ovid may be the favourite author; Horace at forty; and perhaps Tacitus at fifty. Vainly would we, in such cases, endeavour to enter into the sentiments of others, and divest ourselves of those propensities, which are natural to us. We choose our favourite author as we do our friend, from a conformity of humour and disposition. Mirth or passion, sentiment or reflection; whichever of these most predominates in our temper, it gives us a peculiar sympathy with the writer who resembles us.

One person is more pleased with the sublime; another with the tender; a third with raillery. One has a strong sensibility to blemishes, and is extremely studious of correctness: Another has a more lively feeling of beauties, and pardons twenty absurdities and defects for one elevated or pathetic stroke. The ear of this man is entirely turned towards conciseness and energy; that man is delighted with a copious, rich, and harmonious expression. Simplicity is affected by one; ornament by another. Comedy, tragedy, satire, odes, have each its partizans, who prefer that particular species of writing to all others. It is plainly an error in a critic, to confine his approbation to one species or style of writing, and condemn all the rest. But it is almost impossible not to feel a predilection for that which suits our particular turn and disposition. Such preferences are innocent and unavoidable, and can never reasonably be the object of dispute, because there is no standard, by which they can be decided.

For a like reason, we are more pleased, in the course of our reading, with pictures and characters, that resemble objects which are found in our own age or country, than with those which describe a different set of customs. It is not without some effort, that we reconcile ourselves to the simplicity of ancient manners, and behold princesses carrying water from the spring, and kings and heroes dressing their own victuals. We may allow in general, that the representation of such manners is no fault in the author, nor deformity in the piece; but we are not so sensibly touched with them. For this reason, comedy is not easily transferred from one age or nation to another. A Frenchman or Englishman is not pleased with the Andria of Terence, or Clitia of Machiavel; where the fine lady, upon whom all the play turns, never once appears to the spectators, but is always kept behind the scenes, suitably to the reserved humour of the ancient Greeks and modern Italians. A man of learning and reflection can make allowance for these peculiarities of manners; but a common audience can never divest themselves so far of their usual ideas and sentiments, as to relish pictures which no wise resemble them.

But here there occurs a reflection, which may, perhaps, be useful in examining the celebrated controversy concerning ancient and modern learning; where we often find the one side excusing any seeming absurdity in the ancients from the manners of the age, and the other refusing to admit this excuse, or at least, admitting it only as an apology for the author, not for the performance. In my opinion, the proper boundaries in this subject have seldom been fixed between the contending parties. Where any innocent peculiarities of manners are represented, such as those above mentioned, they ought certainly to be admitted; and a man, who is shocked with them, gives an evident proof of false delicacy and refinement. The poet's *monument more durable than brass,* must fall to the ground like common brick or clay, were men to make no allowance for the continual revolutions of manners and customs, and would admit of nothing but what was suitable to the prevailing fashion. Must we throw aside the pictures of our ancestors, because of their ruffs and fardingales? But where the ideas of morality and decency alter from one age to another, and where vicious manners are described, without being marked with the proper characters of blame and disapprobation; this must be allowed to disfigure the poem, and to be a real deformity. I cannot, nor is it proper I should, enter into such sentiments; and however I may excuse the poet, on account of the manners of his age, I never can relish the composition. The want of humanity and of decency, so conspicuous in the characters drawn by several of the ancient poets, even sometimes by Homer and the Greek tragedians, diminishes considerably the merit of their noble performances, and gives modern authors an advantage over them. We are not interested in the fortunes and sentiments of such rough heroes: We are displeased to find the limits of vice and virtue so much confounded: And whatever indulgence we may give to the writer on account of his prejudices, we cannot prevail on ourselves to enter into his sentiments, or bear an affection to characters, which we plainly discover to be blameable.

The case is not the same with moral principles, as with speculative opinions of any kind. These are in continual flux and revolution. The son embraces a different system from the father. Nay, there scarcely is any man, who can boast of great constancy and uniformity in this particular. Whatever speculative errors may be found in the polite writings of any age or country, they detract but little from the value of those compositions. There needs but a certain turn of thought or imagination to make us enter into all the opinions, which then prevailed, and relish the sentiments or conclusions derived from them. But a very violent effort is requisite to change our judgment of manners, and excite sentiments of approbation or blame, love or hatred, different from those to which the mind from long custom has been familiarized. And where a man is confident of the rectitude of that moral standard, by which he judges, he is justly jealous of it, and will not pervert the sentiments of his heart for a moment, in complaisance to any writer whatsoever.

Of all speculative errors, those, which regard religion, are the most excusable in compositions of genius; nor is it ever permitted to judge of the civility or wisdom of any people, or even of single persons, by the grossness or refinement of their theological principles. The same good sense, that directs men in the ordinary occurrences of life, is not hearkened to in religious matters, which are supposed to be placed altogether above the cognizance of human reason. On this account, all the absurdities of the pagan system of theology must be overlooked by every critic, who would pretend to form a just notion of ancient poetry; and our posterity, in their turn, must have the same indulgence to their forefathers. No religious principles can ever be imputed as a fault to any poet, while they remain merely principles, and take not such strong possession of his heart, as to lay him under the imputation of *bigotry* or *superstition*. Where that happens, they confound the sentiments of morality, and alter the natural boundaries of vice and virtue. They are therefore eternal blemishes, according to the principle abovementioned; nor are the prejudices and false opinions of the age sufficient to justify them.

It is essential to the Roman catholic religion to inspire a violent hatred of every other worship, and to represent all pagans, mahometans, and heretics as the objects of divine wrath and vengeance. Such sentiments, though they are in reality very blameable, are considered as virtues by the zealots of that communion, and are represented in their tragedies and epic poems as a kind of divine heroism. This bigotry has disfigured two very fine tragedies of the French theatre, Polieucte and Athalia; where an intemperate zeal for particular modes of worship is set off with all the pomp imaginable, and forms the predominant character of the heroes. 'What is this,' says the sublime Joad to Josabet, finding her in discourse with Mathan, the priest of Baal, 'Does the daughter of David speak to this traitor? Are you not afraid, lest the earth should open and pour forth flames to devour you both? Or lest these holy walls should fall and crush you together? What is his purpose? Why comes that enemy of God hither to poison the air, which we breathe, with his horrid presence?' Such sentiments are received with great applause on the theatre of Paris; but at London the spectators would be full as much pleased to hear Achilles tell Agamemnon, that he was a dog in his forehead, and a deer in his heart, or Jupiter threaten Juno with a sound drubbing, if she will not be quiet.

Religious principles are also a blemish in any polite composition, when they rise up to superstition, and intrude themselves into every sentiment, however remote from any connection with religion. It is no excuse for the poet, that the customs of his country had burthened life with so many religious ceremonies and observances, that no part of it was exempt from that yoke.

It must for ever be ridiculous in Petrarch to compare his mistress, Laura, to Jesus Christ. Nor is it less ridiculous in that agreeable libertine, Boccace, very seriously to give thanks to God Almighty and the ladies, for their assistance in defending him against his enemies.

Source: David Hume, 'Of the Standard of Taste', in *Essays, Moral, Political and Literary*, ed. Eugene F. Miller, Indianapolis 1987, Essay 23, pp. 226–49

TWELVE

THOMAS REID
Beauty and Common Sense

Reid's chapter is a classic statement of the common sense criticism of Hume's doctrine in 'Of the standard of taste'. According to Hume, as we saw in excerpt 11, 'beauty and deformity . . . belong entirely to the sentiment', and Reid sets himself to show that this is a false doctrine, for he believes that Hume makes it impossible for himself to give an adequate account of the normativity or objectivity of aesthetic judgments.

There are distinctions to be made in seeking to analyse an aesthetic judgment. When I perceive or conceive something that I judge to be beautiful, I have an agreeable emotion – the object pleases me. In being pleased I am responding to something in the object, whether or not I can say precisely what it is about the object that causes my pleasure. I can however say at least that I am responding to the beauty, fineness, excellence, or elegance, of the object, or some other aesthetically agreeable quality of it. What is the relation between on the one hand the sensation of pleasure, and on the other the aesthetically pleasing quality?

At this point common sense asserts itself, and does so in a way that informs many of Reid's philosophical moves. He sees in the philosophy of Hume, and his great predecessors George Berkeley, John Locke and René Descartes, a tendency to internalise things that are not truly located in our minds at all, but are in the world outside. And Reid criticises Hume for internalising beauty, for identifying it with a sentiment, a feeling, when in fact it is the cause of the sentiment and not identical with it. Hume held, as did many others, that many qualities that we ascribe to external objects are really in us, existing as sensations. Such a quality considered as a sensation in me, and not as something inherent in the external object, is said to be a 'secondary quality', as opposed to whatever it is in the external object that produces that sensation.

Hume treats aesthetic qualities as secondary qualities in the sense that he believes them really to be sensations in us and not qualities in things. Reid's counter-thesis can be stated as follows: Aesthetic qualities are not secondary qualities; they actually do inhere in the things to which they are ascribed by us when we say of something that it is beautiful, and of something else that it is elegant, and so on. Reid argues that there is ample linguistic evidence for his position. For when we say that a painting is beautiful, it is plain that the term 'beautiful' is being predicated of the painting and not of ourselves. Reid concludes: 'No reason can be given why all mankind should express themselves thus, but that they believe what they say. It is therefore contrary to the universal sense of mankind, expressed by their language, that beauty is not really in the object, but is merely a feeling in the person who is said to perceive it. Philosophers should be very cautious in opposing the common sense of mankind', adds Reid, 'for when they do, they rarely miss going wrong'.

Of course it is true, and philosophically important, that we cannot judge something beautiful without taking pleasure in it. The beautiful, so far as it is beautiful, is enjoyed by us. It is part of the original constitution of our nature that we respond in this way to what we judge beautiful. But the judgment is one thing and the pleasure another thing entirely. Reid is therefore anti-sentimentalist.

A.B.

Of Taste

CHAPTER I *Of Taste in General*

That power of the mind by which we are capable of discerning and relishing the beauties of Nature, and whatever is excellent in the fine arts, is called *taste*.

The external sense of taste, by which we distinguish and relish the various kinds of food, has given occasion to a metaphorical application of its name to this internal power of the mind, by which we perceive what is beautiful and what is deformed or defective in the various objects that we contemplate.

Like the taste of the palate, it relishes some things, is disgusted with others; with regard to many, is indifferent or dubious; and is considerably influenced by habit, by associations, and by opinion. These obvious analogies between external and internal taste, have led men, in all ages, and in all or most polished languages, to give the name of the external sense to this power of discerning what is beautiful with pleasure, and what is ugly and faulty in its kind with disgust.

In treating of this as an intellectual power of the mind, I intend only to make some observations, first on its nature, and then on its objects.

1. In the external sense of taste, we are led by reason and reflection to distinguish between the agreeable sensation we feel, and the quality in the object which occasions it. Both have the same name, and on that account are apt to be confounded by the vulgar, and even by philosophers. The sensation I feel when I taste any sapid body is in my mind; but there is a real quality in the body which is the cause of this sensation. These two things have the same name in language, not from any similitude in their nature, but because the one is the sign of the other, and because there is little occasion in common life to distinguish them.

This was fully explained in treating of the secondary qualities of bodies. The reason of taking notice of it now is, that the internal power of taste bears a great analogy in this respect to the external.

When a beautiful object is before us, we may distinguish the agreeable emotion it produces in us, from the quality of the object which causes that emotion. When I hear an air in music that pleases me, I say, it is fine, it is excellent. This excellence is not in me; it is in the music. But the pleasure it gives is not in the music; it is in me. Perhaps I cannot say what it is in the tune that pleases my ear, as I cannot say what it is in a sapid body that pleases my palate; but there is a quality in the sapid body which pleases my palate, and I call it a delicious taste; and there is a quality in the tune that pleases my taste, and I call it a fine or an excellent air.

This ought the rather to be observed, because it is become a fashion among modern philosophers, to resolve all our perceptions into mere feelings or sensations in the person that perceives, without anything corresponding to those feelings in the external object. According to those philosophers, there is no heat in the fire, no taste in a sapid body; the taste and the heat being only in the person that feels them. In like manner, there is no beauty in any object whatsoever; it is only a sensation or feeling in the person that perceives it.

The language and the common sense of mankind contradict this theory. Even those who hold it, find themselves obliged to use a language that contradicts it. I had occasion to shew, that there is no solid foundation for it when applied to the secondary qualities of body; and the same arguments shew equally, that it has no solid foundation when applied to the beauty of objects, or to any of those qualities that are perceived by a good taste.

But, though some of the qualities that please a good taste resemble the secondary qualities of body, and therefore may be called occult qualities, as we only feel their effect, and have no more knowledge of the cause, but that it is something which is adapted by nature to produce that effect – this is not always the case.

Our judgment of beauty is in many cases more enlightened. A work of art may appear beautiful to the most ignorant, even to a child. It pleases, but he knows not why. To one who understands it perfectly, and perceives how every part is fitted with exact judgment to its end, the beauty is not mysterious; it is perfectly comprehended; and he knows wherein it consists, as well as how it affects him.

2. We may observe, that, though all the tastes we perceive by the palate are either agreeable or disagreeable, or indifferent; yet, among those that are agreeable, there is great diversity, not in degree only, but in kind. And, as we have not generical names for all the different kinds of taste, we distinguish them by the bodies in which they are found.

In like manner, all the objects of our internal taste are either beautiful, or disagreeable, or indifferent; yet of beauty there is a great diversity, not only of degree, but of kind. The beauty of a demonstration, the beauty of a poem, the beauty of a palace, the beauty of a piece of music, the beauty of a fine woman, and many more that might be named, are different kinds of beauty; and we have no names to distinguish them but the names of the different objects to which they belong.

As there is such diversity in the kinds of beauty as well as in the degrees, we need not think it strange that philosophers have gone into different systems in analysing it, and enumerating its simple ingredients. They have made many just observations on the subject; but, from the love of simplicity, have reduced it to fewer principles than the nature of the thing will permit, having had in their eye some particular kinds of beauty, while they overlooked others.

There are moral beauties as well as natural; beauties in the objects of sense, and in intellectual objects; in the works of men, and in the works of God; in things inanimate, in brute animals, and in rational beings; in the constitution of the body of man, and in the constitution of his mind. There is no real excellence which has not its beauty to a discerning eye, when placed in a proper point of view; and it is as difficult to enumerate the ingredients of beauty as the ingredients of real excellence.

3. The taste of the palate may be accounted most just and perfect, when we relish the things that are fit for the nourishment of the body, and are disgusted with things of a contrary nature. The manifest intention of nature in giving us this sense, is, that we may discern what it is fit for us to eat and to drink, and what it is not. Brute animals are directed in the choice of their food merely by their taste. Led by this guide, they choose the food that nature intended for them, and seldom make mistakes, unless they be pinched by hunger, or deceived by artificial compositions. In infants likewise the taste is commonly sound and uncorrupted, and of the simple productions of nature they relish the things that are most wholesome.

In like manner, our internal taste ought to be accounted most just and perfect, when we are pleased with things that are most excellent in their kind, and displeased with the contrary. The intention of nature is no less evident in this internal taste than in the external. Every excellence has a real beauty and charm that makes it an agreeable object to those who have the faculty of discerning its beauty; and this faculty is what we call a good taste.

A man who, by any disorder in his mental powers, or by bad habits, has contracted a relish for what has no real excellence, or what is deformed and defective, has a depraved taste, like one who finds a more agreeable relish in ashes or cinders than in the most wholesome food. As we must acknowledge the taste of the palate to be depraved in this case, there is the same reason to think the taste of the mind depraved in the other.

There is therefore a just and rational taste, and there is a depraved and corrupted taste. For it is too evident, that, by bad education, bad habits, and wrong associations, men may acquire a relish for nastiness, for rudeness, and ill-breeding, and for many other deformities. To say that such a taste is not vitiated, is no less absurd than to say, that the sickly girl who delights in eating charcoal and tobacco-pipes, has as just and natural a taste as when she is in perfect health.

4. The force of custom, of fancy, and of casual associations, is very great both upon the external and internal taste. An Eskimaux can regale himself with a draught of whale-oil, and a Canadian can feast upon a dog. A Kamschatkadale lives upon putrid fish, and is sometimes reduced to eat the bark of trees. The taste of rum, or of green tea, is at first as nauseous as that of ipecacuan, to some persons, who may be brought by use to relish what they once found so disagreeable.

When we see such varieties in the taste of the palate produced by custom and associations, and some, perhaps, by constitution, we may be the less surprised that the same causes should produce like varieties in the taste of beauty; that the African should esteem thick lips and a flat nose; that other nations should draw out their ears, till they hang over their shoulders; that in one nation ladies should paint their faces, and in another should make them shine with grease.

5. Those who conceive that there is no standard in nature by which taste may be regulated, and that the common proverb, 'That there ought to be no dispute about taste,' is to be taken in the utmost latitude, go upon slender and insufficient ground. The same arguments might be used with equal force against any standard of truth.

Whole nations by the force of prejudice are brought to believe the grossest absurdities; and why should it be thought that the taste is less capable of being perverted than the judgment? It must indeed be acknowledged, that men differ more in the faculty of taste than in what we commonly call judgment; and therefore it may be expected that they should be more liable to have their taste corrupted in matters of beauty and deformity, than their judgment in matters of truth and error.

If we make due allowance for this, we shall see that it is as easy to account for the variety of tastes, though there be in nature a standard of true beauty, and consequently of good taste, as it is to account for the variety and contrariety of opinions, though there be in nature a standard of truth, and, consequently, of right judgment.

6. Nay, if we speak accurately and strictly, we shall find that, in every operation of taste, there is judgment implied.

When a man pronounces a poem or a palace to be beautiful, he affirms something of that poem or that palace; and every affirmation or denial expresses judgment. For we cannot better define judgment, than by saying that it is an affirmation or denial of one thing concerning another. I had occasion to shew, when treating of judgment, that it is implied in every perception of our external senses. There is an immediate conviction and belief of the existence of the quality perceived, whether it be colour, or sound, or figure; and the same thing holds in the perception of beauty or deformity.

If it be said that the perception of beauty is merely a feeling in the mind that perceives, without any belief of excellence in the object, the necessary consequence of this opinion is, that when I say Virgil's 'Georgics' is a beautiful poem, I mean not to say anything of the poem, but only something concerning myself and my feelings. Why should I use a language that expresses the contrary of what I mean?

My language, according to the necessary rules of construction, can bear no other meaning but this, that there is something in the poem, and not in me, which I call beauty. Even those who hold beauty to be merely a feeling in the person that perceives it, find themselves under a necessity of expressing themselves as if beauty were solely a quality of the object, and not of the percipient.

No reason can be given why all mankind should express themselves thus, but that they believe what they say. It is therefore contrary to the universal sense of mankind, expressed by their language, that beauty is not really in the object, but is merely a feeling in the person who is said to perceive it. Philosophers should be very cautious in opposing the common sense of mankind; for, when they do, they rarely miss going wrong.

Our judgment of beauty is not indeed a dry and unaffecting judgment, like that of a mathematical or metaphysical truth. By the constitution of our nature, it is accompanied with an agreeable feeling or emotion, for which we have no other name but the sense of beauty. This sense of beauty, like the perceptions of our other senses, implies not only a feeling, but an opinion of some quality in the object which occasions that feeling.

In objects that please the taste, we always judge that there is some real excellence, some superiority to those that do not please. In some cases, that superior excellence is distinctly perceived, and can be pointed out; in other cases, we have only a general notion of some excellence which we cannot describe. Beauties of the former kind may be compared to the primary qualities perceived by the external senses; those of the latter kind, to the secondary.

7. Beauty or deformity in an object, results from its nature or structure. To perceive the beauty, therefore, we must perceive the nature or structure from which it results. In this the internal sense differs from the external. Our external senses may discover qualities which do not depend upon any antecedent perception. Thus, I can hear the sound of a bell, though I never perceived anything else belonging to it. But it is impossible to perceive the beauty of an object without perceiving the object, or, at least, conceiving it. On this account, Dr Hutcheson called the senses of beauty and harmony reflex or secondary senses; because the beauty cannot be perceived unless the object be perceived by some other power of the mind. Thus, the sense of harmony and melody in sounds supposes the external sense of hearing, and is a kind of secondary to it. A man born deaf may be a good judge of beauties of another kind, but can have no notion of melody or harmony. The like may be said of beauties in colouring and in figure, which can never be perceived without the senses by which colour and figure are perceived.

Source: Thomas Reid, *Essays on the Intellectual Powers*, Essay 8, ch. 1, in *The Works of Thomas Reid*, ed. William Hamilton, 6th edn, Edinburgh 1863, vol. 1, pp. 490–2

THIRTEEN

THOMAS REID
The Craft of Painting

Reid distinguishes between a visible object and its visible appearance, that is, the appearance that it makes to an observer. Thus, for example, there is a visible object, say, a round coin, and there is its visible appearance, say, its appearance as an ellipse to an observer who is observing the coin from a given angle. The visible appearance is, for Reid, a sign which by experience we learn to interpret, so that with the aid of the other senses, particularly the sense of touch, we come to read the visible appearance as the appearance of a solid object with given physical properties and lying at a given distance from us. Thus an object appears as an ellipse, but by experience we know that the object is a round coin which, of course, from a given angle, will appear elliptical. There are many things that we know about the objects around us by inferring from appearances, that is, by interpreting what we see. Reid argues that the art of painting is in part a skill at copying what we see and not what we know; a good painter places on canvas a copy not of the object but of its visible appearance. It is then for the spectator to interpret correctly the marks on the two-dimensional canvas. In the following brief excerpts Reid attends to a major obstacle to the acquisition of this skill.

A.B.

Visible Appearance and Painting

In this section we must speak of things which are never made the object of reflection, though almost every moment presented to the mind. Nature intended them only for signs; and in the whole course of life they are put to no other use. The mind has acquired a confirmed and inveterate habit of inattention to them; for they no sooner appear, than quick as lightning the thing signified succeeds, and engrosses all our regard. They have no name in language; and, although we are conscious of them when they pass through the mind, yet their passage is so quick and so familiar, that it is absolutely unheeded; nor do they leave any footsteps of themselves, either in the memory or imagination. That this is the case with regard to the sensations of touch, hath been shewn in the last chapter; and it holds no less with regard to the visible appearances of objects.

I cannot therefore entertain the hope of being intelligible to those readers who have not, by pains and practice, acquired the habit of distinguishing the appearance of objects to the eye, from the judgment which we form by sight of their colour, distance, magnitude, and figure. The only profession in life wherein it is necessary to make this distinction, is that of painting. The painter hath occasion for an abstraction, with regard to visible objects, somewhat similar to that which we here require: and this indeed is the most difficult part of his art. For it is evident, that, if he could fix in his imagination the visible appearance of objects, without confounding it with the things signified by that appearance, it would be as easy for him to paint from the life, and to give every figure its proper shading and relief, and its perspective proportions, as it is to paint from a copy. Perspective, shading, giving relief, and colouring, are nothing else but copying the appearance which things make to the eye. We may therefore borrow some light on the subject of visible appearance from this art.

Let one look upon any familiar object, such as a book, at different distances and in different positions: is he not able to affirm, upon the testimony of his sight, that it is the same book, the same object, whether seen at the distance of one foot or of ten, whether in one position or another; that the colour is the same, the dimensions the same, and the figure the same, as far as the eye can judge? This surely must be acknowledged. The same individual object is presented to the mind, only placed at different distances and in different positions. Let me ask, in the next place, Whether this object has the same appearance to the eye in these different distances? Infallibly it hath not. For,

First, However certain our judgment may be that the colour is the same, it is as certain that it hath not the same appearance at different distances. There is a certain degradation of the colour, and a certain confusion and indistinctness of the minute parts, which is the natural consequence of the removal of the object to a greater distance. Those that are not painters, or critics in painting, overlook this; and cannot easily be persuaded, that the colour of the same object hath a different appearance at the distance of one foot and of ten, in the shade and in the light. But the masters in painting know how, by the degradation of the colour and the confusion of the minute parts, figures which are upon the same canvass, and at the same distance from the eye, may be made to represent objects which are at the most unequal distances. They know how to make the objects appear to be of the same colour, by making their pictures really of different colours, according to their distances or shades.

Secondly, Every one who is acquainted with the rules of perspective, knows that the appearance of the figure of the book must vary in every different position: yet if you ask a man that has no notion of perspective, whether the figure of it does not appear to his eye to be the same in all its different positions? he can with a good conscience affirm that it does. He hath learned to make allowance for the variety of visible figure arising from the difference of position, and to draw the proper conclusions from it. But he draws these conclusions so readily and habitually, as to lose sight of the premises: and therefore where he hath made the same conclusion, he conceives the visible appearance must have been the same.

Thirdly, Let us consider the apparent magnitude or dimensions of the book. Whether I view it at the distance of one foot or of ten feet, it seems to be about seven inches long, five broad, and one thick. I can judge of these dimensions very nearly by the eye, and I judge them to be the same at both distances. But yet it is certain, that, at the distance of one foot, its visible length and breadth is about ten times as great as at the distance of ten feet; and consequently its surface is about a hundred times as great. This great change of apparent magnitude is altogether overlooked, and every man is apt to imagine, that it appears to the eye of the same size at both distances. Further, when I look at the book, it seems plainly to have three dimensions of length, breadth, and thickness: but it is certain that the visible appearance hath no more than two, and can be exactly represented upon a canvass which hath only length and breadth.

In the last place, does not every man, by sight, perceive the distance of the book from his eye? Can he not affirm with certainty, that in one case it is not above one foot distant, that in another it is ten? Nevertheless, it appears certain, that distance from the eye is no immediate object of sight. There are certain things in the visible appearance, which are signs of distance from the eye, and from which, as we shall afterwards shew, we learn by experience to judge of that distance within certain limits; but it seems beyond doubt, that a man born blind, and suddenly made to see, could form no judgment at first of the distance of the objects which he saw. The young man couched by Cheselden thought, at first, that everything he saw touched his eye, and learned only by experience to judge of the distance of visible objects.

I have entered into this long detail, in order to shew that the visible appearance of an object is extremely different from the notion of it which experience teaches us to form by sight; and to enable the reader to attend to the visible appearance of colour, figure, and extension, in visible things, which is no common object of thought, but must be carefully attended to by those who would enter into the philosophy of this sense, or would comprehend what shall be said upon it. To a man newly made to see, the visible appearance of objects would be the same as to us; but he would see nothing at all of their real dimensions, as we do. He could form no conjecture, by means of his sight only, how many inches or feet they were in length, breadth, or thickness. He could perceive little or nothing of their real figure; nor could he discern that this was a cube, that a sphere; that this was a cone, and that a cylinder. His eye could not inform him that this object was near, and that more remote. The habit of a man or of a woman, which appeared to us of one uniform colour, variously folded and shaded, would present to his eye neither fold or shade, but variety of colour. In a word, his eyes, though ever so perfect, would at first give him almost no information of things without him. They would indeed present the same appearances to him as they do to us, and speak the same language; but to him it is an unknown language; and, therefore, he would attend only to the signs, without knowing the signification of them, whereas to us it is a language perfectly familiar; and, therefore, we take no notice of the signs, but attend only to the thing signified by them.

. . .

Visible figure is never presented to the eye but in conjunction with colour: and, although there be no connection between them from the nature of the things, yet, having so invariably kept company together, we are hardly able to disjoin them even in our imagination. What mightily increases this difficulty is, that we have never been accustomed to make visible figure an object of thought. It is only used as a sign, and, having served this purpose, passes away, without leaving a trace behind. The drawer or designer, whose business it is to hunt this fugitive form, and to take a copy of it, finds how difficult his task is, after many years' labour and practice. Happy! if at last he can acquire the art of arresting it in his imagination, until he can delineate it. For then it is evident that he must be able to draw as accurately from the life as from a copy. But how few of the professed masters of designing are ever able to arrive at this degree of perfection! It is no wonder, then, that we should find so great difficulty in conceiving this form apart from its constant associate, when it is so difficult to conceive it at all.

. . .

The difficulty of attending to the visible figure of bodies, and making it an object of thought, appears so similar to that which we find in attending to our sensations, that both have probably like causes. Nature intended the visible figure as a sign of the tangible figure and situation of bodies, and hath taught us, by a kind of instinct, to put it always to this use. Hence it happens, that the mind passes over it with a rapid motion, to attend to the things signified by it. It is as unnatural to the mind to stop at the visible figure, and attend to it, as it is to a spherical body to stop upon an inclined plane. There is an inward principle, which constantly carries it forward, and which cannot be overcome but by a contrary force.

There are other external things which nature intended for signs; and we find this common to them all, that the mind is disposed to overlook them, and to attend only to the things signified by them. Thus there are certain modifications of the human face, which are natural signs of the present disposition of the mind. Every man understands the meaning of these signs, but not one of a hundred ever attended to the signs themselves, or knows anything about them. Hence you may find many an excellent practical physiognomist who knows nothing of the proportions of a face, nor can delineate or describe the expression of any one passion.

An excellent painter or statuary can tell, not only what are the proportions of a good face, but what changes every passion makes in it. This, however, is one of the chief mysteries of his art, to the acquisition of which infinite labour and attention, as well as a happy genius, are required; but when he puts his art in practice, and happily expresses a passion by its proper signs, every one understands the meaning of these signs, without art, and without reflection.

What has been said of painting, might easily be applied to all the fine arts. The difficulty in them all consists in knowing and attending to those natural signs whereof every man understands the meaning.

We pass from the sign to the thing signified, with ease, and by natural impulse; but to go backward from the thing signified to the sign, is a work of labour and difficulty. Visible figure, therefore, being intended by nature to be a sign, we pass on immediately to the thing signified, and cannot easily return to give any attention to the sign.

.   .   .

In order to direct both eyes to an object, the optic axes must have a greater or less inclination, according as the object is nearer or more distant. And, although we are not conscious of this inclination, yet we are conscious of the effort employed in it. By this means we perceive small distances more accurately than we could do by the conformation of the eye only. And, therefore, we find, that those who have lost the sight of one eye are apt, even within arm's-length, to make mistakes in the distance of objects, which are easily avoided by those who see with both eyes. Such mistakes are often discovered in snuffing a candle, in threading a needle, or in filling a tea-cup.

When a picture is seen with both eyes, and at no great distance, the representation appears not so natural as when it is seen only with one. The intention of painting being to deceive the eye, and to make things appear at different distances which in reality are upon the same piece of canvass, this deception is not so easily put upon both eyes as upon one; because we perceive the distance of visible objects more exactly and determinately with two eyes than with one. If the shading and relief be executed in the best manner, the picture may have almost the same appearance to one eye as the objects themselves would have; but it cannot have the same appearance to both. This is not the fault of the artist, but an unavoidable imperfection in the art. And it is owing to what we just now observed, that the perception we have of the distance of objects by one eye is more uncertain, and more liable to deception, than that which we have by both.

The great impediment, and I think the only invincible impediment, to that agreeable deception of the eye which the painter aims at, is the perception which we have of the distance of visible objects from the eye, partly by means of the conformation of the eye, but chiefly by means of the inclination of the optic axes. If this perception could be removed, I see no reason why a picture might not be made so perfect as to deceive the eye in reality, and to be mistaken for the original object. Therefore, in order to judge of the merit of a picture, we ought, as much as possible, to exclude these two means of perceiving the distance of the several parts of it.

In order to remove this perception of distance, the connoisseurs in painting use a method which is very proper. They look at the picture with one eye, through a tube which excludes the view of all other objects. By this method, the principal mean whereby we perceive the distance of the object – to wit, the inclination of the optic axes – is entirely excluded. I would humbly propose, as an improvement of his method of viewing pictures, that the aperture of the tube next to the eye should be very small. If it is as small as a pin-hole, so much the better, providing there be light enough to see the picture clearly. The reason of this proposal is, that, when we look at an object through a small aperture, it will be seen distinctly, whether the conformation of the eye be adapted to its distance or not; and we have no mean left to judge of the distance, but the light and colouring, which are in the painter's power. If, therefore, the artist performs his part properly, the picture will by this method affect the eye in the same manner that the object represented would do; which is the perfection of this art.

Although this second mean of perceiving the distance of visible objects be more determinate and exact than the first, yet it hath its limits, beyond which it can be of no use. For when the optic axes directed to an object are so nearly parallel that, in directing them to an object yet more distant, we are not conscious of any new effort, nor have any different sensation, there our perception of distance stops; and, as all more distant objects affect the eye in the same manner, we perceive them to be at the same distance. This is the reason why the sun, moon, planets, and fixed stars, when seen not near the horizon, appear to be all at the same distance, as if they touched the concave surface of a great sphere. The surface of this celestial sphere is at that distance beyond which all objects affect the eye in the same manner. Why this celestial vault appears more distant towards the horizon, than towards the zenith, will afterwards appear.

The colours of objects, according as they are more distant, become more faint and languid, and are tinged more with the azure of the intervening atmosphere: to this we may add, that their minute parts become more indistinct, and their outline less accurately defined. It is by these means chiefly, that painters can represent objects at very different distances, upon the same canvass. And the diminution of the magnitude of an object would not have the effect of making it appear to be at a great distance, without this degradation of colour, and indistinctness of the outline, and of the minute parts. If a painter should make a human figure ten times less than other human figures that are in the same piece, having the colours as bright, and the outline and minute parts as accurately defined, it would not have the appearance of a man at a great distance, but of a pigmy or Lilliputian.

When an object hath a known variety of colours, its distance is more clearly indicated by the gradual dilution of the colours into one another, than when it is of one uniform colour. In the steeple which stands before me at a small distance, the joinings of the stones are clearly perceptible; the grey colour of the stone, and the white cement are distinctly limited: when I see it at a greater distance, the joinings of the stones are less distinct, and the colours of the stone and of the cement begin to dilute into one another: at a distance still greater, the joinings disappear altogether, and the variety of colour vanishes.

In an apple-tree which stands at the distance of about twelve feet, covered with flowers, I can perceive the figure and the colour of the leaves and petals; pieces of branches, some larger, others smaller, peeping through the intervals of the leaves – some of them enlightened by the sun's rays, others shaded; and some openings of the sky are perceived through the whole. When I gradually remove from this tree, the appearance, even as to colour, changes every minute. First, the smaller parts, then the larger, are gradually confounded and mixed. The colours of leaves, petals, branches, and sky, are gradually diluted into each other, and the colour of the whole becomes more and more uniform. This change of appearance, corresponding to the several distances, marks the distance more exactly than if the whole object had been of one colour.

Dr Smith, in his 'Optics,' gives us a very curious observation made by Bishop Berkeley, in his travels through Italy and Sicily. He observed, That, in those countries, cities and palaces seen at a great distance appeared nearer to him by several miles than they really were: and he very judiciously imputed it to this cause, That the purity of the Italian and Sicilian air, gave to very distant objects that degree of brightness and distinctness which, in the grosser air of his own country, was to be seen only in those that are near. The purity of the Italian air hath been assigned as the reason why the Italian painters commonly give a more lively colour to the sky than the Flemish. Ought they not, for the same reason, to give less degradation of the colours, and less indistinctness of the minute parts, in the representation of very distant objects?

It is very certain that, as in air uncommonly pure, we are apt to think visible objects nearer and less than they really are, so, in air uncommonly foggy, we are apt to think them more distant and larger than the truth. Walking by the sea-side in a thick fog, I see an object which seems to me to be a man on horseback, and at the distance of about half a mile. My companion, who has better eyes, or is more accustomed to see such objects in such circumstances, assures me that it is a sea-gull, and not a man on horseback. Upon a second view, I immediately assent to his opinion; and now it appears to me to be a sea-gull, and at the distance only of seventy or eighty yards. The mistake made on this occasion, and the correction of it, are both so sudden, that we are at a loss whether to call them by the name of *judgment*, or by that of *simple perception*.

It is not worth while to dispute about names; but it is evident that my belief, both first and last, was produced rather by signs than by arguments, and that the mind proceeded to the conclusion in both cases by habit, and not by ratiocination. And the process of the mind seems to have been this – First, Not knowing, or not minding, the effect of a foggy air on the visible appearance of objects, the object seems to me to have that degradation of colour, and that indistinctness of the outline, which objects have at the distance of half a mile; therefore, from the visible appearance as a sign, I immediately proceed to the belief that the object is half a mile distant. Then, this distance, together with the visible magnitude, signify to me the real magnitude, which, supposing the distance to be half a mile, must be equal to that of a man on horseback; and the figure, considering the indistinctness of the outline, agrees with that of a man on horseback. Thus the deception is brought about. But when I am assured that it is a sea-gull, the real magnitude of a sea-gull, together with the visible magnitude presented to the eye, immediately suggests the distance, which, in this case, cannot be above seventy or eighty yards: the indistinctness of the figure likewise suggests the fogginess of the air as its cause; and now the whole chain of signs, and things signified, seems stronger and better connected than it was before; the half mile vanishes to eighty yards; the man on horseback dwindles to a sea-gull; I get a new perception, and wonder how I got the former, or what is become of it; for it is now so entirely gone, that I cannot recover it.

. . .

The original appearance which the colour of an object makes to the eye, is a sensation for which we have no name, because it is used merely as a sign, and is never made an object of attention in common life: but this appearance, according to the different circumstances, signifies various things. If a piece of cloth, of one uniform colour, is laid so that part of it is in the sun, and part in the shade, the appearance of colour, in these different parts, is very different: yet we perceive the colour to be the same; we interpret the variety of appearance as a sign of light and shade, and not as a sign of real difference in colour. But, if the eye could be so far deceived as not to perceive the difference of light in the two parts of the cloth, we should, in that case, interpret the variety of appearance to signify a variety of colour in the parts of the cloth.

Again, if we suppose a piece of cloth placed as before, but having the shaded part so much brighter in the colour that it gives the same appearance to the eye as the more enlightened part, the sameness of appearance will here be interpreted to signify a variety of colour, because we shall make allowance for the effect of light and shade.

When the real colour of an object is known, the appearance of it indicates, in some circumstances, the degree of light or shade; in others, the colour of the circumambient bodies, whose rays are reflected by it; and, in other circumstances, it indicates the distance or proximity of the object – as was observed in the last section; and by means of these, many other things are suggested to the mind. Thus, an unusual appearance in the colour of familiar objects may be the diagnostic of a disease in the spectator. The appearance of things in my room may indicate sunshine or cloudy weather, the earth covered with snow or blackened with rain. It hath been observed, that the colour of the sky, in a piece of painting, may indicate the country of the painter, because the Italian sky is really of a different colour from the Flemish.

Source: Thomas Reid, *An Inquiry into the Human Mind on the Principles of Common Sense*, ch. 6, in *The Works of Thomas Reid*, ed. William Hamilton, Edinburgh 1863, vol. 1, selected passages

PART V
RELIGION

FOURTEEN

ADAM SMITH
The Rules of Morality and the Laws of God

There are several ways in which religion and morality are linked. One is in respect of motivation to act as morality requires, and it is chiefly this link that Smith explores in the following excerpt. The context of his discussion is his explanation of the existence of moral rules, an explanation which runs counter to the common position that moral rules are innate. On Smith's account they are developed by us in response to our capacity to deceive ourselves regarding the merit or demerit of our actions. In order to determine the merit or otherwise of an action we propose to perform, or have already performed, we imagine ourselves into the shoes of an impartial spectator, and ask ourselves what his judgment of the action would be. This imaginative experiment has the advantage of permitting us to transcend the distorting prism of our own passions. Smith describes our capacity for self-deceit as a 'fatal weakness of mankind' and claims that it is the source of half the disorders of human life. He adds: 'If we saw ourselves in the light in which others see us, or in which they would see us if they knew all, a reformation would generally be unavoidable. We could not otherwise endure the sight.' The resonances with Robert Burns, who was familiar with *The Theory of Moral Sentiments*, are unmistakable: 'O wad some Pow'r the giftie gie us / tae see oursels as others see us!' (in 'To a louse').

We are, of course, aware of the danger of self-deception, and the tactic we employ to circumvent it is to construct rules of conduct which declare what it is right or fitting to do, or not to do. The rules, founded on each person's observation of what is judged meritorious or otherwise, proper or otherwise, act as a corrective to the misrepresentations forced on him by his passions. And as Smith affirms, in language we now strongly associate with Immanuel Kant: 'that reverence for the rule which past

experience has impressed upon him, checks the impetuosity
of his passion . . . he cannot throw off altogether the awe
and respect with which he has been accustomed to regard
it'. It should be noted however that, contrary to Kantian
doctrine, Smith holds that in the first instance we do not
judge things to be right or wrong in the light of our moral
rules, but on the contrary we construct our moral rules in
the light of our judgments of what is right or wrong.

A question about motivation naturally arises: Why obey
the rules? Smith's chief answer is that we form a respect
for them, a respect which we also call a sense of duty, and
it is this respect for them that motivates us. That these are
the rules that have been derived from our experience in the
way just described is, for many people most of the time,
quite enough to prompt obedience. Thus for example even
if a person does not feel grateful for help graciously given,
he might, without being in any way hypocritical, act as
though he does feel grateful, and he will act in this way
because he respects the rule regarding gratitude.

For Smith, however, this is not the end of the story, for
it is 'first impressed by nature, and afterwards confirmed by
reasoning and philosophy' that these same rules are the laws
of God. And this fact about them enhances our reverence
for them, and increases the probability of our obedience.

The following excerpt is a key passage for an appreciation
of Smith's theodicy, his doctrine that the universe is
governed by a just God. Smith holds that it is part of
the divinely ordained plan for the universe that we humans
be happy. He also holds that this fact about the plan can
be deduced, first, from an 'abstract consideration of his
infinite perfections', by which Smith may have in mind
a version of the so-called 'ontological argument', that is,
the argument by which God's existence and nature are
established on the basis of our concept of God as possessor
of all the perfections. Secondly, the fact that our happiness
is part of the divinely ordained plan can be determined by
'the examination of the works of Nature'. Thus Smith
commends natural theology as leading from a scientific
investigation of nature to true conclusions concerning the
existence and attributes of God.

The passage in which Smith notes the success of natural
theology is of particular interest in light of the fact that
David Hume's *Dialogues concerning Natural Religion*, the
manuscript of which was, on Hume's death, placed in

Smith's care, contains a powerful attack on natural theology, and by the time Smith was working on later versions of his *Theory of Moral Sentiments* he must have known his close friend's arguments. He does not however attempt, here or elsewhere, to refute them. This does not imply that Smith was really hostile to religion and was merely making conventional noises in its favour, but something of his position regarding religion emerges clearly at the end of the excerpt, where he speaks of the circumstance in which 'the natural principles of religion are not corrupted by the factious and party zeal of some worthless cabal', and condemns those who 'imagine, that by sacrifices and ceremonies, and vain supplications, they can bargain with the Deity for fraud, and perfidy, and violence'. Instead he commends a religion 'wherever the first duty which it requires is to fulfil all the obligations of morality'. Hume would hardly have taken exception to such sentiments and indeed himself said similar things.

A.B.

Of the Influence and Authority of the General Rules of Morality, and that They are Justly Regarded as the Laws of the Deity

The regard to those general rules of conduct, is what is properly called a sense of duty, a principle of the greatest consequence in human life, and the only principle by which the bulk of mankind are capable of directing their actions. Many men behave very decently, and through the whole of their lives avoid any considerable degree of blame, who yet, perhaps, never felt the sentiment upon the propriety of which we found our approbation of their conduct, but acted merely from a regard to what they saw were the established rules of behaviour. The man who has received great benefits from another person, may, by the natural coldness of his temper, feel but a very small degree of the sentiment of gratitude. If he has been virtuously educated, however, he will often have been made to observe how odious those actions appear which denote a want of this sentiment, and how amiable the contrary. Though his heart therefore is not warmed with any grateful affection, he will strive to act as if it was, and will endeavour to pay all those regards and attentions to his patron which the liveliest gratitude could suggest. He will visit him regularly; he will behave to him respectfully; he will never talk of him but with expressions of the highest esteem, and of the many obligations which he owes to him. And what is more, he will carefully embrace every opportunity of making a proper return for past services. He may do all this too without any hypocrisy or blamable dissimulation, without any selfish intention of obtaining new favours, and without any design of imposing either upon his benefactor or the public. The motive of his actions may be no other than a reverence for the established rule of duty, a serious and earnest desire of acting, in every respect, according to the law of gratitude. A wife, in the same manner, may sometimes not feel that tender regard for her husband which is suitable to the relation that subsists between them. If she has been virtuously educated, however, she will endeavour to act as if she felt it, to be careful, officious, faithful, and sincere, and to be deficient in none of those attentions which the sentiment of conjugal affection could have prompted her to perform. Such a friend, and such a wife, are neither of them, undoubtedly, the very best of their kinds; and though both of them may have the most serious and earnest desire to fulfil every part of their duty, yet they will fail in many nice and delicate regards, they will miss many opportunities of obliging, which they could never have overlooked if they had possessed the sentiment that is proper to their situation. Though not the very first of their kinds, however, they are perhaps the second; and if the regard to the general rules of conduct has been very strongly impressed upon them, neither of them will fail in any very essential part of their duty. None but those of the happiest mould are capable of suiting, with exact justness, their sentiments and behaviour to the smallest difference of situation, and of acting upon all occasions with the most delicate and accurate propriety. The coarse clay of which the bulk of mankind are formed, cannot be wrought up to such perfection. There is scarce any man, however, who by discipline, education, and example, may not be so impressed with a regard to general rules, as to act upon almost every occasion with tolerable decency, and through the whole of his life to avoid any considerable degree of blame.

Without this sacred regard to general rules, there is no man whose conduct can be depended upon. It is this which constitutes the most essential difference between a man of principle and honour and a worthless fellow. The one adheres, on all occasions, steadily and resolutely to his maxims, and preserves through the whole of his life one even tenour of conduct. The other, acts variously and accidentally, as humour, inclination, or interest chance to be uppermost. Nay, such are the inequalities of humour to which all men are subject, that without this principle, the man who, in all his cool hours, had the most delicate sensibility to the propriety of conduct, might often be led to act absurdly upon the most frivolous occasions, and when it was scarce possible to assign any serious motive for his behaving in this manner. Your friend makes you a visit when you happen to be in a humour which makes it disagreeable to receive him: in your present mood his civility is very apt to appear an impertinent intrusion; and if you were to give way to the views of things which at this time occur, though civil in your temper, you would behave to him with coldness and contempt. What renders you incapable of such a rudeness, is nothing but a regard to the general rules of civility and hospitality, which prohibit it. That habitual reverence which your former experience has taught you for these, enables you to act, upon all such occasions, with nearly equal propriety, and hinders those inequalities of temper, to which all men are subject, from influencing your conduct in any sensible degree. But if without regard to these general rules, even the duties of politeness, which are so easily observed, and which one can scarce have any serious motive to violate, would yet be so frequently violated, what would become of the duties of justice, of truth, of chastity, of fidelity, which it is often so difficult to observe, and which there may be so many strong motives to violate? But upon the tolerable observance of these duties, depends the very existence of human society, which would crumble into nothing if mankind were not generally impressed with a reverence for those important rules of conduct.

This reverence is still further enhanced by an opinion which is first impressed by nature, and afterwards confirmed by reasoning and philosophy, that those important rules of morality are the commands and laws of the Deity, who will finally reward the obedient, and punish the transgressors of their duty.

This opinion or apprehension, I say, seems first to be impressed by nature. Men are naturally led to ascribe to those mysterious beings, whatever they are, which happen, in any country, to be the objects of religious fear, all their own sentiments and passions. They have no other, they can conceive no other to ascribe to them. Those unknown intelligences which they imagine but see not, must necessarily be formed with some sort of resemblance to those intelligences of which they have experience. During the ignorance and darkness of pagan superstition, mankind seem to have formed the ideas of their divinities with so little delicacy, that they ascribed to them, indiscriminately, all the passions of human nature, those not excepted which do the least honour to our species, such as lust, hunger, avarice, envy, revenge. They could not fail, therefore, to ascribe to those beings, for the excellence of whose nature they still conceived the highest admiration, those sentiments and qualities which are the great ornaments of humanity, and which seem to raise it to a resemblance of divine perfection, the love of virtue and beneficence, and the abhorrence of vice and injustice. The man who was injured, called upon Jupiter to be witness of the wrong that was done to him, and could not doubt, but that divine being would behold it with the same indignation which would animate the meanest of mankind, who looked on when injustice was committed. The man who did the injury, felt himself to be the proper object of the detestation and resentment of mankind; and his natural fears led him to impute the same sentiments to those awful beings, whose presence he could not avoid, and whose power he could not resist. These natural hopes and fears, and suspicions, were propagated by sympathy, and confirmed by education; and the gods were universally represented and believed to be the rewarders of humanity and mercy, and the avengers of perfidy and injustice. And thus religion, even in its rudest form, gave a sanction to the rules of morality, long before the age of artificial reasoning and philosophy. That the terrors of religion should thus enforce the natural sense of duty, was of too much importance to the happiness of mankind, for nature to leave it dependent upon the slowness and uncertainty of philosophical researches.

These researches, however, when they came to take place, confirmed those original anticipations of nature. Upon whatever we suppose that our moral faculties are founded, whether upon a certain modification of reason, upon an original instinct, called a moral sense, or upon some other principle of our nature, it cannot be doubted, that they were given us for the direction of our conduct in this life. They carry along with them the most evident badges of this authority, which denote that they were set up within us to be the supreme arbiters of all our actions, to superintend all our senses, passions, and appetites, and to judge how far each of them was either to be indulged or restrained. Our moral faculties are by no means, as some have pretended, upon a level in this respect with the other faculties and appetites of our nature, endowed with no more right to restrain these last, than these last are to restrain them. No other faculty or principle of action judges of any other. Love does not judge of resentment, nor resentment of love. Those two passions may be opposite to one another, but cannot, with any propriety, be said to approve or disapprove of one another. But it is the peculiar office of those faculties now under our consideration to judge, to bestow censure or applause upon all the other principles of our nature. They may be considered as a sort of senses of which those principles are the objects. Every sense is supreme over its own objects. There is no appeal from the eye with regard to the beauty of colours, nor from the ear with regard to the harmony of sounds, nor from the taste with regard to the agreeableness of flavours. Each of those senses judges in the last resort of its own objects. Whatever gratifies the taste is sweet, whatever pleases the eye is beautiful, whatever soothes the ear is harmonious. The very essence of each of those qualities consists in its being fitted to please the sense to which it is addressed. It belongs to our moral faculties, in the same manner to determine when the ear ought to be soothed, when the eye ought to be indulged, when the taste ought to be gratified, when and how far every other principle of our nature ought either to be indulged or restrained. What is agreeable to our moral faculties, is fit, and right, and proper to be done; the contrary wrong, unfit, and improper. The sentiments which they approve of, are graceful and becoming: the contrary, ungraceful and unbecoming. The very words, right, wrong, fit, improper, graceful, unbecoming, mean only what pleases or displeases those faculties.

Since these, therefore, were plainly intended to be the governing principles of human nature, the rules which they prescribe are to be regarded as the commands and laws of the Deity, promulgated by those vicegerents which he has thus set up within us. All general rules are commonly denominated laws: thus the general rules which bodies observe in the communication of motion, are called the laws of motion. But those general rules which our moral faculties observe in approving or condemning whatever sentiment or action is subjected to their examination, may much more justly be denominated such. They have a much greater resemblance to what are properly called laws, those general rules which the sovereign lays down to direct the conduct of his subjects. Like them they are rules to direct the free actions of men: they are prescribed most surely by a lawful superior, and are attended too with the sanction of rewards and punishments. Those vicegerents of God within us, never fail to punish the violation of them, by the torments of inward shame, and self-condemnation; and on the contrary, always reward obedience with tranquillity of mind, with contentment, and self-satisfaction.

There are innumerable other considerations which serve to confirm the same conclusion. The happiness of mankind, as well as of all other rational creatures, seems to have been the original purpose intended by the Author of nature, when he brought them into existence. No other end seems worthy of that supreme wisdom and divine benignity which we necessarily ascribe to him; and this opinion, which we are led to by the abstract consideration of his infinite perfections, is still more confirmed by the examination of the works of nature, which seem all intended to promote happiness, and to guard against misery. But by acting according to the dictates of our moral faculties, we necessarily pursue the most effectual means for promoting the happiness of mankind, and may therefore be said, in some sense, to co-operate with the Deity, and to advance as far as in our power the plan of Providence. By acting otherways, on the contrary, we seem to obstruct, in some measure, the scheme which the Author of nature has established for the happiness and perfection of the world, and to declare ourselves, if I may say so, in some measure the enemies of God. Hence we are naturally encouraged to hope for his extraordinary favour and reward in the one case, and to dread his vengeance and punishment in the other.

There are besides many other reasons, and many other natural principles, which all tend to confirm and inculcate the same salutary doctrine. If we consider the general rules by which external prosperity and adversity are commonly distributed in this life, we shall find, that notwithstanding the disorder in which all things appear to be in this world, yet even here every virtue naturally meets with its proper reward, with the recompense which is most fit to encourage and promote it; and this too so surely, that it requires a very extraordinary concurrence of circumstances entirely to disappoint it. What is the reward most proper for encouraging industry, prudence, and circumspection? Success in every sort of business. And is it possible that in the whole of life these virtues should fail of attaining it? Wealth and external honours are their proper recompense, and the recompense which they can seldom fail of acquiring. What reward is most proper for promoting the practice of truth, justice, and humanity? The confidence, the esteem, and love of those we live with. Humanity does not desire to be great, but to be beloved. It is not in being rich that truth and justice would rejoice, but in being trusted and believed, recompenses which those virtues must almost always acquire. By some very extraordinary and unlucky circumstance, a good man may come to be suspected of a crime of which he was altogether incapable, and upon that account be most unjustly exposed for the remaining part of his life to the horror and aversion of mankind. By an accident of this kind he may be said to lose his all, notwithstanding his integrity and justice; in the same manner as a cautious man, notwithstanding his utmost circumspection, may be ruined by an earthquake or an inundation. Accidents of the first kind, however, are perhaps still more rare, and still more contrary to the common course of things than those of the second; and it still remains true, that the practice of truth, justice, and humanity is a certain and almost infallible method of acquiring what those virtues chiefly aim at, the confidence and love of those we live with. A person may be very easily misrepresented with regard to a particular action; but it is scarce possible that he should be so with regard to the general tenor of his conduct. An innocent man may be believed to have done wrong: this, however, will rarely happen. On the contrary, the established opinion of the innocence of his manners, will often lead us to absolve him where he has really been in the fault, notwithstanding very strong presumptions. A knave, in the same manner, may escape censure, or even meet with applause, for a particular knavery, in which his conduct is not understood. But no man was ever habitually such, without being almost universally known to be so, and without being even frequently suspected of guilt, when he was in reality perfectly innocent. And so far as vice and virtue can be either punished or rewarded by the sentiments and opinions of mankind, they both, according to the common course of things, meet even here with something more than exact and impartial justice.

But though the general rules by which prosperity and adversity are commonly distributed, when considered in this cool and philosophical light, appear to be perfectly suited to the situation of mankind in this life, yet they are by no means suited to some of our natural sentiments. Our natural love and admiration for some virtues is such, that we should wish to bestow on them all sorts of honours and rewards, even those which we must acknowledge to be the proper recompenses of other qualities, with which those virtues are not always accompanied. Our detestation, on the contrary, for some vices is such, that we should desire to heap upon them every sort of disgrace and disaster, those not excepted which are the natural consequences of very different qualities. Magnanimity, generosity, and justice, command so high a degree of admiration, that we desire to see them crowned with wealth, and power, and honours of every kind, the natural consequences of prudence, industry, and application; qualities with which those virtues are not inseparably connected. Fraud, falsehood, brutality, and violence, on the other hand, excite in every human breast such scorn and abhorrence, that our indignation rouses to see them possess those advantages which they may in some sense be said to have merited, by the diligence and industry with which they are sometimes attended. The industrious knave cultivates the soil; the indolent good man leaves it uncultivated. Who ought to reap the harvest? who starve, and who live in plenty? The natural course of things decides it in favour of the knave: the natural sentiments of mankind in favour of the man of virtue. Man judges, that the good qualities of the one are greatly over-recompensed by those advantages which they tend to procure him, and that the omissions of the other are by far too severely punished by the distress which they naturally bring upon him; and human laws, the consequences of human sentiments, forfeit the life and the estate of the industrious and cautious traitor, and reward, by extraordinary recompenses, the fidelity and public spirit of the improvident and careless good citizen. Thus man is by Nature directed to correct, in some measure, that distribution of things which she herself would otherwise have made. The rules which for this purpose she prompts him to follow, are different from those which she herself observes. She bestows upon every virtue, and upon every vice, that precise reward or punishment which is best fitted to encourage the one, or to restrain the other. She is directed by this sole consideration, and pays little regard to the different degrees of merit and demerit, which they may seem to possess in the sentiments and passions of man. Man, on the contrary, pays regard to this only, and would endeavour to render the state of every virtue precisely proportioned to that degree of love and esteem, and of every vice to that degree of contempt and abhorrence, which he himself conceives for it. The rules which she follows are fit for her, those which he follows for him: but both are calculated to promote the same great end, the order of the world, and the perfection and happiness of human nature.

But though man is thus employed to alter that distribution of things which natural events would make, if left to themselves; though, like the gods of the poets, he is perpetually interposing, by extraordinary means, in favour of virtue, and in opposition to vice, and, like them, endeavours to turn away the arrow that is aimed at the head of the righteous, but to accelerate the sword of destruction that is lifted up against the wicked; yet he is by no means able to render the fortune of either quite suitable to his own sentiments and wishes. The natural course of things cannot be entirely controlled by the impotent endeavours of man: the current is too rapid and too strong for him to stop it; and though the rules which direct it appear to have been established for the wisest and best purposes, they sometimes produce effects which shock all his natural sentiments. That a great combination of men should prevail over a small one; that those who engage in an enterprise with forethought and all necessary preparation, should prevail over such as oppose them without any; and that every end should be acquired by those means only which Nature has established for acquiring it, seems to be a rule not only necessary and unavoidable in itself, but even useful and proper for rousing the industry and attention of mankind. Yet, when, in consequence of this rule, violence and artifice prevail over sincerity and justice, what indignation does it not excite in the breast of every human spectator? What sorrow and compassion for the sufferings of the innocent, and what furious resentment against the success of the oppressor? We are equally grieved and enraged at the wrong that is done, but often find it altogether out of our power to redress it. When we thus despair of finding any force upon earth which can check the triumph of injustice, we naturally appeal to heaven, and hope, that the great Author of our nature will himself execute hereafter, what all the principles which he has given us for the direction of our conduct, prompt us to attempt even here; that he will complete the plan which he himself has thus taught us to begin; and will, in a life to come, render to every one according to the works which he has performed in this world. And thus we are led to the belief of a future state, not only by the weaknesses, by the hopes and fears of human nature, but by the noblest and best principles which belong to it, by the love of virtue, and by the abhorrence of vice and injustice.

'Does it suit the greatness of God,' says the eloquent and philosophical bishop of Clermont, with that passionate and exaggerating force of imagination, which seems sometimes to exceed the bounds of decorum; 'does it suit the greatness of God, to leave the world which he has created in so universal a disorder? To see the wicked prevail almost always over the just; the innocent dethroned by the usurper; the father become the victim of the ambition of an unnatural son; the husband expiring under the stroke of a barbarous and faithless wife? From the height of his greatness ought God to behold those melancholy events as a fantastical amusement, without taking any share in them? Because he is great, should he be weak, or unjust, or barbarous? Because men are little, ought they to be allowed either to be dissolute without punishment, or virtuous without reward? O God! if this is the character of your Supreme Being; if it is you whom we adore under such dreadful ideas; I can no longer acknowledge you for my father, for my protector, for the comforter of my sorrow, the support of my weakness, the rewarder of my fidelity. You would then be no more than an indolent and fantastical tyrant, who sacrifices mankind to his insolent vanity, and who has brought them out of nothing, only to make them serve for the sport of his leisure and of his caprice.'

When the general rules which determine the merit and demerit of actions, come thus to be regarded as the laws of an All-powerful Being, who watches over our conduct, and who, in a life to come, will reward the observance, and punish the breach of them; they necessarily acquire a new sacredness from this consideration. That our regard to the will of the Deity ought to be the supreme rule of our conduct, can be doubted of by nobody who believes his existence. The very thought of disobedience appears to involve in it the most shocking impropriety. How vain, how absurd would it be for man, either to oppose or to neglect the commands that were laid upon him by Infinite Wisdom, and Infinite Power! How unnatural, how impiously ungrateful not to reverence the precepts that were prescribed to him by the infinite goodness of his Creator, even though no punishment was to follow their violation. The sense of propriety too is here well supported by the strongest motives of self-interest. The idea that, however we may escape the observation of man, or be placed above the reach of human punishment, yet we are always acting under the eye, and exposed to the punishment of God, the great avenger of injustice, is a motive capable of restraining the most headstrong passions, with those at least who, by constant reflection, have rendered it familiar to them.

It is in this manner that religion enforces the natural sense of duty: and hence it is, that mankind are generally disposed to place great confidence in the probity of those who seem deeply impressed with religious sentiments. Such persons, they imagine, act under an additional tie, besides those which regulate the conduct of other men. The regard to the propriety of action, as well as to reputation, the regard to the applause of his own breast, as well as to that of others, are motives which they suppose have the same influence over the religious man, as over the man of the world. But the former lies under another restraint, and never acts deliberately but as in the presence of that Great Superior who is finally to recompense him according to his deeds. A greater trust is reposed, upon this account, in the regularity and exactness of his conduct. And wherever the natural principles of religion are not corrupted by the factious and party zeal of some worthless cabal; wherever the first duty which it requires, is to fulfil all the obligations of morality; wherever men are not taught to regard frivolous observances, as more immediate duties of religion, than acts of justice and beneficence; and to imagine, that by sacrifices, and ceremonies, and vain supplications, they can bargain with the Deity for fraud, and perfidy, and violence, the world undoubtedly judges right in this respect, and justly places a double confidence in the rectitude of the religious man's behaviour.

Source: Adam Smith, *The Theory of Moral Sentiments*, ed. D. D. Raphael and A. I. Macfie, Oxford 1976, part 3, ch. 5

FIFTEEN

DAVID HUME
Of Miracles

Miracles were a lively subject among the literati because on the one hand the Church, to speak generally, required people to accept miracle claims on the basis either of eyewitness reports or of reports of such reports, whereas on the other hand the spirit of the Enlightenment required that reason be given its head and that claims be accepted by the sanction of reason rather than on the authority of others.

Hume wrote on miracles some time between 1735 and 1737 while composing his *Treatise of Human Nature*. He was staying in France, at La Flèche, and we know, from a letter he sent to George Campbell dated 7 June 1762, that he discussed miracles with a father at the local Jesuit College. During that discussion Hume thought up the argument that later formed the substance of the essay 'Of miracles'. His intention had been to include a discussion on miracles in the *Treatise* (published 1739) but it was not until 1748 that the argument was first presented to the public, not in the *Treatise* but in the *Enquiry concerning Human Understanding*. He had tactical reasons for not upsetting Scotland's divines beyond necessity, and he believed, correctly as it turned out, that many of them would be upset by his position. In brief, Hume believed he could demonstrate that no report of any miracle was to be trusted. It is clear that Hume thought that no miracle had ever occurred or ever would, but he argues explicitly only for the weaker conclusion that no testimony is sufficient to establish a miracle. The question at issue therefore concerns not the existence of miracles but rather the reliability of testimony to their existence. Since Christianity has at its heart a set of claims regarding miracles, it was to be expected that Hume's views would set him at odds with the Church.

He presents an argument which 'if just, will, with the wise and learned, be an everlasting check to all kinds of superstitious delusion, and consequently, will be useful as long as the world endures'. Hume, who is particularly concerned with the idea of testimony, argues that the credence we place in testimony in general is derived from experience, the experience of the occasions when testimony has turned out to be true as against the occasions when it has turned out not to be. If it were not for this experience of a regular conjunction between testimony and things turning out in fact to be according to the witness's testimony, we should not believe self-proclaimed witnesses. Likewise our belief that an event of a given sort will occur in a given circumstance is also derived from experience. We have experience of regular conjunctions in nature, for example of the sun rising in the east, and of fire burning dry wood, and so we believe that tomorrow's sunrise will be in the east, and that this flame will ignite this dry twig. All our beliefs about how things will turn out rest on the fundamental principle of our nature, that on the basis of our experience of uniformities, of observing A constantly followed by B, we come to believe that B will happen when we experience A.

In 'Of miracles' Hume argues that if the reported event is rather improbable then we have to ask how probable it can be that the witness is speaking the truth given the improbability of the event that he claims to have witnessed. Hume argues that in the case of miracles, where the term is understood to mean a violation of a law of nature, the improbability of their happening is so great that no testimony could tell effectively in their favour. Hume writes: 'A wise man, therefore, proportions his belief to the evidence', and argues that the evidence against a miracle always overwhelms eyewitness evidence in favour of it.

A.B.

Of Miracles

PART I

There is, in Dr. Tillotson's writings, an argument against the *real presence*, which is as concise, and elegant, and strong as any argument can possibly be supposed against a doctrine, so little worthy of a serious refutation. It is acknowledged on all hands, says that learned prelate, that the authority, either of the scripture or of tradition, is founded merely in the testimony of the apostles, who were eye-witnesses to those miracles of our Saviour, by which he proved his divine mission. Our evidence, then, for the truth of the *Christian* religion is less than the evidence for the truth of our senses; because, even in the first authors of our religion, it was no greater; and it is evident it must diminish in passing from them to their disciples; nor can any one rest such confidence in their testimony, as in the immediate object of his senses. But a weaker evidence can never destroy a stronger; and therefore, were the doctrine of the real presence ever so clearly revealed in scripture, it were directly contrary to the rules of just reasoning to give our assent to it. It contradicts sense, though both the scripture and tradition, on which it is supposed to be built, carry not such evidence with them as sense; when they are considered merely as external evidences, and are not brought home to every one's breast, by the immediate operation of the Holy Spirit.

Nothing is so convenient as a decisive argument of this kind, which must at least *silence* the most arrogant bigotry and superstition, and free us from their impertinent solicitations. I flatter myself, that I have discovered an argument of a like nature, which, if just, will, with the wise and learned, be an everlasting check to all kinds of superstitious delusion, and consequently, will be useful as long as the world endures. For so long, I presume, will the accounts of miracles and prodigies be found in all history, sacred and profane.

Though experience be our only guide in reasoning concerning matters of fact; it must be acknowledged, that this guide is not altogether infallible, but in some cases is apt to lead us into errors. One, who in our climate, should expect better weather in any week of June than in one of December, would reason justly, and conformably to experience; but it is certain, that he may happen, in the event, to find himself mistaken. However, we may observe, that, in such a case, he would have no cause to complain of experience; because it commonly informs us beforehand of the uncertainty, by that contrariety of events, which we may learn from a diligent observation. All effects follow not with like certainty from their supposed causes. Some events are found, in all countries and all ages, to have been constantly conjoined together: Others are found to have been more variable, and sometimes to disappoint our expectations; so that, in our reasonings concerning matter of fact, there are all imaginable degrees of assurance, from the highest certainty to the lowest species of moral evidence.

A wise man, therefore, proportions his belief to the evidence. In such conclusions as are founded on an infallible experience, he expects the event with the last degree of assurance, and regards his past experience as a full *proof* of the future existence of that event. In other cases, he proceeds with more caution: He weighs the opposite experiments: He considers which side is supported by the greater number of experiments: to that side he inclines, with doubt and hesitation; and when at last he fixes his judgement, the evidence exceeds not what we properly call *probability*. All probability, then, supposes an opposition of experiments and observations, where the one side is found to overbalance the other, and to produce a degree of evidence, proportioned to the superiority. A hundred instances or experiments on one side, and fifty on another, afford a doubtful expectation of any event; though a hundred uniform experiments, with only one that is contradictory, reasonably beget a pretty strong degree of assurance. In all cases, we must balance the opposite experiments, where they are opposite, and deduct the smaller numbers from the greater, in order to know the exact force of the superior evidence.

To apply these principles to a particular instance; we may observe, that there is no species of reasoning more common, more useful, and even necessary to human life, than that which is derived from the testimony of men, and the reports of eye-witnesses and spectators. This species of reasoning, perhaps, one may deny to be founded on the relation of cause and effect. I shall not dispute about a word. It will be sufficient to observe that our assurance in any argument of this kind is derived from no other principle than our observation of the veracity of human testimony, and of the usual conformity of facts to the reports of witnesses. It being a general maxim, that no objects have any discoverable connexion together, and that all the inferences, which we can draw from one to another, are founded merely on our experience of their constant and regular conjunction; it is evident, that we ought not to make an exception to this maxim in favour of human testimony, whose connexion with any event seems, in itself, as little necessary as any other. Were not the memory tenacious to a certain degree; had not men commonly an inclination to truth and a principle of probity; were they not sensible to shame, when detected in a falsehood: Were not these, I say, discovered by *experience* to be qualities, inherent in human nature, we should never repose the least confidence in human testimony. A man delirious, or noted for falsehood and villany, has no manner of authority with us.

And as the evidence, derived from witnesses and human testimony, is founded on past experience, so it varies with the experience, and is regarded either as a *proof* or a *probability*, according as the conjunction between any particular kind of report and any kind of object has been found to be constant or variable. There are a number of circumstances to be taken into consideration in all judgements of this kind; and the ultimate standard, by which we determine all disputes, that may arise concerning them, is always derived from experience and observation. Where this experience is not entirely uniform on any side, it is attended with an unavoidable contrariety in our judgements, and with the same opposition and mutual destruction of argument as in every other kind of evidence. We frequently hesitate concerning the reports of others. We balance the opposite circumstances, which cause any doubt or uncertainty; and when we discover a superiority on any side, we incline to it; but still with a diminution of assurance, in proportion to the force of its antagonist.

This contrariety of evidence, in the present case, may be derived from several different causes; from the opposition of contrary testimony; from the character or number of the witnesses; from the manner of their delivering their testimony; or from the union of all these circumstances. We entertain a suspicion concerning any matter of fact, when the witnesses contradict each other; when they are but few, or of a doubtful character; when they have an interest in what they affirm; when they deliver their testimony with hesitation, or on the contrary, with too violent asseverations. There are many other particulars of the same kind, which may diminish or destroy the force of any argument, derived from human testimony.

Suppose, for instance, that the fact, which the testimony

endeavours to establish, partakes of the extraordinary and the marvellous; in that case, the evidence, resulting from the testimony, admits of a diminution, greater or less, in proportion as the fact is more or less unusual. The reason why we place any credit in witnesses and historians, is not derived from any *connexion*, which we perceive *a priori*, between testimony and reality, but because we are accustomed to find a conformity between them. But when the fact attested is such a one as has seldom fallen under our observation, here is a contest of two opposite experiences; of which the one destroys the other, as far as its force goes, and the superior can only operate on the mind by the force, which remains. The very same principle of experience, which gives us a certain degree of assurance in the testimony of witnesses, gives us also, in this case, another degree of assurance against the fact, which they endeavour to establish; from which contradiction there necessarily arises a counterpoize, and mutual destruction of belief and authority.

I should not believe such a story were it told me by Cato, was a proverbial saying in Rome, even during the lifetime of that philosophical patriot.[1] The incredibility of a fact, it was allowed, might invalidate so great an authority.

The Indian prince, who refused to believe the first relations concerning the effects of frost, reasoned justly; and it naturally required very strong testimony to engage his assent to facts, that arose from a state of nature, with which he was unacquainted, and which bore so little analogy to those events, of which he had had constant and uniform experience. Though they were not contrary to his experience, they were not conformable to it.[2]

---

1 Plutarch, *In Vita Catonis*.
2 No Indian, it is evident, could have experience that water did not freeze in cold climates. This is placing nature in a situation quite unknown to him; and it is impossible for him to tell *a priori* what will result from it. It is making a new experiment, the consequence of which is always uncertain. One may sometimes conjecture from analogy what will follow; but still this is but conjecture. And it must be confessed, that, in the present case of freezing, the event follows contrary to the rules of analogy, and is such as a rational Indian would not look for. The operations of cold upon water are not gradual, according to the degrees of cold; but whenever it comes to the freezing point, the water passes in a moment, from the utmost liquidity to perfect hardness. Such an event, therefore, may be denominated *extraordinary*, and requires a pretty

But in order to encrease the probability against the testimony of witnesses, let us suppose, that the fact, which they affirm, instead of being only marvellous, is really miraculous; and suppose also, that the testimony considered apart and in itself, amounts to an entire proof; in that case, there is proof against proof, of which the strongest must prevail, but still with a diminution of its force, in proportion to that of its antagonist.

A miracle is a violation of the laws of nature; and as a firm and unalterable experience has established these laws, the proof against a miracle, from the very nature of the fact, is as entire as any argument from experience can possibly be imagined. Why is it more than probable, that all men must die; that lead cannot, of itself, remain suspended in the air; that fire consumes wood, and is extinguished by water; unless it be, that these events are found agreeable to the laws of nature, and there is required a violation of these laws, or in other words, a miracle to prevent them? Nothing is esteemed a miracle, if it ever happen in the common course of nature. It is no miracle that a man, seemingly in good health, should die on a sudden: because such a kind of death, though more unusual than any other, has yet been frequently observed to happen. But it is a miracle, that a dead man should come to life; because that has never been observed in any age or country. There must, therefore, be a uniform experience against every miraculous event, otherwise the event would not merit that appellation. And as a uniform experience amounts to a proof, there is here a direct and full *proof*, from the nature of the fact, against the existence of any miracle; nor can such a proof be destroyed, or the miracle rendered credible, but by an opposite proof, which is superior.[1]

strong testimony, to render it credible to people in a warm climate: But still it is not *miraculous*, nor contrary to uniform experience of the course of nature in cases where all the circumstances are the same. The inhabitants of Sumatra have always seen water fluid in their own climate, and the freezing of their rivers ought to be deemed a prodigy: But they never saw water in Muscovy during the winter; and therefore they cannot reasonably be positive what would there be the consequence.

1 Sometimes an event may not, *in itself, seem* to be contrary to the laws of nature, and yet, if it were real, it might, by reason of some circumstances, be denominated a miracle; because, in *fact*, it is contrary to these laws. Thus if a person, claiming a divine authority, should command a sick person to be well, a

The plain consequence is (and it is a general maxim worthy of our attention), 'That no testimony is sufficient to establish a miracle, unless the testimony be of such a kind, that its falsehood would be more miraculous, than the fact, which it endeavours to establish; and even in that case there is a mutual destruction of arguments, and the superior only gives us an assurance suitable to that degree of force, which remains, after deducting the inferior.' When anyone tells me, that he saw a dead man restored to life, I immediately consider with myself, whether it be more probable, that this person should either deceive or be deceived, or that the fact, which he relates, should really have happened. I weigh the one miracle against the other; and according to the superiority, which I discover, I pronounce my decision, and always reject the greater miracle. If the falsehood of his testimony would be more miraculous, than the event which he relates; then, and not till then, can he pretend to command my belief or opinion.

PART II

In the foregoing reasoning we have supposed, that the testimony, upon which a miracle is founded, may possibly amount to an entire proof, and that the falsehood of that testimony would be a real prodigy: But it is easy to shew, that we have been a great deal too liberal in our concession, and that there never was a miraculous event established on so full an evidence.

> healthful man to fall down dead, the clouds to pour rain, the winds to blow, in short, should order many natural events, which immediately follow upon his command; these might justly be esteemed miracles, because they are really, in this case, contrary to the laws of nature. For if any suspicion remain, that the event and command concurred by accident, there is no miracle and no transgression of the laws of nature. If this suspicion be removed, there is evidently a miracle, and a transgression of these laws; because nothing can be more contrary to nature than that the voice or command of a man should have such an influence. A miracle may be accurately defined, *a transgression of a law of nature by a particular volition of the Deity, or by the interposition of some invisible agent*. A miracle may either be discoverable by men or not. This alters not its nature and essence. The raising of a house or ship into the air is a visible miracle. The raising of a feather, when the wind wants ever so little of a force requisite for that purpose, is as real a miracle, though not so sensible with regard to us.

For *first*, there is not to be found, in all history, any miracle attested by a sufficient number of men, of such unquestioned good-sense, education, and learning, as to secure us against all delusion in themselves; of such undoubted integrity, as to place them beyond all suspicion of any design to deceive others; of such credit and reputation in the eyes of mankind, as to have a great deal to lose in case of their being detected in any falsehood; and at the same time, attesting facts performed in such a public manner and in so celebrated a part of the world, as to render the detection unavoidable: All which circumstances are requisite to give us a full assurance in the testimony of men.

Secondly. We may observe in human nature a principle which, if strictly examined, will be found to diminish extremely the assurance, which we might, from human testimony, have, in any kind of prodigy. The maxim, by which we commonly conduct ourselves in our reasonings, is, that the objects, of which we have no experience, resemble those, of which we have; that what we have found to be most usual is always most probable; and that where there is an opposition of arguments, we ought to give the preference to such as are founded on the greatest number of past observations. But though, in proceeding by this rule, we readily reject any fact which is unusual and incredible in an ordinary degree; yet in advancing farther, the mind observes not always the same rule; but when anything is affirmed utterly absurd and miraculous, it rather the more readily admits of such a fact, upon account of that very circumstance, which ought to destroy all its authority. The passion of *surprise* and *wonder*, arising from miracles, being an agreeable emotion, gives a sensible tendency towards the belief of those events, from which it is derived. And this goes so far, that even those who cannot enjoy this pleasure immediately, nor can believe those miraculous events, of which they are informed, yet love to partake of the satisfaction at second-hand or by rebound, and place a pride and delight in exciting the admiration of others.

With what greediness are the miraculous accounts of travellers received, their descriptions of sea and land monsters, their relations of wonderful adventures, strange men, and uncouth manners? But if the spirit of religion join itself to the love of wonder, there is an end of common sense; and human testimony, in these circumstances, loses all pretension to authority. A religionist may be an enthusiast, and imagine he sees what has no reality: he may know his narrative to be false, and yet persevere in it, with the best intentions in the world, for the sake of promoting so holy a cause: or even where this delusion has not place, vanity, excited by so strong a temptation, operates on him more powerfully than on the rest of mankind in any other circumstances; and self-interest with equal force. His auditors may not have, and commonly have not, sufficient judgement to canvass his evidence: what judgement they have, they renounce by principle, in these sublime and mysterious subjects: or if they were ever so willing to employ it, passion and a heated imagination disturb the regularity of its operations. Their credulity increases his impudence: and his impudence overpowers their credulity.

Eloquence, when at its highest pitch, leaves little room for reason or reflection; but addressing itself entirely to the fancy or the affections, captivates the willing hearers, and subdues their understanding. Happily, this pitch it seldom attains. But what a Tully or a Demosthenes could scarcely effect over a Roman or Athenian audience, every *Capuchin*, every itinerant or stationary teacher can perform over the generality of mankind, and in a higher degree, by touching such gross and vulgar passions.

The many instances of forged miracles, and prophecies, and supernatural events, which, in all ages, have either been detected by contrary evidence, or which detect themselves by their absurdity, prove sufficiently the strong propensity of mankind to the extraordinary and the marvellous, and ought reasonably to beget a suspicion against all relations of this kind. This is our natural way of thinking, even with regard to the most common and most credible events. For instance: There is no kind of report which rises so easily, and spreads so quickly, especially in country places and provincial towns, as those concerning marriages; insomuch that two young persons of equal condition never see each other twice, but the whole neighbourhood immediately join them together. The pleasure of telling a piece of news so interesting, of propagating it, and of being the first reporters of it, spreads the intelligence. And this is so well known, that no man of sense gives attention to these reports, till he finds them confirmed by some greater evidence. Do not the same passions, and others still stronger, incline the generality of mankind to believe and report, with the greatest vehemence and assurance, all religious miracles?

Thirdly. It forms a strong presumption against all supernatural and miraculous relations, that they are observed chiefly to abound among ignorant and barbarous nations; or if a civilized people has ever given admission to any of them, that people will be found to have received them from ignorant and barbarous ancestors, who transmitted them with that inviolable sanction and authority, which always attend received opinions. When we peruse the first histories of all nations, we are apt to imagine ourselves transported into some new world; where the whole frame of nature is disjointed, and every element performs its operations in a different manner, from what it does at present. Battles, revolutions, pestilence, famine and death, are never the effect of those natural causes, which we experience. Prodigies, omens, oracles, judgements, quite obscure the few natural events, that are intermingled with them. But as the former grow thinner every page, in proportion as we advance nearer the enlightened ages, we soon learn, that there is nothing mysterious or supernatural in the case, but that all proceeds from the usual propensity of mankind towards the marvellous, and that, though this inclination may at intervals receive a check from sense and learning, it can never be thoroughly extirpated from human nature.

It is strange, a judicious reader is apt to say, upon the perusal of these wonderful historians, *that such prodigious events never happen in our days*. But it is nothing strange, I hope, that men should lie in all ages. You must surely have seen instances enough of that frailty. You have yourself heard many such marvellous relations started, which, being treated with scorn by all the wise and judicious, have at last been abandoned even by the vulgar. Be assured, that those renowned lies, which have spread and flourished to such a monstrous height, arose from like beginnings; but being sown in a more proper soil, shot up at last into prodigies almost equal to those which they relate.

It was a wise policy in that false prophet, Alexander, who though now forgotten, was once so famous, to lay the first scene of his impostures in Paphlagonia, where, as Lucian tells us, the people were extremely ignorant and stupid, and ready to swallow even the grossest delusion. People at a distance, who are weak enough to think the matter at all worth enquiry, have no opportunity of receiving better information. The stories come magnified to them by a hundred circumstances. Fools are industrious in propagating the imposture; while the wise and learned are contented, in general, to deride its absurdity, without informing themselves of the particular facts, by which it may be distinctly refuted. And thus the impostor above mentioned was enabled to proceed, from his ignorant Paphlagonians, to the enlisting of votaries, even among the Grecian philosophers, and men of the most eminent rank and distinction in Rome: nay, could engage the attention of that sage emperor Marcus Aurelius; so far as to make him trust the success of a military expedition to his delusive prophecies.

The advantages are so great, of starting an imposture among an ignorant people, that, even though the delusion should be too gross to impose on the generality of them (*which, though seldom, is sometimes the case*) it has a much better chance for succeeding in remote countries, than if the first scene had been laid in a city renowned for arts and knowledge. The most ignorant and barbarous of these barbarians carry the report abroad. None of their countrymen have a large correspondence, or sufficient credit and authority to contradict and beat down the delusion. Men's inclination to the marvellous has full opportunity to display itself. And thus a story, which is universally exploded in the place where it was first started, shall pass for certain at a thousand miles distance. But had Alexander fixed his residence at Athens, the philosophers of that renowned mart of learning had immediately spread, throughout the whole Roman empire, their sense of the matter; which, being supported by so great authority, and displayed by all the force of reason and eloquence, had entirely opened the eyes of mankind. It is true; Lucian, passing by chance through Paphlagonia, had an opportunity of performing this good office. But, though much to be wished, it does not always happen, that every Alexander meets with a Lucian, ready to expose and detect his impostures.

I may add as a *fourth* reason, which diminishes the authority of prodigies, that there is no testimony for any, even those which have not been expressly detected, that is not opposed by an infinite number of witnesses; so that not only the miracle destroys the credit of testimony, but the testimony destroys itself. To make this the better understood, let us consider, that, in matters of religion, whatever is different is contrary; and that it is impossible the religions of ancient Rome, of Turkey, of Siam, and of China should, all of them, be established on any solid foundation. Every miracle, therefore, pretended to have been wrought in any of these religions (and all of them abound in miracles), as its direct scope is to establish the particular system to which it is attributed; so has it the same force, though more indirectly, to overthrow every other system. In destroying a rival system, it likewise destroys the credit of those miracles, on which that system was established; so that all the prodigies of different religions are to be regarded as contrary facts, and the evidences of these prodigies, whether weak or strong, as opposite to each other. According to this method of reasoning, when we believe any miracle of Mahomet or his successors, we have for our warrant the testimony of a few barbarous Arabians: And on the other hand, we are to regard the authority of Titus Livius, Plutarch, Tacitus, and, in short, of all the authors and witnesses, Grecian, Chinese, and Roman Catholic, who have related any miracle in their particular religion; I say, we are to regard their testimony in the same light as if they had mentioned that Mahometan miracle, and had in express terms contradicted it, with the same certainty as they have for the miracle they relate. This argument may appear over subtile and refined; but is not in reality different from the reasoning of a judge, who supposes, that the credit of two witnesses, maintaining a crime against any one, is destroyed by the testimony of two others, who affirm him to have been two hundred leagues distant, at the same instant when the crime is said to have been committed.

One of the best attested miracles in all profane history, is that which Tacitus reports of Vespasian, who cured a blind man in Alexandria, by means of his spittle, and a lame man by the mere touch of his foot; in obedience to a vision of the god Serapis, who had enjoined them to have recourse to the Emperor, for these miraculous cures. The story may be seen in that fine historian;[1] where every circumstance seems to add weight to the testimony, and might be displayed at large with all the force of argument and eloquence, if any one were now concerned to enforce the evidence of that exploded and idolatrous superstition. The gravity, solidity, age, and probity of so great an emperor, who, through the whole course of his life, conversed in a familiar manner with his friends and courtiers, and never affected those extraordinary airs of divinity assumed by Alexander and Demetrius. The historian, a cotemporary writer, noted for candour and veracity, and withal, the greatest and most penetrating genius, perhaps, of all antiquity; and so free from any tendency to credulity, that he even lies under the contrary imputation, of atheism and profaneness: The persons, from whose authority he related the miracle, of established character for judgement and veracity, as we may well presume; eye-witnesses of the fact, and confirming their testimony, after the Flavian family was despoiled of the empire, and could no longer give any reward, as the price of a lie. *Utrumque, qui interfuere, nunc quoque memorant, postquam nullum mendacio pretium.* To which if we add the public nature

---

[1] Hist. lib. v. cap. 8. Suetonius gives nearly the same account *In Vita Vesp.*

of the facts, as related, it will appear, that no evidence can well be supposed stronger for so gross and palpable a falsehood.

There is also a memorable story related by Cardinal de Retz, which may well deserve our consideration. When that intriguing politician fled into Spain, to avoid the persecution of his enemies, he passed through Saragossa, the capital of Arragon, where he was shewn, in the cathedral, a man, who had served seven years as a doorkeeper, and was well known to every body in town, that had ever paid his devotions at that church. He had been seen, for so long a time, wanting a leg; but recovered that limb by the rubbing of holy oil upon the stump; and the cardinal assures us that he saw him with two legs. This miracle was vouched by all the canons of the church; and the whole company in town were appealed to for a confirmation of the fact; whom the cardinal found, by their zealous devotion, to be thorough believers of the miracle. Here the relater was also cotemporary to the supposed prodigy, of an incredulous and libertine character, as well as of great genius; the miracle of so *singular* a nature as could scarcely admit of a counterfeit, and the witnesses very numerous, and all of them, in a manner, spectators of the fact, to which they gave their testimony. And what adds mightily to the force of the evidence, and may double our surprise on this occasion, is, that the cardinal himself, who relates the story, seems not to give any credit to it, and consequently cannot be suspected of any concurrence in the holy fraud. He considered justly, that it was not requisite, in order to reject a fact of this nature, to be able accurately to disprove the testimony, and to trace its falsehood, through all the circumstances of knavery and credulity which produced it. He knew, that, as this was commonly altogether impossible at any small distance of time and place; so was it extremely difficult, even where one was immediately present, by reason of the bigotry, ignorance, cunning, and roguery of a great part of mankind. He therefore concluded, like a just reasoner, that such an evidence carried falsehood upon the very face of it, and that a miracle, supported by any human testimony, was more properly a subject of derision than of argument.

There surely never was a greater number of miracles ascribed to one person, than those, which were lately said to have been wrought in France upon the tomb of Abbé Paris, the famous Jansenist, with whose sanctity the people were so long deluded. The curing of the sick, giving hearing to the deaf, and sight to the blind, were every where talked of as the usual effects of that holy sepulchre. But what is more extraordinary; many of the miracles were immediately proved upon the spot, before judges of unquestioned integrity, attested by witnesses of credit and distinction, in a learned age, and on the most eminent theatre that is now in the world. Nor is this all: a relation of them was published and dispersed every where; nor were the *Jesuits*, though a learned body, supported by the civil magistrate, and determined enemies to those opinions, in whose favour the miracles were said to have been wrought, ever able distinctly to refute or detect them. Where shall we find such a number of circumstances, agreeing to the corroboration of one fact? And what have we to oppose to such a cloud of witnesses, but the absolute impossibility or miraculous nature of the events, which they relate? And this surely, in the eyes of all reasonable people, will alone be regarded as a sufficient refutation.

Is the consequence just, because some human testimony has the utmost force and authority in some cases, when it relates the battle of Philippi or Pharsalia for instance; that therefore all kinds of testimony must, in all cases, have equal force and authority? Suppose that the Cæsarean and Pompeian factions had, each of them, claimed the victory in these battles, and that the historians of each party had uniformly ascribed the advantage to their own side; how could mankind, at this distance, have been able to determine between them? The contrariety is equally strong between the miracles related by Herodotus or Plutarch, and those delivered by Mariana, Bede, or any monkish historian.

The wise lend a very academic faith to every report which favours the passion of the reporter; whether it magnifies his country, his family, or himself, or in any other way strikes in with his natural inclinations and propensities. But what greater temptation than to appear a missionary, a prophet, an ambassador from heaven? Who would not encounter many dangers and difficulties, in order to attain so sublime a character? Or if, by the help of vanity and a heated imagination, a man has first made a convert of himself, and entered seriously into the delusion; who ever scruples to make use of pious frauds, in support of so holy and meritorious a cause?

The smallest spark may here kindle into the greatest flame; because the materials are always prepared for it. The *avidum genus auricularum*,[1] the gazing populace, receive greedily, without examination, whatever sooths superstition, and promotes wonder.

1 Lucret.

How many stories of this nature have, in all ages, been detected and exploded in their infancy? How many more have been celebrated for a time, and have afterwards sunk into neglect and oblivion? Where such reports, therefore, fly about, the solution of the phenomenon is obvious; and we judge in conformity to regular experience and observation, when we account for it by the known and natural principles of credulity and delusion. And shall we, rather than have a recourse to so natural a solution, allow of a miraculous violation of the most established laws of nature?

I need not mention the difficulty of detecting a falsehood in any private or even public history, at the place, where it is said to happen; much more when the scene is removed to ever so small a distance. Even a court of judicature, with all the authority, accuracy, and judgement, which they can employ, find themselves often at a loss to distinguish between truth and falsehood in the most recent actions. But the matter never comes to any issue, if trusted to the common method of altercations and debate and flying rumours; especially when men's passions have taken part on either side.

In the infancy of new religions, the wise and learned commonly esteem the matter too inconsiderable to deserve their attention or regard. And when afterwards they would willingly detect the cheat, in order to undeceive the deluded multitude, the season is now past, and the records and witnesses, which might clear up the matter, have perished beyond recovery.

No means of detection remain, but those which must be drawn from the very testimony itself of the reporters: and these, though always sufficient with the judicious and knowing, are commonly too fine to fall under the comprehension of the vulgar.

Upon the whole, then, it appears, that no testimony for any kind of miracle has ever amounted to a probability, much less to a proof; and that, even supposing it amounted to a proof, it would be opposed by another proof; derived from the very nature of the fact, which it would endeavour to establish. It is experience only, which gives authority to human testimony; and it is the same experience, which assures us of the laws of nature. When, therefore, these two kinds of experience are contrary, we have nothing to do but subtract the one from the other, and embrace an opinion, either on one side or the other, with that assurance which arises from the remainder. But according to the principle here explained, this subtraction, with regard to all popular religions, amounts to an entire annihilation; and therefore we may establish it as a maxim, that no human testimony can have such force as to prove a miracle, and make it a just foundation for any such system of religion.

I beg the limitations here made may be remarked, when I say, that a miracle can never be proved, so as to be the foundation of a system of religion. For I own, that otherwise, there may possibly be miracles, or violations of the usual course of nature, of such a kind as to admit of proof from human testimony; though, perhaps, it will be impossible to find any such in all the records of history. Thus, suppose, all authors, in all languages, agree, that, from the first of January 1600, there was a total darkness over the whole earth for eight days: suppose that the tradition of this extraordinary event is still strong and lively among the people: that all travellers, who return from foreign countries, bring us accounts of the same tradition, without the least variation or contradiction: it is evident, that our present philosophers, instead of doubting the fact, ought to receive it as certain, and ought to search for the causes whence it might be derived. The decay, corruption, and dissolution of nature, is an event rendered probable by so many analogies, that any phenomenon, which seems to have a tendency towards that catastrophe, comes within the reach of human testimony, if that testimony be very extensive and uniform.

But suppose, that all the historians who treat of England, should agree, that, on the first of January 1600, Queen Elizabeth died; that both before and after her death she was seen by her physicians and the whole court, as is usual with persons of her rank; that her successor was acknowledged and proclaimed by the parliament; and that, after being interred a month, she again appeared, resumed the throne, and governed England for three years: I must confess that I should be surprised at the concurrence of so many odd circumstances, but should not have the least inclination to believe so miraculous an event. I should not doubt of her pretended death, and of those other public circumstances that followed it: I should only assert it to have been pretended, and that it neither was, nor possibly could be real. You would in vain object to me the difficulty, and almost impossibility of deceiving the world in an affair of such consequence; the wisdom and solid judgement of that renowned queen; with the little or no advantage which she could reap from so poor an artifice: All this might astonish me; but I would still reply, that the knavery and folly of men are such common phenomena, that I should rather believe the most extraordinary events to arise from their concurrence, than admit of so signal a violation of the laws of nature.

But should this miracle be ascribed to any new system of religion; men, in all ages, have been so much imposed on by ridiculous stories of that kind, that this very circumstance would be a full proof of a cheat, and sufficient, with all men of sense, not only to make them reject the fact, but even reject it without farther examination. Though the Being to whom the miracle is ascribed, be, in this case, Almighty, it does not, upon that account, become a whit more probable; since it is impossible for us to know the attributes or actions of such a Being, otherwise than from the experience which we have of his productions, in the usual course of nature. This still reduces us to past observation, and obliges us to compare the instances of the violation of truth in the testimony of men, with those of the violation of the laws of nature by miracles, in order to judge which of them is most likely and probable. As the violations of truth are more common in the testimony concerning religious miracles, than in that concerning any other matter of fact; this must diminish very much the authority of the former testimony, and make us form a general resolution, never to lend any attention to it, with whatever specious pretence it may be covered.

Lord Bacon seems to have embraced the same principles of reasoning. 'We ought,' says he, 'to make a collection or particular history of all monsters and prodigious births or productions, and in a word of every thing new, rare, and extraordinary in nature. But this must be done with the most severe scrutiny, lest we depart from truth. Above all, every relation must be considered as suspicious, which depends in any degree upon religion, as the prodigies of Livy: And no less so, every thing that is to be found in the writers of natural magic or alchimy, or such authors, who seem, all of them, to have an unconquerable appetite for falsehood and fable.'[1]

I am the better pleased with the method of reasoning here delivered, as I think it may serve to confound those dangerous friends or disguised enemies to the *Christian Religion*, who have undertaken to defend it by the principles of human reason. Our most holy religion is founded on *Faith*, not on reason; and it is a sure method of exposing it to put it to such a trial as it is, by no means, fitted to endure. To make this more evident, let us examine those miracles, related in scripture; and not to lose ourselves in too wide a field, let us confine ourselves to such as we find in the *Pentateuch*, which we shall examine, according to

[1] *Nov. Org.* lib. ii. aph. 29.

the principles of these pretended Christians, not as the word or testimony of God himself, but as the production of a mere human writer and historian. Here then we are first to consider a book, presented to us by a barbarous and ignorant people, written in an age when they were still more barbarous, and in all probability long after the facts which it relates, corroborated by no concurring testimony, and resembling those fabulous accounts, which every nation gives of its origin. Upon reading this book, we find it full of prodigies and miracles. It gives an account of a state of the world and of human nature entirely different from the present: Of our fall from that state: Of the age of man, extended to near a thousand years: Of the destruction of the world by a deluge: Of the arbitrary choice of one people, as the favourites of heaven; and that people the countrymen of the author: Of their deliverance from bondage by prodigies the most astonishing imaginable: I desire any one to lay his hand upon his heart, and after a serious consideration declare, whether he thinks that the falsehood of such a book, supported by such a testimony, would be more extraordinary and miraculous than all the miracles it relates; which is, however, necessary to make it be received, according to the measures of probability above established.

What we have said of miracles may be applied, without any variation, to prophecies; and indeed, all prophecies are real miracles, and as such only, can be admitted as proofs of any revelation. If it did not exceed the capacity of human nature to foretell future events, it would be absurd to employ any prophecy as an argument for a divine mission or authority from heaven. So that, upon the whole, we may conclude, that the *Christian Religion* not only was at first attended with miracles, but even at this day cannot be believed by any reasonable person without one. Mere reason is insufficient to convince us of its veracity: And whoever is moved by *Faith* to assent to it, is conscious of a continued miracle in his own person, which subverts all the principles of his understanding, and gives him a determination to believe what is most contrary to custom and experience.

Source: David Hume, *An Enquiry concerning Human Understanding*, section 10, in *Enquiries concerning Human Understanding and concerning the Principles of Morals*, ed. L. A. Selby-Bigge, 3rd edn by P. H. Nidditch, Oxford 1975, pp. 109–31

SIXTEEN

GEORGE CAMPBELL
Of Miracles

Hume's essay 'Of miracles', first published in 1748 (see excerpt 15), prompted a number of responses from enlightened ministers. One response came in 1762 from George Campbell, principal of Marischal College, Aberdeen, and friend of Thomas Reid. Campbell sent his response, the *Dissertation on Miracles*, to Hugh Blair, who passed it on, with Campbell's permission, to Hume. Hume duly wrote to Campbell to say: 'it is impossible for me not to see the ingenuity of your performance, and the great learning which you have displayed against me . . . I owe it to you that I never felt so violent an inclination to defend myself as at present, when I am thus fairly challenged by you; and I think I could find something specious, at least, to say in my own defence.' (See letter 194 in Hume, *The Letters of David Hume*, ed. J.Y.T. Greig.) Hume did not however publish a reply to the *Dissertation*, though we know from a letter Hume wrote to Blair (see letter 188 in *The Letters of David Hume*) regarding the *Dissertation* that Campbell did not change Hume's mind on any matter of significance.

A crucial part of Hume's argument is the premiss that the evidence of testimony is derived solely from experience, and it is against this premiss that Campbell makes his opening move. He argues that Hume is simply wrong about this aspect of human nature, for there is within all human beings a natural tendency to believe other people. This is not a learned response based upon repeated experience. Quite the contrary, as a result of repeated experiences our disposition to credit people with honesty is gradually eroded. A child's natural response is assent. It takes quite a lot to get the child to modify that response, and to become less confident and more diffident. But if this is indeed how we are, then the implication is that for us there is a natural presumption in favour of testimony. Once testimony has been placed before us it becomes the default position. For us it is not false until proved true but, instead, true until proved false. That is how we are by nature.

A.B.

Miracles are Capable of Proof from Testimony, and Religious Miracles are not Less Capable of this Evidence than Others

SECTION I *Mr Hume's Favourite Argument is Founded on a False Hypothesis*

It is not the aim of this author to evince, that miracles, if admitted to be true, would not be a sufficient evidence of a divine mission. His design is solely to prove that miracles which have not been the objects of our own senses, at least such as are said to have been performed in attestation of any religious system, cannot reasonably be admitted by us, or believed on the testimony of others. 'A miracle,' says he, 'supported by any human testimony, is more properly a subject of derision than of argument.' Again, in the conclusion of his essay, 'Upon the whole, it appears that no testimony for *any kind* of miracle can ever possibly amount to a probability, much less to a proof.' Here he concludes against all miracles. '*Any kind* of miracle' are his express words. He seems however immediately sensible, that, in asserting this, he has gone too far; and therefore, in the end of the same paragraph, retracts part of what he had advanced in the beginning. 'We may establish it as a maxim, that no human testimony can have such force, as to prove a miracle, and make it a just foundation for any system of religion.' In the note on this passage, he has these words. 'I beg the limitation here made, may be remarked, when I say, that a miracle can never be proved, so as to be the foundation of a system of religion. For I own that otherwise there may possibly be miracles, or violations of the usual course of nature, of such a kind, as to admit of proof from human testimony.'

So much for that cardinal point, which the essayist labours so strenuously to evince; and which, if true, will not only be subversive of revelation, as perceived by us, on the testimony of the apostles, and prophets, and martyrs; but will directly lead to this general conclusion: 'That it is impossible for God Almighty to give a revelation, attended with such evidence, that it can be reasonably believed in after-ages, or even in the same age, by any person who hath not been an eye-witness of the miracles, by which it is supported.'

Now by what wonderful process of reasoning is this strange

conclusion made out? Several topics have been employed for the purpose by this subtle disputant. Among these there is one principal argument, which he is at great pains to set off to the best advantage. Here indeed he claims a particular concern, having discovered it himself. His title to the honour of the discovery, it is not my business to controvert; I confine myself entirely to the consideration of its importance. To this end I shall now lay before the reader, the unanswerable argument, as he flatters himself it will be found; taking the freedom, for brevity's sake, to compendize the reasoning, and to omit whatever is said merely for illustration. To do otherwise would lay me under the necessity of transcribing the great part of the essay.

'Experience,' says he, 'is our only guide in reasoning concerning matters of fact. Experience is in some things variable, in some things uniform. A variable experience gives rise only to probability; an uniform experience amounts to a proof. Probability always supposes an opposition of experiments and observations, where the one side is found to overbalance the other, and to produce a degree of evidence proportioned to the superiority. In such cases we must balance the opposite experiments, and deduct the lesser number from the greater, in order to know the exact force of the superior evidence. Our belief or assurance of any fact, from the report of eye-witnesses, is derived from no other principle than experience; that is, our observation of the veracity of human testimony, and of the usual conformity of facts to the reports of witnesses. Now if the fact attested partakes of the marvellous, if it is such as has seldom fallen under our observation, here is a contest of two opposite experiences, of which the one destroys the other, as far as its force goes, and the superior can only operate on the mind by the force which remains. The very same principle of experience, which gives us a certain degree of assurance, in the testimony of witnesses, gives us also, in this case, another degree of assurance, against the fact which they endeavour to establish; from which contradiction, there necessarily arises a counterpoise, and mutual destruction of belief and authority. Further, if the fact affirmed by the witnesses, instead of being only marvellous, is really miraculous; if besides, the testimony considered apart and in itself, amounts to an entire proof; in that case there is proof against proof, of which the strongest must prevail, but still with a diminution of its force, in proportion to that of its antagonist. A miracle is a violation of the laws of nature; and as a firm and unalterable experience has established these laws, the proof against a miracle from the very nature of the fact, is as entire, as any argument from experience can possibly be imagined. And if so, it is an undeniable consequence, that, it cannot be surmounted by any proof whatever from testimony. A miracle therefore, however attested, can never be rendered credible, even in the lowest degree.' This, in my apprehension, is the sum of the argument, on which my ingenious opponent rests the strength of his cause.

In answer to this I propose first to prove, that the whole is built upon a false hypothesis. That the evidence of testimony is derived solely from experience, which seems to be an axiom of this writer, is at least not so incontestible a truth as he supposes it; that, on the contrary, testimony has a natural and original influence on belief, antecedent to experience, will, I imagine, easily be evinced. For this purpose let it be remarked, that the earliest assent, which is given to testimony by children, and which is previous to all experience, is in fact the most unlimited; that by a gradual experience of mankind, it is gradually contracted, and reduced to narrower bounds. To say therefore that our diffidence in testimony is the result of experience, is more philosophical, because more consonant to truth, than to say that our faith in testimony has this foundation. Accordingly youth, which is unexperienced, is credulous; age, on the contrary, is distrustful. Exactly the reverse would be the case, were this author's doctrine just.

Perhaps it will be said, If experience is allowed to be the only measure of a logical or reasonable faith in testimony, the question, *Whether the influence of testimony on belief, be original or derived?* if it be not merely verbal, is at least of no importance in the present controversy. But I maintain it is of the greatest importance. The difference between us is by no means so inconsiderable, as to a careless view it may appear. According to his philosophy, the presumption is against the testimony, or (which amounts to the same thing) there is not the smallest presumption in its favour, till properly supported by experience. According to the explication given above, there is the strongest presumption in favour of the testimony, till properly refuted by experience.

If it be objected by the author, that such a faith in testimony as is prior to experience, must be unreasonable and unphilosophical, because unaccountable; I should reply, that there are, and must be, in human nature, some original grounds of belief, beyond which our researches cannot proceed, and of which therefore it is vain to attempt a rational account. I should desire the objector to give a reasonable account of his faith in this principle, that *similar causes always produce similar effects;* or in this, that *the course of nature will be the same to-morrow, that it was yesterday, and is to-day*; Principles, which he himself acknowledges, are neither intuitively evident, nor deduced from premises; and which nevertheless we are under a necessity of presupposing, in all our reasonings from experience. I should desire him to give a reasonable account of his faith in the clearest informations of his memory, which he will find it alike impossible either to doubt, or to explain. Indeed memory bears nearly the same relation to experience, that testimony does. Certain it is that the defects and misrepresentations of memory are often corrected by experience. Yet should any person hence infer, that memory derives all its evidence from experience, he would fall into a manifest absurdity. For, on the contrary, experience derives its origin solely from memory, and is nothing else but the general maxims or conclusions, we have formed, from the comparison of particular facts remembered. If we had not previously given an implicit faith to memory, we had never been able to acquire experience. When therefore we say that memory, which gives birth to experience, may nevertheless, in some instances, be corrected by experience, no more is implied, but that the inferences, formed from the most lively and perspicuous reports of memory, sometimes serve to rectify the mistakes which arise from such reports of this faculty, as are most languid and confused. Thus memory, in these instances, may be said to correct itself. The case is often much the same with experience and testimony, as will appear more clearly in the second section, where I shall consider the ambiguity of the word *experience*, as used by this author.

But how, says Mr Hume, is testimony then to be refuted? Principally in one or other of these two ways: *first*, And most directly, by contradictory testimony; that is, when an equal or greater number of witnesses, equally or more credible, attest the contrary: *secondly*, By such evidence, either of the incapacity or of the bad character of the witnesses, as is sufficient to discredit them. What, rejoins my antagonist, cannot then testimony be confuted by the extraordinary nature of the fact attested? Has this consideration no weight at all? That this consideration has no weight at all, it was never my intention to maintain; that by itself it can very rarely, if ever, amount to a refutation against ample and unexceptionable testimony, I hope to make extremely plain. Who has ever denied, that the uncommonness of an event related, is a presumption against its reality; and that chiefly on account of the tendency, which, experience teaches us, and this author has observed, some people have to sacrifice truth to the love of wonder? The question only is, How far does this presumption extend? In the extent which Mr Hume has assigned it, he has greatly exceeded the limits of nature, and consequently of all just reasoning.

In his opinion, 'When the fact attested is such as has seldom fallen under our observation, there is a contest of two opposite experiences, of which the one destroys the other, as far as its force goes, and the superior can only operate on the mind, by the force which remains.' There is a metaphysical, I had almost said, a magical *balance* and *arithmetic*, for the weighing and subtracting of evidence, to which he frequently recurs, and with which he seems to fancy he can perform wonders. I wish he had been a little more explicit in teaching us how these rare inventions must be used. When a writer of genius and elocution expresses himself in general terms, he will find it an easy matter to give a plausible appearance to things the most unintelligible in nature. Such sometimes is this author's way of writing. In the instance before us, he is particularly happy in his choice of metaphors. They are such as are naturally adapted to prepossess a reader in his favour. What candid person can think of suspecting the impartiality of an inquirer, who is for *weighing* in the *scales* of reason, all the arguments on both sides? Who can suspect his exactness who determines every thing by a *numerical computation?* Hence it is, that to a superficial view his reasoning appears scarcely inferior to demonstration; but, when narrowly canvassed, it is impracticable to find an application, of which, in a consistency with good sense, it is capable.

In confirmation of the remark just now made, let us try how his manner of arguing on this point can be applied to a particular instance. For this purpose I make the following supposition. I have lived for some years near a ferry. It consists with my knowledge, that the passage-boat has a thousand times crossed the river, and as many times returned safe. An unknown man, whom I have just now met, tells me, in a serious manner, that it is lost; and affirms, that he himself, standing on the bank, was a spectator of the scene; that he saw the passengers carried down the stream, and the boat overwhelmed. No person, who is influenced in his judgment of things, not by philosophical subtilties, but by common sense, a much surer guide, will hesitate to declare, that in such a testimony I have probable evidence of the fact asserted. But if leaving common sense, I shall recur to metaphysics, and submit to be tutored in my way of judging by the essayist, he will remind me, 'that there is here a contest of two opposite experiences, of which the one destroys the other, as far as its force goes, and the superior can only operate on the mind by the force which remains.' I am warned, that 'the very

same principle of experience, which gives me a certain degree of
assurance in the testimony of the witness, gives me also, in this case,
another degree of assurance, against the fact, which he endeavours
to establish, from which contradiction there arises a counterpoise,
and mutual destruction of belief and authority.' Well, I would
know the truth, if possible; and that I may conclude fairly and
philosophically, how must I balance these opposite experiences,
as you are pleased to term them? Must I set the thousand, or
rather the two thousand instances of the one side, against the
single instance of the other? In that case, it is easy to see, I have
nineteen hundred and ninety-nine degrees of evidence, that my
information is false. Or is it necessary, in order to make it credible,
that the single instance have two thousand times as much evidence,
as any of the opposite instances, supposing them equal among
themselves; or supposing them unequal, as much as all the two
thousand put together, that there may be at least an equilibrium?
This is impossible. I had for some of those instances, the evidence
of sense, which hardly any testimony can equal, much less exceed.
Once more, must the evidence I have of the veracity of the witness,
be a full equivalent to the two thousand instances, which oppose the
fact attested? By the supposition, I have no positive evidence for or
against his veracity, he being a person whom I never saw before. Yet
if none of these be the balancing, which the essay-writer means, I
despair of being able to discover his meaning.

Is then so weak a proof from testimony incapable of being
refuted? I am far from thinking so; though even so weak a proof
could not be overturned by such a contrary experience. How then
may it be overturned? *First*, by contradictory testimony. Going
homewards I met another person, whom I know as little as I
did the former; finding that he comes from the ferry, I ask him
concerning the truth of the report. He affirms, that the whole is
a fiction; that he saw the boat, and all in it, come safe to land.
This would do more to turn the scale, than fifty thousand such
contrary instances, as were supposed. Yet this would not remove
suspicion. Indeed, if we were to consider the matter abstractly,
one would think, that all suspicion would be removed, that the
two opposite testimonies would destroy each other, and leave the
mind entirely under the influence of its former experience, in the
same state as if neither testimony had been given. But this is by no
means consonant to fact. When once testimonies are introduced,
former experience is generally of no account in the reckoning; it
is but like the dust of the balance, which hath not any sensible
effect upon the scales. The mind hangs in suspense between the

two contrary declarations, and considers it as one to one, or equal in probability, that the report is true, or that it is false. Afterwards a third, and a fourth, and a fifth, confirm the declaration of the second. I am then quite at ease. Is this the only effective way of confuting false testimony? No. I suppose *again*, that instead of meeting with any person who can inform me concerning the fact, I get from some, who are acquainted with the witness, information concerning his character. They tell me, he is notorious for lying; and that his lies are commonly forged, not with a view to interest, but merely to gratify a malicious pleasure, which he takes in alarming strangers. This, though not so direct a refutation as the former, will be sufficient to discredit his report. In the former, where there is testimony contradicting testimony, the author's metaphor of a balance may be used with propriety. The things weighed are homogeneal: And when contradictory evidences are presented to the mind, tending to prove positions which cannot be both true, the mind must decide on the comparative strength of the opposite evidences, before it yield to either.

But is this the case in the supposition first made? By no means. The two thousand instances formerly known, and the single instance attested, as they relate to different facts, though of a contrary nature, are not contradictory. There is no inconsistency in believing both. There is no inconsistency in receiving the last on weaker evidence, (if it be sufficient evidence) not only than all the former together, but even than any of them singly. Will it be said, that though the former instances are not themselves contradictory to the fact recently attested, they lead to a conclusion that is contradictory? I answer, It is true, that the experienced frequency of the conjunction of any two events, leads the mind to infer a similar conjunction in time to come. But let it at the same time be remarked, that no man considers this inference, as having equal evidence with any one of those past events, on which it is founded, and for the belief of which we have had sufficient testimony. Before then the method recommended by this author can turn to any account, it will be necessary for him to compute and determine, with precision, how many hundreds, how many thousands, I might say how many myriads of instances, will confer such evidence on the conclusion founded on them, as will prove an equipoise for the testimony of one ocular witness, a man of probity, in a case of which he is allowed to be a competent judge.

There is in *arithmetic* a rule called Reduction, by which numbers of different denominations are brought to the same denomination. If this ingenious author shall invent a rule in *logic*, analogous to this, for reducing different classes of evidence to the same class, he will bless the world with a most important discovery. Then indeed he will have the honour to establish an everlasting peace in the republic of letters; then we shall have the happiness to see controversy of every kind, theological, historical, philosophical, receive its mortal wound: for though, in every question, we could not even then determine, with certainty, on which side the truth lay, we could always determine (and that is the utmost the nature of the thing admits) with as much accuracy as geometry and algebra can afford, on which side the probability lay, and in what degree. But till this metaphysical *reduction* be discovered, it will be impossible, where the evidences are of different orders, to ascertain by *subtraction* the superior evidence. We could not but esteem him a novice in arithmetic, who being asked, whether seven pounds or elevenpence make the greater sum, and what is the difference? should, by attending solely to the numbers, and overlooking the value, conclude that elevenpence were the greater, and that it exceeded the other by four. Must we not be equal novices in reasoning, if we follow the same method? Must we not fall into as great blunders? Of as little significancy do we find the balance. Is the value of things heterogeneal to be determined merely by weight? Shall silver be weighed against lead, or copper against iron? If, in exchange for a piece of gold, I were offered some counters of baser metal, is it not obvious, that till I know the comparative value of the metals, in vain shall I attempt to find what is equivalent, by the assistance either of scales or of arithmetic?

It is an excellent observation, and much to the purpose, which the late learned and pious Bishop of Durham, in his admirable performance on the analogy of religion to the course of nature, hath made on this subject. 'There is a very strong presumption,' says he, 'against the most ordinary facts, before the proof of them, which yet is overcome by almost any proof. There is a presumption of millions to one against the story of Cæsar, or of any other man. For suppose a number of common facts, so and so circumstanced, of which one had no kind of proof, should happen to come into one's thoughts, every one would, without any possible doubt, conclude them to be false. The like may be said of a single common fact.'[1] What then, I may subjoin, shall be said of an uncommon fact? And that an uncommon fact may be proved by testimony, has not *yet* been made a question. But,

---

[1] *The Analogy of Religion*, Part 2, ch. 2, § 3.

in order to illustrate the observation above cited, suppose, first, one at random mentions, that at such an hour, of such a day, in such a part of the heavens, a comet *will* appear; the conclusion from experience would not be as millions, but as infinite to one, that the proposition is false. Instead of this, suppose you have the testimony of but one ocular witness, a man of integrity, and skilled in astronomy, that at such an hour, of such a day, in such a part of the heavens, a comet *did* appear; you will not hesitate one moment to give him credit. Yet all the presumption that was against the truth of the first supposition, though almost as strong evidence as experience can afford, was also against the truth of the second, before it was thus attested.

Is it necessary to urge further, in support of this doctrine, that as the water in the canal cannot be made to rise higher than the fountain whence it flows, so it is impossible, that the evidence of testimony, if it proceeded from experience, should ever exceed that of experience, which is its source? Yet that it greatly exceeds this evidence, appears not only from what has been observed already, but still more from what I shall have occasion to observe in the sequel. One may safely affirm, that no conceivable conclusion from experience, can possess stronger evidence, than that which ascertains us of the regular succession and duration of day and night. The reason is, the instances on which this experience is founded, are both without number and without exception. Yet even this conclusion, the author admits, as we shall see in the third section, may, in a particular instance, not only be surmounted, but even annihilated by testimony.

Lastly, let it be observed, that the immediate conclusion from experience is always *general*, and runs thus: 'This is the ordinary course of nature.' 'Such an event may reasonably be expected, where all the circumstances are entirely similar.' But when we descend to particulars, the conclusion becomes weaker, being more indirect. For though all the *known* circumstances be similar, all the *actual* circumstances may not be similar; nor is it possible in any case to be assured (our knowledge of things being at best but superficial) that all the *actual* circumstances are *known* to us. On the contrary, the direct conclusion from testimony is always *particular*, and runs thus: 'This is the fact in such an individual dual instance.' The remark now made will serve both to throw light on some of the preceding observations, and to indicate the proper sphere of each species of evidence. *Experience* of the past is the only rule whereby we can judge concerning the *future:* And as when the sun is below the horizon, we must do the best we can by the light of the moon, or even of the stars; so in all cases where we have no testimony, we are under a necessity of recurring to experience, and of balancing or numbering contrary observations.[1] But the evidence resulting hence, even in the clearest cases, is acknowledged to be so weak, compared with that which results from testimony, that the strongest conviction, built merely on the former, may be overturned by the slightest proof exhibited by the latter. Accordingly the future has, in all ages and nations, been denominated the province of conjecture and uncertainty.

1 Wherever such balancing or numbering can take place, the opposite evidences must be entirely similar. It will rarely assist us in judging of facts supported by testimony; for even where contradictory testimonies come to be considered, you will hardly find, that the characters of the witnesses on the opposite sides are so precisely equal, as that an arithmetical operation will evolve the credibility. In matters of pure experience it has often place. Hence the computations that have been made of the value of annuities, insurances, and several other commercial articles. In calculations concerning chances, the degree of probability may be determined with mathematical exactness. I shall here take the liberty, though the matter be not essential to the design of this tract, to correct an oversight in the essayist, who always supposes, that where contrary evidences must be balanced, the probability lies in the remainder or surplus, when the less number is subtracted from the greater. The probability does not consist in the surplus, but in the ratio, or geometrical proportion, which the numbers on the opposite sides bear to each other. I explain myself thus. In favour of one supposed event, there are 100 similar instances, against it 50. In another case under consideration, the favourable instances are 60, and only 10 unfavourable. Though the difference, or arithmetical proportion, which is 50, be the same in both cases, the probability is by no means equal, as the author's way of reasoning implies. The probability of the first event is as 100 to 50, or 2 to 1. The probability of the second is as 60 to 10, or 6 to 1. Consequently on comparing the different examples, though both be probable, the second is thrice as probable as the first. I am sensible that the precise degree of probability is not entirely determined, even by the ratio. There are other circumstances to be considered where the utmost accuracy is requisite: But it does not appear necessary, in the present inquiry, to enter deeper into the subject. See Dr Price's Dissertation, Sect. II.

From what has been said, the attentive reader will easily discover, that the author's argument against *miracles*, has not the least affinity to the argument used by Dr Tillotson against *transubstantiation*, with which Mr Hume has introduced his subject. Let us hear the argument, as it is related in the Essay, from the writings of the Archbishop. 'It is acknowledged on all hands,' says that learned prelate, 'that the authority either of the scripture or of tradition, is founded merely on the testimony of the apostles, who were eye-witnesses to those miracles of our Saviour, by which he proved his divine mission. Our evidence then for the truth of the Christian religion is less than the evidence for the truth of our senses; because even in the first authors of our religion it was no greater; and it is evident, it must diminish in passing from them to their disciples; nor can any one be so certain of the truth of their testimony, as of the immediate objects of his senses. But a weaker evidence can never destroy a stronger; and therefore, were the doctrine of the real presence ever so clearly revealed in scripture, it were directly contrary to the rules of just reasoning to give our assent to it. It contradicts sense, though both the scripture and tradition, on which it is supposed to be built, carry not such evidence with them as sense, when they are considered merely as external evidences, and are not brought home to every one's breast, by the immediate operation of the Holy Spirit.' That the evidence of *testimony* is less than the evidence of *sense*, is undeniable. *Sense* is the source of that evidence, which is first transferred to the *memory* of the individual, as to a general reservoir, and thence transmitted to others by the channel of *testimony*. That the original evidence can never gain any thing, but must lose, by the transmission, is beyond dispute. What has been rightly perceived may be misremembered; what is rightly remembered may, through incapacity, or through ill intention, be misreported; and what is rightly reported may be misunderstood. In any of these four ways therefore, either by defect of memory, of elocution, or of veracity in the relater, or by misapprehension in the hearer, there is a chance, that the truth received by the information of the senses, may be misrepresented or mistaken; now every such chance occasions a real diminution of the evidence. That the sacramental elements are bread and wine, not flesh and blood, our sight and touch and taste and smell concur in testifying. If these senses are not to be credited, the apostles themselves could not have evidence of the mission of their master. For the greatest external evidence they had, or could have, of his mission, was that which their senses gave them, of the reality of his miracles. But whatever strength there is in this argument, with regard to the apostles, the argument, with regard to us, who, for those miracles, have only the evidence, not of our own senses, but of their testimony, is incomparably stronger. In their case, it is sense contradicting sense, in ours, it is sense contradicting testimony. But what relation has this to the author's argument? None at all. Testimony, it is acknowledged, is a weaker evidence than sense. But it has been already evinced, that its evidence for particular facts is infinitely stronger than that which the general conclusions from experience can afford us. Testimony holds directly of memory and sense. Whatever is duly attested must be remembered by the witness; whatever is duly remembered must once have been perceived. But nothing similar takes place with regard to experience, nor can testimony, with any appearance of meaning, be said to hold of it.

Thus I have shown, as I proposed, that the author's reasoning proceeds on a false hypothesis. – It supposes testimony to derive its evidence solely from experience, which is false. – It supposes by consequence, that contrary observations have a weight in opposing testimony, which the first and most acknowledged principles of human reason, or, if you like the term better, common sense, evidently shows that they have not. – It assigns a rule for discovering the superiority of contrary evidences, which, in the latitude there given it, tends to mislead the judgment, and which it is impossible, by any explication, to render of real use.

Source: George Campbell, *A Dissertation on Miracles*, Edinburgh 1796, vol. I, part I, pp. 33–64

SEVENTEEN

HUGH BLAIR
On our Imperfect Knowledge of a Future State

The Scottish Enlightenment, considered as the work of a distinguished band of teachers, preachers and pleaders, owes a particular debt to Hugh Blair for he was outstanding in the first two of these three categories. He was perhaps the greatest pulpit orator of his generation, and the principles of rhetoric which he learned in a practical way in the pulpit of the High Kirk of St Giles were duly taught to generations of students at the University of Edinburgh where he occupied the chair of Rhetoric and Belles Lettres. His two posts, secular and ecclesiastical, are bound tightly together in his *Sermons*. The sermons are artfully constructed, insightful works of high and serious moral tone and with theological learning lightly carried. The emphasis throughout his pulpit writings is on what lies naturally within our power, the exercise of civic virtue, rather than on what is ours by an act of divine grace.

In the pulpit he was principally concerned with educating his flock in the ways of godliness, where godliness is conceived primarily in humanistic terms. We are to be good citizens, faithful friends, and loving to our family. Blair's friend David Hume could have found little to cavil at in Blair's description of a morally well-lived life. He would however have found something to cavil at in Blair's theological point of departure in Sermon 4, for Blair attends to the depth of our ignorance of our future state, while acknowledging that we can look forward to one, whereas Hume acknowledges no such thing. The question at issue really has its background in theodicy, the idea that the world is ruled by a just God. Has God done the right thing by us by leaving us in the dark regarding our future state? Would it not have been better for us had we not been left having to 'see through a glass, darkly'? Blair's strongly argued reply is that the knowledge afforded us if the glass were clear would have a catastrophic effect. We would be so bewitched by the vision that the arts and labours that support social order and promote the happiness of society would be neglected. Each of us would 'sojourn on earth as a melancholy exile . . . no longer a fit inhabitant of this world'. But we have a job to do on Earth, to face up to difficulties and temptations, and in so doing to develop the virtues of fortitude, temperance, self-denial, and so on. The overarching concept with which Blair is working is encapsulated in his phrase, that this life is 'the childhood of existence' – we are being educated for immortality, and will not be fit to receive it if we do not pass through the educative process constituted by life on Earth.

A.B.

On our Imperfect Knowledge of a Future State

1 Corinthians xiii. 12
For now we see through a glass, darkly.

The Apostle here describes the imperfection of our knowledge with relation to spiritual and eternal objects. He employs two metaphors to represent more strongly the disadvantages under which we lie: One, that we see those objects *through a glass*, that is, through the intervention of a medium which obscures their glory; the other, that we see them *in a riddle* or enigma, which our translators have rendered by seeing them *darkly;* that is, the truth in part is discovered, in part concealed, and placed beyond our comprehension.

This description, however just and true, cannot fail to occasion some perplexity to an inquiring mind. For it may seem strange, that so much darkness should be left upon those celestial objects, towards which we are at the same time commanded to aspire. We are strangers in the universe of God. Confined to that spot on which we dwell, we are permitted to know nothing of what is transacting in the regions above us and around us. By much labour, we acquire a superficial acquaintance with a few sensible objects which we find in our present habitation; but we enter, and we depart, under a total ignorance of the nature and laws of the spiritual world. One subject in particular, when our thoughts proceed in this train, must often recur upon the mind with peculiar anxiety; that is, the immortality of the soul, and the future state of man. Exposed as we are at present to such variety of afflictions, and subjected to so much disappointment in all our pursuits of happiness, Why, it may be said, has our gracious Creator denied us the consolation of a full discovery of our future existence, if indeed such an existence be prepared for us? – Reason, it is true, suggests many arguments in behalf of immortality: Revelation gives full assurance of it. Yet even that Gospel, which is said to have *brought life and immortality to light*, allows us to *see only through a glass, darkly. It doth not yet appear what we shall be.* Our knowledge of a future world is very imperfect; our ideas of it are faint and confused. It is not displayed in such a manner as to make an impression suited to the importance of the object. The faith even of the best men is much inferiour, both in clearness and in force, to the evidence of sense; and proves on many occasions insufficient to counterbalance the temptations of the present world. Happy moments indeed there sometimes are in the lives of pious men, when, sequestered from worldly cares, and borne up on the wings of divine contemplation, they rise to a near and transporting view of immortal glory. But such efforts of the mind are rare, and cannot be long supported. When the spirit of meditation subsides, this lively sense of a future state decays; and though the general belief of it remain, yet even good men, when they return to the ordinary business and cares of life, seem to rejoin the multitude, and to reassume the same hopes, and fears, and interests, which influence the rest of the world.

From such reflections a considerable difficulty respecting this important subject either arises, or seems to arise. Was such an obscure and imperfect discovery of another life worthy to proceed from God? Does it not afford some ground, either to tax his goodness, or to suspect the evidence of its coming from him? – This is the point which we are now to consider; and let us consider it with that close attention which the subject merits. Let us inquire whether we have any reason, either to complain of Providence, or to object to the evidence of a future state, because that evidence is not of a more sensible and striking nature. Let us attempt humbly to trace the reasons why, though permitted to know and to see somewhat of the eternal world, we are nevertheless permitted only to *know in part, and to see through a glass, darkly.*

It plainly appears to be the plan of the Deity, in all his dispensations, to mix light with darkness, evidence with uncertainty. Whatever the reasons of this procedure be, the fact is undeniable. He is described in the Old Testament as *a God that hideth himself.*[1] *Clouds and darkness* are said to *surround him. His way is in the sea, and his path in the great waters; his footsteps are not known.* Both the works and the ways of God are full of mystery. In the ordinary course of his government, innumerable events occur which perplex us to the utmost. There is a certain limit to all our inquiries of religion, beyond which if we attempt to proceed, we are lost in a maze of inextricable difficulties. Even that revelation which affords such material instruction to man concerning his duty and his happiness, leaves many doubts unresolved. Why it was not given sooner; why not to all men; why there should be so many things in it *hard to be understood;* are difficulties not inconsiderable, in the midst of that incontestable evidence by which it is supported. If, then, the future state of man be not placed in so full and clear a light as we

[1] Isaiah, xiv. 15.

desire, this is no more than what the analogy of all religion, both natural and revealed, gave us reason to expect.

But such a solution of the difficulty will be thought imperfect. It may, perhaps, not give much satisfaction to show, that all religion abounds with difficulties of a like nature. Our situation, it will be said, is so much the more to be lamented, that not on one side only we are confined in our inquiries, but on all hands environed with mysterious obscurity. – Let us then, if so much dissatisfied with our condition, give scope for once to Fancy, and consider how the plan of Providence might be rectified to our wish. Let us call upon the Sceptic, and desire him to say, what measure of information would afford him entire satisfaction.

This, he will tell us, requires not any long or deep deliberation. He desires only to have his view enlarged beyond the limits of this corporeal state. Instead of resting upon evidence which requires discussion, which must be supported by much reasoning, and which, after all, he alleges, yields very imperfect information, he demands the everlasting mansions to be so displayed, if in truth such mansions there be, as to place faith on a level with the evidence of sense. What noble and happy effects, he exclaims, would instantly follow, if man thus beheld his present and his future existence at once before him! He would then become worthy of his rank in the creation. Instead of being the sport, as now, of degrading passions and childish attachments, he would act solely on the principles of immortality. His pursuit of virtue would be steady; his life would be undisturbed and happy. Superiour to the attacks of distress, and to the solicitations of pleasure, he would advance, by a regular process, towards those divine rewards and honours which were continually present to his view. – Thus Fancy, with as much ease and confidence as if it were a perfect judge of creation, erects a new world to itself, and exults with admiration of its own work. But let us pause, and suspend this admiration, till we coolly examine the consequences that would follow from this supposed reformation of the universe.

Consider the nature and circumstances of man. Introduced into the world in an indigent condition, he is supported at first by the care of others; and, as soon as he begins to act for himself, finds labour and industry to be necessary for sustaining his life, and supplying his wants. Mutual defence and interest give rise to society; and society, when formed, requires distinctions of property, diversity of conditions, subordinations of ranks, and a multiplicity of occupations, in order to advance the general good. The services of the poor, and the protection of the rich, become reciprocally necessary. The governours and the governed must co-operate for general safety. Various arts must be studied; some respecting the cultivation of the mind, others the care of the body; some to ward off the evils, and some to provide the conveniences of life. In a word, by the destination of his Creator, and the necessities of his nature, man commences, at once, an active, not merely a contemplative being. Religion assumes him as such. It supposes him employed in this world, as on a busy stage. It regulates, but does not abolish, the enterprises and cares of ordinary life. It addresses itself to the various ranks in society; to the rich and the poor, to the magistrate and the subject. It rebukes the slothful; directs the diligent how to labour; and requires every man to *do his own business*.

Suppose, now, that veil to be withdrawn which conceals another world from our view. Let all obscurity vanish; let us no longer *see darkly, as through a glass;* but let every man enjoy that intuitive perception of divine and eternal objects which the Sceptic was supposed to desire. The immediate effect of such a discovery would be, to annihilate in our eye all human objects, and to produce a total stagnation in the affairs of the world. Were the celestial glory exposed to our admiring view; did the angelic harmony sound in our enraptured ears; what earthly concerns would have the power of engaging our attention for a single moment? All the studies and pursuits, the arts and labours which now employ the activity of man, which support the order, or promote the happiness of society, would lie neglected and abandoned. Those desires and fears, those hopes and interests, by which we are at present stimulated, would cease to operate. Human life would present no objects sufficient to rouse the mind; to kindle the spirit of enterprise, or to urge the hand of industry. If the mere sense of duty engaged a good man to take some part in the business of the world, the task, when submitted to, would prove distasteful. Even the preservation of life would be slighted, if he were not bound to it by the authority of God. Impatient of his confinement within this tabernacle of dust, languishing for the happy day of his translation to those glorious regions which were displayed to his sight, he would sojourn on earth as a melancholy exile. Whatever Providence has prepared for the entertainment of man, would be viewed with contempt. Whatever is now attractive in society, would appear insipid. In a word, he would be no longer a fit inhabitant of this world, nor be qualified for those exertions which are allotted to him in his present sphere of being. But, all his faculties being sublimated above the measure of humanity, he would be in the condition of a being of superiour order, who, obliged to reside among men, would regard their pursuits with scorn, as dreams, trifles, and puerile amusements of a day.

But to this reasoning it may perhaps be replied, That such consequences as I have now stated, supposing them to follow, deserve not much regard. – For what though the present arrangement of human affairs were entirely changed by a clearer view and a stronger impression of our future state? Would not such a change prove the highest blessing to man? Is not his attachment to worldly objects the great source both of his misery and his guilt? Employed in perpetual contemplation of heavenly objects, and in preparation for the enjoyment of them, would he not become more virtuous, and of course more happy, than the nature of his present employments and attachments permits him to be? – Allowing, for a moment, the consequence to be such, this much is yielded, that, upon the supposition which was made, man would not be the creature which he now is, nor human life the state which we now behold. How far the change would contribute to his welfare, comes to be considered.

If there be any principle fully ascertained by religion, it is, That this life was intended for a state of trial and improvement to man. His preparation for a better world required a gradual purification, carried on by steps of progressive discipline. The situation, therefore, here assigned him was such as to answer this design, by calling forth all his active powers, by giving full scope to his moral dispositions, and bringing to light his whole character. Hence it became proper, that difficulty and temptation should arise in the course of his duty. Ample rewards were promised to virtue; but these rewards were left, as yet, in obscurity and distant prospect. The impressions of sense were so balanced against the discoveries of immortality, as to allow a conflict between faith and sense, between conscience and desire, between present pleasure and future good. In this conflict, the souls of good men are tried, improved, and strengthened. In this field, their honours are reaped. Here are formed the capital virtues of fortitude, temperance, and self-denial; moderation in prosperity, patience in adversity, submission to the will of God, and charity and forgiveness to men, amidst the various competitions of worldly interest.

Such is the plan of Divine wisdom for man's improvement. But put the case that the plans devised by human wisdom were to take place, and that the rewards of the just were to be more fully displayed to view; the exercise of all those graces which I have mentioned, would be entirely superseded. Their very names would be unknown. Every temptation being withdrawn, every worldly attachment being subdued by the overpowering discoveries of eternity, no trial of sincerity, no discrimination of characters, would remain; no opportunity would be afforded for those active exertions, which are the means of purifying and perfecting the good. On the competition between time and eternity, depends the chief exercise of human virtue. The obscurity which at present hangs over eternal objects, preserves the competition. Remove that obscurity, and you remove human virtue from its place. You overthrow that whole system of discipline, by which imperfect creatures are, in this life, gradually trained up for a more perfect state.

This, then, is the conclusion to which at last we arrive: That the full display which was demanded of the heavenly glory, would be so far from improving the human soul, that it would abolish those virtues and duties which are the great instruments of its improvement. It would be unsuitable to the character of man in every view, either as an active being or a moral agent. It would disqualify him for taking part in the affairs of the world; for relishing the pleasures, or for discharging the duties of life: In a word, it would entirely defeat the purpose of his being placed on this earth; and the question, Why the Almighty has been pleased to leave a spiritual world, and the future existence of man, under so much obscurity, resolves in the end into this, Why there should be such a creature as man in the universe of God? – Such is the issue of the improvements proposed to be made on the plans of Providence. They add to the discoveries of the superiour wisdom of God, and of the presumption and folly of man.

From what has been said it now appears, That no reasonable objection to the belief of a future state arises from the imperfect discoveries of it which we enjoy; from the difficulties that are mingled with its evidence; from our *seeing as through a glass, darkly, and being* left to *walk by faith, and not by sight.* It cannot be otherwise, it ought not to be otherwise, in our present state. The evidence which is afforded, is sufficient for the conviction of a candid mind, sufficient for a rational ground of conduct, though not so striking as to withdraw our attention from the present world, or altogether to overcome the impression of sensible objects. In such evidence it becomes us to acquiesce, without indulging either doubts or complaints on account of our not receiving all the satisfaction which we fondly desire, but which our present immaturity of being excludes. For, upon the supposition of immortality, this life is no other than the childhood of existence; and the measures of our knowledge must be proportioned to such a state. To the successive stages of human life, from infancy to old age, belong certain peculiar attachments, certain cares, desires, and interests, which open not abruptly, but by gradual advances, on the mind, as it becomes fit to receive them, and is prepared for acting the part to which, in their order, they pertain. Hence, in the education of a child, no one thinks of inspiring him all at once with the knowledge, the sentiments, and views of a man, and with contempt for the exercises and amusements of childhood. On the contrary, employments suited to his age are allowed to occupy him. By these his powers are gradually unfolded; and advantage is taken of his youthful pursuits, to improve and strengthen his mind; till, step by step, he is led on to higher prospects, and prepared for a larger and more important scene of action.

This analogy, which so happily illustrates the present conduct of the Deity towards man, deserves attention the more, as it is the very illustration used by the Apostle, when treating of this subject in the context. *Now*, says he, *we know in part; but when that which is perfect is come, that which is in part shall be done away. When I was a child, I spoke as a child, I understood as a child, I thought as a child; but when I became a man, I put away childish things. For now we see through a glass, darkly; but then face to face: Now I know in part; but then, I shall know even as I am known.* Under the care of the Almighty, our education is now going on from a mortal to an immortal state. As much light is let in upon us, as we can bear without injury. When the objects become too splendid and dazzling for our sight, the curtain is drawn. Exercised in such a field of action as suits the strength of our unripened powers, we are, at the same time, by proper prospects and hopes, prompted to aspire towards the manhood of our nature, the time when *childish things shall be put away*. But still, betwixt those future prospects, and the impression of present objects, such an accurate proportion is established, as on the one hand shall not produce a total contempt of earthly things, while we aspire to those that are heavenly; and, on the other, shall not encourage such a degree of attachment to our present state, as would render us unworthy of future advancement. In a word, the whole course of things is so ordered, that we neither by an irregular and precipitate education become men too soon, nor by a fond and trifling indulgence are suffered to continue children for ever.

Let these reflections not only remove the doubts which may arise from our obscure knowledge of immortality, but likewise produce the highest admiration of the wisdom of our Creator. The structure of the natural world affords innumerable instances of profound design, which no attentive spectator can survey without wonder. In the moral world, where the workmanship is of much finer and more delicate contexture, subjects of still greater admiration open to view. But admiration must rise to its highest point, when those parts of the moral constitution, which at first were reputed blemishes, which carried the appearance of objections, either to the wisdom or the goodness of Providence, are discovered, on more accurate inspection, to be adjusted with the most exquisite propriety. We have now seen that the darkness of man's condition is no less essential to his well-being, than the light which he enjoys. His internal powers, and his external situation, appear to be exactly fitted to each other. Those complaints which we are apt to make, of our limited capacity and narrow views, of our inability to penetrate further into the future destination of man, are found, from the foregoing observations, to be just as unreasonable, as the childish complaints of our not being formed with a microscopic eye, nor furnished with an eagle's wing; that is, of not being endowed with powers which would subvert the nature, and counteract the laws of our present state.

In order to do justice to the subject, I must observe, that the same reasoning which has been now employed with respect to our knowledge of immortality, is equally applicable to many other branches of intellectual knowledge. Thus, why we are permitted to know so little of the nature of that Eternal Being who rules the universe; why the manner in which he operates on the natural and moral world, is wholly concealed; why we are kept in such ignorance with respect to the extent of his works, to the nature and agency of spiritual beings, and even with respect to the union between our own soul and body: To all these, and several other inquiries of the same kind, which often employ the solicitous researches of speculative men, the answer is the same that was given to the interesting question which makes the subject of our discourse. The degree of knowledge desired, would prove incompatible with the design, and with the proper business of this life. It would raise us to a sphere too exalted; would reveal objects too great and striking for our present faculties; would excite feelings too strong for us to bear; in a word, would unfit us for thinking or acting like human creatures. It is therefore reserved for a more advanced period of our nature; and the hand of Infinite wisdom hath in mercy drawn a veil over scenes which would overpower the sight of mortals.

One instance, in particular, of Divine wisdom is so illustrious, and corresponds so remarkably with our present subject, that I cannot pass it over without notice; that is, the concealment under which Providence has placed the future events of our life on earth. The desire of penetrating into this unknown region has ever been one of the most anxious passions of men. It has often seized the wise as well as the credulous, and given rise to many vain and impious superstitions throughout the whole earth. Burning with curiosity at the approach of some critical event, and impatient under the perplexity of conjecture and doubt, How cruel is Providence (we are apt to exclaim) in denying to man the power of foresight, and in limiting him to the knowledge of the present moment! Were he permitted to look forward into the course of destiny, how much more suitably would he be prepared for the various turns and changes in his life? With what moderation would he enjoy his prosperity under the foreknowledge of an approaching reverse? and with what eagerness be prompted to improve the flying hours, by seeing the inevitable term draw nigh which was to finish his course?

But while Fancy indulges such vain desires and criminal complaints, this coveted foreknowledge must clearly appear to the eye of Reason to be the most fatal gift which the Almighty could bestow. If, in this present mixed state, all the successive scenes of distress through which we are to pass, were laid before us in one view, perpetual sadness would overcast our life. Hardly would any transient gleams of intervening joy be able to force their way through the cloud. Faint would be the relish of pleasures of which we foresaw the close; insupportable the burden of afflictions, under which we were oppressed by a load, not only of present, but of an anticipated sorrow. Friends would begin their union with lamenting the day which was to dissolve it; and, with weeping eye, the parent would every moment behold the child whom he knew that he was to lose. In short, as soon as that mysterious veil, which now covers futurity, was lifted up, all the gaiety of life would disappear; its flattering hopes, its pleasing illusions, would vanish, and nothing but its vanity and sadness remain. The foresight of the hour of death would continually interrupt the course of human affairs, and the overwhelming prospect of the future, instead of exciting men to proper activity, would render them immovable with consternation and dismay. How much more friendly to man is that mixture of knowledge and ignorance which is allotted to him in this state! Ignorant of the events which are to befal us, and of the precise term which is to conclude our life, by this ignorance our enjoyment of present objects is favoured; and knowing that death is certain, and that human affairs are full of change, by this knowledge our attachment to those objects is moderated. Precisely in the same manner, as by the mixture of evidence and obscurity which remains on the prospect of a future state, a proper balance is preserved betwixt our love of this life, and our desire of a better.

The longer that our thoughts dwell on this subject, the more must we be convinced, that in nothing the Divine wisdom is more admirable, than in proportioning knowledge to the necessities of man. Instead of lamenting our condition, that we are permitted only to *see as through a glass, darkly*, we have reason to bless our Creator, no less for what he hath concealed, than for what he hath allowed us to know. He *is wonderful in counsel, as he is excellent in working. He is wise in heart, and his thoughts are deep. How unsearchable are the riches of the wisdom of the knowledge of God!*

From the whole view which we have taken of the subject, this important instruction arises, that the great design of all the knowledge, and in particular of the religious knowledge which God hath afforded us, is, to fit us for discharging the duties of life. No useless discoveries are made to us in religion: No discoveries even of useful truths, beyond the precise degree of information, which is subservient to right conduct. To this great end all our information points. In this centre all the lines of knowledge meet. *Life and immortality are brought to light in the gospel;* yet not so displayed as to gratify the curiosity of the world with an astonishing spectacle; but only so far made known, as to assist and support us in the practice of our duty. If the discovery were more imperfect, it would excite no desire of immortality; if it were more full and striking, it would render us careless of life. On the first supposition, no sufficient motive to virtue would appear; on the second, no proper trial of it would remain. In the one case, we should think and act like men who *have their portion only in this world;* in the other case, like men who have no concern with this world at all. Whereas now, by the wise constitution of Heaven, we are placed in the most favourable situation for acting, with propriety, our allotted part here; and for rising, in due course, to higher honour and happiness hereafter.

Let us then second the kind intentions of Providence, and act upon the plan which it hath pointed out. Checking our inquisitive solicitude about what the Almighty hath concealed, let us diligently improve what he hath made known. Inhabitants of the earth, we are at the same time candidates for heaven. Looking upon these as only different views of one consistent character, let us carry on our preparation for heaven, not by abstracting ourselves from the concerns of this world, but by fulfilling the duties and offices of every station in life. Living *soberly, righteously, and godly in the present world*, let us *look for that blessed hope, and the glorious appearing of the great God, and our Saviour Jesus Christ.*

Before I conclude, it may be proper to observe, That the reasonings in this discourse give no ground to apprehend any danger of our being too much influenced by the belief of a future state. I have shown the hurtful effects which would follow from too bright and full a discovery of the glory of that state; and in showing this, I have justified the decree of Providence, which permits no such discovery. But as our nature is at present constituted, attached by so many strong connexions to the world of sense, and enjoying a communication so feeble and distant with the world of spirits, we need fear no danger from cultivating intercourse with the latter as much as possible. On the contrary, from that intercourse the chief security of our virtue is to be sought. The bias of our nature leans so much towards sense, that from this side the peril is to be dreaded, and on this side the defence is to be provided.

Let us then *walk by faith*. Let us strengthen this principle of action to the utmost of our power. Let us implore the Divine grace to strengthen it within us more and more; that we may thence derive an antidote against that subtle poison, which incessant commerce with the objects of sense diffuses through our souls; that we may hence acquire purity and dignity of manners suited to our divine hopes; and undefiled by the pleasures of the world, unshaken by its terrours, may preserve to the end one constant tenour of integrity. Till at last, having, under the conduct of Christian faith, happily finished the period of discipline, we enter on that state, where a far nobler scene shall open where eternal objects shall shine in their native splendour; where this twilight of mortal life being past, the *Sun of righteousness* shall rise; and *that which is perfect being come, that which is in part shall be done away.*

Source: Hugh Blair, *Sermons*, Edinburgh 1824, vol. 1, sermon 4, pp. 40–53

EIGHTEEN

HENRY HOME, LORD KAMES
The Benevolence of God

Kames's *Essays* caused a stir on their first appearance, prompting accusations of scepticism and impiety, and friendly ministers of the Kirk stepped forward to defend him against the charge of heresy. He was not an obvious target for such a charge, and certainly the material in the chapter on the benevolence of the deity would have caused few qualms among the moderate clergy. In any case a major target of Kames's critical writings was David Hume, who really was an obvious target for the kind of ecclesiastical attack made on Kames. In the following excerpt Kames has Hume in his sights. The reference made at the start, to the eleventh essay 'Of the practical consequences of natural religion' in *Philosophical Essays concerning Human Understanding*, is in fact to the essay 'Of a particular providence and of a future state', which was published as section 11 of Hume's *An Enquiry concerning Human Understanding*.

In the *Enquiry*, and at much greater length in his magisterial *Dialogues Concerning Natural Religion*, Hume deploys the principle that in arguing from effect to cause nothing more ought to be assigned to the cause than is requisite to explain the effect. If for example we wish to argue to the existence and nature of God solely on the basis of what we find in the natural order then we are logically constrained to ascribe to God only such attributes as are necessary to explain those natural phenomena for which we are seeking an explanation. It is inappropriate to draw upon the knowledge of God to which we would be able to lay claim if we had recourse to revelation.

This methodological point is important since, as the title of his book makes clear, Kames is concerned with natural, and not revealed, religion. He wants to know what can be learned about God if we restrict ourselves to reading nature, and therefore do not also read the Bible. But in that case, why not take the Humean line that since ours is a demonstrably imperfect world we are not entitled, on that basis, to conclude that the creator is perfect? For though we need to postulate a perfect cause to explain a perfect effect, we need do no such thing to explain an imperfect effect. Kames does not reject Hume's principle. If anything he sees himself as tightening up its application beyond even the point to which Hume was prepared to go. For example, Kames argues that by reason alone we are not, strictly speaking, entitled to claim that if something comes into existence it must have any cause whatsoever. What prevents Kames slipping into agnosticism, at least as far as natural theology goes, is his conviction that we should listen to the voice of sense and intuition as well as to the voice of reason. There are 'principles implanted in our nature' that permit us to draw conclusions that reason alone does not sanction. At this point Kames comes very close to a common sense approach, understanding 'common sense' as Thomas Reid uses the term. If something is a 'tendency of our nature' then we have to rely on it as a source of truth. It is such a tendency that Kames invokes when he points out that, though we see evil as well as good around us, we do not conclude that the cause also must be a mixture of good and evil: 'it is a tendency of our nature to reject a mixed character of benevolence and malevolence, unless where it is necessarily pressed home upon us by an equality of opposite effects'. In any case Kames sees a world which is predominantly, if not overwhelmingly, good and 'a few cross instances' cannot make him waver, especially as what looks a 'cross instance' to us now might not look so from a more ample perspective. And he looks forward to the day when, after sufficient progress in learning, we will see why the few cross instances are not after all really cross. It is unlikely that any of the arguments in this excerpt would have satisfied Kames's distant kinsman David Hume, but the arguments indicate that Kames occupied a position with which many of the enlightened moderate clergy would have felt entirely comfortable.

A.B.

Benevolence of the Deity

The mixed nature of the events that fall under our observation,
seems to point out a mixed cause, partly good and partly ill. The
author of *Philosophical Essays concerning human understanding*, in
his eleventh essay, *Of the practical consequences of natural religion*,
puts in the mouth of an Epicurean philosopher a very shrewd
argument against the benevolence of the Deity. The sum is what
follows: 'If the cause be known only by the effect, we never ought
to assign to it any qualities, beyond what are precisely requisite to
produce the effect. Allowing, therefore, God to be the author of the
existence and order of the universe; it follows, that he possesses
that precise degree of power, intelligence, and benevolence, which
appears in his workmanship.' And hence, from the present scene
of things, apparently so full of ill and disorder, it is concluded,
'That we have no foundation for ascribing any attribute to the
Deity, but what is precisely commensurate with the imperfection
of this world.' With regard to mankind, he reasons differently.
In works of human art and contrivance, it is admitted that we
can advance from the effect to the cause, and returning back
from the cause, that we conclude new effects, which have not
yet existed. Thus, for instance, from the sight of a half-finished
building, surrounded with heaps of stones and mortar, and all the
instruments of masonry, we naturally conclude, that the building
will be finished, and receive all the farther improvements which
art can bestow upon it. But the foundation of this reasoning
is plainly, that man is a being whom we know by experience,
and whose motives and designs we are acquainted with, which
enables us to draw many inferences, concerning what may be
expected from him. But did we know man only from the single
work or production which we examine, we could not argue in
this manner; because our knowledge of all the qualities which
we ascribe to him, being, upon that supposition, derived from
the work or production, it is impossible they could point any
thing farther, or be the foundation of any new inference.'

Supposing reason to be our only guide in these matters, which
is supposed in this argument, it appears to be just. By no inference
of reason, can I conclude any power or benevolence in the cause,
beyond what is displayed in the effect. But this is no wonderful
discovery. The philosopher might have carried his argument a

greater length: he might have observed, even with regard to a man I am perfectly acquainted with, that I cannot conclude by any chain of reasoning, that he will finish the house he has begun. It is to no purpose to urge his temper and disposition; for from what principle of reason can I infer, that these will continue the same as formerly? He might further have observed, that the difficulty is greater with regard to a man I know nothing of, supposing him to have begun the building. For what foundation have I in reason to transfer the qualities of the persons I am acquainted with to a stranger, which surely is not performed by any process of reasoning? There is still a wider step; which is, that reason will not support me in attributing to the Deity even that precise degree of power, intelligence and benevolence, which appears in his workmanship. I find no inconsistency in supposing, that a blind and undesigning cause may be productive of excellent effects: it will I presume be difficult to produce a demonstration to the contrary. And supposing, at the instant of operation, the Deity to have been endued with these properties, can we make out, by any argument *a priori*, that they are still subsisting in him? Nay, this same philosopher might have gone a great way further, by observing, when any thing comes into existence, that, by no process of reasoning, can we so much as infer any cause of its existence.

But happily for man, where reason fails him, sense and intuition come to his assistance. By means of principles implanted in our nature, we are enabled to make the foregoing conclusions and inferences; as at full length is made out in some of the foregoing Essays. More particularly, power discovered in any object, is intuitively perceived to be a permanent quality, like figure or extension.[1] Upon this account, power discovered by a single effect, is considered as sufficient to produce the like effects, without end. Further, great power may be discovered from a small effect; which holds even in bodily strength, as where an action is performed readily and without effort. This is equally remarkable in wisdom and intelligence: a very short argument may unfold correctness of judgment, and a deep reach. The same holds in art and skill: examining a slight piece of workmanship done with taste, we readily observe, that the artist was equal to a greater task. But it is most of all remarkable in the quality of benevolence; even from a single effect produced by an unknown cause, which appears adapted to some good purpose, we necessarily attribute

1 Essay, 'Knowledge of Future Events.'

to this cause benevolence, as well as power and wisdom.[1] The perception is indeed but weak when it ariseth from a single effect; but still is a perception of pure benevolence, without any mixture of malice; for such contradictory qualities are not readily ascribed to the same cause. There indeed may be a difficulty, where the effect is of a mixed nature, partly ill partly good; or where a variety of effects, having these opposite characters, proceed from the same cause. Such intricate cases cannot fail to embarrass us; but as we must form some sentiment, we ascribe benevolence or malevolence to the cause, from the prevalence of the one or other quality in the effects. If evil make the greater figure, we perceive the cause to be malevolent, notwithstanding opposite instances of goodness. If, upon the whole, goodness be supereminent, we perceive the cause to be benevolent; and are not moved by the cross instances of evil, which for ought we know may be necessary for producing on the whole the greatest quantity of good. In a word, it is the tendency of our nature to reject a mixed character made up of benevolence and malevolence, unless where it is necessarily pressed home upon us by an equality of opposite effects; and in every subject that cannot be reached by the reasoning faculty, we justly rely on the tendency of our nature, as the best proof the subject can admit of.

Such are the conclusions that we can draw; not indeed from reason, but from intuitive perception. So little are we acquainted with the essence or nature of things, that we cannot establish these conclusions upon any argument *a priori*. Nor would it be of great benefit to mankind, to have these conclusions demonstrated to them; few having either leisure or talents to comprehend such profound speculations. It is more wisely ordered, that they appear to us intuitively certain.

This is a solid foundation for our conviction of the benevolence of the Deity. If, from a single effect, pure benevolence in the cause can be perceived; what doubt can there be of the pure benevolence of the Deity, when we survey his works, pregnant with good-will to mankind. Innumerable instances of things wisely adapted to good purposes, give us the strongest conviction of the goodness as well as wisdom of the Deity; which is joined with the firmest persuasion of constancy and uniformity in his operations. A few cross instances cannot make us waver. When we know so little of nature, it would be surprising indeed, if we should be able to account for every event and its final tendency. Unless we were let

1 Essay, 'Power,' at the close.

into the counsels of the Almighty, we can never hope to unravel all the mysteries of the creation.

I shall add some other considerations to confirm our belief of the pure benevolence of the Deity. And first, the independent and all-sufficient nature of the Deity, sets him above all suspicion of being liable either to envy, or to the pursuit of any interest, other than the general interest of his creatures. Wants, weakness, and opposition of interests, are the causes of ill-will among men. From all such influences the Deity is exempted. And therefore, unless we suppose him less perfect than the creatures he hath made, we cannot suppose that there is any degree of malice in his nature.

There is a second consideration, which hath always afforded me great satisfaction. Did natural evil prevail in reality, as much as it doth in appearance, we must expect, that the enlargement of natural knowledge should daily discover new instances of bad, as well as of good intention. But the fact is directly otherways. Our discoveries ascertain us more and more of the benevolence of the Deity, by unfolding beautiful final causes without number; while the appearances of ill intention gradually vanish, like a mist when the sun breaks out. Many things are now found to be curious in their contrivance and productive of good effects, which formerly appeared useless, or perhaps of ill tendency. And, in the gradual progress of learning, we have the strongest reason to expect, that many more discoveries of the kind will be made. This very consideration, had we nothing else to rely on, ought to make us rest with assurance upon the intuitive conviction we have of the benevolence of the Deity; without giving way to the perplexity of a few cross appearances, which, in matters so far beyond our comprehension, ought rationally to be ascribed to our own ignorance, not to any malevolence in the Deity. In the progress of learning, the time may come, we have great reason to hope it will come, when all doubts and perplexities of this kind shall be fully cleared up.

I satisfy myself with suggesting but one other consideration, That inferring a mixed nature in the Deity from events which cannot be clearly reconciled to benevolence, is, at best, new-moulding the Manichean system, by substituting in place of it, one really less plausible. For I can with greater facility form a conception of two opposite powers governing the universe, than of one power endued with great goodness and great malevolence, principles so repugnant to each other.

It thus appears, that our conviction of the attribute of pure benevolence hath a wide and solid foundation. It is impressed upon us by intuitive perception, by every discovery we make in the science of nature, and by every argument suggested by reason and reflection. There is but one objection of any weight that can be moved against it, arising from the difficulty of accounting for natural and moral evil. It is observed above, that the objection, however it may puzzle, ought not to shake our faith in this attribute; because an argument from ignorance can never be a convincing argument in any case. This therefore, in its strongest light, appears but in the shape of a difficulty, not of a solid objection. At the same time, as the utmost labour of thought is well bestowed upon a subject so interesting, I shall proceed to some reflections, which may tend to satisfy us, that the instances commonly given of natural and moral evil, are not so inconsistent with pure benevolence, as at first sight may be imagined.

One preliminary point must be settled, which I presume will be admitted without much hesitation. It certainly will not be thought inconsistent in any degree with the pure benevolence of the Deity, that the world is filled with an endless variety of creatures, gradually ascending in the scale of being, from the most groveling to the most glorious. To think that this affords an argument against pure benevolence, is in effect to think, that all inanimate beings ought to be endued with life and motion, and that all animate beings ought to be angels. If at first view it shall be thought, that infinite power and goodness cannot stop short of absolute perfection in their operations, and that the work of creation must be confined to the highest order of beings, in the highest perfection; this thought will soon be corrected, by considering, that by this supposition a great void is left, which, according to the present system of things, is filled with beings, and with life and motion. And, supposing the world to be replenished with the highest order of beings created in the highest degree of perfection, it is certainly an act of more extensive benevolence, to complete the work of creation by the addition of an infinity of creatures less perfect, than to leave a great blank betwixt beings of the highest order and nothing.

The imperfection then of a created being, abstractly considered, impeaches none of the attributes of the Deity, whether power, wisdom, or benevolence. And if so, neither can pain abstractly considered be an impeachment, as far as it is the natural and necessary consequence of imperfection. The government of the world is carried on by general laws, which produce constancy and uniformity in the operations of nature. Among many reasons for this, we can clearly discover one, which is unfolded in a former Essay,[1] that were not nature uniform and constant, men and other sensible beings would be altogether at a loss how to conduct themselves. Our nature is adjusted to these general laws; and must therefore be subjected to all their varieties, whether beneficial or hurtful. We are made sensitive beings, and therefore equally capable of pleasure and pain. And it must follow from the very nature of the thing, that delicacy of perception, which is the source of much pleasure, may be equally the source of much pain. It is true, we cannot pronounce it to be a contradiction, that a being should be susceptible of pleasure only and not of pain. But no argument can be founded upon this supposition but what will conclude, that a creature such as man ought to have no place in the scale of beings; which surely will not be maintained: for it is still better, that man be as he is, than not to be at all. It is further to be observed in general, that aversion to pain is not so great, at least in mankind, as to counterbalance every other appetite. Most men would purchase an additional share of happiness, at the expence of some pain. And therefore it can afford no argument against the benevolence of the Deity, that created beings from their nature and condition are capable of pain, supposing upon the whole their life to be comfortable. Their state is still preferable to that of inanimate matter, capable neither of pleasure nor pain.

Thus it appears, even from a general view of our subject, that natural evil affords no argument against the benevolence of the Deity. And this will appear in a stronger light, when we go to particulars. It is laid open in the first Essay, that the social affections, even when most painful, are accompanied with no degree of aversion, either in the direct feeling or in subsequent reflection. We value ourselves the more for being so constituted; being conscious that such a constitution is *right* and *meet* for sociable creatures. Distresses therefore of this sort cannot be called evils, when we have no aversion to them, and do not repine at them. And if these be laid aside, what may be justly termed natural evils, are reduced within a small compass. They will be found to proceed necessarily, and by an established train of causes and effects, either from the imperfection of our nature, or from the operation of general laws. Pain is not distributed thro' the world blindly, or with any appearance of malice; but

1 'Knowledge of Future Events'

ends, proportions, and measures, are observed in the distribution. Sensible marks of good tendency are conspicuous, even in the harshest dispensations of Providence; and the good tendency of general laws, is a sure pledge of benevolence, even in those instances where we may be puzzled to explain their good effects. One thing is certain, that there is in man a natural principle to submit to these general laws, and their consequences. And were this principle cultivated as it ought to be, men would have the same consciousness of right conduct in submitting to the laws of the natural world, that they have in submitting to the laws of the moral world, and would as little repine at the distresses of the one kind, as at those of the other.

But justice is not done to the subject, unless we proceed to show, that pain and distress are productive of manifold good ends, and that they are in a measure necessary to the present system. In the first place, pain is necessary, as a monitor of what is hurtful and dangerous to life. Every man is trusted with the care of his own preservation; and he would be ill qualified for that trust, were he left entirely to the guidance of reason: he would die for want of food, were it not for the pain of hunger: and, but for the pain arising from fear, he would precipitate himself every moment into the most destructive enterprises. In the next place, pain is the great sanction of laws, both human and divine: there would be no order nor discipline in the world without it. In the third place, the distresses and disappointments that arise from the uncertainty of seasons, from the variable tempers of those we are connected with, and from other cross accidents, are wonderfully well adapted to our constitution, by keeping our hopes and fears in constant agitation. Man is an active being, and is not in his element but when in variety of occupation. A constant and uniform tenor of life without hopes or fears, would soon bring on satiety and disgust. Pain therefore is necessary, not only to enhance our pleasures, but to keep us in motion. And it is needless to observe a second time, that to complain of man's constitution in this respect, is in other words to complain, that there is such a creature as man in the scale of being. To mention but one other thing, pain and distress have a wonderful tendency to advance the interests of society. Grief, compassion, and sympathy, are strong connecting principles, by which every individual is made subservient to the general good of the whole species.

I shall close this branch of my subject with a general reflection, which is reserved to the last place, because in my apprehension it is a decisive argument for the benevolence of the Deity. When we run over what we know of the formation and government of this world, the instances are without number, of good intention and of consummate wisdom in adjusting things to good ends and purposes. And it is equally true, that as we advance in knowledge, scenes of this kind multiply upon us. This observation is enforced above. But I now observe, that there is not a single instance to be met with, which can be justly ascribed to malevolence or bad intention. Many evils may be pointed out; evils at least as to us. But when the most is made of such instances, they appear to be consequences only from general laws which regard the whole more than particulars; and therefore are not marks of malevolence in the Author and Governor of the world. Were there any doubt about the tendency of such instances, it would be more rational to ascribe them to want of power, than want of benevolence, which is so conspicuous in other instances. But we cannot rationally ascribe them to either, but to the pre-established order and constitution of things, and to the necessary imperfection of all created beings. And after all, laying the greatest weight upon these natural evils that can reasonably be demanded, the account stands thus. Instances without number of benevolence in the frame and government of this world, so direct and clear as not to admit of the slightest doubt. On the other side, natural evils are stated, which at best are very doubtful instances of malevolence, and may be ascribed, perhaps obscurely, to another cause. In balancing this account, where the evil appearances are so far outnumbered by the good, why should we hesitate to ascribe pure benevolence to the Deity, and to conclude these evils to be necessary defects in a good system; especially when it is so repugnant to our natural perceptions, to ascribe great benevolence and great malevolence to the same being?

It will be remarked, that in answering the foregoing objection to the benevolence of the Deity, I have avoided urging any argument from our future existence; though it affords a fruitful field of comfort, greatly overbalancing the transitory evils of this life. But I should scarce think it fair reasoning, to urge such topics upon this subject; which would be arguing in a circle; because the benevolence of the Deity is the only solid foundation upon which we can build a future existence.

Having discussed what occurred upon natural evil, we come now to consider moral evil as an objection against the benevolence of the Deity. And some writers carry this objection so far, as to conclude, that God is the cause of moral evil, since he hath given man a constitution, by which moral evil doth and must abound. It is certainly no satisfying answer to this objection, that moral evil is the necessary consequence of human liberty; when it is a very possible supposition, that man might have been endued with a moral sense, so lively and strong as to be absolutely authoritative over his actions. Waving therefore the argument from human liberty, we must look about for a more solid answer to the objection; which will not be difficult, when we consider this matter as laid down in a former essay.[1] It is there made out, it is hoped, to the satisfaction of the reader, that human actions are all of them directed by general laws, which have an operation no less infallible, than those laws have which govern mere matter. Thus, as all things in the moral as well as material world, proceed according to settled laws established by the Almighty, we have a just ground of conviction, that all matters are by Providence ordered in the best manner; and therefore that even human vices and frailties are made to answer wise and benevolent purposes. Every thing possesses its proper place in the Divine plan. All our actions contribute equally to carry on the great and good designs of our Maker; and therefore there is nothing which in his sight is ill, at least nothing which is ill upon the whole.

Considering the objection in the foregoing light, which is the true one, it loses its force. For it certainly will not be maintained as an argument against the goodness of the Deity, that he endued man with a sense of moral evil; which in reality is one of the greatest blessings bestowed upon him, and which eminently distinguishes him from the brute creation.

But if the objection be turned into another shape, and it be demanded, Why was not every man endued with so strong a sense of morality, as to be completely authoritative over all his principles of action, which would prevent much remorse to himself, and much mischief to others? it is answered, first, That this would not be sufficient for an exact regularity of conduct, unless man's judgment of right and wrong were also infallible. For, as long as we differ about what is *yours* and what is *mine*, injustice must be the consequence in many instances however innocent we be. But in the next place, to complain of a defect in the moral sense, is to complain that we are not perfect creatures. And if this complaint be well founded, we may with equal justice complain, that our understanding is but moderate, and that in general our powers and faculties are limited. Why should imperfection in the moral

[1] Essay, 'Liberty and Necessity'

sense be urged as an objection, when all our senses, internal and external, are imperfect? In short, if this complaint be in any measure just, it must go the length, as above observed, to prove, that it is not consistent with the benevolence of the Deity to create such a being as man.

Source: Henry Home, Lord Kames, *Essays on the Principles of Morality and Natural Religion*, 3rd edn, Edinburgh 1779, pp. 349–67

NINETEEN

DAVID HUME
Dialogues Concerning Natural Religion

Hume had begun writing the *Dialogues* by early 1751. The manuscript was revised first in 1761, then in 1776, the last year of his life, and was finally published in 1779. It is the greatest work on religion to have been produced in the Scottish Enlightenment. The narrator of the *Dialogues* is Pamphilus, a young man present at, though not an active participant in, the conversation. In the Introduction a friend of Pamphilus is reported as saying of the three protagonists that Cleanthes has an accurate philosophical turn, Philo a careless scepticism, and Demea a rigid inflexible orthodoxy. It has been disputed which of the three most closely represents Hume's own position, though it is most likely that Philo is Hume's mouthpiece. Nevertheless in the final lines of the *Dialogues* Pamphilus asserts: 'I confess that, upon a serious review of the whole, I cannot but think that Philo's principles are more probable than Demea's, but that those of Cleanthes approach still nearer to the truth.' However, we learn at the start of the *Dialogues* that Pamphilus is Cleanthes's pupil, and it may be that Hume is reminding his readers of this relationship rather than signalling that Cleanthes is Hume's spokesman. In the following excerpt, covering the first three of the twelve parts of the *Dialogues*, we find battle lines being drawn in relation to the central theological question of what can be learned about God from a consideration of the apparent marks of design in the universe.

Philo begins by doubting whether reason can give a coherent account of the most common objects of experience, such as causation, spatial extension, time and motion, and he asks whether reason, which cannot answer basic questions on these matters, can answer questions concerning religion, concerning for example the origin of worlds. Cleanthes's first response to Philo is to attack his scepticism on the grounds that it is a scepticism contrary to human nature;

it can be proclaimed as a theory but cannot be sustained in practice. Cleanthes is duly challenged by Demea on the grounds that any one with common sense will see that God exists, and that the problems all concern not the existence of God but his nature, and those problems Demea believes insoluble, given 'the infirmities of human understanding'. Cleanthes then presents an argument, based upon the manifest appearance of design in the universe, for the wisdom and intelligence of God. This argument is then subjected to a devastating critique by Philo. It has not been possible, since the publication of Hume's *Dialogues*, to adopt any version of the so-called 'design argument' without at least attempting to build into the version some protection against the kind of attack launched by Philo.

A.B.

Dialogues Concerning Natural Religion

PART I

After I joined the company whom I found sitting in Cleanthes'
library, Demea paid Cleanthes some compliments on the great
care which he took of my education, and on his unwearied
perseverance and constancy in all his friendships. The father
of Pamphilus, said he, was your intimate friend; the son is your
pupil, and may indeed be regarded as your adopted son were we
to judge by the pains which you bestow in conveying to him every
useful branch of literature and science. You are no more wanting,
I am persuaded, in prudence than in industry. I shall, therefore,
communicate to you a maxim which I have observed with regard
to my own children, that I may learn how far it agrees with your
practice. The method I follow in their education is founded on the
saying of an ancient, 'That students of philosophy ought first to
learn logics, then ethics, next physics, last of all the nature of the
gods.'[1] This science of natural theology, according to him, being
the most profound and abstruse of any, required the maturest
judgment in its students; and none but a mind enriched with all
the other sciences can safely be entrusted with it.

Are you so late, says Philo, in teaching your children the principles of religion? Is there no danger of their neglecting or rejecting
altogether those opinions of which they have heard so little during
the whole course of their education? It is only as a science, replied
Demea, subjected to human reasoning and disputation, that I
postpone the study of natural theology. To season their minds
with early piety is my chief care; and by continual precept and
instruction and, I hope, too, by example, I imprint deeply on
their tender minds an habitual reverence for all the principles
of religion. While they pass through every other science, I still
remark the uncertainty of each part; the eternal disputations of
men; the obscurity of all philosophy; and the strange, ridiculous
conclusions which some of the greatest geniuses have derived
from the principles of mere human reason. Having thus tamed
their mind to a proper submission and self-diffidence, I have no
longer any scruple of opening to them the greatest mysteries of
religion, nor apprehend any danger from that assuming arrogance

---

1 Chrysippus *apud* Plut., *De repug. Stoicorum*.

of philosophy, which may lead them to reject the most established doctrines and opinions.

Your precaution, says Philo, of seasoning your children's minds early with piety is certainly very reasonable, and no more than is requisite in this profane and irreligious age. But what I chiefly admire in your plan of education is your method of drawing advantage from the very principles of philosophy and learning which, by inspiring pride and self-sufficiency, have commonly, in all ages, been found so destructive to the principles of religion. The vulgar, indeed, we may remark, who are unacquainted with science and profound inquiry, observing the endless disputes of the learned, have commonly a thorough contempt for philosophy, and rivet themselves the faster, by that means, in the great points of theology which have been taught them. Those who enter a little into study and inquiry, finding many appearances of evidence in doctrines the newest and most extraordinary, think nothing too difficult for human reason and, presumptuously breaking through all fences, profane the inmost sanctuaries of the temple. But Cleanthes will, I hope, agree with me that, after we have abandoned ignorance, the surest remedy, there is still one expedient left to prevent this profane liberty. Let Demea's principles be improved and cultivated; let us become thoroughly sensible of the weakness, blindness, and narrow limits of human reason; let us duly consider its uncertainty and endless contrarieties, even in subjects of common life and practice; let the errors and deceits of our very senses be set before us; the insuperable difficulties which attend first principles in all systems; the contradictions which adhere to the very ideas of matter, cause and effect, extension, space, time, motion, and, in a word, quantity of all kinds, the object of the only science that can fairly pretend to any certainty or evidence – when these topics are displayed in their full light, as they are by some philosophers and almost all divines, who can retain such confidence in this frail faculty of reason as to pay any regard to its determinations in points so sublime, so abstruse, so remote from common life and experience? When the coherence of the parts of a stone, or even that composition of parts which renders it extended; when these familiar objects, I say, are so inexplicable, and contain circumstances so repugnant and contradictory, with what assurance can we decide concerning the origin of worlds or trace their history from eternity to eternity?

While Philo pronounced these words, I could observe a smile in the countenance both of Demea and Cleanthes. That of Demea seemed to imply an unreserved satisfaction in the doctrines delivered; but in Cleanthes' features I could distinguish an air of finesse, as if he perceived some raillery or artificial malice in the reasonings of Philo.

You propose then, Philo, said Cleanthes, to erect religious faith on philosophical scepticism; and you think that, if certainty or evidence be expelled from every other subject of inquiry, it will all retire to these theological doctrines, and there acquire a superior force and authority. Whether your scepticism be as absolute and sincere as you pretend, we shall learn by and by, when the company breaks up; we shall then see whether you go out at the door or the window, and whether you really doubt if your body has gravity or can be injured by its fall, according to popular opinion derived from our fallacious senses and more fallacious experience. And this consideration, Demea, may, I think, fairly serve to abate our ill-will to this humorous sect of the sceptics. If they be thoroughly in earnest, they will not long trouble the world with their doubts, cavils, and disputes; if they be only in jest, they are, perhaps, bad railers, but can never be very dangerous, either to the state, to philosophy, or to religion.

In reality, Philo, continued he, it seems certain that, though a man, in a flush of humour, after intense reflection on the many contradictions and imperfections of human reason, may entirely renounce all belief and opinion, it is impossible for him to persevere in this total scepticism or make it appear in his conduct for a few hours. External objects press in upon him; passions solicit him; his philosophical melancholy dissipates; and even the utmost violence upon his own temper will not be able, during any time, to preserve the poor appearance of scepticism. And for what reason impose on himself such a violence? This is a point in which it will be impossible for him ever to satisfy himself, consistently with his sceptical principles. So that, upon the whole, nothing could be more ridiculous than the principles of the ancient Pyrrhonians if, in reality, they endeavoured, as is pretended, to extend throughout the same scepticism which they had learned from the declamations of their schools, and which they ought to have confined to them.

In this view, there appears a great resemblance between the sects of the Stoics and Pyrrhonians, though perpetual antagonists; and both of them seem founded on this erroneous maxim that what a man can perform sometimes, and in some dispositions, he can perform always and in every disposition. When the mind, by Stoical reflections, is elevated into a sublime enthusiasm of virtue and strongly smit with any *species* of honour or public good, the utmost bodily pain and sufferings will not prevail over such a high sense of duty; and it is possible, perhaps, by its means, even to smile and exult in the midst of tortures. If this sometimes may be the case in fact and reality, much more may a philosopher, in his school or even in his closet, work himself up to such an enthusiasm and support, in imagination, the acutest pain or most calamitous event which he can possibly conceive. But how shall he support this enthusiasm itself? The bent of his mind relaxes and cannot be recalled at pleasure; avocations lead him astray; misfortunes attack him unawares; and the *philosopher* sinks, by degrees, into the *plebeian*.

I allow of your comparison between the Stoics and Sceptics, replied Philo. But you may observe, at the same time, that though the mind cannot, in Stoicism, support the highest flights of philosophy, yet, even when it sinks lower, it still retains somewhat of its former disposition; and the effects of the Stoic's reasoning will appear in his conduct in common life, and through the whole tenor of his actions. The ancient schools, particularly that of Zeno, produced examples of virtue and constancy which seem astonishing to present times.

> Vain Wisdom all and false Philosophy.
> Yet with a pleasing sorcery could charm
> Pain, for a while, or anguish; and excite
> Fallacious Hope, or arm the obdurate breast
> With stubborn Patience, as with triple steel.[1]

In like manner, if a man has accustomed himself to sceptical considerations on the uncertainty and narrow limits of reason, he will not entirely forget them when he turns his reflection on other subjects; but in all his philosophical principles and reasoning, I dare not say in his common conduct, he will be found different from those who either never formed any opinions in the case or have entertained sentiments more favourable to human reason.

To whatever length any one may push his speculative principles of scepticism, he must act, I own, and live, and converse, like other men; and for this conduct he is not obliged to give any other reason than the absolute necessity he lies under of so doing. If he ever carries his speculations farther than this necessity constrains him, and philosophizes either on natural or moral subjects, he

1 Milton, *Paradise Lost*, Book II, lines 565–9.

is allured by a certain pleasure and satisfaction which he finds in employing himself after that manner. He considers, besides, that everyone, even in common life, is constrained to have more or less of this philosophy; that from our earliest infancy we make continual advances in forming more general principles of conduct and reasoning; that the larger experience we acquire, and the stronger reason we are endued with, we always render our principles the more general and comprehensive; and that what we call *philosophy* is nothing but a more regular and methodical operation of the same kind. To philosophize on such subjects is nothing essentially different from reasoning on common life, and we may only expect greater stability, if not greater truth, from our philosophy on account of its exacter and more scrupulous method of proceeding.

But when we look beyond human affairs and the properties of the surrounding bodies; when we carry our speculations into the two eternities, before and after the present state of things: into the creation and formation of the universe, the existence and properties of spirits, the powers and operations of one universal Spirit existing without beginning and without end, omnipotent, omniscient, immutable, infinite, and incomprehensible – we must be far removed from the smallest tendency to scepticism not to be apprehensive that we have here got quite beyond the reach of our faculties. So long as we confine our speculations to trade, or morals, or politics, or criticism, we make appeals, every moment, to common sense and experience, which strengthen our philosophical conclusions and remove, at least in part, the suspicion which we so justly entertain with regard to every reasoning that is very subtile and refined. But, in theological reasonings, we have not this advantage; while at the same time we are employed upon objects which, we must be sensible, are too large for our grasp and, of all others, require most to be familiarized to our apprehension. We are like foreigners in a strange country to whom everything must seem suspicious, and who are in danger every moment of transgressing against the laws and customs of the people with whom they live and converse. We know not how far we ought to trust our vulgar methods of reasoning in such a subject, since, even in common life, and in that province which is peculiarly appropriated to them, we cannot account for them and are entirely guided by a kind of instinct or necessity in employing them.

All sceptics pretend that, if reason be considered in an abstract view, it furnishes invincible arguments against itself, and that we could never retain any conviction or assurance, on any subject, were not the sceptical reasonings so refined and subtile that they are not able to counterpoise the more solid and more natural arguments derived from the senses and experience. But it is evident, whenever our arguments lose this advantage and run wide of common life, that the most refined scepticism comes to be upon a footing with them, and is able to oppose and counterbalance them. The one has no more weight than the other. The mind must remain in suspense between them; and it is that very suspense or balance which is the triumph of scepticism.

But I observe, says Cleanthes, with regard to you, Philo, and all speculative sceptics that your doctrine and practice are as much at variance in the most abstruse points of theory as in the conduct of common life. Wherever evidence discovers itself, you adhere to it, notwithstanding your pretended scepticism; and I can observe, too, some of your sect to be as decisive as those who make greater professions of certainty and assurance. In reality, would not a man be ridiculous who pretended to reject Newton's explication of the wonderful phenomenon of the rainbow because that explication gives a minute anatomy of the rays of light – a subject, forsooth, too refined for human comprehension? And what would you say to one who, having nothing particular to object to the arguments of Copernicus and Galilæo for the motion of the earth, should withhold his assent on that general principle that these subjects were too magnificent and remote to be explained by the narrow and fallacious reason of mankind?

There is indeed a kind of brutish and ignorant scepticism, as you well observed, which gives the vulgar a general prejudice against what they do not easily understand, and makes them reject every principle which requires elaborate reasoning to prove and establish it. This species of scepticism is fatal to knowledge, not to religion; since we find that those who make greatest profession of it give often their assent, not only to the great truths of theism and natural theology, but even to the most absurd tenets which a traditional superstition has recommended to them. They firmly believe in witches, though they will not believe nor attend to the most simple proposition of Euclid. But the refined and philosophical sceptics fall into an inconsistency of an opposite nature. They push their researches into the most abstruse corners of science, and their assent attends them in every step, proportioned to the evidence which they meet with. They are even obliged to acknowledge that the most abstruse and remote objects are those which are best explained by philosophy. Light is in reality anatomized; the true system of the heavenly bodies is discovered and ascertained. But the nourishment of bodies by food is still an inexplicable mystery; the cohesion of the parts of matter is still incomprehensible. These sceptics, therefore, are obliged, in every question, to consider each particular evidence apart, and proportion their assent to the precise degree of evidence which occurs. This is their practice in all natural, mathematical, moral, and political science. And why not the same, I ask, in the theological and religious? Why must conclusions of this nature be alone rejected on the general presumption of the insufficiency of human reason, without any particular discussion of the evidence? Is not such an unequal conduct a plain proof of prejudice and passion?

Our senses, you say, are fallacious; our understanding erroneous; our ideas, even of the most familiar objects – extension, duration, motion – full of absurdities and contradictions. You defy me to solve the difficulties or reconcile the repugnancies which you discover in them. I have not capacity for so great an undertaking; I have not leisure for it. I perceive it to be superfluous. Your own conduct, in every circumstance, refutes your principles, and shows the firmest reliance on all the received maxims of science, morals, prudence, and behaviour.

I shall never assent to so harsh an opinion as that of a celebrated writer,[1] who says that the Sceptics are not a sect of philosophers: they are only a sect of liars. I may, however, affirm (I hope without offence) that they are a sect of jesters or railers. But for my part, whenever I find myself disposed to mirth and amusement, I shall certainly choose my entertainment of a less perplexing and abstruse nature. A comedy, a novel, or, at most, a history seems a more natural recreation than such metaphysical subtilties and abstractions.

In vain would the sceptic make a distinction between science and common life, or between one science and another. The arguments employed in all, if just, are of a similar nature and contain the same force and evidence. Or if there be any difference among them, the advantage lies entirely on the side of theology and natural religion. Many principles of mechanics are founded on very abstruse reasoning, yet no man who has any pretensions to science, even no speculative sceptic, pretends to entertain the

---

1 *L'art de penser* (Antoine the great) Arnauld and others:
  La Logique ou l'art de penser (*Port-Royal Logic*), 1662.

least doubt with regard to them. The Copernican system contains the most surprising paradox, and the most contrary to our natural conceptions, to appearances, and to our very senses, yet even monks and inquisitors are now constrained to withdraw their opposition to it. And shall Philo, a man of so liberal a genius and extensive knowledge, entertain any general undistinguished scruples with regard to the religious hypothesis, which is founded on the simplest and most obvious arguments and, unless it meets with artificial obstacles, has such easy access and admission into the mind of man?

And here we may observe, continued he, turning himself towards Demea, a pretty curious circumstance in the history of the sciences. After the union of philosophy with the popular religion, upon the first establishment of Christianity, nothing was more usual, among all religious teachers, than declamations against reason, against the senses, against every principle derived merely from human research and inquiry. All the topics of the ancient Academics were adopted by the Fathers, and thence propagated for several ages in every school and pulpit throughout Christendom. The Reformers embraced the same principles of reasoning or rather declamation; and all panegyrics on the excellence of faith were sure to be interlarded with some severe strokes of satire against natural reason. A celebrated prelate, too,[1] of the Romish communion, a man of the most extensive learning, who wrote a demonstration of Christianity, has also composed a treatise which contains all the cavils of the boldest and most determined Pyrrhonism. Locke seems to have been the first Christian who ventured openly to assert that *faith* was nothing but a species of *reason;* that religion was only a branch of philosophy; and that a chain of arguments, similar to that which established any truth in morals, politics, or physics, was always employed in discovering all the principles of theology, natural and revealed. The ill use which Bayle and other libertines made of the philosophical scepticism of the Fathers and first Reformers still further propagated the judicious sentiment of Mr. Locke. And it is now in a manner avowed, by all pretenders to reasoning and philosophy, that *atheist* and *sceptic* are almost synonymous. And as it is certain that no man is in earnest when he professes the latter principle, I would fain hope that there are as few who seriously maintain the former.

Don't you remember, said Philo, the excellent saying of Lord

[1] Mons. Huet.

Bacon on this head? That a little philosophy, replied Cleanthes, makes a man an Atheist; a great deal converts him to religion. That is a very judicious remark, too, said Philo. But what I have in my eye is another passage, where, having mentioned David's fool, who said in his heart there is no God, this great philosopher observes that the atheists nowadays have a double share of folly, for they are not contented to say in their hearts there is no God, but they also utter that impiety with their lips, and are thereby guilty of multiplied indiscretion and imprudence. Such people, though they were ever so much in earnest, cannot, methinks, be very formidable.

But though you should rank me in this class of fools, I cannot forbear communicating a remark that occurs to me, from the history of the religious and irreligious scepticism with which you have entertained us. It appears to me that there are strong symptoms of priestcraft in the whole progress of this affair. During ignorant ages, such as those which followed the dissolution of the ancient schools, the priests perceived that atheism, deism, or heresy of any kind, could only proceed from the presumptuous questioning of received opinions, and from a belief that human reason was equal to everything. Education had then a mighty influence over the minds of men, and was almost equal in force to those suggestions of the senses and common understanding by which the most determined sceptic must allow himself to be governed. But at present, when the influence of education is much diminished and men, from a more open commerce of the world, have learned to compare the popular principles of different nations and ages, our sagacious divines have changed their whole system of philosophy and talk the language of Stoics, Platonists, and Peripatetics, not that of Pyrrhonians and Academics. If we distrust human reason we have now no other principle to lead us into religion. Thus sceptics in one age, dogmatists in another – whichever system best suits the purpose of these reverend gentlemen in giving them an ascendant over mankind – they are sure to make it their favourite principle and established tenet.

It is very natural, said Cleanthes, for men to embrace those principles by which they find they can best defend their doctrines, nor need we have any recourse to priestcraft to account for so reasonable an expedient. And surely nothing can afford a stronger presumption that any set of principles are true and ought to be embraced than to observe that they tend to the confirmation of true religion, and serve to confound the cavils of atheists, libertines, and free-thinkers of all denominations.

PART II

I must own, Cleanthes, said Demea, that nothing can more surprise me than the light in which you have all along put this argument. By the whole tenor of your discourse, one would imagine that you were maintaining the Being of a God against the cavils of atheists and infidels, and were necessitated to become a champion for that fundamental principle of all religion. But this, I hope, is not by any means a question among us. No man, no man at least of common sense, I am persuaded, ever entertained a serious doubt with regard to a truth so certain and self-evident. The question is not concerning the *being* but the *nature* of God. This I affirm, from the infirmities of human understanding, to be altogether incomprehensible and unknown to us. The essence of that supreme Mind, his attributes, the manner of his existence, the very nature of his duration – these and every particular which regards so divine a Being are mysterious to men. Finite, weak, and blind creatures, we ought to humble ourselves in his august presence, and, conscious of our frailties, adore in silence his infinite perfections which eye hath not seen, ear hath not heard, neither hath it entered into the heart of man to conceive. They are covered in a deep cloud from human curiosity; it is profaneness to attempt penetrating through these sacred obscurities, and, next to the impiety of denying his existence, is the temerity of prying into his nature and essence, decrees and attributes.

But lest you should think that my *piety* has here got the better of my *philosophy*, I shall support my opinion, if it needs any support, by a very great authority. I might cite all the divines, almost from the foundation of Christianity, who have ever treated of this or any other theological subject; but I shall confine myself, at present, to one equally celebrated for piety and philosophy. It is Father Malebranche who, I remember, thus expresses himself.[1] 'One ought not so much,' says he, 'to call God a spirit in order to express positively what he is, as in order to signify that he is not matter. He is a Being infinitely perfect – of this we cannot doubt. But in the same manner as we ought not to imagine, even supposing him corporeal, that he is clothed with a human body, as the anthropomorphites asserted, under colour that that figure was the most perfect of any, so neither ought we to imagine that the spirit of God has human ideas or bears any resemblance to our spirit, under colour that we know nothing more perfect

---

1 *Recherche de la Vérité*, liv. 3, cap. 9.

than a human mind. We ought rather to believe that as he comprehends the perfections of matter without being material . . . he comprehends also the perfections of created spirits without being spirit, in the manner we conceive spirit: that his true name is *He that is*, or, in other words, Being without restriction, All Being, the Being infinite and universal.'

After so great an authority, Demea, replied Philo, as that which you have produced, and a thousand more which you might produce, it would appear ridiculous in me to add my sentiment or express my approbation of your doctrine. But surely, where reasonable men treat these subjects, the question can never be concerning the *being* but only the *nature* of the Deity. The former truth, as you well observe, is unquestionable and self-evident. Nothing exists without a cause; and the original cause of this universe (whatever it be) we call God, and piously ascribe to him every species of perfection. Whoever scruples this fundamental truth deserves every punishment which can be inflicted among philosophers, to wit, the greatest ridicule, contempt, and disapprobation. But as all perfection is entirely relative, we ought never to imagine that we comprehend the attributes of this divine Being, or to suppose that his perfections have any analogy or likeness to the perfections of a human creature. Wisdom, thought, design, knowledge – these we justly ascribe to him because these words are honourable among men, and we have no other language or other conceptions by which we can express our adoration of him. But let us beware lest we think that our ideas anywise correspond to his perfections, or that his attributes have any resemblance to these qualities among men. He is infinitely superior to our limited view and comprehension, and is more the object of worship in the temple than of disputation in the schools.

In reality, Cleanthes, continued he, there is no need of having recourse to that affected scepticism so displeasing to you in order to come at this determination. Our ideas reach no farther than our experience. We have no experience of divine attributes and operations. I need not conclude my syllogism, you can draw the inference yourself. And it is a pleasure to me (and I hope to you, too) that just reasoning and sound piety here concur in the same conclusion, and both of them establish the adorably mysterious and incomprehensible nature of the Supreme Being.

Not to lose any time in circumlocutions, said Cleanthes, addressing himself to Demea, much less in replying to the pious declamations of Philo, I shall briefly explain how I conceive this matter. Look round the world, contemplate the whole and every part of it: you will find it to be nothing but one great machine, subdivided into an infinite number of lesser machines, which again admit of subdivisions to a degree beyond what human sense and faculties can trace and explain. All these various machines, and even their most minute parts, are adjusted to each other with an accuracy which ravishes into admiration all men who have ever contemplated them. The curious adapting of means to ends, throughout all nature, resembles exactly, though it much exceeds, the productions of human contrivance – of human design, thought, wisdom, and intelligence. Since therefore the effects resemble each other, we are led to infer, by all the rules of analogy, that the causes also resemble, and that the Author of nature is somewhat similar to the mind of man, though possessed of much larger faculties, proportioned to the grandeur of the work which he has executed. By this argument *a posteriori*, and by this argument alone, do we prove at once the existence of a Deity and his similarity to human mind and intelligence.

I shall be so free, Cleanthes, said Demea, as to tell you that from the beginning I could not approve of your conclusion concerning the similarity of the Deity to men, still less can I approve of the mediums by which you endeavour to establish it. What! No demonstration of the Being of God! No abstract arguments! No proofs *a priori!* Are these which have hitherto been so much insisted on by philosophers all fallacy, all sophism? Can we reach no farther in this subject than experience and probability? I will not say that this is betraying the cause of a Deity; but surely, by this affected candour, you give advantages to atheists which they never could obtain by the mere dint of argument and reasoning.

What I chiefly scruple in this subject, said Philo, is not so much that all religious arguments are by Cleanthes reduced to experience, as that they appear not to be even the most certain and irrefragable of that inferior kind. That a stone will fall, that fire will burn, that the earth has solidity, we have observed a thousand and a thousand times; and when any new instance of this nature is presented, we draw without hesitation the accustomed inference. The exact similarity of the cases gives us a perfect assurance of a similar event, and a stronger evidence is never desired nor sought after. But wherever you depart, in the least, from the similarity of the cases, you diminish proportionably the evidence, and may at last bring it to a very weak *analogy*, which is confessedly liable to error and uncertainty. After having experienced the circulation of the blood in human creatures, we make no doubt that it takes place in Titius and Maevius; but from its circulation in frogs and fishes it is only a presumption, though a strong one, from analogy that it takes place in men and other animals. The analogical reasoning is much weaker when we infer the circulation of the sap in vegetables from our experience that the blood circulates in animals; and those who hastily followed that imperfect analogy are found, by more accurate experiments, to have been mistaken.

If we see a house, Cleanthes, we conclude, with the greatest certainty, that it had an architect or builder because this is precisely that species of effect which we have experienced to proceed from that species of cause. But surely you will not affirm that the universe bears such a resemblance to a house that we can with the same certainty infer a similar cause, or that the analogy is here entire and perfect. The dissimilitude is so striking that the utmost you can here pretend to is a guess, a conjecture, a presumption concerning a similar cause; and how that pretension will be received in the world, I leave you to consider.

It would surely be very ill received, replied Cleanthes; and I should be deservedly blamed and detested did I allow that the proofs of a Deity amounted to no more than a guess or conjecture. But is the whole adjustment of means to ends in a house and in the universe so slight a resemblance? the economy of final causes? the order, proportion, and arrangement of every part? Steps of a stair are plainly contrived that human legs may use them in mounting; and this inference is certain and infallible. Human legs are also contrived for walking and mounting; and this inference, I allow, is not altogether so certain because of the dissimilarity which you remark; but does it, therefore, deserve the name only of presumption or conjecture?

Good God! cried Demea, interrupting him, where are we? Zealous defenders of religion allow that the proofs of a Deity fall short of perfect evidence! And you, Philo, on whose assistance I depended in proving the adorable mysteriousness of the Divine Nature, do you assent to all these extravagant opinions of Cleanthes? For what other name can I give them? or, why spare my censure when such principles are advanced, supported by such an authority, before so young a man as Pamphilus?

You seem not to apprehend, replied Philo, that I argue with Cleanthes in his own way, and, by showing him the dangerous consequences of his tenets, hope at last to reduce him to our opinion. But what sticks most with you, I observe, is the representation which Cleanthes has made of the argument *a posteriori;* and, finding that that argument is likely to escape your hold and vanish into air, you think it so disguised that you can scarcely believe it to be set in its true light. Now, however much I may dissent, in other respects, from the dangerous principles of Cleanthes, I must allow that he has fairly represented that argument, and I shall endeavour so to state the matter to you that you will entertain no further scruples with regard to it.

Were a man to abstract from everything which he knows or has seen, he would be altogether incapable, merely from his own ideas, to determine what kind of scene the universe must be, or to give the preference to one state or situation of things above another. For as nothing which he clearly conceives could be esteemed impossible or implying a contradiction, every chimera of his fancy would be upon an equal footing; nor could he assign any just reason why he adheres to one idea or system, and rejects the others which are equally possible.

Again, after he opens his eyes and contemplates the world as it really is, it would be impossible for him at first to assign the cause of any one event, much less of the whole of things, or of the universe. He might set his fancy a rambling, and she might bring him in an infinite variety of reports and representations. These would all be possible, but, being all equally possible, he would never of himself give a satisfactory account for his preferring one of them to the rest. Experience alone can point out to him the true cause of any phenomenon.

Now, according to this method of reasoning, Demea, it follows (and is, indeed, tacitly allowed by Cleanthes himself) that order, arrangement, or the adjustment of final causes, is not of itself any proof of design, but only so far as it has been experienced to proceed from that principle. For aught we can know *a priori*, matter may contain the source or spring of order originally within itself, as well as mind does; and there is no more difficulty in conceiving that the several elements, from an internal unknown cause, may fall into the most exquisite arrangement, than to conceive that their ideas, in the great universal mind, from a like internal unknown cause, fall into that arrangement. The equal possibility of both these suppositions is allowed. But, by experience, we find (according to Cleanthes) that there is a difference between them. Throw several pieces of steel together, without shape or form, they will never arrange themselves so as to compose a watch. Stone and mortar and wood, without an architect, never erect a house. But the ideas in a human mind, we see, by an unknown, inexplicable economy, arrange themselves so as to form the plan of a watch or house. Experience, therefore, proves that there is an original principle of order in mind, not in matter. From similar effects we infer similar causes. The adjustment of means to ends is alike in the universe, as in a machine of human contrivance. The causes, therefore, must be resembling.

I was from the beginning scandalized, I must own, with this resemblance which is asserted between the Deity and human creatures, and must conceive it to imply such a degradation of the Supreme Being as no sound theist could endure. With your assistance, therefore, Demea, I shall endeavour to defend what you justly call the adorable mysteriousness of the Divine Nature, and shall refute this reasoning of Cleanthes, provided he allows that I have made a fair representation of it.

When Cleanthes had assented, Philo, after a short pause, proceeded in the following manner.

That all inferences, Cleanthes, concerning fact are founded on experience, and that all experimental reasonings are founded on the supposition that similar causes prove similar effects, and similar effects similar causes, I shall not at present much dispute with you. But observe, I entreat you, with what extreme caution all just reasoners proceed in the transferring of experiments to similar cases. Unless the cases be exactly similar, they repose no perfect confidence in applying their past observation to any particular phenomenon. Every alteration of circumstances occasions a doubt concerning the event; and it requires new experiments to prove certainly that the new circumstances are of no moment or importance. A change in bulk, situation, arrangement, age, disposition of the air, or surrounding bodies – any of these particulars may be attended with the most unexpected consequences. And unless the objects be quite familiar to us, it is the highest temerity to expect with assurance, after any of these changes, an event similar to that which before fell under our observation. The slow and deliberate steps of philosophers here, if anywhere, are distinguished from the precipitate march of the vulgar, who, hurried on by the smallest similitude, are incapable of all discernment or consideration.

But can you think, Cleanthes, that your usual phlegm and philosophy have been preserved in so wide a step as you have taken when you compared to the universe houses, ships, furniture, machines, and, from their similarity in some circumstances, inferred a similarity in their causes? Thought, design, intelligence, such as we discover in men and other animals, is no more than one of the springs and principles of the universe, as well as heat or cold, attraction or repulsion, and a hundred others which fall under daily observation. It is an active cause by which some particular parts of nature, we find, produce alterations on other parts. But can a conclusion, with any propriety, be transferred from parts to the whole? Does not the great disproportion bar all comparison and inference? From observing the growth of a hair, can we learn anything concerning the generation of a man? Would the manner of a leaf's blowing, even though perfectly known, afford us any instruction concerning the vegetation of a tree?

But allowing that we were to take the *operations* of one part of nature upon another for the foundation of our judgment concerning the *origin* of the whole (which never can be admitted), yet why select so minute, so weak, so bounded a principle as the reason and design of animals is found to be upon this planet? What peculiar privilege has this little agitation of the brain which we call *thought*, that we must thus make it the model of the whole universe? Our partiality in our own favour does indeed present it on all occasions, but sound philosophy ought carefully to guard against so natural an illusion.

So far from admitting, continued Philo, that the operations of a part can afford us any just conclusion concerning the origin of the whole, I will not allow any one part to form a rule for another part if the latter be very remote from the former. Is there any reasonable ground to conclude that the inhabitants of other planets possess thought, intelligence, reason, or anything similar to these faculties in men? When nature has so extremely diversified her manner of operation in this small globe, can we imagine that she incessantly copies herself throughout so immense a universe? And if thought, as we may well suppose, be confined merely to this narrow corner and has even there so limited a sphere of action, with what propriety can we assign it for the original cause of all things? The narrow views of a peasant who makes his domestic economy the rule for the government of kingdoms is in comparison a pardonable sophism.

But were we ever so much assured that a thought and reason resembling the human were to be found throughout the whole universe, and were its activity elsewhere vastly greater and more commanding than it appears in this globe, yet I cannot see why the operations of a world constituted, arranged, adjusted, can with any propriety be extended to a world which is in its embryo state, and is advancing towards that constitution and arrangement. By observation we know somewhat of the economy, action, and nourishment of a finished animal, but we must transfer with great caution that observation to the growth of a fœtus in the womb, and still more to the formation of an animalcule in the loins of its male parent. Nature, we find, even from our limited experience, possesses an infinite number of springs and principles which incessantly discover themselves on every change of her position and situation. And what new and unknown principles would actuate her in so new and unknown a situation as that of the formation of a universe, we cannot, without the utmost temerity, pretend to determine.

A very small part of this great system, during a very short time, is very imperfectly discovered to us; and do we thence pronounce decisively concerning the origin of the whole?

Admirable conclusion! Stone, wood, brick, iron, brass, have not, at this time, in this minute globe of earth, an order or arrangement without human art and contrivance; therefore, the universe could not originally attain its order and arrangement without something similar to human art. But is a part of nature a rule for another part very wide of the former? Is it a rule for the whole? Is a very small part a rule for the universe? Is nature in one situation a certain rule for nature in another situation vastly different from the former?

And can you blame me, Cleanthes, if I here imitate the prudent reserve of Simonides, who, according to the noted story, being asked by Hiero, *What God was?* desired a day to think of it, and then two days more; and after that manner continually prolonged the term, without ever bringing in his definition or description? Could you even blame me if I had answered, at first, *that I did not know*, and was sensible that this subject lay vastly beyond the reach of my faculties? You might cry out sceptic and rallier, as much as you pleased; but, having found in so many other subjects much more familiar the imperfections and even contradictions of human reason, I never should expect any success from its feeble conjectures in a subject so sublime and so remote from the sphere of our observation. When two *species* of objects have always been observed to be conjoined together, I can *infer*, by custom, the existence of one wherever I *see* the existence of the other; and this I call an argument from experience. But how this argument can have place where the objects, as in the present case, are single, individual, without parallel or specific resemblance, may be difficult to explain. And will any man tell me with a serious countenance that an orderly universe must arise from some thought and art like the human because we have experience of it? To ascertain this reasoning it were requisite that we had experience of the origin of worlds; and it is not sufficient, surely, that we have seen ships and cities arise from human art and contrivance.

Philo was proceeding in this vehement manner, somewhat between jest and earnest, as it appeared to me, when he observed some signs of impatience in Cleanthes, and then immediately stopped short. What I had to suggest, said Cleanthes, is only that you would not abuse terms, or make use of popular expressions to subvert philosophical reasonings. You know that the vulgar often distinguish reason from experience, even where the question relates only to matter of fact and existence, though it is found, where that *reason* is properly analyzed, that it is nothing but a species of experience. To prove by experience the origin of the universe from mind is not more contrary to common speech than to prove the motion of the earth from the same principle. And a caviller might raise all the same objections to the Copernican system which you have urged against my reasonings. Have you other earths, might he say, which you have seen to move? Have . . .

Yes! cried Philo, interrupting him, we have other earths. Is not the moon another earth, which we see to turn round its centre? Is not Venus another earth, where we observe the same phenomenon? Are not the revolutions of the sun also a confirmation, from analogy, of the same theory? All the planets, are they not earths which revolve about the sun? Are not the satellites moons which move round Jupiter and Saturn, and along with these primary planets round the sun? These analogies and resemblances, with others which I have not mentioned, are the sole proofs of the Copernican system; and to you it belongs to consider whether you have any analogies of the same kind to support your theory.

In reality, Cleanthes, continued he, the modern system of astronomy is now so much received by all inquirers, and has become so essential a part even of our earliest education, that we are not commonly very scrupulous in examining the reasons upon which it is founded. It is now become a matter of mere curiosity to study the first writers on that subject who had the full force of prejudice to encounter, and were obliged to turn their arguments on every side in order to render them popular and convincing. But if we peruse Galileo's famous *Dialogues*[1] concerning the system of

1 *Dialogo dei due Massimi Sistemi del Mondo* (1632).

the world, we shall find that that great genius, one of the sublimest that ever existed, first bent all his endeavours to prove that there was no foundation for the distinction commonly made between elementary and celestial substances. The schools, proceeding from the illusions of sense, had carried this distinction very far; and had established the latter substances to be ingenerable, incorruptible, unalterable, impassible; and had assigned all the opposite qualities to the former. But Galileo, beginning with the moon, proved its similarity in every particular to the earth: its convex figure, its natural darkness when not illuminated, its density, its distinction into solid and liquid, the variations of its phases, the mutual illuminations of the earth and moon, their mutual eclipses, the inequalities of the lunar surface, etc. After many instances of this kind, with regard to all the planets, men plainly saw that these bodies became proper objects of experience, and that the similarity of their nature enabled us to extend the same arguments and phenomena from one to the other.

In this cautious proceeding of the astronomers you may read your own condemnation, Cleanthes, or rather may see that the subject in which you are engaged exceeds all human reason and inquiry. Can you pretend to show any such similarity between the fabric of a house and the generation of a universe? Have you ever seen nature in any such situation as resembles the first arrangement of the elements? Have worlds ever been formed under your eye, and have you had leisure to observe the whole progress of the phenomenon, from the first appearance of order to its final consummation? If you have, then cite your experience and deliver your theory.

PART III

How the most absurd argument, replied Cleanthes, in the hands of a man of ingenuity and invention, may acquire an air of probability! Are you not aware, Philo, that it became necessary for Copernicus and his first disciples to prove the similarity of the terrestrial and celestial matter because several philosophers, blinded by old systems and supported by some sensible appearances, had denied this similarity? But that it is by no means necessary that theists should prove the similarity of the works of *nature* to those of *art* because this similarity is self-evident and undeniable? The same matter, a like form; what more is requisite to show an analogy between their causes, and to ascertain the origin of all things from a divine purpose and intention? Your objections, I must freely tell you, are no better than the abstruse cavils of those philosophers who denied motion, and ought to be refuted in the same manner – by illustrations, examples, and instances rather than by serious argument and philosophy.

Suppose, therefore, that an articulate voice were heard in the clouds, much louder and more melodious than any which human art could ever reach; suppose that this voice were extended in the same instant over all nations and spoke to each nation in its own language and dialect; suppose that the words delivered not only contain a just sense and meaning, but convey some instruction altogether worthy of a benevolent Being superior to mankind – could you possibly hesitate a moment concerning the cause of this voice, and must you not instantly ascribe it to some design or purpose? Yet I cannot see but all the same objections (if they merit that appellation) which lie against the system of theism may also be produced against this inference.

Might you not say that all conclusions concerning fact were founded on experience; that, when we hear an articulate voice in the dark and thence infer a man, it is only the resemblance of the effects which leads us to conclude that there is a like resemblance in the cause; but that this extraordinary voice, by its loudness, extent, and flexibility to all languages, bears so little analogy to any human voice that we have no reason to suppose any analogy in their causes; and, consequently, that a rational, wise, coherent speech proceeded, you know not whence, from some accidental whistling of the winds, not from any divine reason or intelligence? You see clearly your own objections in these cavils, and I hope too you see clearly that they cannot possibly have more force in the one case than in the other.

But to bring the case still nearer the present one of the universe, I shall make two suppositions which imply not any absurdity or impossibility. Suppose that there is a natural, universal, invariable language, common to every individual of human race, and that books are natural productions which perpetuate themselves in the same manner with animals and vegetables, by descent and propagation. Several expressions of our passions contain a universal language: all brute animals have a natural speech, which, however limited, is very intelligible to their own species. And as there are infinitely fewer parts and less contrivance in the finest composition of eloquence than in the coarsest organized body, the propagation of an *Iliad* or *Æneid* is an easier supposition than that of any plant or animal.

Suppose, therefore, that you enter into your library thus peopled by natural volumes containing the most refined reason and most exquisite beauty; could you possibly open one of them and doubt that its original cause bore the strongest analogy to mind and intelligence? When it reasons and discourses; when it expostulates, argues, and enforces its views and topics; when it applies sometimes to the pure intellect, sometimes to the affections; when it collects, disposes, and adorns every consideration suited to the subject; could you persist in asserting that all this, at the bottom, had really no meaning, and that the first formation of this volume in the loins of its original parent proceeded not from thought and design? Your obstinacy, I know, reaches not that degree of firmness; even your sceptical play and wantonness would be abashed at so glaring an absurdity.

But if there be any difference, Philo, between this supposed case and the real one of the universe, it is all to the advantage of the latter. The anatomy of an animal affords many stronger instances of design than the perusal of Livy or Tacitus; and any objection which you start in the former case, by carrying me back to so unusual and extraordinary a scene as the first formation of worlds, the same objection has place on the supposition of our vegetating library. Choose, then, your party, Philo, without ambiguity or evasion; assert either that a rational volume is no proof of a rational cause or admit of a similar cause to all the works of nature.

Let me here observe, too, continued Cleanthes, that this religious argument, instead of being weakened by that scepticism so much affected by you, rather acquires force from it and becomes more firm and undisputed. To exclude all argument or reasoning of every kind is either affectation or madness. The declared profession of every reasonable sceptic is only to reject abstruse, remote, and refined arguments; to adhere to common sense and the plain instincts of nature; and to assent, wherever any reasons strike him with so full a force that he cannot, without the greatest violence, prevent it. Now the arguments for natural religion are plainly of this kind; and nothing but the most perverse, obstinate metaphysics can reject them. Consider, anatomize the eye, survey its structure and contrivance, and tell me, from your own feeling, if the idea of a contriver does not immediately flow in upon you with a force like that of sensation. The most obvious conclusion, surely, is in favour of design; and it requires time, reflection, and study, to summon up those frivolous though abstruse objections which can support infidelity. Who can behold the male and female of each species, the correspondence of their parts and instincts, their passions and whole course of life before and after generation, but must be sensible that the propagation of the species is intended by nature? Millions and millions of such instances present themselves through every part of the universe, and no language can convey a more intelligible irresistible meaning than the curious adjustment of final causes. To what degree, therefore, of blind dogmatism must one have attained to reject such natural and such convincing arguments?

Some beauties in writing we may meet with which seem contrary to rules, and which gain the affections and animate the imagination in opposition to all the precepts of criticism and to the authority of the established masters of art. And if the argument for theism be, as you pretend, contradictory to the principles of logic, its universal, its irresistible influence proves clearly that there may be arguments of a like irregular nature. Whatever cavils may be urged, an orderly world, as well as a coherent, articulate speech, will still be received as an incontestable proof of design and intention.

It sometimes happens, I own, that the religious arguments have not their due influence on an ignorant savage and barbarian, not because they are obscure and difficult, but because he never asks himself any question with regard to them. Whence arises the curious structure of an animal? From the copulation of its parents. And these whence? From *their* parents? A few removes set the objects at such a distance that to him they are lost in darkness and confusion; nor is he actuated by any curiosity to trace them farther. But this is neither dogmatism nor scepticism, but stupidity: a state of mind very different from your sifting, inquisitive disposition, my ingenious friend. You can trace causes from effects; you can compare the most distant and remote objects; and your greatest errors proceed not from barrenness of thought and invention, but from too luxuriant a fertility which suppresses your natural good sense by a profusion of unnecessary scruples and objections.

Here I could observe, Hermippus, that Philo was a little embarrassed and confounded; but, while he hesitated in delivering an answer, luckily for him, Demea broke in upon the discourse and saved his countenance.

Your instance, Cleanthes, said he, drawn from books and language, being familiar, has, I confess, so much more force on that account; but is there not some danger, too, in this very circumstance, and may it not render us presumptuous, by making us imagine we comprehend the Deity and have some adequate idea of his nature and attributes? When I read a volume, I enter into the mind and intention of the author; I become him, in a manner, for the instant, and have an immediate feeling and conception of those ideas which resolved in his imagination while employed in that composition. But so near an approach we never surely can make to the Deity. His ways are not our ways. His attributes are perfect but incomprehensible. And this volume of nature contains a great and inexplicable riddle, more than any intelligible discourse or reasoning.

The ancient Platonists, you know, were the most religious and devout of all the pagan philosophers, yet many of them, particularly Plotinus, expressly declare that intellect or understanding is not to be ascribed to the Deity, and that our most perfect worship of him consists, not in acts of veneration, reverence, gratitude, or love, but in a certain mysterious self-annihilation or total extinction of all our faculties. These ideas are, perhaps, too far stretched, but still it must be acknowledged that, by representing the Deity as so intelligible and comprehensible, and so similar to a human mind, we are guilty of the grossest and most narrow partiality, and make ourselves the model of the whole universe.

All the *sentiments* of the human mind, gratitude, resentment, love, friendship, approbation, blame, pity, emulation, envy, have a plain reference to the state and situation of man, and are calculated for preserving the existence and promoting the activity of such a being in such circumstances. It seems, therefore, unreasonable to transfer such sentiments to a supreme existence or to suppose him actuated by them; and the phenomena, besides, of the universe will not support us in such a theory. All our *ideas* derived from the senses are confessedly false and illusive, and cannot therefore be supposed to have place in a supreme intelligence. And as the ideas of internal sentiment, added to those of the external senses, compose the whole furniture of human understanding, we may conclude that none of the *materials* of thought are in any respect similar in the human and in the divine intelligence. Now, as to the *manner* of thinking, how can we make any comparison between them or suppose them anywise resembling? Our thought is fluctuating, uncertain, fleeting, successive, and compounded; and were we to remove these circumstances, we absolutely annihilate its essence, and it would in such a case be an abuse of terms to apply to it the name of thought or reason. At least, if it appear more pious and respectful (as it really is) still to retain these terms when we mention the Supreme Being, we ought to acknowledge that their meaning, in that case, is totally incomprehensible, and that the infirmities of our nature do not permit us to reach any ideas which in the least correspond to the ineffable sublimity of the Divine attributes.

Source: David Hume, *Dialogues Concerning Natural Religion*, ed. Henry D. Aitken, New York 1948, parts 1–3, pp. 5–30

PART VI
ECONOMICS

TWENTY

DAVID HUME
Of Commerce

Hume's essay 'Of commerce' was first published in 1752, one of a set of essays mainly on matters economic. All the essays, and this one conspicuously, exemplify Hume's claim, made in the Introduction to his *Treatise of Human Nature*, that all the sciences lead back to the science of human nature. Hume affirms 'that there is a great uniformity among the actions of men, in all nations and ages, and that human nature remains still the same in its principles and operations' (*An Enquiry Concerning Human Understanding*, section 8). In the *Treatise* and the *Enquiries* he investigates human nature, and formulates principles concerning the emotions, reason and human motivation. Now he asks, in the light of that investigation, what can be deduced regarding commercial activity. Hume's study of commerce has an experiential basis, for his account of human nature is developed in the light of his experience of human beings. It should be added that Hume's study of commerce is also informed by a deep knowledge of history. His historical researches, which resulted in his multi-volume *History of England*, gave him ample opportunity to test his theory of human nature and provided him with a kind of proxy experience which helped him greatly to refine that theory.

The historic dimension of the essay 'On commerce' emerges rather early, when Hume focuses on the distinction between husbandmen and manufacturers, two classes which arise as soon as men quit their savage state, where they live chiefly by hunting and fishing. At first husbandmen are much the more numerous, but if manufacturing develops, and Hume describes the situations in which it will, this must lead in time to the development of agricultural science, which is then applied to farming and thus to an increase in produce, which in turn stimulates demand for more manufactured goods.

Thus the two classes, of husbandmen and manufacturers, become mutually supportive.

Hume probes this point with a view to discovering ways in which the power of the state is enhanced in this historic process. He bases himself upon the law that 'manufactures increase the power of the state only as they store up so much labour, and that of a kind to which the public may lay claim, without depriving any one of the necessaries of life. The more labour, therefore, is employed beyond mere necessaries, the more powerful is any state.' In developing this argument Hume focuses on the need for the state to work with the grain of the people, and never against it. It is useless to try to infuse them with passions which do not come naturally to them, for example a passion for public good. Instead, as Hume puts the point: 'It is requisite to govern men by other passions, and animate them with a spirit of avarice and industry, art and luxury.' This analysis is then applied to the subject of foreign trade, and Hume demonstrates that a country with substantial imports and exports will be 'more powerful, as well as richer and happier'.

A.B.

Of Commerce

The greater part of mankind may be divided into two classes; that of *shallow* thinkers, who fall short of the truth; and that of *abstruse* thinkers, who go beyond it. The latter class are by far the most rare: and I may add, by far the most useful and valuable. They suggest hints, at least, and start difficulties, which they want, perhaps, skill to pursue; but which may produce fine discoveries, when handled by men who have a more just way of thinking. At worst, what they say is uncommon; and if it should cost some pains to comprehend it, one has, however, the pleasure of hearing something that is new. An author is little to be valued, who tells us nothing but what we can learn from every coffee-house conversation.

All people of *shallow* thought are apt to decry even those of *solid* understanding, as *abstruse* thinkers, and metaphysicians, and refiners; and never will allow any thing to be just which is beyond their own weak conceptions. There are some cases, I own, where an extraordinary refinement affords a strong presumption of falsehood, and where no reasoning is to be trusted but what is natural and easy. When a man deliberates concerning his conduct in any *particular* affair, and forms schemes in politics, trade, œconomy, or any business in life, he never ought to draw his arguments too fine, or connect too long a chain of consequences together. Something is sure to happen, that will disconcert his reasoning, and produce an event different from what he expected. But when we reason upon *general* subjects, one may justly affirm, that our speculations can scarcely ever be too fine, provided they be just; and that the difference between a common man and a man of genius is chiefly seen in the shallowness or depth of the principles upon which they proceed. General reasonings seem intricate, merely because they are general; nor is it easy for the bulk of mankind to distinguish, in a great number of particulars, that common circumstance in which they all agree, or to extract it, pure and unmixed, from the other superfluous circumstances. Every judgment or conclusion, with them, is particular. They cannot enlarge their view to those universal propositions, which comprehend under them an infinite number of individuals, and include a whole science in a single theorem. Their eye is confounded with such an extensive prospect; and the conclusions, derived from it, even though clearly expressed, seem intricate and obscure. But however intricate they may seem, it is certain, that general principles, if just and sound, must always prevail in the general course of things, though they may fail in particular cases; and it is the chief business of philosophers to regard the general course of things. I may add, that it is also the chief business of politicians; especially in the domestic government of the state, where the public good, which is, or ought to be their object, depends on the concurrence of a multitude of causes; not, as in foreign politics, on accidents and chances, and the caprices of a few persons. This therefore makes the difference between *particular* deliberations and *general* reasonings, and renders subtilty and refinement much more suitable to the latter than to the former.

I thought this introduction necessary before the following discourses on *commerce, money, interest, balance of trade, &c.* where, perhaps, there will occur some principles which are uncommon, and which may seem too refined and subtile for such vulgar subjects. If false, let them be rejected: But no one ought to entertain a prejudice against them, merely because they are out of the common road.

The greatness of a state, and the happiness of its subjects, how independent soever they may be supposed in some respects, are commonly allowed to be inseparable with regard to commerce; and as private men receive greater security, in the possession of their trade and riches, from the power of the public, so the public becomes powerful in proportion to the opulence and extensive commerce of private men. This maxim is true in general; though I cannot forbear thinking, that it may possibly admit of exceptions, and that we often establish it with too little reserve and limitation. There may be some circumstances, where the commerce and riches and luxury of individuals, instead of adding strength to the public, will serve only to thin its armies, and diminish its authority among the neighbouring nations. Man is a very variable being, and susceptible of many different opinions, principles, and rules of conduct. What may be true, while he adheres to one way of thinking, will be found false, when he has embraced an opposite set of manners and opinions.

The bulk of every state may be divided into *husbandmen* and *manufacturers*. The former are employed in the culture of the land; the latter work up the materials furnished by the former, into all the commodities which are necessary or ornamental to human life. As soon as men quit their savage state, where they live chiefly by hunting and fishing, they must fall into these two classes; though the arts of agriculture employ *at first* the most numerous parts of the society. Time and experience improve so much these arts, that the land may easily maintain a much greater number of men, than those who are immediately employed in its culture, or who furnish the more necessary manufactures to such as are so employed.

If these superfluous hands apply themselves to the finer arts, which are commonly denominated the arts of *luxury*, they add to the happiness of the state; since they afford to many the opportunity of receiving enjoyments, with which they would otherwise have been unacquainted. But may not another scheme be proposed for the employment of these superfluous hands? May not the sovereign lay claim to them, and employ them in fleets and armies, to encrease the dominions of the state abroad, and spread its fame over distant nations? It is certain that the fewer desires and wants are found in the proprietors and labourers of land, the fewer hands do they employ; and consequently the superfluities of the land, instead of maintaining tradesmen and manufacturers, may support fleets and armies to a much greater extent, than where a great many arts are required to minister to the luxury of particular persons. Here therefore seems to be a kind of opposition between the greatness of the state and the happiness of the subject. A state is never greater than when all its superfluous hands are employed in the service of the public. The ease and convenience of private persons require, that these hands should be employed in their service. The one can never be satisfied, but at the expence of the other. As the ambition of the sovereign must entrench on the luxury of individuals; so the luxury of individuals must diminish the force, and check the ambition of the sovereign.

Nor is this reasoning merely chimerical; but is founded on history and experience. The republic of Sparta was certainly more powerful than any state now in the world, consisting of an equal number of people; and this was owing entirely to the want of commerce and luxury. The Helotes were the labourers: The Spartans were the soldiers or gentlemen. It is evident, that the labour of the Helotes could not have maintained so great a number of Spartans, had these latter lived in ease and delicacy, and given employment to a great variety of trades and manufactures. The like policy may be remarked in Rome. And indeed, throughout all ancient history, it is observable, that the smallest republics raised and maintained greater armies, than states consisting of triple the number of inhabitants, are able to support at present. It is computed, that, in all European nations, the proportion between soldiers and people does not exceed one to a hundred. But we read, that the city of Rome alone, with its small territory, raised and maintained, in early times, ten legions against the Latins. Athens, the whole of whose dominions was not larger than Yorkshire, sent to the expedition against Sicily near forty thousand men.[1] Dionysius the elder, it is said, maintained a standing army of a hundred thousand foot and ten thousand horse, besides a large fleet of four hundred sail;[2] though his territories extended no farther than the city of Syracuse, about a third of the island of Sicily, and some sea-port towns and garrisons on the coast of Italy and Illyricum. It is true, the ancient armies, in time of war, subsisted much upon plunder. But did not the enemy plunder in their turn? which was a more ruinous way of levying a tax, than any other that could be devised. In short, no probable reason can be assigned for the great power of the more ancient states above the modern, but their want of commerce and luxury. Few artizans were maintained by the labour of the farmers, and therefore more soldiers might live upon it. Livy says, that Rome, in his time, would find it difficult to raise as large an army as that which, in her early days, she sent out against the Gauls and Latins.[3] Instead of those soldiers who fought for liberty and empire in Camillus's time, there were, in Augustus's days, musicians, painters, cooks, players, and tailors; and if the land was equally cultivated at both periods, it could certainly maintain equal numbers in the one profession as in the other. They added nothing to the mere necessaries of life, in the latter period more than in the former.

It is natural on this occasion to ask, whether sovereigns may not return to the maxims of ancient policy, and consult their own interest in this respect, more than the happiness of their

---

1 Thucydides, lib. vii.
2 Diod. Sic. lib. vii. This account, I own, is somewhat
   suspicious, not to say worse; chiefly because this army
   was not composed of citizens, but of mercenary forces.
3 Titi Livii, lib. vii. cap. 24. 'Adeo in quæ laboramus,'
   says he, 'sola crevimus, divitias luxuriemque.' (Livy,
   History of Rome 7.25: '. . . so strictly has our growth
   been limited to the only things for which we strive, –
   wealth and luxury' [B. O. Foster]).

subjects? I answer, that it appears to me, almost impossible; and that because ancient policy was violent, and contrary to the more natural and usual course of things. It is well known with what peculiar laws Sparta was governed, and what a prodigy that republic is justly esteemed by every one, who has considered human nature as it has displayed itself in other nations, and other ages. Were the testimony of history less positive and circumstantial, such a government would appear a mere philosophical whim or fiction, and impossible ever to be reduced to practice. And though the Roman and other ancient republics were supported on principles somewhat more natural, yet was there an extraordinary concurrence of circumstances to make them submit to such grievous burthens. They were free states; they were small ones; and the age being martial, all their neighbours were continually in arms. Freedom naturally begets public spirit, especially in small states; and this public spirit, this *amor patriæ*, must encrease, when the public is almost in continual alarm, and men are obliged, every moment, to expose themselves to the greatest dangers for its defence. A continual succession of wars makes every citizen a soldier: He takes the field in his turn: And during his service he is chiefly maintained by himself. This service is indeed equivalent to a heavy tax; yet is it less felt by a people addicted to arms, who fight for honour and revenge more than pay, and are unacquainted with gain and industry as well as pleasure. Not to mention the great equality of fortunes among the inhabitants of the ancient republics, where every field, belonging to a different proprietor, was able to maintain a family, and rendered the number of citizens very considerable, even without trade and manufactures.

But though the want of trade and manufactures, among a free and very martial people, may *sometimes* have no other effect than to render the public more powerful, it is certain, that, in the common course of human affairs, it will have a quite contrary tendency. Sovereigns must take mankind as they find them, and cannot pretend to introduce any violent change in their principles and ways of thinking. A long course of time, with a variety of accidents and circumstances, are requisite to produce those great revolutions, which so much diversify the face of human affairs. And the less natural any set of principles are, which support a particular society, the more difficulty will a legislator meet with in raising and cultivating them. It is his best policy to comply with the common bent of mankind, and give it all the improvements of which it is susceptible. Now, according to the most natural course of things, industry and arts and trade encrease the power of the sovereign as well as the happiness of the subjects; and that policy is violent, which aggrandizes the public by the poverty of individuals. This will easily appear from a few considerations, which will present to us the consequences of sloth and barbarity.

Where manufactures and mechanic arts are not cultivated, the bulk of the people must apply themselves to agriculture; and if their skill and industry encrease, there must arise a great superfluity from their labour beyond what suffices to maintain them. They have no temptation, therefore, to encrease their skill and industry; since they cannot exchange that superfluity for any commodities, which may serve either to their pleasure or vanity. A habit of indolence naturally prevails. The greater part of the land lies uncultivated. What is cultivated, yields not its utmost for want of skill and assiduity in the farmers. If at any time the public exigencies require, that great numbers should be employed in the public service, the labour of the people furnishes now no superfluities, by which these numbers can be maintained. The labourers cannot encrease their skill and industry on a sudden. Lands uncultivated cannot be brought into tillage for some years. The armies, mean while, must either make sudden and violent conquests, or disband for want of subsistence. A regular attack or defence, therefore, is not to be expected from such a people, and their soldiers must be as ignorant and unskilful as their farmers and manufacturers.

Every thing in the world is purchased by labour; and our passions are the only causes of labour. When a nation abounds in manufactures and mechanic arts, the proprietors of land, as well as the farmers, study agriculture as a science, and redouble their industry and attention. The superfluity, which arises from their labour, is not lost; but is exchanged with manufactures for those commodities, which men's luxury now makes them covet. By this means, land furnishes a great deal more of the necessaries of life, than what suffices for those who cultivate it. In times of peace and tranquillity, this superfluity goes to the maintenance of manufacturers, and the improvers of liberal arts. But it is easy for the public to convert many of these manufacturers into soldiers, and maintain them by that superfluity, which arises from the labour of the farmers. Accordingly we find, that this is the case in all civilized governments. When the sovereign raises an army, what is the consequence? He imposes a tax. This tax obliges all the people to retrench what is least necessary to their subsistence.

Those, who labour in such commodities, must either enlist in the troops, or turn themselves to agriculture, and thereby oblige some labourers to enlist for want of business. And to consider the matter abstractedly, manufactures encrease the power of the state only as they store up so much labour, and that of a kind to which the public may lay claim, without depriving any one of the necessaries of life. The more labour, therefore, is employed beyond mere necessaries, the more powerful is any state; since the persons engaged in that labour may easily be converted to the public service. In a state without manufactures, there may be the same number of hands; but there is not the same quantity of labour, nor of the same kind. All the labour is there bestowed upon necessaries, which can admit of little or no abatement.

Thus the greatness of the sovereign and the happiness of the state are, in a great measure, united with regard to trade and manufactures. It is a violent method, and in most cases impracticable, to oblige the labourer to toil, in order to raise from the land more than what subsists himself and family. Furnish him with manufactures and commodities, and he will do it of himself. Afterwards you will find it easy to seize some part of his superfluous labour, and employ it in the public service, without giving him his wonted return. Being accustomed to industry, he will think this less grievous, than if, at once, you obliged him to an augmentation of labour without any reward. The case is the same with regard to the other members of the state. The greater is the stock of labour of all kinds, the greater quantity may be taken from the heap, without making any sensible alteration in it.

A public granary of corn, a storehouse of cloth, a magazine of arms; all these must be allowed real riches and strength in any state. Trade and industry are really nothing but a stock of labour, which, in times of peace and tranquillity, is employed for the ease and satisfaction of individuals; but in the exigencies of state, may, in part, be turned to public advantage. Could we convert a city into a kind of fortified camp, and infuse into each breast so martial a genius, and such a passion for public good, as to make every one willing to undergo the greatest hardships for the sake of the public; these affections might now, as in ancient times, prove alone a sufficient spur to industry, and support the community. It would then be advantageous, as in camps, to banish all arts and luxury; and, by restrictions on equipage and tables, make the provisions and forage last longer than if the army were loaded with a number of superfluous retainers. But as these principles are too disinterested and too difficult to support, it is requisite to govern men by other passions, and animate them with a spirit of avarice and industry, art and luxury. The camp is, in this case, loaded with a superfluous retinue; but the provisions flow in proportionably larger. The harmony of the whole is still supported; and the natural bent of the mind being more complied with, individuals, as well as the public, find their account in the observance of these maxims.

The same method of reasoning will let us see the advantage of *foreign* commerce, in augmenting the power of the state, as well as the riches and happiness of the subject. It encreases the stock of labour in the nation; and the sovereign may convert what share of it he finds necessary to the service of the public. Foreign trade, by its imports, furnishes materials for new manufactures; and by its exports, it produces labour in particular commodities, which could not be consumed at home. In short, a kingdom, that has a large import and export, must abound more with industry, and that employed upon delicacies and luxuries, than a kingdom which rests contented with its native commodities. It is, therefore, more powerful, as well as richer and happier. The individuals reap the benefit of these commodities, so far as they gratify the senses and appetites. And the public is also a gainer, while a greater stock of labour is, by this means, stored up against any public exigency; that is, a greater number of laborious men are maintained, who may be diverted to the public service, without robbing any one of the necessaries, or even the chief conveniences of life.

If we consult history, we shall find, that, in most nations, foreign trade has preceded any refinement in home manufactures, and given birth to domestic luxury. The temptation is stronger to make use of foreign commodities, which are ready for use, and which are entirely new to us, than to make improvements on any domestic commodity, which always advance by slow degrees, and never affect us by their novelty. The profit is also very great, in exporting what is superfluous at home, and what bears no price, to foreign nations, whose soil or climate is not favourable to that commodity. Thus men become acquainted with the *pleasures* of luxury and the *profits* of commerce; and their *delicacy* and *industry*, being once awakened, carry them on to farther improvements, in every branch of domestic as well as foreign trade. And this perhaps is the chief advantage which arises from a commerce with strangers. It rouses men from their indolence; and presenting the gayer and more opulent part of the nation with objects of luxury, which they never before dreamed of, raises in them a desire of a more splendid way of life than what their ancestors enjoyed. And at the same time, the few merchants, who possess the secret of this importation and exportation, make great profits; and becoming rivals in wealth to the ancient nobility, tempt other adventurers to become their rivals in commerce. Imitation soon diffuses all those arts; while domestic manufactures emulate the foreign in their improvements, and work up every home commodity to the utmost perfection of which it is susceptible. Their own steel and iron, in such laborious hands, become equal to the gold and rubies of the Indies.

When the affairs of the society are once brought to this situation, a nation may lose most of its foreign trade, and yet continue a great and powerful people. If strangers will not take any particular commodity of ours, we must cease to labour in it. The same hands will turn themselves towards some refinement in other commodities, which may be wanted at home. And there must always be materials for them to work upon; till every person in the state, who possesses riches, enjoys as great plenty of home commodities, and those in as great perfection, as he desires; which can never possibly happen. China is represented as one of the most flourishing empires in the world; though it has very little commerce beyond its own territories.

It will not, I hope, be considered as a superfluous digression, if I here observe, that, as the multitude of mechanical arts is advantageous, so is the great number of persons to whose share the production of these arts fall. A too great disproportion among the citizens weakens any state. Every person, if possible, ought to enjoy the fruits of his labour, in a full possession of all the necessaries, and many of the conveniences of life. No one can doubt, but such an equality is most suitable to human nature, and diminishes much less from the *happiness* of the rich than it adds to that of the poor. It also augments the *power of the state*, and makes any extraordinary taxes or impositions be paid with more chearfulness. Where the riches are engrossed by a few, these must contribute very largely to the supplying of the public necessities. But when the riches are dispersed among multitudes, the burthen feels light on every shoulder, and the taxes make not a very sensible difference on any one's way of living.

Add to this, that, where the riches are in few hands, these must enjoy all the power, and will readily conspire to lay the whole burthen on the poor, and oppress them still farther, to the discouragement of all industry.

In this circumstance consists the great advantage of England above any nation at present in the world, or that appears in the records of any story. It is true, the English feel some disadvantages in foreign trade by the high price of labour, which is in part the effect of the riches of their artisans, as well as of the plenty of money: But as foreign trade is not the most material circumstance, it is not to be put in competition with the happiness of so many millions. And if there were no more to endear to them that free government under which they live, this alone were sufficient. The poverty of the common people is a natural, if not an infallible effect of absolute monarchy; though I doubt, whether it be always true, on the other hand, that their riches are an infallible result of liberty. Liberty must be attended with particular accidents, and a certain turn of thinking, in order to produce that effect. Lord Bacon, accounting for the great advantages obtained by the English in their wars with France, ascribes them chiefly to the superior ease and plenty of the common people amongst the former; yet the government of the two kingdoms was, at that time, pretty much alike. Where the labourers and artisans are accustomed to work for low wages, and to retain but a small part of the fruits of their labour, it is difficult for them, even in a free government, to better their condition, or conspire among themselves to heighten their wages. But even where they are accustomed to a more plentiful way of life, it is easy for the rich, in an arbitrary government, to conspire against *them*, and throw the whole burthen of the taxes on their shoulders.

It may seem an odd position, that the poverty of the common people in France, Italy, and Spain, is, in some measure, owing to the superior riches of the soil and happiness of the climate; yet there want not reasons to justify this paradox. In such a fine mould or soil as that of those more southern regions, agriculture is an easy art; and one man, with a couple of sorry horses, will be able, in a season, to cultivate as much land as will pay a pretty considerable rent to the proprietor. All the art, which the farmer knows, is to leave his ground fallow for a year, as soon as it is exhausted; and the warmth of the sun alone and temperature of the climate enrich it, and restore its fertility. Such poor peasants, therefore, require only a simple maintenance for their labour. They have no stock or riches, which claim more; and at the same time, they are for ever dependant on their landlord, who gives no leases, nor fears that his land will be spoiled by the ill methods of cultivation. In England, the land is rich, but coarse; must be cultivated at a great expence; and produces slender crops, when not carefully managed, and by a method which gives not the full profit but in a course of several years. A farmer, therefore, in England must have a considerable stock, and a long lease; which beget proportional profits. The fine vineyards of Champagne and Burgundy, that often yield to the landlord above five pounds *per* acre, are cultivated by peasants, who have scarcely bread: The reason is, that such peasants need no stock but their own limbs, with instruments of husbandry, which they can buy for twenty shillings. The farmers are commonly in some better circumstances in those countries. But the grasiers are most at their ease of all those who cultivate the land. The reason is still the same. Men must have profits proportionable to their expence and hazard. Where so considerable a number of the labouring poor as the peasants and farmers are in very low circumstances, all the rest must partake of their poverty, whether the government of that nation be monarchical or republican.

We may form a similar remark with regard to the general history of mankind. What is the reason, why no people, living between the tropics, could ever yet attain to any art or civility, or reach even any police in their government, and any military discipline; while few nations in the temperate climates have been altogether deprived of these advantages? It is probable that one cause of this phænomenon is the warmth and equality of weather in the torrid zone, which render clothes and houses less requisite for the inhabitants, and thereby remove, in part, that necessity, which is the great spur to industry and invention. *Curis acuens mortalia corda* [sharpening men's minds with cares]. Not to mention, that the fewer goods or possessions of this kind any people enjoy, the fewer quarrels are likely to arise amongst them, and the less necessity will there be for a settled police or regular authority to protect and defend them from foreign enemies, or from each other.

Source: David Hume, 'Of commerce', in *Essays Moral, Political and Literary*, ed. Eugene F. Miller, Indianapolis 1987, essay 1, pp. 253–67

TWENTY-ONE

SIR JAMES STEUART
The Principles of Political Economy

Nothing is more important for a proper appreciation of Sir James Steuart's writings on economics than the fact that among Scots he was in a unique position to bring to bear upon economic theorising an extraordinarily wide and deep range of knowledge, in virtue of the many years he spent on continental Europe, first as a young man on the Grand Tour and then for eighteen years as a Jacobite exile. By the time he was fifty he had passed almost half of his life abroad. During those years he travelled through many countries of Western Europe, mastered four languages (German, French, Spanish and Italian), and noted population distributions, irrigation schemes, famines, regional distributions of poverty, banking procedures, restrictive trade practices, credit schemes, and a thousand other matters, of a macro and micro nature, which found their way into his major work, *An Inquiry into the Principles of Political Oeconomy*. The work itself was completed in 1766, three years after Steuart's return to Scotland from exile, and was published in 1767.

The book, though full of facts of economic significance, particularly facts relating to countries which were, economically speaking, comparatively underdeveloped, is no mere hotch-potch of facts. What we find is a system, with many clearly articulated general principles, arranged in an orderly manner. A distinction, important for an understanding of Steuart's thinking, has to be made here. He provides on the one hand a systematically organised conceptual framework for a discussion of economic phenomena, and provides on the other a detailed content for that framework. The detailed content concerns the way in which people either behave or might be expected to behave in consequence of the operation of the principles of economic behaviour that he presents. But though Steuart was confident of his framework, he was not confident that his principles of economic behaviour would always be acted on. Crudely stated, Steuart was no economic determinist. Even knowing a person's economic circumstances in some detail, we might be proved quite wrong as regards what he will do in those circumstances. Thus Steuart tells us: 'I shall have occasion to make a number of suppositions, and to draw consequences from them, which are abundantly natural, provided a proper · spirit in the people be presupposed, but which would be far from natural without this supposition.' But, sufficiently often his principles are genuinely enlightening, and do have predictive force, as when he affirms: 'From reason it is plain, that industry must give wealth, and wealth will give power, if he who possesses it be left master to employ it as he pleases.'

Elsewhere Steuart affirms: 'The principle of self-interest will serve as a general key to this inquiry; and it may, in one sense, be considered as the ruling principle of my subject, and may therefore be traced throughout the whole. This is the main spring, and only motive which a statesman should make use of, to engage a free people to concur in the plans which he lays down for their government.' He makes it clear that the statesman himself should behave in a public spirited manner; the self-interest at issue is the motive he should assume the subjects to act on. It is this well-founded assumption (the very same assumption as that made by Adam Smith in his *Wealth of Nations*) that allows us to predict human behaviour with some chance of being proved right. But even so, the sheer complexity of circumstances, including that important circumstance, the spirit of the people, is an obstacle to success in prediction.

The spirit of the people looms large in Steuart's discussion of the power of the statesman, 'statesman' being, for Steuart, a technical term for the legislature and supreme power. A crucial part of the great art of governing is 'to consult the spirit of the people, to give way to it in appearance, and in so doing to give it a turn capable of inspiring those sentiments which may induce them to relish the change, which an alteration in circumstances has rendered necessary'. As this quotation makes plain, Steuart is sensitive to the complex set of power relations binding statesman and people. In a sense the statesman wields power over his people, yet is constrained by their spirit. He cannot legislate as he pleases; his legislative acts must be congenial to that same spirit.

The dialectic of political power, as delineated by Steuart, has many interesting features. At the heart of his analysis is the fact that the more the statesman exercises power over the economy the more he is constrained by the product of that exercise, and therefore in a sense the less free he is. As Steuart notes: 'It is the order and regularity in the administration of the complicated modern oeconomy, which alone can put a statesman in a capacity to exert the whole force of his people'; and yet this very order and regularity, because of its universality within the state, establishes limits to the behaviour of the statesman. He is as constrained as his people, and in some ways is far more constrained than was a feudal despot, who was free to act in an arbitrary manner, being uncontrolled by a wide-ranging and detailed system of legislation defining economic activity in the state, for in the feudal state there was no such system. Steuart has at his disposal ample materials, gleaned from his years spent observing the economies of many countries, to be able to argue convincingly that: 'modern oeconomy . . . is the most effectual bridle ever was invented against the folly of despotism'.

A.B.

BOOK I
Of Population and Agriculture
Introduction

Oeconomy, in general, is the art of providing for all the wants of a family, with prudence and frugality.

If any thing necessary or useful be found wanting, if any thing provided be lost or misapplied, if any servant, any animal, be supernumerary or useless, if any one sick or infirm be neglected, we immediately perceive a want of oeconomy. The object of it, in a private family, is therefore to provide for the nourishment, the other wants, and the employment of every individual. In the first place, for the master, who is the head, and who directs the whole; next for the children, who interest him above all other things; and last for the servants, who being useful to the head, and essential to the well-being of the family, have therefore a title to become an object of the master's care and concern.

The whole oeconomy must be directed by the head, who is both lord and steward of the family. It is however necessary, that those two offices be not confounded with one another. As lord, he establishes the laws of his oeconomy; as steward, he puts them in execution. As lord, he may restrain and give his commands to all within the house as he thinks proper; as steward, he must conduct with gentleness and address, and is bound by his own regulations. The better the oeconomist, the more uniformity is perceived in all his actions, and the less liberties are taken to depart from stated rules. He is not so much master, as that he may break through the laws of his oeconomy, although in every respect he may keep each individual within the house, in the most exact subordination to his commands. Oeconomy and government, even in a private family, present therefore two different ideas, and have also two different objects.

What oeconomy is in a family, political oeconomy is in a state: with these essential differences, however, that in a state there are no servants, all are children: that a family may be formed when and how a man pleases, and he may there establish what plan of oeconomy he thinks fit; but states are found formed, and the oeconomy of these depends upon a thousand circumstances. The *statesman* (this is a general term to signify the legislature and supreme power, according to the form of government) is neither master to establish what oeconomy he pleases, or, in the exercise of his sublime authority, to overturn at will the established laws of it, let him be the most despotic monarch upon earth.

The great art therefore of political oeconomy is, first to adapt the different operations of it to the spirit, manners, habits, and customs of the people; and afterwards to model these circumstances so, as to be able to introduce a set of new and more useful institutions.

The principal object of this science is to secure a certain fund of subsistence for all the inhabitants, to obviate every circumstance which may render it precarious; to provide every thing necessary for supplying the wants of the society, and to employ the inhabitants (supposing them to be free-men) in such a manner as naturally to create reciprocal relations and dependencies between them, so as to make their several interests lead them to supply one another with their reciprocal wants.

If one considers the variety which is found in different countries, in the distribution of property, subordination of classes, genius of people, proceeding from the variety of forms of government, laws, climate, and manners, one may conclude, that the political oeconomy in each must necessarily be different, and that principles, however universally true, may become quite ineffectual in practice, without a sufficient preparation of the spirit of a people.

It is the business of a statesman to judge of the expediency of different schemes of oeconomy, and by degrees to model the minds of his subjects so as to induce them, from the allurement of private interest, to concur in the execution of his plan.

The speculative person who, removed from the practice, extracts the principles of this science from *observation* and *reflection*, should divest himself, as far as possible, of every prejudice in favour of established opinions, however reasonable, when examined relatively to particular nations: he must do his utmost to become a citizen of the world, comparing customs, examining minutely institutions which appear alike, when in different countries they are found to produce different effects: he should examine the cause of such differences with the utmost diligence and attention. It is from such inquiries that the true principles are discovered.

He who takes up the pen upon this subject, keeping in his eye the customs of his own or any other country, will fall more naturally into a description of one particular system of it, than into an examination of the principles of the science in general; he will applaud such institutions as he finds rightly administered at home; he will condemn those which are administered with abuse; but, without comparing different methods of executing the same plan in different countries, he will not easily distinguish the disadvantages which are essential to the institution, from those which proceed from the abuse. For this reason a land-tax excites the indignation of a Frenchman, an excise that of an Englishman. One who looks into the execution of both, in each country, and in every branch of their management, will discover the real effects of these impositions, and be able to distinguish what proceeds from abuse, from what is essential to the burden.

Nothing is more effectual towards preparing the spirit of a people to receive a good plan of oeconomy, than a proper representation of it. On the other hand, nothing is better calculated to keep the statesman, who is at the head of affairs, in awe.

When principles are well understood, the real consequences of burdensome institutions are clearly seen: when the purposes they are intended for are not obtained, the abuse of the statesman's administration appears palpable. People then will not so much cry out against the imposition, as against the misapplication. It will not be a land-tax of four shillings in the pound, nor an excise upon wines and tobacco, which will excite the murmurs of a nation; it will be the prodigal dissipation and misapplication of the amount of these taxes after they are laid on. But when principles are not known, all inquiry is at an end, the moment a nation can be engaged to submit to the burden. It is the same with regard to many other parts of this science: while people remain blind they are always mistrustful.

Having pointed out the object of my pursuit, I shall only add, that my intention is to attach myself principally to a clear deduction of principles, and a short application of them to familiar examples, in order to avoid abstraction as much as possible. I farther intend to confine myself to such parts of this extensive subject, as shall appear the most interesting in the general system of modern politics; of which I shall treat with that spirit of liberty, which reigns more and more every day, throughout all the polite and flourishing nations of Europe.

When I compare the elegant performances which have appeared in Great Britain and in France with my dry and abstracted manner of treating the same subject, in a plain language void of ornament,

I own I am discouraged on many accounts. If I be obliged to set out by laying down, as fundamental principles, the most obvious truths, I dread the imputation of pedantry, and of pretending to turn common sense into science. If I follow these principles through a minute detail, I may appear trifling. I therefore hope the reader will believe me, when I tell him, that these defects have not escaped my discernment, but that my genius, the nature of the work, and the connection of the subject, have obliged me to write in an order and in a style, where every thing has been sacrificed to perspicuity.

My principal aim shall be to discover truth, and to enable my reader to touch the very link of the chain where I may at any time go astray.

My business shall not be to seek for new thoughts, but to reason consequentially; and if any thing new shall be found, it will be in the conclusions.

Long steps in political reasoning lead to error: close reasoning is tedious, and to many appears trivial: this, however, must be my plan, and my consolation is, that the farther I advance, I shall become the more interesting.

Every supposition must be considered as strictly relative to the circumstances presupposed; and though, in order to prevent misapplication, and to avoid abstraction as much as possible, I frequently make use of examples for illustrating every principle; yet these, which are taken from matters of fact, must be supposed divested of every foreign circumstance inconsistent with the supposition.

I shall combat no particular opinion in such intricate matters; though sometimes I may pass them in review, in order to point out how I am led to differ from them.

I pretend to form no system, but, by tracing out a succession of principles, consistent with the nature of man and with one another, I shall endeavour to furnish some materials towards the forming of a good one.

CHAPTER I *Of the Government of Mankind*

Man we find acting uniformly in all ages, in all countries, and in all climates, from the principles of self-interest, expediency, duty, or passion. In this he is alike, in nothing else.

These motives of human actions produce such a variety of circumstances, that if we consider the several species of animals in the creation, we shall find the individuals of no class so unlike to one another, as man to man. No wonder then if people differ in opinion with regard to every thing almost which relates to our species.

As this noble animal is a sociable creature, both from necessity and inclination, we find also, in all ages, climates and countries, a certain modification of government and subordination established among them. Here again we are presented with as great a variety, as there are different societies; all however agreeing in this, that the end of a *voluntary* subordination to authority is with a view to promote the general good.

Constant and uninterrupted experience has proved to man, that virtue and justice, in those who govern, are sufficient to render the society happy, under any form of government. Virtue and justice, when applied to government, mean no more than a tender affection for the whole society, and an exact and impartial regard for the interest of every class.

All actions, and all things indeed, are good or bad by relation only. Nothing is so complex as relations when considered with regard to a society, and nothing is so difficult as to discover truth, when involved and blended with these relations.

We are not to conclude from this, that every operation of government must become problematical and uncertain as to its consequences: some are evidently good; others are notoriously bad; those, the tendency of which is less evident, are always the least essential, and the more complex they appear to a discerning eye, the more trivial they are found to be in their immediate consequences.

A government must be continually in action, and one principal object of its attention must be, the consequences and effects of new institutions.

Experience alone will shew, what human prudence could not foresee; and mistakes must be corrected as often as expediency requires.

All governments have what they call their fundamental laws; but fundamental, that is, invariable laws, can never subsist among men, the most variable thing we know: the only fundamental law, *salus populi*, must ever be relative, like every other thing. But this is rather a maxim than a law.

It is however expedient, nay absolutely necessary, that in every state, certain laws be supposed fundamental and invariable: both to serve as a curb to the ambition of individuals, and to point out to the statesman the outlines, or sketch of that plan of government, which experience has proved to be the best adapted to the spirit of his people.

Such laws may even be considered as actually invariable, while a state subsists without convulsions or revolutions; because then the alterations are so gradual, that they become imperceptible to all, but the most discerning, who can compare the customs and manners of the same people in different periods of time and under different circumstances.

As we have taken for granted the fundamental maxim, that every operation of government should be calculated for the good of the people, so we may with equal certainty decide, that in order to make a people happy, they must be governed according to the spirit which prevails among them.

I am next to explain what I mean by the spirit of a people, and to show how far this spirit must be made to influence the government of every society.

CHAPTER II *Of the Spirit of a People*

The spirit of a people is formed upon a set of received opinions relative to three objects; morals, government, and manners: these once generally adopted by any society, confirmed by long and constant habit, and never called in question, form the basis of all laws, regulate the form of every government, and determine what is commonly called the customs of a country.

To know a people, we must examine them under these general heads. We acquire the knowledge of their morals with ease, by consulting the tenets of their religion, and from what is taught among them by authority.

The second, or government, is more disguised, as it is constantly changing from circumstances, partly resulting from domestic and partly from foreign considerations. A thorough knowledge of their history, and conversation with their ministers of state, may give one, who has access to these helps, a very competent knowledge of this branch.

The last, or the knowledge of the manners of a people, is by far the most difficult to acquire, and yet is the most open to every person's observation. Certain circumstances with regard to manners are supposed by every one in the country to be so well known, so generally followed and observed, that it seldom occurs to any body to inform a stranger concerning them. In one country nothing is so injurious as a stroke with a stick, or even a gesture which implies a design or a desire to strike: in another a stroke is not near so offensive as an opprobrious expression. An innocent liberty with the fair sex, which in one country passes without censure, is looked upon in another as the highest indignity. In general, the opinion of a people with regard to injuries is established by custom only, and nothing is more necessary in government, than an exact attention to every circumstance peculiar to the people to be governed.

The kingdom of Spain was lost for a violence committed upon chastity; the city of Genoa for a blow; the kingdoms of Naples and Sicily have ever been ready to revolt; because having been for many ages under the dominion of strangers, the people have never been governed according to the true spirit of their manners. Let us consult the revolutions of all countries, and we shall find, that the most trivial circumstances have had a greater influence on such events, than the more weighty reasons, which are always set forth as the real motives. I need not enlarge upon this subject, my intention is only to suggest an idea which any one may pursue, and which will be applied upon many occasions as we go along; for there is no treating any point which regards the political oeconomy of a nation, without accompanying the example with some supposition relative to the spirit of the people.

I have said, that the most difficult thing to learn concerning a people, is the spirit of their manners. Consequently, the most difficult thing for a stranger to adopt, is their manner. Men acquire the language, nay even lose the foreign accent, before they lose the peculiarity of their manner. The reason is plain. The inclinations must be changed, the taste for amusements must be new-modelled; established maxims upon government, manners, nay even upon some moral actions, must undergo certain new modifications, before the stranger's conversation and behaviour can become consistent with the spirit of the people with whom he lives.

From these considerations, we may find the reason, why nothing is more heavy to bear than the government of conquerors, in spite of all their endeavours to render themselves agreeable to the conquered. Of this, experience has ever proved the truth, and princes are so much persuaded of it, that when a country is subdued in our days, or when it otherwise changes masters, there is seldom any question of altering, but by very slow degrees and length of time, the established laws and customs of the inhabitants. I might safely say, there is no form of government upon earth so excellent in itself, as, necessarily, to make the people happy under it. Freedom itself, *imposed* upon a people groaning under the greatest slavery, will not make them happy, unless it is made to undergo certain modifications, relative to their established habits.

Having explained what I mean by the spirit of a people, I come next to consider, how far this spirit must influence government.

If governments be taken in general, we shall find them analogous to the spirit of the people. But the point under consideration is, how a statesman is to proceed, when expediency and refinement require a change of administration, or when it becomes necessary from a change of circumstances.

The great alteration in the affairs of Europe within these three centuries, by the discovery of America and the Indies, the springing up of industry and learning, the introduction of trade and the luxurious arts, the establishment of public credit, and a general system of taxation, have entirely altered the plan of government every where.

From feudal and military, it is become free and commercial. I oppose freedom in government to the feudal system, to mark only that there is not found now that chain of subordination among the subjects, which made the essential part of the feudal form. The head there had little power, and the lower classes of the people little liberty. Now every industrious man, who lives with oeconomy, is free and independent under most forms of government. Formerly, the power of the barons swallowed up the independency of all inferior classes. I oppose commercial to military; because the military governments now are made to subsist from the consequences and effects of commerce only: that is, from the revenue of the state, proceeding from taxes. Formerly, every thing was brought about by numbers; now, numbers of men cannot be kept together without money.

This is sufficient to point out the nature of the revolution in the political state, and of consequence in the manners of Europe.

The spirit of a people changes no doubt of itself, but by slow degrees. The same generation commonly adheres to the same principles, and retains the same spirit. In every country we find two generations upon the stage at a time; that is to say, we may distribute into two classes the spirit which prevails; the one amongst men between twenty and thirty, when opinions are forming; the other of those who are past fifty, when opinions and habits are formed and confirmed. A person of judgment and observation may foresee many things relative to government, from an exact attention to the rise and progress of new customs and opinions, provided he preserve his mind free from all attachments and prejudices, in favour of those which he himself has adopted, and in that delicacy of sensation necessary to perceive the influence of a change of circumstances. This is the genius proper to form a great minister.

In every new step the spirit of the people should be first examined; and if this be not found ripe for the execution of the plan, it ought to be put off, kept entirely secret, and every method used to prepare the people to relish the innovation.

The project of introducing popery into England was blown before it was put in practice, and so miscarried. Queen Elizabeth kept her own secret, and succeeded in a similar attempt. The scheme of a general excise was pushed with too much vivacity, was made a matter of party, was ill-timed, and the people nowise prepared for it; hence it will be the more difficult to bring about at another time, without the greatest precautions.

In turning and working upon the spirit of a people, nothing is impossible to an able statesman. When a people can be engaged to murder their wives and children, and to burn themselves, rather than submit to a foreign enemy; when they can be brought to give their most precious effects, their ornaments of gold and silver, for the support of a common cause; when women are brought to give their hair to make ropes, and the most decrepit old men to mount the walls of a town for its defence; I think I may say, that by properly conducting and managing the spirit of a people, nothing is impossible to be accomplished. But when I say, nothing is impossible, I must be understood to mean, that nothing essentially necessary for the good of the people is impossible; and this is all that is required in government.

That it requires a particular talent in a statesman to dispose the minds of a people to approve even of the scheme which is the most conducive to their interest and prosperity, appears from this, that we set examples of wise, rich, and powerful nations languishing in inactivity, at a time when every individual is animated with a quite contrary spirit; becoming a prey to their enemies, like the city of Jerusalem, while they are taken up with their domestic animosities, merely because the remedies proposed against these evils contradict the spirit of the times.

The great art of governing is to divest oneself of prejudices and attachments to particular opinions, particular classes, and above all to particular persons; to consult the spirit of the people, to give way to it in appearance, and in so doing to give it a turn capable of inspiring those sentiments which may induce them to relish the change, which an alteration of circumstances has rendered necessary.

Can any change be greater among free men, than from a state of absolute liberty and independence to become subject to constraint in the most trivial actions? This change has however taken place over all Europe within these three hundred years, and yet we think ourselves more free than ever our fathers were. Formerly a gentleman who enjoyed a bit of land, knew not what it was to have any demand made upon him, but in virtue of obligations by himself contracted. He disposed of the fruits of the earth, and of the labour of his servants or vassals, as he thought fit. Every thing was bought, sold, transferred, transported, modified, and composed, for private consumption, or for public use, without ever the state's being once found interested in what was doing. This, I say, was formerly the general situation of Europe, among free nations under a regular administration; and the only impositions commonly known to affect landed men, were made in consequence of a contract of subordination, feudal or other, which had certain limitations; and the impositions were appropriated for certain purposes.

Daily experience shews, that nothing is more against the inclinations of a people than the imposition of taxes; and the less they are accustomed to them, the more difficult it is to get them established.

The great abuse of governors in the application of taxes contributes not a little to entertain and augment this repugnancy in the governed: but besides abuse, there is often too little management used to prepare the spirits of the people for such innovations; for we see them upon many occasions submitting with cheerfulness to very heavy impositions, provided they be well-timed, and consistent with their manners and disposition. A French gentleman, who cannot bear the thought of being put upon a level with a peasant in paying a land-tax, pays contentedly, in time of war, a general tax upon all his effects, under a different name. To pay for your head is terrible in one country; to pay for light appears as terrible in another.

It often happens, that statesmen take the hint of new impositions from the example of other nations, and not from a nice examination of their own domestic circumstances. But when these are rightly attended to, it becomes easy to discover the means of executing the same plan, in a way quite adapted to the spirit, temper, and circumstances of the people. When strangers are employed as statesmen, the disorder is still greater, unless there be extraordinary penetration, temper, and, above all, flexibility and discretion.

Statesmen have sometimes recourse to artifice instead of reason, because their intentions often are not upright. This destroys all confidence between them and the people; and confidence is necessary when you are in a manner obliged to ask a favour, or when what you demand is not indisputably your right. A people thus tricked into an imposition, though expedient for their prosperity, will oppose violently, at another time, a like measure, even when essential to their preservation.

At other times, we see statesmen presenting the allurement of present ease, precisely at the time when people's minds are best disposed to receive a burden. I mean when war threatens, and when the mind is heated with a resentment of injuries. Is it not wonderful, at such a time as this, to increase taxes in proportion only to the interest of money wanted; does not this imply a shortsightedness, or at least an indifference as to what is to come? Is it not more natural, that a people should consent to come under burdens to gratify revenge, than submit to repay a large debt when their minds are restored to a state of tranquility.

From the examples I have given, I hope what I mean by the spirit of a people is sufficiently understood, and I think I have abundantly shewn the necessity of its being properly disposed, in order to establish a right plan of oeconomy. This is so true, that many examples may be found, of a people's rejecting the most beneficial institutions, and even the greatest favours, merely because some circumstance had shocked their established customs. No wonder then, if we see them refuse to come under limitations, restraints, and burdens, when the utmost they can be flattered with from them, is a distant prospect of national good.

I have found it necessary to premise these general reflections, in order to obviate many objections which might naturally enough occur in the perusal of this inquiry. I shall have occasion to make a number of suppositions, and to draw consequences from them, which are abundantly natural, provided a proper spirit in the people be presupposed, but which would be far from being natural without this supposition. I suppose, for example, that a poor man, loaded with many children, would be glad to have the state maintain them; that another, who has waste lands, would be obliged to one who would gratuitously build him a farm-house upon it. Yet in both suppositions I may prove mistaken: for fathers there are, who would rather see their children dead than out of their hands; and proprietors are to be found, who, for the sake of hunting, would lay the finest country in Europe into a waste.

In order to communicate an adequate idea of what I understand by political oeconomy, I have explained the term, by pointing out the object of the art; which is, to provide food, other necessaries, and employment to every one of the society.

This is a very simple and a very general method of defining a most complicated operation.

To provide a proper employment for all the members of a society, is the same as to model and conduct every branch of their concerns.

Upon this idea may be formed, I think, the most extensive basis for an inquiry into the principles of political oeconomy.

The next thing to be done, is to fall upon a distinct method of analysing so extensive a subject, by contriving a train of ideas, which may be directed towards every part of the plan, and which, at the same time, may be made to arise methodically from one another.

For this purpose I have taken a hint from what the late revolutions in the politics of Europe have pointed out to be the regular progress of mankind, from great simplicity to complicated refinement.

This first book shall then set out with taking up society in the cradle, as I may say. I shall here examine the principles which influence their multiplication, the method of providing for their subsistence, the origin of their labour, the effects of their liberty and slavery, the distribution of them into classes, with some other topics which relate to mankind in general.

Here we shall find the principles of industry influencing the multiplication of mankind, and the cultivation of the soil. This I have thrown in on purpose to prepare my reader for the subject of the second book; where he will find the same principle (under the wings of liberty) providing an easy subsistence for a numerous populace, by the means of trade, which sends the labour of an industrious people over the whole world.

From the experience of what has happened these last two hundred years, we find to what a pitch the trade and industry of Europe has increased alienations, and the circulation of money. I shall therefore closely adhere to these, as the most immediate consequences of the preceding improvement; and, by analysing them, I shall form my third and fourth books, in which I intend to treat of money and credit.

We see also how credit has engaged nations to avail themselves of it in their wars, and how, by the use of it, they have been led to contract debts; which they never can satisfy and pay, without imposing taxes. The doctrine, then, of debts and taxes will very naturally follow that of credit in this great chain of political consequences.

By this kind of historical clue, I shall conduct myself through the great avenues of this extensive labyrinth; and in my review of every particular district, I shall step from consequence to consequence, until I have penetrated into the inmost recesses of my own understanding.

When a subject is broken off, I shall render my transitions as gradual as I can, by still preserving some chain of connexion; and although I cannot flatter myself (in such infinite variety of choice, as to order and distribution) to hit at all times on that method, which may appear to every reader the most natural and the most correct, yet I shall spare no pains in casting the materials into different forms, so as to make the best distribution of them in my power.

BOOK II
Of Trade and Industry

CHAPTER XIII *How far the Form of Government of a particular Country may be favourable or unfavourable to a Competition with other Nations, in matters of Commerce*

The question before us, though relative to another science, is not altogether foreign to this. I introduce it in this place, not so much for the sake of connexion, as by way of an illustration, which at the same time that it may serve as an exercise upon general principles, may also prove a relaxation to the mind, after so long a chain of close reasoning.

In setting out, I informed my readers that I intended to treat of the political oeconomy of free nations only; and upon every occasion where I have mentioned slavery, I have pointed out how far the nature of it is contrary to the advancement of private industry, the inseparable concomitant of foreign and domestic trade.

No term is less understood than that of *liberty*, and it is not my intention, at present, to enter into a particular inquiry into all the different acceptations of it.

By a people's being free, I understand no more than their being governed by general laws, well known, not depending upon the ambulatory will of any man, or any set of men, and established so as not to be changed, but in a regular and uniform way; for reasons which regard the body of the society, and not through favour or prejudice to particular persons, or particular classes. So far as a power of dispensing with, restraining or extending general laws, is left in the hands of any governor, so far I consider public liberty as precarious. I do not say it is hereby hurt; this will depend upon the use made of such prerogatives. According to this definition of liberty, a people may be found to enjoy freedom under the most despotic forms of government; and perpetual service itself, where the master's power is limited according to natural equity, is not altogether incompatible with liberty in the servant.

Here new ideas present themselves concerning the general principles of *subordination* and *dependence* among mankind; which I shall lay before my reader before I proceed, submitting the justness of them to his decision.

As these terms are both relative, it is proper to observe, that by *subordination* is implied an authority which superiors have over inferiors; and by *dependence*, is implied certain advantages which the inferiors draw from their subordination: a servant is under *subordination* to his master, and *depends* upon him for his subsistence.

Dependence is the only bond of society; and I have observed, in the fourth chapter of the first book, that the dependence of one man upon another for food, is a very natural introduction to slavery. This was the first contrivance mankind fell upon, in order to become useful to one another.

Upon the abolishing of slavery, from a principle of christianity, the next step taken was the establishment of an extraordinary subordination between the different classes of the people; this was the principle of the feudal government.

The last refinement, and that which has brought liberty to be generally extended to the lowest denominations of a people, without destroying that dependence necessary to serve as a band of society, was the introduction of industry: by this is implied, the circulation of an adequate equivalent for every service, which procures to the rich every advantage they could expect to reap, either from the servitude or dependence of the poor; and to these again, every comfort they could wish to enjoy under the mildest slavery, or most gentle subordination.

From this exposition, I divide dependence into three kinds. The first natural, between parents and children; the second political between masters and servants, lords and vassals, Princes and subjects; the third commercial, between the rich and the industrious.

May I be allowed to transgress the limits of my subject for a few lines, and to dip so far into the principles of the law of nature, as to enquire, how far subordination among men is thereby authorized? I think I may decide, *that so far as the subordination is in proportion to the dependence, so far it is reasonable and just.* This represents an even balance. If the scale of subordination is found too weighty, tyranny ensues; and licentiousness is implied, in proportion as it rises above the level. From this let me draw some conclusions.

First, He who depended upon another, for the preservation of a life justly forfeited, and at all times in the power of him who spared it, was, by the civil law, called a slave. This surely is the highest degree of dependence.

Secondly, He who depends upon another for every thing necessary for his subsistence, seems to be in the second degree; this is the dependence of children upon their parents.

Thirdly, He who depends upon another for the means of procuring subsistence to himself by his own labour, stands in the third degree: this I take to have been the case between the feudal lords, and the lowest classes of their vassals, the labourers of the ground.

Fourthly, He who depends totally upon the sale of his own industry, stands in the fourth degree: this is the case of tradesmen and manufacturers, with respect to those who employ them.

These I take to be the different degrees of subordination between man and man, considered as members of the same society.

In proportion, therefore, as certain classes, or certain individuals become more dependent than formerly, in the same proportion ought their just subordination to increase: and in proportion as they become less dependent than formerly, in the same proportion ought this just subordination to diminish. This seems to be a rational principle: next for the application.

I deduce the origin of the great subordination under the feudal government, from the necessary dependence of the lower classes for their subsistence. They consumed the produce of the land, as the price of their subordination, not as the reward of their industry in making it produce.

I deduce modern liberty from the independence of the same classes, by the introduction of industry, and circulation of an adequate equivalent for every service.

If this doctrine be applied in order to resolve the famous

question so much debated, concerning the origin of supreme authority, so far as it is a question of the law of nature, I do not find the decision so very difficult: *All authority is in proportion to dependence, and must vary according to circumstances.*

I think it is as rational to say, that the fatherly power proceeded originally from the act of the children, as to say, that the great body of the people who were fed, and protected by a few great lords, was the fountain of power, and creator of subordination. Those who have no other equivalent to give for their food and protection, must pay in personal service, respect, and submission; and so soon as they come to be in a situation to pay a proper equivalent for these dependences, so far they acquire a title to liberty and independence. The feudal lords, therefore, who, with reason, had an entire authority over many of their vassals, being subdued by their King; the usurpation was upon *their* rights, not upon the rights of the lower classes: but when a King came to extend the power he had over the vassals of the lords, to the inhabitants of cities, who had been independent of this subordination, his usurpation became evident.

The rights of Kings, therefore, are to be sought for in history; and not founded upon the supposition of tacit contracts between them and their people, inferred from the principles of an imaginary law of nature, *which makes all mankind equal*: nature can never be in opposition to common reason.

The general principle I have laid down, appears, in my humble opinion, more rational than this imaginary contract; and as consonant to the full with the spirit of free government. If the original tacit contract of government between Prince and people is admitted universally, then all governments ought to be similar; and every subordination, which appears contrary to the entire liberty and independence of the lowest classes, ought to be construed as tyrannical: whereas, according to my principle, the subordination of classes may, in different countries, be vastly different; the prerogative of one sovereign may, from different circumstances, be far more extended than that of another.

May not one have attained the sovereignty (by the free election of the people, I suppose) because of the great extent of his possessions, number of his vassals and dependents, quantity of wealth, alliances and connexions with neighbouring sovereigns? Had not, for example, such a person as Hugh Capet, the greatest feudal lord of his time, a right to a much more extensive jurisdiction over his subjects, than could reasonably be aspired to by a King of Poland, sent from France, or from

Germany, and set at the head of a republic, where he has not one person depending upon him for any thing?

The power of Princes, as *Princes*, must then be distinguished from the power they derive from other circumstances, which do not necessarily follow in consequence of their elevation to the throne. It would, I think, be the greatest absurdity to advance, that the title of King abolishes, of itself, the subordination due to the person who exercises the office of that high magistracy.

Matter of fact, which is stronger than all reasoning, demonstrates the force of the principle here laid down. Do we not see how subordination rises and falls under different reigns, under a rich Elizabeth, and a necessitous Charles, under a powerful Austrian, and a distressed Bavarian Emperor? I proceed no farther in the examination of this matter: perhaps my reader has decided that I have gone too far already.

From these principles may be deduced the boundaries of subordination. A people who depend upon nothing but their own industry for their subsistence, ought to be under no farther subordination than what is necessary for their protection. And as the protection of the whole body of such a people implies the protection of every individual, so every political subordination should there be general and equal: no person, no class should be under a greater subordination than another. This is the subordination of the laws; and whenever laws establish a subordination more than what is proportionate to the dependence of those who are subordinate, so far such laws may be considered as contrary to natural equity, and arbitrary.

These things premised, I come to the question proposed, namely, How far particular forms of government are favourable or unfavourable to a competition with other nations, in point of commerce?

If we reason from facts, and from experience, we shall find, that trade and industry have been found to flourish best under the republican form, and under those which have come the nearest to it. May I be allowed to say, that, perhaps, one principal reason for this has been, that under these forms the administration of the laws has been the most uniform, and consequently, that most liberty has *actually* been there enjoyed: I say actually, because I have said above, that in my acceptation of the term, liberty is equally compatible with monarchy as with democracy; I do not say the enjoyment of it is equally secure under both; because under the first it is much more liable to be destroyed.

The life of the democratical system is equality. Monarchy

conveys the idea of the greatest inequality possible. Now, if, on one side, the equality of the democracy secures liberty; on the other, the moderation in expence discourages industry; and if, on one side, the inequality of the monarchy endangers liberty, the progress of luxury encourages industry on the other. From whence we may conclude, that the democratical system is naturally the best for giving birth to foreign trade; the monarchical, for the refinement of the luxurious arts, and for promoting a rapid circulation of inland commerce.

The danger which liberty is exposed to under monarchy, and the discouragement to industry, from the frugality of the democracy, are only the natural and immediate effects of the two forms of government; and these inconveniences will take place only, while statesmen neglect the interest of commerce, so far as not to make it an object of administration.

The disadvantage, therefore, of the monarchical form, in point of trade and industry, does not proceed from the inequality it establishes among the citizens, but from the consequence of this inequality, which is very often accompanied with an arbitrary and undeterminate subordination between the individuals of the higher classes, and those of the lower; or between those vested with the execution of the laws, and the body of the people. The moment it is found that any subordination within the monarchy, between subject and subject, is left without proper bounds prescribed, liberty is so far at an end. Nay monarchy itself is hereby hurt, as this undeterminate subordination implies an arbitrary power in the state, not vested in the monarch. *Arbitrary* power never can be delegated; for if it be *arbitrary*, it may be turned against the monarch, as well as against the subject.

I might therefore say, that when such a power in individuals is constitutional in the monarchy, such monarchy is not a government, but a tyranny, and therefore falls without the limits of our subject; and when such a power is anti-constitutional, and yet is exercised, that it is an abuse, and should be overlooked. But as the plan of this inquiry engages me to investigate the operations of general principles, and the consequences they produce, I cannot omit, in this place, to point out those which flow from an indeterminate subordination, from whatever cause it may proceed.

Whether this indeterminate subordination between individuals, be a *vice* in the constitution of the government, or an *abuse*, it is the same thing as to the consequences which result from it. It is this which checks and destroys industry, and which in a great measure prevents its progress from being equal in all countries. This difference in the form or administration of governments, is the only one which it is essentially necessary to examine in this inquiry; and so essential it is, in my opinion, that I imagine it would be less hurtful, in a plan for the establishment of commerce, fairly, and at once to enslave the lower classes of the inhabitants, and to make them vendible like other commodities, than to leave them nominally free, burthened with their own maintenance, charged with the education of their children, and at the same time under an irregular subordination; that is, liable at every moment to be loaded with new prestations or impositions, either in work or otherwise, and to be fined or imprisoned at will by their superiors.

It produces no difference, whether these irregularities be exercised by those of the superior classes, or by the statesman and his substitutes. It is the irregularity of the exactions more than the extent of them which ruins industry. It renders living precarious, and the very idea of industry should carry along with it, not only an assured livelihood, but a certain profit over and above.

Let impositions be ever so high, provided they be proportional, general, gradually augmented, and permanent, they may have indeed the effect of stopping foreign trade, and of starving the idle, but they never will ruin the industrious; as we shall have occasion to shew in treating of taxation. Whereas, when they are arbitrary, falling unequally upon individuals of the same condition, sudden, and frequently changing their object, it is impossible for industry to stand its ground. Such a system of oeconomy introduces an unequal competition among those of the same class, it stops industrious people in the middle of their career, discourages others from exposing to the eyes of the public *the ease of their circumstances*, consequently encourages hoarding; this again excites rapaciousness upon the side of the statesman, who sees himself frustrated in his schemes of laying hold of private wealth.

From this a new set of inconveniences follow. He turns his views upon solid property. This inspires the landlords with *indignation* against *him* who can load *them* at will; and with envy against the *monied interest*, who can baffle his attempts. This class again is constantly upon the catch to profit of the public distress for want of money. What is the consequence of all this? It is that the lowest classes of the people, who ought by industry to enrich the state, find on one hand the monied interest constantly amassing, in order to lend to the state, instead of distributing among *them*, by seasonable loans, their superfluous income, with a view to share the reasonable profits of their ingenuity; and on the other hand, they find the emissaries of taxation robbing them of the seed before it is sown, instead of waiting for a share in the harvest.

Under the feudal form of government, liberty and independence were confined to the nobility. Birth opened the door of preferment to some, and birth as effectually shut it against others. I have often observed how, by reason and from experience, such a form of government must be unfavourable both to trade and industry.

From reason it is plain, that industry must give wealth, and wealth *will* give power, if he who possesses it be left the master to employ it as he pleases. A government could not therefore encourage a system which tended to throw power into the hands of those who were made to obey only. It was consequently very natural for the nobility to be jealous of wealthy merchants, and of every one who became easy and independent by means of his own industry; experience proved how exactly this principle regulated their administration.

A statesman ought, therefore, to consider attentively every circumstance of the constitution of his country, before he sets on foot the modern system of trade and industry. I am far from being of opinion that this is the only road to happiness, security, and ease; though, from the general taste of the times I live in, it be the system I am principally employed to examine. A country may be abundantly happy, and sufficiently formidable to those who come to attack it, without being extremely rich. Riches indeed are forbid to all who have neither mines, or foreign trade.

If a country be found labouring under many natural disadvantages from inland situation, barren soil, distant carriage, it would be in vain to attempt a competition with other nations in foreign markets. All that can be then undertaken is a passive trade, and that so far only as it can bring in additional wealth. When little money can be acquired, the statesman's application must be, to make that already acquired to circulate as much as possible, in order to give bread to every one in the society.

In countries where the government is vested in the hands of the great lords, as is the case in all aristocracies, as was the case under the feudal government, and as it still is the case in many countries in Europe, where trade, however, and industry are daily gaining ground; the statesman who sets the new system of political oeconomy on foot, may depend upon it, that either his attempt will fail, or the constitution of the government will change. If he destroys all arbitrary dependence between individuals, the wealth of the industrious will share, if not totally root out the power of the grandees. If he allows such a dependence to subsist, his project will fail.

While Venice and Genoa flourished, they were obliged to open the doors of their senate to the wealthy citizens, in order to prevent their being broken down. What is venal nobility? The child of commerce, the indispensible consequence of industry, and a middle term, which our Gothic ancestors found themselves obliged to adopt, in order not entirely to lose their own rank in the state. Money, they found, must carry off the fasces, (sic), so they chose rather to adopt the wealthy plebeians, and to clothe ignoble shoulders with their purple mantle, than to allow these to wrest all authority out of the hands of the higher class. By this expedient, a sudden revolution has often been prevented. Some kingdoms have been quit for a bloody rebellion or a long civil war. Other countries have likewise demonstrated the force of the principles here laid down: a wealthy populace has broken their chains to pieces, and overturned the very foundations of the feudal system.

All these violent convulsions have been owing to the short-sightedness of statesmen; who, inattentive to the consequences of growing wealth and industry, foolishly imagined that hereditary subordination was to subsist among classes, whose situation, with respect to each other, was entirely changed.

The pretorian cohorts were at first subordinate to the orders of the Emperors, and were the guards of the city of Rome. The Janissaries are understood to be under the command of the principal officers of the Port. So soon as the leading men of Rome and Constantinople, who naturally were entitled to govern the state, applied to these tumultuous bodies for their protection and assistance, they in their turn, made sensible of their own importance, changed the constitution, and shared in the government.

A milder revolution, entirely similar, is taking place in modern times; and an attentive spectator may find amusement in viewing the progress of it in many states of Europe. *Trade* and *industry* are in vogue; and their establishment is occasioning a wonderful fermentation with the remaining fierceness of the feudal constitution.

Trade and industry owed their establishment to *war* and to

ambition; and perhaps mankind may hope to see the day when this establishment will put an end to the first, by exposing the expensive folly of the latter.

Trade and industry, I say, owed their establishment to the ambition of princes who supported and favoured the plan in the beginning, principally with a view to enrich themselves, and thereby to become formidable to their neighbours. But they did not discover, until experience taught them, that the wealth they drew from such fountains was but the overflowing of the spring; and that an opulent, bold, and spirited people, having the fund of the prince's wealth in their own hands, have it also in their own power, when it becomes strongly their inclination, to shake off his authority. The consequence of this change has been the introduction of a more mild, and a more regular plan of administration. The money gatherers are become more useful to princes, than the great lords; and those who are fertile in expedients for establishing public credit, and for drawing money from the coffers of the rich, by the imposition of taxes, have been preferred to the most wise and most learned counsellors.

As this system is new, no wonder if it has produced phenomena both new and surprising. Formerly, the power of Princes was employed to destroy liberty, and to establish arbitrary subordination; but in our days, we have seen those who have best comprehended the true principles of the new plan of politics, arbitrarily limiting the power of the higher classes, and thereby applying their authority towards the extension of public liberty, by extinguishing every subordination, but that due to the established laws.

The fundamental maxim of some of the greatest ministers, has been to restrain the power of the great lords. The natural inference that people drew from such a step, was, that the minister thereby intended to make every thing depend on the prince's will only. This I do not deny. But what use have we seen made of this new acquisition of power? Those who look into events with a political eye, may perceive several acts of the most arbitrary authority exercised by some late European sovereigns, with no other view than to establish public liberty upon a more extensive bottom.

And although the prerogative of some princes be increased considerably beyond the bounds of the ancient constitution, even to such a degree as perhaps justly to deserve the name of usurpation; yet the consequences resulting from the revolution, cannot every where be said, upon the whole, to have impaired what I call *public liberty*. I should be at no loss to prove this assertion from matters of fact, and by examples, did I think it proper: it seems better to prove it from reason.

When once a state begins to subsist by the consequences of industry, there is less danger to be apprehended from the power of the sovereign. The mechanism of his administration becomes more complex, and, as was observed in the introduction to the first book, he finds himself so bound up by the laws of his political oeconomy, that every transgression of them runs him into new difficulties.

I speak of governments only which are conducted systematically, constitutionally, and by general laws; and when I mention princes, I mean their councils. The principles I am enquiring into, regard the cool administration of their government; it belongs to another branch of politics, to contrive bulwarks against their passions, vices and weaknesses, as men.

I say, therefore, that from the time states have begun to be supported by the consequences of industry, the plan of administration has become more moderate; has been changing and refining by degrees; and every change, as has been often observed, must be accompanied with inconveniences.

It is of governments as of machines, the more they are simple, the more they are solid and lasting; the more they are artfully composed, the more they become useful; but the more apt they are to be out of order.

The Lacedemonian form may be compared to the wedge, the most solid and compact of all the mechanical powers. Those of modern states to watches, which are continually going wrong; sometimes the spring is found too weak, at other times too strong for the machine: and when the wheels are not made according to a determinate proportion, by the able hands of a Graham, or a Julien le Roy, they do not tally well with one another; then the machine stops, and if it be forced, some part gives way; and the workman's hand becomes necessary to set it right.

CHAPTER XXII *Preliminary Reflections upon inland Commerce*

I resume the subject, which, as a rest to the mind, I dropt at the end of the 19th chapter.

I am now to treat directly of inland commerce, which has been sufficiently distinguished from infant, and foreign trade.

We are to consider ourselves now as transported into a new country, where foreign trade had been carried to the greatest height possible; until the luxury of the inhabitants, the care-lessness, perhaps, of the statesman, and the natural advantages of other nations, added to the progress of their industry and refinement, had concurred to cut it off, and thereby to dry up the source which had till then been constantly augmenting the national opulence.

We must examine the natural effects of this revolution; we must point out how every inconvenience proceeding from it may be avoided, and how a statesman may regulate his conduct, so as to prevent the exportation of any part of that wealth which the nation may have heaped up within herself, during the prosperity of her foreign trade. How he may keep the whole of his people constantly employed, and by what means he may promote an equable circulation of domestic wealth, through the hands of the lower classes, which will prove an adequate equivalent given by the rich, for the services rendered them by the industrious poor. How, by a judicious imposition of taxes, he may draw together an equitable proportion of every man's annual income, without reducing any one below the standard of a full physical-necessary. How he may, with this public fund, preserve in vigour every branch of industry, and be enabled also, by the means of it, to profit of the smallest revolution in the situation of other nations, so as to re-establish the foreign trade of his own people. And lastly, how the society may be thereby sufficiently defended against foreign enemies, by a body of men regularly supported and maintained at the public charge, without occasioning any sudden revolution hurtful to industry, either when it becomes necessary to increase their numbers, in order to carry on an unavoidable war, or to diminish them, upon the return of peace and tranquility. This is, in few words, the object of a statesman's attention when he finds himself at the head of a people living upon their own wealth without any mercantile connections with strangers.

How hurtful soever the natural and immediate effects of political revolutions may have been formerly, when the mechanism of government was more simple than at present, they are now brought under such restrictions, by the complicated system of modern oeconomy, that the evil which might otherwise result from them may be guarded against with ease.

As often, therefore, as we find a notable prejudice resulting to a state, from a change of their circumstances, *gradually taking place*, we may safely conclude, that negligence, or want of abilities, in those who have the direction of public affairs, has more than any other cause been the occasion of it.

It was observed, in the second chapter of the first book, that before the introduction of modern oeconomy, which is made to subsist by the means of taxes, a state was seldom found to be interested in watching over the actions of the people. They bought and sold, transferred, transported, modified, and compounded productions and manufactures, for public use, and private consumption, just as they thought fit. Now it is precisely in these operations that a modern state is chiefly interested; because proportional taxes are made to affect a people on every such occasion.

The interest the state has in levying these impositions, gives a statesman an opportunity of laying such operations under certain restrictions; by the means of which, upon every change of circumstances, he can produce the effect he thinks fit. Do the people buy from foreigners what they can find at home? he imposes a duty upon importation. Do they sell what they ought to manufacture? he shuts the gates of the country. Do they transfer or transport at home? he accelerates or retards the operation, as best suits the common interest. Do they modify or compound what the public good requires to be consumed in its simple state? he can either prevent it by a positive prohibition, or he may permit such consumption to the more wealthy only, by subjecting it to a duty.

So powerful an influence over the operations of a whole people, vests an authority in a modern statesman, which in former ages, even under the most absolute governments, was utterly unknown. The truth of this remark will appear upon reflecting on the force of some states, at present in Europe, where the sovereign power is extremely limited, in every *arbitrary* exercise of it, and where, at the same time, it is found to operate over the wealth of the inhabitants, in a manner far more efficacious than the most despotic and arbitrary authority possibly can do.

It is the order and regularity in the administration of the complicated modern oeconomy, which alone can put a statesman in a capacity to exert the whole force of his people. The more he has their actions under his influence, the easier it is for him to make them concur in advancing the general good.

Here it is objected, that any free people who invest a statesman with a power to control their most trivial actions, must be out of their wits, and considered as submitting to a voluntary slavery of the worst nature, as it must be the most difficult to be shaken off. This I agree to; supposing the power vested to be of an arbitrary nature, such as we have described in the thirteenth chapter of this book. But while the legislative power is exerted in acquiring an influence only over the actions of individuals, in order to promote a scheme of political oeconomy, uniform and consistent in all its parts, the consequence will be so far from introducing slavery among the people, that the execution of the plan will prove absolutely inconsistent with every arbitrary or irregular measure.

The power of a modern prince, let it be by the constitution of his kingdom, ever so absolute, immediately becomes limited so soon as he establishes the plan of oeconomy which we are endeavouring to explain. If his authority formerly resembled the solidity and force of the wedge (which may indifferently be made use of, for splitting of timber, stones and other hard bodies, and which may be thrown aside and taken up again at pleasure), it will at length come to resemble the delicacy of the watch, which is good for no other purpose than to mark the progression of time, and which is immediately destroyed, if put to any other use, or touched with any but the gentlest hand.

As modern oeconomy, therefore, is the most effectual bridle ever was invented against the folly of despotism; so the wisdom of so great a power never shines with greater lustre, than when we see it exerted in planning and establishing this oeconomy, as a bridle against the wanton exercise of itself in succeeding generations. I leave it to my reader to seek for examples in the conduct of our modern Princes, which may confirm what, I think, reason seems to point out: were they less striking, I might be tempted to mention them.

The part of our subject we are now to treat of, will present us with a system of political oeconomy, still more complicated than any thing we have hitherto met with.

While foreign trade flourishes and is extended, the wealth of a nation increases daily; but force is not so easily exerted, as after this wealth begins to circulate more at home, as we shall easily shew. But, on the other hand, the force she exerts is much more easily recruited. In the first case, her frugality enables her to draw new supplies out of the coffers of her neighbours; in the last, her luxury affords a resource from the wealth of her own citizens.

In opening my chapter, I have introduced my reader into a new country; or indeed I may say, that I have brought him back into that which we had under our consideration in the first book.

Here luxury and superfluous consumption will strike his view almost at every step. He will naturally compare the system of frugality, which we have dismissed, with that of dissipation, which we are now to take up; and he may very naturally conclude, that the introduction of the latter, must prove a certain forerunner of destruction. The examples found in history of the greatest monarchies being broken to pieces, so soon as the taste for simplicity was lost, seem to justify this conjecture. It is, therefore, necessary to examine circumstances a little, that we may compare, in this particular also, the oeconomy of the ancients with our own; in order to discover whether the introduction of luxury be as hurtful at present, as it formerly proved to those states which made so great a figure in the world; and which are known from history only, and judged of from the few scattered ruins, which remain to bear testimony of their former greatness.

Luxury is the child of wealth; and wealth is acquired by states, as by private people, either by a lucrative, or by an onerous title, as the civilians speak. The lucrative title, by which a state acquires, is either by rapine, or from her mines; the onerous title, or that for a valuable consideration, is by industry.

The wealth of the ancient monarchs of Babylon, Persia, Greece, and Rome, was the effect of rapine; whereas industry enriched the cities of Sydon, Tyre, Carthage, Athens, and Alexandria. The luxury of the first, proved the ruin of the luxurious; the luxury of the last, advanced their grandeur: because they had no rivals to take advantage of the natural effects of this luxury, in cutting off the profits of their foreign trade. Peace was as hurtful to the plunderers, as war was destructive to the industrious.

When an empire was at war, its wealth was thereby made to circulate for an equivalent in services performed. So soon as peace was restored, every one returned, as it were, to a state of slavery. The monarch then possessed himself of all the wealth, and distributed it by caprice. Fortunes were made in an instant, and no body knew how: they were lost again by transitions equally violent and sudden. The luxury of those days was attended with the most excessive oppression. Extraordinary consumption was no proof of the circulation of any adequate equivalent in favour of the industrious: it had not the effect of giving bread to the poor, nor of proportionally diminishing the wealth of the rich. The great remained constantly great; and the more they were prodigal, the more the small were brought into distress. In one word, luxury had nothing to recommend it, but that quality which *solely* constitutes the abuse of it in modern times; to wit, the excessive gratification of the passions of the great, which frequently brought on the corruption of their manners.

When such a state became luxurious, public affairs were neglected because it was not from a right administration that wealth was to be procured. War, under such circumstances, worked effects almost similar to the springing up of industry in modern times; it procured employment, and this produced a more regular circulation, as has been said.

On the other hand, the wealth and luxury of the trading cities above mentioned, which was of the same species with that of modern times, proceeded from the alienation of their work; that is, from their industry. Nothing was got for nothing, and when they were forced to go to war, they found themselves obliged either to dissipate their wealth, by hiring troops, or to abandon the resources of it, the labour of their industrious citizens. Thus the punic wars exalted the grandeur of plundering Rome, and blotted out the existence of industrious Carthage. I do not here pretend to vindicate the justness of these reflections in every circumstance, and it is foreign to my present purpose to be more particular; all I seek for, is to point out the different effects of luxury in ancient and modern times.

Ancient luxury was quite *arbitrary*; consequently could be laid under no limitations, but produced the worst effects, which *naturally* and *mechanically* could proceed from it.

Modern luxury is *systematical*; it cannot make one step, but at the expence of an adequate equivalent, acquired by those who stand the most in need of the protection and assistance of their fellow citizens; and without producing a vibration in the balance of their wealth. This balance is in the hands of the statesman, who may receive a contribution upon every such vibration. He has the reins in his hand, and may turn, restrain, and direct the luxury of his people, towards whatever object he thinks fit.

Luxury here is so far from drawing on a neglect of public affairs, that it requires the closest application to the administration of them, in order to support it. When these are neglected, the industrious will be brought to starve, consumption and taxes will diminish; that is, luxury will insensibly disappear, and hoarding will succeed it. These and similar consequences will undoubtedly take place, and *mechanically* follow one another, when a skilful hand is not applied to prevent them.

It is impossible not to perceive the advantages of supporting a flourishing inland trade, after the extinction of foreign commerce. By such means elegance of taste, and the polite arts, may be carried to the highest pitch. The whole of the inhabitants may be employed in working and consuming; all may be made to live in plenty and in ease, by the means of a swift calculation, which will produce a reasonable equality of wealth among all the inhabitants. Luxury can never be the cause of inequality, though it may be the effect of it. Hoarding and parsimony form great fortunes, luxury dissipates them and restores equality.

Such a situation would surely be of all others the most agreeable, and the most advantageous, were all mankind collected into one society, or were the country where it is established cut off from every communication with other nations.

The balance between work and demand would then only influence the balance of wealth among individuals, and the subversions of it would do little harm. If hands became scarce, the balance would turn the quicker in favour of the laborious, and the idle would grow poor. If hands became too plentiful (which indeed is hardly to be expected) every thing would be bought the cheaper; but the same quantity of national wealth would still remain without any diminution.

Where is, therefore, the great advantage of foreign trade?

I answer by putting another question. Where is the great advantage of a person's making a large fortune in his own country? A man of a small estate may, no doubt, be as happy as another with a great one; and the same thing would be true of nations, were all equally inspired with a spirit of peace and justice; or were they subordinate to a higher temporal power, which could protect the weak against the violence and injustice of the strong.

It is, therefore, the separate interests of nations who incline to communicate together, and consume part of one another's commodities, which renders the consideration of the principles of trade, a matter of great importance.

While nations contented themselves with their own productions, while the difference of their customs, and contrast of their prejudices were great, the connections between them were not very intimate.

From this proceeds the great diversity of languages and dialects. When a traveller finds a sudden transition from one language to another, or from one dialect to another, it is a proof that the manners of such people have been long different, and that they have had little communication with one another. On the contrary, when dialects change by degrees, as in the provinces of the same country, it is a proof that there has been no great repugnancy in their customs. In like manner, when we find several languages, at present different, but plainly deriving from the same source, we may conclude, that there was a time when such nations were connected by correspondence, or that the language has been transplanted from one to the other, by the migration of colonies. But I insensibly wander from my subject.

I have said, that when nations contented themselves with their own productions, connections between them were not very intimate. While trade was carried on by the exchange of consumable commodities, this operation also little interested the state: consumption then was equal on both sides; and no balance was found upon either. But so soon as the precious metals became an object of commerce, and when, by being rendered an universal equivalent for everything; they become also the measure of power between nations, then the acquisition, or at least the preservation of a proportional quantity of them, became to the more prudent, an object of the last importance.

We have seen how a foreign trade, well conducted, has the necessary effect of drawing wealth from all other nations. We have seen in what manner the benefit resulting from this trade may come to a stop, and how the balance of it may come round to the other side. We are now to examine how the same prudence which set foreign trade on foot, and supported it as long as possible, may put an effectual stop to it, and at the same time guard against a sudden revolution; to the end that a nation enriched by commerce may not, by blindly or mechanically carrying it on, when the balance is against her, fall into those inconveniences which other nations must have experienced during her prosperity.

Source: Sir James Steuart, *An Inquiry into the Principles of Political Oeconomy*, 2 vols, ed. A. S. Skinner, Edinburgh and Chicago 1966, Book 1, chs 1, 2, pp. 20–9; Book 2, ch. 13, pp. 206–17; Book 2, ch. 22, pp. 276–83

TWENTY-TWO

ADAM SMITH
The Division of Labour
and the Provision of Education

The first sentence of the *Wealth of Nations* refers to an *improvement* in the productive power of labour. Smith signals thereby that one of the major themes of the book is economic growth. He therefore places especial emphasis on the concept of the division of labour for, as he argues conclusively, without such division there is little, if any, opportunity for even the smallest degree of economic growth. Smith's famous example of ten men able to produce 48,000 pins in one day, where labour is divided efficiently among them, compared with the one pin that each could produce in a day when working alone, greatly understates the case, as Smith is aware. For the workman making his one pin per day does not make his own tools; they are made by other workers upon whose labour he is relying. The link between economic improvement and division of labour is, then, plain.

This is not to say that a division of labour is equally appropriate in all industries. For example, in agriculture, and in other industries where the seasonal dimension has to be considered, seasonality is a constraint on the extent to which labour can be divided. For sound economic reasons a worker will have several jobs. It is for example the same man that ploughs, harrows, sows and reaps.

A further constraint on division of labour is the size of the market. Division of labour involves by definition a process of specialisation, and the more specialised a person's job is the wider the market he needs. Portering is a viable occupation in a town, but not in a small village. As Smith adds: 'In the lone houses and very small villages which are scattered about in so desert a country as the Highlands of Scotland, every farmer must be butcher, baker and brewer to his own family.'

The advantage of division of labour is threefold. First,

it leads to an increase in dexterity, due to the repetitiveness of the task. Secondly, it reduces time by eliminating the passage from one task to another. And thirdly, it leads to the invention of machinery. Since division of labour results in the simplification of tasks, the problem of how to mechanise the tasks is an easier one to tackle. And Smith observes that often the solution is provided by the workmen themselves, who in the nature of the case will have better insight into what is required. Of course, one thinks contrariwise of the innovations made by James Watt and other geniuses of the Enlightenment. But while it can be granted that beyond a certain level of sophistication the large advances, such as Watt's improvements to the Newcomen engine, are in the main due to those who do not spend every hour at some small repetitive task at the work place, Smith might still be entirely correct as regards the early stages in the process of mechanisation. Who else are better placed to detect means to the improvement of a process than those who daily carry out the process?

This suggests that division of labour can be a stimulant to intellectual activity, but Smith strikes a note of caution elsewhere in the *Wealth of Nations* on precisely this point. He was aware of the mind-numbing quality of many jobs which owe their existence to the division of labour, and commends as a solution the provision of education, particularly an education in reading, writing and arithmetic. While he saw this provision as justified on economic grounds, he recognised the moral basis of the provision. An economic system that would stunt the minds of its workers is morally unacceptable if defences against this danger are not in place within that same system. Any modern tendency that there might be to construct economic models without regard to their moral defensibility would have been condemned by Smith. For him, economic activity, like all other human activity, has to have a sound moral basis. It is therefore significant that Smith's lectures on economics, delivered at the University of Glasgow, formed part of his course on moral philosophy.

Division of labour leads inevitably to interdependence. Plainly the more specialised a person's work the less he produces for himself what he needs to consume in order to live. He lives by exchanging that part of his produce surplus to his needs for something of the surplus that others produce. The economic system is thus a system of mutual support in which the products of different talents form a common stock. The motivation which drives people to truck, barter and exchange is self-interest. We do not rely on the benevolence or common humanity of others, but on their seeing that it is in their interest to exchange something of their surplus produce for something of ours.

Some have seen a problem in this position, when it is considered in relation to the teaching on sympathy in Smith's *Theory of Moral Sentiments*. On the one hand, it has been said, Smith founds morality on sympathy, and on the other his economic theory assumes the self-interestedness of people. Surely this means that Smith's moral philosophy and his economic theory have mutually incompatible bases. But this charge is based on a false interpretation of his teaching on sympathy in *The Theory of Moral Sentiments*. There sympathy is a technical term for a feature of human psychology that underlies the cohesiveness of society. It also, and relatedly, signifies a concept which Smith uses in his analysis of moral judgment. Smith has rather little to say about sympathy in the ordinary sense of that term, where it is considered as a motive for human acts. But it is only in this latter sense that one might make any progress with the claim that Smith's moral philosophy and his economic theory are mutually incompatible. Even so, progress would amount to very little, probably to nothing, precisely because sympathy in the ordinary sense is a very minor player indeed in Smith's moral philosophy, while at the same time he regarded enlightened self-interest as a moral virtue.

A.B.

BOOK I

Of the Causes of Improvement in the Productive
Powers of Labour, and of the Order According to
which its Produce is Naturally Distributed
among the Different Ranks of the People

CHAPTER I *Of the Division of Labour*

The greatest improvement in the productive powers of labour,
and the greater part of the skill, dexterity, and judgment with
which it is any where directed, or applied, seem to have been
the effects of the division of labour.

The effects of the division of labour, in the general business
of society, will be more easily understood, by considering in
what manner it operates in some particular manufactures. It is
commonly supposed to be carried furthest in some very trifling
ones; not perhaps that it really is carried further in them than
in others of more importance: but in those trifling manufactures
which are destined to supply the small wants of but a small number
of people, the whole number of workmen must necessarily be
small; and those employed in every different branch of the work
can often be collected into the same workhouse, and placed at
once under the view of the spectator. In those great manufactures,
on the contrary, which are destined to supply the great wants of
the great body of the people, every different branch of the work
employs so great a number of workmen, that it is impossible to
collect them all into the same workhouse. We can seldom see
more, at one time, than those employed in one single branch.
Though in such manufactures, therefore, the work may really be
divided into a much greater number of parts, than in those of a
more trifling nature, the division is not near so obvious, and has
accordingly been much less observed.

To take an example, therefore, from a very trifling manufacture;
but one in which the division of labour has been very often taken
notice of, the trade of the pin-maker; a workman not educated to
this business (which the division of labour has rendered a distinct
trade), nor acquainted with the use of the machinery employed
in it (to the invention of which the same division of labour has
probably given occasion), could scarce, perhaps, with his utmost
industry, make one pin in a day, and certainly could not make

twenty. But in the way in which this business is now carried on, not only the whole work is a peculiar trade, but it is divided into a number of branches, of which the greater part are likewise peculiar trades. One man draws out the wire, another straights it, a third cuts it, a fourth points it, a fifth grinds it at the top for receiving the head; to make the head requires two or three distinct operations; to put it on, is a peculiar business, to whiten the pins is another; it is even a trade by itself to put them into the paper; and the important business of making a pin is, in this manner, divided into about eighteen distinct operations, which, in some manufactories, are all performed by distinct hands, though in others the same man will sometimes perform two or three of them. I have seen a small manufactory of this kind where ten men only were employed, and where some of them consequently performed two or three distinct operations. But though they were very poor, and therefore but indifferently accommodated with the necessary machinery, they could, when they exerted themselves, make among them about twelve pounds of pins in a day. There are in a pound upwards of four thousand pins of a middling size. Those ten persons, therefore, could make among them upwards of forty-eight thousand pins in a day. Each person, therefore, making a tenth part of forty-eight thousand pins, might be considered as making four thousand eight hundred pins in a day. But if they had all wrought separately and independently, and without any of them having been educated to this peculiar business, they certainly could not each of them have made twenty, perhaps not one pin in a day; that is, certainly, not the two hundred and fortieth, perhaps not the four thousand eight hundredth part of what they are at present capable of performing, in consequence of a proper division and combination of their different operations.

In every other art and manufacture, the effects of the division of labour are similar to what they are in this very trifling one; though, in many of them, the labour can neither be so much subdivided, nor reduced to so great a simplicity of operation. The division of labour, however, so far as it can be introduced, occasions, in every art, a proportionable increase of the productive powers of labour. The separation of different trades and employments from one another, seems to have taken place, in consequence of this advantage. This separation too is generally carried furthest in those countries which enjoy the highest degree of industry and improvement; what is the work of one man, in a rude state of society, being generally that of several in an improved one. In every improved society, the farmer is generally nothing but a farmer;

the manufacturer, nothing but a manufacturer. The labour too which is necessary to produce any one complete manufacture, is almost always divided among a great number of hands. How many different trades are employed in each branch of the linen and woollen manufacturers, from the growers of the flax and the wool, to the bleachers and smoothers of the linen, or to the dyers and dressers of the cloth! The nature of agriculture, indeed, does not admit of so many subdivisions of labour, nor of so complete a separation of one business from another, as manufactures. It is impossible to separate so entirely, the business of the grazier from that of the corn-farmer, as the trade of the carpenter is commonly separated from that of the smith. The spinner is almost always a distinct person from the weaver; but the ploughman, the harrower, the sower of the seed, and the reaper of the corn, are often the same. The occasions for those different sorts of labour returning with the different seasons of the year, it is impossible that one man should be constantly employed in any one of them. This impossibility of making so complete and entire a separation of all the different branches of labour employed in agriculture, is perhaps the reason why the improvement of the productive powers of labour in this art, does not always keep pace with their improvement in manufactures. The most opulent nations, indeed, generally excel all their neighbours in agriculture as well as in manufactures; but they are commonly more distinguished by their superiority in the latter than in the former. Their lands are in general better cultivated, and having more labour and expence bestowed upon them, produce more, in proportion to the extent and natural fertility of the ground. But this superiority of produce is seldom much more than in proportion to the superiority of labour and expence. In agriculture, the labour of the rich country is not always much more productive than that of the poor; or, at least, it is never so much more productive, as it commonly is in manufactures. The corn of the rich country, therefore, will not always, in the same degree of goodness, come cheaper to market than that of the poor. The corn of Poland, in the same degree of goodness, is as cheap as that of France, notwithstanding the superior opulence and improvement of the latter country. The corn of France is, in the corn provinces, fully as good, and in most years nearly about the same price with the corn of England, though, in opulence and improvement, France is perhaps inferior to England. The corn-lands of England, however, are better cultivated than those of France, and the corn-lands of France are said to be much better cultivated than those of Poland. But though the poor country, notwithstanding the inferiority of its cultivation, can, in some measure, rival the rich in the cheapness and goodness of its corn, it can pretend to no such competition in its manufactures; at least if those manufactures suit the soil, climate, and situation of the rich country. The silks of France are better and cheaper than those of England, because the silk manufacture, at least under the present high duties upon the importation of raw silk, does not so well suit the climate of England as that of France. But the hard-ware and the coarse woollens of England are beyond all comparison superior to those of France, and much cheaper too in the same degree of goodness. In Poland there are said to be scarce any manufactures of any kind, a few of those coarser household manufactures excepted, without which no country can well subsist.

This great increase of the quantity of work, which, in consequence of the division of labour, the same number of people are capable of performing, is owing to three different circumstances; first, to the increase of dexterity in every particular workman; secondly, to the saving of the time which is commonly lost in passing from one species of work to another; and lastly, to the invention of a great number of machines which facilitate and abridge labour, and enable one man to do the work of many.

First, the improvement of the dexterity of the workman necessarily increases the quantity of the work he can perform, and the division of labour, by reducing every man's business to some one simple operation, and by making this operation the sole employment of his life, necessarily increases very much the dexterity of the workman. A common smith, who, though accustomed to handle the hammer, has never been used to make nails, if upon some particular occasion he is obliged to attempt it, will scarce, I am assured, be able to make above two or three hundred nails in a day, and those too very bad ones. A smith who has been accustomed to make nails, but whose sole or principal business has not been that of a nailer, can seldom with his utmost diligence make more than eight hundred or a thousand nails in a day. I have seen several boys under twenty years of age who had never exercised any other trade but that of making nails, and who, when they exerted themselves, could make, each of them, upwards of two thousand three hundred nails in a day. The making of a nail, however, is by no means one of the simplest operations. The same person blows the bellows, stirs or mends the fire as there is occasion, heats the iron, and forges every part of the nail: In forging the head too he is obliged to change his tools. The different operations into which the making of a pin, or of a metal button, is subdivided, are all of them much more simple, and the dexterity of the person, of whose life it has been the sole business to perform them, is usually much greater. The rapidity with which some of the operations of those manufactures are performed, exceeds what the human hand could, by those who had never seen them, be supposed capable of acquiring.

Secondly, the advantage which is gained by saving the time commonly lost in passing from one sort of work to another, is much greater than we should at first view be apt to imagine it. It is impossible to pass very quickly from one kind of work to another, that is carried on in a different place, and with quite different tools. A country weaver, who cultivates a small farm, must lose a great deal of time in passing from his loom to the field, and from the field to his loom. When the two trades can be carried on in the same workhouse, the loss of time is no doubt much less. It is even in this case, however, very considerable. A man commonly saunters a little in turning his hand from one sort of employment to another. When he first begins the new work he is seldom very keen and hearty; his mind, as they say, does not go to it, and for some time he rather trifles than applies to good purpose. The habit of sauntering and of indolent careless application, which is naturally, or rather necessarily acquired by every country workman who is obliged to change his work and his tools every half hour, and to apply his hand in twenty different ways almost every day of his life; renders him almost always slothful and lazy, and incapable of any vigorous application even on the most pressing occasions. Independent, therefore, of his deficiency in point of dexterity, this cause alone must always reduce considerably the quantity of work which he is capable of performing.

Thirdly, and lastly, every body must be sensible how much labour is facilitated and abridged by the application of proper machinery. It is unnecessary to give any example. I shall only observe, therefore, that the invention of all those machines by which labour is so much facilitated and abridged, seems to have been originally owing to the division of labour. Men are much more likely to discover easier and readier methods of attaining any object, when the whole attention of their minds is directed towards that single object, than when it is dissipated among a great variety of things. But in consequence of the division of labour, the whole of every man's attention comes naturally to be directed towards some one very simple object. It is naturally to be expected, therefore, that some one or other of those who are employed in each particular branch of labour should soon find out easier and readier methods of performing their own particular work, wherever the nature of it admits of such improvement. A great part of the machines made use of in those manufactures in which labour is most subdivided, were originally the inventions of common workmen, who, being each of them employed in some very simple operation, naturally turned their thoughts towards finding out easier and readier methods of performing it. Whoever has been much accustomed to visit such manufactures, must frequently have been shewn very pretty machines, which were the inventions of such workmen, in order to facilitate and quicken their own particular part of the work. In the first fire-engines, a boy was constantly employed to open and shut alternately the communication between the boiler and the cylinder, according as the piston either ascended or descended. One of those boys, who loved to play with his companions, observed that, by tying a string from the handle of the valve, which opened this communication, to another part of the machine, the valve would open and shut without his assistance, and leave him at liberty to divert himself with his play-fellows. One of the greatest improvements that has been made upon this machine, since it was first invented, was in this manner the discovery of a boy who wanted to save his own labour.

All the improvements in machinery, however, have by no means been the inventions of those who had occasion to use the machines. Many improvements have been made by the ingenuity of the makers of the machines, when to make them became the business of a peculiar trade; and some by that of those who are called philosophers or men of speculation, whose trade it is, not to do any thing, but to observe every thing; and who, upon that account, are often capable of combining together the powers of the most distant and dissimilar objects. In the progress of society, philosophy or speculation becomes, like every other employment, the principal or sole trade and occupation of a particular class of citizens. Like every other employment too, it is subdivided into a great number of different branches, each of which affords occupation to a peculiar tribe or class of philosophers; and this subdivision of employment in philosophy, as well as in every other business, improves dexterity, and saves time. Each individual becomes more expert in his own peculiar branch, more work is done upon the whole, and the quantity of science is considerably increased by it.

It is the great multiplication of the productions of all the different arts, in consequence of the division of labour, which occasions, in a well-governed society, that universal opulence which extends itself to the lowest ranks of the people. Every workman has a great quantity of his own work to dispose of beyond what he himself has occasion for; and every other workman being exactly in the same situation, he is enabled to exchange a great quantity of his own goods for a great quantity, or, what comes to the same thing, for the price of a great quantity of theirs. He supplies them abundantly with what they have occasion for, and they accommodate him as amply with what he has occasion for, and a general plenty diffuses itself through all the different ranks of the society.

Observe the accommodation of the most common artificer or day-labourer in a civilized and thriving country, and you will perceive that the number of people of whose industry a part, though but a small part, has been employed in procuring him this accommodation, exceeds all computation. The woollen coat, for example, which covers the day-labourer, as coarse and rough as it may appear, is the produce of the joint labour of a great multitude of workmen. The shepherd, the sorter of the wool, the wool-comber or carder, the dyer, the scribbler, the spinner, the weaver, the fuller, the dresser, with many others, must all join their different arts in order to complete even this homely production. How many merchants and carriers, besides, must have been employed in transporting the materials from some of those workmen to others who often live in a very distant part of the country! How much commerce and navigation in particular, how many ship-builders, sailors, sail-makers, rope-makers, must have been employed in order to bring together the different drugs made use of by the dyer, which often come from the remotest corners of the world! What a variety of labour too is necessary in order to produce the tools of the meanest of those workmen! To say nothing of such complicated machines as the ship of the sailor, the mill of the fuller, or even the loom of the weaver, let us consider only what a variety of labour is requisite in order to form that very simple machine, the shears with which the shepherd clips the wool. The miner, the builder of the furnace for smelting the ore, the feller of the timber, the burner of the charcoal to be made use of in the smelting-house, the brick-maker, the brick-layer, the workmen who attend the furnace, the mill-wright, the forger, the smith, must all of them join their different arts in order to produce them. Were we to examine, in the same manner, all the different parts of his dress and household furniture, the coarse linen shirt which he wears next his skin, the shoes which cover his feet, the bed which he lies on, and all the different parts which compose it, the kitchen-grate at which he prepares his victuals, the coals which he makes use of for that purpose, dug from the bowels of the earth, and brought to him perhaps by a long sea and a long land carriage, all the other utensils of his kitchen, all the furniture of his table, the knives and forks, the earthen or pewter plates upon which he serves up and divides his victuals, the different hands employed in preparing his bread and his beer, the glass window which lets in the heat and the light, and keeps out the wind and the rain, with all the knowledge and art requisite for preparing that beautiful and happy invention, without which these northern parts of the world could scarce have afforded a very comfortable habitation, together with the tools of all the different workmen employed in producing those different conveniences; if we examine, I say, all these things, and consider what a variety of labour is employed about each of them, we shall be sensible that without the assistance and co-operation of many thousands, the very meanest person in a civilized country could not be provided, even according to, what we very falsely imagine, the easy and simple manner in which he is commonly accommodated. Compared, indeed, with the more extravagant luxury of the great, his accommodation must no doubt appear extremely simple and easy; and yet it may be true, perhaps, that the accommodation of an European prince does not always so much exceed that of an industrious and frugal peasant, as the accommodation of the latter exceeds that of many an African king, the absolute master of the lives and liberties of ten thousand naked savages.

CHAPTER II *Of the Principle which gives Occasion to the Division of Labour*

This division of labour, from which so many advantages are derived, is not originally the effect of any human wisdom, which foresees and intends that general opulence to which it gives occasion. It is the necessary, though very slow and gradual consequence of a certain propensity in human nature which has in view no such extensive utility; the propensity to truck, barter, and exchange one thing for another.

Whether this propensity be one of those original principles in human nature, of which no further account can be given; or whether, as seems more probable, it be the necessary consequence of the faculties of reason and speech, it belongs not to our present subject to enquire. It is common to all men, and to be found in no other race of animals, which seem to know neither this nor any other species of contracts. Two greyhounds, in running down the same hare, have sometimes the appearance of acting in some sort of concert. Each turns her towards his companion, or endeavours to intercept her when his companion turns her towards himself. This, however, is not the effect of any contract, but of the accidental concurrence of their passions in the same object at that particular time. Nobody ever saw a dog make a fair and deliberate exchange of one bone for another with another dog. Nobody ever saw one animal by its gestures and natural cries signify to another, this is mine, that yours; I am willing to give this for that. When an animal wants to obtain something either of a man or of another animal, it has no other means of persuasion but to gain the favour of those whose service it requires. A puppy fawns upon its dam, and a spaniel endeavours by a thousand attractions to engage the attention of its master who is at dinner, when it wants to be fed by him. Man sometimes uses the same arts with his brethren, and when he has no other means of engaging them to act according to his inclinations, endeavours by every servile and fawning attention to obtain their good will. He has not time, however, to do this upon every occasion. In civilized society he stands at all times in need of the co-operation and assistance of great multitudes, while his whole life is scarce sufficient to gain the friendship of a few persons. In almost every other race of animals each individual, when it is grown up to maturity, is intirely independent, and in its natural state has occasion for the assistance of no other living creature. But man has almost constant occasion for the help of his brethren, and it is in vain for him to expect it from their benevolence only. He will be more likely to prevail if he can interest their self-love in his favour, and shew them that it is for their own advantage to do for him what he requires of them. Whoever offers to another a bargain of any kind, proposes to do this. Give me that which I want, and you shall have this which you want, is the meaning of every such offer; and it is in this manner that we obtain from one another the far greater part of those good offices which we stand in need of. It is not from the benevolence of the butcher, the brewer, or the baker, that we expect our dinner, but from their regard to their own interest. We address ourselves, not to their humanity but to their self-love, and never talk to them of our own necessities but of their advantages. Nobody but a beggar chuses to depend chiefly upon the benevolence of his fellow-citizens. Even a beggar does not depend upon it entirely. The charity of well-disposed people, indeed, supplies him with the whole fund of his subsistence. But though this principle ultimately provides him with all the necessaries of life which he has occasion for, it neither does nor can provide him with them as he has occasion for them. The greater part of his occasional wants are supplied in the same manner as those of other people, by treaty, by barter, and by purchase. With the money which one man gives him he purchases food. The old cloaths which another bestows upon him he exchanges for other old cloaths which suit him better, or for lodging, or for food, or for money, with which he can buy either food, cloaths, or lodging, as he has occasion.

As it is by treaty, by barter, and by purchase, that we obtain from one another the greater part of those mutual good offices which we stand in need of, so it is this same trucking disposition which originally gives occasion to the division of labour. In a tribe of hunters or shepherds a particular person makes bows and arrows, for example, with more readiness and dexterity than any other. He frequently exchanges them for cattle or for venison with his companions; and he finds at last that he can in this manner get more cattle and venison, than if he himself went to the field to catch them. From a regard to his own interest, therefore, the making of bows and arrows grows to be his chief business, and he becomes a sort of armourer. Another excels in making the frames and covers of their little huts or moveable houses. He is accustomed to be of use in this way to his neighbours, who reward him in the same manner with cattle and with venison, till at last he finds it his interest to dedicate himself entirely to this employment, and to become a sort of house-carpenter. In the same manner a third becomes a smith or a brazier, a fourth a tanner or dresser of hides or skins, the principal part of the clothing of savages. And thus the certainty of being able to exchange all that surplus part of the produce of his own labour, which is over and above his own consumption, for such parts of the produce of other men's labour as he may have occasion for, encourages every man to apply himself to a particular occupation, and to cultivate and bring to perfection whatever talent or genius he may possess for that particular species of business.

The difference of natural talents in different men is, in reality, much less than we are aware of; and the very different genius which appears to distinguish men of different professions, when grown up to maturity, is not upon many occasions so much the cause, as the effect of the division of labour. The difference between the most dissimilar characters, between a philosopher and a common street porter, for example, seems to arise not so much from nature, as from habit, custom, and education. When they came into the world, and for the first six or eight years of their existence, they were, perhaps, very much alike, and neither their parents nor play-fellows could perceive any remarkable difference. About that age, or soon after, they come to be employed in very different occupations. The difference of talents comes then to be taken notice of, and widens by degrees, till at last the vanity of the philosopher is willing to acknowledge scarce any resemblance. But without the disposition to truck, barter and exchange, every man must have procured to himself every necessary and conveniency of life which he wanted. All must have had the same duties to perform, and the same work to do, and there could have been no such difference of employment as could alone give occasion to any great difference of talents.

As it is this disposition which forms that difference of talents, so remarkable among men of different professions, so it is this same disposition which renders that difference useful. Many tribes of animals acknowledged to be all of the same species, derive from nature a much more remarkable distinction of genius, than what, antecedent to custom and education, appears to take place among men. By nature a philosopher is not in genius and disposition half so different from a street porter, as a mastiff is from a greyhound, or a greyhound from a spaniel, or this last from a shepherd's dog. Those different tribes of animals, however, though all of the same species, are of scarce any use to one another. The strength of the mastiff is not, in the least, supported either by the swiftness of the greyhound, or by the sagacity of the spaniel, or by the docility of the shepherd's dog. The effects of those different geniuses and talents, for want of the power or disposition to barter and exchange, cannot be brought into a common stock, and do not in the least contribute to the better accommodation and conveniency of the species. Each animal is still obliged to support and defend itself, separately and independently, and derives no sort of advantage from that variety of talents with which nature has distinguished its fellows. Among men, on the contrary, the most dissimilar geniuses are of use to one another; the different produces of their respective talents, by the general disposition to truck, barter, and exchange, being brought, as it were, into a common stock, where every man may purchase whatever part of the produce of other men's talents he has occasion for.

CHAPTER III *That the Division of Labour is limited by the Extent of the Market*

As it is the power of exchanging that gives occasion to the division of labour, so the extent of this division must always be limited by the extent of that power, or, in other words, by the extent of the market. When the market is very small, no person can have any encouragement to dedicate himself entirely to one employment, for want of the power to exchange all that surplus part of the produce of his own labour, which is over and above his own consumption, for such parts of the produce of other men's labour as he has occasion for.

There are some sorts of industry, even of the lowest kind, which can be carried on no where but in a great town. A porter, for example, can find employment and subsistence in no other place. A village is by much too narrow a sphere for him; even an ordinary market town is scarce large enough to afford him constant occupation. In the lone houses and very small villages which are scattered about in so desert a country as the Highlands of Scotland, every farmer must be butcher, baker and brewer for his own family. In such situations we can scarce expect to find even a smith, a carpenter, or a mason, within less than twenty miles of another of the same trade. The scattered families that live at eight or ten miles distance from the nearest of them, must learn to perform themselves a great number of little pieces of work, for which, in more populous countries, they would call in the assistance of those workmen. Country workmen are almost every where obliged to apply themselves to all the different branches of industry that have so much affinity to one another as to be employed about the same sort of materials. A country carpenter deals in every sort of work that is made of wood: a country smith in every sort of work that is made of iron. The former is not only a carpenter, but a joiner, a cabinet-maker, and even a carver in wood, as well as a wheel-wright, a plough-wright, a cart and waggon maker. The employments of the latter are still more various. It is impossible there should be such a trade as even that of a nailer in the remote and inland parts of the Highlands of Scotland. Such a workman at the rate of a thousand nails a day, and three hundred working days in the year, will make three hundred thousand nails in the year. But in such a situation it would be impossible to dispose of one thousand, that is, of one day's work in the year.

As by means of water-carriage a more extensive market is

opened to every sort of industry than what land-carriage alone
can afford it, so it is upon the sea-coast, and along the banks of
navigable rivers, that industry of every kind naturally begins to
subdivide and improve itself, and it is frequently not till a long
time after that those improvements extend themselves to the
inland parts of the country. A broad-wheeled waggon, attended
by two men, and drawn by eight horses, in about six weeks
time carries and brings back between London and Edinburgh
near four ton weight of goods. In about the same time a ship
navigated by six or eight men, and sailing between the ports
of London and Leith, frequently carries and brings back two
hundred ton weight of goods. Six or eight men, therefore, by
the help of water-carriage, can carry and bring back in the same
time the same quantity of goods between London and Edinburgh,
as fifty broad-wheeled waggons, attended by a hundred men,
and drawn by four hundred horses. Upon two hundred tons
of goods, therefore, carried by the cheapest land-carriage from
London to Edinburgh, there must be charged the maintenance
of a hundred men for three weeks, and both the maintenance,
and, what is nearly equal to the maintenance, the wear and
tear of four hundred horses as well as of fifty great waggons.
Whereas, upon the same quantity of goods carried by water,
there is to be charged only the maintenance of six or eight men,
and the wear and tear of a ship of two hundred tons burden,
together with the value of the superior risk, or the difference of
the insurance between land and water-carriage. Were there no
other communication between those two places, therefore, but
by land-carriage, as no goods could be transported from the one
to the other, except such whose price was very considerable in
proportion to their weight, they could carry on but a small part
of that commerce which at present subsists between them, and
consequently could give but a small part of that encouragement
which they at present mutually afford to each other's industry.
There could be little or no commerce of any kind between the
distant parts of the world. What goods could bear the expence
of land-carriage between London and Calcutta? Or if there were
any so precious as to be able to support this expence, with what
safety could they be transported through the territories of so many
barbarous nations? Those two cities, however, at present carry on
a very considerable commerce with each other, and by mutually
affording a market, give a good deal of encouragement to each
other's industry.

Since such, therefore, are the advantages of water-carriage, it is natural that the first improvements of art and industry should be made where this conveniency opens the whole world for a market to the produce of every sort of labour, and that they should always be much later in extending themselves into the inland parts of the country. The inland parts of the country can for a long time have no other market for the greater part of their goods, but the country which lies round about them, and separates them from the sea-coast, and the great navigable rivers. The extent of their market, therefore, must for a long time be in proportion to the riches and populousness of that country, and consequently their improvement must always be posterior to the improvement of that country. In our North American colonies the plantations have constantly followed either the sea-coast or the banks of the navigable rivers, and have scarce any where extended themselves to any considerable distance from both.

The nations that, according to the best authenticated history, appear to have been first civilized, were those that dwelt round the coast of the Mediterranean sea. That sea, by far the greatest inlet that is known in the world, having no tides, nor consequently any waves except such as are caused by the wind only, was, by the smoothness of its surface, as well as by the multitude of its islands, and the proximity of its neighbouring shores, extremely favourable to the infant navigation of the world; when, from their ignorance of the compass, men were afraid to quit the view of the coast, and from the imperfection of the art of ship-building, to abandon themselves to the boisterous waves of the ocean. To pass beyond the pillars of Hercules, that is, to sail out of the Streights of Gibraltar, was, in the antient world, long considered as a most wonderful and dangerous exploit of navigation. It was late before even the Phenicians and Carthaginians, the most skilful navigators and shipbuilders of those old times, attempted it, and they were for a long time the only nations that did attempt it.

Of all the countries on the coast of the Mediterranean sea, Egypt seems to have been the first in which either agriculture or manufactures were cultivated and improved to any considerable degree. Upper Egypt extends itself nowhere above a few miles from the Nile, and in Lower Egypt that great river breaks itself into many different canals, which, with the assistance of a little art, seem to have afforded a communication by water-carriage, not only between all the great towns, but between all the considerable villages, and even to many farm-houses in the country; nearly in the same manner as the Rhine and the Maese do in Holland at present. The extent and easiness of this inland navigation was probably one of the principal causes of the early improvement of Egypt.

The improvements in agriculture and manufactures seem likewise to have been of very great antiquity in the provinces of Bengal in the East Indies, and in some of the eastern provinces of China; though the great extent of this antiquity is not authenticated by any histories of whose authority we, in this part of the world, are well assured. In Bengal the Ganges and several other great rivers form a great number of navigable canals in the same manner as the Nile does in Egypt. In the Eastern provinces of China too, several great rivers form, by their different branches, a multitude of canals, and by communicating with one another afford an inland navigation much more extensive than that either of the Nile or the Ganges, or perhaps than both of them put together. It is remarkable that neither the antient Egyptians, nor the Indians, nor the Chinese, encouraged foreign commerce, but seem all to have derived their great opulence from this inland navigation.

All the inland parts of Africa, and all that part of Asia which lies any considerable way north of the Euxine and Caspian seas, the antient Scythia, the modern Tartary and Siberia, seem in all ages of the world to have been in the same barbarous and uncivilized state in which we find them at present. The sea of Tartary is the frozen ocean which admits of no navigation, and though some of the greatest rivers in the world run through that country, they are at too great a distance from one another to carry commerce and communication through the greater part of it. There are in Africa none of those great inlets, such as the Baltic and Adriatic seas in Europe, the Mediterranean and Euxine seas in both Europe and Asia, and the gulphs of Arabia, Persia, India, Bengal, and Siam, in Asia, to carry maritime commerce into the interior parts of that great continent: and the great rivers of Africa are at too great a distance from one another to give occasion to any considerable inland navigation. The commerce besides which any nation can carry on by means of a river which does not break itself into any great number of branches or canals, and which runs into another territory before it reaches the sea, can never be very considerable; because it is always in the power of the nations who possess that other territory to obstruct the communication between the upper country and the sea. The navigation of the Danube is of very little use to the different states of Bavaria, Austria and Hungary, in comparison of what it would be if any of them possessed the whole of its course till it falls into the Black Sea.

CHAPTER IV *Of the Origin and Use of Money*

When the division of labour has been once thoroughly established, it is but a very small part of a man's wants which the produce of his own labour can supply. He supplies the far greater part of them by exchanging that surplus part of the produce of his own labour, which is over and above his own consumption, for such parts of the produce of other men's labour as he has occasion for. Every man thus lives by exchanging, or becomes in some measure a merchant, and the society itself grows to be what is properly a commercial society.

But when the division of labour first began to take place, this power of exchanging must frequently have been very much clogged and embarrassed in its operations. One man, we shall suppose, has more of a certain commodity than he himself has occasion for, while another has less. The former consequently would be glad to dispose of, and the latter to purchase, a part of this superfluity. But if this latter should chance to have nothing that the former stands in need of, no exchange can be made between them. The butcher has more meat in his shop than he himself can consume, and the brewer and the baker would each of them be willing to purchase a part of it. But they have nothing to offer in exchange, except the different productions of their respective trades, and the butcher is already provided with all the bread and beer which he has immediate occasion for. No exchange can, in this case, be made between them. He cannot be their merchant, nor they his customers; and they are all of them thus mutually less serviceable to one another. In order to avoid the inconveniency of such situations, every prudent man in every period of society, after the first establishment of the division of labour, must naturally have endeavoured to manage his affairs in such a manner, as to have at all times by him, besides the peculiar produce of his own industry, a certain quantity of some one commodity or other, such as he imagined few people would be likely to refuse in exchange for the produce of their industry.

Many different commodities, it is probable, were successively both thought of and employed for this purpose. In the rude ages of society, cattle are said to have been the common instrument of commerce; and, though they must have been a most inconvenient one, yet in old times we find things were frequently valued according to the number of cattle which had been given in exchange for them. The armour of Diomede, says Homer, cost only nine oxen; but that of Glaucus cost an hundred oxen. Salt is said to be the common instrument of commerce and exchanges in Abyssinia; a species of shells in some parts of the coast of India; dried cod at Newfoundland; tobacco in Virginia; sugar in some of our West India colonies; hides or dressed leather in some other countries; and there is at this day a village in Scotland where it is not uncommon, I am told, for a workman to carry nails instead of money to the baker's shop or the ale-house.

In all countries, however, men seem at last to have been determined by irresistible reasons to give the preference, for this employment, to metals above every other commodity. Metals can not only be kept with as little loss as any other commodity, scarce any thing being less perishable than they are, but they can likewise, without any loss, be divided into any number of parts, as by fusion those parts can easily be re-united again; a quality which no other equally durable commodities possess, and which more than any other quality renders them fit to be the instruments of commerce and circulation. The man who wanted to buy salt, for example, and had nothing but cattle to give in exchange for it, must have been obliged to buy salt to the value of a whole ox, or a whole sheep at a time. He could seldom buy less than this, because what he was to give for it could seldom be divided without loss; and if he had a mind to buy more, he must, for the same reasons, have been obliged to buy double or triple the quantity, the value, to wit, of two or three oxen, or of two or three sheep. If, on the contrary, instead of sheep or oxen, he had metals to give in exchange for it, he could easily proportion the quantity of the metal to the precise quantity of the commodity which he had immediate occasion for.

Different metals have been made use of by different nations for this purpose. Iron was the common instrument of commerce among the antient Spartans; copper among the antient Romans; and gold and silver among all rich and commercial nations.

Those metals seem originally to have been made use of for this purpose in rude bars, without any stamp or coinage. Thus we are told by Pliny, upon the authority of Timaeus, an antient historian, that, till the time of Servius Tullius, the Romans had no coined money, but made use of unstamped bars of copper to purchase whatever they had occasion for. These rude bars, therefore, performed at this time the function of money.

The use of metals in this rude state was attended with two very considerable inconveniences; first, with the trouble of weighing;

and, secondly, with that of assaying them. In the precious metals, where a small difference in the quantity makes a great difference in the value, even the business of weighing, with proper exactness, requires at least very accurate weights and scales. The weighing of gold in particular is an operation of some nicety. In the coarser metals, indeed, where a small error would be of little consequence, less accuracy would, no doubt, be necessary. Yet we should find it excessively troublesome, if every time a poor man had occasion either to buy or sell a farthing's worth of goods, he was obliged to weigh the farthing. The operation of assaying is still more difficult, still more tedious, and, unless a part of the metal is fairly melted in the crucible, with proper dissolvents, any conclusion that can be drawn from it, is extremely uncertain. Before the institution of coined money, however, unless they went through this tedious and difficult operation, people must always have been liable to the grossest frauds and impositions, and instead of a pound weight of pure silver, or pure copper, might receive in exchange for their goods, an adulterated composition of the coarsest and cheapest materials, which had, however, in their outward appearance, been made to resemble those metals. To prevent such abuses, to facilitate exchanges, and thereby to encourage all sorts of industry and commerce, it has been found necessary, in all countries that have made any considerable advances towards improvement, to affix a publick stamp upon certain quantities of such particular metals, as were in those countries commonly made use of to purchase goods. Hence the origin of coined money, and of those publick offices called mints; institutions exactly of the same nature with those of the aulnagers and stampmasters of woollen and linen cloth. All of them are equally meant to ascertain, by means of a publick stamp, the quantity and uniform goodness of those different commodities when brought to market.

The first publick stamps of this kind that were affixed to the current metals, seem in many cases to have been intended to ascertain, what it was both most difficult and most important to ascertain, the goodness or fineness of the metal, and to have resembled the sterling mark which is at present affixed to plate and bars of silver, or the Spanish mark which is sometimes affixed to ingots of gold, and which being struck only upon one side of the piece, and not covering the whole surface, ascertains the fineness, but not the weight of the metal. Abraham weighs to Ephron the four hundred shekels of silver which he had agreed to pay for the field of Machpelah. They are said however to be the current money of the merchant, and yet are received by weight and not by tale, in the same manner as ingots of gold and bars of silver are at present. The revenues of the antient Saxon kings of England are said to have been paid, not in money but in kind, that is, in victuals and provisions of all sorts. William the Conqueror introduced the custom of paying them in money. This money, however, was, for a long time, received at the exchequer, by weight and not by tale.

The inconveniency and difficulty of weighing those metals with exactness gave occasion to the institution of coins, of which the stamp, covering entirely both sides of the piece and sometimes the edges too, was supposed to ascertain not only the fineness, but the weight of the metal. Such coins, therefore, were received by tale as at present, without the trouble of weighing.

The denominations of those coins seems originally to have expressed the weight or quantity of metal contained in them. In the time of Servius Tullius, who first coined money at Rome, the Roman As or Pondo contained a Roman pound of good copper. It was divided in the same manner as our Troyes pounds, into twelve ounces, each of which contained a real ounce of good copper. The English pound sterling, in the time of Edward I., contained a pound, Tower weight, of silver of a known fineness. The Tower pound seems to have been something more than the Roman pound, and something less than the Troyes pound. This last was not introduced into the mint of England till the 18th [year] of Henry VIII. The French livre contained in the time of Charlemagne a pound, Troyes weight, of silver of a known fineness. The fair of Troyes in Champaign was at that time frequented by all the nations of Europe, and the weights and measures of so famous a market were generally known and esteemed. The Scots money pound contained, from the time of Alexander the First to that of Robert Bruce, a pound of silver of the same weight and fineness with the English pound sterling. English, French, and Scots pennies too, contained all of them originally a real pennyweight of silver, the twentieth part of an ounce, and the two-hundred-and-fortieth part of a pound. The shilling too seems originally to have been the denomination of a weight. *When wheat is at twelve shillings the quarter*, says an antient statute of Henry III. *then wastel bread of a farthing shall weigh eleven shillings and four pence*. The proportion, however, between the shilling and either the penny on the one hand, or the pound on the other, seems not to have been so constant and uniform as that between the penny and the pound. During the first race of the kings of France, the French sou or shilling appears upon different occasions to have contained five, twelve, twenty, and forty pennies. Among the antient Saxons a shilling appears at one time to have contained only five pennies, and it is not improbable that it may have been as variable among them as among their neighbours, the antient Franks. From the time of Charlemagne among the French, and from that of William the Conqueror among the English, the proportion between the pound, the shilling, and the penny, seems to have been uniformly the same as at present, though the value of each has been very different. For in every country of the world, I believe, the avarice and injustice of princes and sovereign states, abusing the confidence of their subjects, have by degrees diminished the real quantity of metal, which had been originally contained in their coins. The Roman As, in the latter ages of the Republick, was reduced to the twenty-fourth part of its original value, and, instead of weighing a pound, came to weigh only half an ounce. The English pound and penny contain at present about a third only; the Scots pound and penny about a thirty-sixth; and the French pound and penny about a sixty-sixth part of their original value. By means of those operations the princes and sovereign states which performed them were enabled, in appearance, to pay their debts and to fulfil their engagements with a smaller quantity of silver than would otherwise have been requisite. It was indeed in appearance only; for their creditors were really defrauded of a part of what was due to them. All other debtors in the state were allowed the same privilege, and might pay with the same nominal sum of the new and debased coin whatever they had borrowed in the old. Such operations, therefore, have always proved favourable to the debtor, and ruinous to the creditor, and have sometimes produced a greater and more universal revolution in the fortunes of private persons, than could have been occasioned by a very great publick calamity.

It is in this manner that money has become in all civilized nations the universal instrument of commerce, by the intervention of which goods of all kinds are bought and sold, or exchanged for one another.

What are the rules which men naturally observe in exchanging them either for money or for another, I shall now proceed to examine. These rules determine what may be called the relative or exchangeable value of goods.

The word 'value,' it is to be observed, has two different meanings, and sometimes expresses the utility of some particular object, and sometimes the power of purchasing other goods which the possession of that object conveys. The one may be called 'value in use;' the other, 'value in exchange.' The things which have the greatest value in use have frequently little or no value in exchange; and, on the contrary, those which have the greatest value in exchange have frequently little or no value in use. Nothing is more useful than water: but it will purchase scarce any thing; scarce any thing can be had in exchange for it. A diamond, on the contrary, has scarce any value in use; but a very great quantity of other goods may frequently be had in exchange for it.

In order to investigate the principles which regulate the exchangeable value of commodities, I shall endeavour to shew,

First, what is the real measure of this exchangeable value; or, wherein consists the real price of all commodities,

Secondly, what are the different parts of which this real price is composed or made up.

And, lastly, what are the different circumstances which sometimes raise some or all of these different parts of price above, and sometimes sink them below their natural or ordinary rate; or, what are the causes which sometimes hinder the market price, that is, the actual price of commodities, from coinciding exactly with what may be called their natural price.

I shall endeavour to explain, as fully and distinctly as I can, those three subjects in the three following chapters, for which I must very earnestly entreat both the patience and attention of the reader: his patience in order to examine a detail which may perhaps in some places appear unnecessarily tedious; and his attention in order to understand what may, perhaps, after the fullest explication which I am capable of giving of it, appear still in some degree obscure. I am always willing to run some hazard of being tedious in order to be sure that I am perspicuous; and after taking the utmost pains that I can to be perspicuous, some obscurity may still appear to remain upon a subject in its own nature extremely abstracted.

BOOK V

Of the Expenses of the Sovereign or Commonwealth

CHAPTER I *Of the Expenses of the Sovereign or Commonwealth*

In the progress of the division of labour, the employment of the far greater part of those who live by labour, that is, of the great body of the people, comes to be confined to a few very simple operations; frequently to one or two. But the understandings of the greater part of men are necessarily formed by their ordinary employments. The man whose whole life is spent in performing a few simple operations, of which the effects too are, perhaps, always the same, or very nearly the same, has no occasion to exert his understanding, or to exercise his invention in finding out expedients for removing difficulties which never occur. He naturally loses, therefore, the habit of such exertion, and generally becomes as stupid and ignorant as it is possible for a human creature to become. The torpor of his mind renders him, not only incapable of relishing or bearing a part in any rational conversation, but of conceiving any generous, noble, or tender sentiment, and consequently of forming any just judgment concerning many even of the ordinary duties of private life. Of the great and extensive interests of his country, he is altogether incapable of judging; and unless very particular pains have been taken to render him otherwise, he is equally incapable of defending his country in war. The uniformity of his stationary life naturally corrupts the courage of his mind, and makes him regard with abhorrence the irregular, uncertain, and adventurous life of a soldier. It corrupts even the activity of his body, and renders him incapable of exerting his strength with vigour and perseverance, in any other employment than that to which he has been bred. His dexterity at his own particular trade seems, in this manner, to be acquired at the expence of his intellectual, social, and martial virtues. But in every improved and civilized society this is the state into which the labouring poor, that is, the great body of the people, must necessarily fall, unless government takes some pains to prevent it.

It is otherwise in the barbarous societies, as they are commonly called, of hunters, of shepherds, and even of husbandmen in that rude state of husbandry which precedes the improvement of manufactures, and the extension of foreign commerce. In such societies the varied occupations of every man oblige every man to exert his capacity, and to invent expedients for removing difficulties which are continually occurring. Invention is kept alive, and the mind is not suffered to fall into that drowsy stupidity, which, in a civilized society, seems to benumb the understanding of almost all the inferior ranks of people. In those barbarous societies, as they are called, every man, it has already been observed, is a warrior. Every man too is in some measure a statesman, and can form a tolerable judgment concerning the interest of the society, and the conduct of those who govern it. How far their chiefs are good judges in peace, or good leaders in war, is obvious to the observation of almost every single man among them. In such a society indeed, no man can well acquire that improved and refined understanding, which a few men sometimes possess in a more civilized state. Though in a rude society there is a good deal of variety in the occupations of every individual, there is not a great deal in those of the whole society. Every man does, or is capable of doing, almost every thing which any other man does, or is capable of doing. Every man has a considerable degree of knowledge, ingenuity, and invention; but scarce any man has a great degree. The degree, however, which is commonly possessed, is generally sufficient for conducting the whole simple business of the society. In a civilized state, on the contrary, though there is little variety in the occupations of the greater part of individuals, there is an almost infinite variety in those of the whole society. These varied occupations present an almost infinite variety of objects to the contemplation of those few, who, being attached to no particular occupation themselves, have leisure and inclination to examine the occupations of other people. The contemplation of so great a variety of objects necessarily exercises their minds in endless comparisons and combinations, and renders their understandings, in an extraordinary degree, both acute and comprehensive. Unless those few, however, happen to be placed in some very particular situations, their great abilities, though honourable to themselves, may contribute very little to the good government or happiness of their society. Notwithstanding the great abilities of those few, all the nobler parts of the human character may be, in a great measure, obliterated and extinguished in the great body of the people.

The education of the common people requires, perhaps, in a civilized and commercial society, the attention of the publick more than that of people of some rank and fortune. People of some rank and fortune are generally eighteen or nineteen years of age before they enter upon that particular business, profession, or trade, by which they propose to distinguish themselves in the world. They have before that full time to acquire, or at least to fit themselves for afterwards acquiring, every accomplishment which can recommend them to the publick esteem, or render them worthy of it. Their parents or guardians are generally sufficiently anxious that they should be so accomplished, and are, in most cases, willing enough to lay out the expence which is necessary for that purpose. If they are not always properly educated, it is seldom from the want of expence laid out upon their education; but from the improper application of that expence. It is seldom from the want of masters; but from the negligence and incapacity of the masters who are to be had, and from the difficulty, or rather from the impossibility which there is, in the present state of things, of finding any better. The employments too in which people of some rank or fortune spend the greater part of their lives, are not, like those of the common people, simple and uniform. They are almost all of them extremely complicated, and such as exercise the head more than the hands. The understandings of those who are engaged in such employments can seldom grow torpid for want of exercise. The employments of people of some rank and fortitude, besides, are seldom such as harass them from morning to night. They generally have a good deal of leisure, during which they may perfect themselves in every branch either of useful or ornamental knowledge of which they may have laid the foundation, or for which they may have acquired some taste in the earlier part of life.

It is otherwise with the common people. They have little time to spare for education. Their parents can scarce afford to maintain them even in infancy. As soon as they are able to work, they must apply to some trade by which they can earn their subsistence. That trade too is generally so simple and uniform as to give little exercise to the understanding; while, at the same time, their labour is both so constant and so severe, that it leaves them little leisure and less inclination to apply to, or even to think of any thing else.

But though the common people cannot, in any civilized society, be so well instructed as people of some rank and fortune, the most essential parts of education, however, to read, write, and account, can be acquired at so early a period of life, that the greater part even of those who are to be bred to the lowest occupations, have time to acquire them before they can be employed in those occupations. For a very small expence the publick can facilitate, can encourage, and can even impose upon almost the whole body of the people, the necessity of acquiring those most essential parts of education.

The publick can facilitate this acquisition by establishing in every parish or district a little school, where children may be taught for a reward so moderate, that even a common labourer may afford it; the master being partly, but not wholly paid by the publick; because if he was wholly, or even principally paid by it, he would soon learn to neglect his business. In Scotland the establishment of such parish schools has taught almost the whole common people to read, and a very great proportion of them to write and account. In England the establishment of charity schools has had an effect of the same kind, though not so universally, because the establishment is not so universal. If in those little schools the books, by which the children are taught to read, were a little more instructive than they commonly are: and if, instead of a little smattering of Latin; which the children of the common people are sometimes taught there, and which can scarce ever be of any use to them: they were instructed in the elementary parts of geometry and mechanicks, the literary education of this rank of people would perhaps be as complete as it can be. There is scarce a common trade which does not afford some opportunities of applying to it the principles of geometry and mechanicks, and which would not therefore gradually exercise and improve the common people in those principles, the necessary introduction to the most sublime as well as to the most useful sciences.

The publick can encourage the acquisition of those most essential parts of education by giving small premiums, and little badges of distinction, to the children of the common people who excel in them.

The publick can impose upon almost the whole body of the people the necessity of acquiring those most essential parts of education, by obliging every man to undergo an examination or probation in them before he can obtain the freedom in any corporation, or be allowed to set up any trade either in a village or town corporate.

It was in this manner, by facilitating the acquisition of their military and gymnastic exercises, by encouraging it, and even by imposing upon the whole body of the people the necessity of learning those exercises, that the Greek and Roman republicks maintained the martial spirit of their respective citizens. They facilitated the acquisition of those exercises by appointing a certain place for learning and practising them, and by granting to certain masters the privilege of teaching in that place. Those masters do not appear to have had either salaries or exclusive privileges of any kind. Their reward consisted altogether in what they got from their scholars; and a citizen who had learnt his exercises in the publick Gymnasia, had no sort of legal advantage over one who had learnt them privately, provided the latter had learnt them equally well. Those republicks encouraged the acquisition of those exercises, by bestowing little premiums and badges of distinction upon those who excelled in them. To have gained a prize in the Olympic, Isthmian or Nemaean games, gave illustration, not only to the person who gained it, but to his whole family and kindred. The obligation which every citizen was under to serve a certain number of years, if called upon, in the armies of the republick, sufficiently imposed the necessity of learning those exercises without which he could not be fit for that service.

That in the progress of improvement the practice of military exercises, unless government takes proper pains to support it, goes gradually to decay, and, together with it, the martial spirit of the great body of the people, the example of modern Europe sufficiently demonstrates. But the security of every society must always depend, more or less, upon the martial spirit of the great body of the people. In the present times, indeed, that martial spirit alone, and unsupported by a well-disciplined standing army, would not, perhaps, be sufficient for the defence and security of any society. But where every citizen had the spirit of a soldier, a smaller standing army would surely be requisite. That spirit, besides, would necessarily diminish very much the dangers to liberty, whether real or imaginary, which are commonly apprehended from a standing army. As it would very much facilitate the operations of that army against a foreign invader, so it would obstruct them as much if unfortunately they should ever be directed against the constitution of the state.

The antient institutions of Greece and Rome seem to have been much more effectual, for maintaining the martial spirit of the great body of the people, than the establishment of what are called the militias of modern times. They were much more simple. When they were once established, they executed themselves, and it required little or no attention from government to maintain them in the most perfect vigour. Whereas to maintain even in tolerable execution the complex regulations of any modern militia, requires the continual and painful attention of government, without which they are constantly falling into total neglect and disuse. The influence, besides, of the antient institutions was much more universal. By means of them the whole body of the people was compleatly instructed in the use of arms. Whereas it is but a very small part of them who can ever be so instructed by the regulations of any modern militia; except, perhaps, that of Switzerland. But a coward, a man incapable either of defending or of revenging himself, evidently wants one of the most essential parts of the character of a man. He is as much mutilated and deformed in his mind, as another is in his body, who is either deprived of some of its more essential members, or has lost the use of them. He is evidently the more wretched and miserable of the two; because happiness and misery, which reside altogether in the mind, must necessarily depend more upon the healthful or unhealthful, the mutilated or entire state of the mind, than upon that of the body. Even though the martial spirit of the people were of no use towards the defence of the society, yet to prevent that sort of mental mutilation, deformity and wretchedness, which cowardice necessarily involves in it, from spreading themselves through the great body of the people, would still deserve the most serious attention of government; in the same manner as it would deserve its most serious attention to prevent a leprosy or any other loathsome and offensive disease, though neither mortal nor dangerous, from spreading itself among them; though, perhaps, no other publick good might result from such attention besides the prevention of so great a publick evil.

The same thing may be said of the gross ignorance and stupidity which, in a civilized society, seem so frequently to benumb the understandings of all the inferior ranks of people. A man, without the proper use of the intellectual faculties of a man, is, if possible, more contemptible than even a coward, and seems to be mutilated and deformed in a still more essential part of the character of human nature. Though the state was to derive no advantage from the instruction of the inferior ranks of people, it would still deserve its attention that they should not be altogether uninstructed. The state, however, derives no inconsiderable advantage from their instruction. The more they are instructed, the less liable they are to the delusions of enthusiasm and superstition, which, among ignorant nations, frequently occasion the most dreadful disorders. An instructed and intelligent people besides are always more decent and orderly than an ignorant and stupid one. They feel themselves, each individually, more respectable, and more likely to obtain the respect of their lawful superiors, and they are therefore more disposed to respect those superiors. They are more disposed to examine, and more capable of seeing through, the interested complaints of faction and sedition, and they are, upon that account, less apt to be misled into any wanton or unnecessary opposition to the measures of government. In free countries, where the safety of government depends very much upon the favourable judgment which the people may form of its conduct, it must surely be of the highest importance that they should not be disposed to judge rashly or capriciously concerning it.

Source: Adam Smith, *An Inquiry in the Nature and Causes of the Wealth of Nations*, 2 vols, ed. R. H. Campbell and A. S. Skinner; textual editor W. B. Todd, Oxford 1976, Indianapolis 1981, Book 1, chs 1–4, pp. 13–46; Book 5, ch. 1, part 3, art. 2, pp. 781–8

TWENTY-THREE

SIR JOHN SINCLAIR
Statistical Account of Forfar

The preceding three excerpts are all on the theory of economics; the present one is on the kind of statistical information required by economic theorists. By far the greatest source of statistical information on the Scottish economy for the latter half of the eighteenth century is Sir John Sinclair's *The Statistical Account of Scotland* (see excerpt 32 for further details). The second half of the eighteenth century was a period of rapid industrial development, and agricultural improvement, and it was, relatedly, a time of high inflation. These national changes are well exemplified in this excerpt from the Forfar account.

A.B.

Parish of Forfar
(County and Presbytery of Forfar, Synod of Angus and Mearns)

By the Rev. Mr. John Bruce

Town of Forfar. Forfar is a royal burgh of considerable antiquity, and the capital of the county of Angus or Forfar; the sheriff whereof has held his court for upwards of two hundred years in this town, which is pretty centrically situated for the administration of justice. It is also the seat of the presbytery of Forfar; consisting in all of eleven parishes, the churches of which lie around it, at, or within the distance of four computed miles, except that of Cortachie which is rather more than five.

The ground on which it stands, with that for a considerable way around, is uncommonly uneven, and covered, as it were, with hillocks of various sizes, as if nature had here, at some period, suffered a convulsion. Though low with respect to the circumjacent ground on every side excepting the West, it is high in comparison to the general level of the country. The lakes and springs, a mile to the east of it, run eastward and empty themselves into the German ocean at Lunan Bay. Its own springs, and those on the west side of it, run directly west through the fertile valley of Strathmore, till they join the Tay near Perth; and such is level of the country, that it has been thought practicable, and by some an object worthy of commercial attention, to open a communication by a canal between Forfar and the sea in either of these directions.

Forfar commands a fine view of the Seedlaw hills and the valley of Strathmore, terminated by the Grampians on the west, the most considerable of which is about 50 miles distant. In that direction is the famous Schihallion.

Forfar is perhaps a singular instance in Scotland, of a town of any note, built at a distance from running water; but the vicinity of the lake with its numerous springs, and the protection of the castle, a place in former times of considerable strength, must have first invited the inhabitants of the country to settle and form a village, which afterwards becoming the occasional residence of Majesty, was distinguished by considerable numbers of royal favours, the memory of which is preserved in the names of places and fields within the royalty, such as the King's muir, the Queen's well, the Queen's manor, the palace-dykes, the guard-breads, &c.

The burgh is governed by a provost, two bailies, and twelve common counsellors, who are elected annually by themselves with the assistance of four deacons of crafts, who are also members of council, (but chosen by the members of the respective corporations,) and fifteen other burgesses nominated for the occasion, by the retiring provost and bailies. The annual council, thus consisting of nineteen members, have the privilege of electing a delegate, to vote for the election of one representative in Parliament for the burghs of Perth, Dundee, St. Andrews, Forfar, and Cupar in Fife. The revenue of the burgh, arising from lands, customs, &c. is supposed, *communibus annis*, to be little below L. 400 sterling clear, and it is yearly increasing.

The incorporation of shoemakers, which is still the richest in the town, was, previous to the year 1745, the most numerous; and the wealth of the place arose chiefly from their industry in manufacturing a peculiar fabric of shoes, which they still carry on to a great extent, it being well adapted to the uses of the country people, particularly in the braes of Angus. About the year 1745 or 1746 the manufactory of Osnaburgh was introduced here, which from very small beginnings has grown into a great trade, and has become the staple of the place; and the happy influence of which, particularly of late years, is visible in the amazing increase of population and wealth, and the consequent improvement of every thing. This branch of manufacture was brought to Forfar by a gentleman still living there, who has acquired by it a comfortable independence. His brother, a weaver in or near Arbroath, (about the year 1738 or 1739) having got a small quantity of flax unfit for the kind of cloth then usually brought to market, made it into a web, and offered it to his merchant as a piece on which he thought he should, and was willing to, lose. The merchant, who had been in Germany, immediately remarked the similarity between this piece of cloth and the fabric of Osnaburgh, and urged the weaver to attempt other pieces of the same kind, which he reluctantly undertook. The experiment however succeeded to a wish. Many hands were soon employed in the neighbourhood of Arbroath, where a Company was established to promote the business, and from whence the discovery was brought to Forfar at the period above mentioned. Before that time the flax was dressed by women; there was no cloth made at Forfar, but a few yard-wides, called Scrims; the number of incorporated weavers did not exceed 40, nor were there above 60 looms employed in the town. But in consequence of the act for encouraging weavers, the trade increased so rapidly, that, before the year 1750, there were upwards of 140 looms going in Forfar, and at present there are between 400 and 500.

The knowledge of this art is so easily acquired, the call for hands so great, that almost every young man here betakes himself to it. He receives a part of the profit of his work from the very day his apprenticeship begins; in a year or two he is qualified to carry on business for himself, and able to support a family, and so he marries and multiplies; and this facility of acquiring a living at an early period of life is one great cause of the rapid increase of population. To this also it is owing, perhaps, that other professions, less profitable and more difficult to acquire, are seldomer pursued by the young men of this place; and it is a fact worthy of notice, that there has not been above one or two apprentice taylors in Forfar these seven years past.

The Osnaburgh trade is indeed a fluctuating one, and when the demand for that fabric slackens at any time, it brings many of the young and unprovident into difficulties, and oftentimes adds to the number of the poor. But when the trade is good (and it has been for sometimes past more stable and more flourishing than ever it was known before), the profits of it, with the government bounty, are sufficient to support the sober and industrious weaver against the influence of a falling market. Manufacturers are just now giving from 15s. to 20s. for working the piece of ten dozen of yards, which a man of good execution will accomplish in nearly as many days; and a man working his own web, has been known to produce 18 such pieces by his own hands in the space of 19 weeks. This however is allowed by all to be extraordinary, though it shews what sobriety and diligence may do.

The trade and wealth of Forfar having increased so rapidly since the year 1745, must naturally be supposed to have produced great alterations in the appearance of the place and the manners of its inhabitants. Accordingly their buildings, their expence of living, and their dress are almost totally changed since that period. And there is a remarkable difference, even within these 10 years, not only in all these respects, but also in their amusements.

About and before the year 1745 there were few private houses covered with slate, and the masonry of almost all of them was of a very inferior kind; since that time almost every new house has been covered with slates of a coarse kind, of which there are plenty in quarries within the royalty, and several of the principal ones with Easdale. A thatched house is scarcely to be seen, and the masonry of such houses as have been built of late years is neat and substantial; the inhabitants appearing to have caught a new taste in building from the pattern set them in the new Town-house and new Church, which are of neat modern architecture.

Like most towns in Scotland, Forfar had been built without any regular design, as every man's fancy dictated the situation of his house; now more attention is bestowed in regulating the streets in the extended parts of the town, as well as in removing irregularities in rebuilding houses in the old-street. There are no uninhabited houses, new ones are extending the town in almost every direction, and house rents are rather on the rise. Most of the houses built for trades-people consist of two stories, having four apartments of about 16 feet square each, one of which, with a portion of the garret, is sufficient to accommodate a weaver with his loom, his furniture and his fuel, and he pays for it, and a few feet of garden ground, from 20s. to 45s. *per annum*, according to its distance from the market-place or its other advantages or disadvantages. The weaver generally prefers the low flat for his operations, and an open exposure, if possible, to the heart of the town.[1]

1 About 50 or 60 years ago there were not above 7 tea-kettles, as many hand-bellows, and as many watches in Forfar: now tea-kettles and hand-bellows are the necessary furniture of the poorest house in the parish, and almost the meanest menial servant must have his watch.

About the same period, a leg of good beef weighing 4 stone might have been purchased for 5s.; a leg of tolerable veal for 5d. the highest for 1s. and some so low as 2d1/2.; mutton from 8d. to 1s. per leg; a smaller sort from the Grampians, but of excellent flavour, from 4d. to 5d. per leg. Previous to 1745 there was no meat sold in Forfar by weight, and very seldom was an ox killed till the greater part of the carcase had been bespoken. A little before that two work oxen, weighing about 30 stone each, were sold in one of the Forfar fairs for 50 merks Scots the head; and both the size of the cattle and the price of them were thought a wonder.

An ox, worth at that time about 40s. supplied the flesh-market of Forfar eight days or a fortnight, except on extraordinary occasions, from Christmas to Lammas. Between Hallowmass and Christmas, when the people laid in their winter provisions, about 24 beeves were killed in a week; the best not exceeding 16 or 20 stone. A man who had bought a shillings worth of beef or an ounce of tea would have concealed it from his

About 1745 the common rent of an acre of burgh land was L. 10 Scotch, including 40d. for ministers stipend. An acre of the same land is now often let at from 50s. to L. 3 *per annum*: Several of them near the town bring more than twice as much, and the whole of them have been lately found by a decreet arbitral to be worth 25s. per acre, if let *in cumulo* for a lease of 19 years.

General Character of the Inhabitants. The general character of the inhabitants is that of industry and enterprise. As in other large assemblages of men, instances of dissipation are not wanting, and failures among trading people now and then happen; effects, which a sudden influx of wealth, and inexperience in the paths of extended commerce, seldom fail to produce and multiply; but it has been observed, to the honour of the merchants of Forfar, by the people from a distance who have had long and extensive dealings in this country, that there is no town in Angus, where they find fewer bankruptcies and more punctual payments.

Articles of commerce are greatly more numerous within these few years. Wine of various sorts, which was formerly brought from Dundee in dozens, and seldom used but as a medicine, is

neighbours like murder. Eggs were bought for 1d. per dozen, butter from 3d. to 4d. per lb. and a good hen was thought high at a groat.

The gradual advancement of population, trade, and agricultural improvement, has produced the gradual rise in the price and consumption of all these articles, which within these last twenty years are some of them doubled, and many of them trebled; oat meal too has risen, but not in the same proportion with most other articles. And there are few artificers who cannot well afford to treat themselves and their families frequently with meat and wheaten bread, considerable quantities of both being consumed by them. At an average, there is not less than L. 50. worth of meat sold in the flesh market of Forfar every week throughout the year. Good meat brings from 3d. to 4d. and sometimes 5d. per lb. and can seldom be purchased in quantities, even at the cheapest periods, for less than 4s. per stone. Eggs which ten years ago sold at 2d. per dozen are now risen to 4d. and sometimes 6d. Hens are from 10d. to 1s. Butter from 8d. to 10d.½ per pound of 24 ounces English – and other articles in proportion. Though this bears hard upon annuitants, yet it is universally allowed that labouring people purchase more of these articles now, and are better able to do it, than when provisions were cheaper.

now imported in pipes, and is a very common drink at private as well as at public entertainments. Porter, which, about 20 years ago was scarcely known, is now brought from London in great quantities and is becoming a common beverage with the lowest of the people. Table-beer is seldom made by private families, but by the brewers in the town, who are a flourishing class of men; from 1600 to 2000 bolls of malt are consumed annually, but the consumpt of this article is lessened since the introduction of porter.

Superfine cloths, and all kinds of cotton, cloth and many other articles formerly got from Dundee, are now to be had in plenty in many shops in Forfar.

Dundee is the nearest sea-port town, and with which Forfar has most frequent intercourse, but it also carries on a trade with Arbroath and Montrose. The communication with all these places will be greatly facilitated when the turnpike roads leading to them are finished. The turnpike act for this county commenced in June 1789, and the roads to Dundee and Arbroath are now nearly completed. Though the popular prejudice was at first against them, every one begins to see his interest in them now, since as much can be drawn by one horse as could formerly have been done with two, and the toll exigible for a one horse cart per day from Forfar to Arbroath or Dundee, is no more than 4½ on either road. The turnpike road from Forfar to Perth is likewise in great forwardness, and will soon be compleated, to the general improvement of the estates through which it passes and the towns to and from which it leads.

One great drawback on the property of Forfar is the scarcity of fuel. Peats have indeed for several years past been obtained from the lands gained by draining the loch of Forfar; these are now nearly exhausted, and a new moss has been opened by the draining Loch Restenet, which, in its turn, a few years will see to an end: at any rate the peats got from thence, though a convenient, are by no means a cheap article of fuel; for the poor man, could he afford the money all at once, would be much cheaper, and if cheaper he must be more comfortable, with coal. A considerable quantity of thriving firs are rising on the town's property, and on some of the estates in the neighbourhood; but their number seems by no means adequate to the probable demand for firing, when the mosses shall be exhausted; so that the community's sole dependence for this article, at some future period, will be on coal, which at present is obtained from Arbroath and Dundee, at a very great expence, not less than from 9s. to 10s. 6d. per boll of 70 stone Dutch. In some places of the slate quarries in this neighbourhood, strata of culm-stone have been found, such as indicate the vicinity of coal, and they excited no little expectation some years that this useful fossil might be discovered here. Some feeble attempts towards a discovery were made by the proprietor of one of these quarries, and a few acres around it; but his finances were unequal to the expence, and he met with no support from the public.

There are few places within the royalty, in which a quarry of some kind may not easily be found, so that both stone and slate are comparatively cheap; but the expence of lime and wood, neither of which can be had but from the sea port towns or an equal distance, will probably continue, with the high price of fuel, to obstruct in some measure the growing prosperity of this burgh, till wealth and the spirit of enterprize shall open a communication by water between it and the sea.

In spite of these disadvantages, however, Forfar is, and is likely to continue, a thriving place; situated in the centre of a well cultivated county, the seat of the court of justice, the members of which at a moderate computation bring L. 1500 a year to the town; the place of resort for the free-holders, not only for transacting the business of the country, but for the enjoyment of society in clubs, assemblies, &c. laying on a great road through the kingdom, and open by the turnpikes to a ready intercourse with all her neighbours, possessed also of several substantial manufactures, conducted by men of spirit and industry, who daily stretching out new paths of art and commerce, she must rise, in the nature of things, to greater eminence than she has yet attained.

Many things doubtless are necessary to the accomplishment of this desirable end. A well regulated police, and the suppression of a multiplicity of ale houses, so dangerous to the morals of the people, are particularly requisite. The clearing and lighting of the streets, and the introduction of water in pipes, are also objects worthy of attention, to which, it is hoped, in time, the people in power may well apply their care. It is also universally allowed, that nothing can contribute more to the civil and religious interests of any society, than a sacred attention to the education of youth. And where the funds of a parish admit of it, as well as those of this district can, there ought to be at least three established schools, one for Latin-grammar, and the other learned or foreign tongues, one for English solely, and one for writing and arithmetic. There are at present two established schools in Forfar, with tolerable appointments, in each of which the master is permitted to teach all the branches of education promiscuously, a method calculated to perplex himself and obstruct the improvement of his pupils. The schools about the middle of this century were in considerable reputation; but the town for many years past has been rather unfortunate in the appointments made to these important offices. The magistrates and council have, however, of late taken such measures as it is hoped shall in future secure the good institution of youth, and raise the schools to some degree of celebrity.[1]

Poor. The number of poor in the town is very considerable; they are supported by money arising from lands purchased with the donations of Messrs Robert and William Strangs mentioned in the preceding note, about the year 1654, amounting to about L. 96 yearly; and the money collected weekly at the church door, which with the interests of certain savings in former times of plenty, amounts to about L. 100 yearly. Out of these sums, besides a monthly distribution of about L. 6 or L. 7 and occasional supplies in cases of urgent necessity, the poor are furnished with shoes, clothing, and house rent. Since the scarcity in the year 1783, when oat-meal was 20s. per boll, through the increase of the number of poor and the rise of provisions, the funds which before were accumulating have been scarcely adequate to the expenditure; and new methods are now trying to render the supply of the industrious poor more effectual, without increasing the burden of the community. The fact seems to be, that over-grown charity funds, are enemies to industry, as they encourage the idle and improvident, to depend upon them as a security against want in the evening of life. And so they will neither work nor save. For many years preceding the year 1788, provisions were more easily obtained by the poor, than now, by the great quantities of fresh fish with which the market of Forfar was supplied at very reasonable prices, by carriers who gained a livelyhood by bringing them almost daily from the sea-port towns. A supply which had

1 Within these few years the manse has been repaired
  at a considerable expence at two thirds of the money
  which would have built a commodious one from the
  foundation; and yet it is a manse still standing in need
  of repair; a proof among many of the inattention of
  heritors to their own interest. Were such public works
  finished substantially at once, they would cost them less
  trouble and less expense.

its influence also on the price of meat. But since the year 1788 fish have been very scarce; the haddocks particularly have left our coasts entirely, and one great article for the subsistance of the poor, as well as a luxury for the rich, is withdrawn.

There is a weekly market held in Forfar every Saturday; it is well attended, and a great deal of country business is transacted there. A branch of the Dundee Banking Company, and one of the commercial Bank Company of Aberdeen, have been established here for these two or three years, and both have considerable employ.

There are several well frequented fairs kept on the muir adjoining to the town; the custom of one of them was purchased some time ago from the Earl of Strathmore, and all make a considerable addition to the revenue of the burgh. From Martinmas to Candlemass there is a weekly market on Wednesday, free of custom, held on the street for the sale of fat cattle; and during the feed-time there is one weekly on the same day for the sale of work horses, all of which are well frequented, and occasion the spending a great deal of money in the town, by the country people who attend them.

Source: Sir John Sinclair (ed.), *The Statistical Account of Scotland*, Edinburgh 1791–9, vol. 6, pp. 511–26

PART VII

SOCIAL THEORY AND POLITICS

TWENTY-FOUR

ADAM SMITH
The Four Stages of Society

The fact that Smith's famous statement of the four stages of society, the stages of hunting, shepherding, agriculture, and commerce, occurs in the context of a set of lectures on jurisprudence is important for an understanding of the four-stages theory. Smith is interested in the question of the origin and development of our property rights, and since he thinks that the rules concerning the methods by which we acquire property 'vary considerably according to the state or age society is in at that time', he must first give an account of the stages through which society passes if he is to be in a position to trace the development of those property rights. So Smith's aim is to understand how we, in this commercial age, have the property rights we do.

It is to be noted at once that Smith says that the regulations concerning the methods by which property is acquired *must*, not may, vary according to the stage society is at. We are therefore not dealing here with any accident of history, but with a necessity. But this necessity concerns not so much the move of society from one stage to the next as the role that property plays at each stage in this process. There is no inexorability here. A society can, for any one of many reasons, get stuck at one stage or another, and it can also possess simultaneously the characteristics of adjacent stages. These considerations point to the fact that the four stages are not to be judged in terms of whether they are in detail historical events; instead it is more helpful to think of Smith's descriptions as having the status of what Max Weber was to call ideal types. They form a conceptual framework rather than an accurate account of events on the ground. Smith is aware that he is not giving a description of things as they must develop, as witness his report that the American Indians have some notion of agriculture though they have no conception of herding, whereas he places herding before agriculture in his ordering of the stages of society.

In the first stage, hunters have practically no property; they own the creatures they kill and the fruit and plants they pluck, and that is all. Neither do they have any accumulated property rights, for what they kill or pluck is promptly eaten; it cannot be stored because it will not stay fresh. In such a society there are no significant differences in wealth, nor therefore any authority-subordination relations based upon relative wealth. By the same token there is no possibility of inherited wealth bringing inherited power.

The second stage, the age of the shepherds, is distinguished in one respect by its relative absence of mobility, at least compared with the age of the hunters, though it is still broadly speaking nomadic. The second stage is in another respect different from the first, in that herdsmen can accumulate wealth in the form of herds, and this creates the possibility of great inequality of fortune, which in turn leads to power relations based upon wealth. In the second stage people have goods to protect, and therefore their attitude to theft is quite different from the attitude to theft in the first stage, for hunters have almost no property and therefore almost nothing to be stolen, and they can therefore take a more relaxed attitude to theft.

The third stage of society is the agricultural, which is less mobile than either of the others, and permanent housing becomes a major contributor to the lifestyle. Such a society requires a wide variety of laws, in virtue of the wide variety of property that can be held. It also permits even greater inequalities of fortune than does the second stage, which, again, affects the distribution of power within the society. And finally the fourth stage, the commercial, much the most complex of the four stages, requires yet more laws to regulate property. Thus we see that property, and the legal framework governing property, are functions of the stage of production within which property is held. In particular, it becomes clear why Smith chose to present his account of the four stages of society within the context of his lectures on jurisprudence.

In view of the Scottish Enlightenment preoccupation with *improvement*, it should be borne in mind that Smith did not believe that all historical change was for the better. A spectacular reversal that he elsewhere highlights is the collapse of the Roman Empire, which was followed by a culturally impoverished period. An underlying optimism is, nevertheless, to be found in the writings of Smith, and he assuredly thought that the moves from the first through to the fourth stages of human society were moves for the better, in view of the steadily increasing opportunities for the development of the rich cultural life, structured by civilised values, of which we are all capable.

A.B.

The Origin and Development
of our Property Rights

The first thing that comes to be considered in treating of rights
is the originall or foundation from whence they arise.

Now we may observe that the original of the greatest part of
what are called natural rights, or those which are competent to
a man merely as a man, need not be explained. That a man has
received an injury when he is wounded or hurt any way is evident
to reason, without any explanation; and the same may be said
of the injury done one when his liberty is any way restrain'd;
any one will at first perceive that there is an injury done in this
case. That one is injured when he is defamed, and his good
name hurt amongst men, needs not be proved by any great
discussion. One of the chief studies of a mans life is to obtain
a good name, to rise above those about and render himself some
way their superiors. When therefore one is thrown back not only
to a level, but even degraded below the common sort of men,
he receives one of the most affecting and atrocious injuries that
possibly can be inflicted on him. The only case where the origin
of naturall rights is not altogether plain, is in that of property. It
does not at first appear evident that, e.g. any thing which may
suit another as well or perhaps better than it does me, should
belong to me exclusively of all others barely because I have got
it into my power; as for instance, that an apple, which no doubt
may be as agreable and as usefull to an other as it is to me, should
be altogether appropriated to me and all others excluded from it
merely because I had pulled it of the tree.

We will find that there are five causes from whence property
may have its occasion. First, occupation, by which we get any
thing into our power that was not the property of another before.
Secondly, tradition, by which property is voluntarily transferred
from one to an other. Thirdly, accession, by which the property
of any part that adheres to a subject and seems to be of small
consequences as compared to it, or to be a part of it, goes to
the proprieter of the principall, as the milk or young of beasts.
Fourthly, prescription or Usucapio, by which a thing that has
been for a long time out of the right owners possession and in
the possession of an other, passes in right to the latter. Fifthly,
succession, by which the nearest of kin or the testamentary heir

has a right of property to what was left him by the testator. Of these in order.

Of Occupation

Before we consider exactly this or any of the other methods by which property is acquired it will be proper to observe that the regulations concerning them must vary considerably according to the state or age society is in at that time. There are four distinct states which mankind pass thro: first, the Age of Hunters; secondly, the Age of Shepherds; thirdly, the Age of Agriculture; and fourthly, the Age of Commerce.

If we should suppose 10 or 12 persons of different sexes settled in an uninhabited island, the first method they would fall upon for their sustenance would be to support themselves by the wild fruits and wild animalls which the country afforded. Their sole business would be hunting the wild beasts or catching the fishes. The pulling of a wild fruit can hardly be called an imployment. The only thing amongst them which deserved the appellation of a business would be the chase. This is the age of hunters. In process of time, as their numbers multiplied, they would find the chase too precarious for their support. They would be necessitated to contrive some other method whereby to support themselves. At first perhaps they would try to lay up at one time when they had been successful what would support them for a considerable time. But this could go no great length. The contrivance they would most naturally think of, would be to tame some of those wild animalls they caught, and by affording them better food than what they could get elsewhere they would enduce them to continue about their land themselves and multiply their kind. Hence would arise the age of shepherds. They would more probably begin first by multiplying animalls than vegetables, as less skill and observation would be required. Nothing more than to know what food suited them. We find accordingly that in almost all countries the age of shepherds preceded that of agriculture. The Tartars and Arabians subsist almost entirely by their flocks and herds. The Arabs have a little agriculture, but the Tartars none at all. The whole of the savage nations which subsist by flocks have no notion of cultivating the ground. The only instance that has the appearance of an objection to this rule is the state of the North American Indians. They, tho they have no conception of flocks and herds, have nevertheless some notion of agriculture. Their women plant a few stalks of Indian corn at the back of their huts. But this can hardly be called agriculture.

This corn does not make any considerable part of their food; it serves only as a seasoning or something to give a relish to their common food; the flesh of those animalls they have caught in the chase. Flocks and herds therefore are the first resource men would take themselves to when they found difficulty in subsisting by the chase.

But when a society becomes numerous they would find a difficulty in supporting themselves by herds and flocks. Then they would naturally turn themselves to the cultivation of land and the raising of such plants and trees as produced nourishment fit for them. They would observe that those seeds which fell on the dry bare soil or on the rocks seldom came to any thing, but that those which entered the soil generally produced a plant and bore seed similar to that which was sown. These observations they would extend to the different plants and trees they found produced agreable and nourishing food. And by this means they would gradually advance in to the age of agriculture. As society was farther improved, the severall arts, which at first would be exercised by each individual as far as was necessary for his welfare, would be seperated; some persons would cultivate one and others others, as they severally inclined. They would exchange with one an other what they produced more than was necessary for their support, and get in exchange for them the commodities they stood in need of and did not produce themselves. This exchange of commodities extends in time not only betwixt the individualls of the same society but betwixt those of different nations. Thus we send to France our cloths, iron work, and other trinkets and get in exchange their wines. To Spain and Portugall we send our superfluous corn and bring from thence the Spanish and Portuguese wines. Thus at last the age of commerce arises. When therefore a country is stored with all the flocks and herds it can support, the land cultivated so as to produce all the grain and other commodities necessary for our subsistance it can be brought to bear, or at least as much as supports the inhabitants when the superfluous products whether of nature or art are exported and other necessary ones brought in exchange, such a society has done all in its power towards its ease and convenience.

It is easy to see that in these severall ages of society, the laws and regulations with regard to property must be very different. In Tartary, where as we said the support of the inhabitants consists in herds and flocks, *theft* is punished with immediate death; in North America, again, where the age of hunters subsists, theft is not much regarded. As there is almost no property amongst them, the only injury that can be done is the depriving them of their game. Few laws or regulations will be requisite in such an age of society, and these will not extend to any great length, or be very rigorous in the punishments annexed to any infringements of property. Theft as we said is not much regarded amongst a people in this age or state of society; there are but few opportunities of committing it, and these too can not hurt the injured person in a considerable degree. But when flocks and herds come to be reared property then becomes of a very considerable extent; there are many opportunities of injuring one another and such injuries are extremely pernicious to the sufferer. In this state many more laws and regulations must take place; theft and robbery being easily committed, will of consequence be punished with the utmost rigour. In the age of agriculture, they are not perhaps so much exposed to theft and open robbery, but then there are many ways added in which property may be interrupted as the subjects of it are considerably extended. The laws therefore tho perhaps not so rigorous will be of a far greater number than amongst a nation of shepherds. In the age of commerce, as the subjects of property are greatly increasd the laws must be proportionally multiplied. The more improved any society is and the greater length the severall means of supporting the inhabitants are carried, the greater will be the number of their laws and regulations necessary to maintain justice, and prevent infringements of the right of property.

Having premised this much, we proceed as we proposed to consider property acquired by occupation. The first thing to be attended to is how occupation, that is, the bare possession of a subject, comes to give us an exclusive right to the subject so acquired. How is it that a man by pulling an apple should be imagined to have a right to that apple and a power of excluding all others from it – and that an injury should be conceived to be done when such a subject is taken from the possessor. From the system I have already explain'd, you will remember that I told you we may conceive an injury was done one when an impartial spectator would be of opinion he was injured, would join with him in his concern and go along with him when he defended the subject in his possession against any violent attack, or used force to recover what had been thus wrongfully wrested out of his hands. This would be the case in the abovementioned circumstances. The spectator would justify the first possessor in defending and even in avenging himself when injured, in the manner we mentioned. The cause of this sympathy or concurrence betwixt the spectator and the possessor is, that he enters into his thoughts and concurrs in his opinion that he may form a reasonable expectation of using the fruit or whatever it is in what manner he pleases. This expectation justifies in the mind of the spectator, the possessor both when he defends himself against one who would deprive him of what he has thus acquired and when he endeavours to recover it by force. The spectator goes along with him in his expectation, but he can not enter into the designs of him who would take the goods from the first possessor. The reasonable expectation therefore which the first possessor furnishes is the ground on which the right of property is acquired by occupation. You may ask indeed, as this apple is as fit for your use as it is for mine, what title have I to detain it from you. You may go to the forest (says one to me) and pull another. You may go as well as I, replied I. And besides it is more reasonable that you should, as I have gone already and bestowed my time and pains in procuring the fruit.

Having explain'd the foundation on which occupancy gives the property to the occupant, the next thing to be considered is at what time property is conceived to begin by occupation. Whether it be when we have got a sight of the subject, or when we have got into our actual possession. In most cases the property in a subject is not conceived to commence till we have actually got possession of it. A hare started does not appear to be altogether in our power; we may have an expectation of obtaining it but still it may happen that it shall escape us. The spectator does not go along with us so far as to conceive we could be justified in demanding satisfaction for the injury done us in taking such a booty out of our power. We see however that in this point lawyers have differed considerably. Trebatius, as Justinian informs us, conceived that an animall began to be our property when ever it was wounded; that this gave us a just title to it, and that one might claim it from any possessor rei vindicatio compelere ei judicabat.[1] Other more strict lawyers, as Proculus and Sabinus, were of opinion that it did not become ours till it came into our actual possession. Frederic Barbarossa, refining still more on Trebatius doctrine, made a distinction with regard to the manner in which the wound was given. If it was given with a missile weapon he judged that it did not immediately convey property; but if it was with a weapon held in ones hand,

1 Corrupt passage. The gist is that the owner's action
  was available to the wounder of the animal to compel a
  possessor to restore it.

as a spear or sword, he judged that the beast, e.g. a wild boar, came immediately under the property of the person who gave the wound. It was without doubt very near being in his power and he conceived it to have been altogether. In different countries there are different constitutions on this head. It was enacted by a law of the Lombards that a hart which was wounded, if killed in 24 hours after he received the wound, should belong partly to the person who gave the wound and partly to him who killd him, as the former was conceived to have had a hand in the catching him. The part given to the wounder was I think a leg and 4 ribs. In the same manner, at this day, the ships which go to the Greenland fishery share the whale that was wounded betwixt the ship who wounded and that which killed the whale. If the harpoon of any ship that was at the fishing the same season be found in the fish, a certain part is alotted to that ship as having by the wound contributed to the taking of the fish. In most cases however property was conceived to commence when the subject comes into the power of the captor.

The next thing in order which comes to be treated of is, how long and in what circumstances property continues and at what time it is supposed to be at an end.

At first property was conceived to end as well as to begin with possession. They conceived that a thing was no longer ours in any way after we had lost the immediate property of it. A wild beast we had caught, when it gets out of our power is considered as ceasing to be ours. But as there is some greater connection betwixt the possessor who loses the possession of the thing he had obtained than there was before he had obtain'd it, property was considered to extend a little farther, and to include not only those animalls we then possessed but also those we had once possessed though they were then out of our hands, that is, so long as we pursued them, and had a probability of recovering them.

If I was desirous of pulling an apple and had stretched out my hand towards it, but an other who was more nimble comes and pulls it before me, an impartial spectator would conceive this was a very great breach of good manners and civility but would not suppose it an incroachment on property. If after I had got the apple into my hand I should happen to let it fall, and an other should snatch it up, this would be still more uncivil and a very heinous affront, bordering very near on a breach of the right of property. But if one should attempt to snatch it out of my hand when I had the actuall possession of it, the bystander would immediately agree that my property was incroached on, and would go along with me in recovering it or preventing the injury before hand, even suppose I should use violence for the accomplishing my design. Let us now apply this to the case of the hunters. When I start a hare, I have only a probability of catching it on my side. It may possibly escape me; the bystander does not go along with me altogether in an expectation that I must catch it; many accidents may happen that may prevent my catching it. If one in this case should come and take the game I had started and was in pursuit of, this would appear a great tresspass on the laws of fair hunting; I can not however justly take satisfaction of the transgressor. The forester may in some countries impose a fine on such an offender. If after I had taken the hare or other wild beast it should chance to escape, if I continued to pursue it and kept it in my view, the spectator would more easily go along with my expectations; one who should prevent me in this pursuit would appear to have trespassed very heinously against the rules of fair hunting and to have approached very near to an infringement of the right of property. But after it is out of my power, even tho I may possibly see it, there is no longer any connection betwixt it and me; I can have no longer any claim to it any more than to any other wild animall, as there is no greater probability I should catch it. But if he had violently or theftuously taken from me what I had actually in my possession, this would evidently be an atrocious transgression of the right of property such as might justify, in the eyes of the beholder, my endeavours to recover what I had been so wrongfully deprived of. In this age of society therefore property would extend no farther than possession.

But when men came to think of taming these wild animalls and bringing them up about themselves, property would necessarily be extended a great deal farther. We may consider animalls to be of three sorts. First, Ferae, such as are always in a wild state. Secondly, Mansuefactae, which are those which have been tamed so as to return back to us after we have let them out of our power, and do thus habitually; tho there be others of the same sort, as stags, hares, ducks, etc. of which there are some wild and others tame. Thirdly, Mansuetae, which are such as are only to be found tame, as oxen. When men first began to rear domestick animalls, they would be all under the class of the mansuefactae, as there must have been others still wild. But even in this case it would be absolutely necessary that property should not cease immediately when possession was at an end. The proprietor could not have all those animalls about him which he had tamed; it was necessary for the very being of any property of this sort that it should continue some what farther. They considered therefore all animalls to remain in the property of him to whom they apertaind at first, as long as they retain'd the habit of returning into his power at certain times. And this continues still to be the case with regard to those animalls that are mansuetae, or what we properly call tamed. Hawks, stags, etc. when they no longer return into the power of their owner are supposed to cede to the occupant. But in process of time, when some species of animalls came to be nowhere met with but in the state of mansuefactae, they lost that name and became mansuetae. A farther extension was by this means introduced into the notion of property, so as that all these animalls were esteemd to be in the property of their master as long as they could be distinguished to be his; altho they had for a long time ceased to come into his power, yet still they were considered as fully his property. This was no doubt a great extention of the notion of property. But a still greater followed on the introduction of agriculture. It seems probable that at first, after the cultivation of land, there was no private property of that sort; the fixing of their habitations and the building of cities first introduced the division of land amongst private persons. The notion of property seems at first to have been confined to what was about ones person, his cloaths and any instruments he might have occasion for. This would naturally be the custom amongst hunters, whose occupation lead them to be continually changing their place of abode. Charlevois tells us that a certain Canadian woman having a great string of wampum which serves for money amongst them was so extremely fond of it that she could never let it out of her sight. One day it happened that she carried it with her to a field where she was to reap her corn. There was no tree in her field, but one in that of her neighbour hard by. In this tree she hung up her string. Another woman, observing her, went and took it off. The owner of the string demanded it from her, she refused, the matter was referred to one of the chief men of the village, who gave it as his opinion that in strict law the string belonged to the woman who took it off the tree, and that the other had lost all claim of property to it by letting it out of her possession. But that if the other woman did not incline to do very scandalous action and get the character of excessive avarice (a most reproachfull term in that country), she ought to restore it to the owner, which she accordingly did.

The introduction of shepherds made their habitation somewhat more fixed but still very uncertain. The huts they put up have been by the consent of the tribe allowed to be the property of the builder. For it would not appear at first why a hut should be the property of one after he had left it more than of another. A cave or grotto would be considered as belonging to him who had taken possession of it as long as he continued in it; but it would not appear that one had any right to it tomorrow night because he had lodged there this night. The introduction of the property of houses must have therefore been by the common consent of the severall members of some tribe or society. Hence in time the house and the things in it became to be considered as the property of the builder. Hence the Greek and Latin words for property, dominium and οικειον. But still property would not be extended to land or pasture. The life of a shepherd requires that he should frequently change his situation, or at least the place of his pasturing, to find pasture for his cattle. The property of the spot he built on would be conceived to end as soon as he had left it, in the same manner as the seats in a theatre or a hut on the shore belong no longer to any person than they are possessed by him. They would not easily conceive a subject of such extent as land is, should belong to an object so little as a single man. It would more easily be conceived that a large body such as a whole nation should have property in land. Accordingly we find that in many nations the different tribes have each their peculiar territory on which the others dare not encroach (as the Tartars and inhabitants of the coast of Guinea). But here the property is conceived to continue no longer in a private person than he actually possessed the subject. A field that had been pastured on by one man would be considered to be his no longer than he actually staid on it. Even after the invention of agriculture it was some time before the land was divided into particular properties. At first the whole community cultivated a piece of ground in common; they divided the crops produced by this piece of ground amongst the severall inhabitants according to the numbers in each family and the rank of the severall individualls. The inclination of any single person would not be sufficient to constitute his property in any parcel of land if it were but for one season; the rest of the community would cry out against him as incroaching on and appropriating to himself what ought to be in common amongst them all. In the same manner as any corporation or society amongst us would not permit any of their body to set appart for his own use any part of their common field or any tree in it, etc., as they ought to reap in common the fruit of these common'd subjects. As a confirmation of this, we learn from Tacitus that each nation who had any agriculture amongst them cultivated some spot of ground the product of which was divided amongst the members of the community. The first origin of private property would probably be mens taking themselves to fixt habitations and living together in cities, which would probably be the case in every improved society. The field they would cultivate when living together in this manner would be that which lies most contiguous to them. As their place of abode was now become fixt, it would readily appear to them to be the easiest method to make a division of the land once for all, rather than be put to the unnecessary trouble of dividing the product every year. In consequence of this design the principall persons of such a community, or state, if you please to denominate a set of men in this condition by that honourable appellation, would divide the common land into seperate portions for each individuall or family. We find accordingly that Homer and Aristotle, whenever they give us an account of the settling of any colony, the first thing they mention is the dividing of the land. Aristotle too mentions the manner in which this was done. He tells us that the ground lying nearest to the new built city was divided into seperate parcells as it was most convenient for each, but that which was more remote was still allowed to remain common.

One thing which strengthens the opinion that the property of land was settled by the chief magistrate posterior to the cultivation is that, in this country, as soon as the crop is off the ground the cattle are no longer kept up or looked after but are turnd out on what they call the long tether; that is, they are let out to roam about as they incline. Tho this be contrary to Act of Parliament yet the country people are so wedded to the notion that property in land continues no longer than the crop is on the ground that there is no possibility of getting them to observe it, even by the penalty which is appointed to be exacted against them.

This last species of property, viz. in land, is the greatest extention it has undergone.

Source: Adam Smith, *Lectures on Jurisprudence*, ed. R. L. Meek, D. D. Raphael and P. G. Stein, Oxford 1978, pp. 13–23

TWENTY-FIVE

JOHN MILLAR
The Origin of the Distinction of Ranks

Millar describes his treatise as an illustration of the 'natural history of mankind', by which he has in mind particularly the way in which 'the gradual progress of civilization and improvement' affects 'the manners, laws, and the government of a people'. Among the topics he explores, as a pioneer, under the heading of 'natural history' are the rank and condition of women in pastoral and agricultural ages and at times of great opulence, and the form of authority that a master has over his servant in primitive and subsequent ages. If this task is to be accomplished, the author must take a view regarding the stages through which society naturally passes, and also a view regarding the way in which variations in the circumstances of a society affect in detail the shape that the society takes at each stage in its development.

Nevertheless there are constraints on the range of variations, the chief constraint being the uniformity of human nature. It is less the differences among people than the differences of the circumstances within which they operate that produce the different systems of law and different social structures that we see today, though of course, as Millar stresses, our ideas and feelings are strongly affected by those same circumstances, and constitute, though at a lower level of abstraction, a degree of diversity among people.

The idea that human nature is essentially uniform is a common position of the Enlightenment, informing, for example, much of Hume's economic, political and historical work. The view is much enhanced by Newton's demonstration that the great variety of changes in the universe can be brought under a few principles, in the end under a single one, the inverse square law. The process of understanding nature is therefore a process of grand simplification. The point about a principle of change is that it is applicable to many individual changes; the principle that explains why a change of a particular kind occurs can also explain why many others of that kind also occur.

Millar, in search of this principle, seeks it in the uniformity of human nature. His starting point is this, that there is in man 'a disposition and capacity for improving his condition, by the exertion of which, he is carried on from one degree of advancement to another', and since we are similar in respect of our wants and of the faculties by means of which those wants are satisfied, the successive steps of our progress are also 'remarkably uniform'. The steps he outlines, which are reminiscent of steps outlined by Adam Smith (see excerpt 24), take us from the primitive hunter–gatherer stage to commercial life. Millar stresses a corresponding development in moral insight and activity. For example, he notes that as society develops and we become less oppressed by our wants, we are more at liberty to cultivate the feelings of humanity. Likewise, the rights of mankind become recognised and protected, and more complex forms of government, and more complex systems of law, are put in place in response to the need for the distribution of justice, especially in respect of the greater quantity of property, and more complicated forms of ownership of it.

These various changes Millar describes as 'a natural progress'; what he offers here is a natural history of humankind. There is a kind of determinism implicit in the picture he draws, but it is tempered by his view that accidents can and do happen, in particular that people of genius arise who make a difference which cannot be anticipated because it depends on the precise character of the genius, and the precise circumstances, especially the social circumstances in which they operate. Nevertheless, Millar is doubtful about the extent to which even a genius can effect changes in society, unless he works along, and not against, the grain of society. It is plain that Millar believes that climate has a much greater impact on the development of a society than is ever made by the great persons in its midst.

A.B.

The Origin of the Distinction of Ranks

Those who have examined the manners and customs of nations have had chiefly two objects in view. By observing the systems of law established in different parts of the world, and by remarking the consequences with which they are attended, men have endeavoured to reap advantage from the experience of others, and to make a selection of such institutions and modes of government as appear most worthy of being adopted.

To investigate the causes of different usages has been likewise esteemed an useful as well as an entertaining speculation. When we contemplate the amazing diversity to be found in the laws of different countries, and even of the same country at different periods, our curiosity is naturally excited to enquire in what manner mankind have been led to embrace such different rules of conduct; and at the same time it is evident, that, unless we are acquainted with the circumstances which have recommended any set of regulations, we cannot form a just notion of their utility, or even determine, in any case, how far they are practicable.

In searching for the causes of those peculiar systems of law and government which have appeared in the world, we must undoubtedly resort, first of all, to the differences of situation, which have suggested different views and motives of action to the inhabitants of particular countries. Of this kind, are the fertility or barrenness of the soil, the nature of its productions, the species of labour requisite for procuring subsistence, the number of individuals collected together in one community, their proficiency in arts, the advantages which they enjoy for entering into mutual transactions, and for maintaining an intimate correspondence. The variety that frequently occurs in these, and such other particulars, must have a prodigious influence upon the great body of a people; as, by giving a peculiar direction to their inclinations and pursuits, it must be productive of correspondent habits, dispositions, and ways of thinking.

When we survey the present state of the globe, we find that, in many parts of it, the inhabitants are so destitute of culture, as to appear little above the condition of brute animals; and even when we peruse the remote history of polished nations, we have seldom any difficulty in tracing them to a state of the same rudeness and barbarism. There is, however, in man a disposition and capacity for improving his condition, by the exertion of which, he is carried on from one degree of advancement to another; and the similarity of his wants, as well as of the faculties by which those wants are supplied, has every where produced a remarkable uniformity in the several steps of his progression. A nation of savages, who feel the want of almost every thing requisite for the support of life, must have their attention directed to a small number of objects, to the acquisition of food and clothing, or the procuring shelter from the inclemencies of the weather; and their ideas and feelings, in conformity to their situation, must, of course, be narrow and contracted. Their first efforts are naturally calculated to increase the means of subsistence, by catching or ensnaring wild animals, or by gathering the spontaneous fruits of the earth; and the experience, acquired in the exercise of these employments, is apt, successively, to point out the methods of taming and rearing cattle, and of cultivating the ground. According as men have been successful in these great improvements, and find less difficulty in the attainment of bare necessaries, their prospects are gradually enlarged, their appetites and desires are more and more awakened and called forth in pursuit of the several conveniencies of life; and the various branches of manufacture, together with commerce, its inseparable attendant, and with science and literature, the natural offspring of ease and affluence, are introduced, and brought to maturity. By such gradual advances in rendering their situation more comfortable, the most important alterations are produced in the state and condition of a people: their numbers are increased; the connections of society are extended; and men, being less oppressed with their own wants, are more at liberty to cultivate the feelings of humanity: property, the great source of distinction among individuals, is established; and the various rights of mankind, arising from their multiplied connections, are recognised and protected: the laws of a country are thereby rendered numerous; and a more complex form of government becomes necessary, for distributing justice, and for preventing the disorders which proceed from the jarring interests and passions of a large and opulent community. It is evident, at the same time, that these, and such other effects of improvement, which have so great a tendency to vary the state of mankind, and their manner of life, will be productive of suitable variations in their taste and sentiments, and in their general system of behaviour.

There is thus, in human society, a natural progress from ignorance to knowledge, and from rude, to civilized manners, the several stages of which are usually accompanied with peculiar laws and customs. Various accidental causes, indeed, have contributed to accelerate, or to retard this advancement in different countries. It has even happened that nations, being placed in such unfavourable circumstances as to render them long stationary at a particular period, have been so habituated to the peculiar manners of that age, as to retain a strong tincture of those peculiarities, through every subsequent revolution. This appears to have occasioned some of the chief varieties which take place in the maxims and customs of nations equally civilized.

The character and genius of a nation may, perhaps, be considered as nearly the same with that of every other in similar circumstances; but the case is very different with respect to individuals, among whom there is often a great diversity, proceeding from no fixed causes that are capable of being ascertained. Thus, in a multitude of dice thrown together at random, the result, at different times, will be nearly equal; but in one or two throws of a single die, very different numbers may often be produced. It is to be expected, therefore, that, though the greater part of the political system of any country be derived from the combined influence of the whole people, a variety of peculiar institutions will sometimes take their origin from the casual interposition of particular persons, who happen to be placed at the head of a community, and to be possessed of singular abilities, and views of policy. This has been regarded, by many writers, as the great source of those differences which are to be found in the laws, and government of different nations. It is thus that Brama is supposed to have introduced the peculiar customs of Indostan; that Lycurgus is believed to have formed the singular character of the Lacedemonians; and that Solon is looked upon as the author of that very different style of manners which prevailed at Athens. It is thus, also, that the English constitution is understood to have arisen from the uncommon genius, and patriotic spirit of King Alfred. In short, there is scarcely any people, ancient or modern, who do not boast of some early monarch, or statesman, to whom it is pretended they owe whatever is remarkable in their form of government.

But, notwithstanding the concurring testimony of historians, concerning the great political changes introduced by the lawgivers of a remote age, there may be reason to doubt, whether the effect of their interpositions has ever been so extensive as is generally supposed. Before an individual can be invested with so much authority, and possessed of such reflection and foresight as would induce him to act in the capacity of a legislator, he must, probably, have been educated and brought up in the knowledge of those natural manners and customs, which, for ages perhaps, have prevailed among his countrymen. Under the influence of all the prejudices derived from ancient usage, he will commonly be disposed to prefer the system already established to any other, of which the effects have not been ascertained by experience; or if in any case he should venture to entertain a different opinion, he must be sensible that, from the general prepossession in favour of the ancient establishment, an attempt to overturn it, or to vary it in any considerable degree, would be a dangerous measure, extremely unpopular in itself, and likely to be attended with troublesome consequences.

As the greater part of those heroes and sages that are reputed to have been the founders and modellers of states, are only recorded by uncertain tradition, or by fabulous history, we may be allowed to suspect that, from the obscurity in which they are placed, or from the admiration of distant posterity, their labours have been exaggerated, and misrepresented. It is even extremely probable, that those patriotic statesmen, whose existence is well ascertained, and whose laws have been justly celebrated, were at great pains to accommodate their regulations to the situation of the people for whom they were intended; and that, instead of being actuated by a projecting spirit, or attempting from visionary speculations of remote utility, to produce any violent reformation, they confined themselves to such moderate improvements as, by deviating little from the former usage, were in some measure supported by experience, and coincided with the prevailing opinions of the country. All the ancient systems of legislation that have been handed down to us with any degree of authenticity, show evident marks of their having been framed with such reasonable views; and in none of them is this more remarkable than in the regulations of the Spartan Lawgiver, which appear, in every respect, agreeable to the primitive manners of that simple and barbarous people, for whose benefit they were promulgated.

Among the several circumstances which may affect the gradual improvements of society, the difference of climate is one of the most remarkable. In warm countries, the earth is often extremely fertile, and with little culture is capable of producing whatever is necessary for substance. To labour under the extreme heat of the sun is, at the same time, exceedingly troublesome and oppressive. The inhabitants, therefore, of such countries, while they enjoy a degree of affluence, and, while by the mildness of the climate they are exempted from many inconveniences and wants, are seldom disposed to any laborious exertion, and thus, acquiring habits of indolence, become addicted to sensual pleasure, and liable to all those infirmities which are nourished by idleness and sloth. The people who live in a cold country find, on the contrary, that little or nothing is to be obtained without labour; and being subjected to numberless hardships, while they are forced to contend with the ruggedness of the soil, and the severity of the seasons, in earning their scanty provision, they become active and industrious, and acquire those dispositions and talents which proceed from the constant and vigorous exercise both of the mind and body.

Some philosophers are of opinion, that the difference of heat and cold, of moisture and dryness, or other qualities of the climate, have a more immediate influence upon the character and conduct of nations, by operating insensibly upon the human body, and by effecting correspondent alterations in the temper. It is pretended that great heat, by relaxing the fibres, and by extending the surface of the skin, where the action of the nerves is chiefly performed, occasions great sensibility to all external impressions; which is accompanied with proportionable vivacity of ideas and feelings. The inhabitants of a hot country are, upon this account, supposed to be naturally deficient in courage, and in that steadiness of attention which is necessary for the higher exertions of judgment; while they are no less distinguished by their extreme delicacy of taste, and liveliness of imagination. The weakness, too, of their bodily organs prevents them from consuming a great quantity of food, though their excessive perspiration, the effect of the climate, requires continual supplies of such thin liquors as are proper to repair the waste of their fluids. In this situation, therefore, temperance in eating and drinking becomes a constitutional virtue.

The inhabitants of a cold region, are said, on the other hand, to acquire an opposite complexion. As cold tends to brace the fibres, and to contract the operation of the nerves, it is held to produce a vigorous constitution of body, with little sensibility or vivacity; from which we may expect activity, courage, and resolution, together with such calm and steady views of objects, as are usually connected with a clear understanding. The vigorous constitutions of men, in a cold climate, are also supposed to demand great supplies of strong food, and to create a particular inclination for intoxicating liquors.

In some such manner as this, it is imagined that the character of different nations arises, in a great measure, from the air which they breathe, and from the soil upon which they are maintained. How far these conjectures have any real foundation, it seems difficult to determine. We are too little acquainted with the structure of the human body, to discover how it is affected by such physical circumstances, or to discern the alterations in the state of the mind, which may possibly proceed from a different conformation of bodily organs; and in the history of the world, we see no regular marks of that secret influence which has been ascribed to the air and climate, but, on the contrary, may commonly explain the great differences in the manners and customs of mankind from other causes, the existence of which is capable of being more clearly ascertained.

How many nations are to be found, whose situation in point of climate is apparently similar, and, yet, whose character and political institutions are entirely opposite? Compare, in this respect, the mildness and moderation of the Chinese, with the rough manners and intolerant principles of their neighbours in Japan. What a contrast is exhibited by people at no greater distance than were the ancient Athenians and Lacedemonians? Can it be conceived that the difference between the climate of France and that of Spain, or between that of Greece and of the neighbouring provinces of the Turkish empire, will account for the different usages and manners of the present inhabitants? How is it possible to explain those national peculiarities that have been remarked in the English, the Irish, and the Scotch, from the different temperature of the weather under which they have lived?

The different manners of people in the same country, at different periods, are no less remarkable, and afford evidence yet more satisfactory, that national character depends very little upon the immediate operation of climate. The inhabitants of Sparta are, at present, under the influence of the same physical circumstances as in the days of Leonidas. The modern Italians live in the country of the ancient Romans.

The following Inquiry is intended to illustrate the natural history of mankind in several important articles. This is attempted, by pointing out the more obvious and common improvements which gradually arise in the state of society, and by showing the influence of these upon the manners, the laws, and the government of a people.

With regard to the facts made use of in the following discourse, the reader, who is conversant in history, will readily perceive the difficulty of obtaining proper materials for speculations of this nature. Historians of reputation have commonly overlooked the transactions of early ages, as not deserving to be remembered; and even in the history of later and more cultivated periods, they have been more solicitous to give an exact account of battles, and public negotiations, than of the interior police and government of a country. Our information, therefore, with regard to the state of mankind in the rude parts of the world, is chiefly derived from the relations of travellers, whose character and situation in life, neither set them above the suspicion of being easily deceived, nor of endeavouring to misrepresent the facts which they have related. From the number, however, and the variety of those relations, they acquire, in many cases, a degree of authority, upon which we may depend with security, and to which the narration of any single person, how respectable soever, can have no pretension. When illiterate men, ignorant of the writings of each other, and who, unless upon religious subjects, had no speculative systems to warp their opinions, have, in distant ages and countries, described the manners of people in similar circumstances, the reader has an opportunity of comparing their several descriptions, and from their agreement or disagreement is enabled to ascertain the credit that is due to them. According to this method of judging, which throws the veracity of the relater very much out of the question, we may be convinced of the truth of extraordinary facts, as well as of those that are more agreeable to our own experience. It may even be remarked, that in proportion to the singularity of any event, it is the more improbable that different persons, who design to impose upon the world, but who have no concert with each other, should agree in relating it. When to all this, we are able to add the reasons of those particular customs which have been uniformly reported, the evidence becomes as complete as the nature of the thing will admit. We cannot refuse our assent to such evidence, without falling into a degree of scepticism by which the credibility of all historical testimony would be in a great measure destroyed. This observation, it is hoped, will serve as an apology for the multiplicity of facts that are sometimes stated in confirmation of the following remarks. At the same time, from an apprehension of being tedious, the author has, on other occasions, selected only a few, from a greater number to the same purpose, that might easily have been procured.

Source: John Millar, *The Origin of the Distinction of Ranks*, Introduction, in William C. Lehmann, *John Millar of Glasgow*, Cambridge 1960, pp. 175–81

TWENTY-SIX

ADAM FERGUSON
The Origins of Civil Society

Although the concepts of improvement and of progress were much in the air during the Scottish Enlightenment, many of the leading thinkers were aware that in many areas progress has a price tag, as witness, for example, Adam Smith's discussion (see excerpt 22) of the threat to the spiritual well-being of the citizens that is posed by the extreme application of the principle of the division of labour. In a sense what is called progress often involves new cures for new ailments.

Adam Ferguson takes much the same measured view as Adam Smith of the way a forward step of social progress is so often accompanied by a backward step. Indeed Ferguson is sceptical as to whether there is progress at all if progress is to be measured in terms of an increasing disproportion of happiness over unhappiness in society. Each person accommodates himself to the conditions of his own society, and the fact that we can hardly, if at all, imagine ourselves happy in most positions in any earlier society does not amount to serious proof that people reared in those societies were not as happy, more or less, as we are in ours. As against our totally unscientific conjectures about how we would feel if we lived in a society so unlike our own that we have practically no relevant experience to support our conjectures, Ferguson proposes a scientific methodology. Whereof there are no records, there is no point in offering descriptions. Ferguson refers to 'boundless regions of ignorance', and among the unscientific descriptions that he has in his sights are those by Thomas Hobbes and Jean-Jacques Rousseau. He also has in his sights Hume, whose *Treatise of Human Nature* is declared in its subtitle to be 'an attempt to introduce the experimental method of reasoning into the moral sciences', but whose account of the formation of society is a conjectural piece concerning the natural appetite between the sexes. In other words Hume is attempting to read off the origins of society from a consideration of human nature as manifested in beings who are social to the core. His account therefore is every bit as conjectural and unscientific as are Hobbes's account of the state of nature as a state of war of every man against every man, and Rousseau's account of the noble savage who is corrupted by the encroachment of society. Both Hobbes and Rousseau looked back to a pre-social state of nature, while disagreeing utterly in their accounts of that state. Ferguson, noting that there is not a shred of evidence to support the claim that human beings ever did live, or even ever could have lived, in a pre-social state, restricts himself to the evidence, and the evidence suggests that we are by nature social animals, and therefore in living socially we live even now, no less than in previous ages, in a state of nature. Non-human animals also live in a state of nature, but there is this difference, that by an inner dynamic of human nature the human species has a great tendency to change, with successive generations adopting new social forms and new values, and no such thing can be said of other sorts of animal. A mouse or wolf 'attains', as Ferguson puts the point, 'in the compass of a single life, to all the perfection his nature can reach: but in the human kind, the species has a progress as well as the individual'. This progress is charted as a natural history of civil society, through the course of the *Essay*. In this excerpt Ferguson's scientific methodology is spelt out with great clarity.

A.B.

Of the Question Relating to the State of Nature

Natural productions are generally formed by degrees. Vegetables grow from a tender shoot, and animals from an infant state. The latter being destined to act, extend their operations as their powers increase: they exhibit a progress in what they perform, as well as in the faculties they acquire. This progress in the case of man is continued to a greater extent than in that of any other animal. Not only the individual advances from infancy to manhood, but the species itself from rudeness to civilization. Hence the supposed departure of mankind from the state of their nature; hence our conjectures and different opinions of what man must have been in the first age of his being. The poet, the historian, and the moralist, frequently allude to this ancient time; and under the emblems of gold, or of iron, represent a condition, and a manner of life, from which mankind have either degenerated, or on which they have greatly improved. On either supposition, the first state of our nature must have borne no resemblance to what men have exhibited in any subsequent period; historical monuments, even of the earliest date, are to be considered as novelties; and the most common establishments of human society are to be classed among the incroachments which fraud, oppression, or a busy invention, have made upon the reign of nature, by which the chief of our grievances or blessings were equally with-held.

Among the writers who have attempted to distinguish, in the human character, its original qualities, and to point out the limits between nature and art, some have represented mankind in their first condition, as possessed of mere animal sensibility, without any exercise of the faculties that render them superior to the brutes, without any political union, without any means of explaining their sentiments, and even without possessing any of the apprehensions and passions which the voice and the gesture are so well fitted to express. Others have made the state of nature to consist in perpetual wars, kindled by competition for dominion and interest, where every individual had a separate quarrel with his kind, and where the presence of a fellow-creature was the signal of battle.

The desire of laying the foundation of a favourite system, or a fond expectation, perhaps, that we may be able to penetrate the secrets of nature, to the very source of existence, have, on this subject, led to many fruitless inquiries, and given rise to many wild suppositions. Among the various qualities which mankind possess, we select one or a few particulars on which to establish a theory, and in framing our account of what man was in some imaginary state of nature, we overlook what he has always appeared within the reach of our own observation, and in the records of history.

In every other instance, however, the natural historian thinks himself obliged to collect facts, not to offer conjectures. When he treats of any particular species of animals, he supposes, that their present dispositions and instincts are the same they originally had, and that their present manner of life is a continuance of their first destination. He admits, that his knowledge of the material system of the world consists in a collection of facts, or at most, in general tenets derived from particular observations and experiments. It is only in what relates to himself, and in matters the most important, and the most easily known, that he substitutes hypothesis instead of reality, and confounds the provinces of imagination and reason, of poetry and science.

But without entering any farther on questions either in moral or physical subjects, relating to the manner or to the origin of our knowledge; without any disparagement to that subtilty which would analyze every sentiment, and trace every mode of being to its source; it may be safely affirmed, that the character of man, as he now exists, that the laws of this animal and intellectual system, on which his happiness now depends, deserve our principal study; and that general principles relating to this, or any other subject, are useful only so far as they are founded on just observation, and lead to the knowledge of important consequences, or so far as they enable us to act with success when we would apply either the intellectual or the physical powers of nature, to the great purposes of human life.

If both the earliest and the latest accounts collected from every quarter of the earth, represent mankind as assembled in troops and companies; and the individual always joined by affection to one party, while he is possibly opposed to another: employed in the exercise of recollection and foresight; inclined to communicate his own sentiments, and to be made acquainted with those of others; these facts must be admitted as the foundation of all our reasoning relative to man. His mixed disposition to friendship or enmity, his reason, his use of language and articulate sounds, like the shape and the erect position of his body, are to be considered as so many attributes of his nature: they are to be retained in his description, as the wing and the paw are in that of the eagle and the lion, and as different degrees of fierceness, vigilance, timidity, or speed, are made to occupy a place in the natural history of different animals.

If the question be put, What the mind of man could perform, when left to itself, and without the aid of any foreign direction? we are to look for our answer in the history of mankind. Particular experiments which have been found so useful in establishing the principles of other sciences, could probably, on this subject, teach us nothing important, or new: we are to take the history of every active being from his conduct in the situation to which he is formed, not from his appearance in any forced or uncommon condition; a wild man therefore, caught in the woods, where he had always lived apart from his species, is a singular instance, not a specimen of any general character. As the anatomy of an eye which had never received the impressions of light, or that of an ear which had never felt the impulse of sounds, would probably exhibit defects in the very structure of the organs themselves, arising from their not being applied to their proper functions; so any particular case of this sort would only shew in what degree the powers of apprehension and sentiment could exist where they had not been employed, and what would be the defects and imbecilities of a heart in which the emotions that pertain to society had never been felt.

Mankind are to be taken in groups, as they have always subsisted. The history of the individual is but a detail of the sentiments and thoughts he has entertained in the view of his species: and every experiment relative to this subject should be made with entire societies, not with single men. We have every reason, however, to believe, that in the case of such an experiment made, we shall suppose, with a colony of children transplanted from the nursery, and left to form a society apart, untaught, and undisciplined, we should only have the same things repeated, which, in so many different parts of the earth, have been transacted already. The members of our little society would feed and sleep, would herd together and play, would have a language of their own, would quarrel and divide, would be to one another the most important objects of the scene, and, in the ardour of their friendships and competitions, would overlook their personal danger, and suspend the care of their self-preservation. Has not the human race been planted like the colony in question? Who has directed their course? whose instruction have they heard? or whose example have they followed?

Nature, therefore, we shall presume, having given to every animal its mode of existence, its dispositions and manner of life, has dealt equally with those of the human race; and the natural historian who would collect the properties of this species, may fill up every article now, as well as he could have done in any former age. Yet one property by which man is distinguished, has been sometimes overlooked in the account of his nature, or has only served to mislead our attention. In other classes of animals, the individual advances from infancy to age or maturity; and he attains, in the compass of a single life, to all the perfection his nature can reach: but, in the human kind, the species has a progress as well as the individual; they build in every subsequent age on foundations formerly laid; and, in a succession of years, tend to a perfection in the application of their faculties, to which the aid of long experience is required, and to which many generations must have combined their endeavours. We observe the progress they have made; we distinctly enumerate many of its steps; we can trace them back to a distant antiquity; of which no record remains, nor any monument is preserved, to inform us what were the openings of this wonderful scene. The consequence is, that instead of attending to the character of our species, where the particulars are vouched by the surest authority, we endeavour to trace it through ages and scenes unknown; and, instead of supposing that the beginning of our story was nearly of a piece with the sequel, we think ourselves warranted to reject every circumstance of our present condition and frame, as adventitious, and foreign to our nature. The progress of mankind from a supposed state of animal sensibility, to the attainment of reason, to the use of language, and to the habit of society, has been accordingly painted with a force of imagination, and its steps have been marked with a boldness of invention, that would tempt us to admit, among the materials of history, the suggestions of fancy, and to receive, perhaps, as the model of our nature in its original state, some of the animals whose shape has the greatest resemblance to ours.

It would be ridiculous to affirm, as a discovery, that the species of the horse was probably never the same with that of the lion; yet, in opposition to what has dropped from the pens of eminent writers, we are obliged to observe, that men have always appeared among animals a distinct and a superior race; that neither the possession of similar organs, nor the approximation of shape, nor the use of the hand, nor the continued intercourse with this sovereign artist, has enabled any other species to blend their nature or their inventions with his; that in his rudest state, he is found to be above them; and in his greatest degeneracy, never descends to their level. He is, in short, a man in every condition; and we can learn nothing of his nature from the analogy of other animals. If we would know him, we must attend to himself, to the course of his life, and the tenor of his conduct. With him the society appears to be as old as the individual, and the use of the tongue as universal as that of the hand or the foot. If there was a time in which he had his acquaintance with his own species to make, and his faculties to acquire, it is a time of which we have no record, and in relation to which our opinions can serve no purpose, and are supported by no evidence.

We are often tempted into these boundless regions of ignorance or conjecture, by a fancy which delights in creating rather than in merely retaining the forms which are presented before it: we are the dupes of a subtilty, which promises to supply every defect of our knowledge, and, by filling up a few blanks in the story of nature, pretends to conduct our apprehension nearer to the source of existence. On the credit of a few observations, we are apt to presume, that the secret may soon be laid open, and that what is termed *wisdom* in nature, may be referred to the operation of physical powers. We forget that physical powers, employed in succession, and combined to a salutary purpose, constitute those very proofs of design from which we infer the existence of God; and that this truth being once admitted, we are no longer to search for the source of existence; we can only collect the laws which the author of nature has established; and in our latest as well as our earliest discoveries, only come to perceive a mode of creation or providence before unknown.

We speak of art as distinguished from nature; but art itself is natural to man. He is in some measure the artificer of his own frame, as well as his fortune, and is destined, from the first age of his being, to invent and contrive. He applies the same talents to a variety of purposes, and acts nearly the same part in very different scenes. He would be always improving on his subject, and he carries this intention where-ever he moves, through the streets of the populous city, or the wilds of the forest. While he appears equally fitted to every condition, he is upon this account unable to settle in any. At once obstinate and fickle, he complains of innovations, and is never sated with novelty. He is perpetually busied in reformations, and is continually wedded to his errors. If he dwell in a cave, he would improve it into a cottage; if he has already built, he would still build to a greater extent. But he does not propose to make rapid and hasty transitions; his steps are progressive and slow; and his force, like the power of a spring, silently presses on every resistance; an effect is sometimes produced before the cause is perceived; and with all his talent for projects, his work is often accomplished before the plan is devised. It appears, perhaps, equally difficult to retard or to quicken his pace; if the projector complain he is tardy, the moralist thinks him unstable; and whether his motions be rapid or slow, the scenes of human affairs perpetually change in his management: his emblem is a passing stream, not a stagnating pool. We may desire to direct his love of improvement to its proper object, we may wish for stability of conduct; but we mistake human nature, if we wish for a termination of labour, or a scene of repose.

The occupations of men, in every condition, bespeak their freedom of choice, their various opinions, and the multiplicity of wants by which they are urged: but they enjoy, or endure, with a sensibility, or a phlegm, which are nearly the same in every situation. They possess the shores of the Caspian, or the Atlantic, by a different tenure, but with equal ease. On the one they are fixed to the soil, and seem to be formed for settlement, and the accommodation of cities: The names they bestow on a nation, and on its territory, are the same. On the other they are mere animals of passage, prepared to roam on the face of the earth, and with their herds, in search of new pasture and favourable seasons, to follow the sun in his annual course.

Man finds his lodgment alike in the cave, the cottage, and the palace; and his subsistence equally in the woods, in the dairy, or the farm. He assumes the distinction of titles, equipage, and dress; he devises regular systems of government, and a complicated body of laws: or, naked in the woods, has no badge of superiority but the strength of his limbs and the sagacity of his mind; no rule of conduct but choice; no tie with his fellow-creatures but affection, the love of company, and the desire of safety. Capable of a great variety of arts, yet dependent on none in particular for the preservation of his being; to whatever length he has carried his artifice, there he seems to enjoy the conveniencies that suit his nature, and to have found the condition to which he is destined. The tree which an American, on the banks of the Oroonoko, has chosen to climb for the retreat, and the lodgement of his family, is to him a convenient dwelling. The sopha, the vaulted dome, and the colonade, do not more effectually content their native inhabitant.

If we are asked therefore, Where the state of nature is to be found? we may answer, It is here; and it matters not whether we are understood to speak in the island of Great Britain, at the Cape of Good Hope, or the Straits of Magellan. While this active being is in the train of employing his talents, and of operating on the subjects around him, all situations are equally natural. If we are told, That vice, at least, is contrary to nature; we may answer, It is worse; it is folly and wretchedness. But if nature is only opposed to art, in what situation of the human race are the footsteps of art unknown? In the condition of the savage, as well as in that of the citizen, are many proofs of human invention; and in either is not any permanent station, but a mere stage through which this travelling being is destined to pass. If the palace be unnatural, the cottage is so no less; and the highest refinements of political and moral apprehension, are not more artificial in their kind, than the first operations of sentiment and reason.

If we admit that man is susceptible of improvement, and has in himself a principle of progression, and a desire of perfection, it appears improper to say, that he has quitted the state of his nature, when he has begun to proceed; or that he finds a station for which he was not intended, while, like other animals, he only follows the disposition, and employs the powers that nature has given.

The latest efforts of human invention are but a continuation of certain devices which were practised in the earliest ages of the world, and in the rudest state of mankind. What the savage projects, or observes, in the forest, are the steps which led nations, more advanced, from the architecture of the cottage to that of the palace, and conducted the human mind from the perceptions of sense, to the general conclusions of science.

Acknowledged defects are to man in every condition matter of dislike. Ignorance and imbecility are objects of contempt: penetration and conduct give eminence, and procure esteem. Whither should his feelings and apprehensions on these subjects lead him? To a progress, no doubt, in which the savage, as well as the philosopher, is engaged; in which they have made different advances, but in which their ends are the same. The admiration Cicero entertained for literature, eloquence, and civil accomplishments, was not more real than that of a Scythian for such a measure of similar endowments as his own apprehension could reach. 'Were I to boast,' says a Tartar prince,[1] 'it would be of that wisdom I have received from God. For as, on the one hand, I yield to none in the conduct of war, in the disposition of armies, whether of horse or of foot, and in directing the movements of great or small bodies; so, on the other, I have my talent in writing, inferior perhaps only to those who inhabit the great cities of Persia or India. Of other nations, unknown to me, I do not speak.'

Man may mistake the objects of his pursuit; he may misapply his industry, and misplace his improvements. If under a sense of such possible errors, he would find a standard by which to judge of his own proceedings, and arrive at the best state of his nature, he cannot find it perhaps in the practice of any individual, or of any nation whatever; not even in the sense of the majority, or the prevailing opinion of his kind. He must look for it in the best conceptions of his understanding, in the best movements of his heart; he must thence discover what is the perfection and the happiness of which he is capable. He will find, on the scrutiny, that the proper state of his nature, taken in this sense, is not a condition from which mankind are for ever removed, but one to which they may now attain; not prior to the exercise of their faculties, but procured by their just application.

Of all the terms that we employ in treating of human affairs, those of *natural* and *unnatural* are the least determinate in their meaning. Opposed to affectation, forwardness, or any other defect of the temper of character, the natural is an epithet of praise; but employed to specify a conduct which proceeds from the nature of man, can serve to distinguish nothing: for all the actions of men are equally the result of their nature. At most, this language can only refer to the general and prevailing sense or practice of mankind; and the purpose of every important inquiry on this subject may be served by the use of a language equally familiar and more precise. What is just, or unjust? What is happy, or wretched, in the manners of men? What, in their various situations, is favourable or adverse to their amiable qualities? are questions to which we may expect a satisfactory answer; and whatever may have been the original state of our species, it is of more importance to know the condition to which we ourselves should aspire, than that which our ancestors may be supposed to have left.

Source: Adam Ferguson, *An Essay on the History of Civil Society*, ed. D. Forbes, Edinburgh 1966, part 1, section 1

TWENTY-SEVEN

DAVID HUME
Of the First Principles of Government

In speaking about 'the first principles of government' Hume has in mind the explanation for the fact, which he considers a surprising fact, that the many allow themselves to be governed by the few. Force must always be on the side of the many; why then do they allow themselves to be governed by the few? The answer, that they do so because they think the government is entitled to their loyalty, prompts the question as to why they think this. There were two common answers to this latter question. One, associated with toryism, is that allegiance to government is owed in virtue of the governor's divine right to govern. This is not an answer that could appeal to Hume, since it immediately prompts questions about the existence and nature of God, and about the veracity of alleged signs of divine right. Who knows what the signs are, and what evidence can be provided in support of the claim to speak with authority on this matter?

On the other hand, the characteristic answer of whiggism is in terms of a social contract, an act by which a number of individuals willed a government into existence where previously there had been no government. This answer however invokes something, an original contract, whose existence cannot be verified, and whose existence could not, even if verified, explain how it could have any force for subsequent generations who were, in the nature of the case, not party to that original contract. Furthermore a point arises concerning why the original contractors should give their allegiance to a government if the government is not already in place and already due their allegiance. But the question we are looking to answer concerns precisely why any government should be considered as due allegiance.

Hume answers his basic question, that concerning the willingness of the many to be governed by the few, in terms of two opinions. One opinion concerns interest, particularly the interest in the general advantage to be gained by having that government in position, and the other opinion concerns right, in particular the right to power and to property. Hume has distinctive things to say here on the relation between right to power and to property. The 'noted author' invoked by Hume, who 'has made property the foundation of all government', is probably James Harrinton (1611–77) who argued that balance of power is dependent on balance of property. Hume however thinks that this claim is contradicted by the historical facts, such as that in 1701 the people sided with William III against the Commons, though the balance of property was overwhelmingly on the side of the Commons.

A.B.

Of the First Principles of Government

Nothing appears more surprizing to those, who consider human affairs with a philosophical eye, than the easiness with which the many are governed by the few; and the implicit submission, with which men resign their own sentiments and passions to those of their rulers. When we enquire by what means this wonder is effected, we shall find, that, as Force is always on the side of the governed, the governors have nothing to support them but opinion. It is therefore, on opinion only that government is founded; and this maxim extends to the most despotic and most military governments, as well as to the most free and most popular. The soldan of Egypt, or the emperor of Rome, might drive his harmless subjects, like brute beasts, against their sentiments and inclination: But he must, at least, have led his *mamalukes*, or *prætorian bands*, like men, by their opinion.

Opinion is of two kinds, to wit, opinion of interest, and opinion of right. By opinion of interest, I chiefly understand the sense of the general advantage which is reaped from government; together with the persuasion, that the particular government, which is established, is equally advantageous with any other that could easily be settled. When this opinion prevails among the generality of a state, or among those who have the force in their hands, it gives great security to any government.

Right is of two kinds, right to Power and right to Property. What prevalence opinion of the first kind has over mankind, may easily be understood, by observing the attachment which all nations have to their ancient government, and even to those names, which have had the sanction of antiquity. Antiquity always begets the opinion of right; and whatever disadvantageous sentiments we may entertain of mankind, they are always found to be prodigal both of blood and treasure in the maintenance of public justice. There is, indeed, no particular, in which, at first sight, there may appear a greater contradiction in the frame of the human mind than the present. When men act in a faction, they are apt, without shame or remorse, to neglect all the ties of honour and morality, in order to serve their party; and yet, when a faction is formed upon a point of right or principle, there is no occasion, where men discover a greater obstinacy, and a more determined sense of justice and equity. The same social disposition of mankind is the cause of these contradictory appearances.

It is sufficiently understood, that the opinion of right to property is of moment in all matters of government. A noted author has made property the foundation of all government; and most of our political writers seem inclined to follow him in that particular. This is carrying the matter too far; but still it must be owned, that the opinion of right to property has a great influence in this subject.

Upon these three opinions, therefore, of public *interest*, of *right to power*, and of *right to property*, are all governments founded, and all authority of the few over the many. There are indeed other principles, which add force to these, and determine, limit, or alter their operation; such as *self-interest*, *fear*, and *affection*: But still we may assert, that these other principles can have no influence alone, but suppose the antecedent influence of those opinions above-mentioned. They are, therefore, to be esteemed the secondary, not the original principles of government.

For, *first*, as to *self-interest*, by which I mean the expectation of particular rewards, distinct from the general protection which we receive from government, it is evident that the magistrate's authority must be antecedently established, at least be hoped for, in order to produce this expectation. The prospect of reward may augment his authority with regard to some particular persons; but can never give birth to it, with regard to the public. Men naturally look for the greatest favours from their friends and acquaintance; and therefore, the hopes of any considerable number of the state would never center in any particular set of men, if these men had no other title to magistracy, and had no separate influence over the opinions of mankind. The same observation may be extended to the other two principles of *fear* and *affection*. No man would have any reason to *fear* the fury of a tyrant, if he had no authority over any but from fear; since, as a single man, his bodily force can reach but a small way, and all the farther power he possesses must be founded either on our own opinion, or on the presumed opinion of others. And though *affection* to wisdom and virtue in a *sovereign* extends very far, and has great influence; yet he must antecedently be supposed invested with a public character, otherwise the public esteem will serve him in no stead, nor will his virtue have any influence beyond a narrow sphere.

A Government may endure for several ages, though the balance of power, and the balance of property do not coincide. This chiefly happens, where any rank or order of the state has acquired a large share in the property; but from the original constitution of the government, has no share in the power. Under what pretence would any individual of that order assume authority in public affairs? As men are commonly much attached to their ancient government, it is not to be expected, that the public would ever favour such usurpations. But where the original constitution allows any share of power, though small, to an order of men, who possess a large share of the property, it is easy for them gradually to stretch their authority, and bring the balance of power to coincide with that of property. This has been the case with the house of commons in England.

Most writers, that have treated of the British government, have supposed, that, as the lower house represents all the commons of Great Britain, its weight in the scale is proportioned to the property and power of all whom it represents. But this principle must not be received as absolutely true. For though the people are apt to attach themselves more to the house of commons, than to any other member of the constitution; that house being chosen by them as their representatives, and as the public guardians of their liberty; yet are there instances where the house, even when in opposition to the crown, has not been followed by the people; as we may particularly observe of the *tory* house of commons in the reign of king William. Were the members obliged to receive instructions from their constituents, like the Dutch deputies, this would entirely alter the case; and if such immense power and riches, as those of all the commons of Great Britain, were brought into the scale, it is not easy to conceive, that the crown could either influence that multitude of people, or withstand that overbalance of property. It is true, the crown has great influence over the collective body in the elections of members; but were this influence, which at present is only exerted once in seven years, to be employed in bringing over the people to every vote, it would soon be wasted; and no skill, popularity, or revenue, could support it. I must, therefore, be of opinion, that an alteration in this particular would introduce a total alteration in our government, and would soon reduce it to a pure republic; and, perhaps, to a republic of no inconvenient form. For though the people, collected in a body like the Roman tribes, be quite unfit for government, yet when dispersed in small bodies, they are more susceptible both of reason and order; the force of popular currents and tides is, in a great measure, broken; and the public interest may be pursued with some method and constancy. But it is needless to reason any farther concerning a form of government, which is never likely to have place in Great Britain, and which seems not to be the aim of any party amongst us. Let us cherish and improve our ancient government as much as possible, without encouraging a passion for such dangerous novelties.

Source: David Hume, 'Of the first principles of government', in *Essays Moral, Political and Literary*, ed. Eugene F. Miller, Indianapolis 1987, essay 4, pp. 32–6

TWENTY-EIGHT

DAVID HUME
Of the Origin of Government

Justice is necessary for the maintenance of peace and order, and peace and order are necessary for the maintenance of civil society. There can therefore be few things more important to us than justice, which prompts a question as to why, utterly dependent as we are upon justice, we are ever unjust. The answer which Hume gives in this, the last of his essays, seems obvious enough, namely that we are a frail and perverse species; and so also his further point seems obvious enough, that as we need the duty of justice to be established among human beings for the sake of civil society, so also we need the establishment of a further duty, of obedience of the law, for the sake of justice. For obedience to be established we need government. Hume speculates that government arose first in war time with the ascendancy of a person of special personal qualities, and that obedience gradually became established by the sheer habituation of the practice of obedience; we simply became accustomed to living under those constraints. In focusing upon the role of custom or habit, Hume draws into his discussion one of the main elements in his account of human nature.

But is there not a problem posed by the development of government, namely its encroachment upon our freedom? Hume's answer is that there is not. Admittedly there is a sense in which each new law constitutes an additional restriction on our behaviour. On the other hand, in the absence of the authority of government there can be no civil society. And in the absence of civil society all those kinds of act that we think of as expressing our freedom would be quite impossible. A balance has to be struck between authority and freedom, but for Hume there is no doubt that it is authority that has primacy.

One crucial point regarding the relation between freedom and the maintenance of civil society concerns the rule of law. Hume stresses the importance of the universality of the law. It is the law not only of the subjects but also of the legislators; all are equally obliged to obey it. What is at stake is the degree of our freedom; random acts by the government are an obstacle to the development of a free society. It is not sufficient that the legislators obey the law; the citizens must be able to find out whether or not the legislators are being obedient. Only in such conditions is there the constitutional basis for the kind of civic stability that Hume especially prized.

A.B.

Of the Origin of Government

Man, born in a family, is compelled to maintain society, from necessity, from natural inclination, and from habit. The same creature, in his farther progress, is engaged to establish political society, in order to administer justice; without which there can be no peace among them, nor safety, nor mutual intercourse. We are, therefore, to look upon all the vast apparatus of our government, as having ultimately no other object or purpose but the distribution of justice, or, in other words, the support of the twelve judges. Kings and parliaments, fleets and armies, officers of the court and revenue, ambassadors, ministers, and privy-counsellors, are all subordinate in their end to this part of administration. Even the clergy, as their duty leads them to inculcate morality, may justly be thought, so far as regards this world, to have no other useful object of their institution.

All men are sensible of the necessity of justice to maintain peace and order; and all men are sensible of the necessity of peace and order for the maintenance of society. Yet, notwithstanding this strong and obvious necessity, such is the frailty or perverseness of our nature! it is impossible to keep men, faithfully and unerringly, in the paths of justice. Some extraordinary circumstances may happen, in which a man finds his interests to be more promoted by fraud or rapine, than hurt by the breach which his injustice makes in the social union. But much more frequently, he is seduced from his great and important, but distant interests, by the allurement of present, though often very frivolous temptations. This great weakness is incurable in human nature.

Men must, therefore, endeavour to palliate what they cannot cure. They must institute some persons, under the appellation of magistrates, whose peculiar office it is, to point out the decrees of equity, to punish transgressors, to correct fraud and violence, and to oblige men, however reluctant, to consult their own real and permanent interests. In a word, Obedience is a new duty which must be invented to support that of Justice; and the tyes of equity must be corroborated by those of allegiance.

But still, viewing matters in an abstract light, it may be thought, that nothing is gained by this alliance, and that the factitious duty of obedience, from its very nature, lays as feeble a hold of the human mind, as the primitive and natural duty of justice. Peculiar interests and present temptations may overcome the one as well as the other. They are equally exposed to the same inconvenience. And the man, who is inclined to be a bad neighbour, must be led by the same motives, well or ill understood, to be a bad citizen and subject. Not to mention, that the magistrate himself may often be negligent, or partial, or unjust in his administration.

Experience, however, proves, that there is a great difference between the cases. Order in society, we find, is much better maintained by means of government; and our duty to the magistrate is more strictly guarded by the principles of human nature, than our duty to our fellow-citizens. The love of dominion is so strong in the breast of man, that many, not only submit to, but court all the dangers, and fatigues, and cares of government; and men, once raised to that station, though often led astray by private passions, find, in ordinary cases, a visible interest in the impartial administration of justice. The persons, who first attain this distinction by the consent, tacit or express, of the people, must be endowed with superior personal qualities of valour, force, integrity, or prudence, which command respect and confidence: and after government is established, a regard to birth, rank, and station has a mighty influence over men, and enforces the decrees of the magistrate. The prince or leader exclaims against every disorder, which disturbs his society. He summons all his partizans and all men of probity to aid him in correcting and redressing it: and he is readily followed by all indifferent persons in the execution of his office. He soon acquires the power of rewarding these services; and in the progress of society, he establishes subordinate ministers and often a military force, who find an immediate and a visible interest, in supporting his authority. Habit soon consolidates what other principles of human nature had imperfectly founded; and men, once accustomed to obedience, never think of departing from that path, in which they and their ancestors have constantly trod, and to which they are confined by so many urgent and visible motives.

But though this progress of human affairs may appear certain and inevitable, and though the support which allegiance brings to justice, be founded on obvious principles of human nature, it cannot be expected that men should beforehand be able to discover them, or foresee their operation. Government commences more casually and more imperfectly. It is probable, that the first ascendant of one man over multitudes begun during a state of war; where the superiority of courage and of genius discovers itself most visibly, where unanimity and concert are most requisite, and where the pernicious effects of disorder are most sensibly felt. The long continuance of that state, an incident common among savage tribes, enured the people to submission; and if the chieftain possessed as much equity as prudence and valour, he became, even during peace, the arbiter of all differences, and could gradually, by a mixture of force and consent, establish his authority. The benefit sensibly felt from his influence, made it be cherished by the people, at least by the peaceable and well disposed among them; and if his son enjoyed the same good qualities, government advanced the sooner to maturity and perfection; but was still in a feeble state, till the farther progress of improvement procured the magistrate a revenue, and enabled him to bestow rewards on the several instruments of his administration, and to inflict punishments on the refractory and disobedient. Before that period, each exertion of his influence must have been particular, and founded on the peculiar circumstances of the case. After it, submission was no longer a matter of choice in the bulk of the community, but was rigorously exacted by the authority of the supreme magistrate.

In all governments, there is a perpetual intestine struggle, open or secret, between Authority and Liberty; and neither of them can ever absolutely prevail in the contest. A great sacrifice of liberty must necessarily be made in every government; yet even the authority, which confines liberty, can never, and perhaps ought never, in any constitution, to become quite entire and uncontroulable. The sultan is master of the life and fortune of any individual; but will not be permitted to impose new taxes on his subjects: a French monarch can impose taxes at pleasure; but would find it dangerous to attempt the lives and fortunes of individuals. Religion also, in most countries, is commonly found to be a very intractable principle; and other principles or prejudices frequently resist all the authority of the civil magistrate; whose power, being founded on opinion, can never subvert other opinions, equally rooted with that of his title to dominion. The government, which, in common appellation, receives the appellation of free, is that which admits of a partition of power among several members, whose united authority is no less, or is commonly greater than that of any monarch; but who, in the usual course of administration, must act by general and equal laws, that are previously known to all the members and to all their subjects. In this sense, it must be owned, that liberty is the perfection of civil society; but still authority must be acknowledged essential to its very existence: and in those contests, which so often take place between the one and the other, the latter may, on that account, challenge the preference. Unless perhaps one may say (and it may be said with some reason) that a circumstance, which is essential to the existence of civil society, must always support itself, and needs be guarded with less jealousy, than one that contributes only to its perfection, which the indolence of men is so apt to neglect, or their ignorance to overlook.

Source: David Hume, 'Of the origin of government', in *Essays Moral, Political and Literary*, ed. Eugene F. Miller, Indianapolis 1987, essay 5, pp. 37–41

TWENTY-NINE

HENRY HOME, LORD KAMES
The Rise and Fall of Patriotism

Patriotism was a common topic in the Scottish Enlightenment. The subject was no doubt particularly likely to be on people's minds in light of the need to define their position in relation to Jacobitism. Of course one could be anti-Jacobite and a patriotic Scot, and many were, including many who sought to remove all traces of Scotticisms from their writings. Patriotism was considered a virtue, love not of oneself but of one's country, and there is therefore no question here of taking it, in the manner of Thomas Hobbes, as derivative upon selfishness, so that selfish interests demand of us that we take seriously the public good when acting.

Patriotism is not merely a matter of acting in the public interest; it is classed by Kames as a passion, love of one's country for its own sake. Patriotism does of course also imply a disposition to act, but the motive is love of country, never of self. It therefore has a tendency to annihilate selfish concerns, and since selfishness was seen as the great obstacle to morally sound behaviour, it is not surprising to find Kames saying of patriotism: 'Wherever it prevails, the morals of the people are found to be pure and correct.'

Kames employs the concept of four stages of society, namely, the stages of hunting, pasturing, agriculture and finally commerce. It is only in the third stage that patriotism can arise, for the people have to have stopped wandering, and to have settled in communities. At that stage therefore they occupy territory that collectively they call their own. Once patriotism is in place it is a bulwark against two reprehensible states which are in a sense mutually opposed. First is despotism, which seeks to deny people's civil liberties, and the other is licentiousness, in which people claim too much liberty. The danger of the licentious person is that he tends to encroach upon the liberties of other people. Licentiousness is therefore indifferent to the public or common interest, and is also a natural enemy in relation to patriotism.

Karnes had a lively interest in the concepts of improvement and progress, and his sketch on the rise and fall of patriotism makes rather bleak reading in relation to those concepts. A nation's prosperity is never to be taken for granted. Kames is particularly complimentary about the Dutch: 'Such was the inherent virtue of that people that their patriotism resisted very long the contagion of wealth.' But even they eventually caved in. An important conclusion of this tale is that progress on a national scale, whether economic or, more importantly, moral has always to be fought for. The fight is uphill, and on one obvious reading of Kames's analysis all the cards are stacked against the nation. Kames thinks it will be defeated. Hence his comment after a brief survey of fallen great powers: 'Such is the rise and fall of patriotism among the nations mentioned; and such will be its rise and fall among all nations in like circumstances.' Kames's whole analysis is shot through with pessimism.

A.B.

The Rise and Fall of Patriotism

The members of a tribe, in their original state of hunting and fishing, being little united but by a common language, have no notion of a patria; and scarce any notion of society, unless when they join in an expedition against an enemy, or against wild beasts. The shepherd-state, where flocks and herds are possessed in common, gives a clear notion of a common interest; but still none of a patria. The sense of a patria begins to unfold itself, when a people leave off wandering, to settle upon a territory which they call their own. Agriculture connects them together; and government still more: they become fellow-citizens; and the territory is termed the patria of every person born in it. It is so ordered by Providence, that a man's country, and his countrymen, are to him in conjunction an object of a peculiar affection, termed amor patriæ, or patriotism: an affection that rises high among a people intimately connected by regular government, by husbandry, by commerce, and by a common interest. 'Cari sunt parentes, cari liberi, propinqui, familiares; sed omnes omnium caritates patria una complexa est: pro qua quis bonus dubitet mortem oppetere.'[1]

Social passions and affections, beside being greatly more agreeable than selfish, are those only which command our esteem. Patriotism stands at the head of social affections; and stands so high in our esteem, that no actions but what proceed from it are termed grand or heroic. When that affection appears so agreeable in contemplation; how sweet, how elevating, must it be in those whom it inspires! Like vigorous health, it beats constantly with an equal pulse: like the vestal fire, it never is extinguished. No source of enjoyment is more plentiful than patriotism, where it is the ruling passion: it triumphs over every selfish motive, and is a firm support to every virtue. In fact, wherever it prevails, the morals of the people are found to be pure and correct.

These are illustrious effects of patriotism with respect to private happiness and virtue; and yet its effects with respect to the public are still more illustrious. A nation in no other period of its progress

[1] 'Our parents are dear to us; so are our children,
our relations, and our friends: all these our country
comprehends; and shall we fear to die for our country?'

is so flourishing, as when patriotism is the ruling passion of every member: during that period, it is invincible. Atheneus remarks, that the Athenians were the only people in the world, who, though clothed in purple, put formidable armies to flight at Marathon, Salamine, and Platea. But at that period patriotism was their ruling passion; and success attended them in every undertaking. Where patriotism rules, men do wonders, whatever garb they wear. The fall of Saguntum is a grand scene; a people exerting the utmost powers of nature, in defence of their country. The city was indeed destroyed; but the citizens were not subdued. The last effort of the remaining heroes was, to burn themselves, with their wives and children, in one great funeral pile. Numantia affords a scene not less grand. The citizens, such as were able to bear arms, did not exceed 8000; and yet braved all the efforts of 60,000 disciplined soldiers commanded by Scipio Nasica. So high was their character for intrepidity, that even when but a few of them were left alive, the Romans durst not attempt to storm the town. And they stood firm till, subdued by famine, they were no longer able to crawl. While the Portuguese were eminent for patriotism, Lopez Carasco, one of their sea-captains, in a single ship with but forty men, stumbled upon the King of Achin's fleet of twenty gallies, as many junks, and a multitude of small vessels. Resolute to perish rather than yield, he maintained the fight for three days, till his ship was pierced through and through with cannon shot, and not a single man left unwounded. And yet, after all, the King's fleet found it convenient to sheer off.

Patriotism at the same time is the great bulwark of civil liberty: equally abhorrent of despotism on the one hand, and of licentiousness on the other. While the despotic government of the Tudor family subsisted, the English were too much depressed to have any affection for their country. But when manufactures and commerce began to flourish in the latter end of Elizabeth's reign, a national spirit broke forth, and patriotism made some figure. That change of disposition was perhaps the chief cause, though not the most visible, of the national struggles for liberty, which were frequent during the government of the Stewart family, and which ended in a free government at the Revolution.

Patriotism is too much cramped in a very small state, and too much relaxed in an extensive monarchy. But that topic has already been discussed in the first sketch of this book.

Patriotism is enflamed by a struggle for liberty, by a civil war, by resisting a potent invader, or by any incident that forcibly draws the members of a state into strict union for their common interest. The resolute opposition of the seven provinces to Philip II. of Spain, in the cause of liberty, is an illustrious instance of the patriotic spirit rising to a degree of enthusiasm. Patriotism, roused among the Corsicans by the oppression of the Genoese, exerted itself upon every proper object. Even during the heat of the war, they erected an university for arts and sciences, a national bank, and a national library; improvements that would not have been thought of in their torpid state. Alas! they have fallen a victim to thirst of power, not to superior valour. Had Providence favoured them with success, their figure would have been considerable in peace as in war.

But violent commotions cannot be perpetual: one party prevails, and prosperity follows. What effect may this have on patriotism? I answer, that nothing is more animating than success after a violent struggle: a nation in that state resembles a comet, which in passing near the sun, has been much heated, and continues full of motion. Patriotism made a capital figure among the Athenians, when they became a free people, after expelling the tyrant Pisistratus. Every man exerted himself for his country: every man endeavoured to excel those who went before him: and hence a Miltiades, an Aristides, a Themistocles, names that for ever will figure in the annals of time. While the Roman republic was confined within narrow bounds, austerity of manners, and disinterested love to their country, formed the national character. The elevation of the Patricians above the Plebeians, a source of endless discord, was at last remedied by placing all the citizens upon a level. This signal revolution excited an animating emulation between the Patricians and Plebeians; the former, by heroic actions, labouring to maintain their superiority; the latter straining every nerve to equal them: the republic never at any other period produced so great men in the art of war.

But such variety there is in human affairs, that though men are indebted to emulation for their heroic actions, yet actions of that kind never fail to suppress emulation in those who follow. An observation is made above, that nothing is more fatal to the progress of an art, than a person of superior genius, who damps emulation in others: witness the celebrated Newton, to whom the decay of mathematical knowledge in Britain is justly attributed. The observation holds equally with respect to action. Those actions only that flow from patriotism are deemed grand and heroic; and such actions, above all others, rouse a national spirit. But beware of a Newton in heroism: instead of exciting emulation, he will damp it: despair to equal the great men who are the admiration of all men, puts an end to emulation. After the illustrious achievements of Miltiades, and after the eminent patriotism of Aristides, we hear no more in Greece of emulation or of patriotism. Pericles was a man of parts, but he sacrificed Athens to his ambition. The Athenians sunk lower and lower under the Archons, who had neither parts nor patriotism; and were reduced at last to slavery, first by the Macedonians, and next by the Romans. The Romans run the same course, from the highest exertions of patriotic emulation, down to the most abject selfishness and effeminacy.

And this leads to other causes that extinguish patriotism, or relax it. Factious disorders in a state never fail to relax it; for there the citizen is lost, and every person is beheld in the narrow view of a friend or an enemy. In the contests between the Patricians and Plebeians of Rome, the public was totally disregarded: the Plebeians could have no heart-affection for a country where they were oppressed; and the Patricians might be fond of their own order, but they could not sincerely love their country, while they were enemies to the bulk of their countrymen. Patriotism did not shine forth in Rome, till all equally became citizens.

To support patriotism, it is necessary that a people be in a train of prosperity: when a nation becomes stationary, patriotism subsides. The ancient Romans upon a small foundation erected a great empire; so great indeed, that it fell to pieces by its unwieldiness. But the plurality of nations, whether from their situation, from the temper of their people, or from the nature of their government, are confined within narrower limits; beyond which their utmost exertions avail little, unless they happen to be extraordinary favourites of fortune. When a nation becomes thus stationary, its pushing genius is at an end: its plan is to preserve, not to acquire: the members, even without any example of heroism to damp emulation, are infected with the languid tone of the state: patriotism subsides; and we hear no more of bold or heroic actions. The Venetians are a pregnant instance of the observation. Their trade with Aleppo and Alexandria did for centuries introduce into Europe the commodities of Syria, Egypt, Arabia, Persia, and India. The cities of Nuremberg and Augsburgh in particular, were supplied from Venice with these commodities; and by that traffick became populous and opulent. Venice, in a word, was for centuries the capital trading town of Europe, and powerful above all its neighbours, both at sea and land. A passage to the East Indies by the Cape of Good Hope was indeed an animating discovery to the Portuguese; but it did not entitle them to exclude the Venetians. The greater distance of Venice from the Cape, a trifle in itself, is more than balanced by its proximity to Greece, Germany, Hungary, Poland, and to the rest of Italy. But the Portuguese at that period were in the spring of prosperity; and patriotism envigorated them to make durable establishments on the Indian coast, overpowering every nation that stood in opposition. The Venetians, on the contrary, being a nation of merchants, and having been long successful in commerce, were become stationary, and unqualified for bold adventures. Being cut out of their wonted commerce to India, and not having resolution to carry on commerce in a new channel, they sunk under the good fortune of their rivals, and abandoned the trade altogether.

No cause hitherto mentioned hath such influence in depressing patriotism, as inequality of rank and of riches in an opulent monarchy. A continual influx of wealth into the capital, generates show, luxury, avarice, which are all selfish vices; and selfishness, enslaving the mind, eradicates every fibre of patriotism. Asiatic luxury, flowing into Rome in a plentiful stream, produced an universal corruption of manners, and metamorphosed into voluptuousness the warlike genius of that great city. The dominions of Rome were now too extensive for a republican government, and its generals too powerful to be disinterested. Passion for glory wore out of fashion, as austerity of manners had done formerly: power and riches were now the only objects of ambition; virtue seemed a farce; honour, a chimera; and fame, mere vanity: every Roman, abandoning himself to sensuality, flattered himself, that he, more wise than his forefathers, was pursuing the cunning road to happiness. Corruption and venality became general, and maintained their usurpation in the provinces as well as in the capital, without ever losing a foot of ground. Pyrrhus attempted by presents to corrupt the Roman senators, but made not the slightest impression. Deplorable was the change of manners in the days of Jugurtha: – 'Pity it is,' said he, 'that no man is so opulent as to purchase a people so willing to be sold.' Cicero, mentioning an oracle of Apollo, that Sparta would never be destroyed but by avarice, justly observes, that the prediction holds in every nation as well as in Sparta. The Greek empire, sunk in voluptuousness without a remaining spark of patriotism, was no match for the Turks, enflamed with a new religion, that promised paradise to those who should die fighting for their prophet. How many nations, like those mentioned, illustrious formerly for vigour of mind, and love to their country, are now sunk by contemptible vices as much below brutes as they ought to be elevated above them: brutes seldom deviate from the perfection of their nature, men frequently.

Successful commerce is not more advantageous by the wealth and power it immediately bestows, than it is hurtful ultimately by introducing luxury and voluptuousness, which eradicates patriotism. In the capital of a great monarchy, the poison of opulence is sudden; because opulence there is seldom acquired by reputable means: the poison of commercial opulence is slow, because commerce seldom enriches without industry, sagacity, and fair dealing. But by whatever means acquired, opulence never fails soon or late to smother patriotism under sensuality and selfishness. We learn from Plutarch and other writers that the Athenians, who had long enjoyed the sunshine of commerce, were extremely corrupt in the days of Philip, and of his son Alexander. Even their chief patriot and orator, a professed champion for independence, was not proof against bribes. While Alexander was prosecuting his conquests in India, Harpalus, to whom his immense treasure was intrusted, fled with the whole to Athens. Demosthenes advised his fellow-citizens to expell him, that they might not incur Alexander's displeasure. Among other things of value, there was the King's cup of massy gold, curiously engraved. Demosthenes, surveying it with a greedy eye, asked Harpalus what it weighed. To you, said Harpalus smiling, it shall weigh twenty talents; and that very night he sent privately to Demosthenes twenty talents with the cup. Demosthenes came next day into the assembly with a cloth rolled about his neck; and his opinion being demanded about Harpalus, he made signs that he had lost his voice. The Capuans, the Tarentines, and other Greek colonies in the lower parts of Italy, when invaded by the Romans, were no less degenerate than their brethren in Greece when invaded by Philip of Macedon; the same depravation of manners, the same luxury, the same passion for feasts and spectacles, the same intestine factions, the same indifference about their country, and the same contempt of its laws. The Portuguese, enflamed with love to their country, when they discovered a passage to the Indies by the Cape of Good Hope, made great and important settlements in that very distant part of the globe; and of their immense commerce there is no parallel in any age or country. Prodigious riches in gold, precious stones, spices, perfumes, drugs, and manufactures, were annually imported into Lisbon from their settlements on the coasts of Malabar and Coromandel, from the kingdoms of Camboya, Decan, Malacca, Patana, Siam, China,

&c. from the islands of Ceylon, Sumatra, Java, Borneo, Moluccas, and Japan: and to Lisbon all the nations in Europe resorted for these valuable commodities. But the downfall of the Portuguese was no less rapid than their exaltation; unbounded power and immense wealth having produced a total corruption of manners. If sincere piety, exalted courage, and indefatigable industry, made the original adventurers more than men; indolence, sensuality, and effeminacy, rendered their successors less than women. Unhappy it was for them to be attacked at that critical time by the Dutch, who, in defence of liberty against the tyranny of Spain, were enflamed with love to their country, as the Portuguese had been formerly. The Dutch, originally from their situation a temperate and industrious people, became heroes in the cause of liberty as just now mentioned; and patriotism was their ruling passion. Prosperous commerce spread wealth through every corner; and yet such was the inherent virtue of that people, that their patriotism resisted very long the contagion of wealth. But as appetite for riches increases with their quantity, patriotism sunk in proportion, till it was totally extinguished; and now the Dutch never think of their country, unless as subservient to private interest. With respect to the Dutch East-India company in particular, it was indebted for its prosperity to the fidelity and frugality of its servants, and to the patriotism of all. But these virtues were undermined, and at last eradicated, by luxury, which Europeans seldom resist in a hot climate. People go from Europe in the service of the company, bent before-hand to make their fortune per fas aut nefas [by fair means or foul]; and their distance from their masters renders every check abortive. The company, eat up by their servants, is rendered so feeble, as to be incapable of maintaining their ground against any extraordinary shock. A war of any continuance with the Indian potentates, or with the English company, would reduce them to bankruptcy. They are at present as ripe for being swallowed up by any rival power as the Portuguese were formerly for being swallowed up by them. Quæritur, Is the English East India company in a much better condition? Such is the rise and fall of patriotism among the nations mentioned; and such will be its rise and fall among all nations in like circumstances.

It grieves me, that the epidemic distempers of luxury and selfishness are spreading wide in Britain. It is fruitless to dissemble, that profligate manners must in Britain be a consequence of too great opulence, as they have been in every other part of the globe. Our late distractions leave no room for a doubt. Listen to a man of figure, thoroughly acquainted with every machination for court-preferment.

> Very little attachment is discoverable in the body of our people to our excellent constitution: no reverence for the customs nor for the opinions of our ancestors; no attachment but to private interest, nor any zeal but for selfish gratifications. While party-distinctions of Whig and Tory, high church and low church, court and country, subsisted, the nation was indeed divided, but each side held an opinion, for which he would have hazarded every thing; for both acted from principle: if there were some who sought to alter the constitution, there were many who would have spilt their blood to preserve it from violation: if divine hereditary right had its partisans, there were multitudes to stand up for the superior sanctity of a title founded on an act of parliament, and the consent of a free people. But the abolition of party-names has destroyed all public principles. The power of the crown was indeed never more visibly extensive over the great men of the nation; but then these men have lost their influence over the lower orders: even parliament has lost much of its authority; and the voice of the multitude is set up against the sense of the legislature: an impoverished and heavily burdened public, a people luxurious and licentious, impatient of rule, and despising all authority, government relaxed in every sinew, and a corrupt selfish spirit pervading the whole.[1]

It is a common observation, that when the belly is full, the mind is at ease. That observation, it would appear, holds not in London; for never in any other place did riot and licentiousness rise to such a height, without a cause, and without even a plausible pretext.

It is deplorable, that in English public schools, patriotism makes no branch of education; young men, on the contrary, are trained up to selfishness. Keep what you get, and get what you can, is the chief lesson inculcated at Westminster, Winchester, and Eaton. Students put themselves in the way of receiving vails from strangers; and that dirty practice continues, though far more poisonous to manners, than the giving vails to menial servants, which the nation is now ashamed of. The Eaton scholars are at times sent to the highway to rob passengers. The strong, without controul, tyrannize over the weak, subjecting them to every servile office, wiping shoes not excepted. They are permitted to trick and deceive one another; and the finest fellow is he who is the most artful. Friendship indeed is cultivated, but such as we find among

1 The Honourable George Grenville.

robbers: a boy would be run down, if he had no associate. In a word, the most determined selfishness is the capital lesson.

When a nation, formerly warlike and public spirited, is depressed by luxury and selfishness, doth nature afford no means for restoring it to its former state? The Emperor Hadrian declared the Greeks a free people; not doubting, but that a change so animating, would restore the fine arts to their pristine lustre – A vain attempt: for the genius of the Greeks vanished with their patriotism; and liberty to them was no blessing. With respect to the Portuguese, the decay of their power and of their commerce, have reduced them to a much lower condition, than when they rose as it were out of nothing. At that time they were poor, but innocent: at present they are poor, but corrupted with many vices. Their pride in particular swells as high when masters of the Indies. The following ridiculous instance is a pregnant proof: shoes and stockings are prohibited to their Indian subjects; though many of them would pay handsomely for the privilege. There is one obvious measure for reviving the Portuguese trade to India; but they have not so much vigour of mind remaining, as even to think of execution. They still possess in that country the town and territory of Goa, the town and territory of Diu, with some other ports, all admirably situated for trade. What stands in the way but indolence merely, against declaring the places mentioned free ports, with liberty of conscience to traders of whatever religion? Free traders flocking there, under protection of the Portuguese, would undermine the Dutch and English companies, which cannot trade upon an equal footing with private merchants; and by that means, the Portuguese trade might again flourish. But that people are not yet brought so low as to be compelled to change their manners, though reduced to depend on their neighbours even for common necessaries. The gold and diamonds of Brasil are a plague that corrupt all. Spain and Portugal afford instructive political lessons: the latter has been ruined by opulence; the former, as will be seen afterward, by taxes no less impolitic than oppressive. To enable these nations to recommence their former course, or any nation in the same situation, I can discover no means but pinching poverty. Commerce and manufactures taking wing, may leave a country in a very distressed condition: but a people may be very distressed, and yet very vitious; for vices generated by opulence are not soon eradicated. And though other vices should at last vanish with the temptations that promoted them, indolence and pusillanimity will remain for ever, unless by some powerful cause the opposite virtues be introduced. A very poor man, however indolent, will be tempted for bread to exert some activity; and he may be trained gradually from less to more by the same means. Activity at the same time produces bodily strength; which will restore courage and boldness. By such means a nation may be put in motion with the same advantages it had originally; and its second progress may prove as successful as the first. Thus nations go round in a circle, from weakness to strength, and from strength to weakness. The first part of the progress is verified in a thousand instances; but the world has not subsisted long enough to afford any clear instance of the other.

I close this sketch with two illustrious examples of patriotism; one ancient, one modern, one among the whites, and one among the blacks. Aristides the Athenian is famed above all the ancients for love to his country. Its safety and honour were the only objects of his ambition; and his signal disinterestedness made it the same to him, whether these ends were accomplished by himself or by others, by his friends or his foes. One conspicuous instance occurred before the battle of Marathon. Of the ten generals chosen to command the Athenian army, he was one: but sensible that a divided command is subjected to manifold inconveniences, he exerted all his influence for delegating the whole power to Miltiades; and at the same time zealously supported the proposal of Miltiades, of boldly meeting the Persians in the field. His disinterestedness was still more conspicuous with regard to Themistocles, his bitter enemy. Suspending all enmity, he cordially agreed with him in every operation of the war; assisting him with his counsel and credit, and yet suffering him to engross all the honours of victory. In peace he was the same, yielding to Themistocles in the administration of government, and contenting himself with a subordinate place. In the senate and in the assembly of the people, he made many proposals in a borrowed name, to prevent envy and opposition. He retired from public business in the latter part of his life; passing his time in training young men for serving the state, instilling into them principles of honour and virtue, and inspiring them with love to their country. His death unfolded a signal proof of the contempt he had for riches; he who had been treasurer of Greece during the lavishment of war, left not sufficient to defray the expence of his funeral: a British commissary in like circumstances acquires the riches of Crœsus.

The scene of the other example is Fouli, a negro kingdom in Africa. Such regard is paid there to royal blood, that no man can succeed to the crown, but who is connected with the first monarch, by an uninterrupted chain of females: a connection by males would give no security, as the women of that country are prone to gallantry. In the last century, the Prince of Sambaboa, the King's nephew by his sister, was invested with the dignity of Kamalingo, a dignity appropriated to the presumptive heir. A liberal and generous mind, with undaunted courage, rivetted him in the affections of the nobility and people. They rejoiced in the expectation of having him for their King. But their expectation was blasted. The King, fond of his children, ventured a bold measure, which was to invest his eldest son with the dignity of Kamalingo, and to declare him heir to the crown. Tho' the Prince of Sambaboa had for him the laws of the kingdom, and the hearts of the people, yet he retired in silence to avoid a civil war. He could not however prevent men of rank from flocking to him; which the King interpreting to be a rebellion, raised an army in order to put them all to the sword. As the King advanced, the Prince retired, resolving not to draw a sword against an uncle, whom he was accustomed to call father. But finding that the command of the King's army was bestowed on his rival, he made ready for battle. The Prince obtained a complete victory: but his heart was not elated: the horrors of a civil war stared him in the face: he bid farewell to his friends, dismissed his army, and retired into a neighbouring kingdom; relying on the affections of the people to be placed on the throne after his uncle's death. During banishment, which continued thirty tedious years, frequent attempts upon his life put his temper to a severe trial; for while he existed, the king had no hopes that his son would reign in peace. He had the fortitude to stand every trial: when, in the year 1702, beginning to yield to age and misfortunes, his uncle died. His cousin was deposed; and he was called by the unanimous voice of the nobles, to reign over a people who adored him.

Source: Henry Home, Lord Kames, 'Rise and fall of patriotism', in *Sketches of the History of Man*, Glasgow 1802, Book 2, sketch 7, in vol. 2, pp. 194–208

THIRTY

JOHN MILLAR
The Powers of the Sovereign

Millar believed perfect equality in society to be a chimera. As soon as people begin to move from a savage or rude state to one that is polished, power relations emerge. Some take advantage of natural talents or advantageous circumstances and secure the upper hand, particularly by appropriating land but also property of other sorts. Others occupy a variety of subordinate positions in relation to those in power, and inequality is already established, built into the system from day one. Millar detects in humans a natural desire for power. Those, therefore, in a superordinate position have a natural desire not to move to a lower rank, and those in a subordinate position have a natural desire to rise. Millar's doctrine is of course highly nuanced, but from the foregoing it follows that the process of social differentiation must also be a process of conflict.

One aspect of this conflict is worked out in some detail in our excerpt, for Millar demonstrates both that there are circumstances which tend to increase the sovereign's power and also that in those same circumstances people of subordinate rank have, and duly exploit, an opportunity to rise. The sovereign acquires an army paid for and maintained by him, an army therefore willing to remain in his service as long as he chooses to retain it. It is by virtue of certain improvements in society, improvements in the direction of affluence, that the sovereign becomes able to set up a standing army. It is in virtue of those same improvements, as Millar argues, that the sovereign becomes able to set up and maintain a professional system for the distribution of justice, manned by those educated and qualified for the job. These institutions, a professional army and a professional judiciary, are very expensive and can only be maintained if a system of general taxation is in place. Such a system itself requires the employment of public officers, a further professional force. The result of this process of division of labour is that the sovereign 'is enabled thereby to give subsistence to a great number of persons, who, in times of faction and disorder, will naturally adhere to his party, and whose interest, in ordinary cases, will be employed to support and to extend his authority'.

Yet the very circumstances of growing opulence in society can also be shown to contribute to a wide distribution of political power and the emergence of a popular government. Millar provides a brilliant analysis of a dialectical situation, in which the luxury enjoyed by the ruling class also leads to its destruction, while growing wealth in the community at large not only leads the people to aspire to liberty and independence but also enables them to acquire these qualities with the help of the destructive effect that luxury has on the ruling class.

In the final section of the excerpt Millar seeks to identify some of the factors that help to produce victory for one side or the other, sovereign or people, in this conflict. It is however plain that Millar believes that any victory is only a holding operation for the victor, and that deeply imbedded features of human nature ensure that there will always be another round to fight.

A.B.

The Changes Produced in the Government of a People, by their Progress in Arts, and in Polished Manners

SECTION I *Circumstances, in a Polished Nation, which Tend to Increase the Power of the Sovereign*

The advancement of a people in the arts of life, is attended with various alterations in the state of individuals, and in the whole constitution of their government.

Mankind, in a rude age, are commonly in readiness to go out to war, as often as their circumstances require it. From their extreme idleness, a military expedition is seldom inconvenient for them; while the prospect of enriching themselves with plunder, and of procuring distinction by their valour, renders it always agreeable. The members of every clan are no less eager to follow their chief, and to revenge his quarrel, than he is desirous of their assistance. They look upon it as a privilege, rather than a burden, to attend upon him, and to share in the danger, as well as in the glory and profit of all his undertakings. By the numberless acts of hostility in which they are engaged, they are trained to the use of arms, and acquire experience in the military art, so far as it is then understood. Thus, without any trouble or expense, a powerful militia is constantly maintained, which, upon the slightest notice, can always be brought into the field, and employed in the defence of the country.

When Caesar made war upon the Helvetii they were able to muster against him no less than ninety-two thousand fighting men, amounting to a fourth part of all the inhabitants.

Hence those prodigious swarms which issued, at different times, from the ill cultivated regions of the north, and over-ran the several provinces of the Roman empire. Hence too, the poor but superstitious princes of Europe were enabled to muster such numerous forces under the banner of the cross, in order to attack the opulent nations of the east, and to deliver the holy sepulchre from the hands of the infidels.

The same observation will, in some measure, account for those immense armies which we read of in the early periods of history; or at least may incline us to consider the exaggerated relations of ancient authors, upon that subject, as not entirely destitute of real foundation.

These dispositions, arising from the frequent disorders incident to a rude society, are of course laid aside when good order and tranquillity begin to be established. When the government acquires so much authority as to protect individuals from oppression, and to put an end to the private wars which subsisted between different families, the people, who have no other military enterprises but those which are carried on in the public cause of the nation, become gradually less accustomed to fighting, and their martial ardour is proportionately abated.

The improvement of arts and manufactures, by introducing luxury, contributes yet more to enervate the minds of men, who, according as they enjoy more ease and pleasure at home, feel greater aversion to the hardships and dangers of a military life, and put a lower value upon that sort of reputation which it affords. The increase of industry, at the same time, creates a number of lucrative employments which require a constant attention, and gives rise to a variety of tradesmen and artificers, who cannot afford to leave their business for the transient and uncertain advantages to be derived from the pillage of their enemies.

In these circumstances the bulk of a people become at length unable or unwilling to serve in war, and when summoned to appear in the field, according to the ancient usage, are induced to offer a sum of money instead of their personal attendance. A composition of this kind is readily accepted by the sovereign or chief magistrate, as it enables him to hire soldiers among those who have no better employment, or who have contracted a liking to that particular occupation. The forces which he has raised in this manner receiving constant pay, and having no other means of procuring a livelihood, are entirely under the direction of their leader, and are willing to remain in his service as long as he chooses to retain them. From this alteration of circumstances, he has an opportunity of establishing a proper subordination in the army, and according as it becomes fitter for action, and, in all its motions, capable of being guided and regulated with greater facility, he is encouraged to enter upon more difficult enterprises, as well as to meditate more distant schemes of ambition. His wars, which were formerly concluded in a few weeks, are now gradually protracted to a greater length of time, and occasioning a greater variety of operations, are productive of suitable improvements in the military art.

After a numerous body of troops have been levied at considerable expense, and have been prepared for war by a long course of discipline and experience, it appears highly expedient to the sovereign that, even in time of peace, some part of them, at least, should be kept in pay, to be in readiness whenever their service is required. Thus, the introduction of mercenary forces is soon followed by that of a regular standing army. The business of a soldier becomes a distinct profession, which is appropriated to a separate order of men; while the rest of the inhabitants, being devoted to their several employments, become wholly unaccustomed to arms; and the preservation of their lives and fortunes, is totally devolved upon those whom they are at the charge of maintaining for that purpose.

This important revolution, with respect to the means of national defence, appears to have taken place in all the civilized and opulent nations of antiquity. In all the Greek states, even in that of Sparta, we find that the military service of the free citizens came, from a change of manners, to be regarded as burdensome, and the practice of employing mercenary troops was introduced. The Romans too, before the end of the republic, had found it necessary to maintain a regular standing army in each of their distant provinces.

In the modern nations of Europe, the disuse of the feudal militia was an immediate consequence of the progress of the people in arts and manufactures; after which the different sovereigns were forced to hire soldiers upon particular occasions, and at last to maintain a regular body of troops for the defence of their dominions. In France, during the reign of Lewis XIII, and in Germany, about the same period, the military system began to be established upon that footing, which it has since acquired in all the countries of Europe.

The tendency of a standing mercenary army to increase the power and prerogative of the crown, which has been the subject of much declamation, is sufficiently obvious. As the army is immediately under the conduct of the monarch; as the individuals of which it is composed depend entirely upon him for preferment; as, by forming a separate order of men they are apt to become indifferent about the rights of their fellow-citizens; it may be expected that, in most cases, they will be disposed to pay an implicit obedience to his commands, and that the same force which is maintained to suppress insurrections, and to repel invasions, may often be employed to subvert and destroy the liberties of the people.

The same improvements in society, which give rise to the maintenance of standing forces, are usually attended with similar changes in the manner of distributing justice. It has been already observed that, in a large community, which has made but little progress in the arts, every chief or baron is the judge over his own tribe, and the king, with the assistance of his great council, exercises a jurisdiction over the members of different tribes or baronies. From the small number of law-suits which occur in the ages of poverty and rudeness, and from the rapidity with which they are usually determined among a warlike and ignorant people, the office of a judge demands little attention, and occasions no great interruption to those pursuits in which a man of rank and distinction is commonly engaged. The sovereign and the nobility, therefore, in such a situation, may continue to hold this office, though, in their several courts, they should appoint a deputy-judge to assist them in discharging the duties of it. But when the increase of opulence has given encouragement to a variety of tedious litigation, they become unwilling to bestow the necessary time in hearing causes, and are therefore induced to devolve the whole business upon inferior judges, who acquire by degrees the several branches of the judicial power, and are obliged to hold regular courts for the benefit of the inhabitants. Thus the exercise of jurisdiction becomes a separate employment, and is committed to an order of men, who require a particular education to qualify them for the duties of their office, and who, in return for their service, must therefore be enabled to earn a livelihood by their profession.

A provision for the maintenance of judges is apt, from the natural course of things, to grow out of their employment; as, in order to procure an indemnification for their attendance, they have an opportunity of exacting fees from the parties who come before them. This is analogous to what happens with respect to every sort of manufacture, in which an artificer is commonly paid by those who employ him. We find, accordingly, that this was the early practice in all the feudal courts of Europe, and that the perquisites drawn by the judges, in different tribunals, yielded a considerable revenue both to the king and the nobles. It is likely that similar customs, in this respect, have been adopted in most parts of the world, by nations in the same period of their advancement. The impropriety, however, of giving a permission to these exactions, which tend to influence the decisions of a judge, to render him active in stirring up law-suits, and in multiplying the forms of his procedure, in order to increase his perquisites; these pernicious consequences with which it is inseparably connected, could not fail to attract the notice of a polished people, and at length produced the more perfect plan of providing for the maintenance of judges by the appointment of a fixed salary in place of their former precarious emoluments.

It cannot be doubted that these establishments, of such mighty importance, and of so extensive a nature, must be the source of great expense to the public. In those early periods, when the inhabitants of a country are in a condition to defend themselves, and when their internal disputes are decided by judges who claim no reward for their interpositions, or at least no reward from government, few regulations are necessary with respect to the public revenue. The king is enabled to maintain his family, and to support his dignity, by the rents of his own estate; and, in ordinary cases, he has no farther demand. But when the disuse of the ancient militia has been succeeded by the practice of hiring troops, these original funds are no longer sufficient; and other resources must be provided in order to supply the deficiency. By the happy disposition of human events, the very circumstance that occasions this difficulty appears also to suggest the means of removing it. When the bulk of a people become unwilling to serve in war, they are naturally disposed to offer a composition in order to be excused from that ancient personal service which, from long custom, it is thought they are bound to perform. Compositions of this nature are levied at first, in consequence of an agreement with each individual: to avoid the trouble arising from a multiplicity of separate transactions, they are afterwards paid in common by the inhabitants of particular districts, and at length give rise to a general *assessment*, of the first considerable taxation that is commonly introduced into a country.

If this tax could always be laid upon the people in proportion to their circumstances, it might easily be augmented in such a manner as to defray all the expenses of government. But the difficulty of ascertaining the wealth of individuals makes it impossible to push the assessment to a great height, without being guilty of oppression, and renders it proper that other methods of raising money should be employed to answer the increasing demands of the society. In return for the protection which is given to merchants in carrying their goods from one country to another, it is apprehended that some recompence is due to the government, and that certain duties may be levied upon the exportation and importation of commodities. The security enjoyed by tradesmen and manufacturers, from the care and vigilance of the magistrate, is held also to lay a foundation for similar exactions upon the retail of goods, and upon the inland trade of a nation. Thus the payment of *customs*, and of what, in a large sense, may be called *excise*, is introduced and gradually extended.

It is not proposed to enter into a comparison of these different taxes, or to consider the several advantages and disadvantages of each. Their general effects in altering the political constitution of a state are more immediately the object of the present enquiry. With respect to this point, it merits attention that, as the sovereign claims a principal share at least, in the nomination of public officers, as he commonly obtains the chief direction in collecting and disposing of the revenue which is raised upon their account, he is enabled thereby to give subsistence to a great number of persons, who, in times of faction and disorder, will naturally adhere to his party, and whose interest, in ordinary cases, will be employed to support and to extend his authority. These circumstances contribute to strengthen the hands of the monarch, to undermine and destroy every opposite power, and to increase the general bias towards the absolute dominion of a single person.

SECTION II *Other Circumstances, which Contribute to Advance the Privileges of the People*

After viewing those effects of opulence and the progress of arts which favour the interest of the crown, let us turn our attention to other circumstances, proceeding from the same source, that have an opposite tendency, and are manifestly conducive to a popular form of government.

In that early period of agriculture when manufactures are unknown, persons who have no landed estate are usually incapable of procuring subsistence otherwise than by serving some opulent neighbour, by whom they are employed, according to their qualifications, either in military service, or in the several branches of husbandry. Men of great fortune find that the entertaining a multitude of servants, for either of these purposes, is highly conducive both to their dignity and their personal security; and in a rude age, when people are strangers to luxury, and are maintained from the simple productions of the earth, the number of retainers who may be supported upon any particular estate is proportionably great.

In this situation, persons of low rank, have no opportunity of acquiring an affluent fortune, or of raising themselves to superior stations; and remaining for ages in a state of dependence, they naturally contract such dispositions and habits are as suited to their circumstances. They acquire a sacred veneration for the person of their master, and are taught to pay an unbounded submission to his authority. They are proud of that servile obedience by which they seem to exalt his dignity, and consider it as their duty to sacrifice their lives and their possessions in order to promote his interest, or even to gratify his capricious humour.

But when the arts begin to be cultivated in a country, the labouring part of the inhabitants are enabled to procure subsistence in a different manner. They are led to make proficiency in particular trades and professions; and, instead of becoming servants to any body, they often find it more profitable to work at their own charges, and to vend the product of their labour. As in this situation their gain depends upon a variety of customers, they have little to fear from the displeasure of any single person; and, according to the good quality and cheapness of the commodity which they have to dispose of, they may commonly be assured of success in their business.

The farther a nation advances in opulence and refinement, it has occasion to employ a greater number of merchants, of tradesmen and artificers; and as the lower people, in general, become thereby more independent in their circumstances, they begin to exert those sentiments of liberty which are natural to the mind of man, and which necessity alone is able to subdue. In proportion as they have less need of the favour and patronage of the great, they are at less pains to procure it; and their application is more uniformly directed to acquire those talents which are useful in the exercise of their employments. The impressions which they received in their former state of servitude are therefore gradually obliterated, and give place to habits of a different nature. The long attention and perseverance, by which they become expert and skilful in their business, render them ignorant of those decorums and of that politeness which arises from the intercourse of society; and that vanity which was formerly discovered in magnifying the power of a chief, is now equally displayed in sullen indifference, or in contemptuous and insolent behaviour to persons of superior rank and station.

While, from these causes, people of low rank are gradually advancing towards a state of independence, the influence derived from wealth is diminished in the same proportion. From the improvement of arts and manufactures, the ancient simplicity of manners is in a great measure destroyed; and the proprietor of a landed estate, instead of consuming its produce in hiring retainers, is obliged to employ a great part of it in purchasing those comforts and conveniences which have become objects of attention, and which are thought suitable to his condition. Thus while fewer persons are under the necessity of depending upon him, he is daily rendered less capable of maintaining dependents; till at last his domestics and servants are reduced to such as are merely subservient to luxury and pageantry, but are of no use in supporting his authority.

From the usual effects of luxury and refinement, it may at the same time be expected that old families will often be reduced to poverty and beggary. In a refined and luxurious nation those who are born to great affluence, and who have been bred to no business, are excited, with mutual emulation, to surpass one another in the elegance and refinement of their living. According as they have the means of indulging themselves in pleasure, they become more addicted to the pursuit of it, and are sunk in a degree of indolence and dissipation which renders them incapable of any active employment. Thus the expense of the landed gentleman is apt to be continually increasing, without any proportional addition to his income. His estate therefore, being more and more incumbered with debts, is at length alienated, and brought into the possession of the frugal and industrious merchant, who, by success in trade, has been enabled to buy it, and who is desirous of obtaining that rank and consequence which landed property is capable of bestowing. The posterity, however, of this new proprietor, having adopted the manners of the landed gentry, are again led, in a few generations, to squander their estate, with a heedless extravagance equal to the parsimony and activity by which it was acquired.

This fluctuation of property, so observable in all commercial countries, and which no prohibitions are capable of preventing, must necessarily weaken the authority of those who are placed in the higher ranks of life. Persons who have lately attained to riches, have no opportunity of establishing that train of dependence which is maintained by those who have remained for ages at the head of a great estate. The hereditary influence of family is thus, in a great measure, destroyed; and the consideration derived from wealth is often limited to what the possessor can acquire during his own life. Even this too, for the reasons formerly mentioned, is greatly diminished. A man of great fortune having dismissed his retainers, and spending a great part of his income in the purchase of commodities produced by tradesmen and manufacturers, has no ground to expect that many persons will be willing either to fight for him, or to run any great hazard for promoting his interest. Whatever profit he means to obtain from the labour and assistance of others, he must give a full equivalent for it. He must buy those personal services which are no longer to be performed either from attachment or from peculiar connexions. Money, therefore, becomes more and more the only means of procuring honours and dignities; and the sordid pursuits of avarice are made subservient to the nobler purposes of ambition.

It cannot be doubted that these circumstances have a tendency to introduce a democratical government. As persons of inferior rank are placed in a situation which, in point of subsistence, renders them little dependent upon their superiors; as no one order of men continues in the exclusive possession of opulence; and as every man who is industrious may entertain the hope of gaining a fortune; it is to be expected that the prerogatives of the monarch and of the ancient nobility will be gradually undermined, that the privileges of the people will be extended in the same proportion, and that power, the usual attendant of wealth, will be in some measure diffused over all the members of the community.

SECTION III *Result of the Opposition between these Different Principles*

So widely different are the effects of opulence and refinement, which, at the same time that they furnish the king with a standing army, the great engine of tyranny and oppression, have also a tendency to inspire the people with notions of liberty and independence. It may thence be expected that a conflict will arise between these two opposite parties, in which a variety of accidents may contribute to cast the balance upon either side.

With respect to the issue of such a contest, it may be remarked that, in a small state, the people have been commonly successful in their efforts to establish a free constitution. When a state consists only of a small territory, and the bulk of the inhabitants live in one city, they have frequently occasion to converse together, and to communicate their sentiments upon every subject of importance. Their attention therefore is roused by every instance of oppression in the government; and as they easily take the alarm, so they are capable of quickly uniting their forces in order to demand redress of their grievances. By repeated experiments they become sensible of their strength, and are enabled by degrees to enlarge their privileges, and to assume a greater share of the public administration.

In large and extensive nations, the struggles between the sovereign and his people are, on the contrary, more likely to terminate in favour of despotism. In a wide country, the encroachments of the government are frequently over-looked; and, even when the indignation of the people has been roused by flagrant injustice, they find it difficult to combine in uniform and vigorous measures for the defence of their rights. It is also difficult, in a great nation, to bring out the militia with that quickness which is requisite in case of a sudden invasion; and it becomes necessary, even before the country has been much civilized, to maintain such a body of mercenaries as is capable of supporting the regal authority.

It is farther to be considered that the revenue of the monarch is commonly a more powerful engine of authority in a great nation than in a small one. The influence of a sovereign seems to depend, not so much upon his absolute wealth, as upon the proportion which it bears to that of the other members of the community. So far as the estate of the king does not exceed that of the richest of his subjects, it is no more than sufficient to supply the ordinary expense of living, in a manner suitable to the splendour and dignity of the crown; and it is only the surplus of that estate which can be directly applied to the purposes of creating dependence. In this view the public revenue of the king will be productive of greater influence according to the extent and populousness of the country in which it is raised. Suppose in a country, like that of ancient Attica, containing about twenty thousand inhabitants, the people were, by assessment or otherwise, to pay at the rate of twenty shillings each person, this would produce only twenty thousand pounds; a revenue that would probably not exalt the chief magistrate above many private citizens. But in a kingdom, containing ten millions of people, the taxes, being paid in the same proportion, would in all probability render the estate of the monarch superior to the united wealth of many hundreds of the most opulent individuals. In these two cases therefore, the disproportion of the armies maintained in each kingdom should be greater than that of their respective revenues; and if in the one, the king was enabled to maintain two hundred and fifty thousand men, he would in the other, be incapable of supporting the expense of five hundred. It is obvious, however, that even five hundred regular and well disciplined troops will not strike the same terror into twenty thousand people, that will be created, by an army of two hundred and fifty thousand, over a nation composed of ten millions.

Most of the ancient republics, with which we are acquainted, appear to have owed their liberty to the narrowness of their territories. From the small number of people, and from the close intercourse among all the individuals in the same community, they imbibed a spirit of freedom even before they had made considerable progress in arts; and they found means to repress or abolish the power of their petty princes, before their effeminacy or industry had introduced the practice of maintaining mercenary troops.

The same observation is applicable to the modern states of Italy, who, after the decay of the western empire, began to flourish in trade, and among whom a republican form of government was early established.

In France, on the other hand, the introduction of a great mercenary army, during the administration of Cardinal Richelieu, which was necessary for the defence of the country, enabled the monarch to establish a despotical power. In the beginning of the reign of Lewis XIII was called the last convention of the states general which has ever been held in that country: and the monarch has, from that period, been accustomed to exercise almost all the different powers of government. Similar effects have arisen from the establishment of standing forces in most of the great kingdoms of Europe.

The fortunate situation of Great Britain, after the accession of James I, gave her little to fear from any foreign invasion, and superseded the necessity of maintaining a standing army, when the service of the feudal militia had gone into disuse. The weakness and bigotry of her monarchs, at that period, prevented them from employing the only expedient capable of securing an absolute authority. Charles I saw the power exercised, about his time, by the other princes of Europe; but he did not discover the means by which it was obtained. He seems to have been so much convinced of his divine indefeasible right as, at first, to think that no force was necessary, and afterwards, that every sort of duplicity was excuseable, in support of it. When at the point of a rupture with his parliament, he had no military force upon which he could depend; and he was therefore obliged to yield to the growing power of the commons.

The boldness and dexterity, joined to the want of public spirit, and the perfidy of Oliver Cromwell, rendered abortive the measures of that party, of which he obtained the direction; but the blood that had been shed, and the repeated efforts that were made by the people in defence of their privileges, cherished and spread the love of liberty, and at last produced a popular government, after the best model, perhaps, which is practicable in an extensive country.

Many writers appear to take pleasure in remarking that, as the love of liberty is natural to man, it is to be found in the greatest perfection among barbarians, and is apt to be impaired according as people make progress in civilization and in the arts of life. That mankind, in the state of mere savages, are in great measure unacquainted with government, and unaccustomed to any sort of constraint, is sufficiently evident. But their independence, in that case, is owing to the wretchedness of their circumstances, which afford nothing that can tempt any one man to become subject to another. The moment they have quitted this primitive situation, and, by endeavouring to supply their natural wants, have been led to accumulate property, they are presented with very different motives of action, and acquire a new set of habits and principles. In those rude ages when the inhabitants of the earth are divided into tribes of shepherds, or of husbandmen, the usual distribution of property renders the bulk of the people dependent upon a few chiefs, to whom fidelity and submission becomes the principal point of honour, and makes a distinguishing part of the national character. The ancient Germans, whose high notions of freedom have been the subject of many a well-turned period, were accustomed, as we learn from Tacitus, to stake their persons upon the issue of a game of hazard, and after an unlucky turn of fortune, to yield themselves up to a voluntary servitude. Where-ever men of inferior condition are enabled to live in affluence by their own industry, and, in procuring their livelihood, have little occasion to court the favour of their superiors, there we may expect that ideas of liberty will be universally diffused. This happy arrangement of things, is naturally produced by commerce and manufactures; but it would be as vain to look for it in the uncultivated parts of the world, as to look for the independent spirit of an English waggoner, among persons of low rank in the highlands of Scotland.

Source: John Millar, *Origin of the Distinction of Ranks*, ch. 5, in William C. Lehmann, *John Millar of Glasgow*, Cambridge 1960, pp. 284–95

THIRTY-ONE

ADAM FERGUSON
Liberty and the Law

In some sense or other, liberty is something that people in the rudest and in the most polished nations can enjoy. But for Ferguson liberty in its fullest sense is only possible under a system of law which protects the rights of citizens. However, the wording of the law is not enough to protect the citizens; the psychological state of those involved in interpreting and administering the law is crucially important. Those involved in the law in these ways might be corrupted in spirit. One sign of corruption is the bestowal of liberty as a favour, when it should be bestowed as a right.

Two points of particular interest in Ferguson's analysis of the process of corruption, in so far as the corruption leads to enslavement of the state, concern moderation and the division of labour, two concepts at the heart of the Scottish Enlightenment. From Ferguson's perspective a polite society is not immune from the encroachment of despotism. Ferguson writes: 'We have reason to dread the political refinements of ordinary men, when we consider, that repose or inaction itself, is in a great measure their object; and that they would frequently model their governments, not merely to prevent injustice and error, but to prevent agitation and bustle; and by the barriers they raise against the evil actions of men, would prevent them from acting at all.' Here Ferguson has in his sights that intellectual élite, the polite society of the Enlightenment, whose virtues Hume, among others, praised so highly. Civil disorder might well be looked upon with fear, and the imposition of laws limiting freedom to act in so uncivil a manner might be fully supported by polite society, who would thereby be condoning an intrusion into civil liberty – though of course they would consider the intrusion to be a means of defending enlightened values. Ferguson on the contrary would consider the polite people to be yielding blindly to despotism. The despot himself might, in the situation Ferguson envisages, be congratulating himself on the way he has brought enlightened values to bear on a tricky situation to bring some less than civil members of the nation under proper civic control. But the fact remains that the civic commotion might have been a demonstration of vigorous and independent spirit provoked by a perceived injustice on the part of the civic authorities, and the demonstration would therefore have been a manifestation of the values and spirit that produced the polite society. On this analysis there is always a danger that polite society will betray its own values.

The concept of division of labour, though playing a central role in Adam Smith's *Wealth of Nations* (see excerpt 22), was recognised by him as having a moral dimension in so far as division of labour has a destructive influence on the human spirit, and society has to take suitable measures, particularly educative measures, to counteract the damage. Ferguson agrees with Smith regarding the dangers of division of labour, and refers in the present excerpt to a further danger, namely that of division into civil and military professions. The military protect the liberty that the rest of us enjoy. Ferguson warns of what would arise if the military became allied with a particular political faction and faced an unarmed civilian population. Whatever the economic arguments for encouraging division of labour, Ferguson is as clear sighted as Smith regarding its inherent destructiveness and the need to have policies in place to protect society against its worst consequences.

A.B.

Of Corruption, as it tends to Political Slavery

Liberty, in one sense, appears to be the portion of polished nations alone. The savage is personally free, because he lives unrestrained, and acts with the members of his tribe on terms of equality. The barbarian is frequently independent from a continuance of the same circumstances, or because he has courage and a sword. But good policy alone can provide for the regular administration of justice, or constitute a force in the state, which is ready on every occasion to defend the rights of its members.

It has been found, that, except in a few singular cases, the commercial and political arts have advanced together. These arts have been in modern Europe so interwoven, that we cannot determine which were prior in the order of time, or derived most advantage from the mutual influences with which they act and re-act upon one another. It has been observed, that in some nations the spirit of commerce, intent on securing its profits, has led the way to political wisdom. A people, possessed of wealth, and become jealous of their properties, have formed the project of emancipation, and have proceeded, under favour of an importance recently gained, still farther to enlarge their pretensions, and to dispute the prerogatives which their sovereign had been in use to employ. But it is in vain that we expect in one age, from the possession of wealth, the fruit which it is said to have borne in a former. Great accessions of fortune, when recent, when accompanied with frugality, and a sense of independence, may render the owner confident in his strength, and ready to spurn at oppression. The purse which is open, not to personal expence, or to the indulgence of vanity, but to support the interests of a faction, to gratify the higher passions of party, render the wealthy citizen formidable to those who pretend to dominion; but it does not follow, that in a time of corruption, equal, or greater, measures of wealth should operate to the same effect.

On the contrary, when wealth is accumulated only in the hands of the miser, and runs to waste from those of the prodigal; when heirs of family find themselves straitened and poor, in the midst of affluence; when the cravings of luxury silence even the voice of party and faction; when the hopes of meriting the rewards of compliance, or the fear of losing what is held at discretion, keep men in a state of suspense and anxiety; when fortune, in short, instead of being considered as the instrument of a vigorous spirit, becomes the idol of a covetous or a profuse, of a rapacious or a timorous mind; the foundation on which freedom was built, may serve to support a tyranny; and what, in one age, raised the pretensions, and fostered the confidence of the subject, may, in another, incline him to servility, and furnish the price to be paid for his prostitutions. Even those, who, in a vigorous age, gave the example of wealth, in the hands of the people, becoming an occasion of freedom, may, in times of degeneracy, verify likewise the maxim of Tacitus, That the admiration of riches leads to despotical government.

Men who have tasted of freedom, and who have felt their personal rights, are not easily taught to bear with incroachments on either, and cannot, without some preparation, come to submit to oppression. They may receive this unhappy preparation, under different forms of government, from different hands, and arrive at the same end by different ways. They follow one direction in republics, another in monarchies, and in mixed governments. But where-ever the state has, by means that do not preserve the virtue of the subject, effectually guarded his safety; remissness, and neglect of the public, are likely to follow; and polished nations of every description, appear to encounter a danger, on this quarter, proportioned to the degree in which they have, during any continuance, enjoyed the uninterrupted possession of peace and prosperity.

Liberty results, we say, from the government of laws; and we are apt to consider statutes, not merely as the resolutions and maxims of a people determined to be free, not as the writings by which their rights are kept on record; but as a power erected to guard them, and as a barrier which the caprice of man cannot transgress.

When a basha, in Asia, pretends to decide every controversy by the rules of natural equity, we allow that he is possessed of discretionary powers. When a judge in Europe is left to decide, according to his own interpretation of written laws, is he in any sense more restrained than the former? Have the multiplied words of a statute an influence over the conscience, and the heart, more powerful than that of reason and nature? Does the party, in any judicial proceeding, enjoy a less degree of safety, when his rights are discussed, on the foundation of a rule that is open to the understandings of mankind, than when they are referred to an intricate system, which it has become the object of a separate profession to study and to explain?

If forms of proceeding, written statutes, or other constituents of law, cease to be enforced by the very spirit from which they arose; they serve only to cover, not to restrain, the iniquities of power: they are possibly respected even by the corrupt magistrate, when they favour his purpose; but they are contemned or evaded, when they stand in his way: And the influence of laws, where they have any real effect in the preservation of liberty, is not any magic power descending from shelves that are loaded with books, but is, in reality, the influence of men resolved to be free; of men, who, having adjusted in writing the terms on which they are to live with the state, and with their fellow-subjects, are determined, by their vigilance and spirit, to make these terms be observed.

We are taught, under every form of government, to apprehend usurpations, from the abuse, or from the extension of the executive power. In pure monarchies, this power is commonly hereditary, and made to descend in a determinate line. In elective monarchies, it is held for life. In republics, it is exercised during a limited time. Where men, or families, are called by election to the possession of temporary dignities, it is more the object of ambition to perpetuate, than to extend their powers. In hereditary monarchies, the sovereignty is already perpetual; and the aim of every ambitious prince, is to enlarge his prerogative. Republics, and, in times of commotion, communities of every form, are exposed to hazard, not from those only who are formally raised to places of trust, but from every person whatever, who is incited by ambition, and who is supported by faction.

It is no advantage to a prince, or other magistrate, to enjoy more power than is consistent with the good of mankind; nor is it of any benefit to a man to be unjust: but these maxims are a feeble security against the passions and follies of men. Those who are intrusted with any measures of influence, are disposed, from a mere aversion to constraint, to remove opposition. Not only the monarch who wears a hereditary crown, but the magistrate who holds his office for a limited time, grows fond of his dignity. The very minister, who depends for his place on the momentary will of his prince, and whose personal interests are, in every respect, those of a subject, still has the weakness to take an interest in the growth of prerogative, and to reckon as gain to himself the incroachments he has made on the rights of a people, with whom he himself and his family are soon to be numbered.

Even with the best intentions towards mankind, we are inclined to think, that their welfare depends, not on the felicity of their own inclinations, or the happy employment of their own talents, but on their ready compliance with what we have devised for their good. Accordingly, the greatest virtue of which any sovereign has hitherto shown an example, is not a desire of cherishing in his people the spirit of freedom and independence; but what is in itself sufficiently rare, and highly meritorious, a steady regard to the distribution of justice in matters of property, a disposition to protect and to oblige, to redress the grievances, and to promote the interest of his subjects. It was from a reference to these objects, that Titus computed the value of his time, and judged of its application. But the sword, which in this beneficent hand was drawn to protect the subject, and to procure a speedy and effectual distribution of justice, was likewise sufficient in the hands of a tyrant, to shed the blood of the innocent, and to cancel the rights of men. The temporary proceedings of humanity, though they suspended the exercise of oppression, did not break the national chains: the prince was even the better enabled to procure that species of good which he studied; because there was no freedom remaining, and because there was no where a force to dispute his decrees, or to interrupt their execution.

Was it in vain, that Antoninus became acquainted with the characters of Thrasea, Heividius, Cato, Dion, and Brutus? Was it in vain, that he learned to understand the form of a free community, raised on the basis of equality and justice; or of a monarchy, under which the liberties of the subject were held the most sacred object of administration?[1] Did he mistake the means of procuring to mankind what he points out as a blessing? Or did the absolute power with which he was furnished, in a mighty empire, only disable him from executing what his mind had perceived as a national good? In such a case, it were vain to flatter the monarch or his people. The first cannot bestow liberty, without raising a spirit, which may, on occasion, stand in opposition to his own designs; nor the latter receive this blessing, while they own that it is in the right of a master to give or to with-hold it. The claim of justice is firm and peremptory. We receive favours with a sense of obligation and kindness; but we would inforce our rights, and the spirit of freedom in this exertion cannot take the tone of supplication, or of thankfulness, without betraying itself. 'You have intreated Octavius,' says Brutus to Cicero, 'that he would spare those who stand foremost among the citizens of Rome. What if he will not? Must we perish? Yes; rather than owe our safety to him.'

[1] M. Antoninus, lib. 1.

Liberty is a right which every individual must be ready to vindicate for himself, and which he who pretends to bestow as a favour, has by that very act in reality denied. Even political establishments, though they appear to be independent of the will and arbitration of men, cannot be relied on for the preservation of freedom; they may nourish, but should not supersede that firm and resolute spirit, with which the liberal mind is always prepared to resist indignities, and to refer its safety to itself.

Were a nation, therefore, given to be moulded by a sovereign, as the clay is put into the hands of the potter, this project of bestowing liberty on a people who are actually servile, is, perhaps, of all others, the most difficult, and requires most to be executed in silence, and with the deepest reserve. Men are qualified to receive this blessing, only in proportion as they are made to apprehend their own rights; and are made to respect the just pretensions of mankind; in proportion as they are willing to sustain, in their own persons, the burden of government, and of national defence; and are willing to prefer the engagements of a liberal mind, to the enjoyments of sloth, or the delusive hopes of a safety purchased by submission and fear.

I speak with respect, and, if I may be allowed the expression, even with indulgence, to those who are intrusted with high prerogatives in the political system of nations. It is, indeed, seldom their fault that states are inslaved. What should be expected from them, but that being actuated by human desires, they should be averse to disappointment, or even to delay; and in the ardour with which they pursue their object, that they should break through the barriers that would stop their career? If millions recede before single men, and senates are passive, as if composed of members who had no opinion or sense of their own; on whose side have the defences of freedom given way, or to whom shall we impute their fall? to the subject, who has deserted his station; or to the sovereign, who has only remained in his own; and who, if the collateral or subordinate members of government shall cease to question his power, must continue to govern without any restraint?

It is well known, that constitutions framed for the preservation of liberty, must consist of many parts; and that senates, popular assemblies, courts of justice, magistrates of different orders, must combine to balance each other, while they exercise, sustain, or check the executive power. If any part is struck out, the fabric must totter, or fall; if any member is remiss, the others must incroach. In assemblies constituted by men of different talents, habits, and apprehensions, it were something more than human that could make them agree in every point of importance; having different opinions and views, it were want of integrity to abstain from disputes: our very praise of unanimity, therefore, is to be considered as a danger to liberty. We wish for it, at the hazard of taking in its place, the remissness of men grown indifferent to the public; the venality of those who have sold the rights of their country; or the servility of others, who give implicit obedience to a leader by whom their minds are subdued. The love of the public, and respect to its laws, are the points in which mankind are bound to agree; but if, in matters of controversy, the sense of any individual or party is invariably pursued, the cause of freedom is already betrayed.

He whose office it is to govern a supine or an abject people, cannot, for a moment, cease to extend his powers. Every execution of law, every movement of the state, every civil and military operation, in which his power is exerted, must serve to confirm his authority, and present him to the view of the public, as the sole object of consideration, fear, and respect. Those very establishments which were devised, in one age, to limit, or to direct the exercise of an executive power, will serve, in another, to settle its foundations, and to give it stability; they will point out the channels in which it may run, without giving offence, or without exciting alarms, and the very councils which were instituted to check its incroachments, will, in a time of corruption, furnish an aid to its usurpations.

The passion for independence, and the love of dominion, frequently arise from a common source: There is, in both, an aversion to controul; and he, who, in one situation, cannot bruik a superior, must, in another, dislike to be joined with an equal.

What the prince, under a pure or limited monarchy, is, by the constitution of his country, the leader of a faction would willingly become in republican governments. If he attains to this envied condition, his own inclination, or the tendency of human affairs, seem to open before him the career of a royal ambition: but the circumstances in which he is destined to act, are very different from those of a king. He encounters with men who are unused to disparity; he is obliged, for his own security, to hold the dagger continually unsheathed. When he hopes to be safe, he possibly means to be just; but is hurried, from the first moment of his usurpation, into every exercise of despotical power. The heir of a crown has no such quarrel to maintain with his subjects: his situation is flattering; and the heart must be uncommonly bad, that does not glow with affection to a people, who are, at once, his admirers, his support, and the ornaments of his reign. In him, perhaps, there is no explicit design of trespassing on the rights of his subjects; but the forms intended to preserve their freedom, are not, on this account, always safe in his hands.

Slavery has been imposed upon mankind in the wantonness of a depraved ambition, and tyrannical cruelties have been committed in the gloomy hours of jealousy and terror: yet these demons are not necessary to the creation, or to the support of an arbitrary power. Although no policy was ever more successful than that of the Roman republic in maintaining a national fortune; yet subjects, as well as their princes, frequently imagine that freedom is a clog on the proceedings of government: they imagine, that despotical power is best fitted to procure dispatch and secrecy in the execution of public councils; to maintain what they are pleased to call *political order*,[1] and to give a speedy redress of complaints. They even sometimes acknowledge, that if a succession of good princes could be found, despotical government is best calculated for the happiness of mankind. While they reason thus, they cannot blame a sovereign who, in the confidence that he is to employ his power for good purposes, endeavours to extend its limits; and, in his own apprehension, strives only to shake off the restraints which stand in the way of reason, and which prevent the effects of his friendly intentions.

Thus prepared for usurpation, let him, at the head of a free state, employ the force with which he is armed, to crush the seeds of apparent disorder in every corner of his dominions; let him effectually curb the spirit of dissension and variance among his people; let him remove the interruptions to government,

1 Our notion of order in civil society is frequently false: it is taken from the analogy of subjects inanimate and dead; we consider commotion and action as contrary to its nature; we think it consistent only with obedience, secrecy, and the silent passing of affairs through the hands of a few. The good order of stones in a wall, is their being properly fixed in the places for which they are hewn; were they to stir the building must fall: but the order of men in society, is their being placed where they are properly qualified to act. The first is a fabric made of dead and inanimate parts, the second is made of living and active members. When we seek in society for the order of mere inaction and tranquillity, we forget the nature of our subject, and find the order of slaves, not that of free men.

arising from the refractory humours and the private interests of his subjects; let him collect the force of the state against its enemies, by availing himself of all it can furnish in the way of taxation and personal service: it is extremely probable, that, even under the direction of wishes for the good of mankind, he may break through every barrier of liberty, and establish a despotism, while he flatters himself, that he only follows the dictates of sense and propriety.

When we suppose government to have bestowed a degree of tranquillity, which we sometimes hope to reap from it, as the best of its fruits, and public affairs to proceed, in the several departments of legislation and execution, with the least possible interruption to commerce and lucrative arts; such a state, like that of China, by throwing affairs into separate offices, where conduct consists in detail, and in the observance of forms, by superseding all the exertions of a great or a liberal mind, is more akin to despotism than we are apt to imagine.

Whether oppression, injustice, and cruelty, are the only evils which attend on despotical government, may be considered apart. In the mean time it is sufficient to observe that liberty is never in greater danger than it is when we measure national felicity by the blessings which a prince may bestow, or by the mere tranquillity which may attend on equitable administration. The sovereign may dazzle with his heroic qualities; he may protect his subjects in the enjoyment of every animal advantage or pleasure: but the benefits arising from liberty are of a different sort; they are not the fruits of a virtue, and of a goodness, which operate in the breast of one man, but the communication of virtue itself to many; and such a distribution of functions in civil society, as gives to numbers the exercises and occupations which pertain to their nature.

The best constitutions of government are attended with inconvenience; and the exercise of liberty may, on many occasions, give rise to complaints. When we are intent on reforming abuses, the abuses of freedom may lead us to incroach on the subject from which they are supposed to arise. Despotism itself has certain advantages, or at least, in time of civility and moderation, may proceed with so little offence, as to give no public alarm. These circumstances may lead mankind, in the very spirit of reformation, or by mere inattention, to apply or to admit of dangerous innovations in the state of their policy.

Slavery, however, is not always introduced by mere mistake; it is sometimes imposed in the spirit of violence and rapine. Princes become corrupt as well as their people; and whatever may have been the origin of despotical government, its pretensions, when fully explained, give rise to a contest between the sovereign and his subjects, which force alone can decide. These pretensions have a dangerous aspect to the person, the property, or the life of every subject; they alarm every passion in the human breast; they disturb the supine; they deprive the venal of his hire; they declare war on the corrupt as well as the virtuous; they are tamely admitted only by the coward; but even to him must be supported by a force that can work on his fears. This force the conqueror brings from abroad; and the domestic usurper endeavours to find in his faction at home.

When a people is accustomed to arms, it is difficult for a part to subdue the whole; or before the establishment of disciplined armies, it is difficult for any usurper to govern the many by the help of a few. These difficulties, however, the policy of civilized and commercial nations has sometimes removed; and by forming a distinction between civil and military professions, by committing the keeping and the enjoyment of liberty to different hands, has prepared the way for the dangerous alliance of faction with military power, in opposition to mere political forms, and the rights of mankind.

A people who are disarmed in compliance with this fatal refinement, have rested their safety on the pleadings of reason and justice at the tribunal of ambition and of force. In such an extremity, laws are quoted, and senates are assembled, in vain. They who compose a legislature, or who occupy the civil departments of state, may deliberate on the messages they receive from the camp or the court; but if the bearer, like the centurion who brought the petition of Octavius to the Roman senate, shew the hilt of his sword, they find that petitions are become commands, and that they themselves are become the pageants, not the repositories of sovereign power.

The reflections of this section may be unequally applied to nations of unequal extent. Small communities, however corrupted, are not prepared for despotical government: their members, crouded together, and contiguous to the seats of power, never forget their relation to the public; they pry, with habits of familiarity and freedom, into the pretensions of those who would rule; and where the love of equality, and the sense of justice, have failed, they act on motives of faction, emulation, and envy. The exiled Tarquin had his adherents at Rome; but if by their means he had recovered his station, it is probable, that in the exercise of his royalty, he must have entered on a new scene of contention with the very party that restored him to power.

In proportion as territory is extended, its parts lose their relative importance to the whole. Its inhabitants cease to perceive their connection with the state, and are seldom united in the execution of any national, or even of any factious, designs. Distance from the seats of administration, and indifference to the persons who contend for preferment, teach the majority to consider themselves as the subjects of a sovereignty, not as the members of a political body. It is even remarkable, that enlargement of territory, by rendering the individual of less consequence to the public, and less able to intrude with his counsel, actually tends to reduce national affairs within a narrower compass, as well as to diminish the numbers who are consulted in legislation, or in other matters of government.

The disorders to which a great empire is exposed, require speedy prevention, vigilance, and quick execution. Distant provinces must be kept in subjection by military force; and the dictatorial powers, which, in free states, are sometimes raised to quell insurrections, or to oppose other occasional evils, appear, under a certain extent of dominion, at all times equally necessary to suspend the dissolution of a body, whose parts were assembled, and must be cemented, by measures forcible, decisive, and secret. Among the circumstances, therefore, which in the event of national prosperity, and in the result of commercial arts, lead to the establishment of despotism, there is none, perhaps, that arrives at this termination, with so sure an aim, as the perpetual enlargement of territory. In every state, the freedom of its members depends on the balance and adjustment of its interior parts; and the existence of any such freedom among mankind, depends on the balance of nations. In the progress of conquest, those who are subdued are said to have lost their liberties; but from the history of mankind, to conquer, or to be conquered, has appeared, in effect, the same.

Source: Adam Ferguson, 'Of corruption, as it tends to political slavery', in *An Essay on the History of Civil Society*, ed. D. Forbes, Edinburgh 1966, part 6, section 5, pp. 261–72

THIRTY-TWO

SIR JOHN SINCLAIR
The Statistical Account of Scotland

The *Statistical Account* was published over a period of nine years from 1791, and gives a picture of Scotland parish by parish at a level of detail far greater than is to be found in any earlier study of Scotland. There had been statistical accounts in other countries, but Sinclair was dissatisfied with them, if only because, as he says, 'they have uniformly been instituted, with a view of ascertaining the state of the country, for the purpose of taxation and of war, and not of national improvement'. The implication of this is that statistics sufficient to serve the purposes of taxation and war will be insufficient to serve the purpose of national improvement. It is to national improvement, a major motive of the Scottish Enlightenment, that Sinclair's *Statistical Account* is dedicated, as is further evidenced by his statement that, as regards the term 'statistical', 'the idea I annex to the term, is an enquiry into the state of the country, *for the purpose of ascertaining the* quantum *of happiness enjoyed by its inhabitants, and the means of its future improvement*'.

At the start of the Address here excerpted, when Sinclair comments on the fact that modern philosophy is superior to ancient in virtue of its sure basis in investigation and experiment, the kind of philosophy he has in mind is natural philosophy, the science of nature, supremely exemplified in the work of Newton. Sinclair, however, does not see himself as a Newton, but as a painstaking compiler of the facts that have to be gathered if the science of government is to be brought to the same height of perfection as that achieved by Newton for the science of nature. To that end Sinclair wrote to the ministers of all the parishes enclosing a list of questions, and the Kirk rose to the challenge; by the end of the exercise, Sinclair had received accounts of all nine hundred and thirty eight parishes. (There were nine hundred and thirty six parishes at the end of the exercise, since two amalgamations had by then been effected.) Sir

George Dempster of Dunnichen wrote to Sinclair: 'This is a most valuable and useful work. It is a real Dooms-Day Book, and promises to be more read and quoted than any book printed since Dooms-Day Book. The older it grows, the more valuable it will prove.'

A.B.

The Statistical Account of Scotland

Address to the Reader

The superiority, which the philosophy of modern times has attained over the antient, is justly attributed to that anxious attention to facts, by which it is so peculiarly distinguished. Resting not on visionary theory, but on the sure basis of investigation, and of experiment, it has arisen to a degree of certainty and pre-eminence, of which it was supposed incapable. It is by pursuing the same method, in regard to political disquisitions, by analysing the real state of mankind, and examining, with anatomical accuracy and minuteness, *the internal structure of society*, that the science of government can alone be brought to the same height of perfection.

Many inquiries, it is certain, have, at various periods, been made, into the political circumstances of nations: Unfortunately, however, they have uniformly been instituted, with a view of ascertaining the state of the country, for the purposes of taxation and of war, and not of national improvement. Their object has been, not to meliorate the condition of the people, but to fill the exchequer, or the armies of the state; and the utmost that could be expected from them, was to render taxation, and other public burdens, less unequal. But, in modern times, more extensive and more important objects of investigation have been pointed out. Real statesmen, and true patriots, no longer satisfied with partial and defective views of the situation of a country, are now anxious to ascertain the real state of its agriculture, its manufactures, and its commerce, – the means of improvement, of which they are respectively capable – the amount of the population of a state, and the causes of its increase or decrease – the manner in which the territory of a country is possessed and cultivated – the nature and amount of the various productions of the soil – the value of the personal wealth or stock of the inhabitants, and how it can be augmented – the diseases to which the people are subject, their causes and their cure – the occupations of the people – where they are entitled to encouragement, and where they ought to be suppressed – the condition of the poor, the best mode of maintaining them, and of giving them employment – the state of schools, and other institutions, formed for purposes of public utility – the state of the villages and towns, and the regulations best calculated for their police and good government – the state of the manners, the morals, and the religious principles of the people, and the means by which their temporal and eternal interests can best be promoted.

Impressed with these ideas, in the month of May 1790, I circulated amongst the clergy of the Church of Scotland, a number of Queries, for the purpose of elucidating the political state of my native country. Nothing could be more flattering than the reception they met with, from that learned and respectable body. Scotland is divided into about 950 parochial districts; and, in less than eighteen months, reports were received from above one half of that number. The returns that were transmitted, also, were not trifling or superficial; but, in general, such as might be expected from men of extensive knowledge, and of sound abilities, acquainted with the various topics to which their attention was directed. With so much zeal, indeed, have they entered into this inquiry, that, in less than three or four years from its commencement, this great and extensive survey will probably be completed.

.   .   .

If similar surveys were instituted in the other kingdoms of Europe, it might be the means of establishing, on sure foundations, the principles of that most important of all sciences, to wit, *political* or *statistical philosophy*. That is the science, which, in preference to every other ought to be held in reverence. No science can furnish, to any mind capable of receiving useful information, so much real entertainment; none can yield such important hints, for the improvement of agriculture, for the extension of commercial industry, for regulating the conduct of individuals, or for extending the prosperity of the state; none can tend so much to promote the general happiness of the species.

.   .   .

First Circular Letter to the Clergy of the Church of Scotland
SIR,
I take the liberty of transmitting the inclosed Queries to you, in hopes that a plan, which has been fortunate enough to meet with the approbation of some of the most respectable and distinguished characters in these kingdoms, will be favoured with your assistance.

To procure information with regard to the real political situation of a country, is what wise Statesmen in every age have thought desirable, but which in these enlightened times is justly held of the most essential public importance.

In many parts of the Continent, more particularly in Germany, Statistical Inquiries, as they are called, have been carried to a very great extent; but in no country, it is believed, can they be brought to such perfection as in Scotland, which boasts of an ecclesiastical establishment, whose members will yield to no description of men, for public zeal, as well as for private virtue, for intelligence, and for ability.

I flatter myself, that upon this occasion, they will not be backward in contributing their aid, to promote an attempt, which may prove of considerable service to the country at large, and cannot fail to add to the reputation and character, which the Church of Scotland has already so deservedly acquired for public utility.

> I have the honour to be,
> > Sir, your very obedient,
> > > And faithful humble servant,
> > > > JOHN SINCLAIR

Edinburgh,
May 25, 1790

N. B. It is not expected, that all the inclosed Queries should be answered by any individual; nor is minute exactness looked for: but it is requested, that as many questions may be attended to, as circumstances will admit of.

Copy of the QUERIES drawn up for the purpose of elucidating the Natural History and Political State of Scotland, which were inclosed in the preceding letter.

I   Questions respecting the Geography and Natural History of the Parish

1. What is the ancient and modern name of the Parish?
2. What is the origin and etymology of the name?
3. In what county is it situated?
4. In what presbytery and synod?
5. What is the extent and form of the parish?
6. What its length and breadth?
7. By what parishes is it bounded?
8. What is the general appearance of the country? Is it flat or hilly, rocky or mountainous?
9. What is the nature of the soil? Is it fertile or barren, deep or shallow?

10. What is the nature of the air? Is it moist or dry, unhealthy or otherwise?

11. What are the most prevalent distempers? and to what circumstances are they to be attributed?

12. Are there any mineral springs? and in what diseases are they serviceable?

13. Are there any considerable lakes or rivers in the parish?

14. What species of fish do they produce? In what quantities? What prices do they fetch on the spot? And in what seasons are they in the greatest perfection?

15. Are the rivers navigable? or might they be rendered useful in navigation?

16. Are there any navigable canals in the parish?

17. What is the extent of sea-coast?

18. Is the shore flat, sandy, high, or rocky?

19. What sorts of fish are caught on the coast? In what quantity? At what prices sold? When most in season? How taken? And to what markets sent?

20. What other sea animals, plants, sponges, corals, shells, &c. are found on or near the coast?

21. Are there any remarkable sea weeds used for manuring land, or curious on any other account?

22. Is there any kelp? And what quantity, at an average, is annually made?

23. What are the courses of the tides on the shore or at sea? and are there any rocks, currents, &c. worthy of notice?

24. Are there any light-houses, beacons, or land-marks? or could any be erected that would be of service?

25. What are the names of the principal creeks, bays, harbours, headlands, sands, or islands, near the coast?

26. Have there been any battles or sea fights near the coast? and when did any remarkable wrecks or accidents happen, which can give light to any historical fact?

27. Are there any remarkable mountains? and what are their heights?

28. Are the hills covered with heath, green, or rocky?

29. Are there any volcanic appearances in the parish?

30. Are there any figured stones, or any having the impression of plants or fishes upon them?

31. Are there any fossil marine bodies, such as shells, corals, &c. or any petrified part of animals? or any petrifying springs or waters?

32. Are there any marble, moor-stone, free-stone, slate, or other stones? How are they got at, and what use is made of them?

33. Are there any mines, particularly coal-mines? What are they? To whom do they belong? And what do they produce?

34. Is any part of the parish subject to inundations or land-floods? When did any remarkable event of that nature happen?
35. Hath there been any remarkable mischief done by thunder and lightning, water-spouts or whirlwinds?
36. Are there any remarkable echoes?
37. Have any remarkable phenomena been observed in the air?
38. Are there any remarkable caves or grottos, natural or artificial?
39. What quadrupeds and birds are there in the parish? What migratory birds? and at what times do they appear and disappear?
40. Is the parish remarkable for breeding any species of cattle, sheep, horses, hogs, or goats, of peculiar quality, size, or value?

II   Questions respecting the Population of the Parish

41. What was the ancient state of the population of the parish, so far as it can be traced?
42. What is now the amount of its population?
43. What may be the number of males?
44. What of females?
45. How many reside in towns?
46. —————— villages?
47. —————— the country?
48. What is the annual average of births?
49. What is the annual average of deaths?[1]
50. —————— marriages?
51. —————— souls under 10 years of age?
52. —————— from 10 to 20?
53. —————— 20 to 50?

1 It is of peculiar importance to have the questions 48 and 49 distinctly answered; for it is generally understood, at least on the Continent, that the population of any district or country, may be known with sufficient accuracy, by multiplying the number of births by 26, or the number of deaths by 36. In Scotland, on the other hand, Mr Wilkie, minister of Cults, supposes, that the number either of births and burials, if they are equal, should be multiplied by 40; or, if there is any difference, the half of the whole, (both the births and the burials), should be multiplied by the expectation of an infant's life, adapted to the particular district, in order to ascertain its population. See Statistical Account, vol. II. p. 415. It appears, from Mr Wilkie's calculations, that the expectation of a life in Scotland, is much greater than in England, or on the Continent.

54. ————— 50 to 70?
55. ————— 70 to 100?
56. Above 100?
57. Are there any instances of long lives well authenticated?
58. What may be the number of farmers and their families?
59. ————— manufacturers?
60. ————— handycraftsmen?
61. ————— apprentices?
62. ————— seamen?
63. ————— fishermen?
64. ————— ferrymen?
65. ————— miners?
66. ————— household servants, male and female?
67. ————— labouring servants, male and female?
68. ————— students at colleges and universities?
69. ————— merchants, citizens or tradesmen?
70. ————— artists?
71. ————— Jews?
72. ————— negroes?
73. ————— gipsies?
74. ————— foreigners?
75. ————— persons born in England, Ireland, or the British colonies?
76. What may be the number of persons born in other districts or parishes in Scotland?
77. What may be the number of the nobility and their families?
78. ————— gentry?
79. ————— clergy?
80. ————— lawyers, and writers or attornies?
81. What may be the number of physicians, surgeons, and apothecaries?
82. ————— the established church?
83. ————— seceders?
84. ————— episcopalians?
85. ————— Roman catholics?
86. Is the population of the parish materially different from what it was 5, 10, or 25 years ago? and to what causes is the alteration attributed?
87. What is the proportion between the annual births and the whole population?
88. What is the proportion between the annual marriages and the whole population?
89. What is the proportion between the annual deaths and the whole population?
90. What is the proportion between the batchelors and the married men, widowers included?

91. How many children does each marriage at an average produce?
92. What may be the causes of depopulation?
93. Are there any destructive epidemical distempers?
94. Have any died from want?
95. Have any murders or suicides been committed?
96. Have many emigrated from the parish?
97. Have any been banished from it?
98. Have any been obliged to leave the parish for want of employment?
99. Are there any uninhabited houses?
100. What may be the number of inhabited houses, and the number of persons at an average to each inhabited house?

III Questions respecting the Productions of the Parish

101. What kinds of vegetables, plants, and trees, does the parish produce?
102. What kinds of animals?
103. What at an average is supposed to be the number of cattle, sheep, horses, hogs, and goats, in the district?
104. Is there any map of the parish? and has the number of acres in it been ascertained?
105. How many acres at an average may be employed in raising corn, roots, &c.?
106. What number of acres to each sort respectively, as wheat, barley, rye, oats, potatoes, turnip, cabbage, &c.?
107. Does the parish supply itself with provisions?
108. Does it in general export or import articles of provision?
109. How many acres are employed in raising hemp or flax?
110. How many in sown or artificial grasses?
111. How many in pasture?
112. When do they in general sow and reap their different crops?
113. What quantity of ground may lie waste or in common?
114. What in woods, forests, marshes, lakes, and rivers?
115. Is there any chalk, marl, fullers earth, potters earth, ochre, &c.?
116. Are there any bitumen, naptha, or other substances of that nature found in the soil?

IV Miscellaneous Questions

117. Has the parish any peculiar advantages or disadvantages?
118. What language is principally spoken in it?
119. From what language do the names of places in the parish seem to be derived?
120. What are the most remarkable instances of such derivations?

121. What may the land rent of the parish be?
122. What the rent of houses, fishings, &c.
123. What is the value of the living, including the glebe? and who is the patron?
124. Who is now minister of the parish?
125. How long has he been settled in it?
126. What are the names of his predecessors as far back as they can now be traced, and the time they respectively held that office?
127. Is the minister married, a widower, or single?
128. If with a family, how many sons, and how many daughters?
129. When were the church and the manse built or repaired?
130. What is the number of heritors, or possessors of landed property in the parish?
131. How many of them reside in it?
132. What is the number of the poor in the parish receiving alms?
133. What is the annual amount of the contributions for their relief, and the produce of alms, legacies, or of any other fund destined for that purpose?
134. What are the present or ancient prices of provisions, beef, veal, mutton, lamb, pork, pigs, geese, ducks, chickens, rabbits, butter, cheese, wheat, barley, oats, &c.?
135. What is generally a day's wages for labourers in husbandry, and other work? and what *per* day for carpenters, bricklayers, masons, tailors, &c.?
136. What is the fuel commonly made use of? Is it coal, wood, heath, peat, furze, or whins? What are the prices paid on the spot; and whence is the fuel procured?
137. What, at an average, may be the expence of a common labourer, when married? and is the wages he receives sufficient to enable him to bring up a family?
138. What are the usual wages of male and female servants in the different branches of husbandry?
139. What the wages of domestic servants?
140. How many ploughs are there in the parish? and of what kinds?
141. How many carts and waggons?
142. How many carriages; and of what sorts?
143. Are there any villages in the parish? and how are they situated?
144. Are there any crosses or obelisks erected in the parish?
145. Are there any remains or ruins of monasteries or religious houses?
146. Are there any Roman, Saxon, Danish, or Pictish castles, camps, altars, roads, forts, or other remains of antiquity?

and what traditions or historical accounts are there of them?

147. Have there been any medals, coins, arms, or other pieces of antiquity dug up in the parish? When were they found? And in whose custody are they now?

148. Are there any barrows, or tumuli? Have any been opened? And what has been found therein?

149. Have there been any remarkable battles fought in the parish? On what spot? At what time? By whom? And what traditions are there respecting the same?

150. Has the parish either given birth or burial to any man eminent for learning, or distinguished for any other valuable qualification?

151. Are the people of the country remarkable for strength, size, complexion, or any other personal or mental qualities?

152. What is the general size of the people?

153. What is the greatest height which any individual in the parish has attained, properly authenticated?

154. Are the people disposed to industry? What manufactures are carried on in the parish? And what number of hands are employed therein?

155. Are the people fond of a sea-faring life? What is the number of boats and of larger vessels belonging to the parish? And what number of seamen have entered into the navy during any preceding war?

156. Are the people fond of a military life? Do many inlist in the army? And principally in what corps?

157. Are the people economical, or expensive and luxurious for their circumstances? Is property, particularly in land, often changing? And at what prices is it in general sold?

158. Are the people disposed to humane and generous actions; to protect and relieve the shipwrecked, &c.? and are there any events which have happened in the parish, which do honour to human nature?

159. Do the people, on the whole, enjoy, in a reasonable degree, the comforts and advantages of society? and are they contented with their situation and circumstances?

160. Are there any means by which their condition could be ameliorated?

ADDENDA

1. What is the state of the roads and bridges in the parish? How were they originally made? How are they kept in repair? Is the statute labour exacted in kind, or commuted? Are there any turnpikes? and what is the general opinion of the advantages of turnpike roads?

2. What is in general the rent of the best arable and the best

pasture or meadow grounds, *per* acre? What the rent of inferior?

3. What in general is the size and the average rent of the farms in the parish? And is the number of farms increasing or diminishing?

4. Is the parish in general inclosed, or uninclosed? And are the people convinced of the advantages of inclosures?

5. What was the situation of the parish *anno* 1782 and 1783? Please state any curious or important circumstances connected with that era, or with any other season of scarcity.

6. Are there any curious or important facts tending to prove any great alteration in the manners, customs, dress, stile of living, &c. of the inhabitants of the parish, now, and 20 or 50 years ago?

N.B. If you reside in a town or city, please give an account of the history and antiquities of the place; of its buildings, age, walls, sieges, charters, privileges, immunities, gates, streets, markets, fairs; the number of churches, wards, guilds, companies, fraternities, clubs, &c.: How the town is governed: if it is represented in parliament, to whom does the right of election belong, and what the number of electors? together with a comparison between its ancient and modern state, in regard to population, commerce, shipping, fisheries, manufactures, more particularly at the following periods, about the time of the Union, since the year 1745, and at present.

It may be proper to add, that many important facts and observations may occur to those to whom this paper is addressed, not hinted at in the queries, which it would be particularly obliging in any gentleman to add to any answer which he may take the trouble of drawing up.

Edinburgh,
May 25, 1790

Second printed Circular Letter to the Clergy, with a Specimen of Four Parishes

. . .

Sir,

Some districts, such as the parish of Hounam, furnish little room for statistical investigation. In that case, the state of population, and facts connected with the political circumstances of the country, are all that is necessary. Full accounts are desirable; but, at the same time, no minister ought to hesitate about sending a short one, when there are not means of supplying more important materials.

In the queries formerly sent, some particulars were omitted, of which I should be glad to be informed, even from those gentlemen who have already favoured me with their answers: as,

1. What is the state of the schools in the parish; the salary and perquisites of the schoolmaster; and the number of his scholars?
2. What is the number of alehouses, inns, &c.; and what effect have they on the morals of the people?
3. What is the number of new houses or cottages which have been built within these ten years past; and how many old ones have been pulled down, or have become uninhabitable?
4. What has been the effect of employing cottagers in agriculture, or of working by hired servants in their stead? and,
5. What has been the number of prisoners in any jail in the district, in the course of the year 1790; and for what causes were they imprisoned?

Tables of births, marriages, and deaths, kept in any particular parish, would be very desirable. Nor can the information respecting all points connected with the population of the country, be too accurate and minute.

Edinburgh,
Jan. 25, 1791

Source: Sir John Sinclair (ed.), *The Statistical Account of Scotland*, Edinburgh 1791–9, vol. 3, pp. (xii)–(xvi); vol. 20, pp. xxvi–xxxvi

THIRTY-THREE

SIR JOHN SINCLAIR
Memorial of the Parish Schoolmasters of Scotland

This is an edited version of a text first printed in the *Scots Magazine*, vol. 46, 1784, pp. 1–4, and said to have been circulated to all Scots MPs 'as introductory to a bill for relief of the parish schoolmasters'. Paragraphs 14–19 of the original version were omitted from the version Sinclair published; someone (presumably Sir John Sinclair) has omitted from the original version all matter which was critical of the Scottish parish clergy; and there are curious re-arrangements of the text, presumably – as with some interpolations – to make the text more punchy in an effort to persuade Parliament in 1799 (when the final volume of the *Statistical Account* was published) to move to augment parochial teachers' stipends, as was to be done in 1803. The second last paragraph to the Memorial, beginning 'The memorialist, who is himself no parochial schoolmaster', is rather puzzling. This is not in the original, and again, may be Sir John Sinclair himself, providing a suitable finishing touch to it.

A.B.

Appendix to the Statistical Account

It is thought advisable to reprint the following Memorial, drawn up for the parochial schoolmasters in Scotland, anno 1782. It presents a melancholy picture of their situation; and it gives us, at the same time, a high idea of the dignity and importance of their office. It is proper to observe, that if their situation was then so uncomfortable, their distress must have been much heightened by the rise which has taken place, in the price of provisions, since that time.

The education of youth, in every civilized state, has always been considered as an object of the first importance: because not only the future happiness, but the future existence of the state, in a great measure, depends upon it.

Where a right education is established and universally encouraged, early habits of virtue and good principles contribute more to the safety, peace, and happiness of society, than the most perfect civil and criminal laws can do, where education is neglected.

Every man who has accustomed himself to reflect, must be convinced, that the strength and prosperity of every state depend on the number of virtuous citizens; and that good morals are absolutely necessary to the increase of mankind: and, therefore, by a right institution of youth cannot be meant what is commonly called a learned education, but chiefly that moral discipline which habituates the mind of the pupil in his early youth to discern the beauty of prudence, temperance, justice, fortitude, and charity; to avoid sloth as an enemy, to embrace industry as a friend; to love truth, to abhor falsehood, and universally to refuse the evil and choose the good.

The knowledge of the dead languages, and also of the principal living languages of Europe founded thereon, are both useful and ornamental branches of education for the principal citizens: but to spell, to read and to write our mother tongue with ease, and to understand the common and fundamental rules of arithmetic, is a very necessary addition to the above mentioned moral education of every citizen, male and female.

Without this early education, the understanding can never be opened to the arts of civil life; the vigour of mind that prompts to discovery, to commerce, and to every improvement, must fail; and society itself must languish and decay.

In every civilized country, and especially in our own, there are men whose minds are enlarged enough to see and wish to promote the happiness of their fellow citizens; and these men, who are the supports and ornaments of society, have only to turn their attention to this object for a few moments, and they will readily acknowledge, that the right education of youth is the first and great mean of turning the wilderness into a fruitful field, and the fruitful field into a garden, where innocence, industry, beneficence, and happiness prevail.

From the revival of letters in Europe to the present time, is but a short period in the history of mankind; and yet that period, short as it is, exhibits to the pleased reader a greater portion of public and private happiness, than is to be found in the history of the whole preceding thousand years.

Scotland, or North Britain, struggles with many natural disadvantages; the climate is cold, the sky seldom serene, the weather variable, the soil unfruitful, the mountains bleak, barren, rocky, often covered with snows, and the appearance of the country in many places very forbidding to strangers; yet, by an early attention to the education of youth, to form good men and good citizens, she has uniformly maintained a high character among the nations, has always been deemed an excellent nurse of the human species, and has furnished, not soldiers only, but divines, generals, statesmen, and philosophers, to almost every nation of Europe.

Our ancestors, towards the end of the last century, turning their attention to this subject, beheld with pleasure the progress already made in useful knowledge and arts. They saw that the laws of nature and religion required of parents the virtuous education of their offspring; but they saw also that the increasing cares and avocations of civil life, together with the ignorance of many parents, rendered it necessary to call to their assistance a body of men appointed by the state to attend upon this one thing.

The schoolmasters, thus legally established, were supposed to be men who had turned their attention to the improvement of their minds, to the dignity, virtue, and happiness of human nature, to the distinctions between right and wrong in human conduct; and who were, besides, 'apt to teach,' patient, diligent, and faithful.

The encouragement appointed by the state for this respectable and useful body of men, though not great, was yet well suited to the times, the funds, and distinction of rank at the period. The emoluments of their office placed them above day-labourers, and the poorer class of mechanics and farmers; nay, raised them to an equality with the more opulent farmers, respectable tradesmen and citizens; among whom their employment, their manners, and prospects in life, procured them a degree of respect very advantageous to their profession.

Ninety years have produced such a change, and so great improvements, in the agriculture, navigation, commerce, arts, and riches of this country, that 15l. sterling per annum, at the end of the last century, may be considered as a better income than 45l. sterling per annum at this present time.

Suppose, then, that in Scotland there are 900 parochial schoolmasters, which is very near the truth; 800 of these will be found struggling with indigence, inferior in point of income to 800 day-labourers in the best-cultivated parts of this island, and receiving hardly half the emoluments of the menial servants of country gentlemen and wealthy citizens.

It seems a reproach to the enlightened minds and enlarged views of the present age, that nine hundred of their fellow citizens, selected to form the tempers and characters of a million, by conveying to them the first principles of literature, morality, and religion, should in the last century have been placed in a respectable station, possessing, not merely necessaries, but comforts and conveniences; and, by the progress of improvements, which they themselves have been the means of introducing, that so many of their successors, chosen, like them, out of the great body of the people, to form the minds and manners of more than a million and a half of their fellow subjects to the love of justice, temperance, integrity, industry, and every virtue, and likewise to instruct them in the rudiments of useful literature – should, in this century, be reduced so low as to want the very necessaries of life.

The established clergy of Scotland, who possess a great share of polite and useful learning, and are as virtuous, faithful, and diligent teachers of Christianity, as are now to be found on earth, are all to a man convinced, that unless the minds of children are opened by a right education, *their* instructions from the pulpit will never be understood, and cannot profit the hearers: and therefore, they justly consider it as incumbent on them to superintend the schools; but from the various, laborious, and complicated duties of their office, they cannot engage in the arduous task of teaching children. Many of the clergy too, having spent the first years of manhood in teaching children the elements of literature and of the Christian religion, and struggled with all the difficulties above mentioned, will cheerfully give their best advice and assistance in providing a remedy for the growing evil.

The common people of North Britain have long possessed a

degree of education, both in morals and in letters, unknown to any other subjects of the same rank in the British empire; and hence they have been much employed and much approved in the active departments of life throughout all Europe. The neighbouring nations are all ready to confess, that no servants are more faithful, sober, honest, and industrious; no sailors more hardy and resolute; no soldiers more patient of discipline, or less licentious; and no citizens, who know better both how to command, and how to obey. It is hoped, we shall long retain our national character; and that we may do this the more easily, we ought to give such encouragement to the teachers of youth, as will excite the most virtuous and best educated among the people to embrace this profession.

If no remedy be provided, the unavoidable consequence must be, that few men in any degree qualified to teach will undertake that laborious employment; the citizens from age to age will become more ignorant and less virtuous; and the state will exhibit all the symptoms of a society verging towards destruction.

The memorialist, who is himself no parochial schoolmaster, and can have no expectation of any private emolument, nor any motive for writing this, but the good of his country, has the honour to be known to several noblemen and gentlemen of great property, as well as to many other public-spirited citizens, who have liberal ideas and love their country, and whose sentiments he knows to be the same with his own. Nor does he presume to dictate the provision that ought to be made by law for parochial schoolmasters; but only to suggest, that the present salaries and quarterly payments, received by the established teachers of youth, are totally inadequate to the education which public teachers ought to have, the rank in civil society which they ought to hold, and the pains and labours which they must endure.

If the attention of the public first, and then of the legislature, be turned to this subject, resources will not be wanting for putting the parochial schoolmasters of Scotland on a footing as respectable in regard to emoluments, as their labours are necessary and useful to the virtue and happiness both of individuals, and of the community at large.

Source: Sir John Sinclair (ed.), *The Statistical Account of Scotland*, Edinburgh 1791–9, vol. 21, pp. 336–41

PART VIII

LAW

THIRTY-FOUR

DAVID HUME
Of Justice

According to Hume, justice is not natural but artificial, in a real sense a human invention whose existence is due to certain calculations regarding the appropriate constraints we have to impose upon ourselves to achieve an end universally desired. Justice is thus to be contrasted with the affection a person has for a friend, with the love a parent has for a child, with the compassion we feel for a person in pain. All these feelings are fine and meritorious, and indeed without them there could be no recognisably human society. However, they are none of them contrived; they well up naturally. Hume contends that there is no such thing as a feeling of justice that wells up naturally; it is not by a law of our nature that we respect the property of others and refrain from using it without their permission and return it to them if it has been loaned to us. A system of justice is instituted because public utility is best served by this means.

To establish this claim Hume starts at his invariable starting point, human nature, our emotional no less than our rational nature, and asks what practical judgments human beings would make in extreme circumstances. In circumstances of superabundance of all the things that anyone could want there would be no room for rules governing property. If we suppose the opposite scenario, namely such scarcity of essentials that many will perish and the life of everyone is precarious, then again, argues Hume, we will see that the laws of justice do not operate. A person shipwrecked does not refrain from grabbing and using a buoyant object merely because it is not his to use. The question of whose it is is irrelevant in this life-or-death situation.

We however live in an intermediate circumstance between a superabundance of all we might want, and a serious scarcity of bare necessities. It is only in such circumstances that the concept of property can arise, because it is only in those circumstances that public utility can be served by a practical distinction between mine and thine.

It is noteworthy that, in his discussion of these two extremes and their intermediate, Hume restricts himself to questions concerning property. Other writers of that period regarded the concept of justice as embracing not only property but also equality, human rights, and so on. Despite this point of mild criticism, Hume's discussion of justice in relation to property remains of great interest.

A.B.

Of Justice

PART I

That Justice is useful to society, and consequently that *part* of its merit, at least, must arise from that consideration, it would be a superfluous undertaking to prove. That public utility is the *sole* origin of justice, and that reflections on the beneficial consequences of this virtue are the *sole* foundation of its merit; this proposition, being more curious and important, will better deserve our examination and enquiry.

Let us suppose that nature has bestowed on the human race such profuse *abundance* of all *external* conveniencies, that, without any uncertainty in the event, without any care or industry on our part, every individual finds himself fully provided with whatever his most voracious appetites can want, or luxurious imagination wish or desire. His natural beauty, we shall suppose, surpasses all acquired ornaments: the perpetual clemency of the seasons renders useless all clothes or covering: the raw herbage affords him the most delicious fare; the clear fountain, the richest beverage. No laborious occupation required: no tillage: no navigation. Music, poetry, and contemplation form his sole business: conversation, mirth, and friendship his sole amusement.

It seems evident that, in such a happy state, every other social virtue would flourish, and receive tenfold increase; but the cautious, jealous virtue of justice would never once have been dreamed of. For what purpose make a partition of goods, where every one has already more than enough? Why give rise to property, where there cannot possibly be any injury? Why call this object *mine*, when upon the seizing of it by another, I need but stretch out my hand to possess myself to what is equally valuable? Justice, in that case, being totally useless, would be an idle ceremonial, and could never possibly have place in the catalogue of virtues.

We see, even in the present necessitous condition of mankind, that, wherever any benefit is bestowed by nature in an unlimited abundance, we leave it always in common among the whole human race, and make no subdivisions of right and property. Water and air, though the most necessary of all objects, are not challenged as the property of individuals; nor can any man commit injustice by the most lavish use and enjoyment of these blessings. In fertile extensive countries, with few inhabitants, land is regarded on the same footing. And no topic is so much insisted on by those, who defend the liberty of the seas, as the unexhausted use of them in navigation. Were the advantages, procured by navigation, as inexhaustible, these reasoners had never had any adversaries to refute; nor had any claims ever been advanced of a separate, exclusive dominion over the ocean.

It may happen, in some countries, at some periods, that there be established a property in water, none in land;[1] if the latter be in greater abundance than can be used by the inhabitants, and the former be found, with difficulty, and in very small quantities.

Again; suppose, that, though the necessities of human race continue the same as at present, yet the mind is so enlarged, and so replete with friendship and generosity, that every man has the utmost tenderness for every man, and feels no more concern for his own interest than for that of his fellows; it seems evident, that the use of justice would, in this case, be suspended by such an extensive benevolence, nor would the divisions and barriers of property and obligation have ever been thought of. Why should I bind another, by a deed or promise, to do me any good office, when I know that he is already prompted, by the strongest inclination, to seek my happiness, and would, of himself, perform the desired service; except the hurt, he thereby receives, be greater than the benefit accruing to me? in which case, he knows, that, from my innate humanity and friendship, I should be the first to oppose myself to his imprudent generosity. Why raise land-marks between my neighbour's field and mine, when my heart has made no division between our interests; but shares all his joys and sorrows with the same force and vivacity as if originally my own? Every man, upon this supposition, being a second self to another, would trust all his interests to the discretion of every man; without jealousy, without partition, without distinction. And the whole human race would form only one family; where all would lie in common, and be used freely, without regard to property; but cautiously too, with as entire regard to the necessities of each individual, as if our own interests were most intimately concerned.

In the present disposition of the human heart, it would, perhaps, be difficult to find complete instances of such enlarged affections; but still we may observe, that the case of families approaches towards it; and the stronger the mutual benevolence is among the

1 Genesis, chaps. xiii and xxi.

individuals, the nearer it approaches; till all distinction of property be, in a great measure, lost and confounded among them. Between married persons, the cement of friendship is by the laws supposed so strong as to abolish all division of possessions; and has often, in reality, the force ascribed to it. And it is observable, that, during the ardour of new enthusiasms, when every principle is inflamed into extravagance, the community of goods has frequently been attempted; and nothing but experience of its inconveniences, from the returning or disguised selfishness of men, could make the imprudent fanatics adopt anew the ideas of justice and of separate property. So true is it, that this virtue derives its existence entirely from its necessary *use* to the intercourse and social state of mankind.

To make this truth more evident, let us reverse the foregoing suppositions; and carrying everything to the opposite extreme, consider what would be the effect of these new situations. Suppose a society to fall into such want of all common necessaries, that the utmost frugality and industry cannot preserve the greater number from perishing, and the whole from extreme misery; it will readily, I believe, be admitted, that the strict laws of justice are suspended, in such a pressing emergence, and give place to the stronger motives of necessity and self-preservation. Is it any crime, after a shipwreck, to seize whatever means or instrument of safety one can lay hold of, without regard to former limitations of property? Or if a city besieged were perishing with hunger; can we imagine, that men will see any means of preservation before them, and lose their lives, from a scrupulous regard to what, in other situations, would be the rules of equity and justice? The use and tendency of that virtue is to procure happiness and security, by preserving order in society: but where the society is ready to perish from extreme necessity, no greater evil can be dreaded from violence and injustice; and every man may now provide for himself by all the means, which prudence can dictate, or humanity permit. The public, even in less urgent necessities, opens granaries, without the consent of proprietors; as justly supposing, that the authority of magistracy may, consistent with equity, extend so far: but were any number of men to assemble, without the tie of laws or civil jurisdiction; would an equal partition of bread in a famine, though effected by power and even violence, be regarded as criminal or injurious?

Suppose, likewise, that it should be a virtuous man's fate to fall into the society of ruffians, remote from the protection of laws and government; what conduct must he embrace in that melancholy situation? He sees such a desperate rapaciousness prevail; such a disregard to equity, such contempt of order, such stupid blindness to future consequences, as must immediately have the most tragical conclusion, and must terminate in destruction to the greater number, and in a total dissolution of society to the rest. He, meanwhile, can have no other expedient than to arm himself, to whomever the sword he seizes, or the buckler, may belong: To make provision of all means of defence and security: And his particular regard to justice being no longer of use to his own safety or that of others, he must consult the dictates of self-preservation alone, without concern for those who no longer merit his care and attention.

When any man, even in political society, renders himself by his crimes, obnoxious to the public, he is punished by the laws in his goods and person; that is, the ordinary rules of justice are, with regard to him, suspended for a moment, and it becomes equitable to inflict on him, for the *benefit* of society, what otherwise he could not suffer without wrong or injury.

The rage and violence of public war; what is it but a suspension of justice among the warring parties, who perceive, that this virtue is now no longer of any *use* or advantage to them? The laws of war, which then succeed to those of equity and justice, are rules calculated for the *advantage* and *utility* of that particular state, in which men are now placed. And were a civilized nation engaged with barbarians, who observed no rules even of war, the former must also suspend their observance of them, where they no longer serve to any purpose; and must render every action or rencounter as bloody and pernicious as possible to the first aggressors.

Thus, the rules of equity or justice depend entirely on the particular state and condition in which men are placed, and owe their origin and existence to that utility, which results to the public from their strict and regular observance. Reverse, in any considerable circumstance, the condition of men: Produce extreme abundance or extreme necessity: Implant in the human breast perfect moderation and humanity, or perfect rapaciousness and malice: By rendering justice totally *useless*, you thereby totally destroy its essence, and suspend its obligation upon mankind.

The common situation of society is a medium amidst all these extremes. We are naturally partial to ourselves, and to our friends; but are capable of learning the advantage resulting from a more equitable conduct. Few enjoyments are given us from the open and liberal hand of nature; but by art, labour, and industry, we can extract them in great abundance. Hence the ideas of property become necessary in all civil society: Hence justice derives its usefulness to the public: And hence alone arises its merit and moral obligation.

These conclusions are so natural and obvious, that they have not escaped even the poets, in their descriptions of the felicity attending the golden age or the reign of Saturn. The seasons, in that first period of nature, were so temperate, if we credit these agreeable fictions, that there was no necessity for men to provide themselves with clothes and houses, as a security against the violence of heat and cold: The rivers flowed with wine and milk: The oaks yielded honey; and nature spontaneously produced her greatest delicacies. Nor were these the chief advantages of that happy age. Tempests were not alone removed from nature; but those more furious tempests were unknown to human breasts, which now cause such uproar, and engender such confusion. Avarice, ambition, cruelty, selfishness, were never heard of: Cordial affection, compassion, sympathy, were the only movements with which the mind was yet acquainted. Even the punctilious distinction of *mine* and *thine* was banished from among that happy race of mortals, and carried with it the very notion of property and obligation, justice and injustice.

This *poetical* fiction of the *golden age* is, in some respects, of a piece with the *philosophical* fiction of the *state of nature*; only that the former is represented as the most charming and most peaceable condition, which can possibly be imagined; whereas the latter is painted out as a state of mutual war and violence, attended with the most extreme necessity. On the first origin of mankind, we are told, their ignorance and savage nature were so prevalent, that they could give no mutual trust, but must each depend upon himself and his own force or cunning for protection and security. No law was heard of: No rule of justice known: No distinction of property regarded: Power was the only measure of right; and a perpetual war of all against all was the result of men's untamed selfishness and barbarity.[1]

1 This fiction of a state of nature, as a state of war,
was not first started by Mr. Hobbes, as is commonly
imagined. Plato endeavours to refute an hypothesis
very like it in the second, third, and fourth books
de republica. Cicero, on the contrary, supposes it
certain and universally acknowledged in the following
passage. 'Quis enim vestrum, judices, ignorat, ita
naturam rerum tulisse, ut quodam tempore homines,
nondum neque naturali neque civili jure descripto, fusi

Whether such a condition of human nature could ever exist, or if it did, could continue so long as to merit the appellation of a *state*, may justly be doubted. Men are necessarily born in a family-society, at least; and are trained up by their parents to some rule of conduct and behaviour. But this must be admitted, that, if such a state of mutual war and violence was ever real, the suspension of all laws of justice, from their absolute inutility, is a necessary and infallible consequence.

The more we vary our views of human life, and the newer and more unusual the lights are in which we survey it, the more shall we be convinced, that the origin here assigned for the virtue of justice is real and satisfactory.

Were there a species of creatures intermingled with men, which, though rational, were possessed of such inferior strength, both of body and mind, that they were incapable of all resistance, and could never, upon the highest provocation, make us feel the effects of their resentment; the necessary consequence, I think, is that we should be bound by the laws of humanity to give gentle usage to these creatures, but should not, properly speaking, lie under any restraint of justice with regard to them, nor could they possess any right or property, exclusive of such arbitary lords. Our intercourse with them could not be called society, which supposes a degree of equality; but absolute command on the one side, and servile obedience on the other. Whatever we covet, they must instantly resign: Our permission is the only tenure, by which they hold their possessions: Our compassion and kindness the only check,

per agros ac dispersi vagarentur tantumque haberent
quantum manu ac viribus, per caedem ac vulnera,
ant eripere aut retinere potuissent? Qui igitur primi
virtute & consilio praestanti extiterunt, ii perspecto
genere humanae docilitatis atque ingenii, dissipatos
unum in locum congregarunt, eosque ex feritate illa ad
justitiam ac mansuetudinem transduxerunt. Tum res ad
communem utilitatem, quas publicas appellamus, tum
conventicula hominum, quae postea civitates nominatae
sunt, tum domicilia conjuncta, quas urbes dicamus,
invento & divino & humano jure, moenibus sepserunt.
Atque inter hanc vitam, perpolitam humanitate, &
illam immanem, nihil tam interest quam JUS atque
VIS. Horum utro uti nolimus, altero est utendum. Vim
volumus extingui. Jus valeat necesse est, id est, judicia,
quibus omne jus continetur. Judicia displicent, aut nulla
sunt. Vis dominetur necesse est. Haec vident omnes.'
Pro Sext. §. 42.

by which they curb our lawless will: And as no inconvenience ever results from the exercise of a power, so firmly established in nature, the restraints of justice and property, being totally *useless*, would never have place in so unequal a confederacy.

This is plainly the situation of men, with regard to animals; and how far these may be said to possess reason, I leave it to others to determine. The great superiority of civilized Europeans above barbarous Indians, tempted us to imagine ourselves on the same footing with regard to them, and made us throw off all restraints of justice, and even of humanity, in our treatment of them. In many nations, the female sex are reduced to like slavery, and are rendered incapable of all property, in opposition to their lordly masters. But though the males, when united, have in all countries bodily force sufficient to maintain this severe tyranny, yet such are the insinuation, address, and charms of their fair companions, that women are commonly able to break the confederacy, and share with the other sex in all the rights and privileges of society.

Were the human species so framed by nature as that each individual possessed within himself every faculty, requisite both for his own preservation and for the propagation of his kind: Were all society and intercourse cut off between man and man, by the primary intention of the supreme Creator: It seems evident, that so solitary a being would be as much incapable of justice, as of social discourse and conversation. Where mutual regards and forbearance serve to no manner of purpose, they would never direct the conduct of any reasonable man. The headlong course of the passions would be checked by no reflection on future consequences. And as each man is here supposed to love himself alone, and to depend only on himself and his own activity for safety and happiness, he would, on every occasion, to the utmost of his power, challenge the preference above every other being, to none of which he is bound by any ties, either of nature or of interest.

But suppose the conjunction of the sexes to be established in nature, a family immediately arises; and particular rules being found requisite for its subsistence, these are immediately embraced; though without comprehending the rest of mankind within their prescriptions. Suppose that several families unite together into one society, which is totally disjoined from all others, the rules, which preserve peace and order, enlarge themselves to the utmost extent of that society; but becoming then entirely useless, lose their force when carried one step farther. But again suppose, that several distinct societies maintain a kind of intercourse for mutual convenience and advantage, the boundaries of justice still grow large, in proportion to the largeness of men's views, and the force of their mutual connexions. History, experience, reason sufficiently instruct us in this natural progress of human sentiments, and in the gradual enlargement of our regards to justice, in proportion as we become acquainted with the extensive utility of that virtue.

PART II

If we examine the *particular* laws, by which justice is directed, and property determined; we shall still be presented with the same conclusion. The good of mankind is the only object of all these laws and regulations. Not only it is requisite, for the peace and interest of society, that men's possessions should be separated; but the rules, which we follow, in making the separation, are such as can best be contrived to serve farther the interests of society.

We shall suppose that a creature, possessed of reason, but unacquainted with human nature, deliberates with himself what rules of justice or property would best promote public interest, and establish peace and security among mankind: His most obvious thought would be, to assign the largest possessions to the most extensive virtue, and give every one the power of doing good, proportioned to his inclination. In a perfect theocracy, where a being, infinitely intelligent, governs by particular volitions, this rule would certainly have place, and might serve to the wisest purposes: But were mankind to execute such a law; so great is the uncertainty of merit, both from its natural obscurity, and from the self-conceit of each individual, that no determinate rule of conduct would ever result from it; and the total dissolution of society must be the immediate consequence. Fanatics may suppose, *that dominion is founded on grace,* and *that saints alone inherit the earth*; but the civil magistrate very justly puts these sublime theorists on the same footing with common robbers, and teaches them by the severest discipline, that a rule, which, in speculation, may seem the most advantageous to society, may yet be found, in practice, totally pernicious and destructive.

That there were *religious* fanatics of this kind in England, during the civil wars, we learn from history; though it is probable, that the obvious *tendency* of these principles excited such horror in mankind, as soon obliged the dangerous enthusiasts to renounce, or at least conceal their tenets. Perhaps the *levellers*, who claimed an equal distribution of property, were a kind of *political* fanatics, which arose from the religious species, and more openly avowed their pretensions; as carrying a more plausible appearance, of being practicable in themselves, as well as useful to human society.

It must, indeed, be confessed, that nature is so liberal to mankind, that, were all her presents equally divided among the species, and improved by art and industry, every individual would enjoy all the necessaries, and even most of the comforts of life; nor would ever be liable to any ills, but such as might accidentally arise from the sickly frame and constitution of his body. It must also be confessed, that, wherever we depart from this equality, we rob the poor of more satisfaction than we add to the rich, and that the slight gratification of a frivolous vanity, in one individual, frequently costs more than bread to many families, and even provinces. It may appear withal, that the rule of equality, as it would be highly *useful*, is not altogether *impracticable*; but has taken place, at least in an imperfect degree, in some republics; particularly that of Sparta; where it was attended, it is said, with the most beneficial consequences. Not to mention that the Agrarian laws, so frequently claimed in Rome, and carried into execution in many Greek cities, proceeded, all of them, from a general idea of the utility of this principle.

But historians, and even common sense, may inform us, that, however specious these ideas of *perfect* equality may seem, they are really, at bottom, *impracticable*; and were they not so, would be extremely *pernicious* to human society. Render possessions ever so equal, men's different degrees of art, care, and industry will immediately break that equality. Or if you check these virtues, you reduce society to the most extreme indigence; and instead of preventing want and beggary in a few, render it unavoidable to the whole community. The most rigorous inquisition too is requisite to watch every inequality on its first appearance; and the most severe jurisdiction, to punish and redress it. But besides, that so much authority must soon degenerate into tyranny, and be exerted with great partialities; who can possibly be possessed of it, in such a situation as is here supposed? Perfect equality of possessions, destroying all subordination, weakens extremely the authority of magistracy, and must reduce all power nearly to a level, as well as property.

We may conclude, therefore, that in order to establish laws for the regulation of property, we must be acquainted with the nature and situation of man; must reject appearances, which may be false, though specious; and must search for those rules, which are, on the whole, most *useful* and *beneficial*. Vulgar sense and slight experience are sufficient for this purpose; where men give not way to too selfish avidity, or too extensive enthusiasm.

Who sees not, for instance, that whatever is produced or improved by a man's art or industry ought, for ever, to be secured to him, in order to give encouragement to such *useful* habits and accomplishments? That the property ought also to descend to children and relations, for the same *useful* purpose? That it may be alienated by consent, in order to beget that commerce and intercourse, which is so *beneficial* to human society? And that all contracts and promises ought carefully to be fulfilled, in order to secure mutual trust and confidence, by which the general *interest* of mankind is so much promoted?

Examine the writers on the laws of nature; and you will always find, that, whatever principles they set out with, they are sure to terminate here at last, and to assign, as the ultimate reason for every rule which they establish, the convenience and necessities of mankind. A concession thus extorted, in opposition to systems, has more authority than if it had been made in prosecution of them.

What other reason, indeed, could writers ever give, why this must be *mine* and that *yours*; since uninstructed nature surely never made any such distinction? The objects which receive those appellations are, of themselves, foreign to us; they are totally disjoined and separated from us; and nothing but the general interests of society can form the connexion.

Sometimes the interests of society may require a rule of justice in a particular case; but may not determine any particular rule, among several, which are all equally beneficial. In that case, the slightest *analogies* are laid hold of, in order to prevent that indifference and ambiguity, which would be the source of perpetual dissension. Thus possession alone, and first possession, is supposed to convey property, where no body else has any preceding claim and pretension. Many of the reasonings of lawyers are of this analogical nature, and depend on very slight connexions of the imagination.

Does any one scruple, in extraordinary cases, to violate all regard to the private property of individuals, and sacrifice to public interest a distinction, which had been established for the sake of that interest? The safety of the people is the supreme law: All other particular laws are subordinate to it, and dependent on it: And if, in the *common* course of things, they be followed and regarded; it is only because the public safety and interest *commonly* demand so equal and impartial an administration.

Sometimes both *utility* and *analogy* fail, and leave the laws of justice in total uncertainty. Thus, it is highly requisite, that prescription or long possession should convey property; but what number of days or months or years should be sufficient for that purpose, it is impossible for reason alone to determine. *Civil laws* here supply the place of the natural *code*, and assign different terms for prescription, according to the different *utilities*, proposed by the legislator. Bills of exchange and promissory notes, by the laws of most countries, prescribe sooner than bonds, and mortgages, and contracts of a more formal nature.

In general we may observe that all questions of property are subordinate to the authority of civil laws, which extend, restrain, modify, and alter the rules of natural justice, according to the particular *convenience* of each community. The laws have, or ought to have, a constant reference to the constitution of government, the manners, the climate, the religion, the commerce, the situation of each society. A late author of genius, as well as learning, has prosecuted this subject at large, and has established, from these principles, a system of political knowledge, which abounds in ingenious and brilliant thoughts, and is not wanting in solidity.[1]

---

[1] The author of *L'Esprit des Loix*. This illustrious writer, however, sets out with a different theory, and supposes all right to be founded on certain *rapports* or relations; which is a system, that, in my opinion, never will be reconciled with true philosophy. Father Malebranche, as far as I can learn, was the first that started this abstract theory of morals, which was afterwards adopted by Cudworth, Clarke, and others; and as it excludes all sentiment, and pretends to found everything on reason, it has not wanted followers in this philosophic age. See Section I, Appendix I. With regard to justice, the virtue here treated of, the inference against this theory seems short and conclusive. Property is allowed to be dependent on civil laws; civil laws are allowed to have no other object, but the interest of society: This therefore must be allowed to be the sole foundation of property and justice. Not to mention, that our obligation itself to obey the magistrate and his laws is founded on nothing but the interests of society.

If the ideas of justice, sometimes, do not follow the dispositions of civil law; we shall find, that these cases, instead of objections, are confirmations of the theory delivered above. Where a civil law is so perverse as to cross all the interests of society, it loses all its authority,

What is a man's property? Anything which it is lawful for him, and for him alone, to use. *But what rule have we, by which we can distinguish these objects?* Here we must have recourse to statutes, customs, precedents, analogies, and a hundred other circumstances; some of which are constant and inflexible, some variable and arbitrary. But the ultimate point, in which they all professedly terminate, is the interest and happiness of human society. Where this enters not into consideration, nothing can appear more whimsical, unnatural, and even superstitious, than all or most of the laws of justice and of property.

Those who ridicule vulgar superstitions, and expose the folly of particular regards to meats, days, places, postures, apparel, have an easy task; while they consider all the qualities and relations of the objects, and discover no adequate cause for that affection or antipathy, veneration or horror, which have so mighty an influence over a considerable part of mankind. A Syrian would have starved rather than taste pigeon; an Egyptian would not have approached bacon: But if these species of food be examined by the senses of sight, smell, or taste, or scrutinized by the sciences of chemistry, medicine, or physics, no difference is ever found between them and any other species, nor can that precise circumstance be pitched on, which may afford a just foundation for the religious passion. A fowl on Thursday is lawful food; on Friday abominable: Eggs in this house and in this diocese, are permitted during Lent; a hundred paces farther, to eat them is a damnable sin. This earth or building, yesterday was profane; to-day, by the muttering of

and men judge by the ideas of natural justice, which are conformable to those interests. Sometimes also civil laws, for useful purposes, require a ceremony or form to any deed; and where that is wanting, their decrees run contrary to the usual tenour of justice; but one who takes advantage of such chicanes, is not commonly regarded as an honest man. Thus, the interests of society require, that contracts be fulfilled; and there is not a more material article either of natural or civil justice: But the omission of a trifling circumstance will often, by law, invalidate a contract, *in foro humano*, but not *in foro conscientiae*, as divines express themselves. In these cases, the magistrate is supposed only to withdraw his power of enforcing the right, not to have altered the right. Where his intention extends to the right, and is conformable to the interests of society; it never fails to alter the right; a clear proof of the origin of justice and of property, as assigned above.

certain words, it has become holy and sacred. Such reflections as these, in the mouth of a philosopher, one may safely say, are too obvious to have any influence; because they must always, to every man, occur at first sight; and where they prevail not, of themselves, they are surely obstructed by education, prejudice, and passion, not by ignorance or mistake.

It may appear to a careless view, or rather a too abstracted reflection, that there enters a like superstition into all the sentiments of justice; and that, if a man expose its object, or what we call property, to the same scrutiny of sense and science, he will not, by the most accurate enquiry, find any foundation for the difference made by moral sentiment. I may lawfully nourish myself from this tree; but the fruit of another of the same species, ten paces off, it is criminal for me to touch. Had I worn this apparel an hour ago, I had merited the severest punishment; but a man, by pronouncing a few magical syllables, has now rendered it fit for my use and service. Were this house placed in the neighbouring territory, it had been immoral for me to dwell in it; but being built on this side the river, it is subject to a different municipal law, and by its becoming mine I incur no blame or censure. The same species of reasoning it may be thought, which so successfully exposes superstition, is also applicable to justice; nor is it possible, in the one case more than in the other, to point out, in the object, that precise quality or circumstance, which is the foundation of the sentiment.

But there is this material difference between *superstition* and *justice*, that the former is frivolous, useless, and burdensome; the latter is absolutely requisite to the well-being of mankind and existence of society. When we abstract from this circumstance (for it is too apparent ever to be overlooked) it must be confessed, that all regards to right and property, seem entirely without foundation, as much as the grossest and most vulgar superstition. Were the interests of society nowise concerned, it is as unintelligible why another's articulating certain sounds implying consent, should change the nature of my actions with regard to a particular object, as why the reciting of a liturgy by a priest, in a certain habit and posture, should dedicate a heap of brick and timber, and render it, thenceforth and for ever, sacred.[1]

1 It is evident, that the will or consent alone never
  transfers property, nor causes the obligation of a
  promise (for the same reasoning extends to both) but
  the will must be expressed by words or signs, in

These reflections are far from weakening the obligations of justice, or diminishing anything from the most sacred attention to property. On the contrary, such sentiments must acquire new force from the present reasoning. For what stronger foundation can be desired or conceived for any duty, than to observe, that human society, or even human nature, could not subsist without the establishment of it; and will still arrive at greater degrees of

order to impose a tie upon any man. The expression being once brought in as subservient to the will, soon becomes the principal part of the promise; nor will a man be less bound by his word, though he secretly give a different direction to his intention, and withhold the assent of his mind. But though the expression makes, on most occasions, the whole of the promise, yet it does not always so; and one who should make use of any expression, of which he knows not the meaning, and which he uses without any sense of the consequences, would not certainly be bound by it. Nay, though he know its meaning, yet if he use it in jest only, and with such signs as evidently show, that he has no serious intention of binding himself, he would not lie under any obligation of performance; but it is necessary, that the words be a perfect expression of the will, without any contrary signs. Nay, even this we must not carry so far as to imagine, that one, whom, by our quickness of understanding, we conjecture, from certain signs, to have an intention of deceiving us, is not bound by his expression or verbal promise, if we accept of it; but must limit this conclusion to those cases where the signs are of a different nature from those of deceit. All these contradictions are easily accounted for, if justice arise entirely from its usefulness to society; but will never be explained on any other hypothesis.

It is remarkable, that the moral decisions of the *Jesuits* and other relaxed casuists, were commonly formed in prosecution of some such subtilties of reasoning as are here pointed out, and proceed as much from the habit of scholastic refinement as from any corruption of the heart, if we may follow the authority of Mons. Bayle. See his Dictionary, article Loyola. And why has the indignation of mankind risen so high against these casuists; but because every one perceived, that human society could not subsist were such practices authorized, and that morals must always be handled with a view to public interest, more than philosophical regularity? If the secret division of the intention, said every man of sense, could invalidate a contract; where is our security? And yet a metaphysical happiness and perfection, the more inviolable the regard is, which is paid to that duty?

The dilemma seems obvious: As justice evidently tends to promote public utility and to support civil society, the sentiment of justice is either derived from our reflecting on that tendency, or like hunger, thirst, and other appetites, resentment, love of life, attachment to offspring, and other passions, arises from a simple original instinct in the human breast, which nature has implanted for like salutary purposes. If the latter be the case, it follows, that property, which is the object of justice, is also distinguished by a simple original instinct, and is not ascertained by any argument or reflection. But who is there that ever heard of such an instinct? Or is this a subject in which new discoveries can be made? We may as well expect to discover, in the body, new senses, which had before escaped the observation of all mankind.

But farther, though it seems a very simple proposition to say, that nature, by an instinctive sentiment, distinguishes property, yet in reality we shall find, that there are required for that purpose ten thousand different instincts, and these employed

schoolman might think, that, where an intention was supposed to be requisite, if that intention really had not place, no consequence ought to follow, and no obligation be imposed. The casuistical subtilties may not be greater than the subtilties of lawyers, hinted at above; but as the former are *pernicious*, and the latter *innocent* and even *necessary*, this is the reason of the very different reception they meet with from the world.

It is a doctrine of the Church of Rome, that the priest, by a secret direction of his intention, can invalidate any sacrament. This position is derived from a strict and regular prosecution of the obvious truth, that empty words alone, without any meaning or intention in the speaker, can never be attended with any effect. If the same conclusion be not admitted in reasonings concerning civil contracts, where the affair is allowed to be of so much less consequence than the eternal salvation of thousands, it proceeds entirely from men's sense of the danger and inconvenience of the doctrine in the former case: And we may thence observe, that however positive, arrogant, and dogmatical any superstition may appear, it never can convey any thorough persuasion of the reality of its objects, or put them, in any degree, on a balance with the common incidents of life, which we learn from daily observation and experimental reasoning.

about objects of the greatest intricacy and nicest discernment. For when a definition of *property* is required, that relation is found to resolve itself into any possession acquired by occupation, by industry, by prescription, by inheritance, by contract, &c. Can we think that nature, by an original instinct, instructs us in all these methods of acquisition?

These words too, inheritance and contract, stand for ideas infinitely complicated; and to define them exactly, a hundred volumes of laws, and a thousand volumes of commentators, have not been found sufficient. Does nature, whose instincts in men are all simple, embrace such complicated and artificial objects, and create a rational creature, without trusting anything to the operation of his reason?

But even though all this were admitted, it would not be satisfactory. Positive laws can certainly transfer property. Is it by another original instinct, that we recognize the authority of kings and senates, and mark all the boundaries of their jurisdiction? Judges too, even though their sentence be erroneous and illegal, must be allowed, for the sake of peace and order, to have decisive authority, and ultimately to determine property. Have we original innate ideas of praetors and chancellors and juries? Who sees not, that all these institutions arise merely from the necessities of human society?

All birds of the same species in every age and country, built their nests alike: In this we see the force of instinct. Men, in different times and places, frame their houses differently: Here we perceive the influence of reason and custom. A like inference may be drawn from comparing the instinct of generation and the institution of property.

How great soever the variety of municipal laws, it must be confessed, that their chief out-lines pretty regularly concur; because the purposes, to which they tend, are everywhere exactly similar. In like manner, all houses have a roof and walls, windows and chimneys; though diversified in their shape, figure, and materials. The purposes of the latter, directed to the conveniencies of human life, discover not more plainly their origin from reason and reflection, than do those of the former, which point all to a like end.

I need not mention the variations, which all the rules of property receive from the finer turns and connexions of the imagination, and from the subtilties and abstractions of law-topics and reasonings. There is no possibility of reconciling this observation to the notion of original instincts.

What alone will beget a doubt concerning the theory, on which I insist, is the influence of education and acquired habits, by which we are so accustomed to blame injustice, that we are not, in every instance, conscious of any immediate reflection on the pernicious consequences of it. The views the most familiar to us are apt, for that very reason, to escape us; and what we have very frequently performed from certain motives, we are apt likewise to continue mechanically, without recalling, on every occasion, the reflections, which first determined us. The convenience, or rather necessity, which leads to justice is so universal, and everywhere points so much to the same rules, that the habit takes place in all societies; and it is not without some scrutiny, that we are able to ascertain its true origin. The matter, however, is not so obscure, but that even in common life we have every moment recourse to the principle of public utility, and ask, *What must become of the world, if such practices prevail? How could society subsist under such disorders?* Were the distinction or separation of possessions entirely useless, can any one conceive, that it ever should have obtained in society?

Thus we seem, upon the whole, to have attained a knowledge of the force of that principle here insisted on, and can determine what degree of esteem or moral approbation may result from reflections on public interest and utility. The necessity of justice to the support of society is the sole foundation of that virtue; and since no moral excellence is more highly esteemed, we may conclude that this circumstance of usefulness has, in general, the strongest energy, and most entire command over our sentiments. It must, therefore, be the source of a considerable part of the merit ascribed to humanity, benevolence, friendship, public spirit, and other social virtues of that stamp; as it is the sole source of the moral approbation paid to fidelity, justice, veracity, integrity, and those other estimable and useful qualities and principles. It is entirely agreeable to the rules of philosophy, and even of common reason; where any principle has been found to have a great force and energy in one instance, to ascribe to it a like energy in all similar instances. This indeed is Newton's chief rule of philosophizing.[1]

Source: David Hume, *An Enquiry concerning the Principles of Morals*, section 3 'Of justice', in *Enquiries concerning Human Understanding and concerning the Principles of Morals*, ed. L. A. Selby-Bigge, 3rd edn by P. H. Nidditch, Oxford 1975, pp. 183–204

1 *Principia*, Lib. iii.

THIRTY-FIVE

JOHN ERSKINE OF CARNOCK
Of Laws in General

In this excerpt Erskine provides the framework for a detailed presentation of Scots law. The framework is the theory of natural law, which focuses upon orderliness in the world, patterns of change which enable us to deal with the world in a reasonably confident way. The orderliness of the world can also be described as its lawlike behaviour. All nature operates under the law of nature, which is a law promulgated by God for everything in nature, but a distinction is to be drawn between on the one hand intelligent beings with consciousness and free will and on the other hand everything else. Free beings are free to reject God's law; all other beings obey God's law because they can do nothing else.

Erskine states that the law God promulgated for us free spirits, that we can discover either by reading Scripture or by reading the law 'written in our hearts', is law in the 'strict' sense, and the law for all material creation, from which things cannot deviate, is law in the 'large' sense. The terminology used here, though traditional, is misleading, since law in the strict sense is not a more precisely or more narrowly defined version of law in the large sense. They are instead two sorts of law applying to different sorts of being, to free spirits and non-free beings.

Positive law, law promulgated by a human authority, ought to be consonant with natural law. But even when it is consonant with it, positive law is not simply a more closely or narrowly defined version of natural law. There are many kinds of act to which natural law is indifferent, and it is within this area that positive law has room to operate. In many fields it is necessary for society to agree about the practice it will follow though it does not matter precisely what is agreed; all that matters is the agreement itself. The rule of the road is a conspicuous example; so far as natural law is concerned we can agree to drive on the left or on the right, but we cannot allow a free-for-all. On this matter Erskine follows Aristotle who said of positive law that it treats of things which are indifferent before enactment and necessary after. In that sense natural law provides the space within which positive law can grow.

A.B.

Of Laws in General

The word Law is frequently made use of, both by divines and philosophers, in a large acceptation to express the settled method of God's providence, by which he preserves the order of the material world in such a manner that nothing in it may deviate from that uniform course which he has appointed for it; and as brute matter is merely passive, without the least degree of choice upon its part, these laws are inviolably observed in the material creation, every part of which continues to act, immutably, according to the rules that were from the beginning prescribed to it by infinite wisdom. Thus, philosophers have given the appellation of law to that motion which incessantly pervades and agitates the universe, and is ever changing the form and substance of things, dissolving some, and raising others, as from their ashes, to fill up the void; yet so that, amidst all the fluctuations by which particular things are affected, the universe is still preserved without diminution; *Gravina, de jure nat.* Thus also they speak of the laws of fluids, of gravitation, etc.; and the word is used in this sense in several passages of the sacred writings: in the book of Job, and in Prov. viii. 29, where God is said to have given his law to the seas, that they should not pass his commandment. But law, in the strict meaning of the word, is peculiar to intelligent beings, endued with consciousness and liberty of will, who consequently have an inward power of acting and forbearing, and by disregarding the prescriptions of the law contract guilt, and render themselves obnoxious to punishment. In this restricted meaning, God directs his laws, either to pure spirits or to the human race. But as the law of pure spirits has no immediate relation to the conduct of man, nor indeed falls within the reach of human capacity, the subject of this treatise is to be confined to laws which are prescribed to mankind.

2. Law, even when it is thus limited, is an equivocal word, sometimes denoting the science which teacheth what things are or are not just, styled by the Romans *jurisprudentia*, and sometimes what is contained in that science; or, in other words, the particular rules to which the science is applied. In this last acceptance, law may be defined the command of a sovereign, containing a common rule of life for his subjects, and obliging them to obedience. By a sovereign is understood the supreme power, whether it be lodged in the hands of one or of many.

3. Laws must be directed to those alone whom the lawgiver has a right to command; for the obligation to obey, on the part of the person commanded, can have no other foundation than his dependence on the lawgiver, and the lawgiver's just power of directing his actions. That cannot be a rule of life which is impossible or unintelligible, or of which one cannot be assured whether it be truly commanded. The thing prescribed as a law, therefore, must be in itself possible to be performed; it must be so distinctly exhibited as to convey a precise knowledge of its meaning to those who are to be bound by it; and it must be notified to them in such a way as they may know it to be the will of their sovereign. As the end of law is an equal distribution of justice, on which the happiness of every society depends, all laws ought to be in themselves just. This character is inseparable from the laws of God, who is justice itself; and human laws, when they prescribe anything repugnant to natural justice, have no coercive force.

4. Justice, when it is ascribed, not to laws, but to persons, consists in the conformity of one's actions to law. Ulpian, indeed, copying after the stoic philosophy, has defined it to be a constant and uniform disposition of mind to give every man his due; L. 10, *pr. de just. et jur.* But though this definition may pass without censure from the pen of a divine or a moralist, who considers persons according to the judgment of God, not merely by their actions, but by the inward springs which move to action, yet human tribunals cannot judge by the affections of the mind. If a man act conformably to law, he must be accounted just, whatever his motives to action may have been. On the contrary, if one fail to make good his engagements in any matter of civil right, *ex. gr.* to discharge his debts; though this may have been owing to unavoidable misfortune, yet he is in the judgment of law unjust, and therefore subjected to imprisonment, or such other penalty as the law has inflicted on that constructive transgression.

5. When laws have a tendency to promote the real happiness of the subjects, that alone creates an obligation to obedience, called by Heineccius and other writers, the internal obligation of law. This, however, would be insufficient of itself for enforcing obedience, if these laws were not also guarded by a commination of some punishment or evil which is not the natural consequence of the transgression. That part of the law which inflicts the punishment upon disobedience is called its sanction, from *sancire*, 'to confirm,' because it is that which gives the enactment full force and authority, and chiefly preserves it from being violated by perverse men, who would disregard the true grounds of obedience. Hence it

follows that a sanction, though it should not be expressed in the law, is implied; so that a magistrate or judge to whom the execution of the law is committed may inflict a punishment on the transgressor, greater or less, according to the demerit of the offence. This doctrine seems to be admitted by all writers, even by Hobbes (*De Cive*, ch. 14, §. 8), and is taken for granted in several of our statutes, enjoining certain things to be done for the police of the country, in which, though no special penalty is annexed to the enactment, it is recommended to the judge to see the law carried into execution (1661, c. 41, etc.); and how this can be done effectually without punishing the breach of the law is hard to imagine.

6. Under the sanction of the law may be also included that part of it which proposes rewards as encouragements to obedience. Cumberland (c. 5, *de. leg. nat.*, § 40) maintains that this is the chief and most proper sanction of a law. But his reasoning appears too subtile, and it is certain that this species of sanction is but little in the power of earthly lawgivers. No state can possibly furnish out a stock sufficient for rewarding all who may live in a due observance of the laws; it is God alone, who can not only inflict the severest pains upon transgressors, but also, from the inexhaustible treasures of his power and goodness, animate his creatures to obedience by the highest rewards.

7. Law is divided into the law of Nature, the law of Nations, and Civil or Municipal law. The law of nature may be defined after Grotius, the dictate of reason, by which we discover whether an action be morally good or evil, by its agreement or disagreement with the rational and social nature of man. That there is such a law cannot be denied, without denying the essential attributes of the Deity. Man is endued by his Creator with intellectual faculties, capable of distinguishing between truth and error, between real and apparent happiness; and with a power either of acting immediately, if his judgment shall so direct him, or of suspending the execution of his purposes in cases which require deliberation, till he shall, by a thorough examination, be satisfied of their rectitude. The infinitely wise and good God hath not thus enlightened the soul of man merely to enable him, by an abuse of his understanding, to range more expertly, and with greater success, in the paths of violence and oppression, without being accountable for his wickedness. God necessarily wills what is just and good; and that divine will which we are capable of discerning by natural light, truly constitutes a law to us. The law of nature, therefore, has the God of Nature for its author; and it is not made known

to us by any formal or external notification of His will, but is impressed on our minds by the internal suggestion of reason; and is therefore elegantly said by St Paul to be written by God upon the heart of every one of us.

8. The law of nature hath for its objects, God, our neighbour, and ourselves, according to Tully, *Tusc. Quæst.* l. 1, c. 26. Its duties are known by attending to the relations in which man stands to his Creator, to his fellow-creatures of mankind, and to the other beings that surround him, and by considering the nature and frame of the human constitution. Thus the essential reason of things teaches us to reverence and obey God, who, as our Creator and Preserver, hath the highest title to our worship and obedience; to honour and obey our parents, to whom, under God, we owe our being; to adhere strictly to our obligations and engagements; to perform all the friendly offices we can to those with whom nature hath intended that we should live together in a state of society, as mutual helps to one another; to do to them whatever we might reasonably expect they should do to us in the like circumstances; to take a proper care of our own preservation; to restrain our natural passions and appetites within due bounds; and to cultivate and improve our faculties to the utmost of our power, etc.

9. As a necessary consequence of this, the law of nature lays an indispensable obligation to obedience on the whole human race who have the exercise of their reason, without exception; for all men are alike subject to the command of their Maker, and the frame of the human constitution is the same in every individual. As that constitution, therefore, and the relations of men to other beings must always continue what God at first made them, the duties of natural law must also be of unchangeable obligation. 'It is not therefore one law in Rome and another in Athens, one to-day and another to-morrow; but it is ever the same, exerting its obligatory force over all nations, and throughout all ages;' as Cicero expresses himself in a beautiful fragment preserved by Lactantius, l. 6, c. 8.

10. The observance of the law of nature is strongly enforced by that faculty of the mind called Conscience, by which we are not only informed of what we ought to do, but enabled to turn our eyes inward upon ourselves; and after recollecting and examining our past actions by the test of reason, to pass judgment, either approving or condemning them. The terrors which take fast hold of wicked men upon a sense of their guilt, though they should be placed beyond the reach of human censure, or concealed from

the view of their fellow-creatures, clearly prove their knowledge, not only of the law itself, but of its being fenced with the heaviest penalties. On the other hand, that inward serenity of mind, on the reflection of having led a virtuous life, or of having performed any act of disinterested justice, humanity, or self-denial, is the reward which God hath been pleased to bestow, even in this life, upon those who give a willing obedience to his law.

11. The Romans have, with great impropriety, ascribed this law to the brute part of the creation; L. 1, § 3, *de just. et jur.* Creatures which are merely sensitive have no faculties which can be influenced by motives above sense; they act from necessity, and so are not capable of proper obedience, nor consequently of the obligations of law. On this account also, infants, before they have attained the use of reason, and idiots, who either never had reason, or have lost the use of it, are not to be accounted moral agents, or subjected to punishment as transgressors; for where there is no law there can be no transgression.

12. Writers divide the law of nature into the primary and the secondary. The primary is that which regards men, simply considered, or in their state of nature, previous to any human act or establishment. To this branch of the division the instances already given of natural law may be applied. The secondary respects men as they are formed into several distinct and independent states; and it arises from the nature of society, and from the necessities of mankind as members of it. Because this sort can have no room till men be placed in particular circumstances; Puffendorf, and some writers after him, have chosen to call it the hypothetical law of nature.

13. From this secondary law of nature the right of property hath arisen. By the first or original law all things were common. The few who inhabited the earth were, for some time after the creation, served abundantly with such of its fruits as sprang up without culture or industry; so that no person needed to take possession of more than served his present necessities. But as men multiplied, experience soon taught that society could not long subsist if this common use of things continued. A right of property was therefore established, whereby every man had a certain portion of ground appropriated to him, which he might hold for ever if he did not himself abandon it, or transfer it to another. From hence hath proceeded that mutual intercourse among men which branches out into the contracts of barter, sale, hire, loan, and most of the others mentioned in law books. It is evident that this secondary law is derived by necessary consequence from the primary; and

that it is nothing more in effect than the first and most obvious principles of natural law applied to the state of civil society; for civil government is so far from destroying the essential relations of men and things that it enables us to discharge the duties of that primary law to one another, with greater advantage to the community.

14. The law of nations in its proper sense is that which comprises in it all the duties which one independent state or body-politic owes to another. Both the law of nature and of nations derive their coercive power from reason alone, and so both may be justly said to be prescribed by God himself; for as independent nations may be considered with respect to each other as so many political persons in a state of equality among themselves, the same duties which nature has laid on individuals must be also binding upon states in their mutual intercourse. That, therefore, which is the law of nature when applied to men considered in their first condition, is truly the law of nations when applied to two or more independent kingdoms. Hence, Mr Hobbes not improperly divides the law of nature into the natural law of men and the natural law of states, which last is, in other words, the law of nations. Under this law may be classed the rights of war, the security of ambassadors, the obligations arising from treaties, etc.

15. But the law of nations is frequently understood in a very different sense. It is made to signify those rules that are generally received by sovereign powers for fixing the order of their mutual correspondence, whether in times of war or of peace; *ex. gr.* the form of declaring war previous to any acts of hostility; the regulations relating to reprisals, to contraband goods found aboard neutral ships, to the exchange of prisoners, and to suspension of arms or negotiations of peace, the ceremonial of receiving and entertaining ambassadors, the privileges indulged to their servants and domestics, etc. But these rules make no part of the law of nations in its proper acceptation; for they are arbitrary, and may, without violating the law of nature, be changed for others equally agreeable to right reason. If therefore they are to be accounted laws, they ought to be thrown into the class of positive, which derive their sole authority either from express treaties, or from the tacit agreement of nations, and whereof the obligation can last no longer than the agreement on which it is grounded. And, in fact, several of those rules, where they have been established merely by usage, without express stipulation, are frequently altered by a kingdom or state, without consulting with or giving previous notice to the neighbouring powers.

16. There are certain laws of nature of the greatest importance to society, the observance of which is not enforced by the positive law of any country; either because they consist in the affections of the mind, which are beyond the reach of earthly judges, or because the wisest and best constituted policy cannot settle their measures and degrees by special rules. Of this sort are benevolence to our neighbours, charity to the poor, protection of innocence, gratitude for benefits received, temperance, etc. All these are left entirely to the conscience, without any aid from human penalties, and are therefore said to have God alone for their avenger.

17. The law of nature, of which God is the author, must needs be perfect in its kind. The depravity of men's minds, however, often leads them to pervert that law in its application to particular cases. Hence it hath become necessary for the supreme power in all civilized states to superadd certain rules to it for explaining its true extent where that appears doubtful, and adapting it with some degree of precision to the several exigencies of the state; that so all the members of the community, instead of being left to their own partial reasonings, may be tied down by a set of laws that speak the same uniform language to every individual. To illustrate this by an instance or two; by one of the laws of nature fathers are bound to leave at their death some part at least of their substance to their children; and by another, every man has a right to dispose of his property to whom he will. That neither of those laws may be stretched beyond its just limits, it is highly expedient that special rules be prescribed for fixing the particular proportions of the father's estate which he is disabled from leaving to strangers to the prejudice of his own issue; that so every member of the state may be taught to give to both of these laws their due weight. Again, it is without doubt a breach of the law of nature to take the smallest advantage of the seller's necessity in a contract of sale; but as the greatest human sagacity cannot discover whether the buyer hath done so, unless in so far as outward circumstances may make it presumable, it was highly expedient for the supreme power to fix a standard, as has been done by most states, by which judges might presume whether the bargain was fair or not.

18. That law which is thus superadded to the law of nature by the legislative power of any sovereign state is called civil, and sometimes positive, or municipal. It hath the name of civil because it is enacted by a *civitas*, or state. It is styled positive, in contradistinction to that law which is impressed on us by nature itself, without positive enactment. The appellation of municipal

was, in the original acceptation of the word among the Romans, proper to such laws as obliged *municipia*, or dependent states, which, though they could of themselves claim no right of legislation, being subject to the Roman power, yet had certain magistrates invested with a limited power of enacting laws that were binding upon their own community; L. 21, § 7; L. 25, *ad munic*; L. 6, *de decr. ab ord. fac.* But that word hath by degrees been drawn to signify also laws enacted by sovereign states.

19. The right of legislation is vested in the sovereign alone, or the supreme power of the state; for none other but the supreme power has a right to exact our obedience. No independent state can subsist without a supreme power, or a right of commanding in the last resort; and supreme power cannot restrain itself. No enactment, therefore, of the legislative power in one age can fetter that power in any succeeding age; for the legislature of every age, as it has the unlimited power of making laws, must have the same right of abrogating or altering former laws, otherwise it would cease to be supreme; and from hence the rule arises, *Posteriora derogant prioribus*; L. 4, *de const. princip.* Where the supreme power resides in one person, as in an absolute monarchy, the sovereign is the only lawgiver. If it be vested jointly in the king and the states of the kingdom, as in Britain, the people cannot be bound by an enactment in which the king and the states do not concur. A nation subject to the dominion of a foreign prince, can have no supreme power within itself; and consequently no right of legislation, except in so far as the state on which it depends has granted a permission; L. 9, *de leg. Rhod.* Such was the case of the Roman *municipia*, and other tributary kingdoms. But this doctrine cannot be justly applied to feudatory kings or princes; who, though they are bound to do homage for their crowns to the sovereigns of whom they are holden, have nevertheless an unlimited right of prescribing laws to their own subjects, so long as they take care not to forfeit that right by any feudal delinquency.

20. The supreme power may not only superadd, but even circumscribe or set bounds to the law of nature, without violating its authority. On this head doctors generally distinguish between the preceptive and the concessive law of nature. By the preceptive is meant that which the law of nature either expressly commands or forbids. Concessive is that which gives a man a right without obliging him to exercise it. What the law of nature has commanded cannot be forbidden, or even dispensed with, by positive law; and in like manner what it prohibits cannot be commanded, or even permitted, by human authority. The law of nature being indeed

the command of God, to whom all his creatures owe absolute obedience, no earthly lawgiver who is himself subject to that law hath a right of abrogating or controlling it. Obedience, therefore, to any enactment which is plainly adverse to the preceptive law of nature is rebellion against God. But where the law of nature is barely concessive, bestowing upon a person a right of acting, without obliging him to make use of it, he may not only give it up by compact, but, by entering into civil society, he is understood to vest the legislature with a power of taking it from him, either in whole or in part, if the common interest shall so require. Hence it may be concluded that things which natural law has left mankind at liberty either to do or to forbear, and these only, are the matter of positive law; which is therefore defined by Aristotle, that which treats of things which were indifferent before the enactment, but become necessary afterwards. This points out the true reason why positive law is not, like the law of nature, immutable, but may, and indeed in many cases ought to be, altered or abrogated, according to the changes wrought by time on the riches, commerce, or manners of the people.

21. Though the laws of nature require no formal or external notification (*supr.* § 7), positive law, which, however agreeable it may be to reason, is not discoverable by it, cannot possibly be known, nor consequently serve for a rule of life, till it be promulged to those whose conduct it is to regulate; L. 9, C. *de legib.* After the law is promulged no pretence of ignorance can justify the breach of it, according to the rule *Ignorantia juris neminem excusat*; L. 9, *pr. et* § 3, *de jur. et fac. ign.* And though this may bear hard upon such individuals as from their way of life, have no access to be apprised of it, even after its promulgation; yet if any such excuse were to be admitted it would be pleaded by every transgressor.

22. Laws are given as a common rule of life for the whole people of a kingdom or state, and hence they are called *communia præcepta* and *communes reipublicæ sponsiones.* Nor are they obligatory only upon the natural subjects of the state by birth, but likewise, upon those who are merely temporary subjects by residence; for the civil rights, even of foreigners, must be determined by the laws of that country where they reside for the time. From this property of law it follows, that rules made only for one person, or for a particular corporation, or body of men, are not proper laws; L. 8. *de legib.* Of this kind are gifts, pardons, exemptions, monopolies. They are commonly called privileges; *privæ leges;* and judges are not obliged to take notice of them, if they are not pleaded upon in judgment by the party interested.

23. If laws are given for a rule of life, they must consequently look forward, and can regulate future cases only; for past actions are not in our power, and so admit no rule. Sir George Mackenzie (§ 11, h. t.) excepts from this conclusion laws which, without any new enactment, declare what was formerly law. But that exception is improper; for the only purpose of a declaratory law is, to explain the meaning of a prior statute in a doubtful point – so that it has no retrospect. It is the first law which obliges; the last does no more than give to that first a just interpretation, and it is included in the notion of interpretation, that it must draw back to the date of the law interpreted.

24. It has been doubted whether statutes which, without either commanding or forbidding, simply allow persons to do certain things, are proper laws; because all laws lay by their nature an obligation upon those to whom they are directed; whereas, in actions which the law declares indifferent, no necessity is laid upon any one to act. Nevertheless, even permissive laws imply a positive right in certain persons to have or enjoy the use of certain things, which necessarily draws after it a prohibition that no other shall hinder or obstruct the exercise of it; so that a law of this sort, though it lays no obligation on him to whom the permission is granted, is still a prohibitory law as to others.

25. Civil law is either barely such – mere civil – or mixed. That is barely civil which derives its whole force from the arbitrary will of the lawgiver, without any obvious foundation in nature; as the Roman laws of adoption, and most of those which have been calculated for the forming and perfecting of the feudal system. Mixed civil law is that which is plainly founded in the law of nature, but which, by adding to, or varying from, that law, gives a particular modification to things which nature had left undetermined. Of this sort are the laws of marriage, tutory, testaments, contracts, etc., which are, by the peculiar civil law of each state, clothed with proper forms, that their use may become fixed and certain to the whole community.

26. Positive or civil law may be also divided into divine and human. God himself delivered to the Jews a law, distinct from the law of nature, not only in relation to their ritual observances, but with respect to their public polity and private right, the last of which is called the judicial law of Moses. Some have affirmed that this law, being enacted by an infallible lawgiver, ought to be copied, in so far as it goes, by every other state; and it must be admitted that no part of it is contrary to the law of nature; for God, who is the author of both, cannot contradict himself. But

no positive law, let it be ever so agreeable to the law of nature, can oblige those to whom it is not directed. The ordinances of the Jewish law, in as far as they are the necessary result of reason, and so make part of the preceptive law of nature, must without doubt be binding universally; not because God prescribed them as a rule to the Jews, but because natural law had enjoined their observance antecedently to all enactment. But whatever in that law is adapted specially to the Jewish constitution, or framed with a particular view to the genius of that people, may be disregarded by the legislature of other states, without any want of reverence to its great Author. And indeed most of the Jewish laws will be found, on strict examination, to be either wholly or in part of this last kind.

27. Among all the systems of human law which now exist, the Roman so well deserves the first place, on account of the equity of its precepts and the justness of its reasonings, that wherever the civil law is mentioned, without the addition of any particular state, the Roman law is always understood by way of excellency, though that epithet is alike applicable to the laws of every state. Great weight therefore is given to it, not only in Scotland (of which afterwards), but in most of the nations in Europe. In England, it is of considerable authority in the Courts of Chancery, Admiralty, and Arches; and several axioms of their common law are borrowed from the old Roman jurisconsults. This law was from an immense bulk brought down to a moderate size, and reduced into method, by the Emperor Justinian, who, in the year 533, caused compile an institute of it, under the name of the Pandects or Digests; and immediately after an abridgment or breviary, which he called Institutions. In 534 he published the Code, or a collection of the constitutions of the emperors his predecessors, from Adrian down to his own time; and these, joined to such as were afterwards enacted occasionally by himself, and a few of his successors, called the Novels, make up the body of the Roman law. Upon the repeated inroads made into Italy soon after Justinian's death by the Goths, Lombards, and other barbarous nations, the Roman law declined fast in its authority, and the books of it either suffered by the fate of war, or lay concealed in private libraries till towards the middle of the twelfth century, when a copy of the Pandects having been found at Amalphi, that law was again publicly taught by authority in the schools of Italy, and from thence quickly spread over all the nations of Europe.

28. Soon after the recovery of the Pandects at Amalphi, a body

of law began to be composed, under the direction of the Bishop of Rome, styled the Canon law, from *canon*, a rule, the name given to the ordinances of churchmen assembled in councils or synods, to distinguish them from the constitutions of temporal sovereigns. It was formed to conciliate authority to that extensive jurisdiction which the pope had usurped over the civil rights as well as the consciences of men; and it contains rules, not only for informing the conscience, but for the fixing of private property, civil as well as ecclesiastical. It is compounded, on the one hand, of beautiful principles of equity, chiefly borrowed from the Roman law; and, on the other, of a collection of absurd canons and rescripts, extolling church-authority above the highest secular powers. The body of the canon law consists, *first*, of the *Decretum*, a collection made by Gratian, a Benedictine monk, after the middle of the twelfth century, drawn from the opinions of the fathers, popes, and church-councils, in imitation of the Roman Pandects, which were gathered from the opinions of their jurisconsults; *secondly*, the *Decretalia*, which were collected by Pope Gregory IX. near a century after, from the decretal rescripts or epistles of the popes, as Justinian's Code was from the imperial constitutions, to which decretals new collections were added by several succeeding popes. It may be observed, that when mention is made of the common law in our statutes, the Roman is understood, either by itself (1540, c. 69; 1585, c. 18; 1587, c. 31), or in conjunction with the canon law (1540, c. 80; 1551, c. 22). When the expression is fuller, the common laws of the realm, our ancient usages are meant, whether derived from the Roman law, the feudal customs, or whatever other source; 1503, c. 79; 1584, c. 131, etc. The epithet of Common Law is used by English lawyers nearly in this last sense, to denote their most ancient customary law anterior to statute.

29. Positive law may be divided into public and private. The public law is that which hath more immediately in view the public weal, and the preservation and good order of society; as laws concerning the constitution of the state, the administration of the government, the police of the country, public revenues, trade and manufactures, the punishment of crimes, etc. Private law is that which is chiefly intended for ascertaining the civil rights of individuals. The private law of Scotland is to be the proper subject of this treatise; to which a general sketch of that part of the public law that relates to crimes shall be subjoined in the last Title.

30. The municipal law of Scotland may be divided, after the example of the Romans, into written and unwritten. Written or

statutory law is enacted by the express authority of the supreme power, and is always reduced into writing. Unwritten or customary law derives force wholly from the legislature's tacit or presumed consent, and is generally transmitted from one age to another, by oral tradition and universal usage. Where the customary law of a state is, by the sovereign's order, collected into one body to preserve its remembrance the more incorrupt, and confirmed by him, it becomes thereby the explicit enactment of the supreme power, and consequently makes part of the written law of that state.

.   .   .

50. On this head [the interpretation of a statute – see para. 3 above] it may be premised, *first*, That statutes can in no case be explained into a sense which infers injustice or absurdity, or which, if admitted, would render them of no effect; for laws enacted by the wisdom of a nation must be presumed to be agreeable to the immutable laws of nature, consistent in themselves, and made for some salutary purpose; L. 19, *de legib. Secondly*, That properly there is place for interpretation with regard to those statutes only, the words of which are either obscure, or admit of two different senses; arg. L. 25, § 1, *de legat. Thirdly*, Where the words of a statute are incapable of a double meaning, they must be explained in that only sense which they can bear, whatever hardship this may draw after it; L. 12, § 1, *qui et a quib.* By the precise words in which the statute is conceived every interpretation is excluded except that which necessarily arises from the words themselves; and a judge who should, under the pretence of equity, explain a law in a sense inconsistent with the words, would assume the character of a lawgiver rather than that of a judge.

51. The interpretation of laws ought not to depend on critical learning, or the subtile distinctions of schoolmen: for they are directed to the whole body of the people; and therefore ought to be construed in that sense which the words most obviously suggest to the understanding, L. 67, *de reg. jur.*; otherwise the lower part of mankind would be obliged by laws which, for want of acquired parts, they are not able to comprehend. As a consequence of this, no statute ought to be explained figuratively, where the proper meaning of the words is as commodious, and equally suited to its subject. This rule holds more especially where the statute treats of matters concerning which persons do not usually advise with lawyers, but trust to their own judgment; for there the lawgiver is presumed to speak *ad captum vulgi*, in a popular style; Bacon, *ibid.* aphor. 68. But where any term of law which hath a known legal signification occurs in a statute, it is to be interpreted not

according to the popular use of the word, but in its legal sense: for lawgivers, when they make use of technical words, are presumed to enact in the style of law.

52. Where the words of a statute are dark, the obscurity may be removed, and the true meaning of the law discovered, by comparing them with other parts of the same statute, where the lawgiver hath expressed his mind more clearly. It is therefore recommended to judges (L. 24, *de legib.*) to have the whole tenor of the law under view, and not to cull out detached words or sentences from it, which may pervert its true meaning. Former statutes also are of considerable use in interpretation; for posterior laws ought, in doubtful articles, to be explained most agreeably to former enactments on the same subject; L. 28, *de legib.* If there be none, the usage of our own country, and the laws even of neighbouring kingdoms, may throw light on the difficulty. *Lastly*, Doubtful laws ought to receive that interpretation which suits best with the intention of the lawgiver; L. 17, 18, *ibid.* Indeed to this every rule of interpretation delivered in systems may be reduced; for they are all drawn, either more immediately or more remotely, from his presumed will. Where, therefore, the strict letter seems contrary to the spirit of law, or to equity, judges ought not to regard the proper or received signification of the words so much as that meaning which appears most consonant to the design of the law.

Source: John Erskine of Carnock, *An Institute of the Law of Scotland*, 2 vols, 8th edn, 1871, reprinted with introduction by W. W. McBryde, Edinburgh 1989, Book 1, title 1, pp. 1–11, 22–23

THIRTY-SIX

ADAM SMITH
Duties of the Sovereign

Smith holds that the first two paramount duties of the sovereign are (i) to protect society from violence and invasion by other independent societies, and (ii) as far as possible, to protect every member of the society from the injustice or oppression of every other member (See *Wealth of Nations*, pp. 689, 708). These two duties are related immediately to the three supreme powers of the sovereign, discussed in this excerpt: the federative, the judicial and the legislative. The first of the sovereign's paramount duties relates to the federative power, exercised by the sovereign in so far as the state, in unity, faces outward to other states. In this mode of activity the most important tasks are to wage war and to make and maintain peace with other states. The second power exercised by the sovereign is the power to set up and maintain a judicial system, thereby contributing to peace at home by ensuring, among other things, that citizens resort to the courts, rather than to private vengeance, to get justice. This power is plainly related to the second of the paramount duties of the sovereign, to protect the citizens from each other.

Smith, who always has a historical perspective on the concepts he analyses, claims that the judicial power is antecedent to the third power, the legislative, and is exercised because of the sheer dangerousness of the power of the judges. He is engaging at this point in what Dugald Stewart terms 'conjectural history' (see excerpt 39). Smith's claim is supported by argument, of course, but the claim is, all the same, conjectural, in the sense that it is not supported by direct evidence such as written records. At a very early stage of society somebody would be brought in, or would simply appoint himself, to pass judgment on the basis of a natural feeling of justice, and while this was on the whole a better way of handling disputes than letting people kill each other, there remained both a large degree of uncertainty as regards the outcome of the judge's deliberations, and also the possibility of serious disagreement as to the quality of the judge's intuitions about justice. What was needed, according to Smith, was legislation which would place constraints upon the judge's decisions by educating his intuitions about justice. It would also reduce the degree of uncertainty. The law imposed by the legislative power is therefore as much a form of protection for each citizen who stands before the judge as it is for each citizen in relation to each other.

This point prompts a question regarding the duties of the sovereign in relation to the subjects. The question is difficult to answer because of the relations between legislator and judiciary. One way to find out what the law means is to see what happens in law courts. We can say a great deal about the meaning of laws concerning the relation of subject to subject and of subject to sovereign. But sovereigns hardly ever, if ever, stand before a properly constituted court. Hence even if there are constraints on the behaviour of sovereigns, these are not tested in a court of law but by other means, principally by violence or the threat of it.

If the sovereign loses in a fight against his subjects he is then branded a tyrant and a despot, with the implication that he was duty bound not to be either of these things. But what justifies this implication? In his Jurisprudence lecture of 22 March 1763 Smith sets out to answer this question and begins by setting to one side the view that the sovereign power owes its origin to a contract by which that power is entrusted by the people to a person or persons committed to working for the benefit of the people. But Smith notes that there is no evidence that there ever was such a contract, and adds that even if there had been it cannot also bind the present generation who cannot have participated in it in any way.

Instead of focusing on the myth of the original contract Smith focuses on the principles on which civil states rest. There are two: the principle of authority and the principle of common or general interest. These principles Smith associates respectively with Tories and Whigs; the Tories hold that kingly authority is divinely instituted and that it is therefore an impiety to resist, while the Whigs hold that the government is established for the sake of the people and it is therefore proper to resist the sovereign power if it greatly abuses its position. Nevertheless Tories and Whigs agree that there can come a point at which the sovereign has to be resisted, for example if he becomes a lunatic.

There is one point stressed by Smith in the *Wealth of Nations* that is not explicit in the present excerpt but is I think assumed in it, and that is the need to keep the power of the judiciary out of the hands of the federal or executive power. An executive power which also has judicial power may have the best of intentions; it may recognise on occasion a real necessity to sacrifice, for the sake of state interests, the civil rights of private individuals. But for Smith the liberty of every individual, and his sense of his own security, depend upon the impartial administration of justice. There is no impartial administration of justice if its administration is subordinated to the interests of the state; the judiciary would inevitably be politicised. There is a financial dimension to this political/legal position, which is stressed in the *Wealth of Nations* (p. 723): 'The judge should not be liable to be removed from his office according to the caprice of that [executive] power. The regular payment of his salary should not depend upon the good-will, or even upon the good oeconomy of that power.' This point concerning the separation of the executive and the judicial powers is in effect an application of the principle of the division of labour which lies at the heart of Smith's thinking on economics (see excerpt 22) and on much else besides.

A.B.

On Jurisprudence

Monday March 21, 1763

. . .

I come now to consider the second part of publick law, viz the duties of the sovereign towards his subjects and the crimes he may be guilty of against them. This is a question which I can not pretend to answer with such precision as the others. The nature of this branch of public law, as well as that of the law of nations, is such that we can not pretend to such precision in it as in the private laws amongst subjects, or in the other part of publick law which comprehends the duties of subjects to their sovereigns. Both of these have been frequently canvassed, and laws have regulated and courts have fairly examind and settled precedents both with regard to the duty of subject to subject and of the subject to the sovereign. Laws and the proceedings of judges ascertain them; but there is no court which can try the sovereigns themselves, no authority sovereign to the sovereign, and which has examind and ascertaind how far the actions of the sovereigns to the subject or of one sovereign to another are justifiable and how far their power extends. The precise limits have been little considered and are very difficult to ascertain to which the power of the sovereign extends. In England the exact boundaries of the kings power have been pretty well known since the Revolution; one can tell exactly what he can do. But then we are to consider that the king is not here the sovereign. The sovereign power is lodged in the king and Parliament together, and no one can tell what they can not do. And in the same manner where the king is the sovereign no one can pretend to ascertain how far this power may go, as in France, Spain, Turkey, etc. There are without doubt certain limits, but no one has yet considered them with the same candor and composure as a court does the private affairs of individualls. So that one who is to consider this matter must set out anew and upon his own bottom. All disputes of this sort have been decided by force and violence. If the sovereign got the better of the subjects, then they were condemned as traitors and rebells; and if the subjects have got the better of the sovereign, he is declared to be a tyrant and oppressor not to be endured. Sometimes the decision has been right and sometimes wrong, but they can never be of such weight as the decisions of a cool and impartial court. The three branches of the supreme power are now fully established in the hands of the sovereign; but there are still some things which must be unlawful even for the sovereign. The most necessary branches of this power were at first exercised precariously.

The first part of the supreme power which is exercised in society is the federative power. But as I already mentioned this is altogether precarious in the beginnings of society. The majority of the state determine with regard to peace and war, but then this binds themselves only; the others are conceived to be at full liberty to carry on the war after the others have concluded peace, or to be at peace with those the others are at war with. I observd too that those who continue the war after the body of the people have made the peace are hardly ever punished, tho those are who do not engage in the common quarrel. The reason as I said is that the motives or passions which prompt men to make peace are cool and deliberate, whereas those which prompt them to make war are hot and impetuous and hurry men to the avenging themselves on those who will not engage in the revenging the injuries or affronts they have received; and by this means it happens that the minority who desire to continue the war generally act in the same manner as the majority would were they not hindered by certain prudential reasons. This earliest branch of the supreme power is therefore at first exercised precariously, tho now it is altogether absolute, and one who continues the war after the nations have made peace is liable to be punished not only by the country against whom the injury was committed but also by the laws of his own country; and in the same manner all communication and intercourse betwixt the subjects is stopped as soon as war is declared betwixt the two nations. The judiciall power was also originally altogether precarious, and was in order of time much later of being established than the federative or executive power; and tho in many countries we cant discover a time when the sovereign had not the power of making peace and war, yet there are none in which we cannot discover certain remains and marks which plainly point out to us that this power also was precarious. There was a time when the judge was considered merely as a mediator in criminall cases and an arbiter voluntarily chosen in civill ones; tho' they have at length become absolute, so that whatever they determine must be adhered to, be it right or be it wrong, and no reference can be made from their sentence. The judges at first did not require the parties to come before them and submit to their sentence.

They might instead of putting themselves on their judge and their country put themselves to the judicial combat, the triall by fire ordial or by boiling water, etc., and thus evade the sentence of the judge. Nor were they bound to adhere to the sentence of the judge. They could not indeed fight their opponents after the sentence was passed, but they might then fight their judge if they did not like his sentence, and their quarrell was then turned upon him. All that was done by the sentence was to put it in their power to agree to the decision if it seemed equitable. For they had it still in their power to draw back and falsify the sentence of the judge in the same way as they had before done the claim of the opponents. The judge at this time decided all affronts or contempts done to his authority by force of arms. They asked the dissobedient persons why they did not obey their orders and then challenged and fought them. This sufficiently shews that the judicial power was then very precarious, and that mankind thought themselves bound neither to submit to the authority of the judge in appearing before him nor in adhering to his sentence; but now their authority is so establishd that no one complains, whatever injustice he may think he suffers, as they are absolute and without appeal. All resistance is unlawfull, and tho perhaps it is naturall enough to make resistance yet it is altogether prohibited, in the same progress as that by which it is now unlawfull either to continue in war or to continue correspondence after war with the enemy, after the publick have agreed to the discontinuance of war or peace.

The legislative power also comes in time to be absolute. There is at first in the ruder periods of society no legislative power, nor for some considerable time. Tho one was ready to stand by the sentence of an arbiter chosen perhaps out of the whole body of the people, as the heads of families, yet they would be altogether unwilling they should lay down laws for their conduct. He has no notion of any one having this power over him. No more than a member of a club will submit himself to the rules they may lay down, no more would a savage when he agrees to be a member of a society would think that he was bound to obey all their regulations. The thing which has given occasion to the establishment of laws has always been the generall or partiall institution of judges. When any nation has retaind its liberty, and property has been established amongst them, judges must soon be appointed to determine the many disputes which must occurr concerning it. A judge will to such an early nation appear very terrible. A judge is now rather a comfortable than a terrible sight as he is the source of our liberty, our independence, and our security. Savages do not feel the want of judges; and tho they must be liable to many inconveniencies on that account, yet one who has been accustomed to trust to the strength of his own arm and his own manly prowess is confident and bold to trust to it in future occasions. But for him to think that whenever he is guilty of any trespass, as he knows he has often been, there is one who has the power to call him to trial, and if the fact is proved against him to condemn him to any punishment he thinks proper, appears to be altogether terrible and unsufferable. Savages of all things hate a judge set over their heads. Of this the story of Varus recorded by Tacitus is a striking instance. By all we can learn of him he appears to have been a most amiable man and of very gentle manners, so that we now can hardly conceive how it should have happened that he should have incenced the Germans to such a height. That which incensed them more than all the tyranny, extorsion, and oppression of the Romans was the regular courts of justice which Varus established every where in the country, who tried and punished all offences with the same rigour and severity as had been customary at the Roman courts. This it was which provoked the Germans and in revenge of which they massacred the whole Roman army. The courts of justice when established appear to a rude people to have an authority altogether insufferable; and at the same time when property is considerably advanced judges can not be wanted. The judge is necessary and yet is of all things the most terrible. What shall be done in this case? The only way is to establish laws and rules which may asertain his conduct; This was the case at Athens, Sparta, and other places where the people demanded laws to regulate the conduct of the judge for when it is known in what manner he is to proceed the terror will be in a great measure removed. Laws are in this manner posterior to the establishment of judges. At the first establishment of judges there are no laws; every one trusts to the naturall feeling of justice he has in his own breast and expects to find in others. Were laws to be established in the beginnings of society prior to the judges, they would then be a restraint upon liberty, but when established after them they extend and secure it, as they do not ascertain or restrain the actions of private persons so much as the power and conduct of the judge over the people. In this manner the legislative power is established, which in time, as well as the others, grows up to be absolute; but notwithstanding that the subjects are bound to obedience to all these powers there are some cases in which they may break thro them.

Tuesday March 22, 1763

In yesterdays lecture I begun to explain the rights of the subject against the sovereign; that is, what are the limits of the sovereign power, and in what cases it is proper for the subjects to make resistance. At first all the branches of this power were extremely limited and held precariously; even the federative power was under a precarious tenure. The judiciall power was no less precarious, and the legislative power was at first so far from being absolute that there was hardly any such thing. The growth of the judicial power was what gave occasion to the institution of a legislative power, as that first made them think of restraining the power of judicial officers. Laws instituted at the beginning of a society would never be agreed to; they would appear to be the greatest restraint imaginable on the liberty and security of the subjects; but afterwards they evidently appear to tend to the security of the people by restraining the arbitrary power of the judges, who are then become absolute or nearly so. The legislative power thus constituted must from the very nature and design of it be absolute from the moment of its institution; and the other powers in time become so also. There is now no power of resistance, whether the sentence of the judge appear to the person to be just or not; and in the same manner there is no remedy against a law which appears to be unjust unless it be repealed; private persons must obey and judges give sentence agreeably to it. Those persons who are entrusted with the severall parts of the supreme power in the constitution must be relied on without hesitation. The authority of the Parliament in some things, of the king and Parliament in others, and of the king alone in some, are incontestible, and if they act amiss there is no regular right of resisting them as sovereigns in any way. So that the limits of the sovereign power are extremely doubtfull. The limits of the kings power are in this country well enough known, but the king is far from having the sovereign power. The legislative power he shares with the Parliament, who have now almost the whole of it. He is said indeed to be the fountain of justice; which is indeed so far true that all the ordinary judges are of his appointment; but then these judges are intirely independent of him after their constitution; nor has he in his own person any judicial power. And besides this the House of Lords, who are the supreme judges, are altogether independent on him either with respect to their appointment or their proceedings. He has indeed the whole of executive or federative power; but as the people have a power of impeaching any of his ministers who have given him bad advice, this too is somewhat limited, tho the king and his ministers have the disposall of peace and war in all ordinary cases. There is no doubt then but the power of the king may be resisted; but the question is, when is it lawfull or allowable to resist the power of the king and Parliament. They would never have any thoughts of making any laws which should tell us that, when they went beyond such and such limits, the people were not bound to obey them but might resist. That they should do this can not be imagined. In whatever place there is a sovereign, from the very nature of things the power must be absolute; and no power regularly established of calling the sovereign to account, as the sovereign has an undoubted title to the obedience of the subjects. The foundation of this obedience of the subjects has often been controverted. But whatever it be, there are certain limits to the power of the sovereign, which if he exceeds, the subject may with justice make resistance.

If we shall suppose with the generallity of writers on this subject (as Locke and Sidney, etc.) that the government owes its origin to a voluntary contract in which the people gave over the sovereign power in its different parts, the judiciall or the legislative, to another body, and so of the executive, and promised obedience and submission to this power; even on this submission, which from what has been already explaind concerning the progress of government can hardly be supposed to have ever been the case, even here the subjects must have a right of resistance. The power of the sovereign is in this case a trust reposed in him by the people; he is the great magistrate to whom they have promised obedience as long as he rules with a middling degree of equity; but when he has abused this power in a very violent manner, for it is only a violent abuse of it which can call for such violent measures, then undoubtedly he may be resisted as he is guilty of a breach of the trust reposed in him. When he abuses his power and does not exert it for the benefit of the people for whose advantage it was given him, but turns it to the aggrandizing and exalting of himself, then he may be turned out of his office; in the same manner as a tutor who abuses to his own interest the goods of his pupil committed to his care may be turned out and another put in his room. But indeed this does not seem to be the foundation of the power of the sovereign and the obedience of the people; and supposing that it had originally been the foundation of the authority of the sovereign it can not now be so; and nevertheless we find that in all ordinary cases they are bound to obey the king. Besides, this doctrine of obedience as founded on contract is confined to

Britain and has never been heard of in any other country, so that there it can not be the foundation of the obedience of the people; and even here it can have influence with a very small part of the people, such as have read Locke, etc. The far greater part have no notion of it, and nevertheless they have the same notion of the obedience due to the sovereign power, which can not proceed from any notion of contract. Again, if the first members of the society had entered into a contract with certain persons to whom they entrusted the sovereign power, their obedience would indeed have been founded on a contract in a great measure; but this can not be the case with their posterity; they have entered into no such contract. The contract of ones predecessors never binds one merely because it was his. The heir indeed is bound to pay the debts contracted by his predecessors to whom he has fallen heir, not because their promise is any way binding on him but because by possessing their money he would be *locupletior factus aliena jactura*.[1] One is not bound to personall service promised by his ancestors; their promise has no influence upon him. But if the whole hire or price of his fathers service has been paid beforehand, then he will be bound for the reason above mentioned to make restitution of the value of the part not performed; and so in all other cases. And what makes this entirely evident is that one is bound for the debts of his predecessors no more than what the estate left by them will amount to, altho it be greatly less; which overturns the old fancy of the heirs being eadem persona cum defuncto. But to this they may answer that tho one is not bound by the contract of his ancestors, nor here by any express deed of his own, yet he is bound by his own tacit promise. His staying in the country shews that he inclines to submit to the government established in it. Hence, say they, every one who stays in the country must submit to the government. But this is a very fallacious argument. A very ingenious gentleman exposed the deceit of it very clearly by the following example. If one who was carried on board of a ship when asleep was to be told that having continued afterwards on board he was bound to submit to the rules of the crew, any one would see the unreasonableness of it, as he was absolutely forced to stay on board. He had not his coming on board at his own choice, and after he was on board it was folly to tell him he might have gone away when the ocean surrounded him on all hands. Such is the case with every subject of the state. They came into the world without having the place of their birth

---

[1] 'Enriched at the expense of another.'

of their own choosing, so that we may say they came asleep into the country; nor is it in the power of the greater part to leave the country without the greatest inconveniences. So that there is here no tacit consent of the subjects. They have no idea of it, so that it can not be the foundation of their obedience. Again, if this was the case one by leaving the country would free himself from all duty to the government; and yet we see that all nations claim the power of calling back their subjects either by proclamation or by a private mandate (as a writ of the privy seal), and punish all those who do not obey as traitors; and in generall every one who is born under the government is considered as being bound to submit to it. Again, of all the cases where one is bound to submit to the government that of an alien comes the nearest to a voluntary or tacit contract. He comes into the country not asleep but with his eyes open, inlists himself under the protection of this government preferably to all others; and if the principle of allegiance and obedience is ever founded on contract it must be in this case. Yet we see that aliens have always been suspected by the government, and have always been laid under great dissabilities of different sorts and never have any trust or employment in the state; and yet they have shewn more strong and evident signs of an inclination to submit to the government than any others; and the obligations they are under to obedience are to those of a native subject as that of one who voluntarily enlists into the fleet compared to that of a pressed man. So that upon the whole this obedience which every one thinks is due to the sovereign does not arise from any notion of a contract.

This principle or duty of allegiance seems to be founded on two principles. The first we may call the principle of authority, and the second the principall of common or general interest. With regard to the principle of authority, we see that every one naturally has a disposition to respect an established authority and superiority in others, whatever they be. The young respect the old, children respect their parents, and in generall the weak respect those who excell in power and strength. Whatever be the foundation of government this has a great effect. One is born and bred up under the authority of the magistrates; he finds them demanding the obedience of all those about him and he finds that they always submit to their authority; he finds they are far above him in the power they possess in the state; he sees they expect his obedience and he sees also the propriety of obeying and the unreasonableness of disobeying. They have a naturall superiority over him; they have more followers who are ready to support their authority over the disobedient. There is the same propriety in submitting to them as to a father, as all of those in authority are either naturally or by the will of the state who lend them their power placed far above you.

With regard to the other principle, every one sees that the magistrates not only support the government in generall but the security and independency of each individuall, and they see that this security can not be attained without a regular government. Every one therefor thinks it most advisable to submitt to the established government, tho perhaps he may think that it is not disposed in the best manner possible; and this too is strengthened by the naturall modesty of mankind, who are not generally inclined to think they have a title to dispute the authority of those above them. Each of these principles takes place in some degree in every government, tho one is generally predominant. The principle of authority is that which chiefly prevails in a monarchy. Respect and deference to the monarchy, the idea they have that there is a sort of sinfullness or impiety in dissobedience, and the duty they owe to him, are what chiefly influence them. No doubt but the expediency of such obedience may also have its effect on some persons. In a republican government, particularly in a democraticall one, utility is that which chiefly, nay allmost entirely, occasions the obedience of the subject. He feels and is taught from his childhood to feel the excellency of the government he lives under; how much more desirable it is to have the affairs of the state under the direction of the whole than that it should be confined to one person; that in the one case it can hardly ever be abused and in the other it can hardly miss of being so. This recommends the government to the people, who are all bread to understand it. In such governments the principle of authority is as it were in some measure proscribed. A successfull leader, obtaining the good graces of the people, will get every thing he can ask from them; they know no bounds in their affections. Such persons would therefore be very dangerous in the state and might overturn with ease the established government. This principle is therefore discouraged, as it is in the interest of the state that no one should be much distinguished above the others. However even here the principle of authority has some influence in procuring the obedience of the subjects. This respect is not indeed paid to persons, the naturall objects of it, but to offices. Any one who was chosen consul at Rome had great honour and respect paid him, tho inferior to that of a hereditary sovereign. This respect which is paid to the persons in power in every country makes the wheels of the government go on more smoothly. In an aristocracy the principle of authority is the leading one, tho there is no doubt but the other has also some effect.

In Britain the sovereign power is partly entrusted to the king, partly to the people, and partly to the nobles. As it is therefore partly monarchicall the principle of authority takes place in a considerable degree, as also because there is some small part of the government aristocraticall. But as the government is in great part democraticall, by the influence of the House of Commons, the principle of utility is also found in it. Some persons are more directed by the one and others by the other. And to these different principles were owing the distinctions betwixt Whig and Tory. The principle of authority is that of the Tories, as that of utility is followd by the Whigs. They say that as the government was established not for the benefit of the rulers but of the people, and that therefore it is proper to resist their power whenever they abuse it in a great degree and turn it to their own advantages, and that they have no authority unless what they derive from the people. This is their principle, tho they do not explain it very distinctly, endeavouring to reconcile it to the notion of a contract. The Torys again go on the principle of authority, tho they also make still more confused work of it on the supposition of a contract. The Tories pretend that the kingly authority is of divine institution, that the kings derive their authority immediately from God, and that therefore it must be an impiety to resist him; that he has as it were a patriarchall authority and is a sort of father to his people, and as it is unlawfull for children in any case to rebell against their father, so is it for subjects to rebell against their sovereigns. These principles affect people of different casts. The bustling, spirited, active folks, who can't brook oppression and are constantly endeavouring to advance themselves, naturally join in with the democraticall part of the constitution and favour the principle of utility only, that is, the Whig interest. The calm, contented folks of no great spirit and abundant fortunes which they want to enjoy at their own ease, and dont want to be disturbd nor to disturb others, as naturally join with the Tories and found their obedience on the less generous principle of authority. But whatever be the foundation of the obedience of the subjects, there are some things which it is unlawfull for the sovereign to attempt and entitle the subjects to make resistance. Some certain degrees of absurdity and outrage, either in a single person or an assembly, will entirely destroy all their claim of obedience. An assembly indeed is less apt to fall into this absurdity than a single person, for tho there may be the greatest difference betwixt the behaviour of one man and another, an assembly of 4 or 500 taken out of the people will be much the same as any other 500 and will be no more liable to err. Yet even here it will sometimes happen, and from this it was that all the old aristocracies became democracies, the council of the nobles having incensed the people against them. There can be no doubt that one by a certain degree of absurdity and outrage in his conduct may lose his authority altogether. All agree that lunacy, nonnage [i.e. non-age or minority], or ideotism entirely destroy the authority of a prince. Now there are degrees of absurdity and impropriety in the conduct of a sovereign which, tho they do not equall that of lunacy or ideotism, entitle the subjects to resistance in the eyes of every unprejudiced person. Who is there that in reading the Roman history does not acknowledge that the conduct of Nero, Caligula, or Domitian was such as entirely took away all authority from them? No one but must enter into the designs of the people, go along with them in all their plots and conspiracys to turn them out, is rejoiced at their success, and grieves when they fail. So that even on this principle resistance must be permitted. In the principle of utility there can be still less doubt but it is lawfull. If the good of the publick is that on which the obedience [is based?], then this obedience is no longer due than it is usefull; and wherever the confusion which must arise on an overthrow of the established govt. is less than the mischief of allowing it to continue, then resistance is proper and allowable. And that such cases may occur their can be no doubt. Absurdity and impropriety of conduct and great perverseness destroy obedience, whether it be due from authority or the sense of the common good.

Source: Adam Smith, *Lectures on Jurisprudence*, ed. R. L. Meek, D. D. Raphael and P. G. Stein, Oxford 1978, pp. 311–21

THIRTY-SEVEN

HENRY HOME, LORD KAMES
Rewards, Reparations and Final Causes

Lord Kames, one of the major Scottish jurists of the eighteenth century, had a good deal to say about the relation between morality and law, and about what is commonly termed the practicality of our knowledge of morality, that is, the fact that our knowing we ought to perform a given act is by itself sufficient to motivate us to perform it. Nevertheless it is one thing to know what one's duty is, and another to act on that knowledge; and it is possible to succeed in the first of them and fail in the second. As to why we do not always behave as we ought, the chief culprit, in Kames's view, falling here into line with most commentators on the subject, is passion, which therefore has to be controlled since each passion is a totally egoistic motivator seeking its own gratification at whatever cost to the person, and to the society he lives in.

There has therefore to be an institution of reward and punishment which will ensure both that wrong is redressed and also that repetition of that wrong is prevented. But in virtue of what aspect of the performance is a person to be rewarded or punished? Are we to focus upon the intention of the agent or upon the outcome of the act? Suppose someone with the best will in the world does harm by accident. Suppose someone with evil intention does good by accident. Would it be just to punish the former, or to reward the latter? Furthermore is it just to punish a person who does harm knowing that harm will be the outcome of his act, though he does it only because he is, as Kames puts it, 'overawed by fear'? These are all questions of the first importance for the just administration of a system of rewards and punishments, and Kames's sensitive discussion places the overwhelming weight where no doubt it ought to be, on the side of the agent's intention rather than on the outcome of the act.

A distinction has to be made between virtues of two sorts,

those of the primary and of the secondary sort, for reward and punishment are related in quite different ways to the two, and it is interesting to note how the virtue of justice fares in relation to the distinction. On the one hand there are virtues, among which justice is pre-eminent, of such a nature that acts which conflict with them are thought to merit punishment though the contrary acts, those that are just, are not thought worthy of reward. For we are entitled to just treatment, and it is therefore failure to act justly that calls forth a response from us. On the other hand there are virtues such as kindness, generosity and magnanimity, of such a nature that acts embodying them are thought worthy of reward though the contrary acts, acts displaying lack of generosity and so on, are not thought worthy of punishment. The secondary virtues are expressed in acts all of which go beyond the call of duty. The primary virtues are expressed in acts which one is not permitted to omit.

The topic Kames takes up next, that of the law of reparation, is related to the foregoing discussion for in so far as the aim of reparation is to redress a wrong which is not a criminal wrong, reparation is a form of punishment, and in so far as the aim of reparation is to make up for a loss of whatever sort, it is an act of justice. And just as in the earlier discussion particular attention was paid to the inner aspect of actions, namely the goodness or the badness of the intention was good or bad, so also in the discussion of reparation attention is particularly directed to an inner aspect of actions, namely our belief regarding whether or not harm will result from our act. For clearly we might wonder whether a victim is due reparation if the agent who caused harm had no idea that harm was a certain or even a likely consequence of his act. If the agent was plain unlucky in being the cause of harm to another then should this not make a difference to whether or not he ought to make reparation? But if it should make a difference ought we also to take into account the fact, if it be one, that he ought to have foreseen the harm? These matters are discussed by Kames in a sharp and penetrating fashion. One can also detect a liveliness in his discussion which reminds us that he is reputed to have been eager to secure convictions.

Kames's third topic concerns 'final causes' of certain moral phenomena. To know their final cause is to know their purpose, why they exist. In the subtle and complex discussion several pointers to Kames's place in the Scottish

Enlightenment are detectable. Three may be mentioned here. First there is the emphasis on the role of common sense in the moral aspects of our lives. Secondly there is an emphasis on moral sense, as when he tells us that 'we are directed by the moral sense to perform certain plain and simple acts, which are obvious to us by intuitive perception', and here Kames lines himself up with a major strand in the thought of Francis Hutcheson. And finally there is an emphasis by Kames on the fact that we carry society about with us even in our most covert acts. Thus, when I am tempted to perform a bad act I ask myself how that act would appear to my acquaintances: 'I imagine my friends expostulating, my enemies reviling'; and that is enough to discourage me from performing the act. This part of Kames's discussion is strongly reminiscent of Adam Smith (see excerpt 7), who was in many ways, personal as well as intellectual, close to Kames.

A.B.

Morality and Law

Laws respecting Rewards and Punishments

Reflecting on the moral branch of our nature, qualifying us for society in a manner suited to our capacity, we cannot overlook the hand of our Maker; for means so finely adjusted to an important end, never happen by chance. It must however be acknowledged, that in many individuals, the principle of duty has not vigour nor authority sufficient to stem every tide of unruly passion: by the vigilance of some passions, we are taken unguarded; deluded by the sly insinuations of others; or overwhelmed with the stormy impetuosity of a third sort. Moral evil is thus introduced, and much wrong is done. This new scene suggests to us, that there must be some article still wanting, to complete the moral system. The means provided for directing us in the road of duty have been explained: but as in deviating from the road wrongs are committed, nothing hitherto has been said, about redressing such wrongs, nor about preventing the reiteration of them. To accomplish these important ends, there are added to the moral system, laws relative to rewards and punishments, and to reparation; of which in their order.

Many animals are qualified for society by instinct merely; such as beavers, sheep, monkeys, bees, rooks. But men are seldom led by instinct: their actions are commonly prompted by passions; of which there is an endless variety, social and selfish, benevolent and malevolent. And were every passion equally intitled to gratification, man would be utterly unqualified for society: he would be a ship without a rudder, obedient to every wind, and moving at random, without any ultimate destination. The faculty of reason would make no opposition: for were there no sense of wrong, it would be reasonable to gratify every desire that harms not ourselves: and to talk of punishment would be absurd; for punishment, in its very idea, implies some wrong that ought to be redressed. Hence the necessity of the moral sense, to qualify us for society: by instructing us in our duty, it renders us accountable for our conduct, and makes us susceptible of rewards and punishments. The moral sense fulfils another valuable purpose: it erects in man an unerring standard for the application and measure of rewards and punishments.

To complete the system of rewards and punishments, it is

necessary that a provision be made, both of power and of willingness to reward and punish. The Author of our nature hath provided amply for the former, by entitling every man to reward and punish as his native privilege. And he has provided for the latter, by a noted principle in our nature, prompting us to exercise the power. Impelled by that principle, we reward the virtuous with approbation and esteem, and punish the vicious with disapprobation and contempt. So prevalent is the principle, that we have great satisfaction in rewarding, and no less in punishing.

As to punishment in particular, an action done intentionally to produce mischief, is criminal, and merits punishment. Such an action, being disagreeable, raises my resentment, even where I have no connection with the person injured; and the principle under consideration impels me to chastise the delinquent with indignation and hatred. An injury done to myself raises my resentment to a higher tone: I am not satisfied with so slight a punishment as indignation and hatred: the author must by my hand suffer mischief, as great as he has made me suffer.

Even the most secret crimes escapes not punishment. The delinquent is tortured with remorse: he even desires to be punished; sometimes so ardently, as himself to be the executioner. There cannot be imagined a contrivance more effectual, to deter one from vice; for remorse is itself a grievous punishment. Self-punishment goes still farther: every criminal, sensible that he ought to be punished, dreads punishment from others; and this dread, however smothered during prosperity, breaks out in adversity, or in depression of mind; his crime stares him in the face, and every accidental misfortune is in his disturbed imagination interpreted to be a punishment. 'And they said one to another, We are verily guilty concerning our brother, in that we saw the anguish of his soul, when he besought us; and we would not hear: therefore is this distress come upon us. And Reuben answered them, saying, spake I not unto you saying, do not sin against the child, and ye would not hear? therefore behold also his blood is required.'[1]

No transgression of self-duty escapes punishment, more than transgression of duty to others. The punishments, though not the same, differ in degree more than in kind. Injustice is punished with remorse: impropriety with shame, which is remorse in a lower degree. Injustice raises indignation in the beholder, and so doth every flagrant impropriety: slighter improprieties receive a milder

[1] Genesis xlii. 21.

punishment, being rebuked with some degree of contempt, and commonly with derision.[1]

So far we have been led in a beaten track; but in attempting to proceed, we are entangled in mazes and intricacies. An action well intended, may happen to produce no good; and an action ill intended may happen to produce no mischief: a man over-awed by fear, may be led to do mischief against his will; and a person, mistaking the standard of right and wrong, may be innocently led to do acts of injustice. By what rule, in such cases, are rewards and punishments to be applied? Ought a man to be rewarded when he does no good, or punished when he does no mischief: ought he to be punished for doing mischief against his will, or for doing mischief when he thinks he is acting innocently? These questions suggest a doubt, whether the standard of right and wrong be applicable to rewards and punishments.

We have seen that there is an invariable standard of right and wrong, which depends not in any degree on private opinion or conviction. By that standard, all pecuniary claims are judged, all claims of property, and, in a word, every demand founded on interest, not excepting reparation, as will afterward appear. But with respect to the moral characters of men, and with respect to rewards and punishments, a different standard is erected in the common sense of mankind, neither rigid nor inflexible; which is, the opinion that men have of their own actions. It is mentioned above, that a man is esteemed innocent in doing what he himself thinks right, and guilty in doing what he himself thinks wrong. In applying this standard to rewards and punishments, we reward those who in doing wrong are however convinced that they are innocent; and punish those who in doing right are however convinced that they are guilty.[2] Some it is true, are so perverted by bad education, or by superstition, as to espouse numberless absurd tenets, contradictory to the standard of right and wrong; and yet such men are no exception from the general rule: if they act according to conscience, they are innocent, and safe against punishment, however wrong the action may be; and if they act against conscience, they are guilty and punishable, however right the action may be: it is abhorrent to every moral perception, that

---

1 See *Elements of Criticism*, chap. 10.
2 Virtuous and vicious, innocent and guilty, signify qualities both of men and of their actions. Approbation and disapprobation, praise and blame, signify certain emotions or sentiments of those who see or contemplate men and their actions.

a guilty person be rewarded, or an innocent person punished. Further, if mischief be done contrary to will, as where a man is compelled by fear, or by torture, to reveal the secrets of his party; he may be grieved for yielding to the weakness of his nature, contrary to his firmest resolves; but he has no check of conscience, and upon that account is not liable to punishment. And, lastly, in order that personal merit and demerit may not in any measure depend on chance, we are so constituted as to place innocence and guilt, not on the event, but on the intention of doing right or wrong; and accordingly, whatever be the event, a man is praised for an action well intended, and condemned for an action ill intended.

But what if a man intending a certain wrong, happen by accident to do a wrong he did not intend; as, for example, intending to rob a warren by shooting the rabbits, he accidentally wounds a child unseen behind a bush? The delinquent ought to be punished for intending to rob; and he is also subjected to repair the hurt done to the child; but he cannot be punished for the accidental wound, because our nature regulates punishment by the intention, and not by the event.

A crime against any primary virtue is attended with severe and never-failing punishment, more efficacious than any that have been invented to enforce municipal laws: on the other hand, the preserving primary virtues inviolate, is attended with little merit. The secondary virtues are directly opposite: the neglecting them is not attended with any punishment; but the practice of them is attended with illustrious rewards. Offices of undeserved kindness, returns of good for ill, generous toils and sufferings for our friends or for our country, are attended with consciousness of self-merit, and with universal praise and admiration; the highest rewards human nature is susceptible of.

From what is said, the following observation will occur: The pain of transgressing justice, fidelity, or any duty, is much greater than the pleasure of performing; but the pain of neglecting a generous action, or any secondary virtue, is as nothing compared with the pleasure of performing. Among the vices opposite to the primary virtues, the most striking moral deformity is found; among the secondary virtues, the most striking moral beauty.

Laws respecting Reparation

The principle of reparation is made a branch of the moral system for accomplishing two ends; which are, to repress wrongs that are not criminal, and to make up the loss sustained by wrongs of whatever kind. With respect to the former, reparation is a species of punishment: with respect to the latter, it is an act of justice. These ends will be better understood, after ascertaining the nature and foundation of reparation; to which the following division of actions is necessary. First, actions that we are bound to perform. Second, actions that we perform in prosecution of a right or privilege. Third, indifferent actions, described above. Actions of the first kind subject not a man to reparation, whatever damage ensues: because it is his duty to perform them, and it would be inconsistent with morality that a man should be subjected to reparation for doing his duty. The laws of reparation that concern actions of the second kind, are more complex. The social state, highly beneficial by affording opportunity for mutual good offices, is attended with some inconveniences; as where a person happens to be in a situation of necessarily harming others by exercising a right or privilege. If the foresight of harming another, restrain me not from exercising my right, the interest of that other is made subservient to mine: on the other hand, if such foresight restrain me from exercising my right, my interest is made subservient to his. What doth the moral sense provide in that case? To preserve as far as possible an equality among persons born free, and by nature equal in rank, the moral sense lays down a rule, no less beautiful than salutary; which is, That the exercising a right will not justify me for doing direct mischief; but will justify me, though I foresee that mischief may possibly happen. The first branch of the rule resolves into a proposition established above, viz. That no interest of mine, not even life itself, will authorise me to hurt an innocent person. The other branch is supported by expediency: for if the bare possibility of hurting others were sufficient to restrain a man from prosecuting his rights and priviledges, men would be too much cramped in action: or rather would be reduced to a state of absolute inactivity. With respect to the first branch, I am criminal, and liable even to punishment: with respect to the other, I am not even culpable, nor bound to repair the mischief that happens to ensue.

With respect to the third kind, viz. indifferent actions, the moral sense dictates, that we ought carefully to avoid mischief, either direct or consequential. As we suffer no loss by forbearing actions that are done for pastime merely, such an action is *culpable* or *faulty*, if the consequent mischief was foreseen or might have been foreseen; and the actor of course is subjected to reparation. As this is a cardinal point in the doctrine of reparation, I shall endeavour to explain it more fully. Without intending any harm, a man may foresee, that what he is about to do will probably or possibly produce mischief; and sometimes mischief follows that which was neither intended nor foreseen. The action in the former case is not criminal; because ill intention is essential to a crime: but it is culpable or faulty; and if mischief ensues, the actor blames himself, and is blamed by others, for having done what he ought not to have done. Thus a man who throws a large stone among a croud of people, is highly culpable; because he must foresee that mischief will probably ensue, though he has no intention to hurt any person. As to the latter case, though mischief was neither intended nor foreseen, yet if it might have been foreseen, the action is rash or uncautious, and consequently culpable or faulty in some degree. Thus, if a man in pulling down an old house, happen to wound one passing accidentally, without calling aloud to keep out of the way, the action is in some degree culpable, because the mischief might have been foreseen. But though mischief ensue, an action is not culpable or faulty if all reasonable precautions have been adhibited: the moral sense declares the author to be innocent[1] and blameless; the mischief is accidental, and the action may be termed *unlucky*, but comes not under the denomination of either right or wrong. In general, when we act merely for amusement, our nature makes us answerable for the harm that ensues, if it was either foreseen, or might with due attention have been foreseen. But our rights and privileges would profit us little, if their exercise were put under the same restraint: it is more wisely ordered, that the probability of mischief, even foreseen, should not restrain a man from prosecuting his concerns which may often be of consequence to him. He proceeds accordingly with a safe conscience, and is not afraid of being blamed either by God or man.

With respect to rash or uncautious actions, where the mischief might have been foreseen though not actually foreseen, it is not sufficient to escape blame, that a man, naturally rash or inattentive, acts according to his character: a degree of precaution is required, both by himself and by others, such as is natural to the generality of men: he perceives that he might and *ought* to have acted more cautiously; and his conscience reproaches him for his inattention,

---

1 *Innocent* here is opposed to *culpable*: in a broader sense
it is opposed to *criminal*. With respect to punishment,
an action tho' culpable is innocent, if it be not criminal:
with respect to reparation, it is not innocent if it be
culpable.

no less than if he were naturally more sedate and attentive. Thus the circumspection natural to mankind in general, is applied as a standard to every individual; and if they fall short of that standard, they are culpable and blameable, however unforeseen by them the mischief may have been.

What is said upon culpable actions is equally applicable to culpable omissions; for by these also mischief may be occasioned, entitling the sufferer to reparation. If we forbear to do our duty with an intention to occasion mischief, the forbearance is criminal. The only question is, how far forbearance without such intention is culpable. Supposing the probability of mischief to have been foreseen, though not intended, the omission is highly culpable: and though neither intended nor foreseen, yet the omission is culpable in a lower degree, if there have been less care and attention than are proper for performing the duty required. But supposing all due care, the omission of extreme care and diligence is not culpable.

By ascertaining what acts and omissions are culpable or faulty, the doctrine of reparation is rendered extremely simple; for it may be laid down as a rule without a single exception, That every culpable act, and every culpable omission, binds us in conscience to repair the mischief occasioned by it. The moral sense binds us no farther; for it loads not with reparation the man who is blameless and innocent: the harm is accidental; and we are so constituted as not to be responsible in conscience for what happens by accident. But here it is requisite, that the man be in every respect innocent: for if he intend harm, though not what he has done, he will find himself bound in conscience to repair the accidental harm he has done; as, for example, when aiming a blow unjustly at one in the dark, he happens to wound another whom he did not suspect to be there. And hence it is a rule in all municipal laws, That one *versans in illicito* is liable to repair every consequent damage. That these particulars are wisely ordered by the Author of our nature for the good of society, will appear afterwards. In general, the rules above mentioned are dictated by the moral sense; and we are compelled to obey them by the principle of reparation.

We are now prepared for a more particular inspection of the two ends of reparation above mentioned, viz. the repressing wrongs that are not criminal, and the making up what loss is sustained by wrongs of whatever kind. With respect to the first, it is clear, that punishment, in its proper sense, cannot be inflicted for a wrong that is culpable only; and if nature did not provide some means for repressing such wrongs, society would scarce be a comfortable state. Laying conscience aside, pecuniary reparation is the only remedy that can be provided against culpable omissions: and with respect to culpable commissions, the necessity of reparation is still more apparent; for conscience alone, without the sanction of reparation, would seldom have authority sufficient to restrain us from acting rashly or uncautiously, even where the possibility of mischief is foreseen, and far less where it is not foreseen.

With respect to the second end of reparation, my conscience dictates to me, that if a man suffer by my fault, whether the mischief was foreseen or not foreseen, it is my duty to make up his loss: and I perceive intuitively, that the loss ought to rest ultimately upon me, and not upon the sufferer, who has not been culpable in any degree.

In every case where the mischief done can be estimated by a pecuniary compensation, the two ends of reparation coincide. The sum is taken from the one as a sort of punishment for his fault, and is bestowed on the other to make up the loss he has sustained. But in numberless cases where mischief done cannot be compensated with money, reparation is in its nature a sort of punishment. Defamation, contemptuous treatment, personal restraint, the breaking one's peace of mind, are injuries that cannot be repaired by money; and the pecuniary reparation decreed against the wrong-doer, can only be a sort of punishment, in order to deter him from reiterating such injuries: the sum, it is true, is awarded to the person injured; but not as sufficient to make up his loss, which money cannot do, but only as a *solatium* for what he has suffered.

Hitherto it is supposed, that the man who intends a wrong action, is, at the same time, conscious of its being so. But a man may intend a wrong action, thinking erroneously that it is right; or a right action, thinking erroneously that it is wrong; and the question is, What shall be the consequence of such errors with respect to reparation. The latter case is clear: the person who occasionally suffers loss by a right action, has not a claim for reparation, because he has no just cause of complaint. On the other hand, if the action be wrong, the innocence of the author, for which he is indebted to an error in judgment, will not relieve him from reparation. When he is made sensible of his error, he feels himself bound in conscience to repair the harm he has done by a wrong action: and others, sensible of his error from the beginning, have the same feeling: nor will his obstinacy in resisting conviction, or his dullness in not apprehending his error, mend the matter! it is well that these defects relieve him from punishment, without wronging others by denying a claim for reparation. A man's errors ought to affect himself only, and not those who have not erred. Hence in general, reparation always follows wrong; and is not affected by any erroneous opinion of a wrong action being right, more than of a right action being wrong.

But this doctrine suffers an exception with respect to a man, who having undertaken a trust, is bound in duty to act. A judge is in that situation: it is his duty to pronounce sentence in every case that comes before him; and if he judge according to the best of his knowledge he is not liable for consequences. A judge cannot be subjected to reparation, unless it can be verified, that the judgment he gave was intentionally wrong. An officer of the revenue is in the same predicament. Led by a doubtful clause in a statute, he makes a seizure of goods as forfeited to the crown, which afterwards, in the proper court, are found not to be seizable. The officer ought not to be subjected to reparation, if he has acted to the best of his judgment. This rule however must be taken with a limitation; a public officer who is grossly erroneous, will not be excused; for he ought to know better.

Reparation is due, though the immediate act be involuntary, provided it be connected with a preceding voluntary act. Example: 'If A ride an unruly horse in Lincolns-inn fields, to tame him, and the horse breaking from A, run over B, and grievously hurt him; B shall have an action against A: for though the mischief was done against the will of A, yet since it was his fault to bring a wild horse into a frequented place, where mischief might ensue, he must answer for the consequences.' Gaius seems to carry this rule still farther, holding in general, that if a horse, by the weakness or unskilfulness of the rider, break away and do mischief, the rider is liable. But Gaius probably had in his eye a frequented place, where the mischief might have been foreseen. Thus in general a man is made liable for the mischief occasioned by his voluntary deed, though the immediate act that occasioned the mischief be involuntary.

Final Causes of the foregoing Laws of Nature

Several final causes have been occasionally mentioned in preceding parts of this essay, which could not conveniently be reserved for the present section, being necessary to explain the subjects to which they relate, the final cause for instance of erecting a standard of morals upon the common sense of mankind. I proceed now to what have not been mentioned, or but slightly mentioned.

The final cause that presents itself first to view, respects man considered as an accountable being. The sense of being accountable, is one of the most vigilant guards against the silent attacks of vice. When a temptation moves me, it immediately occurs. What will the world say? I imagine my friends expostulating, my enemies reviling – I dare not dissemble, my spirits sink – the temptation vanishes. Secondly, Praise and blame, especially from those we regard, are strong incentives to virtue: but if we were not accountable for our conduct, praise and blame would be seldom well directed; for how should a man's intentions be known, without calling him to account? And praise or blame, frequently ill directed, would lose their influence. Thirdly, This branch of our nature, is the corner stone of the criminal law. Did not a man think himself accountable to all the world, and to his judge in a peculiar manner, it would be natural for him, to think, that the justest sentence pronounced against him is oppression, not justice. Fourthly, This branch is a strong cement to society. If we were not accountable beings, those connected by blood or by country, would be no less shy and reserved, than if they were mere strangers to each other.

The final cause that next occurs, being simple and obvious, is mentioned only that it may not seem to have been overlooked. All right actions are agreeable, all wrong actions disagreeable. This is a wise appointment of Providence. We meet with so many temptations against duty, that it is not always an easy task to persevere in the right path: would we persevere, were duty disagreeable? And were acts of pure benevolence disagreeable, they would be extremely rare, however worthy of praise.

Another final cause respects duty, in contradistinction to pure benevolence. All the moral laws are founded on intuitive perception; and are so simple and plain, as to be perfectly apprehended by the most ignorant. Were they in any degree complex or obscure, they would be perverted by selfishness and prejudice. No conviction inferior to what is afforded by intuitive perception, could produce in mankind a common sense with respect to moral duties. Reason would afford no general conviction; because that faculty is distributed in portions so unequal, as to bar all hopes from it of uniformity either in practice or in opinion. At the same time, we are taught by woeful experience, that reason has little influence over the greater part of men. Reason, it is true, aided by experience, supports morality, by convincing us, that we cannot be happy if we abandon duty for any other interest. But conviction seldom weighs much against imperious passion; to control which the vigorous and commanding principles of duty is requisite, directed by the shining light of intuition.

A proposition laid down above appears to be a sort of mystery in the moral system, viz. That though evidently all moral duties are contrived for promoting the general good, yet that choice is not permitted among different goods, or between good and ill; and that we are strictly tied down to perform or forbear certain particular acts, without regard to consequences; or, in other words, that we must not do wrong, whatever good it may produce. The final cause, which I am about to unfold, will clear this mystery, and set the beauty of the moral system in a conspicuous light. I begin with observing, that as the general good of mankind, or even of the society we live in, results from many and various circumstances intricately combined, it is far above the capacity of man, to judge in every instance what particular actions will tend the most to that end. The authorising therefore a man to trace out his duty, by weighing endless circumstances good and ill, would open a wide door to partiality and passion, and often lead him unwittingly to prefer the preponderating ill, under a false appearance of being the greater good. At that rate, the opinions of men about right and wrong, would be as various as their faces; which, as observed above, would totally unhinge society. It is better ordered by Providence, even for the general good, that, avoiding complex and obscure objects, we are directed by the moral sense to perform certain plain and simple acts, which are obvious to us by intuitive perception.

In the next place, To permit ill in order to produce greater good, may suit a being of universal benevolence; but is repugnant to the nature of man, composed of selfish and benevolent principles. We have seen above, that the true moral balance depends on a subordination of self-love to duty, and of arbitrary benevolence to self-love; and accordingly every man is sensible of injustice when he is hurt in order to benefit another. Were it a rule in society, That a greater good to any other would make it an act of justice to deprive me of my life, of my reputation, or of my property, I should renounce the society of men, and associate with more harmless animals.

Thirdly, the true moral system, that which is displayed above, is not only better suited to the nature of man, and to his limited capacity and intelligence, but contributes more to the general good, which I now proceed to demonstrate. It would be losing time to prove, that a man entirely selfish is ill fitted for society; and we have seen, that universal benevolence, were it a duty, would contribute to the general good perhaps less than an absolute selfishness. Man is too limited in capacity and in power for universal benevolence. Even the greatest monarch has not power to exercise his benevolence but within a very small compass; and if so, how unfit would such a duty be for private persons, who have very little power? Serving only to distress them by inability of performance, they would endeavour to smother it altogether, and give full scope to selfishness. Man is much better qualified for doing good, by a constitution in which benevolence is duly blended with self-love. Benevolence, as a duty, takes place of self-love; a regulation essential to society. Benevolence, as a virtue, not a duty, gives place to self-love; because as every man has more power, knowledge and opportunity, to promote his own good than that of others, a greater quantity of good is produced, than if benevolence were our principle of action. This holds, even supposing no harm done to any person: much more would it hold, were we permitted to hurt some, in order to produce more good to others.

The foregoing final causes respect morality in general. We shall now proceed to particulars: and the first and most important is the law of restraint. Man is evidently framed for society: and as there can be no society among creatures who prey upon each other, it was necessary to provide against mutual injuries; which is effectually done by this law. Its necessity with respect to personal security is self-evident; and with respect to property, its necessity will appear from what follows. In the nature of every man, there is a propensity to hoard or store up things useful to himself and family. But this natural propensity would be rendered ineffectual, were he not secured in the possession of what he thus stores up; for no man will toil to accumulate what he cannot securely possess. This security is afforded by the moral sense, which dictates that the first occupant of goods provided by nature for the subsistence of man, ought to be secure in his possession, and that such goods ought to be inviolable as his property. Thus, by the great law of restraint, men have a protection for their goods, as well as for their persons; and are no less secure in society, than if they were separated from each other by impregnable walls.

Several other duties are little less essential than that of restraint to the existence of society. Mutual trust and confidence, without which society would be an uncomfortable state, enter into the character of the human species; to which the duties of veracity and fidelity correspond. The final cause of these corresponding duties, is obvious: the latter would be of no use in society without the former; and the former without the latter would be hurtful, by laying men open to fraud and deceit.

With respect to veracity in particular, man is so constituted, that he must be indebted to information for the knowledge of most things that benefit or hurt him; and if he could not depend upon information, society would be very little beneficial. Further, it is wisely ordered, that we should be bound by the moral sense always to speak truth, even where we perceive no harm in transgressing that duty; because it is sufficient that harm may ensue, though not foreseen. At the same time falsehood always does mischief: it may happen not to injure us externally in our reputation, or in our goods: but it never fails to injure us internally; for one great blessing of society is, a candid intercourse of sentiments, of opinions, of desires, of wishes; and to admit any falsehood in such intercourse, would poison the most refined pleasures of life.

Because man is the weakest of all animals in a state of separation; and the very strongest in society, by mutual aid and support to which covenants and promises greatly contribute, these are made binding by the moral sense.

The final cause of the law of propriety, which enforces the duty we owe to ourselves, comes next in order. In discoursing upon those laws of nature which concern society, there is no occasion to mention any self-duty but what relates to society; of which kind are prudence, temperance, industry, firmness of mind. And that such qualities should be made our duty, is wisely ordered in a double respect; first, as qualifying us to act a proper part in society, and next, as intitling us to good-will from others. It is the interest, no doubt, of every man, to suit his behaviour to the dignity of his nature, and to the station allotted him by Providence; for such rational conduct contributes to happiness, by preserving health, procuring plenty, gaining the esteem of others, and, which of all is the greatest blessing, by gaining a justly founded self-esteem. But here interest solely is not relied on: the powerful authority of duty is added, that in a matter of the utmost importance to ourselves, and of some importance to the society we live in, our conduct may be regular and steady. These duties tend not only to render a man happy in himself, but also by procuring the good-will and esteem of others, to command their aid and assistance in time of need.

I proceed to the final causes of natural rewards and punishments. It is laid down above, that controversies about property and about other matters of interest, must be adjusted by the standard of right and wrong. But to bring rewards and punishments under the same standard, without regard to private conscience, would be a plan unworthy of our Maker. It is extremely clear, that to reward one who is not conscious of merit, or to punish one who is not conscious of guilt, cannot answer any good end; and in particular, cannot tend either to improvement, or to reformation of manners. How much more like the Deity is the plan of nature, which rewards no man who is not conscious that he merits reward, and punishes no man who is not conscious that he merits punishment! By that plan, and by that only, rewards and punishments accomplish every good end; a final cause most illustrious! The rewards and punishments that attend the primary and secondary virtues, are finely contrived for supporting the distinction between them, set forth above. Punishment must be confined to the transgression of primary virtues, it being the intention of nature, that secondary virtues be entirely free. On the other hand, secondary virtues are more highly rewarded than primary; generosity, for example, makes a greater figure than justice; and magnanimity, heroism, undaunted courage, a still greater figure. One would imagine, at first view, that primary virtues, being more essential, should be intitled to the first place in our esteem, and be more amply rewarded than secondary; and yet in elevating the latter above the former, peculiar wisdom and foresight are conspicuous. Punishment is appropriated to enforce primary virtues; and if these virtues were also attended with high rewards, secondary virtues, degraded to a lower rank, would be deprived of that enthusiastic admiration which is their chief support: self-interest would universally prevail over benevolence, and banish those numberless favours we receive from each other in society, which are beneficial in point of interest, and still more so by generating affection and friendship.

In our progress through final causes we come at last to reparation, one of the principles destined by Providence for redressing wrongs committed, and for preventing the reiteration of them. The final cause of this principle, when the mischief arises from intention, is clear: for to protect individuals in society, it is not sufficient that the delinquent be punished; it is necessary over and above, that the mischief be repaired.

Secondly, Where the act is wrong or unjust, though not understood by the author to be so, it is wisely ordered that reparation should follow; which will thus appear. Considering the fallibility of man, it would be too severe to permit advantage to be taken of one's error in every circumstance. On the other hand, to make it a law in our nature, never to take advantage of error, would be giving too much indulgence to indolence and remission of mind, tending to make us neglect the improvement of our rational faculties. Our nature is so happily framed, as to avoid these extremes by distinguishing between gain and loss. No man is conscious of wrong, when he takes advantage of an error committed by another to save himself from loss: if there must be a loss, common sense dictates, that it ought to rest upon the person who has erred, however innocently, rather than upon the person who has not erred. Thus, in a competition among creditors about the state of their bankrupt debtor, every one is at liberty to avail himself of every error committed by his competitor, in order to recover payment. But *in lucro captando*, the moral sense teacheth a different lesson; which is, that no man ought to lay hold of another's error to make gain by it. Thus, an heir finding a rough diamond in the repositories of his ancestor, gives it away, mistaking it for a common pebble: the purchaser is in conscience and equity bound to restore it, or to pay a just price.

Thirdly, The following considerations unfold a final cause, no less beautiful than that last mentioned. Society could not subsist in any tolerable manner, were full scope given to rashness and negligence, and to every action that is not strictly criminal; whence it is a maxim founded no less upon utility than upon justice, that men in society ought to be extremely circumspect, as to every action that may possibly do harm. On the other hand, it is also a maxim, That as the prosperity and happiness of man depend on action, activity ought to be encouraged, instead of being discouraged by dread of consequences. These maxims, seemingly in opposition, have natural limits that prevent their incroaching upon each other. There is a certain degree of attention and circumspection that men generally bestow upon affairs, proportioned to their importance: if that degree were not sufficient to defend against a claim of reparation, individuals would be too much cramped in action; which would be a great discouragement to activity: if a less degree were sufficient, there would be too great scope for rash or remiss conduct, which would prove the bane of society. These limits, which evidently tend to the good of society, are adjusted by the moral sense; which dictates, as laid down in the section of Reparation, that the man who acts with foresight of the probability of mischief, or acts rashly and uncautiously without such foresight, ought to be liable for consequences: but that the man who acts cautiously, without foreseeing or suspecting any mischief, ought not to be liable for consequences.

In the same section it is laid down, that the moral sense requires from every man, not his own degree of vigilance and attention, which may be very small, but that which belongs to the common nature of the species. The final cause of that regulation will appear upon considering, that were reparation to depend upon personal circumstances, there would be a necessity of enquiring into the characters of men, their education, their manner of living, and the extent of their understanding; which would render judges arbitrary, and such lawsuits inextricable. But by assuming the common nature of the species as a standard, by which every man in conscience judges of his own actions, lawsuits about reparation are rendered easy and expeditious.

Source: Henry Home, Lord Kames, *Sketches of the History of Man*, Glasgow 1802, Book 3, sketch 2, sections 5, 6, 7, from vol. 4, pp. 24–45

PART IX

HISTORIOGRAPHY

THIRTY-EIGHT

ADAM SMITH
A History of Historians

David Hume speaks of history as 'so many collections of experiments by which the moral philosopher fixes the principles of his science'. Smith concurred with this and believed that the economic theorist benefits from knowledge of history no less than the moral philosopher does, and in the same way: as helping him to fix the principles of his science. At every turn in the *Wealth of Nations* Smith is to be found invoking the past in support of his affirmations concerning some aspect or other of his economic theory. He displays a formidable knowledge of historical texts, and also a formidable ability to present in concentrated form a vast mass of historical material on a restricted topic, as witness his chapter 'Of the rise and progress of cities and towns, after the fall of the Roman Empire' (*Wealth of Nations*, Book 3, ch. 3).

Smith is also interested in theoretical questions concerning the writing of history, and develops his ideas in this field most systematically in his *Lectures on Rhetoric and Belles Lettres*. Those ideas themselves are systematically related to other major themes of Smith's, for example, the doctrine of sympathy which he develops in *The Theory of Moral Sentiments* (see excerpt 7), the idea of improvement, which pervades Smith's thought – see for example the first sentence of the first chapter of the *Wealth of Nations* (see excerpt 22) – and the account of scientific discovery presented in the 'Essay on Astronomy' (see excerpt 44).

A.B.

On Rhetoric

LECTURE XVII *Wednesday January 5,* 1763

Having now given those observations I think necessary to the describing single objects both externall and internall, and the more important complex ones, as the characters of men and the more important and interesting actions; I might now proceed to Shew how these are to be applied to the Oratoricall Composition; what objects, and what manner of describing them, and what circumstances were most Proper to interest us and fixing our attention on one side perswade us to be of that opinion.

But as the particular directions already laid down naturally lead us to consider how they are to be applied in the most distinct manner, and where they are all conjoin'd, I shall first consider how they are to be applied to the historicall stile. Besides the narration makes a considerable part in every Oration. It requires no small art to narrate properly those facts which are necessary for the Groundwork of the Oration. So that I would be necessitated to lay down rules for narration in generall, that is for the historicall Stile, before I could thoroughly explain The Rhetoricall composition.

The End of every discourse is either to narrate some fact or prove some proposition. When the design is to set the case in the clearest light; to give every argument its due force, and by this means persuade us no farther than our unbiassed judgement is Convinced; this is not to make use of the Rhetoricall Stile. But when we propose to persuade at all events, and for this purpose adduce those arguments that make for the side we have espoused, and magnify these to the utmost of our power; and on the other hand make light of and extenuate all those which may be brought on the other side, then we make use of the Rhetoricall Stile.

But when we narrate transactions as they happened without being inclined to any party, we then write in the narrative Stile. The Didactic and the oratoricall compositions consist of two parts, the proposition which we lay down and the proof that is brought to confirm this; whether this proof be a strict one applyed to our reason and sound judgement, or one adapted to affect our passions and by that means persuade us at any rate. But in the narrative Stile there is only one Part, that is, the narration of the facts. There is no proposition laid down or proof to confirm it. When a historian brings anything to confirm the truth of a fact it is only a quotation in the margin or a parenthesis and as this makes no part of the work it can not be said to be a part of the didactick. But when a historian sets himself to compare the evidence that is brought for the proof of any fact and way the arguments on both Sides this is assuming the Character of a Didactick writer.

The facts which are most commonly narrated and will be most adapted to the taste of the generality of men will be those that are interesting and important. Now these must be the actions of men; The most interesting and important of these are such as have contributed to great revolutions and changes in States and Governments. The changes or accidents that have happened to innanimate or irrationall beings can not greatly interest us; we look upon them to be guided in a great measure by chance, and undesigning instinct; Design and Contrivance is what chiefly interests us, and the more of this we conceive to be in any transaction the more we are concerned in it. A history of earthquakes or other naturall Phenomena, tho it might Contain great variety of incidents, and be very agreable to a naturallist who had entered deeply into these matters, and by that means conceived them to be of considerable importance, as we do of everything that we have gone so far into as to have some notion of its extent, yet it would appear very dull and uninteresting to the generallity of mankind. The accidents that befall irrationall objects affect us merely by their externall appearance, their Novelty, Grandeur etc. but those which affect the human Species interest us greatly by the Sympatheticall affections they raise in us. We enter into their misfortunes, grieve when they grieve, rejoice when they rejoice, and in a word feel for them in some respect as if we ourselves were in the same condition.

The design of historicall writing is not merely to entertain; (this perhaps is the intention of an epic poem) besides that it has in view the instruction of the reader. It sets before us the more interesting and important events of human life, points out the causes by which these events were brought about and by this means points out to us by what manner and method we may produce similar good effects or avoid Similar bad ones.

Should one lay down certain principles which he afterwards confirmed by examples This work would have the same end as a history but the means would be different, it would not be a narrative but a didactick writing.

In this it differs from a Romance the Sole view of which is to entertain. This being the end, it is of no consequence whether the incidents narrated be true or false. A well contrived Story may be as interesting and entertaining as any real one: the causes which brought about the several incidents that are narrated may all be very ingeniously contrived and well adapted to their severall ends, but still as the facts are not such as have realy existed, the end proposed by history will not be answered. The facts must be real, otherwise they will not assist us in our future conduct, by pointing out the means to avoid or produce any event. Feigned Events and the causes contrived for them, as they did not exist, can not inform us of what happened in former times, nor of consequence assist us in a plan of future conduct.

Some hints of this Sort, pointing out the view with which the author undertook his Work, whether he was induced to it by the importance of the facts or whether it was to remedy the innaccuracy or partiallity of former writers, and also showing us what we may expect to find in the work, would form a much better subject for the preface or beginning of the work (where Tacitus has applied them) than Commonplace-morality as that with which Sallust introduces his works. These however pretty have no connection with the matter in hand, and might have been anywhere else as well as where they are. This much with regard to the preface.

The next thing that comes to be considered in the course of the history is the Causes which brought about the effects that are to be narrated. And here it may be questioned whether we are to relate the remoter causes or only the more immediate ones which preceded the events. If the events are very interesting they will so far attract our attention that we can not be satisfied unless we know something of the causes which brought them about. If these causes again be very important, we for the same reason require to have some account of the causes which produced them. But these need not be so accurately explaind as the more immediate ones, and so on gradually diminishing the importance of the cause till at last we satisfy the Reader.

In general the more remote any cause is the less circumstantially it may be described. Thus Sallust in his Jugurthan war, where the immediate cause of that event was the character of that Prince and the State of the Numidian affairs at the death of Micipsa, dwells but little on the events that preceded that Reign. These he points out more minutely but less so than those that happened in Jugurthas life; and in it too those that happen'd in his infancy or when he was in the Roman Camp are much less accurately explained than those which immediately preceded and were intimately connected with the Chief events. Had he dwelt more on the events that happend before Micipsa's reign, he would have been necessitated to have explained those that preceded them and so on in infinitum. By not attending to this method the Introduction to the history fills a whole folio volume; Gordon who translated Tacitus tells us that when he set about writing the Life of Oliver Cromwell he found the Events in that Period so connected with those before the Reformation and those again with the former Reigns that he was obliged to go as far back as the Conquest, and by going on in the same way he would have found himself reduced to the necessity of tracing the whole back even to the fall of Adam. It is always however necessary to give some reason for the events which more immediately preceded the Chief cause, but this may often be done in such a manner as to prevent any farther Curiosity. Thus Sallust when he tells us that the Cause of the Cataline conspiracy was the Temper and character of that man and the circumstances of his life, join'd with the corrupt manners of the people. Here we naturally demand how it came to pass that a people once so strictly virtuous and sober should have degenerated so much, he tells us that it was owing to the Luxury introduced by their Asiatick conquests. This altogether satisfies us; as those conquests and their circumstances however interesting appear no way connected with the matters in hand.

The more lively and shocking the impression is which any Phænomenon makes on the mind the greater curiosity does it excite to know its Causes, tho perhaps the Phænomenon may not be intrinsically half so grand or important as another less Striking. Thus it is that we have a greater Curiosity to pry into the cause of thunder and Lightning and of the Cœlestiall Motions than of Gravity because they naturally make a greater impression on us. Hence it is that we have naturally a greater curiosity to examine the Causes and Relations of those things which pass without us than of those which pass within us, the latter naturally making very little impression. The associations of our Ideas, the progress and origin of our Passions, are what very few think of enquiring into. But when one has turned his thoughts that way and made some enquiries he begins to think these matters to be of importance and is therefore interested in them.

A Historian therefore is to expose the causes of every thing only in proportion to the impression it makes. Now the Cause of the Event makes a less impression than the Event itself and so excites less curiosity with regard to its Cause; that cause therefore is to be touched upon more slightly, and by being so it excites but very little Curiosity about its Cause, which therefore may be still more superficially mentioned. It is thus that Salust ascribes the Conspiracy of Cataline to the Characters and Circumstances of

Certain Persons in the State; these he traces to the Generall profligacy and Luexury then prevailing in Rome, which at length he deduces from the Conquest of Asia, where he leaves us fully satisfied that we know all that is necessary of the matter and not disposed to enter into the origin of these conquests, however convinced that the enquiry would be curious at a proper time.

The causes that may be assigned for any event are of two Sorts; either the externall causes which directly produced it, or the internall ones, that is those causes that tho' they no way affected the event yet had an influence on the minds of the chief actors so as to alter their conduct from what it would otherwise have been . . . We may observe on this head that those who have been engaged in the transactions they relate or others of the same Sort, generally dwell on those of the first Sort. Thus Cæsar, Polybius and Thucydides, who had all been engaged in most of the battles they describe, account for the fate of the battle by the Situation of the two armies, the nature of the Ground, the weather etc. Those on the other hand who have little acquaintance with the particular incidents of this sort that determine events, but have made enquiries into the nature of the human mind and the severall passions, endeavour by means of the circumstances that would influence them, to account for the fate of battles and other events, which they could not have done by those causes that immediately determine them. Thus Tacitus who seems to have been but little versant in Military or indeed publick affairs of any sort, always accounts for the event of a battle by the circumstances that would influence the mind of the Combatants.

This difference in the manner of accounting for events is very plainly seen in the Description of a battle in the night; one by Thucydides and the other by Tacitus. The former mentions all the causes the nature of the circumstances would have on the armies: whereas the Other has entirely omitted these and mentioned solely those that would affect the minds of the Combatants with lesser courage etc. The first is the account of the attack of Syracuse by the Athenians and the latter of the battle betwixt Vespasian and Vitellius generall.

The describing of characters is no essentiall part of a historicall narration: The temper of the person of the actors at the different times will be sufficient. Xenophon in his account of the Retreat of the 10000 Greeks describes very accurately the Characters of the 3 commanders who were betrayed by Artaxerxes. (Xenophon is almost the only antient Historian who professedly draws characters.) In his Greek history likewise tho he does not enter on purpose on the describing of characters but by the different circumstances and particular incidents he relates the characters are sufficiently plain. Herodotus and Thucydides hardly describe any characters. Herodotus indeed has some exclamations on the characters of the different persons, but such generall ones as are not to be called characters, and might be equally applicable to 100 others (as in the Exclamations on the virtues of Pericles. A man of grave or a merry, of a good nature, or morose temper, may advance to battle or scale the walls with equall intrepidity.) Tis not the degrees of virtue or vice, of courage, good nature etc. that distinguish a character, as the particular turns they have received from the temper and turn of the mind of the severall individualls. Thucydides gives us no account of characters at all. This we can not attribute to want of ability, as he was personally acquainted with most of the characters he would have had occasion to describe and has shewn his skill in this art, in the admirable Characters he has given of whole communities, as of the Athenians after the [text missing in original] which is still more difficult than the describing of characters of single persons; we must then attribute this conduct to an opinion that it was not at all necessary.

There is no author who has more distinctly explained the causes of events than Thucydides. He is in this respect far superior to Polybius, who is at such great pains in minutely explaining all the externall causes of any event that his labour appears visibly in his works and is not only tiresome but at the same time is less pleasant by the constraint the author seems to have been in. Thucydides on the other hand often expresses all that he labours so much in a word or two, sometimes placed in the middle of the narration but in such a manner as not in the least to confound it. Next to Thucydides come Xenophon and Tacitus; This last has often been censured as being too deep a Politician. The author of this remark was I think Trajan Boccalini, an Italian, who has been implicitly followed by all the petty cricks since his time. This remark was very naturall at that time when such subtility prevailed and Machiavelian politicks were in fashion; but does not seem at all suitable to the ingenuous temper of Tacitus, nor is it confirmed by his writings. In the beginning of his history of the affaires in the Reign of Tiberius he gives us some politicall remarks on the Genius and temper of that Prince, but this is sufficiently justified by the character of cunning and design given him by other authors. In other parts of his work the pains he is at to explain the causes of events from the internall causes seems to point out a conterary temper.

Livy seldom endeavours to account for events in either way, by the external or internal causes, and those who are acquainted with millitary affairs affirm that he is not altogether clear in his accounts of battles or sieges. He supports the dignity of his narration by the interesting manner in which he relates the severall events: which he does so admirably that we enter into all the concerns of the parties and are allmost as much affected with them as if we ourselves had been concerned in them.

Events as we before observed may be described either in a direct or indirect manner. We observed also that in most cases the indirect method is much preferable, even when the objects were inanimate; much more then will it be to be chosen when we describe the actions of men where the effects are so much stronger; as the actions themselves are more interesting. 'Tis the proper use of this method that makes most of the ancient historians, as Thucydides, so interesting; and the neglecting it that has rendered the modern historians for the most part so dull and so lifeless. The ancients carry us as it were into the very circumstances of the actors, we feel for them as it were for ourselves. They show us the feelings and agitation of Mind in the Actors previous to and during the Event. They Point to us also the Effects and Consequences of the Event not only in the intrinsick change it made on the Situation of the Actors but the manner of behaviour with which they supported them.

One method which most modern historians and all the Romance writers take to render their narration interesting is to keep their event in Suspense. Whenever the story is beginning to point to the grand event they turn to something else and by this means get us to read thro a number of dull nonsensicall stories, our curiosity prompting us to get at the important event, as Ariosto in his Orlando Furioso. This method the ancients never made use of, they trusted not to the readers Curiosity alone, but relied on the importance of the facts and the interesting manner in which they narrated them. Livy when he relates the affecting catastrophe of the Fabii and the Battle of Cannæ does not endeavour to conceall the event but on the other hand gives us a plain intimation what will be the event of those expeditions before they are related. (In cassum misse Preces [prayers sent in vain]). Yet this does not in the least diminish our concern on the relation, which by the lively manner in which he has executed it engages us as much as if it had been intirely unknown. This method has besides this advantage that we can then with patience attend to the less important intervening accidents, which if the great event had been intirely concealed, our curiosity would make us hurry over; We would count the pages we had to read to get to the event, as we generally do in a Novel. Nay in some cases this warning has a very manifest and considerable advantage. Thus after being given to know that the Generous attempt of the Fabii was to fail we read every future circumstance and the progress of their expedition with a melancholy which is extremely pleasing. Livy seems almost with design to give Warning of the Event of his battles as of Thrasymene and Cannæ.

As newness is the only merit in a Novel and curiosity the only motive which induces us to read them, the writers are necessitated to make use of this method to keep it up. Even the Antient Poets who had not reality on their side never have recourse to this method, the importance of the naration they trust will keep us interested. Virgil in the beginning of the Æneid and Homer in both his heroick poems inform us in the beginning of the chief events that are told in the whole poem.

Even in Tragedy where it is reckoned an essentiall part to keep the plot in Suspence this is not so necessary as in Romance. A tragedy can bear to be read again and again, tho the incidents be not new to us they are new to the actors and by this means interest us as well as by their own importance.

The graduall and just developement of the Catastrophe constitutes a great beauty in any Tragedy yet is it not a necessary one, otherwise we could never with any pleasure hear or see acted a play for the Second time; yet that pleasure often grows by Repetition.

Euripides often in his Prologues by means of a God or a Ghost makes us acquainted with the Events and puts us on our Guard that we may be free to attend to the Sentiments and Action of each Scene, some of which he has laboured greatly.

LECTURE XVIII *Friday January* 7, 1763

The order in which I proposed to treat of historicall Composition was first to treat of the End; next of the means of accomplishing that End, of the Materialls of history; next of the arrangement of these materials; next of the Expression; and lastly of those who have most excelled in this Subject.

The next thing in order that comes to be considered with regard to historicall composition is the arrangement in which the severall parts of the narration are to be placed. In generall the narration is to be carried on in the same order as that in which the events themselves happened. The mind naturally conceives that the facts happened in the order they are related, and when they are by this

means suited to our naturall conceptions the notion we form
of them is by that means rendered more distinct. This rule is
quite evident and accordingly few Historians have tresspassed
against it.

But when severall of the events that are to be related happened
in different places at the same time, the difficulty in this case is to
determine in what order they are to be related: the best method is to
observe the connection of place, that is relate those that happen'd
in the same place for some considerable succession of time without
interrupting the thread of the narration by introducing those that
happened in a different place. 'Tis in this manner that Herodotus
after having followed the course of events in one Country to some
remarkable Æra passes on to those that happened during a Period
nearly of the same length in another country, Resuming afterwards
the former by itself where he had left it off.

But tho the connection of time and place are very strong, yet
they are not to be so invariably observed as to supercede the
observance of all others. There is another connection still more
striking than any of the former, I mean that of cause and Effect.
There is no connection with which we are so much interested as
this of cause and effect; we are not satisfied when we have a fact
told us which we are at a loss to conceive what it was that brought
it about. Now there is often such a connection betwixt the facts
that have happened at different times in different countries that
the one can not be explaind distinct from the other. They would
appear altogether unintelligible unless those which produced
them were also understood. The Difficulty of Accommodating
the explaining the causes that have produced the different events
with the distinctness which is necessary to give one a clear notion of
any one series of events, has lead different authors into error in both
the distinctness of events and the connection of causes with events.
Diodorus of Halicarnassus accuses Thucydides of having adhered
so much to the connection of time that the different events he relates
to have happen'd in different places at the same time are so jumbled
together that it is impossible to form a distinct notion of what passed
in any one place. This observation of the Halicarnassian is not
perhaps altogether just with regard to Thucydides. The History
he writes is that of a war; and the events of one campaign in each
place he narrates by themselves; this period is not so short but one
may form a distinct enough notion of the Events that happen'd
in each place. The Criticism may however serve to shew what
disadvantages would attend the writing a history with too close
an attention to the connection of time. Had Thucydides chosen

much shorter periods, as a month, which the compilers of the history of Europe a work publishd some Years ago did, no one could form any conception of the events any more than from a chronologicall table.

Mr Rapin on the other hand having adhered too much to the connection of Place has often rendered the causes of the events altogether obscure. In his account of the Saxon Heptarchy, he relates the whole affairs of each of those seperate states by themselves, in one continued account from their first establishment till their subversion by the West Saxons. The transactions that pass in any of these are so connected with what passed at the same time or a little before in another part of England that one can not perceive by what means they were brought about unless he is before informed of what passed in the neighbouring states. So that one can not form any notions of the history of any one of these till he has read thro the whole severall times and that with no small attention. The same may be observed of his account of the disputes betwixt the people and King Charles I, which for distinctness sake as he says he relates in the same manner, and the obscurity and incoherence that follows it is still greater as the affairs are still more nearly connected. For distinctness sake says he I will relate separately the affair of the Bishops, of the Militia and of the Earl of Stafford. These are unluckily so Interwoven that to understand what is done in one of them we must know what is doing in the others.

The best method therefore is to adhere to the succession of time as long as it does not introduce an inconvenience from the want of connection; and that when there are a number of simultaneous events to be related we should relate by themselves those that happen'd in each place, recapitulating under each those concerning the others so far as is necessary to keep up the connection betwixt the Cause and the event, and place the former always in order before the latter.

I shall only observe two things farther with regard to the arrangement of the narration; the first is that there is an other way of keeping up with the connection besides the two abovementioned; That is, the Poeticall method, which connects the different facts by some slight circumstances which often had nothing in the bringing about the series of the events, or by some relation that appears betwixt them. This is the method which Livy generally has made use of, and to such good purpose that he has never been condemned for want of connection. Thucydides on the other hand never observes any sort of connection in the circumstances he

brings in. Those mentioned in his description of the battle in the
night would do equally well in whatever order they were placed:
Tacitus, describing the distress an army was in says: They were
without tents and in want of bandages.

The second is that, We should never leave any chasm or Gap in
the thread of the narration even tho there are no remarkable events
to fill up that space. The very notion of a gap makes us uneasy for
what should have happened in that time. Tacitus is often guilty of
this fault. He tells us that the army of Germanicus being attacked
in their camp gained a great victory over the enemy; this is in the
middle of Germany and in the next sentence we find them across
the Rhine, supported by the assiduity and Care of Agrippina when
they were in the utmost hazard.

I shall now proceed to make some observations on the Manner
in which the narration is to be expressed and the difference betwixt
the didactick, oratoricall and the Historicall Stile.

An historian as well as an orator may excite our love or esteem
for the persons he treats of, but then the methods they take are very
different. The Rhetorician will not barely set forth the character of
a person as it realy existed but will magnify every particular that
may tend to excite the Strongest emotions in us. He will also seem
to be deeply affected with that affection which he would have us feel
towards any object. He will exclaim, for example, on the amiable
Character, the sweet temper and behaviour of the man towards
whom he would have us to feel those affections. The Historian
on the conterary can only excite our affection by the narration of
the facts and setting them in as interesting a view as he possibly
can. But all exclamations in his own person would not suit with
the impartiality he is to maintain and the design he is to have
in view of narrating facts as they are without magnifying them
or diminishing them. An historian in the same way may excite
grief or compassion but only by narrating facts which excite those
feelings; whereas the orator heightens every incident and pretends
at least to be deeply affected by them himself, often exclaiming on
the wretched condition of those he talks of etc. (I could almost say
damn it.)

Few historians accordingly have run in this error. Tacitus indeed
has a passionate exclamation in the latter part of his character of
Agricola. The Elder Pliny too has severall times been guilty of this
foolish affectation as it certainly is in him who in other respects
is a very grave author, and the more so on the subject he writes
on, which is naturall history, a subject which tho' it may be very
amusing does not appear to be very animating. Besides these there

is no historian who has used them unless it be Valerius maximus, and Florus (if he deserves the name of a historian) who is full of them from the beginning to the end.

As the historian is not to make use of the Oratoricall Stile so neither has he any occasion for the didactick. It is not his business to bring proofs for propositions but to narrate facts. The only thing he can be under any necessity of proving is the events he relates. The best way in this case is not to set a labourd and formall demonstration but barely mentioning the authorities on both sides, to shew for what reason he had chosen to be of the one opinion rather than of the other. Long demonstrations as they are no part of the historians province are seldom made use of by the ancients. The modern authors have often brought them in. Historicall truths are now in much greater request than they ever were in the ancient times. One thing that has contributed to the increase of this curiosity is that there are now severall sects in Religion and politicall disputes which are greatly dependent on the truth of certain facts. This it is that has induced almost all historians for some time past to be at great pains in the proof of those facts on which the claims of the parties they favoured depended. These proofs however besides that they are inconsistent with the historicall stile, are likewise of bad consequence as they interrupt the thread of the narration, and that most commonly in the parts that are most interesting. They withdraw our attention from the main facts, and before we can get thro them they have so far weakened our concern for the issue of the affair that was broke off that we are never again so much interested in them.

The Dissertations which are everywhere interwoven into Modern Histories contribute among other things and that not a little to render them less interesting than those wrote by the Antients. To avoid a dissertation about the Truth of a Fact a Historian might first Relate the Event according to the most likely opinion and when he had done so give the others by saying that such or such a Circumstance had occasiond such or such a mistake or that such a misrepresentation had been propagated by such a person for such Ends. This would be making a fact of it. The Truth and Evidence of Historicall facts is now in much more request and more critically Examined than among the Antients because of all the Numerous Sects among us whether Civil or Religious, there is hardly one the reasonableness of whose Tenets does not depend on some historicall fact.

Besides no fact that is called in question interests us so much or makes so lasting impression, as those of whose truth we are altogether satisfied. Now all proofs of this sort show that the matter is somewhat dubious; so that on the whole it would be more proper to narrate these facts without mentioning the doubt, than to bring in any long proof.

The same objections that have been mentioned against Long Demonstrations hold equally against Reflexions and observations that exceed the length of too or three sentences. If one was to point out to us some interesting spectacle, it would surely be very disagreable in the most engaging part to interupt us and turn our attention from it by desiring us to attend to the fine contrivance of the parts of the object or the admirable exactness with which the whole was carried on. We would be uneasy by being thus withdrawn from what we were so much concerned in. The historian who brings in long reflections acts precisely in the same manner, he withdraws us from the most interesting part of the narration; and in such interruptions we always imagine that we lose some part of the transaction; Tho' the narration is broken off we cannot conceive that the action is interrupted. The short Reflexions and observations made use of by The Cardinal de Rhetz and by Tacitus are not liable to the same objections. Of these Two Tacitus has evidently the superiority: his observations do not stand out from the narration but often appear to make a part of it, whereas those of the Cardinall, tho not too long are intirely separate from the narration.

I saw, says the Cardinall, the whole extent of my danger and I saw nothing but what was terrible. There is in great dangers a Certain charm etc. etc.

Speeches interspersed in the narration do not appear so faulty (tho they may be of considerable length) as long observations or Rhetoricall declamations. The Stile indeed is altogether different from that of the Historian as they are oratoricall compositions; But then they are not in the authors own person, and therefore do not contradict the impartiality he is to maintain. Neither do they interrupt the thread of the narration as they are not considered as the authors, but make a part of the facts related. They give also an opportunity of introducing those observations and reflections which we observed are not so properly made in the person of the writer. Livy often makes this use of them; Thus he introduces his reflection on the hazard, the importance and generosity of the undertaking of the Fabii not in his own person but by making their design the subject of Debate in the Senate, which also adds to the sentiments he would inspire us with.

The only objection then that can be made against the using

speeches in this manner is, That tho they be represented as facts, they are not genuine ones. But neither does he desire you to consider them as such, but only as being brought in to illustrate the narration.

LECTURE XIX *Monday January* 10, 1763

Having in the preceding lectures given ye an account of the principall things necessary to be observed in the writing of history, I proceed to *The History of Historians*.

The Poets were the first Historians of any. They recorded those accounts that were most apt to surprise and strike the imagination such as the mythological history and adventures of their Deities. We find accordingly all the most ancient writings were ballads or Hymns in honour of their Gods recording the most amazing parts of their conduct. As their Subject was the marvellous, so they naturally expressed themselves in the Language of wonder, that is in Poetry, for in that Stile amazement and surprise naturally break forth.

Of the actions of men, again, military exploits would be the first subject of the Poets as they are most fraught with adventures that are fit to amaze and gratify the desire men have especially in the early periods for what is marvellous. Homer accordingly has recorded the most remarkable war that his countrymen had been engaged in before those days. All the other poets he mentions, for he mentions no writers but what were poets, had also followed the same plan; they related the most surprising adventures and warlike exploits of the great men in or before their time. In all Countries we find poetry has been the first Species of writing, as the marvellous is that which first draws the attention of unimproved men. The oldest originall Writings in Latin, Italian, French, English and Scots, are all poets. There are indeed other writings perhaps as old as any of these Poems, that are wrote in Prose; but these are only Monkish Legends or others of that sort; which as they are wrote in a foreign Language, and in a different way from that naturally to the country, are evidently copied from the works of authors of an other Country (and are not to be numbred with the Productions of that Country).

The next Species of Historians were Poets in every respect except the form of the Language. Their language was prose but their Subject altogether Poeticall – Furies, Harpys, Animalls, half men and half Bird, or snake, Centaurs, and other half fish and half man that were bread in Tartarus and swam about in the Sea; The intercourse of Gods with Women, and Goddesses with men, and the Heroes that Sprung from them, and their exploits, were the subject of their Works according to Dionysius of Halicarnassus. When one reads his account it will immediately put him in mind of the Geoffry of Monmouth and the other earlier writers, their Elves and Fairies, Dragons, Griffins and other monsters with the accounts of which the greatest part of their Books were filled, The Creatures of an imagination engendered by the terror and Superstitious fear which is allways found in the ruder state of Mankind. These writers that followed this method amongst the ancients confined their accounts to the memorable Stories of some one country or province; and in the same manner the monkish legends are confin'd to one town or perhaps to one monastery.

The first author who formed the Design of extending the plan of history was Herodotus. He chose for this reason a period of 240 Years before his time, and comprehends the history not only of all the Grecian States but also of all the Barbarous nations. These he has connected together in such an easy and naturall manner, as to leave no gap nor chasm in his narration. The stile is gracefull and easy; his narration Crowded with memorable facts and those the most extraordinary that happened in each country. He does not however confine himself to those that produced any memorable change or alteration in each country but chooses out whatever is most agreable. He has not near so many of those fabulous and marvellous accounts as we are told the authors who preceded him had but then he has still a good number scattered in his work. His design indeed seems to have been rather to amuse than to instruct. This is confirmed by the long period he has chosen and the wide tract of Country which he has made the Subjects of his history; by this means his facts could be more easily rendered amusing and he has accordingly picked from the history of each country those which are most intertaining whether they be of importance or not. We can learn from him rather the Customs of the different nations and the series of events, than any account of the internall government or the causes that brought about the events he relates; but in this way too we may learn a great deal.

History continued in the same state as Herodotus left it till Thucydides undertook a history of the Peloponesian war. His design was different from that of former historians, and was that which is the proper design of historicall writing. He tells us that he undertook that work that by recording in the truest manner the various incidents of that war and the causes that produced it, posterity may learn how to produce the like events or shun others, and know what is to be expected from such and such circumstances. In this design he has succeeded better perhaps than any preceding or succeeding writer. His Stile is Strong and Nervous, his narration crouded with the most important events. The Subject of his work is the history of a war which he relates in the distinctest manner, giving the history of each campaign by itself so as that we have a compleat notion of the progress of the war in each place. He never introduces any circumstances that do not some way contribute to the producing some remarkable change in the affairs of the two contending states; This is a fault most other historians are often guilty of. Tacitus and many others introduce all those circumstances which give them an opportunity of displaying their Eloquence. Thus Tacitus in one place stops short to describe a Temple Titus happen'd to visit, and in another the particular circumstances of the disorder in Verres army. The only place where Thucydides is guilty of it is in describing the concern of the Soldiers at the recall of a favourite generall, and for this too he makes an apology acknowledging that such matters are not the subject of a history. His Events are all chosen so as to be of consequence to the narration, and in his account of them he abundantly satisfies his design, accounting for every event by the externall causes that produced it, pointing out what circumstances of time, place, etc. in the side of either party determin'd the success of the enterprize they were engaged in. He renders his narration at the same time interesting by the internall effects the events produced as in that before mention'd of the Battle in the night, and also by the great number of speeches he introduces into his works, and by which he opens up the different circumstances of the affairs at each time. His narration is by this means very crouded and tho perhaps it is not so amusing as that of Herodotus, yet (as he himself says) one who desires to know the truth and the causes of the different success of the war will be pleased with it. He gives a good deal more of the Politicall and Civill History of the two States engaged in the war than Herodotus, but neither does he seem to have had it much in his view.

Thucydides is the first who pays any attention at all to Civill History, all who preceded him had attached themselves merely to the military.

The next author we come to is Xenophon. His Stile is easy and agreable, not so strong as that of Thucydides but perhaps more pleasant; Nor is his narration so crouded as he often condescends to intermix circumstances that do not tend much to the chief events in the history. His retreat of the Ten thousand Grecians is commonly Compared to Cæsar's Commentaries as they are the accounts of the conduct of two generalls wrote by themselves without the least ostentation. In this point indeed they bear a great resemblance, but in other matters they differ very widely. The Plainness of Xenophon is very different from that of Cæsar, and displays an ingenuity and openness of heart that does not appear in the writings of the other. Cæsars Stile is constantly crouded, he hurrys from one fact of importance to another without touching on anything that is not of importance betwixt them. It is not easy to convey a notion of Xenophons beauties, there are no passages which taken by themselves could shew his manner, and his peculiar excellencies (as he uses but a few circumstances in comparison of Thucidides in his description. The precedent is always so much connected with every passage that we cannot enter into the beauties of any passage unless we are acquainted with what precedes.) He must be read through to perceive his beauties and enter into his manner. In his Expedition Of Cyrus he is at pains in all the circumstances of the narration which would otherwise often have been of little consequence, that tended to conciliate the affections of the Soldiers to their commander, and by this means he engages us so much in his favour that we are no less affected by the description he gives of the fate of the battle, tho' it be very plain and void of ornament, than we would have been by one of the most interesting of those drawn by Thucydides, with all the circumstances he brings in of the effect the events had on the actors both in the action and afterwards. By thus drawing us gradually on he becomes one of the most engaging tho not one of the most passionate and interesting of authors. (To Speak in the Painters Stile; tho neither the Lines nor the Colouring or expression be very strong yet the ordonnance of the piece is such that it is on the whole very engaging and attractive.) He does not raise those violent emotions that Thucydides does but he pleases and engages fully as much. It is evident from this that no one passage can make us acquainted with his beauties. On the other hand there are many passages in Cæsar which will give us a compleat notion of his manner and his beauties. As all the events he describes are important, he is often induced to describe them in a striking and interesting manner. Xenophon too has given us severall descriptions of characters in his works, not indeed of set purpose but by the circumstances he mentions of the persons that occur in the Course of his history. This he does particularly in his treatise of the Grecian affairs, in which he takes up the history where Thucydides left it off, and by this means he gives us more insight into Politicall affairs of Greece than the fore-mentioned historians do.

The first writer however who enters into the Civil history of the Nations he treats of is Polybius. This author tho inferior to Herodotus in Grace, and to Thucydides in Strength and Xenophon in Sweetness; and tho his manner be not very interesting; Yet by the distinctness and accuracy with which he has related a series of events, which would by their importance have been interesting tho handled by a less able author; as well as by the views he has given us of the Civill constitution of the Romans, is rendered not only instructing but agreable.

Of all the Latin historians Livy is without doubt the best; and if to be agreable were the chief view of an author he would merit the chief Rank amongst the whole number. He does not indeed enter deeply into the causes of things, in the same manner as the Greek historians do; but on the other hand he renders his descriptions extremely interesting by the great number of affecting circumstances he has thrown together, and that not without any connection, as is the method of Thucydides, but in an order naturall to the times in which they happend and the circumstances themselves. The circumstances mentiond in the night battle are narated in such a manner as if they had all happened at the same time; but those Livy relates in the Confusion at Rome after the battle of [Cannae] are all related in the order they must have succeeded.

But that which is the peculiar excellency of Livy's Stile is the Grandeur and majesty which he maintains thro' the whole of his works and in which he excells all other historians tho' perhaps he is inferiour in many other respects. Tis probably to keep up this gravity, that he pays so much attention to the ceremonies of Religion and the omens and Portents, which he never omitts. For it is not to be supposed that he had any belief in them himself in an age when the vulgar Religion was altogether disregarded except as a Politicall Institution by the wiser Sort.

Livy is generally accused of being very inaccurate in his accounts of military affairs, but I imagine he is not so faulty in this respect as common fame reports. He gives us too a very good account of the Roman constitution not indeed so particular as that of the Halicarnassian; but there is enough thro the work to make us tollerably acquainted with it. It is to be considered too that Livy wrote to Romanes to whom it would have been impertinent to give a minute account of their own Customs; Whereas Dionysius of Halicarnassus wrote for Greeks unacquainted with those matters.

Livy is compared by Quintilian with Herodotus and Sallust with Thucydides. But Livy without question far excells Herodotus and

Sallust on the other hand falls no less short of Thycidides. He resembles him indeed in the conciseness of his manner and the suddeness of his transitions but then he has neither his strength nor his accuracy. Nor is narration so crouded in the Cataline conspiracy (induced perhaps by the subject which furnished him with no very wide field), he has thrown in severall digressions of considerable length very little connected with his subject. In both the works that are now remaining he is very defective in his descriptions, his circumstances are often so far from being adapted to the matter in hand that they are what we may call common place and such as would do equally well in any account of the same nature tho the State of the affairs were considerably different. His Description of the battle with Jugurtha would in allmost all the circumstances suit equally to any other battle; it signifies indeed nothing more than that there was a great confusion. Thucydides in his description of the night battle, tho he represents nothing more than the confusion, yet it is such a confusion as in no other place, nor in no other conditions could possibly have happened. That described by Sallust is such as happen in every battle. In the same way the circumstances by which he represents the Luxury of the Romans and their depraved moralls are such as attend Luxury in every country. But those by which Thucydides points out the effect of the Sedition in Greece are such as no other sort of sedition, no other state of a country could have occasioned. Besides this, his conciseness which it is plain he copied from Thucydides is rather apparent than real. For tho his sentences are always very short, Yet the one signifies nothing more than was implied by the former and in the following one. In the Description of the battle abovementioned the first Sentence implies all the following ones. He supports (however) his narration by the aptness of his expression in which perhaps he surpasses all the other historians, and by the variety of his Speeches which as well as those of Thucydides shall be considered when we come to Deliberative Eloquence. But from his descriptions, one would imagine that he had enquired rather into the events, than into the different Circumstances, with any accuracy. And as, by this means, he was necessitated to contrive Incidents, he would naturally fall upon Common-place ones such as would occur in every affair of the same Sort . . .

Source: Adam Smith, *Lectures on Rhetoric and Belles Lettres*, ed. J. C. Bryce, Oxford 1983, Lectures 17–19, pp. 89–110

THIRTY-NINE

DUGALD STEWART
Conjectural History

In this excerpt we find Stewart putting into the public arena
for the first time a crucial piece of Scottish Enlightenment
terminology, 'theoretical or conjectural history'. Although
he invented the terminology primarily to speak about Smith's
writings, the genre Stewart had in mind attracted many of the
Scottish literati, including David Hume, as is acknowledged
by Stewart when he comments that the term 'conjectural
history . . . coincides pretty nearly in its meaning with
that of *Natural History*, as employed by Mr Hume'. The
work by Hume is *The Natural History of Religion*, which
certainly contains conjectural history, but Stewart also finds
conjectural history in writings on language, politics, science
and on many other elements and features of human culture.
For example, the Scottish literati discussed the earliest forms
of government, the religious beliefs of ancient peoples, their
interpretations of the movements of the heavenly bodies,
and the origin of language. Here Stewart investigates the
philosophical credentials of these discussions.

A.B.

Theoretical or Conjectural History

The Dissertation on the Origin of Languages, which now forms a part of the same volume with the Theory of Moral Sentiments, was, I believe, first annexed to the second edition of that work. It is an essay of great ingenuity, and on which the author himself set a high value; but, in a general review of his publications, it deserves our attention less, on account of the opinions it contains, than as a specimen of a particular sort of inquiry, which, so far as I know, is entirely of modern origin, and which seems, in a peculiar degree, to have interested Mr Smith's curiosity. Something very similar to it may be traced in all his different works, whether moral, political, or literary; and on all these subjects he has exemplified it with the happiest success.

When, in such a period of society as that in which we live, we compare our intellectual acquirements, our opinions, manners, and institutions, with those which prevail among rude tribes, it cannot fail to occur to us as an interesting question, by what gradual steps the transition has been made from the first simple efforts of uncultivated nature, to a state of things so wonderfully artificial and complicated. Whence has arisen that systematical beauty which we admire in the structure of a cultivated language; that analogy which runs through the mixture of languages spoken by the most remote and unconnected nations; and those peculiarities by which they are all distinguished from each other? Whence the origin of the different sciences and of the different arts; and by what chain has the mind been led from their first rudiments to their last and most refined improvements? Whence the astonishing fabric of the political union; the fundamental principles which are common to all governments; and the different forms which civilized society has assumed in different ages of the world? On most of these subjects very little information is to be expected from history; for long before that stage of society when men begin to think of recording their transactions, many of the most important steps of their progress have been made. A few insulated facts may perhaps be collected from the casual observations of travellers, who have viewed the arrangements of rude nations; but nothing, it is evident, can be obtained in this way, which approaches to a regular and connected detail of human improvement.

In this want of direct evidence, we are under a necessity of supplying the place of fact by conjecture; and when we are unable to ascertain how men have actually conducted themselves upon particular occasions, of considering in what manner they are likely to have proceeded, from the principles of their nature, and the circumstances of their external situation. In such inquiries, the detached facts which travels and voyages afford us, may frequently serve as land-marks to our speculations; and sometimes our conclusions *a priori*, may tend to confirm the credibility of facts, which, on a superficial view, appeared to be doubtful or incredible.

Nor are such theoretical views of human affairs subservient merely to the gratification of curiosity. In examining the history of mankind, as well as in examining the phenomena of the material world, when we cannot trace the process by which an event *has been* produced, it is often of importance to be able to show how it *may have been* produced by natural causes. Thus, in the instance which has suggested these remarks, although it is impossible to determine with certainty what the steps were by which any particular language was formed, yet if we can shew, from the known principles of human nature, how all its various parts might gradually have arisen, the mind is not only to a certain degree satisfied, but a check is given to that indolent philosophy, which refers to a miracle, whatever appearances, both in the natural and moral worlds, it is unable to explain.

To this species of philosophical investigation, which has no appropriated name in our language, I shall take the liberty of giving the title of *Theoretical or Conjectural History*; an expression which coincides pretty nearly in its meaning with that of *Natural History*, as employed by Mr Hume,[1] and with what some French writers have called *Histoire Raisonnée*.

The mathematical sciences, both pure and mixed, afford, in many of their branches, very favourable subjects for theoretical history; and a very competent judge, the late M. d'Alembert, has recommended this arrangement of their elementary principles, which is founded on the natural succession of inventions and discoveries, as the best adapted for interesting the curiosity and exercising the genius of students. The same author points out as a model a passage in Montucla's History of Mathematics, where an attempt is made to exhibit the gradual progress of philosophical speculation, from the first conclusions suggested by a general survey of the heavens, to the doctrines of Copernicus.

[1] See his *Natural History of Religion*.

It is somewhat remarkable, that a theoretical history of this very science (in which we have, perhaps, a better opportunity than in any other instance whatever, of comparing the natural advances of the mind with the actual succession of hypothetical systems) was one of Mr Smith's earliest compositions, and is one of the very small number of his manuscripts which he did not destroy before his death.

I already hinted, that inquiries perfectly analogous to these may be applied to the modes of government, and to the municipal institutions which have obtained among different nations. It is but lately, however, that these important subjects have been considered in this point of view; the greater part of politicians before the time of Montesquieu, having contented themselves with an historical statement of facts, and with a vague reference of laws to the wisdom of particular legislators, or to accidental circumstances, which it is now impossible to ascertain. Montesquieu, on the contrary, considered laws as originating chiefly from the circumstances of society; and attempted to account, from the changes in the condition of mankind, which take place in the different stages of their progress, for the corresponding alterations which their institutions undergo. It is thus that, in his occasional elucidations of the Roman jurisprudence, instead of bewildering himself among the erudition of scholiasts and of antiquaries, we frequently find him borrowing his lights from the most remote and unconnected quarters of the globe, and combining the casual observations of illiterate travellers and navigators, into a philosophical commentary on the history of law and of manners.

The advances made in this line of inquiry since Montesquieu's time have been great. Lord Kames, in his Historical Law Tracts, has given some excellent specimens of it, particularly in his Essays on the History of Property and of Criminal Law, and many ingenious speculations of the same kind occur in the works of Mr Millar.

In Mr Smith's writings, whatever be the nature of his subject, he seldom misses an opportunity of indulging his curiosity, in tracing from the principles of human nature, or from the circumstances of society, the origin of the opinions and the institutions which he describes. I formerly mentioned a fragment concerning the History of Astronomy which he has left for publication; and I have heard him say more than once, that he had projected, in the earlier part of his life, a history of the other sciences on the same plan. In his Wealth of Nations, various disquisitions are introduced which have a like object in view, particularly the theoretical delineation he has given of the natural progress of opulence in a country; and his investigation of the causes which have inverted this order in the different countries of modern Europe. His lectures on jurisprudence seem, from the account of them formerly given, to have abounded in such inquiries.

I am informed by the same gentleman who favoured me with the account of Mr Smith's lectures at Glasgow, that he had heard him sometimes hint an intention of writing a treatise upon the Greek and Roman republics. 'And after all that has been published on that subject, I am convinced (says he), that the observations of Mr Smith would have suggested many new and important views concerning the internal and domestic circumstances of those nations, which would have displayed their several systems of policy, in a light much less artificial than that in which they have hitherto appeared.'

The same turn of thinking was frequently, in his social hours, applied to more familiar subjects; and the fanciful theories which, without the least affectation of ingenuity, he was continually starting upon all the common topics of discourse, gave to his conversation a novelty and variety that were quite inexhaustible. Hence too the minuteness and accuracy of his knowledge on many trifling articles, which, in the course of his speculations, he had been led to consider from some new and interesting point of view; and of which his lively and circumstantial descriptions amused his friends the more, that he seemed to be habitually inattentive, in so remarkable a degree, to what was passing around him.

I have been led into these remarks by the Dissertation on the Formation of Languages, which exhibits a very beautiful specimen of theoretical history, applied to a subject equally curious and difficult. The analogy between the train of thinking from which it has taken its rise, and that which has suggested a variety of his other disquisitions, will, I hope, be a sufficient apology for the length of this digression; more particularly, as it will enable me to simplify the account which I am to give afterwards, of his inquiries concerning political economy.

I shall only observe farther on this head, that when different theoretical histories are proposed by different writers, of the progress of the human mind in any one line of exertion, these theories are not always to be understood as standing in opposition to each other. If the progress delineated in all of them be plausible, it is possible at least, that they may all have been realized; for human affairs never exhibit, in any two instances, a perfect uniformity. But whether they have been realized or no, is often a question of little consequence. In most cases, it is of more importance to ascertain the progress that is most simple, than the progress that is most agreeable to fact; for, paradoxical as the proposition may appear, it is certainly true, that the real progress is not always the most natural. It may have been determined by particular accidents, which are not likely again to occur, and which cannot be considered as forming any part of that general provision which nature has made for the improvement of the race.

Source: Dugald Stewart, 'Account of the Life and Writings of Adam Smith, LL.D.', in Adam Smith, *Essays on Philosophical Subjects*, ed. W. P. D. Wightman, J. C. Bryce and I. S. Ross, Oxford 1980, pp. 292–6

FORTY

WILLIAM ROBERTSON
Comparative History

Robertson aimed to write a scientific history in which he would not only record facts about the past, but also provide explanations for those facts. As regards the numerous reports of past events, which were to be believed? The answer to this must point to a methodology of history, and the answer provided by Robertson and his fellow historians of the Scottish Enlightenment, including and perhaps especially Hume, focuses upon the concept of human nature. Reports of human behaviour are to be placed on a spectrum between the evidently true and the incredible, purely in light of our knowledge of human nature in general, or of our knowledge of the nature of the particular person or persons involved. Since people can act out of character the strangeness of a reported act is not proof that it did not occur, but it is a reason for handling the report with care.

Not only should we bring to bear our knowledge of human nature in considering whether a report is historically accurate; we must also use our historical knowledge in the course of constructing a science of human nature. David Hume writes: 'Its [history's] chief use is only to discover the constant and universal principles of human nature by showing men in all varieties of circumstances and situations and furnishing us with materials from which we may form our observations and become acquainted with the regular springs of human action and behaviour' [*An Enquiry Concerning Human Understanding*, p. 83]. Robertson fully concurs, though he was primarily concerned with the reverse move, using our knowledge of human nature to test historical reports. Thus, for him, the principle that human nature has certain unchanging features is a substantive principle of scientific history.

Even so, that well-established facts of human nature make a given report unlikely is not a reason for disbelieving the report. Here we come to two further substantive principles of scientific history, both of them endorsed and employed by Robertson. The recurrence of reports of events of a certain kind, or of social relations of a certain kind, where the reporters appear to be writing independently of each other, makes it more likely that events or relations of those kinds did indeed occur. This principle is employed in our excerpt, where Robertson invokes Caesar and Tacitus as witnesses of the customs and social and political institutions of the German tribes.

The last of the substantive principles that should be noted is stated in our excerpt as: 'the human mind, whenever it is placed in the same situation, will, in ages the most distant, and in countries the most remote, assume the same form, and be distinguished by the same manners'. Robertson is speaking here of the comparative method of scientific history, vividly illustrated in our excerpt in which the ancient German tribes are compared with the tribes of North America and remarkable similarities are demonstrated. The methodological point is clear. It was reported of the ancient German tribes, which were in a rude or barbaric state, that they had certain customs and social and political institutions. The savage tribes of North America had, according to eighteenth-century eye-witness reports, almost identical customs and social and political institutions. This fact about the North American tribes can, according to Robertson, be treated as corroborative of the reports of Caesar and Tacitus.

The demonstration of the likeness is also a demonstration of the existence of constant and universal principles of human nature. History will have been used, exactly as Hume wished, to show people in all varieties of circumstances and situations and to furnish us with materials 'from which we may form our observations and become acquainted with the regular springs of human action and behaviour'. In a real sense Robertson wrote history as a philosopher. He was a close friend of Hume, who had the greatest respect for Robertson's historical writings. We get a taste of this in a letter Hume wrote to Robertson in February 1759 shortly after the publication of Robertson's *History of Scotland*: 'All the people whose friendship or judgment either of us value, are friends to both, and will be pleased with the success of both, as we will be with that of each other. I declare to you I have not of a long time had a more sensible pleasure than the good reception of your *History* has given me within this fortnight.'

A.B.

Historical Proofs and Illustrations

I have observed, that our only certain information concerning the ancient state of the barbarous nations must be derived from the Greek and Roman writers. Happily an account of the institutions and customs of one people, to which those of all the rest seem to have been in a great measure similar, has been transmitted to us by two authors, the most capable, perhaps, that ever wrote, of observing them with profound discernment, and of describing them with propriety and force. The reader must perceive that Cæsar and Tacitus are the authors whom I have in view. The former gives a short account of the ancient Germans in a few chapters of the sixth book of his Commentaries: the latter wrote a treatise expressly on that subject. These are the most precious and instructive monuments of antiquity to the present inhabitants of Europe. From them we learn,

1. That the state of society among the ancient Germans was of the rudest and most simple form. They subsisted entirely by hunting or by pasturage. Cæs. lib. vi. c. 21. They neglected agriculture, and lived chiefly on milk, cheese, and flesh. Ibid. c. 22. Tacitus agrees with him in most of these points; De morib. Germ. c. 14, 15. 23. The Goths were equally negligent of agriculture. Prisc. Rhet. ap. Byz. Script. v. i. p. 31. B. Society was in the same state among the Huns, who disdained to cultivate the earth, or to touch a plough. Amm. Marcel. lib. xxxi. p. 475. The same manners took place among the Alans; ibid. p. 477. While society remains in this simple state, men by uniting together scarcely relinquish any portion of their natural independence. Accordingly we are informed, 2. That the authority of civil government was extremely limited among the Germans. During times of peace they had no common or fixed magistrate, but the chief men of every district dispensed justice and accommodated differences. Cæs. ibid. c. 23. Their kings had not absolute or unbounded power; their authority consisted rather in the privilege of advising, than in the power of commanding. Matters of small consequence were determined by the chief men; affairs of importance by the whole community. Tacit. c. 7. 11. The Huns, in like manner, deliberated in common concerning every business of moment to the society; and were not subject to the rigour of regal authority. Amm. Marcel. lib. xxxi. p. 474. 3. Every

individual among the ancient Germans was left at liberty to chuse whether he would take part in any military enterprise which was proposed; there seems to have been no obligation to engage in it imposed on him by public authority. 'When any of the chief men proposes an expedition, such as approve of the cause and of the leader rise up, and declare their intention of following him; after coming under this engagement, those who do not fulfil it, are considered as deserters and traitors, and are looked upon as infamous.' Cæs. ibid. c. 23. Tacitus plainly points at the same custom, though in terms more obscure. Tacit. c. 11. 4. As every individual was so independent, and master in so great a degree of his own actions, it became, of consequence, the great object of every person among the Germans, who aimed at being a leader, to gain adherents, and attach them to his person and interest. These adherents Cæsar calls *Ambacti* and *Cliente*, i. e. retainers or clients; Tacitus, *Comites*, or companions. The chief distinction and power of the leaders consisted in being attended by a numerous band of chosen youth. This was their pride as well as ornament during peace, and their defence in war. The leaders gained or preserved the favour of these retainers by presents of armour and of horses; or by the profuse though inelegant hospitality with which they entertained them. Tacit. c. 14, 15. 5. Another consequence of the personal liberty and independence which the Germans retained, even after they united in society, was their circumscribing the criminal jurisdiction of the magistrate within very narrow limits, and their not only claiming but exercising almost all the rights of private resentment and revenge. Their magistrates had not the power either of imprisoning or of inflicting any corporal punishment on a free man. Tacit. c. 7. Every person was obliged to avenge the wrongs which his parents or friends had sustained. Their enemies were hereditary, but not irreconcilable. Even murder was compensated by paying a certain number of cattle. Tacit. c. 21. A part of the fine went to the king, or state, a part to the person who had been injured, or to his kindred. Ibid. c. 12.

Those particulars concerning the institutions and manners of the Germans, though well known to every person conversant in ancient literature, I have thought proper to arrange in this order, and to lay before such of my readers as may be less acquainted with these facts, both because they confirm the account which I have given of the state of the barbarous nations, and because they tend to illustrate all the observations I shall have occasion to make concerning the various changes in their government and customs.

The laws and customs introduced by the barbarous nations into their new settlements, are the best commentary on the writings of Cæsar and Tacitus; and their observations are the best key to a perfect knowledge of these laws and customs.

One circumstance, with respect to the testimonies of Cæsar and Tacitus concerning the Germans, merits attention. Cæsar wrote his brief account of their manners more than an hundred years before Tacitus composed his Treatise De Moribus Germanorum. An hundred years make a considerable period in the progress of national manners, especially if, during that time, those people who are rude and unpolished have had much communication with more civilized states. This was the case with the Germans. Their intercourse with the Romans began when Cæsar crossed the Rhine, and increased greatly during the interval between that event and the time when Tacitus flourished. We may accordingly observe, that the manners of the Germans, in his time, which Cæsar describes, were less improved than those of the same people as delineated by Tacitus. Besides this, it is remarkable that there was a considerable difference in the state of society among the different tribes of Germans. The Suiones were so much improved, that they began to be corrupted. Tacit. cap. 44. The Fenni were so barbarous, that it is wonderful how they were able to subsist. Ibid. cap. 46. Whoever undertakes to describe the manners of the Germans, or to found any political theory upon the state of society among them, ought carefully to attend to both these circumstances.

Before I quit this subject, it may not be improper to observe, that, though successive alterations in their institutions, together with the gradual progress of refinement, have made an entire change in the manners of the various people who conquered the Roman empire, there is still one race of men nearly in the same political situation with theirs, when they first settled in their new conquests; I mean the various tribes and nations of savages in North America. It cannot then be considered either as a digression, or as an improper indulgence of curiosity, to enquire whether this similarity in their political state has occasioned any resemblance between their character and manners. If the likeness turns out to be striking, it is a stronger proof that a just account has been given of the ancient inhabitants of Europe, than the testimony even of Cæsar or of Tacitus.

1. The Americans subsist chiefly by hunting and fishing. Some tribes neglect agriculture entirely. Among those who cultivate some small spot near their huts, that, together with all works

of labour, is performed by the women. P. Charlevoix Journal Historique d'un Voyage de l'Amerique, 4to. Par. 1744. p. 334. In such a state of society, the common wants of men being few, and their mutual dependence upon each other small, their union is extremely imperfect and feeble, and they continue to enjoy their natural liberty almost unimpaired. It is the first idea of an American, that every man is born free and independent, and that no power on earth hath any right to diminish or circumscribe his natural liberty. There is hardly any appearance of subordination either in civil or domestic government. Every one does what he pleases. A father and mother live with their children, like persons whom chance has brought together, and whom no common bond unites. Their manner of educating their children is suitable to this principle. They never chastise or punish them, even during their infancy. As they advance in years, they continue to be entirely masters of their own actions, and seem not to be conscious of being responsible for any part of their conduct. Ibid. p. 272, 273.

2. The power of their civil magistrates is extremely limited. Among most of their tribes, the Sachem, or chief, is elective. A council of old men is chosen to assist him, without whose advice he determines no affair of importance. The Sachems neither possess nor claim any great degree of authority. They propose and intreat, rather than command. The obedience of their people is altogether voluntary. Ibid. p. 266, 268.

3. The savages of America engage in their military enterprises, not from constraint, but choice. When war is resolved, a chief arises, and offers himself to be the leader. Such as are willing (for they compel no person) stand up one after another, and sing their war-song. But if, after this, any of these should refuse to follow the leader to whom they have engaged, his life would be in danger, and he would be considered as the most infamous of men. Ibid. p. 217, 218.

4. Such as engage to follow any leader, expect to be treated by him with great attention and respect; and he is obliged to make them presents of considerable value. Ibid. p. 218.

5. Among the Americans, the magistrate has scarcely any criminal jurisdiction. Ibid. p. 272. Upon receiving any injury, the person or family offended may inflict what punishment they please on the person who was the author of it. Ibid. p. 274. Their resentment and desire of vengeance are excessive and implacable. Time can neither extinguish nor abate it. It is the chief inheritance parents leave to their children; it is transmitted from generation to generation, until an occasion be found of satisfying it. Ibid.

p. 309. Sometimes, however, the offended party is appeased. A compensation is paid for a murder that has been committed. The relations of the deceased receive it; and it consists most commonly of a captive taken in war, who being substituted in place of the person who was murdered, assumes his name, and is adopted into his family. Ibid. p. 274.

The resemblance holds in many other particulars. It is sufficient for my purpose to have pointed out the similarity of those great features which distinguish and characterise both people. Bochart, and other philologists of the last century, who, with more erudition than science, endeavoured to trace the migrations of various nations, and who were apt, upon the slightest appearance of resemblance, to find an affinity between nations far removed from each other, and to conclude that they were descended from the same ancestors, would hardly have failed, on viewing such an amazing similarity, to pronounce with confidence, 'That the Germans and Americans must be the same people.' But a philosopher will satisfy himself with observing, 'That the characters of nations depend on the state of society in which they live, and on the political institutions established among them; and that the human mind, whenever it is placed in the same situation, will, in ages the most distant, and in countries the most remote, assume the same form, and be distinguished by the same manners.'

I have pushed the comparison between the Germans and Americans no further than was necessary for the illustration of my subject. I do not pretend that the state of society in the two countries was perfectly similar in every respect. Many of the German tribes were more civilized than the Americans. Some of them were not unacquainted with agriculture; almost all of them had flocks of tame cattle, and depended upon them for the chief part of their subsistence. Most of the American tribes subsist by hunting, and are in a ruder and more simple state than the ancient Germans. The resemblance, however, between their condition, is greater, perhaps, than any that history affords an opportunity of observing between any two races of uncivilized people, and this has produced a surprising similarity of manners.

.   .   .

When nations subject to despotic government make conquests, these serve only to extend the dominion and power of their master. But armies composed of freemen conquer for themselves, not for their leaders. The people who overturned the Roman Empire, and settled in its various provinces, were of the latter class. Not only the different nations that issued from the north of Europe, which has always been considered as the seat of liberty, but the Huns and Alans who inhabited part of those countries, which have been marked out as the peculiar region of servitude, enjoyed freedom and independence in such a high degree as seems to be scarcely compatible with a state of social union, or with the subordination necessary to maintain it. They followed the chieftain who led them forth in quest of new settlements, not by constraint, but from choice; not as soldiers whom he could order to march, but as volunteers who offered to accompany him.

Source: William Robertson, *History of the Reign of Charles the Fifth*, 2 vols, London 1857, vol. I, pp. 239–48, 14

PART X
LANGUAGE

FORTY-ONE

GEORGE CAMPBELL
The Philosophy of Rhetoric

At the heart of the Scottish Enlightenment was the study of human nature. As part of that study an investigation was made into discourse, people speaking to each other and, especially, trying to persuade each other by the power of speech. Such investigations come under the heading of rhetoric, and the art of rhetoric was a popular subject among the literati, a fact to be expected given that most of them were professors, ministers of the church, or lawyers, whose positions depended in part on their skills as communicators. Though Lord Monboddo, Adam Smith, Thomas Reid and Hugh Blair contributed to the subject, none went so deeply into the matter as George Campbell.

One cannot go far into rhetoric without encountering the concept of a faculty of the mind, for in any rhetorical exercise the faculties of intellect, imagination, emotion (or passion) and will are exercised. It is therefore natural that George Campbell attends to them in *The Philosophy of Rhetoric*. These four faculties are appropriately ordered in the above way in rhetorical studies, for the orator first has an idea, whose location is the intellect. By an act of imagination the idea is then expressed in suitable words. These words produce a response in the form of an emotion in the audience, and the emotion inclines the audience to will the acts that the orator has in mind for them.

Not surprisingly, and following an ancient emphasis, Campbell stresses the power of the orator. As he puts it, the orator's power is greater than that of a despot, for the despot enslaves only the body, whereas nothing is exempted from the dominion of the orator, 'neither judgment nor affection, not even the inmost recesses, the most latent movements of the soul'.

A.B.

The Nature and Foundations of Eloquence

CHAPTER I *Eloquence in the largest Acceptation Defined, its more General Forms Exhibited, with their Different Objects, Ends, and Characters*

In speaking there is always some end proposed, or some effect which the speaker intends to produce in the hearer. The word *eloquence* in its greatest latitude denotes, 'That art or talent by which the discourse is adapted to its end.'

All the ends of speaking are reducible to four; every speech being intended to enlighten the understanding, to please the imagination, to move the passions, or to influence the will.

Any one discourse admits only one of these ends as the principal. Nevertheless, in discoursing on a subject, many things may be introduced, which are more immediately and apparently directed to some of the other ends of speaking, and not to that which is the chief intent of the whole. But then these other and immediate ends are in effect but means, and must be rendered conducive to that which is the primary intention. Accordingly, the propriety or the impropriety of the introduction of such secondary ends, will always be inferred from their subserviency or want of subserviency to that end, which is, in respect of them, the ultimate. For example, a discourse addressed to the understanding, and calculated to illustrate or evince some point purely speculative, may borrow aid from the imagination, and admit metaphor and comparison, but not the bolder and more striking figures, as that called vision or fiction, prosopopœia, and the like, which are not so much intended to elucidate a subject, as to excite admiration. Still less will it admit an address to the passions, which, as it never fails to disturb the operation of the intellectual faculty, must be regarded by every intelligent hearer as foreign at least, if not insidious. It is obvious, that either of these, far from being subservient to the main design, would distract the attention from it.

There is indeed one kind of address to the understanding, and only one, which, it may not be improper to observe, disdains all assistance whatever from the fancy. The address I mean, is mathematical demonstration. As this doth not, like moral reasoning, admit degrees of evidence, its perfection in point of eloquence, if so uncommon an application of the term may be allowed, consists in perspicuity. Perspicuity here results entirely from propriety and simplicity of diction, and from accuracy of method, where the mind is regularly, step by step, conducted forwards in the same track, the attention no way diverted, nothing left to be supplied, no one unnecessary word or idea introduced. On the contrary, an harangue framed for affecting the hearts or influencing the resolves of an assembly, needs greatly the assistance both of intellect and of imagination.

In general it may be asserted, that each preceding species, in the order above exhibited, is preparatory to the subsequent; that each subsequent species is founded on the preceding; and that thus they ascend in a regular progression. Knowledge, the object of the intellect, furnisheth materials for the fancy; the fancy culls, compounds, and, by her mimic art, disposes these materials so as to affect the passions; the passions are the natural spurs to volition or action, and so need only to be right directed. This connexion and dependency will better appear from the following observations.

When a speaker addresseth himself to the understanding, he proposes the *instruction* of his hearers, and that, either by explaining some doctrine unknown, or not distinctly comprehended by them, or by proving some position disbelieved or doubted by them. In other words, he proposes either to dispel ignorance or to vanquish error. In the one, his aim is their *information*; in the other, their *conviction*. Accordingly the predominant quality of the former is *perspicuity*; of the latter *argument*. By that we are made to know, by this to believe.

The imagination is addressed by exhibiting to it a lively and beautiful representation of a suitable object. As in this exhibition, the task of the orator may, in some sort, be said, like that of the painter, to consist in imitation, the merit of the work results entirely from these two sources; dignity, as well in the subject or thing imitated, as in the manner of imitation; and resemblance, in the portrait or performance. Now the principal scope for this class being in narration and description, poetry, which is one mode of oratory, especially epic poetry, must be ranked under it. The effect of the dramatic, at least of tragedy, being upon the passions, the drama falls under another species, to be explained afterwards. But that kind of address of which I am now treating, attains the summit of perfection in the *sublime*, or those great and noble images, which, when in suitable colouring presented to the mind, do, as it were, distend the imagination with some vast conception, and quite ravish the soul.

The sublime, it may be urged, as it raiseth admiration, should be considered as one species of address to the passions. But this objection, when examined, will appear superficial. There are few words in any language (particularly such as relate to the operations and feelings of the mind) which are strictly univocal. Thus admiration, when persons are the object, is commonly used for a high degree of esteem; but when otherwise applied, it denotes solely an internal taste. It is that pleasurable sensation which instantly arises on the perception of magnitude, or of whatever is great and stupendous in its kind. For there is a greatness in the degrees of quality in spiritual subjects, analogous to that which subsists in the degrees of quantity in material things. Accordingly, in all tongues, perhaps without exception, the ordinary terms, which are considered as literally expressive of the latter, are also used promiscuously to denote the former. Now admiration, when thus applied, doth not require to its production, as the passions generally do, any reflex view of motives or tendencies, or of any relation either to private interest, or to the good of others; and ought therefore to be numbered among those original feelings of the mind, which are denominated by some the reflex senses, being of the same class with a taste for beauty, an ear for music, or our moral sentiments. Now the immediate view of whatever is directed to the imagination (whether the subject be things inanimate or animal forms, whether characters, actions, incidents, or manners) terminates in the gratification of some internal taste; as a taste for the wonderful, the fair, the good; for elegance, for novelty, or for grandeur.

But it is evident, that this creative faculty, the fancy, frequently lends her aid in promoting still nobler ends. From her exuberant stores most of those tropes and figures are extracted, which, when properly employed, have such a marvellous efficacy in rousing the passions, and by some secret, sudden, and inexplicable association, awakening all the tenderest emotions of the heart. In this case, the address of the orator is not ultimately intended to astonish by the loftiness of his images, or to delight by the beauteous resemblance which his painting bears to nature; nay, it will not permit the hearers even a moment's leisure for making the comparison, but as it were by some magical spell, hurries them, ere they are aware, into love, pity, grief, terror, desire, aversion, fury, or hatred. It therefore assumes the denomination of *pathetic*,[1] which is the characteristic of the third species of discourse, that addressed to the passions.

Finally, as that kind, the most complex of all, which is calculated to influence the will, and persuade to a certain conduct, is in reality an artful mixture of that which proposes to convince the judgment, and that which interests the passions, its distinguishing excellency results from these two, the argumentative and the pathetic incorporated together. These acting with united force, and, if I may so express myself, in concert, constitute that passionate eviction, that *vehemence* of contention, which is admirably fitted for persuasion, and hath always been regarded as the supreme qualification in an orator. It is this which bears down every obstacle, and procures the speaker an irresistible power over the thoughts and purposes of his audience. It is this which hath been so justly celebrated as giving one man an ascendant over others, superior even to what despotism itself can bestow; since by the latter the more ignoble part only, the body and its members are enslaved; whereas from the dominion of the former, nothing is exempted, neither judgment nor affection, not even the inmost recesses, the most latent movements of the soul. What opposition is he not prepared to conquer, on whose arms reason hath conferred solidity and weight, and passion such a sharpness as enables them, in defiance of every obstruction, to open a speedy passage to the heart?

It is not, however, every kind of pathos, which will give the orator so great an ascendancy over the minds of his hearers. All passions are not alike capable of producing this effect. Some are naturally inert and torpid; they deject the mind, and indispose it for enterprise. Of this kind are sorrow, fear, shame, humility. Others, on the contrary, elevate the soul, and stimulate to action. Such are hope, patriotism, ambition, emulation, anger. These, with the greatest facility, are made to concur in direction with arguments exciting to resolution and activity; and are, consequently, the fittest for producing, what, for want of a better term in our language, I shall henceforth denominate the *vehement*. There is, besides, an intermediate kind of passions, which do not so congenially and directly either restrain us from acting, or incite us to act; but, by the art of the speaker, can, in an oblique manner, be made conducive

---

1 I am sensible that this word is commonly used in
   a more limited sense, for that only which excites
   commiseration. *Perhaps* the word *impassioned* would
   answer better.

to either. Such are joy, love, esteem, compassion. Nevertheless, all these kinds may find a place in suasory discourses, or such as are intended to operate on the will. The first is properest for dissuading; the second, as hath been already hinted, for persuading; the third is equally accommodated to both.

Guided by the above reflections, we may easily trace that connection in the various forms of eloquence, which was remarked on distinguishing them by their several objects. The imagination is charmed by a finished picture, wherein even drapery and ornament are not neglected; for here the end is pleasure. Would we penetrate farther, and agitate the soul, we must exhibit only some vivid strokes, some expressive features, not decorated as for show (all ostentation being both despicable and hurtful here), but such as appear the natural exposition of those bright and deep impressions, made by the subject upon the speaker's mind; for here the end is not pleasure, but emotion. Would we not only touch the heart, but win it entirely to co-operate with our views, those affecting lineaments must be so interwoven with our argument, as that, from the passion excited, our reasoning may derive importance, and so be fitted for commanding attention; and by the justness of the reasoning, the passion may be more deeply rooted and enforced; and that thus, both may be made to conspire in effectuating that persuasion which is the end proposed. For here, if I may adopt the schoolmen's language, we do not argue to gain barely the assent of the understanding, but, which is infinitely more important, the consent of the will.

To prevent mistakes, it will not be beside my purpose further to remark, that several of the terms above explained, are sometimes used by rhetoricians and critics in a much larger and more vague signification, than has been given them here. Sublimity and vehemence, in particular, are often confounded, the latter being considered as a species of the former. In this manner has this subject been treated by that great master Longinus, whose acceptation of the term *sublime* is extremely indefinite, importing an eminent degree of almost any excellence of speech, of whatever kind. Doubtless, if things themselves be understood, it does not seem material what names are assigned them. Yet it is both more accurate, and proves no inconsiderable aid to the right understanding of things, to discriminate by different signs such as are truly different. And that the two qualities above mentioned are of this number is undeniable, since we can produce passages full of vehemence, wherein no image is presented, which, with any propriety, can be termed great or sublime. In matters of criticism, as in the abstract sciences, it is of the utmost consequence to ascertain, with precision, the meanings of words, and, as nearly as the genius of the language in which one writes will permit, to make them correspond to the boundaries assigned by Nature to the things signified. That the lofty and the vehement, though still distinguishable, are sometimes combined, and act with united force, is not to be denied. It is then only that the orator can be said to fight with weapons, which are at once sharp, massive, and refulgent, which, like Heaven's artillery, dazzle while they strike, which overpower the sight and the heart in the same instant. How admirably do the two forenamed qualities, when happily blended, correspond in the rational to the thunder and lightning in the natural world, which are not more awfully majestical in sound and aspect, than irresistible in power.

Thus much shall suffice for explaining the spirit, the intent, and the distinguishing qualities of each of the forementioned sorts of address; all which agree in this, an accommodation to affairs of a serious and important nature.

.   .   .

CHAPTER IV *Of the Relation which Eloquence Bears to Logic and to Grammar*

In contemplating a human creature, the most natural division of the subject is the common division into soul and body, or into the living principle of perception and of action, and that system of material organs, by which the other receives information from without, and is enabled to exert its powers, both for its own benefit and for that of the species. Analogous to this, there are two things in every discourse which principally claim our attention, the sense and the expression; or in other words, the thought, and the symbol by which it is communicated. These may be said to constitute the soul and the body of an oration, or indeed, of whatever is signified to another by language. For, as in man, each of these constituent parts hath its distinctive attributes, and as the perfection of the latter consisteth in its fitness for serving the purposes of the former, so it is precisely with those two essential parts of every speech, the sense and the expression. Now it is by the sense that rhetoric holds of logic, and by the expression that she holds of grammar.

The sole and ultimate end of logic, is the eviction of truth; one important end of eloquence, though, as appears from the first chapter, neither the sole, nor always the ultimate, is the conviction of the hearers. Pure logic regards only the subject, which is examined solely for the sake of information. Truth, as such, is the proper aim of the examiner. Eloquence not only considers the subject, but also the speaker and the hearers, and both the subject and the speaker for the sake of the hearers, or rather for the sake of the effect intended to be produced in them. Now to convince the hearers, is always either proposed by the orator as his end in addressing them, or supposed to accompany the accomplishment of his end. Of the five sorts of discourses above mentioned, there are only two wherein conviction is the avowed purpose. One is that addressed to the understanding, in which the speaker proposeth to prove some position disbelieved or doubted by the hearers; the other is that which is calculated to influence the will, and persuade to a certain conduct; for it is by convincing the judgment, that he proposeth to interest the passions, and fix the resolution. As to the three other kinds of discourses enumerated, which address the understanding, the imagination, and the passions; conviction, though not the end, ought ever to accompany the accomplishment of the end. It is never formally proposed as an end where there are not supposed to be previous doubts or errors to conquer. But when due attention is not paid to it, by a proper management of the subject, doubts, disbelief, and mistake will be raised by the discourse itself, where there were none before, and these will not fail to obstruct the speaker's end, whatever it be. In explanatory discourses, which are of all kinds the simplest, there is a certain precision of manner which ought to pervade the whole, and which, though not in the form of argument, is not the less satisfactory, since it carries internal evidence along with it. In harangues pathetic or panegyrical, in order that the hearers may be moved or pleased, it is of great consequence to impress them with the belief of the reality of the subject. Nay, even in those performances where truth, in regard to the individual facts related, is neither sought nor expected, as in some sorts of poetry, and in romance, truth still is an object to the mind, the general truths regarding character, manners, and incidents. When these are preserved, the piece may justly be denominated true, considered as a picture of life; though false, considered as a narrative of particular events. And even these untrue events must be counterfeits of truth, and bear its image; for in cases wherein the proposed end can be rendered consistent with unbelief, it cannot be rendered compatible with incredibility. Thus, in order to satisfy the mind, in most cases, truth, and in every case, what bears the semblance of truth, must be presented to it. This holds equally, whatever be the declared aim of the speaker. I need scarcely add, that to prove a particular point, is often occasionally necessary in every sort of discourse, as a subordinate end conducive to the advancement of the principal. If then it is the business of logic to evince the truth; to convince an auditory, which is the province of eloquence, is but a particular application of the logician's art. As logic therefore forges the arms which eloquence teacheth us to wield, we must first have recourse to the former, that being made acquainted with the materials of which her weapons and armour are severally made, we may know their respective strength and temper, and when and how each is to be used.

Now, if it be by the sense or soul of the discourse that rhetoric holds of logic, or the art of thinking and reasoning, it is by the expression or body of the discourse, that she holds of grammar, or the art of conveying our thoughts, in the words of a particular language. The observation of one analogy naturally suggests another. As the soul is of heavenly extraction, and the body of earthly, so the sense of the discourse ought to have its source in the invariable nature of truth and right; whereas the expression can derive its energy only from the arbitrary conventions of men, sources as unlike, or rather as widely different, as the breath of the Almighty and the dust of the earth. In every region of the globe, we may soon discover, that people feel and argue in much the same manner, but the speech of one nation is quite unintelligible to another. The art of the logician is accordingly, in some sense, universal, the art of the grammarian is always particular, and local. The rules of argumentation laid down by Aristotle, in his Analytics, are of as much use for the discovery of truth in Britain or in China, as they were in Greece; but Priscian's rules of inflection and construction, can assist us in learning no language but Latin. In propriety there cannot be such a thing as an universal grammar, unless there were such a thing as an universal language. The term hath sometimes, indeed, been applied to a collection of observations on the similar analogies that have been discovered in all tongues, ancient and modern, known to the authors of such collections. I do not mention this liberty in the use of the term with a view to censure it. In the application of technical or learned words, an author hath greater scope, than in the application of those which are in more frequent use, and is only then thought censurable, when he exposeth himself to be misunderstood. But it is to my purpose to observe, that as such collections convey the knowledge of no tongue whatever, the name *grammar*, when applied to them, is used in a sense quite different from that which it has in the common acceptation; perhaps as different, though the subject be language, as when it is applied to a system of geography.

Now, the grammatical art hath its completion in syntax; the oratorical, as far as the body or expression is concerned, in style. Syntax regards only the composition of many words into one sentence; style, at the same time that it attends to this, regards further, the composition of many sentences into one discourse. Nor is this the only difference; the grammarian, with respect to what the two arts have in common, the structure of sentences, requires only purity; that is, that the words employed belong to the language, and that they be construed in the manner, and used in the signification, which custom hath rendered necessary for conveying the sense. The orator requires also beauty and strength. The highest aim of the former is the lowest aim of the latter; where grammar ends, eloquence begins.

Thus the grammarian's department bears much the same relation to the orator's, which the art of the mason bears to that of the architect. There is, however, one difference, that well deserves our notice. As in architecture it is not necessary that he who designs should execute his own plans, he may be an excellent artist in this way, who would handle very awkwardly the hammer and the trowel. But it is alike incumbent on the orator to design and to execute. He must, therefore, be master of the language he speaks or writes, and must be capable of adding to grammatic purity those higher qualities of elocution, which will render his discourse graceful and energetic.

So much for the connexion that subsists between rhetoric and these parent arts, logic and grammar.

Source: George Campbell, *The Philosophy of Rhetoric*, Edinburgh 1808, pp. 21–34, 82–8

FORTY-TWO

ADAM SMITH
Considerations Concerning the First Formation of Languages

There are many instances of theoretical or conjectural history in the literature of the Scottish Enlightenment, and they are to be found in a wide range of fields, including science, economics, politics, religion and language studies. Among those who employed this form of exposition in their discussion of language was Adam Smith. Indeed, when the topic is the first formation of language, it is in the nature of the case difficult, if not impossible, to avoid conjectural history, since at the time that language was being formed people lacked the linguistic tools to describe the process of formation. Did people begin with nouns, or with verbs, and when did prepositions make their first appearance? Was it after nouns or with them? Or did people begin perhaps with whole sentences composed of both nouns and verbs? But then, must the nouns and verbs not already have been in place to be available for those who wished to construct sentences? And so on. There is ample room for conjecture.

There is also room for conjecture concerning the nature of Smith's task. Did he really think that the two savages with whom he starts his *Considerations* invented their language? Some have believed so, but it is also possible to read the *Considerations* as an analysis of a language whose existence is from the outset taken for granted. On this view Smith assumes the parts of a language, the nouns and their declensions, the verbs, the prepositions, pronouns and so on, and discusses the systematic ways in which they are related to each other. On this view, therefore, the format of conjectural history was adopted, and deployed, not so much as a contribution to history but rather as a device to facilitate exposition of a natural language already in use. There is in any case evidence that the order of Smith's exposition is not to be taken too seriously as history, since he begins with a discussion of nouns but later on remarks that he believes language to have begun with impersonal verbs.

A.B.

Considerations concerning
the First Formation of Languages, &c. &c.

The assignation of particular names, to denote particular objects, that is, the institution of nouns substantive, would probably, be one of the first steps towards the formation of language. Two savages, who had never been taught to speak, but had been bred up remote from the societies of men, would naturally begin to form that language by which they would endeavour to make their mutual wants intelligible to each other, by uttering certain sounds, whenever they meant to denote certain objects. Those objects only which were most familiar to them, and which they had most frequent occasion to mention, would have particular names assigned to them. The particular cave whose covering sheltered them from the weather, the particular tree whose fruit relieved their hunger, the particular fountain whose water allayed their thirst, would first be denominated by the words *cave*, *tree*, *fountain*, or by whatever other appellations they might think proper, in that primitive jargon, to mark them. Afterwards, when the more enlarged experience of these savages had led them to observe, and their necessary occasions obliged them to make mention of other caves, and other trees, and other fountains, they would naturally bestow, upon each of these new objects, the same name, by which they had been accustomed to express the similar object they were first acquainted with. The new objects had none of them any name of its own, but each of them exactly resembled another object, which had such an appellation. It was impossible that those savages could behold the new objects, without recollecting the old ones; and the name of the old ones, to which the new bore so close a resemblance. When they had occasion, therefore, to mention, or to point out to each other, any of the new objects, they would naturally utter the name of the correspondent old one, of which the idea could not fail, at that instant, to present itself to their memory in the strongest and liveliest manner. And thus, those words, which were originally the proper names of individuals, would each of them insensibly become the common name of a multitude. A child that is just learning to speak, calls every person who comes to the house its papa or its mama; and thus bestows upon the whole species those names which it had been taught to apply to two individuals. I have known a clown, who did not know the proper name of the river which ran by his own door. It was *the river*, he said, and he never heard any other name for it. His experience, it seems, had not led him to observe any other river. The general word *river*, therefore, was, it is evident, in his acceptance of it, a proper name, signifying an individual object. If this person had been carried to another river, would he not readily have called it a river? Could we suppose any person living on the banks of the Thames so ignorant, as not to know the general word *river*, but to be acquainted only with the particular word *Thames*, if he was brought to any other river, would he not readily call it *a Thames?* This, in reality, is no more than what they, who are well acquainted with the general word, are very apt to do. An Englishman, describing any great river which he may have seen in some foreign country, naturally says, that it is another Thames. The Spaniards, when they first arrived upon the coast of Mexico, and observed the wealth, populousness, and habitations of that fine country, so much superior to the savage nations which they had been visiting for some time before, cried out, that it was another Spain. Hence it was called New Spain; and this name has stuck to that unfortunate country ever since. We say, in the same manner, of a hero, that he is an Alexander; of an orator, that he is a Cicero; of a philosopher, that he is a Newton. This way of speaking, which the grammarians call an Antonomasia, and which is still extremely common, though now not at all necessary, demonstrates how much mankind are naturally disposed to give to one object the name of any other, which nearly resembles it, and thus to denominate a multitude, by what originally was intended to express an individual.

It is this application of the name of an individual to a great multitude of objects, whose resemblance naturally recalls the idea of that individual, and of the name which expresses it, that seems originally to have given occasion to the formation of those classes and assortments, which, in the schools, are called genera and species, and of which the ingenious and eloquent M. Rousseau of Geneva finds himself so much at a loss to account for the origin. What constitutes a species is merely a number of objects, bearing a certain degree of resemblance to one another, and on that account denominated by a single appellation, which may be applied to express any one of them.

When the greater part of objects had thus been arranged under their proper classes and assortments, distinguished by such general names, it was impossible that the greater part of that almost infinite number of individuals, comprehended under each particular assortment or species, could have any peculiar or proper names of their own, distinct from the general name of the species. When there was occasion, therefore, to mention any particular object, it often became necessary to distinguish it from the other objects comprehended under the same general name, either, first, by its peculiar qualities; or, secondly, by the peculiar relation which it stood in to some other things. Hence the necessary origin of two other sets of words, of which the one should express quality; the other, relation.

Nouns adjective[1] are the words which express quality considered as qualifying, or, as the schoolmen say, in concrete with, some particular subject. Thus the word *green* expresses a certain quality considered as qualifying, or as in concrete with, the particular subject to which it may be applied. Words of this kind, it is evident, may serve to distinguish particular objects from others comprehended under the same general appellation. The words *green tree*, for example, might serve to distinguish a particular tree from others that were withered or blasted.

Prepositions are the words which express relation considered, in the same manner, in concrete with the co-relative object. Thus the prepositions *of*, *to*, *for*, *with*, *by*, *above*, *below*, &c. denote some relation subsisting between the objects expressed by the words between which the propositions are placed; and they denote that this relation is considered in concrete with the co-relative object. Words of this kind serve to distinguish particular objects from others of the same species, when those particular objects cannot be so properly marked out by any peculiar qualities of their own. When we say, *the green tree of the meadow*, for example, we distinguish a particular tree, not only by the quality which belongs to it, but by the relation which it stands in to another object.

As neither quality nor relation can exist in abstract, it is natural to suppose that the words which denote them considered in concrete, the way in which we always see them subsist, would be of much earlier invention than those which express them considered in

---

1 The grammatical terms *noun adjective* and *noun substantive*, taken from late Latin *nomen adiectivum* and *nomen substantivum*, were normal usage from the late fourteenth century, but were rivalled from *c.*1500 by the simple *adjective* and *substantive* (the latter eventually almost wholly replaced by *noun*). The first probably sounded a little archaic, and ambiguous, in 1761. 'What is an Adjective? I dare not call it Noun Adjective' (Horne Tooke, *Diversions of Purley*, 1786, II.vi).

abstract, the way in which we never see them subsist. The words *green* and *blue* would, in all probability, be sooner invented than the words *greenness* and *blueness*; the words *above* and *below*, than the words *superiority* and *inferiority*. To invent words of the latter kind requires a much greater effort of abstraction than to invent those of the former. It is probable, therefore, that such abstract terms would be of much later institution. Accordingly, their etymologies generally shew that they are so, they being generally derived from others that are concrete.

But though the invention of nouns adjective be much more natural than that of the abstract nouns substantive derived from them, it would still, however, require a considerable degree of abstraction and generalization. Those, for example, who first invented the words *green*, *blue*, *red*, and the other names of colours, must have observed and compared together a great number of objects, must have remarked their resemblances and dissimilitudes in respect of the quality of colour, and must have arranged them, in their own minds, into different classes and assortments, according to those resemblances and dissimilitudes. An adjective is by nature a general, and in some measure an abstract word, and necessarily presupposes the idea of a certain species or assortment of things, to all of which it is equally applicable. The word *green* could not, as we were supposing might be the case of the word *cave*, have been originally the name of an individual, and afterwards have become, by what grammarians call an Antonomasia, the name of a species. The word *green* denoting, not the name of a substance, but the peculiar quality of a substance, must from the very first have been a general word, and considered as equally applicable to any other substance possessed of the same quality. The man who first distinguished a particular object by the epithet of *green*, must have observed other objects that were not *green*, from which he meant to separate it by this appellation. The institution of this name, therefore, supposes comparison. It likewise supposes some degree of abstraction. The person who first invented this appellation must have distinguished the quality from the object to which it belonged, and must have conceived the object as capable of subsisting without the quality. The invention, therefore, even of the simplest nouns adjective, must have required more metaphysics than we are apt to be aware of. The different mental operations, of arrangement or classing, of comparison, and of abstraction, must all have been employed, before even the names of the different colours, the least metaphysical of all nouns adjective, could be instituted. From all which I infer, that when languages were beginning to be formed, nouns adjective would by no means be the words of the earliest invention.

There is another expedient for denoting the different qualities of different substances, which as it requires no abstraction, nor any conceived separation of the quality from the subject, seems more natural than the invention of nouns adjective, and which, upon this account, could hardly fail, in the first formation of language, to be thought of before them. This expedient is to make some variation upon the noun substantive itself, according to the different qualities which it is endowed with. Thus, in many languages, the qualities both of sex and of the want of sex, are expressed by different terminations in the nouns substantive, which denote objects so qualified. In Latin, for example, *lupus, lupa; equus, equa; juvencus, juvenca; Julius, Julia; Lucretius, Lucretia*, &c. denote the qualities of male and female in the animals and persons to whom such appellations belong, without needing the addition of any adjective for this purpose. On the other hand, the words *forum, pratum, plaustrum*, denote by their peculiar termination the total absence of sex in the different substances which they stand for. Both sex, and the want of all sex, being naturally considered as qualities modifying and inseparable from the particular substances to which they belong, it was natural to express them rather by a modification in the noun substantive, than by any general and abstract word expressive of this particular species of quality. The expression bears, it is evident, in this way, a much more exact analogy to the idea or object which it denotes, than in the other. The quality appears, in nature, as a modification of the substance, and as it is thus expressed, in language, by a modification of the noun substantive, which denotes that substance, the quality and the subject are, in this case, blended together, if I may say so, in the expression, in the same manner as they appear to be in the object and in the idea. Hence the origin of the masculine, feminine, and neutral genders, in all the ancient languages. By means of these, the most important of all distinctions, that of substances into animated and inanimated, and that of animals into male and female, seem to have been sufficiently marked without the assistance of adjectives, or of any general names denoting this most extensive species of qualifications.

There are no more than these three genders in any of the languages with which I am acquainted; that is to say, the formation of nouns substantive can, by itself, and without the accompaniment of adjectives, express no other qualities but those three above mentioned, the qualities of male, of female, of neither male nor female. I should not, however, be surprised, if, in other languages with which I am unacquainted, the different formations of nouns substantive should be capable of expressing many other different qualities. The different diminutives of the Italian, and of some other languages, do, in reality, sometimes, express a great variety of different modifications in the substances denoted by those nouns which undergo such variations.

It was impossible, however, that nouns substantive could, without losing altogether their original form, undergo so great a number of variations, as would be sufficient to express that almost infinite variety of qualities, by which it might, upon different occasions, be necessary to specify and distinguish them. Though the different formation of nouns substantive, therefore, might, for some time, forestall the necessity of inventing nouns adjective, it was impossible that this necessity could be forestalled altogether. When nouns adjective came to be invented, it was natural that they should be formed with some similarity to the substantives, to which they were to serve as epithets or qualifications. Men would naturally give them the same terminations with the substantives to which they were first applied, and from that love of similarity of sound, from that delight in the returns of the same syllables, which is the foundation of analogy in all languages, they would be apt to vary the termination of the same adjective, according as they had occasion to apply it to a masculine, to a feminine, or to a neutral substantive. They would say, *magnus lupus, magna lupa, magnum pratum*, when they meant to express a great *he wolf*, a great *she wolf*, a great *meadow*.

This variation, in the termination of the noun adjective, according to the gender of the substantive, which takes place in all the ancient languages, seems to have been introduced chiefly for the sake of a certain similarity of sound, of a certain species of rhyme, which is naturally so very agreeable to the human ear. Gender, it is to be observed, cannot properly belong to a noun adjective, the signification of which is always precisely the same, to whatever species of substantives it is applied. When we say, *a great man, a great woman*, the word *great* has precisely the same meaning in both cases, and the difference of the sex in the subjects to which it may be applied, makes no sort of difference in its signification. *Magnus, magna, magnum*, in the same manner, are words which express precisely the same quality, and the change of the termination is accompanied with no sort of variation in the meaning. Sex and gender are qualities which belong to substances, but cannot belong to the qualities of substances. In general, no quality, when considered in concrete, or as qualifying some particular subject, can itself be conceived as the subject of any other quality; though when considered in abstract it may. No adjective therefore can qualify any other adjective. A *great good man*, means a man who is both *great* and *good*. Both the adjectives qualify the substantive; they do not qualify one another. On the other hand, when we say, the *great goodness* of the man, the word *goodness* denoting a quality considered in abstract, which may itself be the subject of other qualities, is upon that account capable of being qualified by the word *great*.

If the original invention of nouns adjective would be attended with so much difficulty, that of prepositions would be accompanied with yet more. Every preposition, as I have already observed, denotes some relation considered in concrete with the co-relative object. The preposition *above*, for example, denotes the relation of superiority, not in abstract, as it is expressed by the word *superiority*, but in concrete with some co-relative object. In this phrase, for example, *the tree above the cave*, the word *above* expresses a certain relation between the *tree* and the *cave*, and it expresses this relation in concrete with the co-relative object, *the cave*. A preposition always requires, in order to complete the sense, some other word to come after it; as may be observed in this particular instance. Now, I say, the original invention of such words would require a yet greater effort of abstraction and generalization, than that of nouns adjective. First of all, a relation is, in itself, a more metaphysical object than a quality. Nobody can be at a loss to explain what is meant by a quality; but few people will find themselves able to express, very distinctly, what is understood by a relation. Qualities are almost always the objects of our external senses; relations never are. No wonder, therefore, that the one set of objects should be so much more comprehensible than the other. Secondly, though prepositions always express the relation which they stand for, in concrete with the co-relative object, they could not have originally been formed without a considerable effort of abstraction. A preposition denotes a relation, and nothing but a relation. But before men could institute a word, which signified a relation, and nothing but a relation, they must have been able, in some measure, to consider this relation abstractedly from the related objects; since the idea of those objects does not, in any respect, enter into the signification of the preposition. The invention of such a word, therefore, must have required a considerable degree of abstraction. Thirdly, a preposition is from its nature a general word, which, from its very first institution, must have been considered as equally applicable to denote any other similar relation. The man who first invented the word *above*, must not only have distinguished, in some measure, the relation of *superiority* from the objects which were so related, but he must also have distinguished this relation from other relations, such as, from the relation of *inferiority* denoted by the word *below*, from the relation of *juxtaposition*, expressed by the word *beside*, and the like. He must have conceived this word, therefore, as expressive of a particular sort or species of relation distinct from every other, which could not be done without a considerable effort of comparison and generalization.

Whatever were the difficulties, therefore, which embarrassed the first invention of nouns adjective, the same, and many more, must have embarrassed that of prepositions. If mankind, therefore, in the first formation of languages, seem to have, for some time, evaded the necessity of nouns adjective, by varying the termination of the names of substances, according as these varied in some of their most important qualities, they would much more find themselves under the necessity of evading, by some similar contrivance, the yet more difficult invention of prepositions. The different cases in the ancient languages is a contrivance of precisely the same kind. The genitive and dative cases, in Greek and Latin, evidently supply the place of the prepositions; and by a variation in the noun substantive, which stands for the co-relative term, express the relation which subsists between what is denoted by that noun substantive, and what is expressed by some other word in the sentence. In these expressions, for example, *fructus arboris, the fruit of the tree; sacer Herculi, sacred to Hercules*; the variations made in the co-relative words, *arbor* and *Hercules*, express the same relations which are expressed in English by the prepositions *of* and *to*.

To express a relation in this manner, did not require any effort of abstraction. It was not here expressed by a peculiar word denoting relation and nothing but relation, but by a variation upon the co-relative term. It was expressed here, as it appears in nature, not as something separated and detached, but as thoroughly mixed and blended with the co-relative object.

To express relation in this manner, did not require any effort of generalization. The words *arboris* and *Herculi*, while they involve in their signification the same relation expressed by the English prepositions *of* and *to*, are not, like those prepositions, general words, which can be applied to express the same relation between whatever other objects it might be observed to subsist.

To express relation in this manner did not require any effort of comparison. The words *arboris* and *Herculi* are not general words intended to denote a particular species of relations which the inventors of those expressions meant, in consequence of some sort of comparison, to separate and distinguish from every other sort of relation. The example, indeed, of this contrivance would soon probably be followed, and whoever had occasion to express a similar relation between any other objects would be very apt to do it by making a similar variation on the name of the co-relative object. This, I say, would probably, or rather certainly happen; but it would happen without any intention or foresight in those who first set the example, and who never meant to establish any general rule. The general rule would establish itself insensibly, and by slow degrees, in consequence of that love of analogy and similarity of sound, which is the foundation of by far the greater part of the rules of grammar.

To express relation, therefore, by a variation in the name of the co-relative object, requiring neither abstraction, nor generalization, nor comparison of any kind, would, at first, be much more natural and easy, than to express it by those general words called prepositions, of which the first invention must have demanded some degree of all those operations.

The number of cases is different in different languages. There are five in the Greek, six in the Latin, and there are said to be ten in the Armenian language. It must have naturally happened that there should be a greater or a smaller number of cases, according as in the terminations of nouns substantive the first formers of any language happened to have established a greater or a smaller number of variations, in order to express the different relations they had occasion to take notice of, before the invention of those more general and abstract propositions which could supply their place.

It is, perhaps, worth while to observe that those prepositions, which in modern languages hold the place of the ancient cases, are, of all others, the most general, and abstract, and metaphysical; and of consequence, would probably be the last invented. Ask any man of common acuteness, What relation is expressed by the preposition *above?* He will readily answer, that of *superiority*. By the preposition *below?* He will as quickly reply, that of *inferiority*. But ask him, what relation is expressed by the preposition *of*, and, if he has not beforehand employed his thoughts a good deal upon these subjects, you may safely allow him a week to consider of his answer. The prepositions *above* and *below* do not denote any of the relations expressed by the cases in the ancient languages. But the preposition *of*, denotes the same relation, which is in them expressed by the genitive case; and which, it is easy to observe, is of a very metaphysical nature. The preposition *of*, denotes relation in general, considered in concrete with the co-relative object. It marks that the noun substantive which goes before it, is somehow or other related to that which comes after it, but without in any respect ascertaining, as is done by the preposition *above*, what is the peculiar nature of that relation. We often apply it, therefore, to express the most opposite relations; because, the most opposite relations agree so far that each of them comprehends in it the general idea or nature of a relation. We say, *the father of the son*, and *the son of the father*; *the fir-trees of the forest*; and *the forest of the fir-trees*. The relation in which the father stands to the son, is, it is evident, a quite opposite relation to that in which the son stands to the father; that in which the parts stand to the whole, is quite opposite to that in which the whole stands to the parts. The word *of*, however, serves very well to denote all those relations, because in itself it denotes no particular relation, but only relation in general; and so far as any particular relation is collected from such expressions, it is inferred by the mind, not from the preposition itself, but from the nature and arrangement of the substantives, between which the preposition is placed.

What I have said concerning the preposition *of*, may in some measure be applied to the prepositions *to*, *for*, *with*, *by*, and to whatever other prepositions are made use of in modern languages, to supply the place of the ancient cases. They all of them express very abstract and metaphysical relations, which any man, who takes the trouble to try it, will find it extremely difficult to express by nouns substantive, in the same manner as we may express the relation denoted by the preposition *above*, by the noun substantive *superiority*. They all of them, however, express some specific relation, and are, consequently, none of them so abstract as the preposition *of*, which may be regarded as by far the most metaphysical of all prepositions. The prepositions, therefore, which are capable of supplying the place of the ancient cases, being more abstract than the other prepositions, would naturally be of more difficult invention. The relations at the same time which those prepositions express, are, of all others, those which we have most frequent occasion to mention. The prepositions *above*, *below*, *near*, *within*, *without*, *against*, &c. are much more rarely made use of, in modern languages, than the prepositions *of*, *to*, *for*, *with*, *from*, *by*. A preposition of the former kind will not occur twice in a page; we can scarce compose a single sentence without the assistance of one or two of the latter. If these latter prepositions, therefore, which supply the place of the cases, would be of such difficult invention on account of their abstractedness, some expedient, to supply their place, must have been of indispensable necessity, on account of the frequent occasion which men have to take notice of the relations which they denote. But there is no expedient so obvious, as that of varying the termination of one of the principal words.

It is, perhaps, unnecessary to observe, that there are some of the cases in the ancient languages, which, for particular reasons, cannot be represented by any prepositions. These are the nominative, accusative, and vocative cases. In those modern languages, which do not admit of any such variety in the terminations of their nouns substantive, the correspondent relations are expressed by the place of the words, and by the order and construction of the sentence.

As men have frequently occasion to make mention of multitudes as well as of single objects, it became necessary that they should have some method of expressing number. Number may be expressed either by a particular word, expressing number in general, such as the words *many*, *more*, &c. or by some variation upon the words which express the things numbered. It is this last expedient which mankind would probably have recourse to, in the infancy of language. Number, considered in general, without relation to any particular set of objects numbered, is one of the most abstract and metaphysical ideas, which the mind of man is capable of forming; and, consequently, is not an idea, which would readily occur to rude mortals, who were just beginning to form a language. They would naturally, therefore, distinguish when they talked of a single, and when they talked of a multitude of objects, not by any metaphysical adjectives, such as the English *a*, *an*, *many*, but by a variation upon the termination of the word which signified the objects numbered. Hence the origin of the singular and plural numbers, in all the ancient languages; and the same distinction has likewise been retained in all the modern languages, at least, in the greater part of words.

All primitive and uncompounded languages seem to have a dual, as well as a plural number. This is the case of the Greek, and I am told of the Hebrew, of the Gothic, and of many other languages. In the rude beginnings of society, *one*, *two*, and *more*, might possibly be all the numeral distinctions which mankind would have any occasion to take notice of. These they would find it more natural to express, by a variation upon every particular noun substantive, than by such general and abstract words as *one*, *two*, *three*, *four*, &c. These words, though custom has rendered them familiar to us, express, perhaps, the most subtile and refined abstractions, which the mind of man is capable of forming. Let any one consider within himself, for example, what he means by the word *three*, which signifies neither three shillings, nor three pence, nor three men, nor three horses, but three in general; and he will easily satisfy himself that a word, which denotes so very metaphysical an abstraction, could not be either a very obvious or a very early invention. I have read of some savage nations, whose language was capable of expressing no more than the three first numeral distinctions. But whether it expressed those distinctions by three general words, or by variations upon the nouns substantive, denoting the things numbered, I do not remember to have met with any thing which could determine.

As all the same relations which subsist between single, may likewise subsist between numerous objects, it is evident that there would be occasion for the same number of cases in the dual and in the plural, as in the singular number. Hence the intricacy and complexness of the declensions in all the ancient languages. In the Greek there are five cases in each of the three numbers, consequently fifteen in all.

As nouns adjective, in the ancient languages, varied their terminations according to the gender of the substantive to which they were applied, so did they likewise, according to the case and the number. Every noun adjective in the Greek language, therefore, having three genders, and three numbers, and five cases in each number, may be considered as having five and forty different variations. The first formers of language seem to have varied the termination of the adjective, according to the case and the number of the substantive, for the same reason which made them vary it according to the gender; the love of analogy, and of a certain regularity of sound. In the signification of adjectives there is neither case nor number, and the meaning of such words is always precisely the same, notwithstanding all the variety of termination under which they appear. *Magnus vir, magni viri, magnorum virorum; a great man, of a great man, of great men*; in all these expressions the words *magnus, magni, magnorum*, as well as the word *great*, have precisely one and the same signification, though the substantives to which they are applied have not. The difference of termination in the noun adjective is accompanied with no sort of difference in the meaning. An adjective denotes the qualification of a noun substantive. But the different relations in which that noun substantive may occasionally stand, can make no sort of difference upon its qualification.

If the declensions of the ancient languages are so very complex, their conjugations are infinitely more so. And the complexness of the one is founded upon the same principle with that of the other, the difficulty of forming, in the beginnings of language, abstract and general terms.

Verbs must necessarily have been coëval with the very first attempts towards the formation of language. No affirmation can be expressed without the assistance of some verb. We never speak but in order to express our opinion that something either is or is not. But the word denoting this event, or this matter of fact, which is the subject of our affirmation, must always be a verb.

Impersonal verbs, which express in one word a complete event, which preserve in the expression that perfect simplicity and unity, which there always is in the object and in the idea, and which suppose no abstraction, or metaphysical division of the event into its several constituent members of subject and attribute, would, in all probability, be the species of verbs first invented. The verbs *pluit, it rains*; *ningit, it snows*; *tonat, it thunders*; *lucet, it is day*; *turbatur, there is a confusion*, &c. each of them express a complete affirmation, the whole of an event, with that perfect simplicity and unity with which the mind conceives it in nature. On the contrary, the phrases, *Alexander ambulat, Alexander walks*; *Petrus sedet, Peter sits*, divide the event, as it were, into two parts, the person or subject, and the attribute, or matter of fact, affirmed of that subject. But in nature, the idea or conception of Alexander walking, is as perfectly and completely one simple conception, as that of Alexander not walking. The division of this event, therefore, into two parts, is altogether artificial, and is the effect of the imperfection of language, which, upon this, as upon many other occasions, supplies, by a number of words, the want of one, which could express at once the whole matter of fact that was meant to be affirmed. Every body must observe how much more simplicity there is in the natural expression, *pluit*, than in the more artificial expressions, *imber decidit, the rain falls;* or *tempestas est pluvia, the weather is rainy*. In these two last expressions, the simple event, or matter of fact, is artificially split and divided in the one, into two; in the other, into three parts. In each of them it is expressed by a sort of grammatical circumlocution, of which the significancy is founded upon a certain metaphysical analysis of the component parts of the idea expressed by the word *pluit*. The first verbs, therefore, perhaps even the first words, made use of in the beginnings of language, would in all probability be such impersonal verbs. It is observed accordingly, I am told, by the

Hebrew grammarians, that the radical words of their language, from which all the others are derived, are all of them verbs, and impersonal verbs.

It is easy to conceive how, in the progress of language, those impersonal verbs should become personal. Let us suppose, for example, that the word *venit*, *it comes*, was originally an impersonal verb, and that it denoted, not the coming of something in general, as at present, but the coming of a particular object, such as *the Lion*. The first savage inventors of language, we shall suppose, when they observed the approach of this terrible animal, were accustomed to cry out to one another, *venit*, that is, *the lion comes*; and that this word thus expressed a complete event, without the assistance of any other. Afterwards, when, on the further progress of language, they had begun to give names to particular substances, whenever they observed the approach of any other terrible object, they would naturally join the name of that object to the word *venit*, and cry out, *venit ursus*, *venit lupus*. By degrees the word *venit* would thus come to signify the coming of any terrible object, and not merely the coming of the lion. It would now, therefore, express, not the coming of a particular object, but the coming of an object of a particular kind. Having become more general in its signification, it could no longer represent any particular distinct event by itself, and without the assistance of a noun substantive, which might serve to ascertain and determine its signification. It would now, therefore, have become a personal, instead of an impersonal verb. We may easily conceive how, in the further progress of society, it might still grow more general in its signification, and come to signify, as at present, the approach of any thing whatever, whether good, bad, or indifferent.

It is probably in some such manner as this, that almost all verbs have become personal, and that mankind have learned by degrees to split and divide almost every event into a great number of metaphysical parts, expressed by the different parts of speech, variously combined in the different members of every phrase and sentence. The same sort of progress seems to have been made in the art of speaking as in the art of writing. When mankind first began to attempt to express their ideas by writing, every character represented a whole word. But the number of words being almost infinite, the memory found itself quite loaded and oppressed by the multitude of characters which it was obliged to retain. Necessity taught them, therefore, to divide words into their elements, and to invent characters which should represent, not the words themselves, but the elements of which they were composed. In consequence of this invention, every particular word came to be represented, not by one character, but by a multitude of characters; and the expression of it in writing became much more intricate and complex than before. But though particular words were thus represented by a greater number of characters, the whole language was expressed by a much smaller, and about four and twenty letters were found capable of supplying the place of that immense multitude of characters, which were requisite before. In the same manner, in the beginnings of language, men seem to have attempted to express every particular event, which they had occasion to take notice of, by a particular word, which expressed at once the whole of that event. But as the number of words must, in this case, have become really infinite, in consequence of the really infinite variety of events, men found themselves partly compelled by necessity, and partly conducted by nature, to divide every event into what may be called its metaphysical elements, and to institute words, which should denote not so much the events, as the elements of which they were composed. The expression of every particular event, became in this manner more intricate and complex, but the whole system of the language became more coherent, more connected, more easily retained and comprehended.

When verbs, from being originally impersonal, had thus, by the division of the event into its metaphysical elements, become personal, it is natural to suppose that they would first be made use of in the third person singular. No verb is ever used impersonally in our language, nor, so far as I know, in any other modern tongue. But in the ancient languages, whenever any verb is used impersonally, it is always in the third person singular. The termination of those verbs, which are still always impersonal, is constantly the same with that of the third person singular of personal verbs. The consideration of these circumstances, joined to the naturalness of the thing itself, may serve to convince us that verbs first became personal in what is now called the third person singular.

But as the event, or matter of fact, which is expressed by a verb, may be affirmed either of the person who speaks, or of the person who is spoken to, as well as of some third person or object, it became necessary to fall upon some method of expressing these two peculiar relations of the event. In the English language this is commonly done, by prefixing, what are called the personal pronouns, to the general word which expresses the event affirmed. *I came*, *you came*, *he* or *it came*; in these phrases the event of having come is, in the first, affirmed of the speaker; in the second, of the person spoken to; in the third, of some other person, or object.

The first formers of language, it may be imagined, might have done the same thing, and prefixing in the same manner the two first personal pronouns, to the same termination of the verb, which expressed the third person singular, might have said *ego venit, tu venit*, as well as *ille* or *illud venit*. And I make no doubt but they would have done so, if at the time when they had first occasion to express these relations of the verb, there had been any such words as either *ego* or *tu* in their language. But in this early period of the language, which we are now endeavouring to describe, it is extremely improbable that any such words would be known. Though custom has now rendered them familiar to us, they, both of them, express ideas extremely metaphysical and abstract. The word *I*, for example, is a word of a very particular species. Whatever speaks may denote itself by the personal pronoun. The word *I*, therefore, is a general word, capable of being predicated, as the logicians say, of an infinite variety of objects. It differs, however, from all other general words in this respect; that the objects of which it may be predicated, do not form any particular species of objects distinguished from all others. The word *I*, does not, like the word *man*, denote a particular class of objects, separated from all others by peculiar qualities of their own. It is far from being the name of a species, but, on the contrary, whenever it is made use of, it always denotes a precise individual, the particular person who then speaks. It may be said to be, at once, both what the logicians call, a singular, and what they call, a common term; and to join in its signification the seemingly opposite qualities of the most precise individuality, and the most extensive generalization. This word, therefore, expressing so very abstract and metaphysical an idea, would not easily or readily occur to the first formers of language. What are called the personal pronouns, it may be observed, are among the last words of which children learn to make use. A child, speaking of itself, says, *Billy walks, Billy sits*, instead of *I walk, I sit*. As in the beginnings of language, therefore, mankind seem to have evaded the invention of at least the more abstract prepositions, and to have expressed the same relations which these *now* stand for, by varying the termination of the co-relative term, so they likewise would naturally attempt to evade the necessity of inventing those more abstract pronouns by varying the termination of the verb, according as the event which it expressed was intended to be affirmed of the first, second, or third person. This seems, accordingly, to be the universal practice of all the ancient languages. In Latin, *veni, venisti, venit*, sufficiently denote, without any other addition, the different events expressed by the English phrases, *I came, you came, he* or *it came*. The verb would, for the same reason, vary its termination, according as the event was intended to be affirmed of the first, second, or third persons plural; and what is expressed by the English phrases, *we came, ye came, they came*, would be denoted by the Latin words, *venimus, venistis, venerunt*. Those primitive languages, too, which, upon account of the difficulty of inventing numeral names, had introduced a dual, as well as a plural number, into the declension of their nouns substantive, would probably, from analogy, do the same thing in the conjugations of their verbs. And thus in all those original languages, we might expect to find, at least six, if not eight or nine variations, in the termination of every verb, according as the event which it denoted was meant to be affirmed of the first, second, or third persons singular, dual, or plural. These variations again being repeated, along with others, through all its different tenses, through all its different modes, and through all its different voices, must necessarily have rendered their conjugations still more intricate and complex than their declensions.

Language would probably have continued upon this footing in all countries, nor would ever have grown more simple in its declensions and conjugations, had it not become more complex in its composition, in consequence of the mixture of several languages with one another, occasioned by the mixture of different nations. As long as any language was spoke by those only who learned it in their infancy, the intricacy of its declensions and conjugations could occasion no great embarrassment. The far greater part of those who had occasion to speak it, had acquired it at so very early a period of their lives, so insensibly and by such slow degrees, that they were scarce ever sensible of the difficulty. But when two nations came to be mixed with one another, either by conquest or migration, the case would be very different. Each nation, in order to make itself intelligible to those with whom it was under the necessity of conversing, would be obliged to learn the language of the other. The greater part of individuals too, learning the new language, not by art, or by remounting to its rudiments and first principles, but by rote, and by what they commonly heard in conversation, would be extremely perplexed by the intricacy of its declensions and conjugations. They would endeavour, therefore, to supply their ignorance of these, by whatever shift the language could afford them. Their ignorance of the declensions they would naturally supply by the use of prepositions; and a Lombard, who was attempting to speak Latin, and wanted to express that such a person was a citizen of Rome, or a benefactor to Rome, if he happened not to be acquainted with the genitive and dative cases of the word *Roma*, would naturally express himself by prefixing the prepositions *ad* and *de* to the nominative; and, instead of *Roma*, would say, *ad Roma*, and *de Roma*. *Al Roma* and *di Roma*, accordingly, is the manner in which the present Italians, the descendants of the ancient Lombards and Romans, express this and all other similar relations. And in this manner prepositions seem to have been introduced, in the room of the ancient declensions. The same alteration has, I am informed, been produced upon the Greek language, since the taking of Constantinople by the Turks. The words are, in a great measure, the same as before; but the grammar is entirely lost, prepositions having come in the place of the old declensions. This change is undoubtedly a simplification of the language, in point of rudiments and principle. It introduces, instead of a great variety of declensions, one universal declension, which is the same in every word, of whatever gender, number, or termination.

A similar expedient enables men, in the situation above mentioned, to get rid of almost the whole intricacy of their conjugations. There is in every language a verb, known by the name of the substantive verb: in Latin, *sum*; in English, *I am*. This verb denotes not the existence of any particular event, but existence in general. It is, upon this account, the most abstract and metaphysical of all verbs; and, consequently, could by no means be a word of early invention. When it came to be invented, however, as it had all the tenses and modes of any other verb, by being joined with the passive participle, it was capable of supplying the place of the whole passive voice, and of rendering this part of their conjugations as simple and uniform, as the use of prepositions had rendered their declensions. A Lombard, who wanted to say, *I am loved*, but could not recollect the word *amor*, naturally endeavoured to supply his ignorance, by saying *ego sum amatus*. *Io sono amato*, is at this day the Italian expression, which corresponds to the English phrase above mentioned.

Source: Adam Smith, *Considerations concerning the First Formation of Languages*, in *Lectures on Rhetoric and Belles Lettres*, ed. J. C. Bryce, Oxford 1983, pp. 203–21

FORTY-THREE

JAMES DUNBAR
On Language as a Universal Accomplishment

Historians of the eighteenth century (see for example excerpt 40 by William Robertson) responded to the need to understand their society by placing it in its historical context – we hardly know where, or even who, we are if we do not know where we are from. Likewise insight into the structure and significance of our language depends upon knowledge of where it is from. Just as we can learn a good deal about ourselves by considering contemporaneous societies, especially those distant from ours in various respects, so also we can learn a good deal about our language by considering other languages, especially ones very unlike ours. Granted that there are so many languages, we can ask whether there are universals of language. Knowledge of the universals, if they exist, will certainly yield insights into our present language – and into much more besides, as becomes evident if we recall the way that Thomas Reid (see excerpt 4) refers to the universals of language in support of his account of the fundamental belief system of us human beings. One way to discover the universals is to go back to the beginning, to ask what was in language from the start, and to track the initial elements through subsequent linguistic developments.

In excerpt 42 we see Adam Smith employing the conjecturalist device of imagining two language-free savages taking the very first steps in linguistic communication. In the present excerpt we find Dunbar doing the same, but putting forward a very different set of conjectures. He pays particular attention to our natural faculty for analogical thinking and to our related faculty for extending the range of language by using terms analogically. One particularly interesting example Dunbar provides concerns our vocabulary for the mind and its acts. While he does not go into detail on this point it is plain that he has the following sort of case in mind: we see things by using our corporeal eyes, and we grasp things with our hands. This vocabulary is also applied by analogy to mental acts, for we say that we see a point or that we are in the dark as to its meaning, and that we grasp what someone has said or we fail to grasp it. To explain something is to shed light. And of course the very term 'enlightenment' is applied primarily to something physical, and is then applied by analogy to the life of the mind. Dunbar conjectures that it is by means such as this, means readily available to all, that language develops. He is emphatic that this development was due to 'mankind at large' and hardly, if at all, to the activities of a few geniuses.

A.B.

On Language, as an Universal Accomplishment

In tracing the origin of arts and sciences, it is not uncommon to ascribe to the genius of a few superior minds, what arises necessarily out of the system of man. The efforts of an individual are familiar to the eye. The efforts of the species are more remote from sight, and often too deep for our researches.

The connexion, therefore, of events with an individual, is a more popular idea, while it gratifies an admiration and enthusiasm natural to the human mind. Hence the conduct of historians, who describe the origin of nations. Hence are celebrated among every people, the first inventors of arts, the founders of society, and the institutors of laws and government.

Such revolutions, however, in the condition of the world, are more justly reputed the slow result of situations than of regular design, and have, perhaps, less exercised the talents of superior genius, than those of mankind at large. *Usages* there surely are of mere arbitrary institution; *inventions* there surely are which originate with one only, or with a few authors. But other usages and inventions as necessarily refer themselves to the multitude; nor ought the casual exertions of the former to be confounded with the infallible attainments of the species.

Under this precaution, then, let us introduce the question concerning language. Is language, it may be asked, derived to us at first from the happy invention of a few, or to be regarded as an original accomplishment and investiture of nature, or to be attributed to some succeeding effort of the human mind.

The supposed transition of the species from silence to the free exercise of speech, were a transition indeed astonishing, and might well seem disproportioned to our intellectual abilities. Neither history nor philosophy are decisive upon this point; and religion, with peculiar wisdom, refers the attainment to a divine original. Suitable to this idea, language may be accounted in part *natural*, in part *artificial*: in one view it is the work of Providence, in another it is the work of man. And this dispensation of things is exactly conformable to the whole analogy of the divine government. With respect to the organs of speech, what is there peculiar to boast? The same external apparatus is common to us and to other animals. In both the workmanship is the same. In both are displayed the same mechanical laws. And in order to confer on them similar endowments of speech, nothing more seems necessary than the enlargement of their ideas, without any alteration of anatomical texture. In like manner, to divest, or to abridge mankind of these endowments, seems to imply only the degradation of the mental faculties, without any variation of external form.

It is not then supposed that the organs of man alone are capable of forming speech. The voice of some animals is louder, and the voice of other animals is more melodious than his. Nor is the human ear alone susceptible of such impressions. Animals are often conscious of the import, and even recognize the harmony of sound. Thus far there subsists a near equality. Visible signs are likewise possessed in common; and language, in every species, is the power of maintaining social intercourse among creatures of the same order.

By the same medium man is able to converse, in some sort, with the brute creation; and there the various tribes with each other. But besides some general signs constituted to preserve harmony and correspondence among connected systems, there are others of a more mysterious kind, destined for the use and accommodation of each particular class. In this science the sagacity of the philosopher has hitherto made no discoveries. The mystery of animal correspondence will, probably, be always hid; and it is often no more possible to descend into the recesses of their intercourse, than to open a communication with a higher system.

In the great scale of life, the intelligence of some beings soars, perhaps, as high above man, as the objects of his understanding soar above animal life. Let us then imagine a man in some other planet, to reside among a people of this exalted character.

Instructed in the sounds of their language, as the more docile animals are instructed to articulate ours, he might articulate too, but could acquire no more. He might admire the magnificence of sounds louder or more melodious than he had heard before. But, by reason of a dissimilarity and disproportion of ideas, these sounds could never conduct him to the sense; and the secrets of such a people would be as safe in his ears, as ours in the ears of any of our domestic animals.

For the same reasons, if one of superior race were to drop into our world, our language might be, in some respects, impenetrable even to his understanding, because destitute perhaps of some perceptions essential to our meaner system.

Thus each order possesses something peculiar, which is denied to every other; and it belongs to the Author of the universe alone to exhaust that immensity of knowledge which he has diffused in various kind and proportion through the whole circle of being.

Here is an arrangement of Providence coeval with the birth of things; and, considering the similarity of organical texture, the *taciturnity* of the other animals is a problem to be accounted for, as well as the *loquacity* of man.

Whence comes it that *he* alone so far extends the original grant as almost to consider it as his peculiar and exclusive privilege? Between the lower classes and him there subsists one important distinction. They are formed stationary; he progressive. Had the exact measure of his ideas, as of theirs, been at first assigned, his language must have stood for ever as fixed and immutable as theirs. But time and mutual intercourse presenting new ideas, and the scenes of life perpetually varying, the expression of language must vary in the same proportion; and in order to trace out its original, we must go back to the ruder ages, and, beginning with the early dawn, follow the gradual illuminations of the human mind.

Man, we may observe, is at first possessed of few ideas, and of still fewer desires. Absorbed in the present object of sense, he seldom indulges any train of reflection on the past; and cares not, by anxious anticipation, to antedate futurity.

All his competitions with his fellows are rather exertions of body than trials of mind. He values himself on the command of the former, and is dextrous in the performance of its various functions. Too impatient for slow enterprise; too bold and impetuous for intrigue, he uses the resources of instinct, rather than the lights of the understanding; is scarce capable of abstraction, and a stranger to all the combinations and connexions of systematic thought.

In this situation of the world there is no need for the details of language. The feelings of the heart break forth in visible form: sensations glow in the countenance, and passions flash in the eye. Nor are these silent movements the only vehicles of social intercourse.

Prior to the contexture of language, and the use of arbitrary sign, there is established a mechanical connexion between the feelings of the soul and the enunciation of sound. The emotions of pleasure and pain, hope and fear, commiseration, sorrow, despair, indignation, contempt, joy, exultation, triumph, assume their tones; and independently of art, by an inexplicable mechanism of nature, declare the purposes of man to man. These associations are neither accidental nor equivocal; not formed by compact, or the effect of choice, but are parts of an original establishment, calculated, in the first oeconomy, for all the occasions of social life.

And happy surely, in one respect, was this constitution of things, when men were not only devoid of the inclination, but unfurnished with the means of deceit; and sentiment and expression were thus conjoined, by the indissoluble ties of nature.

Such accents and exclamations compose the first elements of a rising language. And in these distant times, when artificial signs have so far supplanted the natural, *interjection* is a part of speech which retains its primeval character, is scarce articulated in any tongue, and is exempted from arbitrary rule.

After the introduction of artificial signs, the tone and cadence of the natural were long retained; but these fell afterwards into disuse; and it became then the province of art to recal the accents of nature.

The perfection of eloquence is allowed to consist in superadding to sentiment and diction, all the emphasis of voice and gesture. And enunciation, or action, as it is called, is extolled by the most approved judges of antiquity as the capital excellence.

The decisive judgment of Demosthenes is well known: and the Roman orator [Cicero], who records that judgment, expatiates himself in almost every page, on that comprehensive language, which, independently of arbitrary appointment, addresses itself to all nations, and to every understanding.

In a certain period of society, there reigns a natural elocution, which the greatest masters afterwards are proud to imitate, and which art can so seldom supply. At first, the talent of the orator, as of the poet, is an inborn talent. Nor has Demosthenes, or Tully, or Roscius, or Garrick, in their most animated and admired performances, reached, perhaps, that vivacity and force which accompany the rude accents of mankind.

In the same original connexion of things resides the expression of music, or the irresistible tendency of the modulations of sound to stir and agitate the different passions. Hence the astonishing effect ascribed to music in antient times, and the empire it still maintains, in a peculiar manner, over rude and unpolished nations.

A Writer [Charles Burney], who exhausts on his favourite science so much ingenuity and learning, has assigned indeed other causes for the empire of music among the antients, besides its intrinsic excellence.

I oppose not such respectable authority. But though the science of harmony is progressive; though *simultaneous harmony*, or music in parts, is entirely modern, yet the union of sound and sense is an original union; and the most wonderful effects of that union are prior to the age of refinement.

'The recitative in music, according to the observation of an exquisite judge [Congreve] is only a more tuneable speaking: it is a kind of prose in music; its beauty consists in coming nearer nature, and improving the natural accents of words by more pathetic and emphatical tones.' The scale of music in different countries is the same; and all the variety of its expression throughout the earth forms but so many dialects of one universal language as unalterable as the human passions.

Such causes then, in the infancy of mankind, operating alone, or with little aid, seemed to supersede all motives to invention; while affairs, however, were gradually approaching towards a different stage.

Next to the impulses of appetite, and the social passions, the talent of *imitation* displays its force. Nor is this talent the gift of heaven to man alone. He shares it in common with the creatures below him, some of whom avail themselves of its exertions in the pursuit of their prey. That even the musical notes of birds are not altogether innate, but rather acquired by imitation, is a proposition supported by late observations. Yet, in consequence of a predilection, not easily explained, similar or kindred notes appear to be universally characteristic of the same species, varying only in different regions of the globe, like different dialects of the same tongue. One species of birds excels in imitation, and in a variety of note; another in the perfection of musical organs; and hence, by combining the peculiar excellencies of different species, an ingenious naturalist has suggested a method of improving upon the music of the grove.

Among animals, however, the talent of imitation occurs more rarely, or is limited to a few performances, and these resorted to as an expedient, rather than as an ultimate end.

But the performances of man are conspicuous, and various, and almost without bounds. He is prompted to imitation from a love of the effect, and, exclusive of all reference to farther end, enters it into the list of his pleasures. Often this secondary pleasure exceeds the primary. And there are few, I imagine, who would reject an entertainment of this sort, on the same principle with Agesilaus of Sparta. When invited to hear a performer who mimicked the nightingale to great perfection, the fastidious king replied, 'I have heard the nightingale herself.' The entertainment might be unworthy of a king; but it was declined, on a principle that forms an exception to the general taste. And imitation may be justly called the first intellectual amusement congenial with our being: in confirmation of which we might appeal to the first essays of infancy, to the taste for the imitative arts so predominant in youth, and to the earliest compositions of antiquity.

Man alone is capable of imitating every creature, while he is, if I may say so, himself a creature which no other can pretend to imitate. In the indulgence then of this talent, he adopts, as it were, every mode of instinct, and re-echoes every voice in the forest. Even still life attracts his attention; and the application of the same talent to every subject, renders him a master in expression, and ripens his genius while it exercises his mechanical powers.

Thus is he occupied in borrowing not only from his own species, but in transcribing, for his amusement, the appearances of the natural and of the animal world; in collecting materials, without knowing their importance, and in laying, with an active, though undesigning hand, the foundations of all arts and sciences.

This imitative faculty, which, in the school of Aristotle, entered into the definition of man, operates so vigorously on the organs of speech, that, in some cases, sound in general seems to become an object of imitation, without any particular archetype. Hence the mechanical trials of children in the easier expressions, when their organs are incapable of other articulation. And hence the same sounds run uniformly through all languages, to denote either parent, to whom the earliest expressions are presumed to be addressed.

By such exertions are we rendered capable of indicating, by intelligible signs, the more striking and familiar objects. But to give an additional compass to the powers of speech was reserved for another principle allied to the former, and often undistinguished in its operations, which may be denominated the *analogical* faculty. A faculty which has vast power in binding the associations of thoughts, and in all the mental arrangements; but with whose influence on language alone we are at present concerned.

Hitherto language consisted in the voice of instinct, or was drawn by imitation from an actual similarity in the nature of things. *Now* analogical connexions supply the place of real resemblance. *Now* instinct borrows aid from *imagination*; and it is the weakness of this principle which imposes the law of silence, and excludes all possibility of improvement in the animal world. Here commences the reign of invention, and here perhaps we should stop, and draw the boundary of art and nature.

There is not an object that can present itself to the senses, or to the imagination, which the mind, by its analogical faculty, cannot assimilate to something antecedently in its possession. By consequence, a term already appropriated, and in use, will, by no violent transition, be shaped and adjusted to the new idea. And thus the division and composition of the primary signs will constitute relations in sound, correspondent with those relations, real or imaginary, which subsist among the objects of human knowledge. Thus the language of the Chinese consists of a few words only, which, merely by a variation of tone, become the representatives of all the ideas of that enlightened people.

This mode of proceeding is so conspicuous in our first attempts, that it is with reluctance children adopt a word altogether new, so long as they can assimilate the object to any of their former acquaintance. And it is wonderful to observe with what promptitude, facility, and apparent ingenuity, they can draw such various expression out of their little store. It is accordingly no illiberal entertainment in presenting strange objects to their sight, to wait, by way of experiment, for their own conclusions, and to cause them to distinguish each by names of their own invention. This would be, perhaps, no improper exercise in training their infant faculties; and it seems to have been upon the same principle that the first of mankind, at the desire and with the approbation of his Creator, was able to name so readily all the beasts of the field, and the fowls of heaven.

Many subsequent innovations in language may be traced up to the same source; and signs apparently the most arbitrary are either the result of some more refined connexion, or are separated from their primitives by a longer chain of analogy.

By this power the same natural sign, besides its primary, admits of a secondary, and even of various import; and what originally denoted an outward object, is, by a certain subtlety of apprehension, transferred to the qualities of the mind. Thus language becomes figurative; and, without any extension of the vocabulary, takes in the compass of our intellectual ideas. It is this principle likewise which conducts the same sign from the individual to the species, and by the frequent application of it, on similar occasions, confers on it a larger and a larger import, till at last it acquires a general acceptation, without any painful or laborious effort.

This process of the mind accounts for the generation of all the different parts of speech, as might be shewn more particularly in the rise of that essential constituent of language, which by reason of its importance is denominated the *verb*.

Not only are emotions of different kinds excited by the objects of sense, but the same kind of emotion is wonderfully modified, according to the circumstances of its birth. How various, even in the savage breast, are the modes of love! how various the emotion of fear!

Let us then suppose that the lion and the serpent are considered by the savage as the most hostile and formidable among animals. A certain species of terror would be excited by the approach of the one; a different modification of the same emotion would be excited by the approach of the other.

Now, in the first stage of language, the natural signs of these kindred emotions, it is presumed, would be employed to indicate, and to distinguish the approach of these animals. In the mean while, let it be supposed that the other inhabitants of the forest have received their names. In these circumstances it is abundantly natural for the savage to join the term, indicating the dread of the lion or serpent, with a proper name, in order to notify the approach of any other offensive creature. This term, by an easy extension, will be transferred from offensive to other creatures; and hence, by a gradual transition, even to inanimate objects, till it is charged at length with a general affirmation, and possesses all the power of the verb.

Such steps as these, we may believe, have led to the more regular combinations of sound; and, under this aspect of things, we may conceive language strong indeed, and animated, but probably remaining long without much compass, or coherence, or order. It consisted chiefly of detached phrase. And though every sound formed not a complete sentence, as at the beginning, yet the more artificial arrangements were unknown. Those connective particles which intimate the relations of thought were not yet brought into existence; and the relations themselves were rather insinuated to the understanding than expressed in form. Nor is this abrupt mode of expression unsuitable to the circumstances of the simple ages. Sentiment, as well as its dress, hung then extremely loose; and men were not accustomed to a chain of reasoning, or to any complex system of thought. Nor is it less conformable to the experience of our early life, the truest perspective, perhaps, in which to contemplate the rising genius of mankind. In the first dialects of children, the particles are but little attended to, if not totally disregarded. They reject the texture of artificial language, even while they adopt its words, presenting the capital objects in immediate succession, without the intervention of terms which are of a more obscure and abstract original. It is the same mode of proceeding which is so often observable in vehement speakers, who, in the hurry of declamation, or of passion, have no leisure to attend to the rules of grammar, or logic. The language of passion accordingly, which consists of broken periods, has been happily imitated by the poets, and might be here illustrated, were it necessary, by examples from the greatest masters, whose prerogative it is to dispense in favour of nature with the established rules of art.

It is also remarkable in all the antient tongues, that the most important distinctions and relations of objects are indicated by an inflection of the voice, or a slight variation of the same sound, without resorting so often to the little engines, which support the modern systems.

Even this inflexion of voice is not always indispensable; and in the oriental tongues no inconveniency is perceived from the want of the *genitive case*; though there is neither an inflexion, nor any intervening particle to suggest the relation.

Let it not then be imagined, that abstract considerations have entered far into the first formation of speech. Such laborious effort had been ill suited to the genius and circumstances of the first inventors; and even the *particles* themselves, though of more doubtful origin, have crept into existence, without any severe application of metaphysical force.

Those talents alone exercised by every human creature, in acquiring his first language, have been exercised by the original institutors. In both cases the love of imitation is often the prime mover, without any farther design. Taught by parents, children learn to utter sound, to which afterwards they affix a meaning. Taught by instinct, men utter sound at the beginning, which the understanding afterwards renders more significant. In both cases, the act of the understanding is posterior to a sort of organical impulse; and in both cases there seems to be less abstraction than is contended for in the schools of philosophy.

Is a man, for example, to be reputed ignorant of the force of particles, because he is incapable to give a metaphysical account of their origin? And if, without metaphysics, he apprehends these particles, why not invent them too?

If we suppose but one of the most obvious relations to be distinctly marked by any particle, that particle will, as it were spontaneously, offer itself upon all similar occasions; and from the law of analogy will be gradually extended in its signification, until it includes under it a vast variety of relation: for it is transferred from object to object in the *concrete*, without any abstract consideration of its powers.

It is easier for the mind to perceive resemblance, than to specify the minute differences of things. Hence the same particles are used to denote various relations, without our attending to their specific differences. And hence these terms, in all languages, are so liable to be confounded, and carry often a sort of vicarious import, mutually participating of the same powers.

When the analogy loses itself in refinement, new particles are devised, and invested with a different office. And were an ordinary man called upon to define the prepositions, or other little constituents of any modern tongue, without a certain preparation of his faculties, the answer with regard to the greater number would be indefinite, or evasive, or merely negative. This particle, might he say, differs in its import from that other: that other from a third. They severally denote relations altogether dissimilar. It is easier to say what they are not, than what they are.

Should a more explicit answer be required, he refers to others more learned than himself, or involves himself in a labyrinth, in which the primary constructors of language never were involved, and from which the logician or the philologist can hardly extricate him. 'The particles,' says a Writer [Dr Samuel Johnson] in whom these characters are united, 'are among all nations applied with so great latitude, that they are not easily reducible under any regular scheme of application. This difficulty is not less, nor, perhaps, greater in English than in any other language. I have laboured them with diligence, I hope with success; such at least as can be expected in a task, which no man however learned or sagacious has yet been able to perform.'

He must be born then with a texture of brain as strong as that of *Johnson*: he must be a *Hercules* in metaphysics, who can declare, in their metaphysical character, the full import of these elements of speech.

Yet the relations of its own thoughts the mind clearly apprehends. The signs of these relations, when once instituted, it apprehends with equal ease. But these relations, clear as the light in the presence of particular objects, in their absence are involved in obscurity.

The vulgar find little difficulty to apprehend the soul itself in an embodied state; but it is reserved for the philosopher to apprehend its separate and abstract existence. And as well might it be contended that this sublime apprehension had, in every age, entered into the imagination of our forefathers, as that the nicer relations of thought had exhibited themselves naked to the understanding, and received names in artificial language, disjoined from the other members which compose the body of this complex machine.

With reason therefore we conclude, that the laws of analogy, by one gentle and uniform effect, superseding or alleviating the efforts of abstraction, permit language to advance towards its perfection free from the embarrassments which seemed to obstruct its progress.

In most speculations upon this subject, there reigns a fundamental error. It consists in referring the rise of ideas and the invention of language to a different æra, as if a time had ever been when mankind laboured for utterance, yet sought in vain to open intellectual treasures, and to be exonerated from the load of their own conceptions. Under this impression we are apt to imagine some great projectors in an early age, balancing a regular plan for the conveyance of sentiment, and the establishment of general intercourse. In such circumstances, indeed, they must have revolved in imagination all the subtleties of logic, and entered far into the science of grammar, before its objects had any existence. Profound abstraction and generalization must have been constantly exercised; all the relations of thought canvassed with care, compared with accuracy, and arranged with propriety and with order: a design competent, perhaps, to superior beings, but by no means compatible with the limited capacity of the human mind. Now these difficulties and incumbrances, in a great measure, disappear, by contemplating ideas and language as uniformly in close conjunction; and the changes in the former, and the innovations in the latter, of the same chronological date.

A few ideas, in the ruder ages, are subjected to expression with the same facility, as a greater number in succeeding periods. And hence speech, in all its different parts, is already formed, when the vocabulary is exceeding scanty, and there is no variety or abundance in any one class. Thus a Grammar even of the Lapland tongue contains all the grammatical parts of speech. Hence too the ease with which a language is attained in infancy, or early youth, and the difficulty attending it in maturer age. When the idea and the sign are contemporary attainments, and coincide in their first impressions, they take root together, and serve reciprocally the one to suggest the other. But where this coincidence is wanting, it becomes more difficult, if not impossible, for the mind to collect its naked thoughts, and subject them afterwards in all their variety to the arbitrary impositions of language.

A more equal oeconomy, therefore, has been maintained by the direction of that principle of analogy to which we so often refer; and the connexion is more easily established, when, from the simplicity and uniformity of savage life, the same signs return so often; when the whole compass of the vocabulary is exhausted upon familiar objects, and almost comprized in the history of a day's adventures. Thus a vocabulary, consisting of about twenty words, is said to be sufficient, in all their ordinary transactions, for the purposes of some savage nations.

Language then, constructed with such scanty materials, increases with the experience and discernment of mankind. 'Uncultivated people,' says a Writer [Edmund Burke] of genius and refinement, 'are but ordinary observers of things, and not critical in distinguishing them; but, for that reason, they admire more, and are more affected with what they see, and therefore express themselves in a warmer and more passionate manner.' On a more exact survey, the mind discriminates its objects, and breaks the system of analogy by attending to the minute differences of things. As therefore the *analogical faculty* enlarges the sense of words, the *discriminating faculty* augments them in number. It breaks speech into smaller divisions, and bestows a copiousness on language by a more precise arrangement of the objects. Thus, by the distribution of our ideas, as well as by the enlargement of the fund, language is constantly enriched; and its barrenness or fertility among a rising people may be always estimated by the number of the objects, and the accuracy with which they are classed.

At a time when utility was almost regarded as the whole of beauty, and perspicuity was the sole aim of speech, nothing superfluous would ever be admitted there. Afterwards the coalition and interferences of different tribes confounded the simplicity of the institution, by the admission of foreign, identical, and supernumerary terms. The love of novelty and variety established their currency: a species of luxury is indulged in the commerce of words. Each simple institution sustained a shock from the collision of contending systems, and out of these jarrings there arose more copious and mixed establishments.

By such causes is language diversified by degrees, in its words, in its texture, and in its idiom. What is at first only a variety of dialects, produces distinct languages in succeeding generations. And, after separation from the fountain, the differences among them become more considerable in proportion to the length of their course. Thus the English, the French, and Italian tongues have borrowed their vocabulary from the Greeks and Romans, while, in their texture, and idiom they are allied to the Celtic and to the Hebrew, or claim a very distant original.

But the consideration of these differences would carry us beyond the limit of the present design, which permits us only to touch on the gradations of a simple institution, referring to those faculties of the mind which appear principally concerned in conducting its successive improvements. In the execution of the enterprise, the mind, no doubt, has exerted collectively, at all times, various powers; but these are exerted in unequal proportion, according to the circumstances of the world; and the order here assigned appeared to our judgement most consonant to the probability of things, to the experience of early life, and to the genius and complexion of the ruder ages.

By such efforts, or at least by efforts competent to the abilities of every society of mankind, some rude system is constructed on the foundations of nature. The superstructure becomes vast and magnificent, like the conceptions of the human mind; but that superstructure is the work of ages, and is as complicated and various, in the different regions of the globe, as the modes of civil life, as the aspect of nature, and as the genius of arts and sciences.

Having therefore considered speech in its lower forms, we proceed to enquire into those superior marks of refinement and art which constitute the criterion of a polished tongue.

Source: James Dunbar, 'On language, as an universal accomplishment', in *Essays on the History of Mankind in Rude and Cultivated Ages*, London 1781, reprinted with new introduction by Christopher J. Berry, Bristol 1995, pp. 61–100

PART XI
SCIENCE

FORTY-FOUR

ADAM SMITH
Scientific Discovery

Smith's *History of Astronomy* was probably written in large
part (including the sections here excerpted) during his time
as a student at Oxford (1740–6), with the final part completed
before 1758. The full title of the work is *The principles which
lead and direct philosophical inquiries: illustrated by the history
of astronomy*. 'Philosophical' must here be understood in a
sufficiently wide sense to take in not only what is now called
philosophy, but also the empirical sciences, such as physics
(formerly termed 'natural philosophy') and astronomy. It is
'the principles which lead and direct' such enquiries, rather
than the history of astronomy as such, that form the subject
matter of the following excerpt.

The *History*, though devoted mainly to the exposition of
four stages in the development of astronomy, is prefaced by
a discussion of the psychology of scientific enquiry. Such
enquiry has three stages, surprise, wonder and admiration.
Smith tells us: 'Philosophy is the science of the connecting
principles of nature.' We will not find the connecting
principles unless we are prompted to look for them, and what
prompts us is surprise. Surprise is not a distinct emotion, but
the 'violent and sudden change produced in the mind when
an emotion of any kind is brought suddenly upon it'. It is just
such a change that prompts us to ask scientific questions.

Smith speaks of two grounds of surprise. One ground
derives from our natural tendency to classify things.
Occasionally we meet with something that is 'quite new
and singular'. The surprise caused by this experience
produces a movement of the spirit as we seek to find
a class into which the new and singular thing can be
fitted. This movement of the spirit is called 'wonder'.
So although Smith calls wonder a sentiment it is plainly
a sentiment with a cognitive element, for wondering is the
emotional state specifically associated with a person not
knowing something but wanting to find out.

The second ground of surprise concerns not new and singular objects but new and singular sequences of events. Here Smith appropriates for his own purposes a central doctrine of David Hume's philosophy of mind. When one of two events has often been observed to precede the other immediately, and never not to precede it, there is what Smith terms 'a natural career of the imagination' by which the idea of the first event is immediately followed by an idea of the second, and observation of the first event prompts the imagination to produce an idea of the second. The more the events are linked in this way, the more natural the sequence of events seems to be, and the less room there seems to be for questions about why the second follows the first. But if the sequence is broken, if, that is, the first event is not followed by the second, then this produces surprise, and also wonder. For now the question has to be faced: Why did this happen? The two events seem disjointed. How do we show that they are not so? What joins them? The wonder ceases with the discovery of the answer to this question.

Of course what for most people might be a smooth transition in the imagination from one event to another might not be smooth in the imagination of others. Some people might be able to detect a disjointness where the generality of mankind see no such thing. It is among such people that the finest scientific enquirers are to be found – among those looking for solutions where most people do not see that there is a problem. With the discovery of the solution nature presents, in Smith's words, 'a more coherent, and therefore a more magnificent spectacle'. It is this spectacle that prompts our admiration, the third of the three stages of scientific enquiry that Smith discusses.

The excerpt contains a remarkable suggestion that in assessing scientific explanations we should not have regard to 'their absurdity or probability, their agreement or inconsistency with truth and reality'. Instead we should 'content ourselves with inquiring how far each of [the explanations] was fitted to soothe the imagination, and to render the theatre of nature a more coherent, and therefore a more magnificent spectacle'. In this and related passages Smith comes very close to detaching the scientific enterprise from questions of truth and placing all the emphasis instead upon the coherence of our picture of the world.

A.B.

The History of Astronomy

Wonder, Surprise, and Admiration, are words which, though often confounded, denote, in our language, sentiments that are indeed allied, but that are in some respects different also, and distinct from one another. What is new and singular, excites that sentiment which, in strict propriety, is called Wonder; what is unexpected, Surprise; and what is great or beautiful, Admiration.

We wonder at all extraordinary and uncommon objects, at all the rarer phaenomena of nature, at meteors, comets, eclipses, at singular plants and animals, and at every thing, in short, with which we have before been either little or not at all acquainted; and we still wonder, though forewarned of what we are to see.

We are surprised at those things which we have seen often, but which we least of all expected to meet with in the place where we find them; we are surprised at the sudden appearance of a friend, whom we have seen a thousand times, but whom we did not imagine we were to see then.

We admire the beauty of a plain or the greatness of a mountain, though we have seen both often before, and though nothing appears to us in either, but what we had expected with certainty to see.

Whether this criticism upon the precise meaning of these words be just, is of little importance. I imagine it is just, though I acknowledge, that the best writers in our language have not always made use of them according to it. Milton, upon the appearance of Death to Satan, says, that

> The Fiend what this might be admir'd;
> Admir'd, not fear'd.[1]

But if this criticism be just, the proper expression should have been *wonder'd*. Dryden, upon the discovery of Iphigenia sleeping, says, that

> The fool of nature stood with stupid eyes
> And gaping mouth, that testified surprise.[2]

But what Cimon must have felt upon this occasion could not so much be Surprise, as Wonder and Admiration. All that I

1 *Paradise Lost*, ii. 677–8, but Milton wrote 'Th'
undaunted Fiend . . .'.
2 'Cymon and Iphigenia', 107–8.

contend for is, that the sentiments excited by what is new, by what is unexpected, and by what is great and beautiful, are really different, however the words made use of to express them may sometimes be confounded. Even the admiration which is excited by beauty, is quite different (as will appear more fully hereafter) from that which is inspired by greatness, though we have but one word to denote them.

These sentiments, like all others when inspired by one and the same object, mutually support and enliven one another: an object with which we are quite familiar, and which we see every day, produces, though both great and beautiful, but a small effect upon us; because our admiration is not supported either by Wonder or by Surprise: and if we have heard a very accurate description of a monster, our Wonder will be the less when we see it; because our previous knowledge of it will in a great measure prevent our Surprise.

It is the design of this Essay to consider particularly the nature and causes of each of these sentiments, whose influence is of far wider extent than we should be apt upon a careless view to imagine. I shall begin with Surprise.

SECTION I *Of the Effect of Unexpectedness, or of Surprise*

When an object of any kind, which has been for some time expected and foreseen, presents itself, whatever be the emotion which it is by nature fitted to excite, the mind must have been prepared for it, and must even in some measure have conceived it before-hand; because the idea of the object having been so long present to it, must have before-hand excited some degree of the same emotion which the object itself would excite: the change, therefore, which its presence produces comes thus to be less considerable, and the emotion or passion which it excites glides gradually and easily into the heart, without violence, pain, or difficulty.[1]

But the contrary of all this happens when the object is unexpected; the passion is then poured in all at once upon the heart, which is thrown, if it is a strong passion, into the most violent and convulsive emotions, such as sometimes cause immediate death; sometimes, by the suddenness of the extacy, so entirely disjoint the whole frame of the imagination, that it never after returns to its former tone and composure, but falls either into a frenzy or habitual lunacy; and such as almost always

1 Cf. Hume, *Treatise of Human Nature*, I.i.4, 'Of the connexion or association of ideas'.

occasion a momentary loss of reason, or of that attention to other things which our situation or our duty requires.

How much we dread the effects of the more violent passions, when they come suddenly upon the mind, appears from those preparations which all men think necessary when going to inform any one of what is capable of exciting them. Who would choose all at once to inform his friend of an extraordinary calamity that had befallen him, without taking care before-hand, by alarming him with an uncertain fear, to announce, if one may say so, his misfortune, and thereby prepare and dispose him for receiving the tidings?

Those panic terrors which sometimes seize armies in the field, or great cities, when an enemy is in the neighbourhood, and which deprive for a time the most determined of all deliberate judgments, are never excited but by the sudden apprehension of unexpected danger. Such violent consternations, which at once confound whole multitudes, benumb their understandings, and agitate their hearts, with all the agony of extravagant fear, can never be produced by any foreseen danger, how great soever. Fear, though naturally a very strong passion, never rises to such excesses, unless exasperated both by Wonder, from the uncertain nature of the danger, and by Surprise, from the suddenness of the apprehension.

Surprise, therefore, is not to be regarded as an original emotion of a species distinct from all others. The violent and sudden change produced upon the mind, when an emotion of any kind is brought suddenly upon it, constitutes the whole nature of Surprise.

But when not only a passion and a great passion comes all at once upon the mind, but when it comes upon it while the mind is in the mood most unfit for conceiving it, the Surprise is then the greatest. Surprises of joy when the mind is sunk into grief, or of grief when it is elated with joy, are therefore the most unsupportable. The change is in this case the greatest possible. Not only a strong passion is conceived all at once, but a strong passion the direct opposite of that which was before in possession of the soul. When a load of sorrow comes down upon the heart that is expanded and elated with gaiety and joy, it seems not only to damp and oppress it, but almost to crush and bruise it, as a real weight would crush and bruise the body. On the contrary, when from an unexpected change of fortune, a tide of gladness seems, if I may say so, to spring up all at once within it, when depressed and contracted with grief and sorrow, it feels as if suddenly extended and heaved up with violent and irresistible force, and is torn with pangs of all others most exquisite, and which almost always occasion faintings, deliriums, and sometimes instant death. For it may be worth while to observe, that though grief be a more violent passion than joy, as indeed all uneasy sensations seem naturally more pungent than the opposite agreeable ones, yet of the two, Surprises of joy are still more insupportable than Surprises of grief. We are told[1] that after the battle of Thrasimenus, while a Roman lady, who had been informed that her son was slain in the action, was sitting alone bemoaning her misfortunes, the young man who escaped came suddenly into the room to her, and that she cried out and expired instantly in a transport of joy. Let us suppose the contrary of this to have happened, and that in the midst of domestic festivity and mirth, he had suddenly fallen down dead at her feet, is it likely that the effects would have been equally violent? I imagine not. The heart springs to joy with a sort of natural elasticity, it abandons itself to so agreeable an emotion, as soon as the object is presented; it seems to pant and leap forward to meet it, and the passion in its full force takes at once entire and complete possession of the soul. But it is otherways with grief; the heart recoils from, and resists the first approaches of that disagreeable passion, and it requires some time before the melancholy object can produce its full effect. Grief comes on slowly and gradually, nor ever rises at once to that height of agony to which it is increased after a little time. But joy comes rushing upon us all at once like a torrent. The change produced therefore by a Surprise of joy is more sudden, and upon that account more violent and apt to have more fatal effects, than that which is occasioned by a Surprise of grief; there seems too to be something in the nature of Surprise, which makes it unite more easily with the brisk and quick motion of joy, than with the slower and heavier movement of grief. Most men who can take the trouble to recollect, will find that they have heard of more people who died or became distracted with sudden joy, than with sudden grief. Yet from the nature of human affairs, the latter must be much more frequent than the former. A man may break his leg, or lose his son, though he has had no warning of either of these events, but he can hardly meet with an extraordinary piece of good fortune, without having had some foresight of what was to happen.

Not only grief and joy but all the other passions, are more violent, when opposite extremes succeed each other. Is any

[1] Livy, XXII.7.13.

resentment so keen as what follows the quarrels of lovers, or any love so passionate as what attends their reconcilement?

Even the objects of the external senses affect us in a more lively manner, when opposite extremes succeed to, or are placed beside each other. Moderate warmth seems intolerable heat if felt after extreme cold. What is bitter will seem more so when tasted after what is very sweet; a dirty white will seem bright and pure when placed by a jet black. The vivacity in short of every sensation, as well as of every sentiment, seems to be greater or less in proportion to the change made by the impression of either upon the situation of the mind or organ; but this change must necessarily be the greatest when opposite sentiments and sensations are contrasted, or succeed immediately to one another. Both sentiments and sensations are then the liveliest; and this superior vivacity proceeds from nothing but their being brought upon the mind or organ when in a state most unfit for conceiving them.

As the opposition of contrasted sentiments heightens their vivacity, so the resemblance of those which immediately succeed each other renders them more faint and languid. A parent who has lost several children immediately after one another, will be less affected with the death of the last than with that of the first, though the loss in itself be, in this case, undoubtedly greater; but his mind being already sunk into sorrow, the new misfortune seems to produce no other effect than a continuance of the same melancholy, and is by no means apt to occasion such transports of grief as are ordinarily excited by the first calamity of the kind; he receives it, though with great dejection, yet with some degree of calmness and composure, and without any thing of that anguish and agitation of mind which the novelty of the misfortune is apt to occasion. Those who have been unfortunate through the whole course of their lives are often indeed habitually melancholy, and sometimes peevish and splenetic, yet upon any fresh disappointment, though they are vexed and complain a little, they seldom fly out into any more violent passion, and never fall into those transports of rage or grief which often, upon the like occasions, distract the fortunate and successful.

Upon this are founded, in a great measure, some of the effects of habit and custom. It is well known that custom deadens the vivacity of both pain and pleasure, abates the grief we should feel for the one, and weakens the joy we should derive from the other. The pain is supported without agony, and the pleasure enjoyed without rapture: because custom and the frequent repetition of any object comes at last to form and bend the mind or organ to that habitual mood and disposition which fits them to receive its impression, without undergoing any very violent change.

SECTION II *Of Wonder, or of the Effects of Novelty*

It is evident that the mind takes pleasure in observing the resemblances that are discoverable betwixt different objects. It is by means of such observations that it endeavours to arrange and methodise all its ideas, and to reduce them into proper classes and assortments. Where it can observe but one single quality, that is common to a great variety of otherwise widely different objects, that single circumstance will be sufficient for it to connect them all together, to reduce them to one common class, and to call them by one general name. It is thus that all things endowed with a power of self-motion, beasts, birds, fishes, insects, are classed under the general name of Animal; and that these again, along with those which want that power, are arranged under the still more general word Substance: and this is the origin of those assortments of objects and ideas which in the schools are called Genera and Species, and of those abstract and general names, which in all languages are made use of to express them.

The further we advance in knowledge and experience, the greater number of divisions and subdivisions of those Genera and Species we are both inclined and obliged to make. We observe a greater variety of particularities amongst those things which have a gross resemblance; and having made new divisions of them, according to those newly-observed particularities, we are then no longer to be satisfied with being able to refer an object to a remote genus, or very general class of things, to many of which it has but a loose and imperfect resemblance. A person, indeed, unacquainted with botany may expect to satisfy your curiosity, by telling you, that such a vegetable is a weed, or, perhaps in still more general terms, that it is a plant. But a botanist will neither give nor accept of such an answer. He has broke and divided that great class of objects into a number of inferior assortments, according to those varieties which his experience has discovered among them; and he wants to refer each individual plant to some tribe of vegetables, with all of which it may have a more exact resemblance, than with many things comprehended under the extensive genus of plants. A child imagines that it gives a satisfactory answer when it tells you, that an object whose name it knows not is a thing, and fancies that it informs you of something, when it thus ascertains to which of the two most obvious and comprehensive classes of objects a particular impression ought to be referred; to the class of realities or solid substances which it calls *things*, or to that of appearances which it calls *nothings*.

Whatever, in short, occurs to us we are fond of referring to some species or class of things, with all of which it has a nearly exact resemblance; and though we often know no more about them than about it, yet we are apt to fancy that by being able to do so, we show ourselves to be better acquainted with it, and to have a more thorough insight into its nature. But when something quite new and singular is presented, we feel ourselves incapable of doing this. The memory cannot, from all its stores, cast up any image that nearly resembles this strange appearance. If by some of its qualities it seems to resemble, and to be connected with a species which we have before been acquainted with, it is by others separated and detached from that, and from all the other assortments of things we have hitherto been able to make. It stands alone and by itself in the imagination, and refuses to be grouped or confounded with any set of objects whatever. The imagination and memory exert themselves to no purpose, and in vain look around all their classes of ideas in order to find one under which it may be arranged. They fluctuate to no purpose from thought to thought, and we remain still uncertain and undetermined where to place it, or what to think of it. It is this fluctuation and vain recollection, together with the emotion or movement of the spirits that they excite, which constitute the sentiment properly called *Wonder*, and which occasion that staring, and sometimes that rolling of the eyes, that suspension of the breath, and that swelling of the heart, which we may all observe, both in ourselves and others, when wondering at some new object, and which are the natural symptoms of uncertain and undetermined thought. What sort of a thing can that be? What is that like? are the questions which, upon such an occasion, we are all naturally disposed to ask. If we can recollect many such objects which exactly resemble this new appearance, and which present themselves to the imagination naturally, and as it were of their own accord, our Wonder is entirely at an end. If we can recollect but a few, and which it requires too some trouble to be able to call up, our Wonder is indeed diminished, but not quite destroyed. if we can recollect none, but are quite at a loss, it is the greatest possible.

With what curious attention does a naturalist examine a singular plant, or a singular fossil, that is presented to him? He is at no loss to refer it to the general genus of plants or fossils; but this does not satisfy him, and when he considers all the different tribes or species of either with which he has hitherto been acquainted, they all, he thinks, refuse to admit the new object among them. It stands alone in his imagination, and as it were detached from all the other species of that genus to which it belongs. He labours, however, to connect it with some one or other of them. Sometimes he thinks it may be placed in this, and sometimes in that other assortment; nor is he ever satisfied, till he has fallen upon one which, in most of its qualities, it resembles. When he cannot do this, rather than it should stand quite by itself, he will enlarge the precincts, if I may say so, of some species, in order to make room for it; or he will create a new species on purpose to receive it, and call it a Play of Nature, or give it some other appellation, under which he arranges all the oddities that he knows not what else to do with. But to some class or other of known objects he must refer it, and betwixt it and them he must find out some resemblance or other, before he can get rid of that Wonder, that uncertainty and anxious curiosity excited by its singular appearance, and by its dissimilitude with all the objects he had hitherto observed.

As single and individual objects thus excite our Wonder when, by their uncommon qualities and singular appearance, they make us uncertain to what species of things we ought to refer them; so a succession of objects which follow one another in an uncommon train or order, will produce the same effect, though there be nothing particular in any one of them taken by itself.

When one accustomed object appears after another, which it does not usually follow, it first excites, by its unexpectedness, the sentiment properly called Surprise, and afterwards, by the singularity of the succession, or order of its appearance, the sentiment properly called Wonder. We start and are surprised at feeling it there, and then wonder how it came there. The motion of a small piece of iron along a plain table is in itself no extraordinary object, yet the person who first saw it begin, without any visible impulse, in consequence of the motion of a loadstone at some little distance from it, could not behold it without the most extreme Surprise; and when that momentary emotion was over, he would still wonder how it came to be conjoined to an event with which, according to the ordinary train of things, he could have so little suspected it to have any connection.

When two objects, however unlike, have often been observed to follow each other, and have constantly presented themselves to the senses in that order, they come to be so connected together in the fancy, that the idea of the one seems, of its own accord, to call up and introduce that of the other. If the objects are still observed to succeed each other as before, this connection, or, as it has been called, this association of their ideas, becomes stricter and stricter, and the habit of the imagination to pass from the conception of the one to that of the other, grows more and more rivetted and confirmed. As its ideas move more rapidly than external objects, it is continually running before them, and therefore anticipates, before it happens, every event which falls out according to this ordinary course of things. When objects succeed each other in the same train in which the ideas of the imagination have thus been accustomed to move, and in which, though not conducted by that chain of events presented to the senses, they have acquired a tendency to go on of their own accord, such objects appear all closely connected with one another, and the thought glides easily along them, without effort and without interruption. They fall in with the natural career of the imagination; and as the ideas which represented such a train of things would seem all mutually to introduce each other, every last thought to be called up by the foregoing, and to call up the succeeding; so when the objects themselves occur, every last event seems, in the same manner, to be introduced by the foregoing, and to introduce the succeeding. There is no break, no stop, no gap, no interval. The ideas excited by so coherent a chain of things seem, as it were, to float through the mind of their own accord, without obliging it to exert itself, or to make any effort in order to pass from one of them to another.

But if this customary connection be interrupted, if one or more objects appear in an order quite different from that to which the imagination has been accustomed, and for which it is prepared, the contrary of all this happens. We are at first surprised by the unexpectedness of the new appearance, and when that momentary emotion is over, we still wonder how it came to occur in that place. The imagination no longer feels the usual facility of passing from the event which goes before to that which comes after. It is an order or law of succession to which it has not been accustomed, and which it therefore finds some difficulty in following, or in attending to. The fancy is stopped and interrupted in that natural movement or career, according to which it was proceeding. Those two events seem to stand at a distance from each other; it endeavours to bring them together, but they refuse to unite; and it feels, or imagines it feels, something like a gap or interval betwixt them. It naturally hesitates, and, as it were, pauses upon the brink of this interval; it endeavours to find out something which may fill up the gap, which, like a bridge, may so far at least unite those seemingly distant objects, as to render the passage of the thought betwixt them smooth, and natural, and easy. The supposition of a chain of intermediate, though invisible, events, which succeed each other in a train similar to that in which the imagination has been accustomed to move, and which link together those two disjointed appearances, is the only means by which the imagination can fill up this interval, is the only bridge which, if one may say so, can smooth its passage from the one object to the other. Thus, when we observe the motion of the iron, in consequence of that of the loadstone, we gaze and hesitate, and feel a want of connection betwixt two events which follow one another in so unusual a train. But when, with Des Cartes, we imagine certain invisible effluvia to circulate round one of them, and by their repeated impulses to impel the other, both to move towards it, and to follow its motion, we fill up the interval betwixt them, we join them together by a sort of bridge, and thus take off that hesitation and difficulty which the imagination felt in passing from the one to the other. That the iron should move after the loadstone seems, upon this hypothesis, in some measure according to the ordinary course of things. Motion after impulse is an order of succession with which of all things we are the most familiar. Two objects which are so connected seem no longer to be disjoined, and the imagination flows smoothly and easily along them.

Such is the nature of this second species of Wonder, which arises from an unusual succession of things. The stop which is thereby given to the career of the imagination, the difficulty which it finds in passing along such disjointed objects, and the feeling of something like a gap or interval betwixt them, constitute the whole essence of this emotion. Upon the clear discovery of a connecting chain of intermediate events, it vanishes altogether. What obstructed the movement of the imagination is then removed. Who wonders at the machinery of the opera-house who has once been admitted behind the scenes? In the Wonders of nature, however, it rarely happens that we can discover so clearly this connecting chain. With regard to a few even of them, indeed, we seem to have been really admitted behind the scenes, and our Wonder accordingly is entirely at an end. Thus the eclipses of the sun and moon, which once, more than all the other appearances in the heavens, excited the terror and amazement of mankind, seem now no longer to be wonderful, since the connecting chain has been found out which joins them to the ordinary course of things. Nay, in those cases in which we have been less successful, even the vague hypotheses of Des Cartes, and the yet more indetermined notions of Aristotle, have, with their followers, contributed to give some coherence to the appearances of nature, and might diminish, though they could not destroy, their Wonder. If they did not completely fill up the interval betwixt the two disjointed objects, they bestowed upon them, however, some sort of loose connection which they wanted before.

That the imagination feels a real difficulty in passing along two events which follow one another in an uncommon order, may be confirmed by many obvious observations. If it attempts to attend beyond a certain time to a long series of this kind, the continual efforts it is obliged to make, in order to pass from one object to another, and thus follow the progress of the succession, soon fatigue it, and if repeated too often, disorder and disjoint its whole frame. It is thus that too severe an application to study sometimes brings on lunacy and frenzy, in those especially who are somewhat advanced in life, but whose imaginations, from being too late in applying, have not got those habits which dispose them to follow easily the reasonings in the abstract sciences. Every step of a demonstration, which to an old practitioner is quite natural and easy, requires from them the most intense application of thought. Spurred on, however, either by ambition, or by admiration for the subject, they still continue till they become, first confused, then giddy, and at last distracted. Could we conceive a person of the soundest judgment, who had grown up to maturity, and whose imagination had acquired those habits, and that mold, which the constitution of things in this world necessarily impress upon it, to be all at once transported alive to some other planet, where nature was governed by laws quite different from those which take place here; as he would be continually obliged to attend to events, which must to him appear in the highest degree jarring, irregular, and discordant, he would soon feel the same confusion and giddiness begin to come upon him, which would at last end in the same manner, in lunacy and distraction. Neither, to produce this effect, is it necessary that the objects should be either great or interesting, or even uncommon, in themselves. It is sufficient that they follow one another in an uncommon order. Let any one attempt to look over even a game of cards, and to attend particularly to every single stroke, and if he is unacquainted with the nature and rules of the game; that is, with the laws which regulate the succession of the cards; he will soon feel the same confusion and giddiness begin to come upon him, which, were it to be continued for days and months, would end in the same manner, in lunacy and distraction. But if the mind be thus thrown into the most violent disorder, when it attends to a long series of events which follow one another in an uncommon train, it must feel some degree of the same disorder, when it observes even a single event fall out in this unusual manner: for the violent disorder can arise from nothing but the too frequent repetition of this smaller uneasiness.

That it is the unusualness alone of the succession which occasions this stop and interruption in the progress of the imagination, as well as the notion of an interval betwixt the two immediately succeeding objects, to be filled up by some chain of intermediate events, is not less evident. The same orders of succession, which to one set of men seem quite according to the natural course of things, and such as require no intermediate events to join them, shall to another appear altogether incoherent and disjointed, unless some such events be supposed: and this for no other reason, but because such orders of succession are familiar to the one, and strange to the other. When we enter the work-houses of the most common artizans; such as dyers, brewers, distillers; we observe a number of appearances, which present themselves in an order that seems to us very strange and wonderful. Our thought cannot easily follow it, we feel an interval betwixt every two of them, and require some chain of intermediate events, to fill it up, and link them together. But the artizan himself, who has been for many years familiar with the consequences of all the operations of his art, feels no such interval. They fall in with what custom has made the natural movement of his imagination: they no longer excite his Wonder, and if he is not a genius superior to his profession, so as to be capable of making the very easy reflection, that those things, though familiar to him, may be strange to us, he will be disposed rather to laugh at, than sympathize with our Wonder. He cannot conceive what occasion there is for any connecting events to unite those appearances, which seem to him to succeed each other very naturally. It is their nature, he tells us, to follow one another in this order, and that accordingly they always do so. In the same manner bread has, since the world began, been the common nourishment of the human body, and men have so long seen it, every day, converted into flesh and bones, substances in all respects so unlike it, that they have seldom had the curiosity to inquire by what process of intermediate events this change is brought about. Because the passage of the thought from the one object to the other is by custom become quite smooth and easy, almost without the supposition of any such process. Philosophers, indeed, who often look for a chain of invisible objects to join together two events that occur in an order familiar to all the world, have endeavoured to find out a chain of this kind betwixt the two events I have just now mentioned; in the same manner as they have endeavoured, by a like intermediate chain, to connect the gravity, the elasticity, and even the cohesion of natural bodies, with some of their other qualities. These, however, are all of them such combinations of events as give no stop to the imaginations of the bulk of mankind, as excite no Wonder, nor any apprehension that there is wanting the strictest connection between them. But as in those sounds, which to the greater part of men seem perfectly agreeable to measure and harmony, the nicer ear of a musician will discover a want, both of the most exact time, and of the most perfect coincidence: so the more practised thought of a philosopher, who has spent his whole life in the study of the connecting principles of nature, will often feel an interval betwixt two objects, which, to more careless observers, seem very strictly conjoined. By long attention to all the connections which have ever been presented to his observation, by having often compared them with one another, he has, like the musician, acquired, if one may say so, a nicer ear, and a more delicate feeling with regard to things of this nature. And as to the one, that music seems dissonance which falls short of the most perfect harmony; so to the other, those events seem altogether separated and disjointed, which fall short of the strictest and most perfect connection.

Philosophy is the science of the connecting principles of nature. Nature, after the largest experience that common observation can acquire, seems to abound with events which appear solitary and incoherent with all that go before them, which therefore disturb the easy movement of the imagination; which make its ideas succeed each other, if one may say so, by irregular starts and sallies; and which thus tend, in some measure, to introduce those confusions and distractions we formerly mentioned. Philosophy, by representing the invisible chains which bind together all these disjointed objects, endeavours to introduce order into this chaos of jarring and discordant appearances, to allay this tumult of the imagination, and to restore it, when it surveys the great revolutions of the universe, to that tone of tranquillity and composure, which is both most agreeable in itself, and most suitable to its nature. Philosophy, therefore, may be regarded as one of those arts which address themselves to the imagination; and whose theory and history, upon that account, fall properly within the circumference of our subject. Let us endeavour to trace it, from its first origin, up to that summit of perfection to which it is at present supposed to have arrived, and to which, indeed, it has equally been supposed to have arrived in almost all former times. It is the most sublime of all the agreeable arts, and its revolutions have been the greatest, the most frequent, and the most distinguished of all those that have happened in the literary world. Its history, therefore, must, upon all accounts, be the most entertaining and the most instructive. Let us examine, therefore, all the different systems of nature, which, in these western parts of the world, the only parts of whose history we know any thing, have successively been adopted by the learned and ingenious; and, without regarding their absurdity or probability, their agreement or inconsistency with truth and reality, let us consider them only in that particular point of view which belongs to our subject; and content ourselves with inquiring how far each of them was fitted to sooth the imagination, and to render the theatre of nature a more coherent, and therefore a more magnificent spectacle, than otherwise it would have appeared to be. According as they have failed or succeeded in this, they have constantly failed or succeeded in gaining reputation and renown to their authors; and this will be found to be the clew that is most capable of conducting us through all the labyrinths of philosophical history: for, in the mean time, it will serve to confirm what has gone before, and to throw light upon what is to come after, that we observe, in general, that no system, how well soever in other respects supported, has ever been able to gain any general credit on the world, whose connecting principles were not such as were familiar to all mankind. Why has the chemical philosophy in all ages crept along in obscurity, and been so disregarded by the generality of mankind, while other systems, less useful, and not more agreeable to experience, have possessed universal admiration for whole centuries together? The connecting principles of the chemical philosophy are such as the generality of mankind know nothing about, have rarely seen, and have never been acquainted with; and which to them, therefore, are incapable of smoothing the passage of the imagination betwixt any two seemingly disjointed objects. Salts, sulphurs, and mercuries, acids, and alkalis, are principles which can smooth things to those only who live about the furnace; but whose most common operations seem, to the bulk of mankind, as disjointed as any two events which the chemists would connect together by them. Those artists, however, naturally explained things to themselves by principles that were familiar to themselves. As Aristotle observes,[1] that the early Pythagoreans, who first studied arithmetic, explained all things by the properties of numbers; and Cicero tells us,[2] that Aristoxenus, the musician, found the nature of the soul to consist in harmony. In the same manner, a learned physician lately gave a system of moral philosophy upon the principles of his own art,[3] in which wisdom and virtue were the healthful state of the soul; the different vices and follies, the different diseases to which it was subject; in which the causes and symptoms of those diseases were ascertained; and, in the same medical strain, a proper method of cure prescribed. In the same manner also, others have written parallels of painting and poetry, of poetry and music, of music and architecture, of beauty and virtue, of all the fine arts; systems which have universally owed their origin to the lucubrations of those who were acquainted with the one art, but ignorant of the other; who therefore explained to themselves the phaenomena, in that which was strange to them, by those in that which was familiar; and with whom, upon that account, the analogy, which in other writers gives occasion to a few ingenious similitudes, became the great hinge upon which every thing turned.

Source: Adam Smith, *The History of Astronomy*, in *Essays on Philosophical Subjects*, ed. W. P. D. Wightman, J. C. Bryce and I. S. Ross, Oxford 1980, pp. 33–47

1 *Metaphysics*, A985^{b}32–986^{a}6.
2 *Tusculan Disputations*, I.10.19, I.18.41.
3 Probably J. O. de La Mettrie, *Discours sur le bonheur* (1748, 1750, 1751, with different titles for substantially the same work).

FORTY-FIVE

JOHN GREGORY
The Duties and Qualifications of a Physician

While at the University of Edinburgh Gregory held the chair of the practice of physic, and delivered lectures not only on the practice but also on the practitioner. It is specifically the physician that Gregory deals with in this lecture; not the surgeon, who had at the time a different and rather lower status in society, and about whom Gregory would probably have made substantially different points regarding education and personal qualities. Gregory's primary and obvious question concerns the qualities possessed by a physician that make for best practice. His answer articulates Enlightenment values. He emphasises the intellectual virtues of the physician, declaring that no profession requires a greater compass of learning. Apart from anatomy, botany (for an understanding of the powers of herbs) and chemistry, he requires mathematics, natural history and natural philosophy (=physics). He speaks of the value of Latin, Greek and French, a value deriving at least in part from the fact that a good deal of the most important technical literature was written in Latin and French.

Gregory was concerned that his students should be aware of the extent to which the practice of medicine is as much an art as a science, dependent on educated hunches and intuitions, and not to be expounded in the form of a set of rules. Particular emphasis is given in the lecture to the moral qualities that a physician should have. Chief among them is the Roman stoic virtue of humanity, and it was no doubt with this also in mind that Gregory spoke of the importance of the knowledge of Latin for the training of the physician. Students attending the Latin class would have heard a great deal about that virtue.

The portrait of the physician painted in this lecture is of a gentle, humane, highly educated person, of discernment and good judgment, all in all the best sort of citizen, a fine representative of polite society.

A.B.

The Duties and Qualifications of a Physician

LECTURE I

Utility and dignity of the medical art. — Reasons why physicians have been sometimes exposed to ridicule. — Requisites to form the character of a physician. — Opportunities which the profession of medicine gives for the exertion of genius, and for the exercise of humanity. — Enquiry into the duties and offices of a physician. — Division of the subject. — The genius, understanding and temper required in a physician. — Difficulties attending the profession. — Command of temper, presence of mind and resolution necessary. — Moral qualities. — Humanity. — Gentleness of manners. — Flexibility. — Particular tenderness due to nervous patients. — Frequent contrast between the manners of a physician when first setting out, and when established in practice. — Obligations to discretion, secrecy and honour. — Temperance, sobriety. — Candour. — Openness to conviction.

The design of the profession which I have the honour to hold in this university, is to explain the *practice of medicine*, by which I understand, the art of preserving health, of prolonging life, and of curing diseases. This is an art of great extent and importance; and for this all your former medical studies were intended to qualify you.

But before I enter upon the particular business of this course, I shall, agreeable to custom, give some preliminary lectures, in which I shall lay before you some considerations, which though not strictly belonging to my subject, yet deserve the attention of all those who would practise medicine. – On this occasion I think it needless to dwell on the utility and dignity of the medical art. Its utility was never seriously called in question; every man who suffers pain or sickness will very gratefully acknowledge the usefulness of an art which gives him relief. People may dispute, whether physick, on the whole, does more good or harm to mankind; just as they may dispute, whether the faculty of reason, considering how it is often perverted, really contributes to make human life more or less happy; whether a vigorous constitution and an independent fortune are blessings or curses to those who possess them; whether the arts and sciences in general have proved beneficial or detrimental to mankind. – Such questions afford opportunities for the display of eloquence, and for saying plausible and ingenious things; but still nobody doubts of the real and substantial advantages attending those acquisitions, if applied to their natural and proper uses. Much wit has indeed, in all ages, been exerted upon our profession; but after all, we shall find that this ridicule has rather been employed against physicians than physick. There are some reasons for this sufficiently obvious. Physicians, considered as a body of men, who live by medicine as a profession, have an interest separate and distinct from the honour of the science. In pursuit of this interest, some have acted with candour, with honour, with the ingenuous and liberal manners of gentlemen. Conscious of their own worth, they disdained every artifice, and depended for success on their real merit. But such men are not the most numerous in any profession. Some impelled by necessity, some stimulated by vanity, and others anxious to conceal ignorance, have had recourse to various mean and unworthy arts to raise their importance among the ignorant, who are always the most numerous part of mankind. Some of these arts have been an affectation of mystery in all their writings and conversations relating to their profession; an affectation of knowledge, inscrutable to all, except the adepts in the science; an air of perfect confidence in their own skill and abilities; and a demeanor solemn, contemptuous, and highly expressive of self-sufficiency. These arts, however well they might succeed with the rest of mankind, could not escape the censure of the more judicious, nor elude the ridicule of men of wit and humour. The stage, in particular, has used freedom with the professors of the salutary art; but it is evident, that most of the satire is levelled against the particular notions, or manners of individuals, and not against the science itself.

Of the dignity of the profession I need say little. I suppose you are well satisfied that you have chosen a reputable one. Whatever may have been the pride or caprices of a few countries, it has generally been looked upon, and with good reason, as one of the most liberal. To excel in it requires a greater compass of learning than is necessary in any other. A knowledge of mathematicks, at least of the elementary parts of them, of natural history, and natural philosophy, are essentially connected with it; as well as the sciences of anatomy, botany, and chemistry, which are indeed its very foundations. There are likewise some parts of knowledge, which, though not absolutely necessary to the successful practice of medicine, are yet so useful, that no physician who has had a regular education is found without them; such are, an acquaintance with the Latin, Greek, and French languages. If you add to this, that knowledge of men, and of manners, which a physician naturally and insensibly acquires by an extensive intercourse with mankind, I think it will evidently appear, that no profession requires a greater variety of liberal accomplishments than that of physick. This sufficiently establishes its dignity; I say, its dignity, if that is to be estimated by its real usefulness to mankind, and by the variety of talents necessary to practise it with success and reputation.

We have indeed much reason to be pleased with the honourable point of view in which our profession is regarded in every part of the British dominions. They who have seen in how contemptible a light some of its branches are considered in other countries of Europe, will feel more sensibly the just regard paid to them here. One happy consequence, among many others, which results from this, is, that gentlemen of the best families, distinguished for their spirit and their genius, often apply to the study of medicine; and the liberal and ingenuous manners, generally found in men well born and genteelly educated, reflect an additional dignity on the profession.

Besides the general consideration of the utility and dignity of the science of medicine, it may be considered in two different views.

In the first place, as presenting a very ample field for the exertion of genius. – The great extent of the subject, and a variety of causes, which I shall afterwards endeavour to explain, have left it imperfect in many of its parts; and indeed there are some in it hitherto unexplored.

In the second place, medicine presents a no less extensive field for the exercise of humanity. A physician has numberless opportunities of giving that relief to distress, which is not to be purchased by the wealth of India. This, to a benevolent mind, must be one of the greatest pleasures. But besides the good which a physician has it often in his power to do, in consequence of skill in his profession, there are many occasions that call for his assistance as a man, as a man who feels for the misfortunes of his fellow-creatures. In this respect he has many opportunities of displaying patience, good-nature, generosity, compassion, and all the gentler virtues that do honour to human nature. The faculty has often been reproached with hardness of heart, occasioned, as is supposed, by their being so much conversant with human misery. I hope and believe the charge is unjust: for habit may beget a command of temper, and a seeming composure which is often mistaken for absolute insensibility. But, by the way, I must observe, that when this insensibility is real, it is a misfortune to a physician, as it deprives him of one of the most natural and powerful incitements to exert himself for the relief of his patient. On the other hand, a physician of too much sensibility may be rendered incapable of doing his duty from anxiety and excess of sympathy, which cloud his understanding, depress his spirit, and prevent him from acting with that steadiness and vigour, upon which perhaps the life of his patient in a great measure depends.

This naturally leads me to make some observations on the duties and office of a physician; a subject of great importance, but perhaps of so delicate a nature as makes it difficult for one of the profession to treat of it with proper freedom. I shall, however, attempt to do it, without any reserve. The difficulty of treating this subject in such a manner as to give no offence arises from hence, that medicine may be considered either as an art the most beneficial and important to mankind, or as a trade by which a considerable body of men gain their subsistence. These two views, though distinct, are far from being incompatible, though in fact they are too often made so. I shall endeavour to set this matter in such a light as may shew that the system of conduct in a physician, which tends most to the advancement of his art, is such as will most effectually maintain the true dignity and honour of the profession, and even promote the private interest of such of its members as are men of real capacity and merit. I am under less apprehension of discussing this subject before gentlemen at your time of life, than if you were further advanced in years. Youth indeed is the season when every sentiment of liberty, of generosity, and of candour, most easily find their way to the heart. If they do not reach it then, they never will afterwards. Age may improve the understanding by accessions of knowledge and experience; whilst at the same time that warmth of temper and imagination, which so often mislead the judgment, gradually abate. But it unfortunately happens, that this very circumstance attending the decline of life, which in some respects improves the understanding, in others throws a damp upon genius, checks the ardent pursuit of science and truth, and shuts the heart against every manly, enlarged, and generous sentiment.

In the prosecution of this subject, I shall, in the first place, consider, what kind of genius, understanding and temper naturally fit a man for being a physician. – In the second place, what are the moral qualities to be expected from him in the exercise of his profession, viz. the obligation to humanity, patience, attention, discretion, secrecy, and honour, which he lies under to his patients. – In the third place, I shall take notice of the decorums and attentions peculiarly incumbent on him as a physician, and which tend most effectually to support the dignity of the profession; as likewise the general propriety of his manners, his behaviour to his patients, to his brethren, to surgeons, and to apothecaries. – In the fourth place, I shall particularly describe that course of education which is necessary for qualifying a physician to practise with success and reputation; and shall, at the same time, mention those ornamental qualifications expected from the physician as a gentleman of a liberal education, and without which it is difficult to support the honour and rank of the profession.

I begin with an enquiry into the genius, understanding, and temper, which naturally fit a man for being a physician.

Perhaps no profession requires so comprehensive a mind as medicine. In the other learned professions, considered as sciences, there is a certain established standard, certain fixed laws and statutes, to which every question must constantly refer, and by which it must be determined. A knowledge of this established authority may be attained by assiduous application and a good memory. There is little room left for the display of genius, where invention cannot add, nor judgment improve; because the established laws, whether right or wrong, must be submitted to. The only exercise for ingenuity, is in cases where it does not clearly appear what the laws are. But even then, as disputable points must be referred to the determination of judges, whose opinions, being formed from various circumstantial combinations, frequently differ, there is no criterion by which the ingenious reasoner can be judged; and his conclusions, whether well or ill drawn, must still remain undecided. The case is very different in medicine. There we have no established authority to which we can refer in doubtful cases. Every physician must rest on his own judgment, which appeals for its rectitude to nature and experience alone. Among the infinite variety of facts and theories with which his memory has been filled in the course of a liberal education, it is his business to make a judicious separation between those founded in nature and experience, and those which owe their birth to ignorance, fraud, or the capricious systems of a heated and deluded imagination. He will likewise find it necessary to distinguish between important facts, and such as, though they may be founded in truth, are notwithstanding trivial or utterly useless to the main ends of his profession. Supposing all these difficulties surmounted, he will find it no easy matter to apply his knowledge to practice. In teaching a system of the practice of physick, every disease must be considered separately, and as existing by itself; but in fact diseases are found complicated in endless varieties, which no system, has hitherto been able to comprehend. This occasions an embarrassment to a young practitioner, which nothing can remove but a habit of nice discernment, a quickness of apprehension which enables him to perceive real analogies, and, what is rarely united with this, a solidity of judgment, which secures him from being deceived by imaginary ones. A student of much fancy and some learning has no idea of this difficulty. In the pride of his heart he fancies every disease must fly before him; he thinks he not only knows the proximate causes and indications of cure in all distempers, but a variety of remedies that will exactly answer them. It will be unfortunate however for his patients, if a little experience does not humble this pride, and satisfy him that in many cases he neither knows the proximate causes nor the indications of cure, nor how to fulfil these indications when he does know them; or shew him, what is equally humiliating, that the indications are different and contradictory. In this situation his boasted science must stoop, perhaps, for some time to be an idle spectator, or to palliate the violence of particular symptoms, or to proceed with the utmost fear and diffidence, with such lights as he can receive from a precarious analogy. Such are the difficulties which a physician has to encounter in his early practice; to conquer which is required, besides the qualifications of a proper education, the concurrence of a penetrating genius, and a clear solid judgment; and, in many cases, of a quickness of apprehension, instantaneously to perceive where the greatest probability of success lies, and resolution to act accordingly.

But although a physician should possess that enlarged medical genius, which I have just now described, yet talents of another kind are also requisite. A physician has not only for an object, the improvement of his own mind, but he must study the temper, and struggle with the prejudices of his patient, of the relations, and of the world in general; nay, he must guard himself against the ill offices of those, whose interest interferes with his; and it unfortunately happens, that the only judges of his medical merit, are those who have sinister views in concealing or depreciating it. Hence appears the necessity of a physician's having a large share of good sense, and knowledge of the world, as well as a medical genius and learning.

Such are the genius and talents required in a physician; but a certain command of the temper and passions, either natural or acquired, must be added, in order to give them their full advantage. Sudden emergencies occur in practice, and diseases often take unexpected turns, which are apt to flutter the spirits of a man of lively parts and a warm temper. Accidents of this kind may affect his judgment in such a manner as to unfit him for discerning what is proper to be done, or if he does perceive it, may nevertheless render him irresolute. Yet such occasions call for the quickest discernment, and the steadiest and most resolute conduct; and the more, as the sick so readily take the alarm, when they discover any diffidence in their physician. The weaknesses too and bad behaviour of patients, and a number of little difficulties and contradictions which every physician must encounter in his practice, are apt to ruffle his temper, and consequently to cloud his judgment, and make him forget propriety and decency of behaviour. Hence appears the advantage of a physician's possessing presence of mind, composure, steadiness, and an appearance of resolution, even in cases where, in his own judgment, he is fully sensible of the difficulty.

I come now to mention the moral qualities peculiarly required in the character of a physician. The chief of these is humanity; that sensibility of heart which makes us feel for the distresses of our fellow-creatures, and which of consequence incites us in the most powerful manner to relieve them. Sympathy produces an anxious attention to a thousand little circumstances that may tend to relieve the patient; an attention which money can never purchase: hence the inexpressible comfort of having a friend for a physician. Sympathy naturally engages the affection and confidence of a patient, which in many cases is of the utmost consequence to his recovery. If the physician possesses gentleness of manners, and a compassionate heart, and what Shakespeare so emphatically calls 'the milk of human kindness,' the patient feels his approach like that of a guardian angel ministering to his relief: while every visit of a physician who is unfeeling, and rough in his manners, makes his heart sink within him, as at the presence of one, who comes to pronounce his doom. Men of the most compassionate tempers, by being daily conversant with scenes of distress, acquire in process of time that composure and firmness of mind so necessary in the practice of physick. They can feel whatever is amiable in pity, without suffering it to enervate or unman them. Such physicians as are callous to sentiments of humanity, treat this sympathy with ridicule, and represent it either as hypocrisy, or the indication of a feeble mind. That sympathy is often affected, I am afraid is true; but this affectation may be easily seen through. Real sympathy is never ostentatious; on the contrary, it rather strives to conceal itself. But what most effectually detects this hypocrisy, is a physician's different manner of behaving to people in high and people in low life; to those who reward him handsomely, and those who have not the means to do it. A generous and elevated mind is even more shy in expressing sympathy with those of high rank, than with those in humbler life; being jealous of the unworthy construction so usually annexed to it. – The insinuation that a compassionate and feeling heart is commonly accompanied with a weak understanding and feeble mind, is malignant and false. Experience demonstrates, that a gentle and humane temper, so far from being inconsistent with vigour of mind, is its usual attendant; and that rough and blustering manners generally accompany a weak understanding and a mean soul, and are indeed frequently affected by men void of magnanimity and personal courage, in order to conceal their natural defects.

There is a species of good-humour different from the sympathy I have been speaking of, which is likewise amiable in a physician. It consists in a certain gentleness and flexibility, which makes him suffer with patience, and even apparent cheerfulness, the many contradictions and disappointments he is subjected to in his practice. If he is rigid and too minute in his directions about regimen, he may be assured they will not be strictly followed; and if he is severe in his manners, the deviations from his rules will as certainly be concealed from him. The consequence is, that he is kept in ignorance of the true state of his patient; he ascribes to the consequences of the disease, what is merely owing to irregularities in diet, and attributes effects to medicines which were perhaps never taken. The errors which in this way he may be led into, are sufficiently obvious, and might easily be prevented by a prudent relaxation of rules that could not well be obeyed. The government of a physician over his patient should undoubtedly be great, but an absolute government very few patients will submit to. A prudent physician should therefore prescribe such laws, as, though not the best, are yet the best that will be observed; of different evils he should chuse the least, and, at no rate, lose the confidence of his patient, so as to be deceived by him as to his true situation. This indulgence, however, which I am pleading for, must be managed with judgment and discretion; as it is very necessary that a physician should support a proper dignity and authority with his patients, for their sakes as well as his own.

There is a numerous class of patients who put a physician's good-nature and patience to a severe trial; those I mean who suffer under nervous ailments. Although the fears of these patients are generally groundless, yet their sufferings are real; and the disease is as much seated in the constitution as a rheumatism or a dropsy. To treat their complaints with ridicule or neglect, from supposing them the effect of a crazy imagination, is equally cruel and absurd. They generally arise from, or are attended with bodily disorders, obvious enough; but supposing them otherwise, still it is the physician's duty to do every thing in his power for the relief of the distressed. Disorders of the imagination may be as properly the object of a physician's attention as those of the body; and surely they are, frequently, of all distresses the greatest, and demand the most tender sympathy; but it requires address and good sense in a physician to manage them properly. If he seems to treat them slightly, or with unseasonable mirth, the patient is hurt beyond measure; if he is too anxiously attentive to every little circumstance, he feeds the disease. For the patient's sake therefore, as well as his own, he must endeavour to strike the medium between negligence and ridicule on the one hand, and too much solicitude about every trifling symptom on the other. He may sometimes divert the mind, without seeming to intend it, from its present sufferings, and from its melancholy prospects of the future, by insensibly introducing subjects that are amusing or interesting; and sometimes he may successfully employ a delicate and good-natured pleasantry.

We sometimes see a remarkable difference between the behaviour of a physician at his first setting out, and afterwards when he is fully established in reputation and practice. In the beginning he is affable, polite, humane, and assiduously attentive to his patients; but afterwards, when he has reaped the fruits of such a behaviour, and finds himself independent, he assumes a very different tone; he becomes haughty, rapacious, careless, and often somewhat brutal in his manners. Conscious of the ascendency he has acquired, he acts a despotic part, and takes a most ungenerous advantage of the confidence which people have in his abilities.

A physician, by the nature of his profession, has many opportunities of knowing the private characters and concerns of the families in which he is employed. Besides what he may learn from his own observation, he is often admitted to the confidence of those, who perhaps think they owe their life to his care. He sees people in the most disadvantageous circumstances, very different from those in which the world views them; – oppressed with pain, sickness, and low spirits. In these humiliating situations, instead of wonted chearfulness, evenness of temper, and vigour of mind, he meets with peevishness, impatience, and timidity. Hence it appears how much the characters of individuals, and the credit of families, may sometimes depend on the discretion, secrecy, and honour of a physician. Secrecy is particularly requisite where women are concerned. Independent of the peculiar tenderness with which a woman's character should be treated, there are certain circumstances of health, which, though in no respect connected with her reputation, every woman, from the natural delicacy of her sex, is anxious to conceal; and, in some cases, the concealment of these circumstances may be of consequence to her health, her interest, and to her happiness.

Temperance and sobriety are virtues peculiarly required in a physician. In the course of an extensive practice, difficult cases frequently occur, which demand the most vigorous exertion of memory and judgment. I have heard it said of some eminent physicians, that they prescribed as justly when intoxicated as when sober. If there was any truth in this report, it contained a severe reflection against their abilities in their profession. It shewed they practised by rote, or prescribed for some of the more obvious symptoms, without attending to those nice peculiar circumstances, a knowledge of which constitutes the great difference between a physician who has genius, and one who has none. Intoxication implies a defect in the memory and judgment; it implies confusion of ideas, perplexity and unsteadiness; and must therefore unfit a man for every business that requires the lively and vigorous use of his understanding.

I may reckon among the moral duties incumbent on a physician, that candor, which makes him open to conviction, and ready to acknowledge and rectify his mistakes. An obstinate adherence to an unsuccessful method of treating a disease, must be owing to a high degree of self-conceit, and a belief of the infallibility of a system. This error is the more difficult to cure, as it generally proceeds from ignorance. True knowledge and clear discernment may lead one into the extreme of diffidence and humility, but are inconsistent with self-conceit. It sometimes happens too, that this obstinacy proceeds from a defect in the heart. Such physicians see that they are wrong, but are too proud to acknowledge their error, especially if it is pointed out to them by one of the profession. To this species of pride, a pride incompatible with true dignity and elevation of mind, have the lives of thousands been sacrificed.

Source: John Gregory, *Lectures on the Duties and Qualifications of a Physician*, London 1772, Lecture I, pp. 1–29

FORTY-SIX

WILLIAM SMELLIE
Animal, Vegetable and Mineral

Natural history, the history of nature, covered the study of minerals, plants and animals. In the seventeenth and eighteenth centuries the subject made considerable progress, and had a large following, partly because of the greatly increased quantity of information that reached the West as a result of European expansion into the Americas, Asia and Polynesia. In particular, many new species of plants and animals were brought back, and prompted scientific questions concerning the relation of new species to familiar ones. The greatest classifier of all was the Swedish botanist Carolus Linnaeus (1707–78), whose *Systema naturae* (1735) is criticised in the following passage from William Smellie's *Philosophy of Natural History*.

For much of his career William Smellie was interested in natural history, in his early twenties giving papers on botanical topics to the Edinburgh Newtonian Society and later, as editor of the first edition (1768–71) of the *Encyclopaedia Britannica*, providing ample space for articles on natural history. The present excerpt deals principally with the question whether there is a reliable way to distinguish between minerals, plants and animals: are there qualities that all plants possess that no mineral possesses, and are there likewise qualities possessed by all animals that no plant possesses? Smellie held that plant life shades imperceptibly into animal, whereas there is a clear gap between minerals and plants.

A.B.

Distinguishing Characters of Animals, Plants, and Minerals — The Analogies between the plant and animal, arising from their structure and organs, their growth and nourishment, their dissemination and decay

Natural bodies, when viewed as they have a relation to man, are marked with characters so apparent, that they escape not the observation of the most unenlightened minds. In a system where all the constituent parts have a reciprocal dependence, and are connected by relations so subtile as to elude the perception of animals, such obvious characters were indispensible. Without them, neither the affairs of human life, nor the functions of the brute creation, could be carried on. Characters of this kind are accommodated to the apprehension of brutes and of vulgar men.

But, when the productions of nature are more closely examined; when they are scrutinized by the eye of philosophy, the number of their relations and differences is discovered to be almost infinite; and their shades of discrimination are often so delicate, that no sense can perceive them. Nothing, apparently, is more easy than to distinguish an animal from a plant; and yet the proper distinction has puzzled the most acute inquirers, and perhaps exceeds the limits of human capacity.

'A plant,' says Jungius, 'is a *living*, but not a *sentient* body, which is fixed in a determined place, and grows, increases in size, and propagates its species.' In this definition living powers are ascribed to vegetables; but they are denied the faculty of sensation. Life, without some degree of sensation, is an incomprehensible idea. An animal limited to the sense of feeling alone, is the lowest conception we can form of life. Deprive this being of the only sense it possesses, and, though its figure should remain, we would instantly conclude it to be as inanimate as a stone. The life attributed to plants seems to be nothing more than an analogical deduction from their growth, nutrition, continuation of their species, and similar circumstances.

Ludwig defines vegetables to be 'Natural bodies, always endowed with the same form, but deprived of the power of local motion.' Every branch of this definition is, with equal propriety, applicable to precious stones, salts, and some animals; and, therefore, requires no farther attention.

Sir Charles Linnaeus, in his Fundamenta Botanica, intends to discriminate the three kingdoms of Nature in two lines. 'Stones,' says he, '*grow;* vegetables grow and *live;* animals grow, live, and *feel.*' This is an assemblage of words, the meaning of which is entirely perverted. The idea of growth implies nutrition and expansion by the intervention of organs. The magnitude of stones may be augmented by an accretion of new matter. But this is not growth, or expansion of parts. The second definition, 'That vegetables grow and *live,*' is equally inaccurate. Instead of proving the life of plants, Linnaeus takes it for granted, and makes it the characteristic between vegetables and brute matter. The third, 'That animals grow, live, and *feel,*' is not less exceptionable. Growth, life, and mere sensation, convey the most ignoble notions of animated beings. From this definition, we would be led to imagine, that Linnaeus meant to describe the condition of a polypus or an oyster. All animals, it is true, grow, live, and feel: but these are only the passive properties of animals. The definition includes none of those instinctive, intellectual, and active powers which exalt ihe animal above the vegetable, and so eminently distinguish the different tribes from each other.

These and many other abortive attempts have been made to ascertain the precise boundaries between the animal and vegetable. Definitions have been the perpetual aim of most writers on this subject. But definitions, when applied to natural objects, must always be vague and elusory. We know not the principle of animal life. We are equally ignorant of the essential cause of vegetable existence. It is vain, therefore, to dream of being able to define what we never can know. We may, however, discover some qualities common to the animal as well as to the vegetable.

Sensation, motion, and structure of parts, give animals a more extensive range in their connection with external objects. A certain portion of intellect, joined to the vital principle, seem to be the most distinguishing properties of animals, and to constitute their essence or being. Animals will, determine, act, and have a communication with distant objects by their senses. They have the laws of nature, in some measure, at command. They protect themselves from injury by employing force, swiftness, address, and cunning. But vegetables remain fixed in the same place, and are subject to every thing that moves. Animals eat at intervals; their food requires time for digestion, and to answer the complicated purposes of secretion and nutrition. The structure of plants is more simple: They receive perpetual nourishment without injury. Animals search for and select particular kinds of food. But plants must receive whatever is brought to them by the different elements. Animals exist on the surface and in the interior parts of the earth, in the air, in water, in the bodies of men and other animals, in the internal parts of plants, and even in stones. But, if we except a few aquatics, plants are fixed to the earth by roots.

All animals, it has been affirmed, have a heart, or particular fountain for propelling and distributing their fluids to the different parts of their bodies: But caterpillars, and many other insects, have no such general receptacle.

The loco-motive faculty has been considered as peculiar to animals. But even this character is extremely suspicious. Oysters, sea-nettles, the gall-insects, and a variety of other animals, can hardly be said to enjoy the power of local motion. Many species remain for ever fixed to the rocks on which they are produced, and have no motion but that of extending or contracting their bodies. Besides, examples of different kinds of motion are discoverable in the vegetable kingdom. When the roots of a tree meet with a stone, or any other obstruction to their motion, in order to avoid it, they change their former direction. They turn from barren to fertile earth, which indicates something analogous to a selection of food. Like the polypus, plants, when confined in a house, uniformly bend toward the window or aperture through which the rays of light are introduced.

The sensitive plant possesses the faculty of motion in an eminent degree. The slightest touch makes its leaves suddenly shrink, and, together with the branch, bend down toward the earth. But the moving plant, or hedysarum movens, of which there are specimens in the botanic garden of Edinburgh, furnishes the most astonishing example of vegetable motion. It is a native of the East Indies. Its movements are not excited by the contact of external bodies, but solely by the influence of the sun's rays. The motions of this plant are confined to the leaves, which are supported by long flexible foot-stalks. When the sun shines, the leaves move briskly in every direction. Their general motion, however, is upward and downward: But they not unfrequently turn almost round; and then their foot-stalks are evidently twisted. These motions go on incessantly as long as the heat of the sun continues: But they cease during the night, and when the weather is cold and cloudy. Our wonder is excited by the rapidity and constancy of the movements peculiar to this plant. The frequency, however, of similar motions in other plants, renders it probable that the leaves of all vegetables move, or are agitated by the rays of the sun, though many of these movements are too slow for our perception.

The American plant called *dionaea muscipula*, or *Venus's fly-trap*, affords another instance of rapid vegetable motion. Its leaves are jointed, and furnished with two rows of strong prickles. Their surfaces are covered with a number of minute glands, which secrete a sweet liquor, and allure the approach of flies. When these parts are touched by the legs of a fly, the two lobes of the leaf instantly rise up, the rows of prickles lock themselves fast together, and squeeze the unwary animal to death. If a straw or a pin be introduced between the lobes, the same motions are excited.

When a seed is sown in a reversed position, the young root turns downward to enter the earth, and the stem bends upward into the air. Confine a young stem to an inclined position, and its extremity will soon assume its former perpendicular direction. Twist the branches of any tree in such a manner that the inferior surfaces of the leaves are turned toward the sky, and you will, in a short time, perceive that all these leaves resume their original position. These motions are performed sooner or later, in proportion to the degree of heat, and the flexibility of the leaves. Many leaves, as those of the mallow, follow the course of the sun. In the morning, their superior surfaces are presented to the east; at noon, they regard the south; and, when the sun sets, they are directed to the west. During the night, or in rainy weather, these leaves are horizontal; and their inferior surfaces are turned toward the earth.

What has been denominated the Sleep of Plants, affords an instance of another species of vegetable motion. The leaves of many plants fold up during the night; but, at the approach of the sun, they expand with renewed vigour. The common appearances of most vegetables are so changed in the night, that it is difficult to recognize the different kinds, even by the assistance of light.

The modes of folding in the leaves, or of sleeping, are extremely various. But it is worthy of remark, that they all dispose themselves so as to give the best protection to the young stems, flowers, buds, or fruit. The leaves of the tamarind-tree contract round the tender fruit, and protect it from the nocturnal cold. The cassia or senna, the glycine, and many of the papilionaceous plants, contract their leaves in a similar manner. The leaves of the chickweed, of the asclepias, atriplex, &c. are disposed in opposite pairs. During the night, they rise perpendicularly, and join so close at the top, that they conceal the flowers. The leaves of the sida or althaea Theophrasti, of the ayenia, and oenothera, are placed alternately.

Though horizontal, or even depending, during the day, at the approach of night they rise, embrace the stem, and protect the tender flowers. The leaves of the solanum, or nightshade, are horizontal during the day; but, in the night, they rise and cover the flowers. The Egyptian vetch erects its leaves during the night, in such a manner that each pair seem to be one leaf only. The leaves of the white lupine, in the state of sleep, hang down, and protect the young buds from being injured by the nocturnal air.

These and similar motions are not peculiar to the leaves of plants. The flowers have also the power of moving. During the night, many of them are inclosed in their calixes. Some flowers, as those of the German spurge, geranium striatum, and common whitlow grass, when asleep, hang their mouths toward the earth, to prevent the noxious effects of rain or dew.

The cause of those movements which constitute the sleep of plants, has been ascribed to the presence or absence of the sun's rays. In some of the examples I have given, the motions produced are evidently excited by heat. But plants kept in a hot-house, where an equal degree of heat is preserved both day and night, fail not to contract their leaves, or to sleep, in the same manner as when they are exposed to the open air. This fact evinces, that the sleep of plants is rather owing to a peculiar law, than to a quicker or slower motion of their juices.

A stomach and brain have been reckoned essential characteristics of the animal; and plants are said to possess nothing analogous to these organs. But the polypus has no stomach; or rather, like vegetables, its whole body may be considered as a stomach. Its internal cavity contains no viscera; and, when this animal is turned outside in, it still continues to live, and to digest its food, in the same manner as if it had received no injury. The mode by which plants are nourished is extremely analogous. They imbibe food by the roots, the trunk, the branches, the leaves, and the flowers. Instead, therefore, of having no stomach, their whole structure is stomach. With regard to the brain, the polypus, and many other insects, are deprived of that organ. Hence neither stomach nor brain are essential characters which discriminate the animal from the vegetable.

But all animals are endowed with sensation, or at least with irritability, which last has been considered as a distinctive character of animal life. Sensation implies a distinct perception of pleasure and pain. We infer the existence of sensation in organized bodies, when we perceive that they have organs similar to our own, or when they act, in certain circumstances, in the same manner as we act. If an organized being has eyes, ears, and a nose, we naturally conclude that it enjoys the same sensations as these organs convey to us. If we see another being, whose structure exhibits nothing analogous to our organs of sensation, contracting with rapidity when touched, directing its body uniformly to the light, seizing small insects with *tentacula*, or a kind of arms, and conveying them into an aperture placed at its anterior end, we hesitate not to pronounce that it is animated. Cut off its arms, deprive it of the faculty of contracting and extending its body, the nature of this being will not be changed; but we will be unable to determine whether it possesses any portion of life. This is nearly the condition of the small sections of a polypus, before their heads begin to grow. The wheel-animal, the eels in blighted wheat, and the snails recorded in the Philosophical Transactions, afford instances of every appearance of sensation, or even of irritability, being suspended, not for months, but for several years, and yet the life of these animals is not extinguished; for they uniformly revive upon a proper application of moisture.

These and similar facts show, that we are entirely ignorant of the essence and properties of life. What life really is, seems too subtile for our understanding to conceive, or our senses to discern. If we have no other criterions to distinguish life, than motion, sensation, and irritability, the animals just mentioned continued for years in a state which every man would pronounce to have been perfectly dead. It is possible, therefore, that life may exist in many bodies which are commonly thought to be as inanimate as stones. Hence it would be rash to exclude plants from every species of sensation. The degrees of sensation decrease imperceptibly from man to the sea-nettle, gall-insects, and what are called the most imperfect animals. Every vegetable, as well as the sensitive plant, shrinks when wounded. But, in most of them, the motion is too slow for our perception. When trees grow near a ditch, the roots which proceed in a direction that would necessarily bring them into the open air, instead of continuing this noxious progress, sink below the level of the ditch, then shoot across, and regain the soil on the opposite side. When a root is uncovered, without exposing it to much heat, and a wet spunge is placed near it, but in a different direction from that in which the root is proceeding, in a short time the root turns towards the spunge. In this manner the direction of roots may be varied at pleasure. All plants make the strongest efforts, by inclining, turning, and even twisting their stems and branches, to escape from darkness and shade, and to procure the influences of the sun. Place a wet spunge under the leaves of a tree, they soon bend downward, and endeavour to apply their inferior surfaces to the spunge. If a vessel of water be placed within six inches of a growing cucumber, in twenty-four hours the cucumber alters the direction of its branches, bends either to the right or left, and never stops till it comes into contact with the water. When a pole is placed at a considerable distance from an unsupported vine, the branches of which are proceeding in a contrary direction from that of the pole, in a short time, it alters its course, and stops not till it clings around the pole.

Facts of this kind excite our wonder; but they by no means prove that vegetables live, or that they are endowed with sensation, which implies a distinct perception of pleasure and pain.

There is an inferior species of sensation, which is distinguished by the term *irritability*. This term denotes that power by which muscular fibres, even after they are detached from the body, contract upon the application of any stimulating substance, whether solid or fluid. The heart of a frog, when pricked with the point of a pin, continues to beat, or to contract and dilate, for several hours after it has been cut out of the animal's body. The heart of a viper, or of a turtle, beats distinctly from twenty to thirty hours after the death of these animals. The peristaltic motion of the intestines is produced by their irritability. When the intestines of a dog, or any other quadruped, are suddenly cut into different portions, all these portions crawl about like worms, and contract upon the slightest touch. Though irritability be unquestionably a vital principle, yet it is equally certain, that muscular fibres, when separated from the body to which they belong, have no distinct perception of pleasure or pain. Their regular contraction and dilatation are evident symptoms of life, which, in many cases, may lead us to attribute living powers to substances that enjoy neither life nor sensation. Hence, though all plants were irritable, this circumstance would not prove that they are possessed of life. The contraction and dilatation of the sensitive plants, and the various motions of the leaves, branches, flowers, and roots of vegetables formerly mentioned, seem to indicate that most plants are endowed with irritability. Perhaps all vegetables have more or less of this quality. The heart, intestines, and diaphragm, are the most irritable parts of animal bodies: And, to discover whether this quality resides in all plants, experiments should be made chiefly on their leaves, flowers, buds, and the tender fibres of the roots.

From this narration of facts, it appears, that plants make a very near approach to animals; and that this similarity, as well as the difficulty of fixing the precise boundaries by which these two great kingdoms of nature are limited, are direct consequences of the organization of vegetables. It is owing to their organic structure alone, that plants and animals are capable of affording reciprocal nourishment to each other. This organic structure, though greatly diversified in the different species of animals and vegetables, evinces that Nature, in the formation of both, has acted upon the same general plan. May we not presume, therefore, as plants as well as animals are composed of a regular system of organs, that the vegetable part of the creation is not entirely deprived of every quality which we are apt to think peculiar to animated beings? I mean not to insinuate, that plants can perceive pleasure or pain. But, as many of their motions and affections cannot be explained upon any principle of mechanism, I am inclined to think, that they originate from the power of irritability, which, though it implies not the perception of pleasure and pain, is the principle that regulates all the vital or involuntary motions of animals. To ascertain this point, would require a set of very nice experiments. I shall mention one, which might be performed with tolerable ease. It was formerly remarked, that plants kept in a hot-house, where the degree of heat is uniform, never fail to sleep during the night. This is direct evidence, that heat alone is not the cause of their vigilance. But they are deprived of light. Let, therefore, a strong artificial light, without increasing the heat, be thrown upon them. If, notwithstanding this light, the plants are not roused, but continue to sleep as usual, then it may be presumed that their organs, like those of animals, are not only irritable, but require the reparation of some invigorating influence which they have lost while awake, by the agitations of the air and the sun's rays, by the act of growing, or by some other latent cause.

It is almost unnecessary to mark the distinction between vegetables and minerals. The transition from the animal to the plant is effected by shades so imperceptible, as to elude the most acute observers. But, between the plant and the mineral, there is a vast chasm in the chain of being, which may be the source of great discoveries. In bodies purely mineral, not a vestige of organization can be discovered. The fibrous structure of the asbestos has been regarded as an approach toward organization, and as the link which connects the mineral to the vegetable kingdom. But this is one of those strained analogies which are too often employed by theoretical writers. Though the asbestos is composed of a kind of threads or fibres, these fibres are not tubular; neither are they interwoven, like that regular tissue or fabric which so remarkably distinguishes organized from brute matter. Of course, the magnitude of the asbestos can only be increased by the apposition of new matter, and not by any development or expansion of parts. But though, in the mineral kingdom, Nature ceases to organize, she continues to arrange.

The regular configuration of salts, crystals, and other precious stones, has been considered by some authors as the result of an organic process. But the uniform figure of salts and chrystals may be the effect of certain laws of attraction peculiar to each species. None of these particles can be regarded as a germ or bud. They are only the elements or constituent parts, which, when applied to each other, form a whole. They never expand or grow, like the embrios of animals or plants. They remain for ever in the same state without diminution or increase, except when separated by force, or magnified by an accumulation of fresh matter. The chrystalline juice is not assimulated by vessels: It is prepared by a chymical operation of Nature. The bodies of plants and animals are machines, exceedingly elaborate, and more or less complicated. These machines, by means of different organs, have the power of converting other animals and vegetables into their own substance. By this assimilation, all their dimensions are increased; and their various parts uniformly preserve the same proportions with regard to each other, and continue to perform their respective functions. Besides, organized bodies not only multiply their species, but some of them possess the power of reproducing such parts as are forcibly abstracted from them.

In these and many other qualities common to the animal and vegetable, there is not the smallest analogy to be found in the mineral kingdom. Between the most regular fossils, as salts and chrystals, and the most imperfect animal or vegetable, the distance is immense. Figured fossils are not more organized than a column or a portico. In the formation of the former, Nature, in that of the latter, man, is the artist. When no similarity is to be discovered in those fossils which are nearly uniform in their configuration, we are not to expect it in the more loose and irregular parts of brute matter. Here, Nature, regardless of symmetry, conjoins heterogeneous materials, of which she composes irregular masses. Many stones, flints, and other concretions, afford examples of this kind. More art, it must be acknowledged, appears in the formation of metals: But their structure exhibits no vestiges of organization.

Source: William Smellie, *The Philosophy of Natural History*, Edinburgh 1790, vol. 1, ch. 1, pp. 1–14

FORTY-SEVEN

JAMES HUTTON
Theory of the Earth

In excerpt 44 we find Adam Smith speaking about the psychological order of scientific discovery, and focusing upon the sequence: surprise, wonder, and admiration. This sequence is well exemplified in the work of Smith's friend James Hutton. Hutton was surprised at the geological facts, wondered about them, and was filled with admiration, indeed awe, at the workings of the planet once he had identified the principles of change. We noted Smith's declaration that 'Philosophy [i.e. natural science] is the science of the connecting principles of nature', and Hutton's success at establishing certain of the fundamental connecting principles of nature is measured by the extent to which he thereby established also the foundations of the modern science of geology.

He perceived the world to be always changing, yielding to the powers of wind and water, heat and cold. These natural forces produce continual processes of erosion, with particles of matter being deposited in the sea. But there must also be a reverse process, given the marine materials found in the mountains. What are the connecting principles between these phenomena? Hutton argued that the sediment reaching the seabed from the surface is consolidated by heat and uplifted and folded over by the same power. This is a continual cycle, of erosion, deposition, consolidation, elevation and folding. There is therefore nothing, or practically nothing, now to be seen of the primitive material on the surface of the Earth. World has succeeded world and this process will continue as the same forces for change continue to operate. In a famous sentence Hutton writes: 'The result, therefore, of our present enquiry is that we find no vestige of a beginning – no prospect of an end.'

In the seventeenth century, Archbishop James Ussher had calculated the age of the earth on the basis of the Bible and deduced that it was created in 4004 BC. His reckoning of the dates of biblical events came to be published in Bibles and became accepted as Gospel. It was inevitable that Hutton would come into conflict with the Church since he worked with a concept of geological time utterly at odds with Ussher's calculations. Nevertheless, as we see from the start of this excerpt, he has a theological perspective. There seems no other way to interpret the statement in the opening paragraph of the excerpt and of his magnum opus: 'We perceive a fabric, erected in wisdom, to obtain a purpose worthy of the power that is apparent in the production of it.' And some paragraphs later he refers to: 'the presence and efficacy of design and intelligence in the power that conducts the work'. Finally in this catalogue we should note his comment: 'We shall thus also be led to acknowledge an order, not unworthy of Divine wisdom, in a subject which, in another view, has appeared as the work of chance, or as absolute disorder and confusion.' These are not the words of an atheist or agnostic, but of a man who sees the marks of a divine designer in the larger structures of the world. Science does not pose a threat to religion but, on the contrary, gives all the more reason to be in awe of the creator. Hutton delivers up to us, in Adam Smith's resonant phrase, 'a more coherent, and therefore a more magnificent spectacle'.

A.B.

Theory of the Earth –
Prospect of the Subject to be Treated of

When we trace the parts of which this terrestrial system is composed, and when we view the general connection of those several parts, the whole presents a machine of a peculiar construction by which it is adapted to a certain end. We perceive a fabric, erected in wisdom, to obtain a purpose worthy of the power that is apparent in the production of it.

We know little of the earth's internal parts, or of the materials which compose it at any considerable depth below the surface. But upon the surface of this globe, the more inert matter is replenished with plants, and with animal and intellectual beings.

Where so many living creatures are to ply their respective powers, in pursuing the end for which they were intended, we are not to look for nature in a quiescent state; matter itself must be in motion, and the scenes of life a continued or repeated series of agitations and events.

This globe of the earth is a habitable world; and on its fitness for this purpose, our sense of wisdom in its formation must depend. To judge of this point, we must keep in view, not only the end, but the means also by which that end is obtained. These are, the form of the whole, the materials of which it is composed, and the several powers which concur, counteract, or balance one another, in procuring the general result.

The form and constitution of the mass are not more evidently calculated for the purpose of this earth as a habitable world, than are the various substances of which that complicated body is composed. Soft and hard parts variously combine to form a medium consistence, adapted to the use of plants and animals; wet and dry are properly mixed for nutrition, or the support of those growing bodies; and hot and cold produce a temperature or climate no less required than a soil: Insomuch, that there is not any particular, respecting either the qualities of the materials, or the construction of the machine, more obvious to our perception, than are the presence and efficacy of design and intelligence in the power that conducts the work.

In taking this view of things, where ends and means are made the object of attention, we may hope to find a principle upon which the comparative importance of parts in the system of nature may be estimated, and also a rule for selecting the object of our inquiries. Under this direction, science may find a fit subject of investigation in every particular, whether of *form*, *quality*, or *active power*, that presents itself in this system of motion and of life; and which, without a proper attention to this character of the system, might appear anomalous and incomprehensible.

It is not only by seeing those general operations of the globe which depend upon its peculiar construction as a machine, but also by perceiving how far the particulars, in the construction of that machine, depend upon the general operations of the globe, that we are enabled to understand the constitution of this earth as a thing formed by design. We shall thus also be led to acknowledge an order, not unworthy of Divine wisdom, in a subject which, in another view, has appeared as the work of chance, or as absolute disorder and confusion.

To acquire a general or comprehensive view of this mechanism of the globe, by which it is adapted to the purpose of being a habitable world, it is necessary to distinguish three different bodies which compose the whole. These are, a solid body of earth, an aqueous body of sea, and an elastic fluid of air.

It is the proper shape and disposition of these three bodies that form this globe into a habitable world; and it is the manner in which these constituent bodies are adjusted to each other, and the laws of action by which they are maintained in their proper qualities and respective departments, that form the Theory of the machine which we are now to examine.

Let us begin with some general sketch of the particulars now mentioned.

First, There is a central body in the globe. This body supports those parts which come to be more immediately exposed to our view, or which may be examined by our sense and observation. This first part is commonly supposed to be solid and inert; but such a conclusion is only mere conjecture; and we shall afterwards find occasion, perhaps, to form another judgment in relation to this subject, after we have examined strictly, upon scientific principles, what appears upon the surface, and have formed conclusions concerning that which must have been transacted in some more central part.

Secondly, We find a fluid body of water. This, by gravitation, is reduced to a spherical form, and by the centrifugal force of the earth's rotation, is become oblate. The purpose of this fluid body is essential in the constitution of the world; for, besides affording the means of life and motion to a multifarious race of animals, it is the source of growth and circulation to the organized bodies of this earth, in being the receptacle of the rivers, and the fountain of our vapours.

Thirdly, We have an irregular body of land raised above the level of the ocean. This, no doubt, is the smallest portion of the globe; but it is the part to us by far most interesting. It is upon the surface of this part that plants are made to grow; consequently, it is by virtue of this land that animal life, as well as vegetation, is sustained in this world.

Lastly, We have a surrounding body of atmosphere, which completes the globe. This vital fluid is no less necessary, in the constitution of the world, than are the other parts; for there is hardly an operation upon the surface of the earth, that is not conducted or promoted by its means. It is a necessary condition for the sustenance of fire; it is the breath of life to animals; it is at least an instrument in vegetation; and, while it contributes to give fertility and health to things that grow, it is employed in preventing noxious effects from such as go into corruption. In short, it is the proper means of circulation for the matter of this world, by raising up the water of the ocean, and pouring it forth upon the surface of the earth.

Such is the mechanism of the globe: Let us now mention some of those powers by which motion is produced, and activity procured to the mere machine.

First, There is the progressive force, or moving power, by which this planetary body, if solely actuated, would depart continually from the path which it now pursues, and thus be for ever removed from its end, whether as a planetary body, or as a globe sustaining plants and animals, which may be termed a living world.

But this moving body is also actuated by gravitation, which inclines it directly to the central body of the sun. Thus it is made to revolve about that luminary, and to preserve its path.

It is also upon the same principles, that each particular part upon the surface of this globe, is alternately exposed to the influence of light and darkness, in the diurnal rotation of the earth, as well as in its annual revolution. In this manner are produced the vicissitudes of night and day, so variable in the different latitudes from the equator to the pole, and so beautifully calculated to equalise the benefits of light, so variously distributed in the different regions of the globe.

Gravitation, and the *vis insita* [innate power] of matter, thus form the first two powers distinguishable in the operations of our system, and wisely adapted to the purpose for which they are employed.

We next observe the influence of light and heat, of cold and condensation. It is by means of these two powers that the various operations of this living world are more immediately transacted; although the other powers are no less required, in order to produce or modify these great agents in the economy of life, and system of our changing things.

We do not now inquire into the nature of those powers, or investigate the laws of light and heat, of cold and condensation, by which the various purposes of this world are accomplished; we are only to mention those effects which are made sensible to the common understanding of mankind, and which necessarily imply a power that is employed. Thus, it is by the operation of those powers that the varieties of season in spring and autumn are obtained, that we are blessed with the vicissitudes of summer's heat and winter's cold, and that we possess the benefit of artificial light and culinary fire.

We are thus bountifully provided with the necessaries of life; we are supplied with things conducive to the growth and preservation of our animal nature, and with fit subjects to employ and to nourish our intellectual powers.

There are other actuating powers employed in the operations of this globe, which we are little more than able to enumerate; such are those of electricity, magnetism, and subterraneous heat or mineral fire.

Powers of such magnitude or force, are not to be supposed useless in a machine contrived surely not without wisdom; but they are mentioned here chiefly on account of their general effect; and it is sufficient to have named powers, of which the actual existence is well known, but of which the proper use in the constitution of the world is still obscure. The laws of electricity and magnetism have been well examined by philosophers; but the purposes of those powers in the oeconomy of the globe have not been discovered. Subterraneous fire, again, although the most conspicuous in the operations of this world, and often examined by philosophers, is a power which has been still less understood, whether with regard to its efficient or final cause. It has hitherto appeared more like the accident of natural things, than the inherent property of the mineral region. It is in this last light, however, that I wish to exhibit it, as a great power acting a material part in the operations of the globe, and as an essential part in the constitution of this world.

We have thus surveyed the machine in general, with those

moving powers, by which its operations, diversified almost *ad infinitum*, are performed. Let us now confine our view, more particularly, to that part of the machine on which we dwell, that so we may consider the natural consequences of those operations which, being within our view, we are better qualified to examine.

This subject is important to the human race, to the possessor of this world, to the intelligent being Man, who foresees events to come, and who, in contemplating his future interest, is led to inquire concerning causes, in order that he may judge of events which otherwise he could not know.

If, in pursuing this object, we employ our skill in research, not in forming vain conjectures; and if *data* are to be found, on which Science may form just conclusions, we should not long remain in ignorance with respect to the natural history of this earth, a subject on which hitherto opinion only, and not evidence, has decided: For in no subject, perhaps, is there naturally less defect of evidence, although philosophers, led by prejudice, or misguided by false theory, may have neglected to employ that light by which they should have seen the system of this world.

But to proceed in pursuing a little farther our general or preparatory ideas. A solid body of land could not have answered the purpose of a habitable world; for, a soil is necessary to the growth of plants; and a soil is nothing but the materials collected from the destruction of the solid land. Therefore, the surface of this land, inhabited by man, and covered with plants and animals, is made by nature to decay, in dissolving from that hard and compact state in which it is found below the soil; and this soil is necessarily washed away, by the continual circulation of the water, running from the summits of the mountains towards the general receptacle of that fluid.

The heights of our land are thus levelled with the shores; our fertile plains are formed from the ruins of the mountains; and those travelling materials are still pursued by the moving water, and propelled along the inclined surface of the earth. These moveable materials, delivered into the sea, cannot, for a long continuance, rest upon the shore; for, by the agitation of the winds, the tides and currents, every moveable thing is carried farther and farther along the shelving bottom of the sea, towards the unfathomable regions of the ocean.

If the vegetable soil is thus constantly removed from the surface of the land, and if its place is thus to be supplied from the dissolution of the solid earth, as here represented, we may perceive an end to this beautiful machine; an end, arising from no error in its constitution as a world, but from that destructibility of its land which is so necessary in the system of the globe, in the economy of life and vegetation.

The immense time necessarily required for this total destruction of the land, must not be opposed to that view of future events, which is indicated by the surest facts, and most approved principles. Time, which measures every thing in our idea, and is often deficient to our schemes, is to nature endless and as nothing; it cannot limit that by which alone it had existence; and, as the natural course of time, which to us seems infinite, cannot be bounded by any operation that may have an end, the progress of things upon this globe, that is, the course of nature, cannot be limited by time, which must proceed in a continual succession. We are, therefore, to consider as inevitable the destruction of our land, so far as effected by those operations which are necessary in the purpose of the globe, considered as a habitable world; and, so far as we have not examined any other part of the economy of nature, in which other operations and a different intention might appear.

We have now considered the globe of this earth as a machine, constructed upon chemical as well as mechanical principles, by which its different parts are all adapted, in form, in quality, and in quantity, to a certain end; an end attained with certainty or success; and an end from which we may perceive wisdom, in contemplating the means employed.

But is this world to be considered thus merely as a machine, to last no longer than its parts retain their present position, their proper forms and qualities? Or may it not be also considered as an organized body? such as has a constitution in which the necessary decay of the machine is naturally repaired, in the exertion of those productive powers by which it had been formed.

This is the view in which we are now to examine the globe; to see if there be, in the constitution of this world, a reproductive operation, by which a ruined constitution may be again repaired, and a duration or stability thus procured to the machine, considered as a world sustaining plants and animals.

If no such reproductive power, or reforming operation, after due inquiry, is to be found in the constitution of this world, we should have reason to conclude, that the system of this earth has either been intentionally made imperfect, or has not been the work of infinite power and wisdom.

Here is an important question, therefore, with regard to the constitution of this globe; a question which, perhaps, it is in the power of man's sagacity to resolve; and a question which, if satisfactorily resolved, might add some lustre to science and the human intellect.

Animated with this great, this interesting view, let us strictly examine our principles, in order to avoid fallacy in our reasoning; and let us endeavour to support our attention, in developing a subject that is vast in its extent, as well as intricate in the relation of parts to be stated.

The globe of this earth is evidently made for man. He alone, of all the beings which have life upon this body, enjoys the whole and every part; he alone is capable of knowing the nature of this world, which he thus possesses in virtue of his proper right; and he alone can make the knowledge of this system a source of pleasure, and the means of happiness.

Man alone, of all the animated beings which enjoy the benefits of this earth, employs the knowledge which he there receives, in leading him to judge of the intention of things, as well as of the means by which they are brought about; and he alone is thus made to enjoy, in contemplation as well as sensual pleasure, all the good that may be observed in the constitution of this world; he, therefore, should be made the first subject of inquiry.

Now, if we are to take the written history of man for the rule by which we should judge of the time when the species first began, that period would be but little removed from the present state of things. The Mosaic history places this beginning of man at no great distance; and there has not been found, in natural history, any document by which a high antiquity might be attributed to the human race. But this is not the case with regard to the inferior species of animals, particularly those which inhabit the ocean and its shores. We find, in natural history, monuments which prove that those animals had long existed; and we thus procure a measure for the computation of a period of time extremely remote, though far from being precisely ascertained.

In examining things present, we have data from which to reason with regard to what has been; and, from what has actually been, we have data for concluding with regard to that which is to happen hereafter. Therefore, upon the supposition that the operations of nature are equable and steady, we find, in natural appearances, means for concluding a certain portion of time to have necessarily elapsed, in the production of those events of which we see the effects.

It is thus that, in finding the relics of sea-animals of every kind in the solid body of our earth, a natural history of those animals is formed, which includes a certain portion of time; and, for the ascertaining this portion of time, we must again have recourse to the regular operations of this world. We shall thus arrive at facts which indicate a period to which no other species of chronology is able to remount.

In what follows, therefore, we are to examine the construction of the present earth, in order to understand the natural operations of time past; to acquire principles, by which we may conclude with regard to the future course of things, or judge of those operations, by which a world, so wisely ordered, goes into decay; and to learn, by what means such a decayed world may be renovated, or the waste of habitable land upon the globe repaired.

This, therefore, is the object which we are to have in view during this physical investigation; this is the end to which are to be directed all the steps in our cosmological pursuit.

Source: James Hutton, *Theory of the Earth with Proofs and Illustrations*, Edinburgh 1795, reprinted Codicote 1959, ch. 1, pp. 3–20

FORTY-EIGHT

COLIN MACLAURIN
Newtonian Science

Newton's natural philosophy (=physics) was quickly taken up in Scotland, with Colin Maclaurin, a friend of Newton's, working to spread knowledge of Newtonianism. In this excerpt we find a brief exposition of Newton's scientific method. The method has two parts: first an investigation of natural events considered as effects, with a view to determining their causes, till we reach the most general cause; and secondly the deployment of that most general cause in an explanation of particular natural events. The moves are therefore from the particular to the general, thus establishing the general, and then from the general to the particular, thus confirming the general. The first part of the method was termed the analysis, and the second the synthesis. Newton, starting from particular events in the world, such as the falling of heavy objects, and the motion of the planets, argued his way to the law of gravity, and from that law was able to predict the motions of other bodies. Maclaurin's emphasis in his exposition is on the weakness of the chief alternative method, which had been commonly employed before Newton, and consisted in the process of synthesis only. The problem with this method, one which Maclaurin thought especially beset Descartes' scientific work, was that it involves employing a starting point which has not itself been established on the basis of any scientific procedure. It starts therefore with conjecture not with knowledge, and can never rise above conjecture.

A.B.

A general view of Sir Isaac Newton's method, and of his account of the system of the world

1. To describe the *phenomena* of nature, to explain their causes, to trace the relations and dependencies of those causes, and to enquire into the whole constitution of the universe, is the business of natural philosophy. A strong curiosity has prompted men in all times to study nature; every useful art has some connexion with this science; and the unexhausted beauty and variety of things makes it ever agreeable, new and surprizing.

But natural philosophy is subservient to purposes of a higher kind, and is chiefly to be valued as it lays a sure foundation for natural religion and moral philosophy; by leading us, in a satisfactory manner, to the knowledge of the Author and Governor of the universe. To study nature is to search into his workmanship: every new discovery opens to us a new part of his scheme. And while we still meet, in our enquiries, with hints of greater things yet undiscovered, the mind is kept in a pleasing expectation of making a further progress; acquiring at the same time higher conceptions of that great Being, whose works are so various and hard to be comprehended.

Our views of nature, however imperfect, serve to represent to us, in the most sensible manner, that mighty power which prevails throughout, acting with a force and efficacy that appears to suffer no diminution from the greatest distances of space or intervals of time; and that wisdom which we see equally displayed in the exquisite structure and just motions of the greatest and subtilest parts. These, with perfect *goodness*, by which they are evidently directed, constitute the supreme object of the speculations of a philosopher; who, while he contemplates and admires so excellent a system, cannot but be himself excited and animated to correspond with the general harmony of nature.

In order to obtain those great purposes, we must not proceed hastily in our enquiries, but with the utmost caution. False schemes of natural philosophy may lead to atheism, or suggest opinions, concerning the Deity and the universe, of most dangerous consequence to mankind; and have been frequently employed to support such opinions. We have the more reason to be on our guard, because philosophers have, on many occasions, shown an unaccountable disposition to give into extravagant fictions in their accounts of nature. A considerable party adopted, of old, that monstrous system, which, excluding the influences of a Deity, attempted to explain the formation of the universe from the accidental play of atoms, and derived the ineffable beauty of things, even life and thought itself, from a lucky hit in the blind uproar. An horror at the dire effects of superstition may have induced them to have recourse to a doctrine so opposite to common sense and reason; but we have not even this excuse to offer in defence of some modern philosophers of great name, who seem to have copied too much after those masters, in their mechanical accounts of the production of the material system.

While we guard against atheism and opinions that approach towards it, we ought likewise to beware of listening to superstition; which discourages enquiries into nature, lest, by having our views enlarged, we should escape from her bonds, and our discoveries should weaken some darling tenets. If those tenets are true, they will rather be confirmed by our enquiries; and if they are false, surely it is better they should be detected. We may pursue truth steadily, secure that it will be always found consistent with itself, and stand in no need of the jealousies and dark suspicions of the superstitious to support it; in whose hands truth itself is apt to suffer, by the base alloy they mix with it, and by the detested means which they have too often employed to maintain so incongruous a union. The philosophers who have been devoted to so mean views, have never failed to expose themselves to just ridicule, without doing service to the cause which they espoused. *Cosmas Indopleustes* of old, misled by an injudicious zeal, compiled a system of nature from some expressions in the sacred writings; which, against the constant and universal use of language, he would needs understand in the most literal and the very strictest sense.

The earth therefore, according to him, was not globular, but an immense plane of a greater length than breadth, environed by an unpassable ocean. He placed a huge mountain towards the north, around which the sun and stars performed their diurnal revolutions; and from the conical shape which he ascribed to it, with the oblique motion of the sun, he accounted for the inequality of the days and the variation of the seasons. The vault of heaven lean'd upon the earth extended beyond the ocean, being likewise supported by two vast columns: beneath the arch, angels conducted the stars in their various motions. Above it were the celestial waters, and above all he placed the supreme heavens. However absurd the conceits of this author, who wrote in darker times, may appear, we have a more inexcusable instance, in the last century, of the same kind, in what *Kircher* calls his Ecstatic Voyage to the Planets; who, after many great discoveries had been made concerning the celestial bodies, produced nothing worthy of so noble a subject, or of his own extensive learning and invention, having determined to make a sacrifice of both to certain decrees of the church of Rome: he descends even so low as to adopt the folly, or rather impiety, of astrologers, in deriving the good or evil that happens to man from the propitious or malignant influences of planets. True religion requires no such sacrifices; nor are its interests advanced by feigning philosophical systems purposely to favour it: for when we afterwards find these to be ill-grounded, we may be in danger of falling into scepticism.

An entire liberty must be allowed in our enquiries, that natural philosophy may become subservient to the most valuable purposes, and acquire all the certainty and perfection of which it is capable: but we ought not to abuse this liberty by *supposing* instead of *enquiring*, and by imagining systems, instead of learning from observation and experience the true constitution of things. Speculative men, by the force of genius, may invent systems that will perhaps be greatly admired for a time; these however are phantoms which the force of truth will sooner or later dispell: and while we are pleas'd with the deceit, true philosophy, with all the arts and improvements that depend upon it, suffers. The real state of things escapes our observation: or, if it presents itself to us, we are apt either to reject it wholly as fiction, or, by new efforts of a vain ingenuity, to interweave it with our own conceits, and labour to make it tally with our favourite schemes. Thus, by blending together parts so ill suited, the whole comes forth an absurd composition of truth and error.

Of the many difficulties that have stood in the way of philosophy, this vanity perhaps has had the worst effects. The love of the marvellous, and the prejudices of sense, obstructed the progress of natural knowledge; but experience and reflection soon taught men to examine and endeavour to correct these. Tho' philosophers met with great discouragements in the dark and superstitious ages, learning flourished, with liberty, in better times. The disputes amongst the sects, more fond of victory than of truth, produced a talkative sort of philosophy, and a vain ostentation of learning, that prevailed for a long time; but men could not be always diverted from pursuing after more real knowledge. These have not done near so much harm, as that pride and ambition, which has led philosophers to think it beneath them, to offer any thing less to the world than a compleat and finished system of nature; and, in order to obtain this at once, to take the liberty of inventing certain principles and hypotheses, from which they pretend to explain all her mysteries.

2. Sir *Isaac Newton* saw how extravagant such attempts were, and therefore did not set out with any favourite principle or supposition, never proposing to himself the invention of a system. He saw that it was necessary to consult nature herself, to attend carefully to her manifest operations, and to extort her secrets from her by well chosen and repeated experiments. He would admit no objections against plain experience from metaphysical considerations, which, he saw, had often misled philosophers, and had seldom been of real use in their enquiries. He avoided presumption, he had the necessary patience as well as genius; and having kept steadily to the right path, he therefore succeeded.

Experiments and observations, 'tis true, could not alone have carried him far in tracing the causes from their effects, and explaining the effects from their causes: a sublime geometry was his guide in this nice and difficult enquiry. This is the instrument, by which alone the machinery of a work, made with so much art, could be unfolded; and therefore he sought to carry it to the greatest height. Nor is it easy to discern, whether he has shewed greater skill, and been more successful, in improving and perfecting the instrument, or in applying it to use. He used to call his philosophy *experimental philosophy*, intimating, by the name, the essential difference there is betwixt it and those systems that are the product of genius and invention only. These could not long subsist; but his philosophy, being founded on experiment and demonstration, cannot fail till reason or the nature of things are changed.

In order to proceed with perfect security, and to put an end for ever to disputes, he proposed that, in our enquiries into nature, the methods of *analysis* and *synthesis* should be both employed in a proper order; that we should begin with the phænomena, or effects, and from them investigate the powers or causes that operate in nature; that, from particular causes, we should proceed to the more general ones, till the argument end in the most general: this is the method of *analysis*. Being once possest of these causes, we should then descend in a contrary order; and from them, as established principles, explain all the phænomena that are their consequences, and prove our explications: and this is the *synthesis*. It is evident that, as in mathematics, so in natural philosophy, the investigation of difficult things by the method of *analysis* ought ever to precede the method of composition, or the *synthesis*. For in any other way, we can never be sure that we assume the principles which really obtain in nature; and that our system, after we have composed it with great labour, is not mere dream and illusion.

By proceeding according to this method, he demonstrated from observations, analytically, that gravity is a general principle; from which he afterwards explained the system of the world. By *analysis* he discovered new and wonderful properties of light, and, from these, accounted for many curious phænomena in a *synthetic* way. But while he was thus demonstrating a great number of truths, he could not but meet with hints of many other things, that his sagacity and diligent observations suggested to him, which he was not able to establish with equal certainty: and as these were not to be neglected, but to be separated with care from the others, he therefore collected them together, and proposed them under the modest title of *queries*.

By distinguishing these so carefully from each other, he has done the greatest service to this part of learning, and has secured his philosophy against any hazard of being disproved or weakned by future discoveries. He has taken care to give nothing for demonstration but what must ever be found such; and having separated from this what he owns is not so certain, he has opened matter for the enquiries of future ages, which may confirm and enlarge his doctrines, but can never refute them. He knew where to stop when experiments were wanting, and when the subtilty of nature carried things out of his reach: nor would he abuse the great authority and reputation he had acquired, by delivering his opinion, concerning these, otherwise than as matter of question. It was long before he could be prevailed on to propose his opinion or conjectures concerning the cause of gravity; and what he has said of it, and of the other powers that act on the minute particles of matter, is delivered with a modesty and diffidence seldom to be met with amongst philosophers of a less name. Nor do they act in a conformity with the spirit of this philosophy who speak dogmatically on these subjects, till a clearer light from new observations and experiments brings them from the class of queries, and places them on the level of demonstration.

3. Such was the method of our incomparable philosopher, whose caution and modesty will ever do him the greatest honour in the opinion of the unprejudiced. But this strict method of proceeding was not relished by those who had been accustomed to treat philosophy in a very different way, and who saw that, by following it, they must give up their favourite systems. His observations and reasonings were unexceptionable; so, finding

nothing to object to these, they endeavoured to lessen the character of his philosophy by general indirect insinuations, and, sometimes, by unjust calumnies. They pretended to find a resemblance between his doctrines and the exploded tenets of the scholastick philosophy. They triumphed mightily in treating gravity as an occult quality, because he did not pretend to deduce this principle fully from its cause. His extending over all the system a power which is so well known to us on the earth, and explaining by it the motions and influences of the celestial bodies, in the most satisfactory manner; and his determining the measures of the various motions that are consequences of this power, by so skilful an application of geometry to nature; all these had no merit with such philosophers, because he did not assign the mechanical cause of gravity. I know not that ever it was made an objection to the circulation of the blood that there is no small difficulty in accounting for it mechanically; they who first extended gravity to air, vapour, and to all bodies round the earth, had their praise, though the cause of gravity was as obscure as before; or rather appeared more mysterious, after they had shewn that there was no body found near the earth, exempt from gravity, that might be supposed to be its cause. Why then were his admirable discoveries, by which this principle was extended over the universe, so ill relished by some philosophers? The truth is, he had, with great evidence, overthrown the boasted schemes by which they pretended to unravel all the mysteries of nature; and the philosophy he introduced, in place of them, carrying with it a sincere confession of our being far from a complete and perfect knowledge of it, could not please those who had been accustom'd to imagine themselves possess'd of the eternal reasons and primary causes of all things.

But to all such as have just notions of the great author of the universe, and of his admirable workmanship, Sir *Isaac Newton*'s caution and modesty will recommend his philosophy; and even the avowed imperfection of some parts of it will, to them, rather appear a consequence of its conformity with nature. To such, all complete and finished systems must appear very suspicious: they will not be surprized that refined speculations, or even the labours of a few ages, are not sufficient to unfold the whole constitution of things, and trace every phænomenon through all the chain of causes to the first cause. Is the admirable progress which has been made in this arduous pursuit to be despised or neglected, because more remains behind undiscovered? Surely we ought rather to rejoice that so much is opened to us of the consummate art by which all things were made, and ought to be afraid to intermix with it our own extravagant conceits.

The processes of nature lie so deep, that, after all the pains we can take, much, perhaps, will remain undiscovered beyond the reach of human art or skill. But this is no reason why we should give ourselves up to the belief of fictions, be they ever so ingenious, instead of hearkening to the unerring voice of nature: for she alone can guide us in her own labyrinths; and it is a consequence of her real beauty, that the least part of true philosophy is incomparably more beautiful than the most complete systems which have been the product of invention. This is particularly true of Sir *Isaac Newton*'s philosophy; and we may compare it in this respect with those celebrated pieces of *Apelles*, which, though they never received his last hand, were in greater admiration amongst the antients, than the most finished pieces of other artists: and we with posterity may not find cause to say of this philosophy what the antients said of those pieces,—*Ipsum defectum cessisse in gloriam artificis, nec qui succederet operi ad præscripta lineamenta inventum fuisse*. Plin.[1]

4. It was, however, no new thing that this philosophy should meet with opposition. All the useful discoveries that were made in former times, and particularly in the last century, had to struggle with the prejudices of those who had accustomed themselves not so much as to think but in a certain systematic way; who could not be prevailed on to abandon their favourite schemes, while they were able to imagine the least pretext for continuing the dispute: every art and talent was displayed to support their falling cause; no aid seemed foreign to them that could in any manner annoy their adversary; and such often was their obstinacy, that truth was able to make little progress, till they were succeeded by younger persons who had not so strongly imbibed their prejudices.

Sir *Isaac Newton* had very early experience of this temper of philosophers, and appears to have been discouraged by it. He had a particular aversion to disputes, and was with difficulty induced to enter into any controversy. The warm opposition his admirable discoveries in optics met with, in his youth, deprived the world of a full account of them for many years, till there appeared a greater

---

1 The quotation is inaccurate. The original, in translation, is: 'The actual damage contributed to the glory of the artist . . . nor could anyone be found to carry on the task in conformity with the outlines of the sketches prepared.' Pliny *Nat. Hist* 35, sects 91, 92.

disposition amongst the learned to receive them; and induced him to retain other important inventions by him, from an apprehension of the disputes in which a publication might involve him. He thus weighed the reasons of things impartially and coolly, before a publication of them can be suspected to have engaged him in their defence. It is well known how slow he was in publishing: and we cannot but observe that the temper and disposition of mind, as well as the abilities of this great man, fitted him in a particular manner for penetrating far into nature and unfolding her harmony.

Nor did his aversion to disputes proceed from the love of quiet only. Philosophy had been in high esteem of old, but had lost its antient lustre from the endless idle janglings that had arisen amongst the sects; and could never recover it while a faculty of inventing a system readily, and defending it obstinately, were the admired talents of a philosopher. While one age or sect overturned for the most part the laborious productions of another, many of the wiser sort despaired of acquiring certainty in natural knowledge, and chose rather to content themselves with the general view of things, open to all men, than attach themselves to schemes which produced no real fruit, and really led them farther from the truth. Our author therefore proposed that all prejudices should be laid aside, and the genuine method of treating natural philosophy, which we have described from him, should be closely followed. By his adhering to it himself, we are secure that truth and nature are on his side; and by following the excellent models which he has given us, we may be able to make farther advances.

Others have pretended to explain the whole constitution of things by what they call clear ideas, and by mere abstracted speculations. They express a contempt for that knowledge of causes which is derived from the contemplation of their effects, and are unwilling to condescend to any other science than that of effects from their causes. Therefore they set out from the *first cause*; and from their ideas of him pretend to unfold the whole chain, and to trace a complete scheme of his works. This is the philosophy that stands in opposition to our author's to this day. It flatters human vanity so much, and sets out in so pompous a manner, that they who attend not to the unexhaustible variety of nature, and consider not how unequal the human powers are to so arduous an undertaking, are deluded by its promises: it may be doubted if such a philosophy lies within the reach of any created being; and it seems to be very plain that it far surpasses the reach of men. But since many are devoted to this phantom, and use all their art to adorn, and recommend it to more admirers, it will be necessary for the service of truth, that, while we proceed, we have in view likewise the detection of this imposture.

5. The view of nature which is the immediate object of sense is very imperfect, and of a small extent; but by the assistance of art, and the help of our reason, is enlarged till it loses itself in an infinity on either hand. The immensity of things on the one side, and their minuteness on the other, carry them equally out of our reach, and conceal from us the far greater and more noble part of physical operations. As magnitude, of every sort, abstractly considered, is capable of being increased to infinity, and is also divisible without end; so we find that, in nature, the limits of the greatest and least dimensions of things are actually placed at an immense distance from each other. We can perceive no bounds of the vast expanse in which natural causes operate, and can fix no border or termination of the universe; and we are equally at a loss when we endeavour to trace things to their elements, and to discover the limits which conclude the subdivisions of matter. The objects, which we commonly call great vanish when we contemplate the vast body of the earth; the terraqueous globe itself is soon lost in the solar system: in some parts it is seen as a distant star. In great part it is unknown, or visible only at rare times to vigilant observers, assisted, perhaps, with an art like to that by which *Galileo* was enabled to discover so many new parts of the system. The Sun itself dwindles into a star; *Saturn*'s vast orbit, and the orbits of all the comets, croud into a point, when viewed from numberless places between the earth and the nearest fix'd stars. Other suns kindle light to illuminate other systems where our sun's rays are unperceived; but they also are swallowed up in the vast expanse. Even all the systems of the stars that sparkle in the clearest sky must possess a small corner only of that space over which such systems are dispersed, since more stars are discovered in one constellation, by the telescope, than the naked eye perceives in the whole heavens. After we have risen so high, and left all definite measures so far behind us, we find ourselves no nearer to a term or limit; for all this is nothing to what may be displayed in the infinite expanse, beyond the remotest stars that ever have been discovered.

If we descend in the scale of nature, towards the other limit, we find a like gradation from minute objects to others incomparably more subtile, and are led as far below sensible measures as we were before carried above them, by similar steps that soon become hid to us in equal obscurity. We have ground to believe that these subdivisions of matter have a termination, and that the elementary particles of bodies are solid and uncompounded, so as to undergo no alteration in the various operations of nature or of art. But from microscopical observations that discover animals, thousands of which could scarce form a particle perceptible to the unassisted sense, each of which have their proper vessels, and fluids circulating in those vessels; from the propagation, nourishment and growth of those animals; from the subtilty of the effluvia of bodies retaining their particular properties after so prodigious a rarefaction; from many astonishing experiments of chymists; and especially from the inconceivable minuteness of the particles of light, that find a passage equally in all directions through the pores of transparent bodies, and from the contrary properties of the different sides of the same ray; it appears, that the subdivisions of the particles of bodies descend by a number of steps or degrees that surpasses all imagination, and that nature is unexhaustible by us on every side. Nor is it in the magnitude of bodies only that this endless gradation is to be observed. Of motions some are performed in moments of time; others are finished in very long periods: some are too slow, and others too swift, to be perceptible by us. The tracing the chain of causes is the most noble pursuit of philosophy; but we meet with no cause but what is, itself, to be considered as an effect, and are able to number but few links of the chain. In every kind of magnitude, there is a degree or sort to which our sense is proportion'd, the perception and knowledge of which is of greatest use to mankind. The same is the ground-work of philosophy; for tho' all sorts and degrees are equally the object of philosophical speculation; yet it is from those which are proportioned to sense that a philosopher must set out in his enquiries, ascending or descending afterwards as his pursuits may require. He does well indeed to take his views from many points of sight, and supply the defects of sense by a well regulated imagination; nor is he to be confined by any limit in space or time: but as his knowledge of nature is founded on the observation of sensible things, he must begin with these, and must often return to them, to examine his progress by them. Here is his secure hold; and as he sets out from thence, so if he likewise trace not often his steps backwards with caution, he will be in hazard of losing his way in the labyrinths of nature.

6. From this short view of nature, and of the situation of man, considered as a spectator of its phænomena and as an enquirer into its constitution, we may form some judgment of the project of those, who, in composing their systems, begin at the summit of

the scale, and then, by clear ideas, pretend to descend through all its steps with great pomp and facility, so as in one view to explain all things. The processes in experimental philosophy are carried on in a different manner: the beginnings are less lofty, but the scheme improves as we arise from particular observations, to more general and more just views. It must be owned, indeed, that philosophy would be perfect, if our view of nature, from the common objects of sense, to the limits of the universe upwards, and to the elements of things downwards, was complete; and the powers or causes that operate in the whole were known. But if we compare the extent of this scheme with the powers of mankind, we shall be obliged to allow the necessity of taking it in parts, and of proceeding with all the caution and care we are capable of, in enquiring into each part. When we perceive such wonders, as naturalists have discovered, in the minutest objects, shall we pretend to describe so easily the productions of infinite power in space, that is at the same time infinitely extended and infinitely divisible? Surely we may rather imagine, that in the whole, there will be matter for the enquiries and perpetual admiration of much more perfect beings.

It is not therefore the business of philosophy, in our present situation in the universe, to attempt to take in at once, in one view, the whole scheme of nature; but to extend, with great care and circumspection, our knowledge, by just steps, from sensible things, as far as our observations or reasonings from them will carry us, in our enquiries concerning either the greater motions and operations of nature, or her more subtile and hidden works. In this way Sir Isaac Newton proceeded in his discoveries: he established his account of the system of the world upon the best astronomical observations, on the one hand; and performed, himself, on the other, with the greatest address, the experiments by which he was enabled to pry into the more secret operations of nature, amongst the minute particles of matter. On either side he has extended our views very far, and has left valuable hints and intimations of what yet lies involved in obscurity.

For those purposes he has given us two incomparable treatises, the most perfect in their kind, philosophy has to boast of; his Mathematical *Principles* of Natural Philosophy, and his Treatise of *Optics*. In the first, he describes the system of the world, and demonstrates the powers which govern the celestial motions, and produce their mutual influences. These are extended from the centre of the sun to the utmost altitude of the highest comet, and probably to the farthest limits of the universe. Nor are these new or abstruse principles, like to those which never had a being but in the imagination of philosophers, but the same which are most familiar to mankind, and in common use, farther extended and more accurately defined. In the second, he treats of light, which, tho' the most potent agent in nature, that is sensible to us, acts only at the least distances. His admirable discoveries, on this subject, led him to search into the motions that are amongst the minute particles of matter, the most abstruse of all natural phænomena.

In the first, he had the observations of astronomers for many ages to build on, with valuable consequences that had been derived from them, by the laborious calculations of diligent and ingenious men. The constancy and regularity of the celestial motions had contributed, with the observations of some thousands of years, to render astronomy the most exact part of the history of nature; the doctrine of comets only excepted. The vast distances of the great bodies which compose the system, from each other, rather favoured a just *analysis* of the powers by which they act on one another; since by the greatness of the distance, these must be reduced to a few simple principles, and be the more easily discovered. In the second treatise, he enquires into more hidden parts of nature, and had most of the phænomena themselves to trace, as well as their causes. The subject is rather more nice and difficult, because of the inconceivable minuteness of the agents, and the subtilty and quickness of the motions; and the principles combined in producing the phænomena being more various, it could not be expected that they should be so easily subjected to an *analysis*. Hence it is that what he has delivered in the first (tho' still capable of improvement) is more complete and finished in several respects; while his discoveries of the second sort are more astonishing.

After having established the principle of the universal Gravitation of Matter in the first treatise, when he is not able to demonstrate the causes of the phænomena described in the second more evidently, he endeavours to judge of them, by *analogy*, from what he had found in the greater motions of the system; a way of reasoning that is agreeable to the harmony of things, and to the old maxim ascribed to *Hermes*, and approved by the observation and judgment of the best philosophers, 'That what passes in the heavens above is similar and analogous to what passes on the earth below.' He had found that all bodies gravitated towards each other, by a power that acts on all their particles equally at equal distances, and increases according to a stated law when the distance is diminished. From a like principle, acting at less distances, with greater vigour, and with more variety, but insensibly at larger distances, he suspected that the more abstruse phænomena of nature proceeded. It was a great matter in philosophy to be secure of one general principle; and one was sufficient for carrying on the regular motions of the heavenly bodies. A greater variety was necessary for conducting the different operations of nature in particular parts; and these being involved in some obscurity, till better light should appear, he could find no surer ground on which to found a judgment of them, than that principle he had already shewn to take place in nature. But because we often find that phænomena, which, at first sight, appear of a very different sort, flow nevertheless from the same cause, and several such causes are often resolved, on farther enquiry, into one more general principle; the whole constitution of nature (notwithstanding the variety of appearances) manifestly leading to one supreme cause; this great philosopher was hence induced, as well as from several observations he had made, to think that all these powers might proceed from one general instrument or agent, as various branches from one great stem, whose efficacy might be resolved more immediately into the direction or influences of the sovereign cause that rules the universe. But he speaks of this in the manner that became a philosopher who had so much studied nature, and knew how obscure those arduous parts of her scheme must be to us.

7. As the most obvious views of the creation suggest to all men the persuasion of the being and government of a Deity; so every discovery in natural philosophy enforces it: and with this improvement of his discoveries, this great man concludes both those treatises. Nor is his philosophy to be thought of little service for this purpose, tho' he has not been able to explain fully the primary causes themselves.

The great mysterious Being, who made and governs the whole system, has set a part of the chain of causes in our view; but we find that, as he himself is too high for our comprehension, so his more immediate instruments in the universe, are also involved in an obscurity that philosophy is not able to dissipate; and thus our veneration for the supreme author is always increased, in proportion as we advance in the knowledge of his works. As we arise in philosophy towards the first cause, we obtain more extensive views of the constitution of things, and see his influences more plainly. We perceive that we are approaching to him, from the simplicity and generality of the powers or laws we discover; from the difficulty we find to account for them mechanically; from the more and more complete beauty and contrivance, that appears to us in the scheme of his works as we advance; and from the hints we obtain of greater things yet out of our reach: but still we find ourselves at a distance from Him, the great source of all motion, power and efficacy; who, after all our enquiries, continues removed from us and veiled in darkness. He is not the object of sense, his nature and essence are unfathomable; the more immediate instruments of his power and energy are but obscurely known to us; the least part of nature, when we endeavour to comprehend it, perplexes us; even *place* and *time*, of which our ideas seem to be simple and clear, have enough in them to embarrass those who allow nothing to be beyond the reach of their faculties. These things, however, do not hinder but we may learn to form great and just conceptions of him from his sensible works, where an art and skill is express'd that is obvious to the most superficial spectator, surprizes the most experienced enquirer, and many times surpasses the comprehension of the profoundest philosopher. From what we are able to understand of nature, we may entertain the greater expectations of what will be discovered to us, if ever we shall be allowed to penetrate to the first cause himself, and see the whole scheme of his works as they are really derived from him, when our imperfect philosophy shall be completed.

Source: Colin Maclaurin, *An Account of Sir Isaac Newton's Philosophical Discoveries*, London 1748, ch. 1, pp. 3–23

Biographical Sketches of Authors

HUGH BLAIR (1718–1800). Blair was born in Edinburgh, educated there, at the High School and the University, and spent the remainder of his life in Edinburgh teaching and preaching. He was ordained minister in 1742 and served at the Canongate Church from 1743 to 1754, at Lady Yester's church from 1754 to 1758 and then from 1758 to 1800 at the High Kirk of St Giles. He was a famous pulpit orator, and has been described by a modern commentator as 'the greatest Moderate preacher of Christian Stoicism' (Richard B. Sher). His five volumes of sermons were widely read. In 1760 he was appointed professor of rhetoric at the University, and two years later became the first occupant of the chair of rhetoric and belles lettres. In the controversy concerning the authenticity of the Gaelic Ossianic poetry which James Macpherson published in translation, Blair, unlike his friend David Hume, was from the outset on Macpherson's side. Blair was also on friendly terms with Lord Kames, and when the latter was investigated for heresy by the Kirk, Blair came strongly to his defence.

GEORGE CAMPBELL (1719–96). Born in Aberdeen, Campbell was educated at Aberdeen Grammar School, then at Marischal College, Aberdeen, and finally at Edinburgh University where he studied theology. During his stay in Edinburgh he heard many sermons preached by Hugh Blair at the Canongate Church and formed a close and lasting friendship with Blair. He was a minister first in Banchory and then Aberdeen, and in 1758 became, along with Thomas Reid, a member of the Literary Society of Aberdeen, the society to which Campbell delivered, as separate papers, much of his masterpiece *The Philosophy of Rhetoric*. In 1759 he was appointed principal of Marischal College and four years later published his *Treatise on Miracles*, a book which had an immediate impact and was quickly translated into French, Dutch and German. His final appointment was in 1771 to the chair of divinity at Marischal College.

JAMES DUNBAR (1742–98). Born in Nairnshire, Dunbar entered King's College, Aberdeen, in 1757 and graduated four years later. He was appointed to a co-regentship at the college in 1765, by which time King's College was the only university in Scotland at which teaching was still done by regents, that is, by teachers who each taught the entire range of arts subjects. He rose in due course to be professor of philosophy at King's, and remained in that post till his retiral in 1794. Marischal College, in Aberdeen, awarded him a doctorate of laws in 1780. He is thought to have published just two works (the existence of a third work, a poem, is disputed). The first is a pamphlet of 1779 attacking the American policy of the government of the day. His pro-American stance was in sharp contrast to the stance of his Aberdeen colleagues George Campbell and Alexander Gerard. The second work is the *Essays on the History of Mankind in Rude and Cultivated Ages*, published in 1780. In 1765 Dunbar was elected to the Aberdeen Philosophical Society, otherwise known as the 'Wise Club', and remained a member till it ceased in 1773. It is probable that a number of the essays in his second work originated as papers presented to the Club.

JOHN ERSKINE OF CARNOCK (1695–1768). Erskine became an advocate in 1719, and in 1737 was appointed to the chair of Scots Law at Edinburgh University, a position he held till 1765. In 1754 he published his *Principles of the Law of Scotland*. His masterwork *An Institute of the Law of Scotland* was composed during his years as professor of Scots Law at Edinburgh and during his brief retirement. At the time of his death it was close to completion, and the work was eventually published (1773) in an edition prepared by his son David, also a lawyer. The *Institute* is not of merely antiquarian interest; extensive use is still made of it in Scottish cases, with over 150 references to it in the last half century. William W. McBryde sums up Erskine's reputation in these terms: 'The respect accorded to his words is greater than that extended to any twentieth century writer on the law. He was, and he remains, an institutional authority.'

ADAM FERGUSON (1723–1816). Ferguson, the only one of the first-rank literati who was a native Gaelic speaker, was born at Logierait and educated at Perth Grammar School and then at St Andrews University from where he graduated in 1742. After a period of study of divinity at Edinburgh he was appointed in 1745 chaplain to the Highland Black Watch regiment, with whom he saw active service at the Battle of Fontenoy. He followed David Hume as librarian to the Advocates' Library, and then held successively two chairs at Edinburgh University, the chair of natural philosophy (1759–64) and the chair of pneumatics and moral philosophy which he gave up in 1785, to be succeeded by Dugald Stewart. Among his writings were his *History of the Roman Republic* (1783) and his *Principles of Moral and Political Science* (1792). Much the most important of his works is *An Essay on the History of Civil Society* (1767), which went through seven editions during his lifetime, and is primarily responsible for his reputation as the father of modern sociology.

JOHN GREGORY (1724–73). Born in Aberdeen, Gregory studied medicine at Edinburgh and Leiden, becoming professor of medicine at King's College, Aberdeen, where he introduced measures to increase considerably the range of subjects in the faculty's syllabus. In 1758 he became (along with his cousin Thomas Reid) a founder member of the Aberdeen Philosophical Society, the Wise Club, which was a chief centre of Enlightenment discussion in the city. In 1766 he was appointed to the chair of the practice of physic (one of the medical chairs) at the University of Edinburgh, and was appointed also physician to the king in Scotland. Among his publications were *A Comparative View of the State and Faculties of Man with those of the Animal World* (London 1765), and his highly readable *Lectures on the Duties and Qualifications of a Physician*, which paints a clear picture of the 'polite physician' in Enlightenment Scotland.

HENRY HOME, LORD KAMES (1696–1782). Born at Kames in Berwickshire, and educated there, Home taught himself law and was called to the bar in 1723. His most famous case came in 1736 when he defended John Porteous, captain of the town guard of Edinburgh, who was charged with murder after his troops, acting on his orders, fired on a mob and killed or injured scores of citizens. (The story is told in Walter Scott's *The Heart of Midlothian*.) Following the defeat of the Jacobite army in 1746 estates of Jacobites were forfeited, and the estates were managed by a team which included Henry Home. He took the title Lord Kames in 1752 on his appointment as a lord of the Court of Session, and he became a lord of the Justiciary Court in 1763. He remained a judge till a few months before his death aged 86. Kames was a leading figure of the Scottish Enlightenment, on close friendly terms with Hume, Smith, Monboddo and Boswell, and often played host to Thomas Reid at the Kames family home at Blair Drummond. In the midst of his busy life as a lawyer Kames wrote numerous books on law, philosophy and aesthetics.

DAVID HUME (1711–76). Hume was the greatest philosopher of the Scottish Enlightenment, and perhaps its central figure. He was born in Edinburgh, and spent his childhood on the family estate at Ninewells near Berwick. He attended the University of Edinburgh, briefly held a post in the office of a Bristol merchant, and then from 1734 to 1737 lived in France, first in Reims and then in the village of La Flèche, close to the Jesuit College where Descartes had studied a century earlier. During this period he worked on his philosophical masterpiece *A Treatise of Human Nature*, which was published in 1739–40, and which, in Hume's words, 'fell dead-born from the press'. He failed to secure the chair of moral philosophy in Edinburgh (1745) and of logic and rhetoric in Glasgow (1751). In 1748 he published *An Enquiry concerning Human Understanding*, and three years later *An Enquiry concerning the Principles of Morals*, in which he presented a modified version of parts of the *Treatise*. During his period as librarian of the Advocates' Library in Edinburgh he carried out research which came to fruition with the publication of a multi-volume *History of England* (1754–62), which, during his own lifetime, was his most popular work. Hume spent several periods abroad, including a spell 1763–6 during which he was secretary to the British Embassy in Paris. He also spent a brief period as under-secretary of state in London before retiring to Edinburgh in 1769. His *Dialogues concerning Natural Religion* were published posthumously. Adam Smith wrote of him: 'I have always considered him, both in his lifetime and since his death, as approaching as nearly to the idea of a perfectly wise and virtuous man, as perhaps the nature of human frailty will permit.'

FRANCIS HUTCHESON (1694–1746). Born in Drumalig, County Down, Ireland, into a family of Ayrshire origins, Hutcheson studied at a presbyterian academy in Ireland before matriculating in 1710 at the University of Glasgow where he studied arts, graduating in 1712. He remained in Glasgow till 1718, as a theology student and then as a private tutor, before returning to Ireland. Shortly thereafter he set up a presbyterian academy in Dublin, and became closely associated with Viscount Molesworth, a liberal minded aristocrat with a circle of philosophically active friends and an enthusiasm for the ideas of Lord Shaftesbury, the English philosopher who, perhaps more than any other, set Hutcheson's agenda in ethics and aesthetics. The 1720s, spent mainly in Dublin, were philosophically Hutcheson's most productive years. His publications of the period included *An Inquiry into the Original of our Ideas of Beauty and Virtue; An Essay on the Nature and Conduct of the Passions, with Illustrations on the Moral Sense; Reflections upon Laughter*; and *Remarks on the Fable of the Bees*. In 1729 he was invited to take up Glasgow University's chair of moral philosophy, whose previous occupant had been Hutcheson's former teacher Gershom Carmichael. He remained in the chair, active as a university politician and as a liberal voice within the Church, until his death. In a famous phrase his pupil (and successor in the moral philosophy chair) Adam Smith spoke of him as 'the never to be forgotten Hutcheson'. Hutcheson's *System of Moral Philosophy* was published posthumously though most of it had been written between 1734 and 1737.

JAMES HUTTON (1726–97). Born in Edinburgh, Hutton attended the University of Edinburgh, studying chemistry and then medicine. He continued his medical studies at the University of Paris and then at Leiden where he graduated MD in 1749. But he did not practise medicine; instead he farmed, first in Norfolk and then in 1754 in Berwickshire. Always interested in chemistry he helped to develop a process for the production of salammoniac (ammonium chloride) from coal soot, and gained a substantial income from the production of salammoniac at an Edinburgh factory. He was on close terms with (among others) leading figures of the Scottish Enlightenment, Joseph Black, Adam Smith, and John Clerk of Eldin, a geologist and landscape artist whose skill was put at Hutton's service when the latter was travelling round Scotland in search of evidence for his theory of the Earth. Hutton's ideas on geological time conflicted with a common interpretation of the Bible, and brought him into conflict with parts of the religious establishment. He presented his theory of the Earth at meetings of the newly established Royal Society of Edinburgh, and subsequently wrote a much more detailed version, his *Theory of the Earth* (1795). John Playfair (1748–1819), professor of mathematics at Edinburgh, and a founder member of the Royal Society of Edinburgh, published in 1802 *Illustrations of the Huttonian Theory*, which did much to secure acceptance of Hutton's work. Hutton wrote on other fields also, such as agriculture and philosophy, but it is as the founder of modern geology that he is now chiefly remembered.

COLIN MACLAURIN (1698–1746). Born at Kilmodan in Argyllshire, Maclaurin entered the University of Glasgow aged eleven and graduated four years later. He was appointed professor of mathematics at Marischal College, Aberdeen, aged nineteen. During his four-year occupancy of the chair he published his *Geometrica Organica* (London 1720), which revealed him as one of the best mathematicians in Britain. He was elected fellow of the Royal Society in 1719 and in 1725 became professor of mathematics at the University of Edinburgh on the recommendation of Sir Isaac Newton. He made a major contribution to the dissemination of knowledge of Newton in Scotland with such works as his *An Account of Sir Isaac Newton's Philosophical Discoveries* (1748). When the Jacobite army marched on Edinburgh in 1745 Maclaurin helped to prepare the city's defences. He then fled to England, and died the following year on his return to Edinburgh.

JOHN MILLAR (1735–1801). Born at Shotts in Lanarkshire, Millar entered the University of Glasgow, where he studied under (among other professors) Adam Smith, with whom he formed a lasting close friendship. In his early twenties, and probably by the good offices of Smith, Millar went to live with the family of Henry Home, Lord Kames, and to act as tutor to Kames's son. There he met David Hume. As Kames's biographer Tytler reports: 'The tutor of the son became the pupil and companion of the father.' Thereafter Kames played a major role in Millar's advancement. Millar became an advocate in 1760, and in 1761, with the support of Adam Smith and Lord Kames, he became professor of civil law at Glasgow. Among his colleagues at Glasgow were Smith, Thomas Reid, Joseph Black, Millar's son James who occupied the mathematics chair for many years, and his son-in-law James Mylne, who occupied the moral philosophy chair from 1797 till 1839. Millar lectured on a wide range of subjects, legal, political and sociological, spoke out strongly in favour of liberal policies, as witness his support for American independence, for the extension of the electoral franchise, and for the abolition of the slave trade. His most important work *The Origin of the Distinction of Ranks* was published in its earliest form in 1771, and republished after extensive revision in 1779.

THOMAS REID (1710–96). Reid, whose mother was a member of the formidable Gregory family, the most distinguished dynasty of the Scottish Enlightenment, was born in Strachan in Kincardineshire, attended Aberdeen Grammar School, and when aged twelve began the four-year arts course as a student of George Turnbull at Marischal College, Aberdeen. He proceeded to the study of theology and in 1731 became a minister of the Kirk. Reid was thereafter, in turn, librarian at Marischal College, minister of New Machar (an appointment in the gift of King's College, Aberdeen), and regent at King's. In 1758 he helped to found the Aberdeen Philosophical Society, which included among other philosophers George Campbell, Alexander Gerard and James Beattie. In Aberdeen he developed many of the distinctive doctrines of his philosophy of common sense, and a number of them were presented in the form of papers to the Philosophical Society. In 1764, his final year in Aberdeen, he published the first of his three major books, *An Inquiry into the Human Mind on the Principles of Common Sense*, which is in part a powerful critique of Hume's philosophy of perception, though the book is in many ways a constructive, and not merely a destructive, exercise. In 1764 Reid succeeded Adam Smith as professor of moral philosophy at the University of Glasgow, and continued to develop his philosophy of common sense. He retired from teaching in 1780 to prepare his ideas for publication. His *Essays on the Intellectual Powers of Man* appeared in 1785 and the *Essays on the Active Powers of the Human Mind* appeared three years later. For about a century from the 1750s there was a school of common-sense philosophy in Scotland, which included thinkers such as George Campbell, Dugald Stewart and William Hamilton, and Reid's three books were much the most important works produced by the school.

WILLIAM ROBERTSON (1721–93). Born in the manse in Borthwick, Midlothian, Robertson attended school in Dalkeith before going on to Edinburgh University. In 1741, following his student days, he was licensed to preach and two years later became minister of Gladsmuir in East Lothian. Shortly after, on the death of his parents within a few hours of each other, he became the chief means of support for his younger brother and six sisters. When the Jacobites marched on Edinburgh in 1745 Robertson was one of the volunteers who defended the city, and on its surrender he fled to Haddington and tried to join General Cope's army. The attempt failed and Cope went on to fight (and lose) the Battle of Prestonpans without Robertson's help. His *History of Scotland during the Reigns of Queen Mary and King James VI* (1759) chiefly concerns the century of the Reformation in Scotland but it includes a survey of earlier centuries and has been described as 'a major contribution to the Scottish Enlightenment's historical investigation of feudalism' (John Robertson). In 1762 Robertson was appointed principal of the University of Edinburgh and the following year, by which time he was a leader of the moderate party in the Church of Scotland, he became moderator of the General Assembly of the Church. One year later he was appointed historiographer royal for Scotland. In 1769 his *History of the Reign of Charles the Fifth* appeared, followed in 1777 by the *History of America*. Robertson was a founder member of the Royal Society of Edinburgh.

SIR JOHN SINCLAIR (1754–1835). Born at Thurso Castle in Caithness, Sinclair was educated at the High School of Edinburgh, and then successively at the universities of Edinburgh, Glasgow (where he studied under Adam Smith) and Oxford. He was called to both the English and the Scottish bars, and in 1780 he entered Parliament as member for Caithness. An indefatigable figure in public life, he wrote extensively – and influentially – on many matters, but especially on fiscal and banking issues. Following an eight thousand mile tour of Europe (1785–7) he set about the task of agricultural improvement on his estate in Caithness, introducing the Cheviot sheep. Sinclair's major work, however, was the compilation of *The Statistical Account of Scotland*, which he began to plan in 1790, and for which he invited every parish minister in Scotland to provide information relating to the geography, natural history, population and employment of his parish. The resulting *Account*, consisting eventually of twenty one volumes, contained a detailed description of the whole of Scotland, a more comprehensive description than was then available for any other country. He was instrumental in setting up the British Wool Society in 1791, and the Board of Agriculture in 1793. The latter produced a series of reports which did for agriculture what the *Statistical Account* had done for society as a whole. He was responsible for the planning of the new town of Thurso.

WILLIAM SMELLIE (1740–95). Born in Edinburgh and educated at the High School, Smellie became an apprentice at a printing firm, attended classes at Edinburgh University, and mixed with the literati. His clubs included the Newtonian Society, of which he was a founder member and whose president was Hugh Blair. When it was resurrected as the Newtonian Club William Smellie was chosen as its secretary. He formed close friendships with leading figures of the Enlightenment such as Lord Monboddo, Lord Kames and Robert Burns. Kames regularly gave Smellie drafts of his writings for his critical comment, and when Burns came to Edinburgh in 1787 to publish his poems it was Smellie who printed them. The work for which Smellie is now chiefly known is the *Encyclopaedia Britannica*, which appeared in a series of instalments between 1768 and 1771, with Smellie himself masterminding the whole work and writing many of the entries. He had a long-standing interest in natural history, and in 1781 became keeper of the museum of natural history. Volume 1 of his *Philosophy of Natural History* appeared in 1790, the second volume appearing in 1799 four years after his death.

ADAM SMITH (1723–90). Born in Kirkcaldy, Smith was educated at the town's Burgh School, at Glasgow University where he studied under Hutcheson, and at Balliol College, Oxford, where he was Snell Exhibitioner. From Oxford he went in 1746 to Edinburgh and delivered there a series of lectures on rhetoric. In 1751 he was appointed to the chair of logic and rhetoric at the University of Glasgow, and in the following year moved to the moral philosophy chair in the same university. His first book *The Theory of Moral Sentiments* was published in 1759. In 1764 he resigned from the chair and travelled to France as tutor to the third Duke of Buccleuch and his brother, and while there he met some of the leading thinkers, especially economic thinkers, of the country. The duke died two years later, and Smith returned to Kirkcaldy. In 1776 he published *An Inquiry into the Nature and Causes of the Wealth of Nations*, in which he analyses in great detail the market economy, argues in favour of free trade, and criticises alternative economic systems. The book was an immediate success, and its implications for economic policy were noted by the professional politicians – Lord North and Pitt the Younger adopted Smith's recommendations. In the year of its publication Hume died, and Smith's moving tribute to him in which he implied that an atheist could die with his soul in a state of repose 'brought upon me ten times more abuse than the very violent attack I had made upon the whole commercial system of great Britain' (Smith, *Correspondence* p. 251). In 1778 Smith settled in Edinburgh on his appointment as a Commissioner of Customs in Scotland, and his home in the Canongate became a regular meeting place for the literati. On his death his literary executors, Joseph Black and James Hutton, followed his instruction regarding the burning of his papers, but some, with Smith's permission, were preserved, and were duly published as *Essays on Philosophical Studies* (1795). He was buried in the Canongate churchyard quite close to his home.

SIR JAMES STEUART (1713–80). Steuart's grandfather, James (1635–1713), was Lord Advocate, and his father, also named James (1681–1727), was Solicitor-General and a member of Parliament in the newly established Union Parliament. Steuart himself matriculated at Edinburgh University aged twelve, studied law and history and headed for a career in law, passing the Bar Examinations in 1735. He then spent five years (till 1740) on the Grand Tour, visiting the Netherlands, and France where he stayed at Avignon, a Jacobite centre. He went on to Spain, and at Madrid met the Earl Marischal, a noted Jacobite. Thence to Italy where, in Rome, he joined a Jacobite club – all this despite the fact that his family was deeply rooted in Protestantism. Once back in Scotland in 1740 Sir James acted on behalf of the Jacobite cause, and in 1745 was sent by Charles Edward Stewart as ambassador to France, with the task of securing military help for the cause in Scotland. Help was not forthcoming, and with the Jacobite defeat at Culloden in 1746, Steuart found himself legally and politically in an exposed position. He stayed in France for a few years, gradually distancing himself from the Jacobite cause. His further travels took him to Tübingen, where he spent four years working on the *Principles of Political Oeconomy*. Meantime there were persistent efforts to secure his pardon. Believing himself to have received a pardon, at last, Steuart returned to Britain, to Coltness near Glasgow, in 1763. The return was premature, but after eight further years pleading, the pardon finally came in 1771. He was on familiar terms with several of the literati of Edinburgh, including Hume with whom he was on warm terms and who admired his work; unlike Adam Smith, who spoke harshly of the *Principles*. That work can now be seen, however, to have made an important contribution to several areas of economic theory.

DUGALD STEWART (1753–1828). Son of the professor of mathematics at Edinburgh University, Stewart studied at the universities of Edinburgh and Glasgow. At the latter he was a student of Thomas Reid's. During this period, while still only eighteen, he composed an essay on dreaming, which was later to appear in his *Elements of the Philosophy of the Human Mind*. In 1775 he returned to Edinburgh as his father's assistant, and was subsequently appointed to the chair of mathematics. In 1785, on Adam Ferguson's retirement from teaching, Stewart moved to Ferguson's chair of moral philosophy at Edinburgh University. He published biographies of Adam Smith, William Robertson and Thomas Reid. However, the most important of his writings was the *Elements*, in which it becomes plain that Thomas Reid was the dominant influence on Stewart's philosophy. His interest in mathematics did not wane, and long after taking up the moral philosophy chair, he delivered lectures for the mathematics professor, John Playfair (1748–1819), the chief populariser of James Hutton's theory of the Earth.

Bibliography

Allan, David, *Virtue, Learning and the Scottish Enlightenment*, Edinburgh 1993

Berry, Christopher J., *Hume, Hegel, and Human Nature*, The Hague 1982

Berry, Christopher J., *Social Theory of the Scottish Enlightenment*, Edinburgh 1997

Blair, Hugh, *Sermons*, Edinburgh 1824

Broadie, Alexander, *The Tradition of Scottish Philosophy*, Edinburgh 1990

Broadie, Alexander, 'A nation of philosophers', in *Scotland: A Concise Cultural History*, ed. Paul H. Scott, Edinburgh 1993, pp. 61–76

Brookes, Derek (ed.), *Thomas Reid, An Inquiry into the Human Mind on the Principles of Common Sense*, Edinburgh 1997

Brown, Stewart J., *William Robertson and the Expansion of Empire*, Cambridge 1997

Cairns, John, 'Rhetoric, language, and Roman law: Legal education and improvement in eighteenth-century Scotland', *Law and History Review*, vol. 9, 1991, pp. 31–58

Campbell, George, *A Dissertation on Miracles*, Edinburgh 1762; 3rd edn, Edinburgh 1797

Campbell, George, *The Philosophy of Rhetoric*, new edn, 2 vols, Edinburgh 1808

Campbell, R. H. and A. S. Skinner (eds), *The Origins and Nature of the Scottish Enlightenment*, Edinburgh 1982

Campbell, T. D., *Adam Smith's Science of Morals*, London 1971

Davie, George E., *The Democratic Intellect*, Edinburgh 1982

Davie, George E., *The Scottish Enlightenment and other Essays*, Edinburgh 1991

Davie, George E., *A Passion for Ideas*, Edinburgh 1994

Donovan, A. L., *Philosophical Chemistry in the Scottish Enlightenment*, Edinburgh 1975

Downie, R. S., 'Ethics and casuistry in Adam Smith' in *Adam Smith Reviewed*, ed. P. Jones and A. S. Skinner, Edinburgh 1992, pp. 119–41

Drummond, A. L. and J. Bulloch, *The Scottish Church, 1688–1843: The Age of the Moderates*, Edinburgh 1973

Dunbar, James, *Essays on the History of Mankind in Rude and Cultivated Ages*, London 1781; reprinted with new introduction by Christopher J. Berry, Bristol 1995

Dwyer, J. and R. B. Sher (eds), *Sociability and Society in Eighteenth Century Scotland*, Edinburgh 1993

Emerson, Roger L., *Professors, Patronage and Politics: The Aberdeen Universities in the Eighteenth Century*, Aberdeen 1992

Emerson, Roger L., 'Calvinism and the Scottish Enlightenment', in *Literatur im Kontext – Literature in Context*, ed. Joachim Schwend, Susanne Hagemann and Herman Vögel, Frankfurt am Main 1992

Erskine of Carnock, John, *An Institute of the Law of Scotland*, 8th edn, 2 vols, Edinburgh 1871; reprinted with introduction by W. W. McBryde, Edinburgh 1989

Ferguson, Adam, *An Essay on the History of Civil Society*, ed. D. Forbes, Edinburgh 1966

Forbes, Duncan, *Hume's Philosophical Politics*, Cambridge 1975

Fry, Michael, *The Dundas Despotism*, Edinburgh 1992

Gay, Peter, *The Enlightenment*, New York 1973

Grave, S. S., *The Scottish Philosophy of Common Sense*, Oxford 1960

Gregory, John, *Lectures on the Duties and Qualifications of a Physician*, London 1772

Haakonssen, K., *The Science of the Legislator: The Natural Jurisprudence of David Hume and Adam Smith*, Cambridge 1981

Haakonssen, K., *Natural Law and Moral Philosophy, from Grotius to the Scottish Enlightenment*, Cambridge 1995

Home, Henry [Lord Kames], *Essays on the Principles of Morality and Natural Religion*, Edinburgh 1751, 3rd edn, 1779

Home, Henry [Lord Kames], *Sketches of the History of Man*, Glasgow 1802

Hope, Vincent (ed.), *Philosophers of the Scottish Enlightenment*, Edinburgh, 1984

Hope, Vincent, *Virtue by Consensus*, Oxford 1989

Hont, I. and M. Ignatieff (eds), *Wealth and Virtue: The Shaping of Political Economy in the Scottish Enlightenment*, Cambridge 1983

Horkheimer, Max and T. W. Adorno, *Dialectic of Enlightenment*, New York 1995

Hume, David, *Enquiries concerning Human Understanding and concerning the Principles of Morals*, ed. L. A. Selby-Bigge, 3rd edn by P. H. Nidditch, Oxford 1975

Hume, David, *A Treatise of Human Nature*, ed. L. A. Selby-Bigge, 2nd edn by P. H. Nidditch, Oxford 1978

Hume, David, *Essays Moral, Political and Literary*, ed. Eugene F. Miller, Indianapolis 1987

Hume, David, *The Letters of David Hume*, ed. J. Y. T. Greig, 2 vols, Oxford 1932

Hume, David, *Dialogues Concerning Natural Religion*, ed. Norman Kemp Smith, 2nd edn, Edinburgh 1947

Hutcheson, Francis, *Reflections upon Laughter and Remarks upon the Fable of the Bees*, Glasgow 1750

Hutcheson, Francis, *An Inquiry into the Original of our Ideas of Beauty and Virtue; in Two Treatises: I Concerning Beauty, Order, Harmony, Design; II Concerning Moral Good and Evil*, printed from the 4th edition of 1738, Glasgow 1772

Hutcheson, Francis, *Philosophical Writings*, ed. R.S. Downie, London, 1994

Hutton, James, 'The system of the earth, its duration and stability', in Claude C. Albritton, *Philosophy of Geohistory*, Stroudburg, Pa. 1975

Hutton, James, *Theory of the Earth with Proofs and Illustrations*, Edinburgh 1795; reprinted Herts. 1959

Kames, Lord, *see* Home, Henry

Kramnick, Isaac (ed.), *The Portable Enlightenment Reader*, Harmondsworth, 1995

Kuehn, Manfred, *Scottish Common Sense in Germany*, 1768–1800, Montreal 1987

Lehmann, William C., *John Millar of Glasgow*, Cambridge 1960

MacCormick, Neil, 'Law', in *Scotland: A Concise Cultural History*, ed. Paul H. Scott, Edinburgh 1993, pp. 343–55

McIntyre, Donald B. and Alan McKirdy, *James Hutton: The Founder of Modern Geology*, Edinburgh 1977

M'Cosh, James, *The Scottish Philosophy*, London 1875

Maclaurin, Colin, *An Account of Sir Isaac Newton's Philosophical Discoveries*, London 1748

Macmillan, Duncan, *Painting in Scotland: The Golden Age*, Oxford 1986

Macmillan, Duncan, *Scottish Art 1460–1990*, Edinburgh 1990

Millar, John, *see* Lehmann, William C.

Norton, David Fate, *David Hume: Common-Sense Moralist, Sceptical Metaphysician*, Princeton NJ, 1982

Norton, David Fate (ed.), *The Cambridge Companion to Hume*, Cambridge 1993

Outram, Dorinda, *The Enlightenment*, Cambridge 1995

Phillipson, Nicholas, *Hume*, London 1989

Phillipson, Nicholas, 'Manners, morals and characters: Henry Raeburn and the Scottish Enlightenment' in Thomson, Duncan, *Raeburn: The Art of Sir Henry Raeburn 1756–1823*, Edinburgh 1997

Phillipson, Nicholas and R. Mitchison (eds), *Scotland in the Age of Improvement*, Edinburgh 1970

Porter, Roy, *The Enlightenment*, London 1990

Reid, Thomas, *Practical Ethics*, ed. K. Haakonssen, Princeton 1990

Reid, Thomas, *Philosophical Works*, ed. William Hamilton, 6th edn, 2 vols, Edinburgh 1863

Reid, Thomas, *Thomas Reid on the Animate Creation: Papers Relating to the Life Sciences*, ed. P. B. Wood, Edinburgh 1995

Robertson, John, *The Scottish Enlightenment and the Militia Issue*, Edinburgh 1985

Robertson, William, *History of the Reign of Charles the Fifth*, 2 vols, London 1857

Ross, Ian, *Lord Kames and the Scotland of his Day*, Oxford 1972

Ross, Ian, *The Life of Adam Smith*, Oxford 1995

Schneider, Louis, *The Scottish Moralists on Human Nature and Society*, Chicago 1967

Scott, Paul H. (ed.), *Scotland: A Concise Cultural History*, Edinburgh 1993

Sher, R. B., *Church and University in the Scottish Enlightenment: The Moderate Literati of Edinburgh*, Edinburgh 1985

Sinclair, Sir John (ed.), *The Statistical Account of Scotland*, 21 vols, Edinburgh 1791–9; reissued in facsimile, with parishes arranged into counties, ed. Donald J. Withrington and Ian R. Grant, 20 vols, Wakefield 1973–83

Skinner, A. S., 'Adam Smith: Ethics and self-love' in *Adam Smith Reviewed*, ed. P. Jones and A. S. Skinner, Edinburgh 1992, pp. 142–67

Skinner, A. S., *A System of Social Science: Papers Relating to Adam Smith*, 2 edn, Oxford 1996

Smellie, William, *The Philosophy of Natural History*, 2 vols, Edinburgh 1790–9

Smith, Adam, *The Theory of Moral Sentiments*, ed. D. D. Raphael and A. L. Macfie, Oxford 1976

Smith, Adam, *The Correspondence of Adam Smith*, ed. E. C. Mossner and I. S. Ross, Oxford 1977

Smith, Adam, *Lectures on Jurisprudence*, ed. R. L. Meek, D. D. Raphael and P. G. Stein, Oxford 1978

Smith, Adam, *Essays on Philosophical Subjects*, eds. W. P. D. Wightman, J. C. Bryce and I. S. Ross, Oxford 1980

Smith, Adam, *The History of Astronomy*, in *Essays on Philosophical Subjects*, ed. W. P. D. Wightman, J. C. Bryce and I. S. Ross, Oxford 1980

Smith, Adam, *An Inquiry into the Nature and Causes of the Wealth of Nations*, 2 vols, ed. R. H. Campbell and A. S. Skinner, textual editor W. B. Todd, Oxford 1976

Smith, Adam, *Lectures on Rhetoric and Belles Lettres*, ed. J. C. Bryce, Oxford 1983

Smith, Adam, *Considerations concerning the First Formation of Languages*, in *Lectures on Rhetoric and Belles Lettres*, ed. J. C. Bryce, Oxford 1983, pp. 203–26

Steuart, Sir James, *An Inquiry into the Principles of Political Oeconomy*, 2 vols, ed. A. S. Skinner, Edinburgh 1966

Stewart, Dugald, *The Collected Works*, ed. Sir William Hamilton, Edinburgh 1854

Stewart, Dugald, *Elements of the Philosophy of the Human Mind*, London 1867

Stewart, Dugald, 'Account of the Life and Writings of Adam Smith, LL.D.', in Adam Smith, *Essays on Philosophical Subjects*, ed. W. P. D. Wightman, J. C. Bryce and I. S. Ross, Oxford 1980, pp. 269–351

Stewart, M. A. (ed.), *Studies in the Philosophy of the Scottish Enlightenment*, Edinburgh 1991

Stewart, M. A., *The Kirk and the Infidel* (Inaugural Lecture at Lancaster University), Lancaster 1994

Stewart, M. A., 'The Scottish Enlightenment' in *British Philosophy and the Age of Enlightenment*, ed. Stuart Brown, London 1996, pp. 274–308

Stewart, M. A. and J. P. Wright (eds), *Hume and Hume's Connexions*, Edinburgh 1994

Stroud, Barry, *Hume*, London 1978

Telfer, Elizabeth, 'Hutcheson's Reflections Upon Laughter', *Journal of Aesthetics and Art Criticism*, vol. 53, 1995, pp. 359–69

Thomson, Duncan, *Raeburn: The Art of Sir Henry Raeburn 1756–1823*, Edinburgh 1997

Walker, David M., *The Scottish Jurists*, Edinburgh 1985

Waszek, Norbert, *Man's Social Nature*, Frankfurt am Main 1986

Withrington, Donald J. and Ian R. Grant (eds), *The Statistical Account of Scotland 1791–1799*, vol. 1: General, Wakefield 1983

Wood, Paul B., *The Aberdeen Enlightenment: The Arts Curriculum in the Eighteenth Century*, Aberdeen 1993

Yolton, John, Porter, Roy, Rogers, Pat and Stafford, Barbara Maria (eds), *The Blackwell Companion to the Enlightenment*, Oxford 1995

Zachs, W., *Without Regard to Good Manners: A Biography of Gilbert Stuart (1743–86)*, Edinburgh 1992

Index